Praise for the
Jane Yellowrock Novels

"A lot of series seek to emulate Hunter's work, but few come close to capturing the essence of urban fantasy: the perfect blend of intriguing heroine, suspense, [and] fantasy with just enough romance." —SF Site

"Readers eager for the next book in Patricia Briggs's Mercy Thompson series may want to give Faith Hunter a try." —*Library Journal*

"Hunter's very professionally executed, tasty blend of dark fantasy, mystery, and romance should please fans of all three genres." —*Booklist*

"In a genre flooded with strong, sexy females, Jane Yellowrock is unique. . . . Her bold first-person narrative shows that she's one tough cookie, but with a likable vulnerability." —*RT Book Reviews*

"Seriously. Best urban fantasy I've read in years, possibly ever." —C. E. Murphy, author of *Shaman Rises*

"The story is fantastic, the action is intense, the romance sweet, and the characters seep into your soul." —Vampire Book Club

"An action-packed thriller. . . . Betrayal, deception, and heartbreak all lead the way in this roller-coaster ride of infinite proportions." —Smexy Books

"A perfect blend of dark fantasy and mystery with a complex and tough vampire-killing heroine." —All Things Urban Fantasy

"Mixing fantasy with a strong mystery story line and a touch of romance, it ticks all the right urban fantasy boxes." —LoveVampires

"A fabulous tale with a heroine who clearly has the strength to stand on her own." —Darque Reviews

Also by Faith Hunter

The Jane Yellowrock Series

Skinwalker

Blood Cross

Mercy Blade

Cat Tales
(short story compilation)

Raven Cursed

Have Stakes Will Travel
(short story compilation)

Death's Rival

Blood Trade

The Jane Yellowrock World Companion

Black Arts

Broken Soul

Dark Heir

The Rogue Mage Novels

Bloodring

Seraphs

Host

BLOOD IN HER VEINS

Nineteen Stories from the World of Jane Yellowrock

FAITH HUNTER

A ROC BOOK

Published by New American Library,
an imprint of Penguin Random House LLC
375 Hudson Street, New York, New York 10014

This book is an original publication of New American Library.

First Printing, February 2016

LIBRARY OF CONGRESS CATALOGING-IN-PUBLICATION DATA:

Names: Hunter, Faith, author.
Title: Blood in her veins: nineteen stories from the world of Jane
Yellowrock/Faith Hunter.
Description: New York: New American Library, 2016. | Series: Jane Yellowrock | "A ROC book."
Identifiers: LCCN 2015035983 | ISBN 9780451475756 (softcover)
Subjects: LCSH: Vampires—Fiction. | Shape-shifting—Fiction. | BISAC: FICTION/Fantasy/Urban Life.
| FICTION/Fantasy/Contemporary. | FICTION/Fantasy/Paranormal. | GSAFD: Fantasy fiction.
Classification: LCC PS3608.U59278 A6 2016 | DDC 813/.6—dc23
LC record available at https://protect-us.mimecast.com/s/K2WvBxCGV05luR

Printed in the United States of America
10 9 8 7 6 5 4 3 2 1

Penguin
Random
House

Sometimes someone enters your life and, because they believe in you, in your ability and talent, your life changes. Their passion for your work gives you faith in yourself, your stories, your career, and your future. Jessica Wade, my editor at Penguin Random House, is that person. She makes me a better writer. She makes me strive for more action, deeper characters, better stories, darker outcomes, and she accepts nothing but my best. For that reason alone I should dedicate every single thing I write to her.

This is for you, Jess. Thank you for the long hours, the mental gymnastics you do for my stories, and mostly for your belief in me. I couldn't do it without you.

ACKNOWLEDGMENTS

To my fans, *you* made this happen. Thank you!

To my wonderful agent and friend, Lucienne Diver, for her help in putting this compilation together, my great thanks!

To Isabel Farhi, thank you for all you did for this compilation and all the work you shoulder for me and for my stories.

To my editor, Jessica Wade, there are not enough words to say thank you . . . soooo . . .

TABLE OF CONTENTS

Hi, all,

This is a first for me. An almost complete collection of my own short stories—nineteen of them, to be exact. I've been writing shorts since almost the beginning of telling Jane Yellowrock's story. I love them because I can explore things that don't make it to the novels—new ideas, new perspectives, new characters. This is the first time they've all been collected together (with a very few exceptions, plus all the stories I intend to write in the future!).

I hope you find that they help you understand Jane's world better—writing them certainly helped me see her world through new eyes. I've also included a timeline, so you can see where each story fits in relation to the novels.

I gotta tell you, I am psyched about this collection, and it's all totally because of the fans. You asked for all the shorts in one place. And you asked. And asked! And that persistence worked, because now you have them! Thank you! And to make that thanking mean more, I have written two brand-new novellas.

Let me tell you about those stories, "Bound No More" and "Cat Fight." "Bound No More" is about Angie Baby and an arcenciel and the future. We get to see Angie's powers in new, and possibly frightening, ways, because she is growing up fast. It's a fight to save the Everhart/Trueblood clan, and it's downright fun!

In "Cat Fight," Jane is tasked by Leo Pellissier to return to Bayou Oiseau, a pretty little Cajun town on the banks of the bayou of the same name. She takes Eli and Alex Younger—natch—but she also has a tagalong in the person of the undead Edmund Hartley. The four quickly discover themselves in the midst of what looks like a love triangle among a vamp, a witch, and a prickly tempered human. It looks as if Jane is expected to play therapist—and then it all goes to hell in a handbasket.

I had a pure blast writing all of these stories. I hope you love them half as much as I do!

Faith Hunter

TIMELINE

Here's a timeline of the stories in this collection and when they take place in relation to the Jane Yellowrock novels.
   Enjoy!

"*Wesa* and the Lumber King"—Short story from Beast's point of view, set in the Hunger Times

"The Early Years"—Short story about Jane Yellowrock just after she left the children's home

"Snafu"—Jane interviews for an internship with a PI.

"Cat Tats"—Short story about how Rick LaFleur got his tattoos

"Kits"—Short story about Jane, with Molly Everhart Trueblood as a secondary character

"Haint(s)"—Short story from Molly's point of view, with Jane as a secondary character

"Signatures of the Dead"—Short story about Molly, with Jane as a secondary character

Skinwalker—The first Jane Yellowrock novel

"First sight"—From George "Bruiser" Dumas' point of view, when he first sees Jane

Blood Cross—The second Jane Yellowrock novel

Mercy Blade—The third Jane Yellowrock novel

"Blood, Fangs, and Going Furry"—Short story about Rick LaFleur's first full moon after being bitten by a were. From Rick's point of view, with Jane as a secondary character.

"Dance Master"—From Bruiser's point of view. He calls Jane to investigate a problem in the Royal Mojo Blues Company. And, oh my, do they dance . . .

Raven Cursed—The fourth Jane Yellowrock novel

"Golden Delicious"—Rick is in PsyLED school with his dual nemeses Brute and Pea. His fellow students go missing, and everything starts to go wrong.

"Cajun with Fangs"—Jane is stranded in Bayou Oiseau when her Harley, Bitsa, has engine trouble. And she walks right into a war between witches and vampires that seems destined to drag her and her boss, Leo Pellissier, down with them into flames.

Death's Rival—The fifth Jane Yellowrock novel

Blood Trade—The sixth Jane Yellowrock novel

"The Devil's Left Boot"—The Everhart witch sisters are asked to find a missing woman who had great taste in boots.

"Beneath a Bloody Moon"—Jane and her team investigate a series of possible werewolf attacks outside of Houma, Louisiana.

"Black Water"—Jane is back in the Deep South, near Houma, this time chasing a human predator, racing to save the lives of the two women he has kidnapped.

Black Arts—The seventh Jane Yellowrock novel

"Off the Grid"—Jane is in Knoxville to do a favor for her boss, the chief fanghead of the southeast U.S. It's supposed to be an easy investigation, but a very important vampire has gone missing and Jane is drawn into the search. This is where Jane meets Nell Nicholson Ingram for the first time.

Broken Soul—The eighth Jane Yellowrock novel

"Not All as It Seems"—A short story featuring Molly, who gets a surprise visit from vampires looking for a relic their master lost long ago

Dark Heir—The ninth Jane Yellowrock novel

"Cat Fight"—Jane is back in Bayou Oiseau, where the witches and vamps are again at war, this time over a magical talisman called *le breloque*.

"Bound No More"—Angie Baby and Molly come to visit Jane. When an *arcenciel* also shows up, bent on mischief, Angie proves she is growing up—into the most powerful witch in Everhart history.

Shadow Rights—The tenth Jane Yellowrock novel, releasing in April of 2016

BLOOD IN HER VEINS

Wesa and the Lumber King

Author's note: This story takes place in the Hunger Times of the late 1800s–early 1900s.

I/we climbed stunted tree, sat in twisted limb. High on ledge at top of gorge. Hidden by smoke from man fire far below. Man fire burned limbs, leaves cut from trees. Smoke filled air. Sound of axes echoed across gorge. Sound of train whistle split air. Hurt ears. Bad sound. All sound of man was bad sound, but sound of white man was worst sound. No sound of birds. No sound of prey on ground. No good sounds anywhere since white man came to mountains. Below, in gorge, limbs and trees and branches were dropped into water, dropped there by human men. White men.

Wesa, little bobcat, said into back of mind, Yunega *tsiluga tala tlugvi, tsiluga totsi tlugvi*. White man kill white pine trees, kill white oak trees. *Asgina*. Devils.

Alpha devil is there, I thought at her. *White man in gray pelt. Do you understand his words?*

Yunega *talk is not Tsalagi talk*, she said in mind speech. *I do not understand.*

I flicked ears, twitched tail, and said to her, *Alpha devil points with paw to other white men which trees to cut. With paws and tongue, tells them to load dead trees onto flat thing that moves, flat place called* train car. *Tells them to throw dead limbs and branches into river below. River is full of trees and does not run. Fish die. Animals run away and die. Birds fly away and die. Smoke fills air, and I cannot breathe.*

I/we had talked in mind den about this. I said to *wesa* again, *White devils must die. If white alpha devil dies, then all white men will stop killing earth. Yes?*

Wesa did not answer. *Wesa* shivered in back of mind, in cave den of mind, in place she had made her own. We watched white men in gorge. We had watched them for two days. We knew where the den of the alpha devil was. We knew he went there at night, always by the same path. Just as deer once used to take same path to water in gorge below, alpha devil took same path to his train-car den. I had been ambush hunter even before *wesa* came to me. I knew to study prey.

After long time, shadows began to stretch upon ground. *Wesa* stirred and asked, *We will kill* yunega *asgina? Wesa* knew this, but still she thought, silent in mind as we watched white man, *I do not like to kill humans.*

White humans are devils. They kill the earth. I/we will kill them.

But not eat them, wesa said. *Elisi,* grandmother, *say man flesh makes us sick.*

We will not eat him. But I/we will kill killer of hunting territory. Killer of trees and killer of prey.

Man was not good hunter, man was stupid. But man was winning and I/we were losing. After killing alpha male human, I/we would leave this place for deep gorge, many days' walk away. *Wesa* knew this as well. She did not like it, but she understood. *Wesa* had once been human, but not white man human. Tsalagi human—*Cherokee.* Tsalagi understood how to live with earth and not kill it. Some Tsalagi did not protect the earth, some killed her, but not most. All white men killed earth. White man was evil.

I stood up on paws on tree limb and watched as night dropped darkness over all of earth. When shadows were long and human men left from killing trees to go eat food, I leaped to ground. *Wesa* hid in dark of mind den, afraid.

I raced down from ledge and trees on sheer part of gorge, place where white man could not get to easily, place of stunted trees and snakes and rock. I leaped straight down, thick tail whirling for balance. Halfway down gorge fall, I twisted like snake, and whipped tail. Changed direction, and landed on tiny ledge. There was small cave in back of ledge. Had once used this place for den to have kits. Liked this place long ago. White man had ruined it. Killed it. I did not go to den now, but pawpawpaw down across tiny ledges, leaping from ledge to ledge, which white men called *outcropping,* until I reached bottom of gorge. Then I moved in shadows for train car of white man, den of white alpha devil.

Night vision came as sunlight left. Earth turned into silvers and greens and grays. Liked this time of day/night. *Wesa* called it beautiful. I called it safe. Shadows were dark and deep, and *wesa* had explained that humans could not see in dark. I padded through dark over rutted bare earth to den of alpha devil. Curled into darker shadow beneath train car. I waited. I/we are good at waiting. Time passed. Night was dark. No moon stood in sky. Moon had died and would be reborn as kit moon in one night, tiny and shaped like thin claw. I/we had chosen this night for this reason. *Wesa* closed her eyes, afraid.

When night was full, I alone crept up stairs and leaped high, onto roof of train car. It was warm from sun of day. Was good place to ambush hunt. Looked over edge of train car, to path white man took for food. Was like ambush hunting on ledge in high hills before white man came and sent prey away.

Heard man paws on earth, loud and scuffling inside dried skin of cow—boots. Man was not balanced and graceful and should not walk on two legs. Would be more quiet and graceful on four legs. But I was happy that white man was stupid and noisy. Listened and watched as he came closer. He carried in one paw much meat. It was cooked, which was bad, but it was meat and I/we had not eaten in two days. We hungered. White man came closer.

I gathered paws close under belly, balanced and steady as rock on flat land. White man came closer. He put one foot on step, one foot still on ground. Was unbalanced on one foot. I leaped. Landed on white man. *Hard!* Tumbled to ground, tangled in his upper legs. Landed on top of white man. With killing teeth, I ripped out his throat. Then held him by throat as he thrashed. He died. His blood was hot in my mouth. It did not taste good, but I hungered! Wanted to drink!

But *wesa* put her mind on top of my mind. *Tlano!* she said. *Do not eat!*

I snarled, but I did not drink blood or eat white man meat. *Wesa* was smart. Blood tasted like blood of buzzard, full of dead things. I took his cooked meat and carried it into night. In shadows, I ate. And listened to sounds of white men when they found my enemy. They gathered together like wolf pack. Like pack hunters. They shouted into night, many white man words. They grabbed white man sticks and made loud noises.

Guns, wesa whispered.

When all the white man's cooked meat was in my belly, I turned and walked into hills. But that night, the foolish white man pack let fire go free. The hills began to burn and burn and burn. Hunger Times were upon us.

I would not come back to my old hunting grounds for many, many years.

The Early Years

Careful of the big gold-toned hoops that pierced my earlobes, I strapped on my helmet and straddled the beat-up Yamaha. It wasn't my dream bike, but it would do until I could afford the one I really wanted. I glanced back to make sure my saddlebags were latched. The teal compartments were secure, held in place with leather straps tightened by Bobby, who now stood to the side, his face long and his eyes downcast. Everything was in place and ready. A thrill of excitement raced along my skin, prickling like fur. Despite the heat, I pulled on my leather riding jacket and tucked my hip-length braid inside it, out of the way. I touched the gold necklace that I still wore like a talisman and reached for the key to start the engine.

"You don't have to go," Bobby blurted.

I looked up at him: his red hair catching the afternoon sun, his freckles a spatter of cinnamon. He was standing with his arms crossed, his hands tight under his armpits, eyes staring at the asphalt. Afraid. He had always been afraid. *Prey,* the insistent, soft voice whispered in my mind. With long practice, I shoved the presence down deep, ignoring it. It hacked with amusement but subsided, watching. Waiting.

"Yes, I do," I repeated for the thousandth time, trying to keep the impatience out of my tone. "I can't stay. They won't let us stay after we turn eighteen. The funding runs out today. And I have to leave." That wasn't strictly true. The children's home did have a program for their graduates, as they called us, but I didn't fit into it at all. And though they would have found a place for me for a while, I had seen the looks on their faces. They were ready for me to go.

"I'm not going to college or tech school, so there's no money for my housing till fall. The only security firm that wanted a trainee is in Asheville. I have to go." That much was true.

"But it won't be the same, Jane."

I knew what he really meant. Like me, Bobby was different, not like the other kids at Bethel Nondenominational Christian Children's Home. While I was just . . . different, he was a little slower than most, both physically and mentally. Bobby was seventeen going on ten. And he was lonely, just as I had been. Like me, he'd been picked on mercilessly by the other kids. Not when a group home parent was nearby, of course, or when a counselor was watching. Never then. Only when no one was looking. His life had been hell until I'd taken him under my wing in the middle of December more than two years ago.

I already had a rep as a fighter at the school, and had spent more time in detention than any other girl had in the history of Bethel. A record I was happy to leave behind me. But despite how tough I was, from the first day he came to Bethel, something about Bobby had called to me. He was like a day-old kitten, mewling in fear. I had fought for Bobby. Protected him. Made sure the other kids left him alone. With me gone, Bobby would have to fend for himself.

I had done what I could to see him safe, mainly by threatening the ringleaders of cliques that bullied the most. I'd come back to visit. And they didn't want me unhappy when I did.

I wasn't that tough—not really—though the years in the dojo learning street fighting proved I could kick butt when I needed to. While the other girls in the group home were taking ballet, piano, and French, I was getting tossed around by a sensei with black belts in three different martial art forms. I was pretty sure the general manager of the school, the dude who had approved the cost of the lessons, had expected the rigorous training program to knock some sense into me and teach me self-restraint. He had probably also figured Sensei would send me back with my antagonistic tail between my legs. Things had worked out a bit differently.

In the dojo, I had finally found a place where I belonged, where I fit in, with Sensei and the kids he groomed as fighters. I never stood for belt testing, but I stuck out the training program, living with the bruises, sprains, and occasional broken rib. I was good. But mostly, as far as the school counselors and their opposite number, the bully masters, were concerned, I was just really good at looking dangerous.

I also worked after school at the dojo, my first real job, cleaning floors and the workout mats, washing windows, general handyman stuff. Sensei taught me how to do the books, pay the taxes, order supplies. He was my first real friend. Even if he did knock me silly when we sparred.

I took Bobby's hand, his flesh soft and moist, and held it, drawing his unwilling eyes to mine. "As soon as I get the trainee position and get started, I'll schedule a few days off and come back. I promise."

Tears filled his eyes. "Okay," he whispered. "I'm not going anywhere."

And he wasn't. Bobby's parents had been killed in an automobile accident with a drunk driver. Though his grandmother had taken in his three brothers and sisters, she had decided she didn't have the strength to raise a kid with a seventy-four IQ. So she dumped him here, which I understood on one level, but it still made my brain boil. Bobby went home to Gramma's to visit on Christmas, on Easter, and for a week in the summer. That was it. That was as much as his grandmother could take of her less-than-normal grandkid.

Of course, I never went anywhere, but I was used to it. I had always been alone.

Weak. *Prey,* my inner voice whispered. My own personal demon, never acknowledged aloud, never alluded to, never hinted at. The counselors would have thought me insane or possessed, depending on their religious beliefs. Either way, I'd have been medicated and sent to more counseling sessions. And been subjected to more torment by my housemates. Again, I shoved it deep and silent.

"I'll be bringing you a present," I said. "Something from the mountains."

Bobby's eyes lit up. "From your spirit quest?"

I dropped his hand and chucked him on the chin. "Right. See you soon." Before he could delay me more, I turned the key and gave the Yamaha a bit of gas. It spat for a sec and then shot me forward. Into the future. I wove through the grounds of the children's home one last time. I would come back. But Bobby was right. This would never be my home again, and it would always-ever-after be different.

Bethel Nondenominational Christian Children's Home was located near the Sumter National Forest in South Carolina, within spitting distance of Georgia and North Carolina, in a locale with more rednecks than all other ethnic groups put together, and ten times more livestock than people. Maybe a hundred times. Maybe a thousand. The place I was going was a lot less populated and a lot more remote.

I dropped down my face shield, cutting the hot wind but making a steam bath inside with my own breath. Speeding, I passed the main offices and lifted a thumb to the one person standing outside to see me go— Belinda Smith, one of my former houseparents. She smiled and waved, and I knew that of all the people at Bethel—besides Bobby—she really was sad to see me leave. She had liked my essays.

I glanced in the rearview to see her place a hand over her mouth, and I could have sworn that she was crying. Not possible. No way.

I looked back at the street and the road before me. Gunned the motor again. The outer gates neared, passed, and fell behind. The bike tore out of the grounds of Bethel, along the main road, and out of the city.

Soon I was gunning it up the mountains.

The quality of the air changed around every bend, freshening each time the elevation rose. The world changed as I two-wheeled into my future and—I hoped—my past.

I didn't have a history. I had wandered out of the Sumter National Forest when I was somewhere near twelve years of age, traumatized, weak, skinny as a rail, totally unsocialized, and with complete amnesia. The newspaper that captured the story and sent it out on the newswires suggested that I was raised by wolves, an accusation that contributed more than almost anything else to the drubbings I took until I could hold my own. Well, except for the fact that I couldn't speak a word of English. That had brought on a lot of pain and suffering too. I couldn't even remember my own name.

All I had muttered was a Cherokee word that one of the park rangers who found me was able to interpret. Yellow Rock. So I became Jane Yellowrock Doe. Eventually they dropped the Doe and I acquired a birth certificate as Jane Yellowrock, birthday August 15, the day of the month when I had been found, and a presumed birth year that made me twelve. No records of me had ever been located, and no one had ever come forward to claim me.

The only memory I had was of a granite mountain cliff, a sunrise, and a white quartz boulder. It was as if I had been born with the vision of the mountain's rock face as seen from above, standing on the crest and looking down on it, and also from far below it, looking up. The horseshoe-shaped granite had been pitted with perfectly round holes, some large enough to act as a cup holder, some sized as if for candles, all in long strands of eroded or carved holes, like tears across the stone of the mountain face, a confusing gray pattern in the rising sun.

On the Internet, it hadn't been that hard to find a mountain fitting the horseshoe description. Horseshoe Rock was in Jackson County, North Carolina, in the Nantahala National Forest. Not all that far from where I had been found. If the pictures were right, there was a gigantic curving rock face on the eastern front of Wolf Mountain. And if that was really true, then so were my dreams, my possible past, and any hope of a family I might ever have.

The memory of the white quartz boulder was more shadowed, hidden. No mention of the boulder was anywhere on the Internet, which had totally sucked. But at least I had a starting point. A place in my broken and lost memory that matched with reality.

Once I discovered that Horseshoe Rock really existed, I had spent hours in the school library researching the history of the mountain, trying to see why I was drawn there. For whatever reason, I had dreamed of the rock face of the mountain my whole life, though as far as I recalled, I had never seen it in person.

In my visions, the image of the white quartz boulder threaded through with gold had been within sight of the mountain. I touched the gold nugget I wore beneath my clothes. Part of my past. The only thing I had from the "Before Times."

But maybe I had family where I was headed. Who knows. Or maybe I had just been born with the pictures of it all imprinted on my mind. Whatever. But I was drawn there like a pile of metal filings to a magnet. I had harbored the need to go there forever, and now, the day I turned eighteen—according to my fictional birth certificate—I was finally on my way.

I had done my homework on MapQuest and TerraServer. I knew where I was going and how to get there. In the latched saddlebag compartments I had annotated Internet maps, a sleeping bag, enough food—mostly beef jerky—to last a few days, water, a rain-resistant backpack and slicker, and well-worn hiking boots. I was headed to my past.

I reached the Nantahala National Forest before dark and took State

Road 281 through the hills, the coiling blacktop like the ridges of a dragon's back, the bike roaring up and down and around, my excitement growing with each turn. The cooler air dried my sweat-soaked skin. Shadows lengthened and the air darkened. On a hairpin turn, I spotted a sign that read WOLF MOUNTAIN ROAD. It was a narrow, blacktopped side road that curled up and out of sight around a fold of the mountain. Satisfied, I headed back into more commercial areas and a cheap hotel that catered to motorcyclists.

Bedding down, I lay staring at the ceiling. The sheets were older than I was. The room probably hadn't been painted in decades. But the place was surface clean, and for what I wanted to pay, that was probably okay. Still, the carpet smelled of mold, stronger than the reek of the fresheners the housekeeping crew used, and I couldn't turn off my nose or my reflexes. When I finally slept, it was only poorly. I was hyperalert on some deep level, a sensation that seemed to prowl around inside me like a nervous, edgy cat, feeling the excitement still gathering, pulsing through me.

I was up at five, pretty much the only person awake except a waitress/cook at a Huddle House knockoff joint. I was so excited I could hardly think, and the breakfast of eggs and bacon I scarfed stuck about midway down and stayed there.

By dawn, the August heat was already in the high eighties, and I was tooling up 281. The sun, hidden by low clouds, threw diffuse shadows across the blacktop. Morning-cool air raced beneath my riding leathers as I turned onto Wolf Mountain Road, a winding asphalt tertiary street that morphed quickly into an unmarked narrow paved strip, and then to a two-rutted trail. The track was ground down and sloppy with mud from the last rains, scored with tire tracks from four-wheelers and off-road motorbikes. It wasn't something my street bike was built for, but the Yamaha was in a good mood, agreeable to my spirit quest, as Bobby had called it, and I made okay time.

Wolf Mountain's highest peak was more than four thousand feet above sea level, and the trail wound up and down at sharp inclines. I skidded and threw dirt and stone as I alternately gunned and braked my bike, balancing with my feet on my climb to the crest. I passed no one, saw no one. I was alone on the mountain. Totally alone. Climbing hard. Following my nose and some instinct I couldn't name.

Once, when I took a break, I touched the necklace, the gold nugget that was the only thing I still had from the forgotten life before I was twelve. Holding the gold, its rounded shape a perfect match for my palm, I opened my mouth and sucked in the morning air, heavy with promised rain, pulling the scents in over the roof of my mouth, tasting, smelling, feeling in the way that worked so well for me. It was a method that had resulted in the other kids laughing at me until I learned to sniff with my nose only, like they did.

Taking off again, I breathed deeply as I roared along the track, through a low-lying cloud heavy with rain. Mist draped the landscape, hiding and revealing boulders, ferns, green-laden trees. The place smelled familiar. Felt familiar. My excitement grew. In the back of my mind a strange thought whispered, *The world of the white man falls away.*

I reached the crest of the mountain after lunch, sweating in the August heat and humidity even at such a high elevation, with the misty clouds burned away. I keyed off the bike and sat, listening to the hot metal pinging, my booted feet on the stony earth, breathing in the mist, letting it fill my lungs, my heart fluttering like a bird caught in a too-tight fist. Letting memory and reality merge.

The air was noticeably thinner, and the smells of hemlock, pine, fir, maple, and oak were stronger than the lingering smell of bike exhaust. Clouds were thickening in the east, and I knew there would be rain soon.

I stepped off the bike, locked it to a tree with a length of chain, hid my helmet in a pile of bracken, and grabbed up my supplies, sliding them into the backpack. And I walked off the two-track trail to the top of Horseshoe Rock. Standing in the lowering clouds, their mist snaking over the ridge and down into the valley below, I looked out over the world.

Horseshoe Rock was bigger than I had expected. Too big to see its scale in photographs. Bigger than the grandstand in a coliseum. Bigger than Horseshoe Falls in Canada. Bigger than anything I could ever remember seeing. Yet it was familiar. I had been here before. Several . . . no. Many times.

The sensation of a pelt rubbing against my flesh and bones grew.

Rippling, uncomfortable. My breath sped, my heart tripping.

I walked the rock, sure-footed, as a thin rain began to fall. Thunder rumbled overhead. The misty drizzle damped my clothes, sticking them to me. Wet seeped into my braid and trickled along my scalp, adding weight to the long plait. I raised my face to the rain. Unlike the other girls in the group home, I had never cared whether I got rain-wet, because I didn't wear much makeup and my hair had never been styled. It was black and straight, hanging way past my hips, worn most often in a single braid; rainwater didn't cause me the problems it did the more socially upscale, high-maintenance girls.

Now, wet and uncaring, I walked all along the upper ridge of the rock, seeing the surface shapes that had caused such arguments among archeologists.

The cliff was marked with ridges of hard rock, veins of whiter marble, harder than the surrounding gray granite, standing up just a bit higher, running across the curvature like multiple spines ridging the stone. And it was pitted. . . . The pits were all uniform in direction, falling from the top of the stone across the almost-flat side, perpendicular to the marble spines, and down, down, around the curve of the mountain, like tears of rain and pain. Every single pit was flat-bottomed, level, and nearly perfectly circular, though the sizes of each pit trail were different. Some tracks were small, starting the size of a Coke bottle bottom and falling away to holes no bigger than a quarter. Some began the size of a large can of . . . of ravioli, descending to the size of a can of cola. Always larger at the top and growing smaller as they trailed across and down the stone to disappear under the curve of the rock.

Moss grew so thickly in the shaded areas that it was like piled carpets in overlapping shades of green from nearly black to nearly white. A flash of lightning forked across the sky. I looked up, into the face of the brewing storm, violence all around me. Drops of rain pelted my face, cold, washing away my sweat. I shivered.

With a sudden roar, the drizzle increased to a true rain, beating the trees and leaves with a hollow patter, slamming against the bare stone, kicking up into the air again, and cascading back into rivulets, rushing down the bowed rock face, through the pathways of pitted depressions, across the ridged spines, down the mountain, splashing and gurgling, as if the earth drank down the rain.

I followed the downward movement with my eyes and then with my feet, to the far right, where scrub grew, dropping fast from Horseshoe Rock, away from the stable flatter stone to the deep earth and down, sliding and slipping below the curve of the broad cliff face into a narrow gorge. Loping with a gait that felt odd in the hiking boots, I splashed through runnels and rills and slipped through muddy depressions. Leaves tossed pooled rain at me; branches whipped me.

I opened my mouth, scenting, pulling in the world with a harsh sucking sound. My breath came fast, almost painfully, in gasps that resounded off the trees and filled my head with partial memories. *I have been here. I have been here. Home . . .*

The elevation fell away, quickly and furiously, trees and leaves and ferns flashing past as I followed the water down. A deer froze off to the side, and I slowed. Crouched. Stopped. Fixed her with a steady stare. Her scent flooded my mouth and body, and I started to salivate, staring at her. I panted, studying the doe. I don't know what she saw in my gaze, but she whirled and bounded over a fallen tree, moving fast, uphill. My muscles tensed, bunching tight, as if to follow. I held myself still, hands gripping the boles of saplings to either side.

Meat! the voice said.

"No," I whispered.

The presence within me, the voice that spoke to me, the . . . the weirdness that set me so much apart from the other girls, hissed, frustrated. And growled, stirring as if alive. With long practice, I shoved the voice down and moved on, away from the fresh meat. Deeper into the trees, the light dimming into colorless false dusk. Holding on to trees to keep my balance, catching myself when gravity took over and the earth fell away.

Artificial evening took over from the afternoon as the sides of a tight crevice closed in, and the rain became drenching, wetting through to my skin, down into my waterproof boots and the collar of my denim jacket. Shadows dappled and moved as if alive. Rain coursed down the mountain.

Nothing looked the same. Everything looked the same. *I have been here. I have been here. Home . . .*

The trees, which had once been huge and old—older than the ravens and the owls, old as the sky and the earth itself—had been raped by the white man, cut and butchered and carted away on trains, leaving bare earth and eroded soil. Now they had been replaced by saplings. I remembered both—the old, massive trees and the barren earth. I remembered the time of hunger. I remembered young trees, when the world tried to regrow . . . the world before and the world after. And a world of fire, when flames consumed everything and the few remaining animals raced in panic. For a moment I saw fire, red and scorching, the mountainside black with suffocating smoke. And the flood that followed, wiping out what little was left.

I had studied the history of the place. I was remembering the early nineteen hundreds, when white men stripped the entire Appalachian Mountains bare of trees. Matching my memories, there had been a fire . . . here. A time long before I was born. Surely it had been long before I was born. Yet I remembered.

I leaped over a rill of water and vaulted over a fallen tree, my palm abrading on the wet, rough bark. Now the trees were somewhere in between in size, no longer saplings but not yet old, not yet wise. Less than a hundred years in age. So much smaller than my earliest memories. And still I plunged down, into the ravine with the water and the rain. Searching.

Something white caught my eye. I stopped. Frozen. Still. Where had I seen it? What?

Rain rolled down my face to hang on my nose and jaws, to drip from the end of my braid. I was at the bottom. Too far right. I moved left, slightly uphill, my feet squishing with the wet that rolled down my ankles into my boots.

I saw the glimmer of white quartz beneath a matting of soil and decades of leaves. I raced to it, knelt, and brushed away the detritus that hid it. And saw the faint line of gold trailing through the quartz. I touched my necklace. The same gold. The same exact gold: from this place, from this rock.

I sobbed hard, a concussive explosion of trapped agony. It was real. All this time. The memories, the dreams. All real.

Unbalanced, I slid downhill, my feet unsteady on the steeply pitched hillside. Caught myself on trailing branches and an oak trunk. Trying to think. How had white man not seen *dalonige'i*? The yellow rock. The gold he lusted after. How had it remained hidden?

Slightly above me, the ground around the boulder gave way, carrying with it pebbles and dirt and a few fist-sized rocks. Erosion had hidden the boulder. Floods had uncovered it, hidden it, and uncovered it again. And though the trees had been raped from the earth by the white man, though they had trampled all over the chasm, they had missed it. The boulder was still here.

My feet, precariously perched in the mud, slid out from me, and I sat down hard, landing with a *splat* in a runnel of water. A roar of white water sounded nearby, running off Horseshoe Rock above, the runoff grown to a river in the rain. Leaves bowed down, and droplets still drummed, and creeks appeared that had been empty only moments ago. Long minutes passed. I leaned a shoulder against the white quartz stone. Lifted a hand to rest against it, my fingers splayed on the cool stone. *It's real.* . . .

Rain raced over me, dribbled through my fingers onto the quartz. I'd found it. I had found the place of my dream. The only thing I had of my past. The one thing that the voice that possessed me and I agreed upon. This rock.

What had happened here? How long ago?

A shiver caught me up. I was so cold. My fingers were blue gray against the white quartz. I stood and moved uphill to a slightly more level place and stripped, tossing my wet clothes across a branch, careless even with the jacket and boots. I opened my knapsack and pulled out my sleeping bag, glad that the pierced and tattooed greenie who sold it to me had insisted that I buy the best rainproof brand. I dried off as well as I was able and climbed inside the bag, zipped it closed, and tied off the hood that protected my face. A mini-tent.

Encased, I curled into the fetal position and stared at the rock, unable to take my eyes off of it. My shivering eventually eased. The day died. As long as there was light, I stared at the white quartz boulder. With the thin vein of gold running up its side.

Dreams began the moment darkness fell, the night wet and chilly and utterly black. I was so deep in the chasm that there was no sky, no moon, no stars, not even clouds to spit out the rain. Yet rain still fell. My body vibrated, shuddering with tremors that I felt in every muscle, every nerve fiber, every cell. My flesh sparked and tingled, itching and painful, like a bad sunburn.

In my dream I untied the sleeping bag and looked down inside. At my body. If clouds were made of light instead of water vapor, they would look like this, like me, all sparkly silver, thrust through with motes of blackness that danced and whirled. The vaguely human-shaped mist coalesced, thickened, and eddied around me. *Was* me.

In my dream I stared as night rain beat down on the sleeping bag. I saw the snake in my body, deep in my cells, thousands of snakes, millions, each a double helix of snakes, twisted and writhing. And I saw the other snake, in my memory. The snake of the voice. The snake of the presence.

And I . . . shifted. Changed.

The grayness enveloped me. My body bent and flowed like water—or like hot wax, a viscous, glutinous liquid, full of gray light and gray shadows and black motes of power. The bones beneath my flesh popped and cracked. Pain arced through me like lightning. I heard my grunting scream, muted for lack of breath. The agony was a blade, slicing me bone from bone, nerve from nerve, fiber from fiber. Agony that went on and on. Whirling like a tornado of torture.

My breathing changed.

The light that was my body grew brighter, the dark motes within me darker.

Both began to dissipate. I slept.

Day came slowly, rain dropping with sharp *splat*s onto the wet ground. Night bird sounds gave way to morning birds.

Hard to catch. Not enough to eat. My stomach rumbled, low growl of the hunter.

I crawled from bag, leaving behind earrings and gold necklace on wet cloth. I stepped from the sleeping bag, unsteady on four feet. Paws. With claws. I flexed my claws out, happy to see them clean and bright, slightly yellow in pale dawn. It had been long. Many years. Many moons. She was in control too long this time.

I—Beast—stepped down the slope to water, to a pool gathered in a shallow basin below the white boulder. The rock that tied us together as one. She did not remember why. But I—Beast—did. I am good hunter. I forget nothing.

I lapped at pool and then, hungry, snatched at human bag of human food. Bloodless, dead meat. But here. With strong claws, tore into bag and into other bags, scattering smoked meat across ground. Wolfed it down. Salty. Cold. Satisfied for now. Sat, grooming, above the water pool. In its reflection saw a mountain lion sitting, eyes golden, with human-shaped pupils. *Puma concolor.* Mountain lion. Big-cat.

Heard scurrying in leaves. I froze. Slow steps sounded from downhill. Dainty. From upwind. Four legs. Tiny hooves. Smelled deer.

Leisurely sniff. Hunger rumbled. Prey. Slow hunch. I curved into earth. Wary, cautious placement of paw, paw, paw, silent into lee of white rock. Deer came down for water. Paused, head up, eyes going wide. Tensed.

I launched. Up. Claws out. Lips pulled back. Killing fangs exposed. Deer leaped.

In midair, I twisted, a sinuous move, claws out. Sinking deep. Blood flooding like life. Struggle of prey, legs flailing. With a single wrench, snapped neck. Doe quivered. Dying. Flesh in jaws was strong with muscle, wet with blood. Taste flooded my mouth.

I held. Unmoving. Feeling, hearing, tasting, smelling. Long moments later, her heart stopped, I dropped her, licking mouth and bloody paws and claws. Looking around for any who would steal.

Theft happened here once. Theft of prey and theft of life. Now this was a good place. Alone. With blood food. I screamed. Claiming this place. My territory. Mine! Satisfied, I settled to the throat of the deer and ripped into warm meat.

Snafu

Author's note: Fans are always asking me about Jane's early life and training, about how she went from the children's home to rogue-vamp hunter. Well, here's a small insight into how.

I unstrapped my helmet and sat, straddling the beat-up Yamaha and taking in the storefront. It didn't look like much. The dirty display windows were covered on the outside by steel bars, and on the inside by cheap, bent, bowed metal blinds. In the creases of the blinds I could make out wood studs and wallboard on the other side, as if the business wanted to make sure no one could see in. ENDERS SECURITY AND PRIVATE INVESTIGATIONS, INC. was stenciled on the door. My place of internship and on-the-job training for the next six months. I was eighteen and on my own, after spending the past six years in Bethel Nondenominational Christian Children's Home. I couldn't decide whether I was excited at the thought of finally being here or dismayed at the dingy storefront.

Using a steel chain and keyed lock, I attached the Yamaha to the pitted and scored aluminum bike post that was situated near the storm drain. It wasn't my dream bike, but it would do until I could afford the one I really wanted. And there was no point in making it easy for my only transportation to be bike-jacked. This neighborhood looked anything but safe and secure. Lucky me. Knowing nothing about Asheville, I'd picked Enders out of a list of possible PI and security businesses to take my paid internship for my private investigator's license. From the broken-down look of things, I'd picked wrong. Closed businesses, run-down buildings, little traffic, and what traffic there was consisted of pimpmobiles and rusted, dented, kidnapper-style paneled vans.

Eyes on the guys watching me from the street corner, I patted my saddlebags, checking the latches. The teal compartments were secure, held in place with leather straps and small locks. Everything I owned was in the compartments: my toothbrush, shampoo, and a few changes of clothes—jeans and T-shirts. Boots I hadn't been able to pass up in the "gently used clothing" consignment store.

The August heat had laid a slick of sweat down my back, and I unzipped my vintage leather riding jacket, freeing my hip-length braid. I touched the gold necklace that I still wore like a talisman and headed for the door.

The guys on the corner started toward me, both with street swaggers meant to intimidate. Hands loose at their sides. One had a bulge at his navel. Gun, I was guessing. The other slid a hand into his pocket and back out. A short length of rope. Metal on his other fingers. Brass knuckles. *Really?* I thought. *Really?* Two armed teenaged boys, younger than me, tattooed, Gun Boy with blondish dreadlocks and Brass Knucks Boy with an Afro, like from the seventies.

I reached the door and twisted the knob. Locked. Some small part of me wasn't surprised. A slightly bigger part was delighted. *Funnnnn,* it whispered. I ignored it, as always.

Using the storefront windows, I checked behind me. No one watching. No one approaching from behind. Just me and two gangbangers on the street, in view of the security camera of my new place of business. Which was locked. Yeah, really. Was this a test of some kind? An unlucky accident of timing? I retucked my braid, shrugged my shoulders to relax, and came to a stop, my back to the door. The guys separated, coming between me and my bike, a pincer move that cut off my retreat.

Fun, the crazy part of me murmured again. The crazy part of me that I had just discovered turned into an animal. Like my own personal were-lion, except not. The crazy part that had been penned in for years in the children's home, and wanted out now, to play with the humans, *play* being in the eyes of the beholder, like a cat playing—with a couple of stupid rats. Yeah. The crazy part of me, the part that the Christian children's home had worked so hard to knock out of me. It rose and glared at them through my eyes, and I chuffed with laughter, showing my teeth. Wanting them to try something. I couldn't help it.

Knucks Boy hesitated at my grin, just a slight hitch in his get-along, as Brenda, one of my housemothers, would have said. A tell, as my sensei would have said.

I set my bike-booted feet on the cracked sidewalk, the worn treads giving me good traction, much better than the fancy previously owned boots in the saddlebags. Stupid thoughts for a skinny teenage girl facing two armed men. I should run, bang on the security office door, and scream a little. But I didn't want to. *I wanted this.* I pulled in air through my nose and out through my mouth, relaxing further. *Fun,* the crazy voice panted. *Fun . . . fun . . . fun.*

"Hey, baby," Brass Knucks said, coming to a stop about five feet away. "Nice bike. How 'bout we go for a ride on that nice lil' bike?"

"No," I said, sounding bored.

"How 'bout we go for a ride on this?" Gun Boy asked, grabbing his crotch.

"Now, why would I want some scuzzy, flea-infested dude with BO and probably STDs?" I asked.

Gun Boy pulled his gun from his pants with a move that was all elbow and lifted shoulder. Nothing economical about it, nothing graceful. As the gun came free, I stepped up, blading my body, and kicked out. A single fluid kick that shoved his gun back into his gut, but with enough force to hurt. Hurt bad. His air whuffed out with a pained grunt, and his body bent in two. My leg bent and I clocked him with a knee to the face and a quick, follow-up one-two to his nose. Messy.

I backed away as he fell, kicking the gun under the closest van. I gave Knucks Boy a little four-fingered "come and get it" wave and he rushed in with a roundhouse. I ducked and tripped him. Head-butted him with the loose helmet. He landed on the other guy and I followed him down to drop a knee in his back. He made a little squeal as I landed. I caught the loose helmet, and I bopped him in the back of head with it. Kinda hard.

I stole the rope and the brass knuckles from his nerveless fingers and tossed them down the storm drain near the bike. Behind me the lock clicked and the door opened. A laconic voice asked, "You want me to call the police? You know. So you can make a police report?"

I stepped away from my would-be-attackers and considered. "How long do you think they'd be in jail?" I asked. "How much time would they do?"

"Hours and they'll be back out on the streets," the voice said. "Then they'll tie you up in court for weeks, and plea-bargain down to zip."

"You got it all on camera?" I asked.

"Yep."

"I want a copy." I shoved the guys over, out of their pile, and patted them down, removing their ID. I checked the pictures to the IDs and handed them to the man behind me. I said, "Anton Jevers and Wayne Roles Junior." I met the eyes of the one who was still mostly conscious. "There's this new thing called YouTube. You can upload video onto it for the whole world to see. I ever see your faces on this street again, I'll upload the video and everyone who knows you will be able to see you get beat up by a skinny girl in a bike helmet."

I went for the gun and picked it up with two fingers. I handed it too to the guy at the door, taking him in with quick glance. Younger than he sounded. Blondish. Jeans and T. Shoulder holster with a nine-millimeter. Scruffy beard. He smelled of coffee and Irish Spring soap.

"What do you want me to do with this?" the guy asked.

"Whatever PIs do with guns they accidently find on their doorsteps, dropped by inefficient muggers, unsuccessful rapists, and dumb-nuts."

He laughed. It was a nice laugh. "Anton, Wayne, you get on outta here or I'll call the po-lice on you. And I bet you both got a little something-something on you that the local law would like to confiscate. You," he said to me, "come on in. I got Cokes on ice and sandwiches in the microwave. I'd have been here sooner, but I was heating lunch and didn't realize you were in trouble until after the ding."

It sounded satisfactory to me, and I followed him inside. Closed and locked the door behind me. "My intern, I assume," he said as he popped the tops on Coke cans and shoved a foot-long club sandwich with bacon toward me over the desk. I nodded and took it and bit in, the taste so good and the bacon so hot that I almost groaned. I ate two more bites, taking the edge off my hunger, watching him, studying the office. He was prettier than I'd expected from the half glance I'd taken outside. The office was less dingy on the inside than it looked on the outside too. Three small desks, three desk chairs, folding chairs in the corner. One of those blue plastic watercoolers. Coffeemaker. Small brown refrigerator with a microwave on top. Unisex bathroom. Lockers. Gun safe bolted onto the floor in the corner. Closet. Iron-bound back door. Not bad. It smelled of mice and bacon and gunpowder, a combo that smelled unexpectedly great.

"Power of observation is important in this business," he said.

I grunted and kept eating. It had been hours since my last meal, and I'd been eating light since I spent my last twenty on the boots. Stupid move, that. Girly move. But they were killer boots. I grinned at the memory.

"My powers of observation told me that you should have run instead of taking on the neighborhood bullies," he said.

"Thought you said you were busy at the microwave," I said around a mouthful of bacon and lettuce leaves.

He shrugged. "Whatever. What did your powers of observation tell *you*?"

"That you set me up. Most likely," I hedged.

His brow wrinkled up in long horizontal lines that weren't visible until he looked puzzled. Or maybe mad? I wasn't sure. I still wasn't real good at reading people's emotions, but he smelled angry. Which was a really weirded-out thought. "Do I look stupid?" he asked. "Or like the kind of guy who would let a little girl get hurt? I was coming in through the back with sandwiches, and sticking them in to heat, when I saw it going down on the camera."

"Fine," I said. "From outside, I could see the light on through the cracks in the Sheetrock over the windows. The entry door is steel, set in a reinforced steel door casing. Over the door is a camera, the kind that moves. What looks like a water pipe runs up the outside wall in the corner and into the building through a tiny hole bored in the brick. Maybe for a retrofitted sprinkler system.

"Not that I've had much training yet, but the place looks like it was set up to survive attack by small-arms fire, Molotov cocktail fire, and maybe even attack by a rolling dump truck. The people inside might get smoked or crushed, but the files might survive, and the attack would be caught on camera to identify the perpetrators."

I stopped and ate some more. The bacon was really good. The other meat was beef and turkey. Even the lettuce tasted good. I was starving. I licked mayo off my thumb, slurped some Coke, and went on.

"The neighborhood is on the way down, except for the building on the corner, which is undergoing a remodeling, probably because of the way-cool windows on the second and third story." I set down the sandwich and held my hands out to the sides at angles. "Like this, with the whaddya call it, the cornerstone? Capstone? Like this." I reshaped my hands.

"Art Deco. Yeah. The upgrade is the beginning of the end of crime on this street. I'll miss Anton and Wayne."

I spluttered with laughter and held out my hand. "Jane Yellowrock. But I guess you know that, what with your mad powers of observation."

"Charles Davidson, but call me Nomad," he said. "Your boss and teacher for the next few months. You got a place to stay until your next paycheck?"

"Nope."

"Money for a hotel? A furnished room?"

"Nope."

Nomad sighed. "There's an inflatable mattress in the closet. Towels. Sheets. Don't let the cops figure it out—I'm not licensed for renters—but you keep your head down and you can bunk here until you make enough money to get a place. Soon as you get a stash, I know a few people who rent places. You can have cheap and dangerous in a few weeks, or more expensive and safer in a few months. We'll do a drive-by and you can evaluate how much you want privacy. But that's for later. Now we got a case." Nomad stood and wiped his face, gathered up all the papers, and tossed them into a trash can. "Keep the trash emptied. Dumpster out back. Place has roaches. Mice. But you don't look like the kind of woman who runs from either."

I shook my head. "What kind of case?"

"Cheating husband."

"You like domestic cases?"

"Hate 'em. But they make up about seventy percent of a PI's business. Bring your bike inside and we'll keep it locked up. Safer. Anton and Wayne are aggressive and stupid and they might think about revenge. You pass your CC yet?"

I nodded. I had passed the concealed carry permit the week before I passed my classroom training for my PI license. "No gun. No money. Do I get the internship?"

"Despite the little snafu on the street, yeah. And you won't need a gun on this trip." He pointed to the restroom. "Pee while you can. Female anatomy isn't particularly well suited to long-term stakeouts."

I nodded.

"Other than answering questions, you're not very talkative, are you?" he observed, cocking his head.

"Nope." I went into the restroom and closed the door. And smiled at myself in the polished metal mirror over the sink, my amber eyes glowing gold with excitement. "I'm in," I whispered. "I did it. I got the job."

It was in a little run-down storefront security and PI business. The pay sucked. And I loved it. I loved it all.

Cat Tats

Rick raised his head, the tendons in his neck straining. Nausea roiled in his stomach and up his throat at the slight movement, and he dropped his head back. He was lying faceup. The rafters were barely visible over his head in the dusky, gloomy light. The familiar scent of hay and horses was strong in his nostrils, but it wasn't the hay of his parents' barn. There was an acrid undertang to this scent, as if the box stalls hadn't been mucked out in a long while, and it was musty, as if horses hadn't used the premises recently. He rolled his head to the side and saw a shaft of light filtering through dusty air, falling through a wide crack in the wall. No. Not Dad's barn. He'd never let it get in this condition.

This place was abandoned.

He almost called out, but something stopped him, some wise wisp of self that wasn't still hazy from the raspberry Jell-O shooters. He tried to sit up, but pain shot from his hands and pooled in his shoulders like liquid fire. His arms were bound.

He craned to see, blinking to clear his vision. His arms were pulled up high in a V and shackled with old-fashioned iron cuffs chained to rings. His legs were stretched out too, similarly secured, his body making a dual V. He was naked. Instantly his body constricted and his breathing sped. He struggled to rise and discovered that he lay on a wide black square stone, cool to the touch despite the Louisiana heat. On the ground around the stone, touching the four corners, was a circle of metal, black in the light.

Terror shot through his veins, clearing the last of the alcohol out of his system. His heart pounded. His breath came fast, gasping. He broke into a hot sweat, which instantly cooled into a clammy stink.

He jerked his arms and legs hard, giving it all he had to pull himself

free. But nothing gave. The pain multiplied in his legs and arms like lightning agony, at his shoulders and groin with liquid fire. His wrists and
ankles burned, the iron cuffs binding him, cutting into his flesh. He turned
his head to the side and retched, but his stomach was empty and his mouth
dry as desert sand.

When the nausea passed, Rick dropped his head back. Forced himself
to breathe deeply, slowly, despite his racing heart. To analyze. To think. To
be calm. He closed his eyes and mouth, and worked to slow his mind, to
contain his racing fear. Around him the barn was silent. Lifeless. *Where
the hell am I?*

When he was calmer, he raised his head again, and studied everything
he could see, everything he could hear, analyzing it all. The barn was old,
of post-and-beam construction, the frame of twelve-by-twelve beams
fitted together with pegs and notches and the vertical boards of the walls
nailed in place to the frame. There were four box stalls, one on each corner, with a tack room on one side between two stalls, and opposite the
tack room, between the stalls on the other side, was a wide space to saddle
and groom horses. The center area was an open passageway more than
twelve feet wide, with moldy hay stacked on the wall opposite the double
front doors. It had to be more than fifty years old, and the wood showed
signs of termites and the kind of damage only time and disuse will provide.
Foliage grew up close to the sides of the barn, vines and tree limbs reaching into the interior. Part of the tin roof was missing, and birds flew in
and out, twittering and cooing. He could hear no sound of engines, which
meant he was miles from any highway, miles from any airport, from any
city, far from help. He could hear the faint sound of water rippling, echoing, a soft trickle, like a bayou moving sluggishly nearby. Rarely, he could
hear a plop as something fell into the water. All of that was bad. But at
least he was alone. For now. That much was good.

When he was calmer, he looked down at himself. If his body had been
a clock, his arms would have been nearly at ten and two, and his legs close
to eight and four. It looked familiar, and from his alcohol- and drug-fogged
brain came an image: He was positioned like Leonardo da Vinci's Vitru-
vian Man. Like an archetype. Bound in a witches' circle, on a square altar.
Like a goat for slaughter.

Was it the full moon? The new moon? Was he the sacrifice in some black-magic ceremony? A long shiver racked down his spine. Rick had a lot of specialized training under his belt, but nothing he'd learned in his criminal justice classes at Tulane, at the police academy afterward, or in the focused and elite training provided by his current covert employers had prepared him for this.

Judging from the angle of the sunbeam, the sun was setting. Or rising. The beam fell across the barn onto a rat-eaten saddle and bridle, and a bedraggled red horse blanket across a joist. As he watched, a bird alighted on the blanket and pecked, eating whatever it found in the ripped, rotting cloth. It pulled out a bit of stuffing and, with a flutter of wings, carried it away into the darkness of the rafters. To the side, against the nearest stall wall, was a glass of water with a red straw in it. His mouth felt even drier at the sight, but there was no way for him to reach it. Rick dropped back his head.

In the academy, he had attracted the attention of the black suits in the Justice Department. He had been co-opted for an undercover assignment, and given a plausible story and a believable problem that got him "kicked out of NOPD." He'd jumped on the opportunity, even though it had meant a false arrest for assault, even though his family couldn't know. And even though, if successful, he'd be alone with vamps, without backup. On the surface, he was a pariah to the cops, but he'd been working to infiltrate the vamps' organization for the New Orleans Police Department, the local FBI field office, and some high muckety-mucks in the DOJ.

A pretty face and a checkered past, along with the police training and the criminal justice degree from Tulane, had made him the perfect hire as part of a security detail for one of Leo Pellissier's scions, Roman Munoz. Munoz was a low-level vamp scumbag needing muscle for hire. Rick had worked himself up in Munoz's organization, and when his new boss went to jail for tax fraud—the first successful vamp conviction in Louisiana, courtesy of Rick's tips, passed to his handler—Rick had migrated into odd jobs for the vampire community: protection gigs, strong-arm stuff, and security. Watching for the golden opportunity to draw the eyes of the MOC—the Master of the City—Leo Pellissier.

Across the barn, a field mouse with tiny round ears scampered across the floor and into a hole. Above Rick, wings fluttered, sounding larger than the sparrow-sized bird. He tried his bindings again, trying to think. Getting nowhere.

He had proven himself and was now an established and trusted part of the lower-level vampire organization. He knew people. He had skills usually cultivated by thugs and thieves, and yet, thanks to his LaFleur upbringing in New Orleans society, he could blend in almost anywhere, even in the upscale Mithran culture. He was versatile, smart, and willing. The vamps seemed to like him and were using his services. Lately, he had done some work for his uncle, who was security chief and primo blood-servant for Katie of Katie's Ladies, which put him one step closer to Pellissier.

He'd been undercover now for more than two years, a long time by covert standards. When his successful stint undercover was done, he would be perfectly placed to move up quickly in law enforcement. But the most recent assignment had proven complex. He was trying to discover where the Mithrans kept their rogues, the new vampires who were bitten and turned but not yet ready for public view. And he was trying to find out something—anything—about the MOC's financial structure. Both had proven elusive, but he had been making headway.

Until his ego let him think he was about to get lucky with Isleen of the cute smile and the bounteous breasts. And the big fangs. A girl. He had been brought down by a girl. He was so damn stupid.

The last thing he remembered was the bar and Isleen, the girl vamp he'd been trying to pick up. And succeeding. Blond, blue-eyed, about five two, and built to please a man, she had flirted steadily with him, even buying him drinks. . . . When did a gorgeous bombshell ever have to buy a guy drinks? Stupid. Yeah, that was him.

He tried to raise his arms; the shackles burned his wrists. He lifted his head again, studying the stone and the witch circle. The stone was polished smooth, not with a high shine but with a matte luster. But it was dusty, as if it hadn't been used in a long time. And one corner was broken off, with a long crack weaving brokenly toward the center. The circle looked like iron in the dim light, but iron would interfere with any spell casting. So maybe silver, highly tarnished. Or copper? Could some witches use copper? But why had a vampire turned him over to the witches? The two races hated each other.

He checked the shaft of light again. It was less sharply angled, nearly straight across, and tinted with pink. Setting. The sun was setting. He shivered in the warm air. Night was coming. Most witch ceremonies were at night, weren't they? At least the black spells? He had to get out of here. He fought his bonds. The pain in his wrists and ankles was liquid heat. Blood trickled from his flesh as it swelled around the too-tight cuffs. Something crawled up his inner thigh, tickling its way through the hair. Spider. Had to be. He bounced his butt hard and dislodged the bug, landing on it. Crushing it beneath his buttock. A soft laugh escaped his throat. Sounding more sob than amusement.

Taking only minutes, the sunbeam reddened and thinned and grew fainter. And vanished. And night fell. Quickly. It took only seconds for the dark to smother him. Heart pounding, he heard only the twitter of birds in the rafters, the rustle of small rodents, and the sound of his breathing—too fast, too harsh. Choked with fear.

Dark. Very dark. The new moon, then. A new-moon ceremony. He tried to remember what the new moon meant for the black arts. And then he heard singing. A soft melody, unfamiliar, rising and falling, from outside the barn. And footsteps. Brushing the earth. Swishing, like a dress sweeping the ground and foliage with each step. Fear crawled up his throat again, and he was glad his stomach was empty. If he vomited, he would be lost. Too bad he hadn't eaten. Maybe it would be a kinder fate.

Something metallic rattled from the double-barn-door entrance. One door groaned as it opened, the echo of the rusty hinges twanging into the night. It was too dark to see anyone enter, but the soft swishing sounds of fabric moving through grass grew stronger, closer.

"You're awake! Good! I brought you something." Isleen's voice. Childlike, happy, as if he were in her bed and she'd just returned from an errand. "Do you like it?"

Rick licked his lips, dry and cracked, drawing up the short introductory course in hostage negotiation he'd taken at the academy. Keep them talking. Make the kidnapper see you as a person, not a tool. Yeah. Right. That was not gonna work so well with a vamp, especially if she was hungry. Make them do things for you, so they had to associate with you as a person. That one might do. . . .

"I can't see in the dark," he whispered.

"Well, poo. Of course you can't, you dear little human. I'll fix that."

In the dark, he heard the soft *shush* of cloth and the sharper *scritch* of a match. Light so bright it hurt flamed and lit the barn. He saw Isleen holding a dusty Coleman lantern, the logo in red on the gray metal can. The light gleamed on her face, porcelain in the sudden illumination. She was dressed in white, the bodice close fitting, pushing up her breasts like a corset might. The dress was long with a handkerchief hem, pointed, embroidered, and beaded with white pearls, like a dress one of his sisters had worn to the prom, and it caught the light like satin or silk. Her hair was down, brushed to a golden shine, with a wreath of braided flowers on her head. White orchids resting in green leaves.

She set the lantern on the black marble stone and held out her arms. "Better now? Do you like it?" She twirled slowly as if modeling the dress.

"Pretty," he said.

"And me?" she said, sounding just a bit put out. Her lower lip was protruding in a pout.

"Pretty," he said. And his voice croaked with thirst on the word. "Ohhhh. You're thirsty." He heard a little *snick*. The sound of fangs clicking down into place. "So am I." Her voice dropped lower, suggestive, a sensual caress. Isleen was close enough now that he could see her eyes in the lantern light. Pupils blown, black as the devil's heart, resting in the bloody sclera of her eyes. And something in the way she tilted her head, her blond hair falling in a long slow wave, looked . . . not quite right. The little vampire wasn't just thirsty—she was hungry.

But instead of biting him, she brought the glass of water over and— sinking onto the dusty stone at his side—brought the red straw to his lips. He drank, a desperate sucking sound that she seemed to like. Her face softened into desire and she licked her lips, a flick of tongue between inch- and-a-half-long fangs. The straw had a bend, and she set it on the stone so that he could reach it by lifting his head and craning to the side. Curl- ing his lips around the top, he again sucked deeply, and finished the water with a loud sputter of air through the straw, leaving only a dribble in the bottom.

He focused on Isleen. She was bent over his left wrist, her mouth open, breathing in the scent of his blood with a soft *scree* of sound, one with a muted moan of desire in it. Her tongue darted out and licked across the seeping wound, along the sides of his wrist and down the center of his palm. Almost instantly, the pain abated in his wrist. Pleasure trailed up his arm. His heart boomed hard, a bass drum in his chest, in his ears. He dropped his head back to the stone, breathing out a faint gasp of desire. And Isleen filled his field of vision, imprisoning him with her eyes, one hand splayed on his chest. "I like the way you tassste," she hissed. "And you are mine now. Miiiine." Isleen placed a slow kiss to the soft part of his belly where his rib cage ended and his belly began. He could feel his pulse pound there, in the huge artery just beneath her lips. Rick was quite certain that she was mad.

He fought his rising fear, knowing that she could smell it and could hear his heart pound, knowing his reactions would incite her predatory instincts. She laughed, the low, sensual sound vibrating deep through her lips into his belly.

Looking over her shoulder, Rick saw the barn door open. Only a crack, but the silence let him hope—for long, hopeless moments—that he might yet be saved. And then a small voice said, "I am here, mistress."

Isleen rose and whirled so quickly it was dizzying, as if time stuttered and stumbled and he missed some vital second where she moved. She crouched and hissed. Stopped for a second and slowly stood upright. "You are late."

"Yes, mistress. There was traffic." When Isleen didn't respond, the newcomer said, "I have my equipment."

"You may begin. But first I will eat. To your knees, girl."

Rick heard a soft *thud* as knees hit the earth of the old barn. The voice whispered even more softly, "I am yours, mistress. But I thought you wanted him bound to you by the end of the new moon."

Isleen paused again, that otherworldly stillness that was another aspect of the Mithrans, the vampire race. It was a stillness that mimicked death, as inhuman as the speed with which they could move and as strange as the need for human blood. "And my drinking from you will impede this?"

"Even if you allowed me to drink from you, I am weak. You have fed deeply, and my body has not yet recovered. I would not be able to finish in time."

Rick understood. Isleen had taken too much for too many days. The girl—Isleen's blood-servant—was dangerously anemic.

"I shall hunt, then. I will return before dawn." Isleen looked back at him over her shoulder, her head cocking, birdlike, the angle not possible for a human, her hair falling like silk. "And I will have my vengeance on Regina Katarina Fonteneau for taking what was mine."

Regina Katarina Fonteneau . . . had to be Katie of Katie's Ladies. But how would killing him hurt Katie?

Another one of those broken seconds later, Isleen was gone. Night air whooshed in softly to fill the place where she had stood. Rick smelled honeysuckle and wild jasmine from the vines on the barn's walls. In Isleen's place was the new arrival. His new tormentor. She was pale skinned, standing somewhere around five feet, and her hair was dyed Goth black. Dark circles rimmed beneath her eyes, and the flesh of her throat was bruised, with blue veins tracing beneath the surface. Her neck, throat, and upper chest were crusted over with scarring. Some of the wounds were fresh, puckered, and oozing. Vampire bites weren't supposed to do that. Vampire saliva and blood were supposed to have healing properties. Unless something was wrong with Isleen. There had been rumors of vampires with illnesses, notably the long-chained scions he was supposed to find.

The girl lit more lanterns, light flooded the room, and Rick raised his head, looking at where Isleen had licked his left wrist. His wrist, hand, and arm were pain free, but the skin was still inflamed. A pustule was forming on the outer part of his wrist, and red streaks were running up his forearm. He wasn't being healed. He was being made sick. His heart sped up again, and Rick turned his head to the girl.

She was a fragile thing, her clothes dirty, blood dried on the neckline. She lifted a case, one that looked a lot like a gun box but bigger, and set it beside him. When she opened it, he could see needles in sterile packets, and chemicals, and his heart painfully skipped a beat. She was going to torture him. With needles. *Jesus, Mary, and Joseph. She's going to use needles. Son of a bitch.* He hated needles. He struggled again, pulling at the bonds. The sound was muted but for his cursing, which seemed to echo through the deserted barn. His energy was quickly depleted, and he fell back, banging his head on the black stone, gasping, sobbing. He was so dehydrated that his eyes stayed dry. He couldn't break free. He had to use other talents.

Humanize yourself. Talk to the captor. Right . . . "What's your name?" he croaked. Ignoring him, the girl lifted out vials and bottles of chemicals, and set them on a small tray, one she could carry and maneuver easily. When she was satisfied, she stepped back and uncoiled an electrical extension cord. Which meant there was a generator—which he couldn't hear—or a building nearby. Someplace to escape to. Maybe find a phone. "What's your name?" he said again, and when she didn't answer, he said, "My name's Rick."

"I don't care," she whispered. She took out a small clock and opened out little legs on the back, making a stand, placing it so that she could see its face. The time read nine twenty-seven. "I don't care what you do or why she brought you here. I don't care if you rescue puppies and heal the sick with a touch of your hand. I'm going to do what she wants. So shut up." She placed the glass, newly filled with water, at his lips.

He drank, and when he spoke, his voice was stronger. "Why? Why are you going to do what she wants?"

The girl's hands stilled. She was so thin that light from the closest lantern spilled through her flesh, turning her bones dark and red, ghostlike and ephemeral. "She tried to force me as her blood-servant"—she glanced away, and when she swallowed, it looked painful—"but she couldn't bind me. I don't know why. But when she failed, she lost control. She nearly drained me."

"Forcing a blood bond is illegal according to Mithran law. So is draining humans."

"I know."

"We could go to the Master of the City. Leo Pellissier is big on vampire law and order. He would make her stop. Punish her."

"I can't." She tried to take a breath, and it sounded like silk tearing, wet and painful along her throat. "I tried to get away. Three times. And this last time . . ." Her voice broke, mewling like a kitten crushed in a fist. Tears filled her eyes, and she rolled her lips in, as if sealing in a memory and its pain. Her breath was tortured, and she pressed her pale hand to her even paler throat. "This last time . . . she took my brother. He's seven." The girl turned her face away, hiding behind a spill of black hair. "She made me watch as she fed on him."

A first feeding always had sexual overtones. What the girl described was molestation and torture all at once. Rick yanked against his bonds, a growl coming from him, part pain, mostly anger. "Let me loose. We can take her down if we work together."

"No. If she dies, Jason is dead. She hid him with her scions," the girl said, "which she calls the long-chained. I don't know where. And if she doesn't come back, they'll all die. If she lives, and if I don't do what she wants, she'll make me watch him die."

"We can find him in time," he snarled.

"I can't take that chance. But thank you for the anger. No one has been angry for us in . . . in forever."

Rick shoved down his rage. It wouldn't help. Neither would the fight-or-flight instincts that battled through his blood. Forcibly he silenced his fury, tamping it down, sealing it off. "What does she want?" he asked when he could, his voice low and even.

Her movements economical and fiercely determined, the girl positioned the lanterns around him, uncapped a marker, and placed it against his skin at his shoulder. "She wants you bound to her," she whispered. "And if she can't do it with her vampire gift, she'll do it with magic." She began drawing on his skin with the marker, drawing and wiping away most of the ink, leaving only a faint outline.

"You're going to tattoo me?" he asked, incredulous, relief flooding his system. "That's all?"

"A tattoo of binding. Using her blood and animal blood in the final part of the spell. The blood will bind you to her. You'll be a blood-servant. Of sorts." The girl looked at him through her bangs, her eyes smoky brown. "It's an old spell. I think she stole it from my grandmother. And I'm sorry to use it on you." Her voice dropped lower. "So very sorry."

Hot sweat broke out along his skin, and his sphincters pulled in so tight that his belly ached. He swore violently as his hope evaporated. *The girl's a witch.* Rick raised his head and looked at the black marble beneath him. Considered the metal ring. An impressive witches' circle, one used for a long time by powerful witches. Probably the girl's grandmother and her coven. He dropped his head back. "Can your grandmother break it once it's done?"

"She could. But Isleen killed her. Broke her neck and threw her in the bayou." Her voice shook, and there was something dark and terrible in her tone. Rick knew Isleen had made the girl watch.

The cute little vampire, Isleen, needed a stake and a beheading. As soon as he got free. Assuming he could get free before his will was sapped and he was magically bound to the crazy bitch vamp. But if one witch knew how to break the spell, then others would too. Assuming he could find them. Assuming . . . assuming a hell of a lot for a guy stretched out naked in a witches' circle. He concentrated on regulating his breathing, feeling the pen against his skin. Pen, then cool, damp cloth. Pen, then cloth. He had to keep his head if he was going to get out of this. He marshaled the negotiation techniques taught in class. "What's your name?"

"Loriann." She lifted his head and shoved a pillow under his neck so that he could see without strain. She turned her back a moment, and Rick quickly scanned the barn. Nothing. Nothing there to help him at all. Not even an old hoe to fight with.

"Put out a finger. Cut the cards."

When Rick looked at her, she was holding cards, bigger than playing cards. Tarot. "I'm Catholic. I don't read tarot." Which was utterly stupid considering his current position, but refusal was instinct, pounded into him by a lifetime of nuns.

"I don't care. Put out a finger or"—Loriann pulled in a breath and firmed her face, steeled her voice—"or I'll make you wish you had."

Shock spilled through him, an icy chill. "You're not a black witch," he managed.

Loriann closed her eyes. Her skin paled even more, looking almost translucent in the lantern light. "It doesn't matter what I am anymore," she whispered. "White, black, blood, light, or dark." She laughed, the sound broken. "I've lost myself. I've lost my choice. So put out your finger and cut this deck, or I'll hurt you."

Straining to move the blood-deprived digit, Rick put out a finger. Placed his nail into the deck about midway through, parting the cards. Loriann separated the deck and shuffled until the oversized cards were well mixed. Then she laid one out. It was a skeleton riding a horse, and the legend beneath the picture read DEATH. "Great," he said. "This is why I don't do tarot."

Loriann said, "Death isn't usually real death. It means change. Now shut up." After that she ignored him and laid out twelve cards in a circular pattern around Death, mumbling to herself. The last card, at the twelve-o'clock position, was the Hanged Man. Whatever she saw didn't make her happy, and she gathered up the cards and reshuffled them, mumbling, "I never liked Aunt Morella's time reading anyway." Louder, she said, "Stick out a finger."

Again he cut the deck with his fingernail, and Loriann laid out a card. The title at the bottom read KNIGHT OF WANDS; the knight was wearing plate armor and riding a red horse, and carried a stick with leaves growing out of it. "This is you," she said. Over that card, at an angle, she laid out another card. It was Death. Again. "This is the problem."

"No shit." He laughed, and it sounded hopeless even to his own ears. Over that she laid another. The card depicted a woman sitting on a throne between two pillars: one white, one black. She wore a white crown like a nun's wimple and a white dress, with a cross on her chest. The card read HIGH PRIESTESS. "Hmmm. This is the solution or best course of action." Quickly Loriann laid out four cards: the first at the bottom, the next to the left, then the top card, placing the last card to the right, in a cross pattern. She laid down four more cards in a line to the far right. The last card she set down showed two naked people. The Lovers. She studied the cards silently. Then gathered them all up again.

"What?" he asked.

She shuffled and held out the deck. "Again." Rick complied. He figured anything that kept her from sticking a needle into him was a good thing. This time she laid out three rows of seven cards. The far left column came up as three knights, the knights of Swords, Wands, and Cups. "Interesting," she said, surprised. She looked at him quickly, something new in her eyes, and then glanced away. Down the middle column were Death, the Queen of Swords, and the Lovers. Loriann studied the cards up and down, left to right, as the night flowed on. It was now ten twenty-five. Closing in on the witching hour.

Loriann arranged the cards, putting them into an order that must have made sense to her, and shoved them into a box, then into a small tin at her side. It was brightly painted in little dots of color, like a print of stained glass in miniature. On the top, the Virgin Mary stood in a pointed, arched window.

The witch took out another box from the tin, this one larger, the box older. On the front was a painted picture of a shadowy woman standing in front of a cauldron, a cat with a bobbed tail at her feet and cave walls at her back. Stalactites dripped from overhead. A witch. "My grandmother's cards," Loriann said softly. Her cheeks took on a hint of color and she leaned forward, as if hiding behind the fall of her ink black hair. She went through the deck, rearranging the placement of the cards. "No one has used them in . . . in a long time." Loriann separated the cards into three stacks of differing depths.

Two stacks were composed of cards that had titles on them and one stack contained cards with only numbers. She shuffled each stack until each was well mixed, and lifted a small stack toward him. She said, "Major Arcana. Cut."

Rick forced out a nail and directed it into the partial deck. He had lost feeling in his hand. He figured that wasn't a good thing.

"Personages of the Minor Arcana," she said, lifting the second partial deck. "The Court Cards. Cut." He cut the second partial deck and the third, which was larger, containing what looked like nearly half of the total number of cards. Loriann shuffled each stack, made him cut the decks again, then laid the cards out in the same three-row pattern as before. This time some cards were taken from the top of one pile, some from another. "Gramma liked gypsy readings, but she did them the way her mother taught her, with the three rows of seven, each column from a specific stack, and to the side, a cross of the Major Arcana. Her cards were specially painted just for her," Loriann said, "and her deck is different. It has different . . ." Her voice trailed away, as if she had just realized she was speaking aloud. She pressed her lips together and bent her head, her hair sliding forward so that he couldn't see her face.

When Loriann finished laying out the cards, at the four corners and down the center column were the Court Cards. To the left top was the Queen of Pentacles, upside down, a wolf asleep at her feet. At the top right was the King of Swords, an African lion at his feet and his sword made of gold. The left bottom corner was the Page of Pentacles. He was a vampire with a scroll under his arm. The right bottom corner was the King of Wands, and he was a witch with red hair, and with fire exploding from his wand, which was clearly a weapon. A huge owl flew overhead. "No cup cards," she murmured. But she didn't explain.

The center column was also composed of Loriann's Court of the Minor Arcana. The top card was the Queen of Swords—a woman in black, a wildcat with a bobbed tail and yellow eyes on her lap, claws drawing blood on her right thigh. The queen held a sword with a silver blade dripping with blood. The Knight of Wands was the center card: He sat on a rearing black horse, holding a bloodied stake and silver sword, with vampire heads beneath the horse's hooves. A wolf howled in the background, head angled up toward a full moon. The Knight of Swords was at the bottom but was upside down, the first time a knight had appeared that way. His bloodied sword was silver and black, and a huge cat—a black leopard with yellow-gold eyes—sat on the horse's rump.

The cards were so old that paint flecked off them as Loriann worked. The edges were rounded and worn from long use. Despite himself, Rick was intrigued. It was almost as if he could sense meaning in the cards, but it seemed to be just out of reach or around the next corner. As if all he had to do was reach out or take a single step, and he would understand. But the significance was elusive, fragmentary.

On the layout of cards in a cross pattern to the side were the Major Arcana. The Wheel of Fortune was in the middle, with animals racing on the wheel— a wolf, a big black cat, a flying owl, an alligator, a spotted dog, and a bear. Around it in a cross pattern was the Devil—a horned, wolf-headed beast with owl's wings, a horse's legs, and cloven feet. The Devil had bloody fangs, and claws hidden in the wing feathers. The Hanged Man was an American Indian chief in full feathered headdress. He had been tortured before the hanging, and a black leopard was curled up on the hanging branch above him, sleeping. At his feet were a small wolf, or a coyote, watching him and salivating, and a grouping of turkey buzzards staring at his head. A card called Strength was painted with an angry mountain lion, screaming, claw-ing the air, sitting on a dead vampire, both with fangs bared. The last card was the Tower. It was on fire, and people and animals were falling out of it.

Loriann studied the tarot placement for a while, while Rick tried to read something—anything—in the cards. "Animals," Loriann muttered. "Vampires. Change everywhere." And then, "Ahhh. I see."

"Well, I don't."

She gathered up the cards and put them away, then brought her needles and tattooing equipment closer. "Your future is both set and undecided. There are two moments when you will be allowed to choose, and both moments will change the course of your future. One is now, with the tattoo and the blood I'll use to bind you to Isleen. You may choose canines, equines, or felines. Which do you desire?"

He almost said *horses*, but the word that came from his mouth was "Cats." He stopped, surprised, because he detested his sisters' cats, and preferred dogs and horses. He shook that away and asked, "But why me? Isleen said something about revenge on Katarina Fonteneau. Is that Katie of Katie's Ladies?"

Loriann nodded. "Katie did something bad to Isleen a long time ago. I'm not sure what. But she can use this spell to get back at her through your bloodline."

"How?"

Loriann looked at him in true surprise. "Because Katie is your mother's great-great-something-or-other-grandma."

"N—" Rick started to disagree and stopped.

The memories of some weird things returned. Money for his education, deposited into his account, a gift from a distant cousin. His sister's medical bills for leukemia, the huge ones not covered by insurance. They had amounted to nearly four hundred thousand dollars. Paid in full by that same distant cousin. His mother disappearing on Christmas Eve every year for an entire night. The strange French-accented voice on the phone several times, calling for his mother. At night. Always and only at night.

Son of a bitch. He was related to one of the city's most powerful vampires. And the cops had sent him in undercover to find out about her—

"I can tell you don't have tats," Loriann said, drawing him back from his past. He turned his face to hers, trying to hide his shock. She shoved her hair behind an ear and almost smiled. Her eyes flickered down his body and back up, lingering at the V of his legs before she returned to her work. "This may hurt."

The first needle pierced his skin.

At dawn, Loriann put away her torture implements. Rick was sweating, shaking with the continual pain. He had no idea how people could go through this over and over, getting full-sleeve tats, tats on their necks and throats. Under their arms, on their privates, on sensitive, tender skin.

Loriann sighed, and he felt fatigue move through her and into his own skin, a shared exhaustion. Over the course of the night, he had become deeply aware of the little witch, pain bringing them close, making him conscious of her breath, alert to the slightest shift of her posture and position, sensitive to her ever-changing emotions, responsive to her intense concentration. It was as if they were two parts of one creature, sharing energy, breath, and his pain—one part administering pain, the other part enduring it. His blood had sealed the deal, trickling several times across his shoulder to the stone beneath him.

He shuddered as his tormentor unclasped the shackles on his right arm. She stepped to his left arm and unclasped that restraint as well.

He tightened his muscles as he had done over and over in the night to relieve the pain of immobility, contracting and releasing. He dragged his numb arms up and shoved his elbows under him. Groaning, he forced himself upward, reclining on his elbows and forearms. Loriann moved clockwise through the dim dawn to his legs.

"I'm going to let you relieve yourself now," she said softly. "Eat something. Drink. Shower off."

"Clean up my blood on the stone?" he said, mocking.

"No," she whispered. "It stays."

He understood. It was part of the sacrifice.

She clicked his left leg shackle loose. He didn't tense. He didn't let his breathing hitch, knowing that somehow, through the bond established during the night of pain, she would expect what he planned. In a moment he could get away. Disable Loriann. Get to the city's vampire headquarters. Tell the blood-servants what was going on. Get help for the kid, Jason. But no matter what, no way was he lying down again on the black stone.

The shackle fell from his left leg with a heavy *clank*. The witch moved to his right leg. He couldn't feel sensation beyond agony in his limbs, but he forced the toes of both feet to wiggle, and he could see them move in the slowly brightening light. He closed his eyes and breathed in. Brought up his free leg. Tried not to tense in preparation for a lunge.

A *click* sounded, different from the other sounds. He opened his eyes, looked down. And cursed. With a clumsy roll, he rose and stumbled across the barn. Was brought up short. He tumbled to the dusty floor. Loriann had attached a shackle to his right ankle and had run a chain from that to one of the rings in the black stone. The chain was less than ten feet long.

Lying in the dust of the stable floor, Rick started to laugh, the sound hollow and echoing. The peals sounded half-mad. And he couldn't stop.

He rolled to his back and held out his leg, shaking it, the chain's heavy links tinkling low. If he had an axe, he could try to cut through it. Or he could cut off his foot. And bleed to death getting to help. Of course, if he had an axe, he could kill Isleen . . . and thereby kill Loriann's seven-year-old brother, Jason. Rick was as trapped as Loriann was.

His muscles were weak from being tied down; his hands and feet were numb and swollen. The pustule at his wrist had broken open during the night and re-formed larger and flatter than before. Red streaks ran up his arm nearly to his elbow. The lower arm was hot to the touch. Blood poisoning. Gangrene could follow on its heels. He needed antibiotics or he might lose the arm. He had to get out of here. But Loriann wouldn't help, and he was more exhausted than he could ever have imagined, his muscles quivering from stress and immobility.

Sick, aching in ways he had never known a man could hurt, Rick rose and relieved himself in a metal bucket, no longer caring about unimportant things like privacy. Tears smeared through the sweaty, bloody barn dust coating him.

He accepted the food and water that Loriann brought—soup right from the can, cling peaches in heavy syrup, and two liters of water—knowing it might be drugged, but not having any choice. Telling himself it wasn't over. He wasn't dead or blood bound yet. He needed strength to get away, and he had until only eight p.m., when the sun set, to accomplish that goal. Getting drugged from the food was a risk, but no worse than being too drained to attempt an escape if the opportunity presented itself.

He spotted his clothes—boxers, jeans, shirt, socks, and boots—piled in a corner, doing him no good. He couldn't get the pants over the shackle, and he wouldn't be able to wear a shirt anytime soon, not with the tattoo painful on his left shoulder. He studied Loriann's work in the pale light but couldn't make out the picture, not looking down on it. It might have been waves or mountains. Or both.

Loriann went into the shadows of the barn, and when she came back, she was dragging a hose, held kinked off in one hand. "They used it to cool off horses and wash them." She indicated the hose. "It's only cold water, but at least you'll be clean. If you want," she said. When he nodded, she pointed to a corner. "The floor's lower there, and the water will drain."

Naked, no longer caring, Rick clanked to the corner and stood, his back to her, his hands up high, supporting himself against the barn wall. The first gush of water felt icy, and he tensed, his skin pebbling as the spray drenched him from head to toe. But he relaxed as the grime and sweat of the night washed away. He turned slowly, facing the water, wondering what he should be feeling in this moment, as the little witch washed him. The water stopped, and he stood as Loriann kinked the hose again and dragged it away. When she returned, she tossed him a towel. He took it and dried off with the rough, coarse terry cloth. She gave him another bottle of water, which he opened and drank, feeling more human. He took the sheet Loriann offered and wrapped it around himself. It would give him some semblance of protection from bug bites. The insects had come in during the night, attracted by blood and sweat and misery.

"Sit," she said softly, pointing at the black stone circle. "I can help you."

"Like you've been helping me all night?" he said.

She shrugged. "It's up to you."

Too tired to argue, Rick sat on the edge of the stone altar and held his head in his hands. His fingers weren't working well, and his toes were on fire, aching with the return of blood supply. Prickles of electric pain ran up and down his limbs. Body limp, spirit dejected, he looked through his too-long, lank hair at the barn door, his way out if he could make it that far, before closing his eyes.

Loriann put her hands on his shoulders, and a moment later a cool release, like a salve, washed over him, passing through his skin into his muscles and deeper into his bones. He took a breath and let it out. He hated to feel grateful to his torturer, but he did. Grudgingly he said, "Thank you. That feels better."

"I'm sorry," she whispered. "I don't have a choice."

"We always have a choice," he said. "Always." He raised his head. "You have a choice now. You could go to Katie, or to my parents, or to the cops, or to Leo Pellissier. You have a choice."

"And my brother would die."

"She's going to kill your brother anyway, Loriann. And you know it." She didn't answer. When he looked up again, Loriann was gone.

He was pretty sure the food or water was drugged, but not enough to knock him out, just enough to leave him sluggish and woozy. The beams holding up the roof seemed faraway, shifting with shadows like bird wings; the wing shadows lightened, changed position, and lengthened again as the day moved past. Insects swarmed around Rick, biting and buzzing, gnats attacking his eyes and dive-bombing his breathing passages. His mouth and nose covered by an edge of the sheet, he slept until noon, surprisingly dreamless, or with no dreams worth remembering. Maybe the unconscious mind just couldn't compete with a reality like sitting through needle torture for hours, torture that made less sense than any dream.

Loriann had left him water, and he forced himself to drink every time he woke. Toward what he judged was midafternoon, the drugs wore off and the nerves in his muscles and flesh began to protest, itching and burning, tight with the futile resistance of the night before. He stood and began to stretch, trying to remember the moves his youngest sister had made when she took up yoga and vegetarianism at age thirteen. Surprisingly the slow stretching helped. When he could move without too much pain, he shoved an edge of his sheet between the shackle and his skin, and began to walk the length of his chain. It clanked hollowly as he moved; the dust beneath him was fine, almost soothing, as it slid around his feet.

Pulling the chain to its full length, Rick searched the parts of the barn he could reach. He found a rake head, the kind with five thick tines for throwing hay. One tine was broken, but he could wrap the fingers of his left hand around the handle's base and slide those of his right through the tines. It was a pretty good weapon against a lesser being than a vampire. For Isleen, the handle would have made a better weapon, a stake to plunge into her black heart. But there was no handle.

I could kill the girl, though.

The thought shocked, like a bucket of icy water. He stood unmoving, his thigh muscles trembling, his stomach cramping with hunger. The iron cool between his fingers.

A weapon. He could kill Loriann. Kill her and take her key. And go to the Master of the City. He turned the rake head over in his hands. The iron was hard and deadly, rusted at the break. The tines were sharp, still showing flakes of green paint between them. *I could kill the girl.*

The nuns had made it clear to them that all men could kill. Cain and Abel had been objects of lecture—the very first sibling rivalry and the very first murder. *I could kill the girl. Grab her. Throw her to the ground. Plunge the tines into her abdomen, just below her rib cage.* The idea turned his stomach. But . . . *I could kill the girl.*

He swiped experimentally at the air. It was a clumsy weapon. If he killed Loriann, her little brother would likely die before Rick could get to Pellissier and convince the MOC to go after one of his own. And, of course, he'd have to live with himself after.

I could kill the girl.

Rick took the weapon and sat on the black stone, trying to use the remaining tines to pick the lock on the shackle. They were too big for the tiny keyhole, but a nail might work. Excitement buzzed through him. Horses were shod with nails.

He set the rake head aside and fell to his hands and knees, his fingers sifting through the fine dust. He concentrated on the area near the walls, as a good farrier would never leave a shoeing nail lying in the center of the barn, where it might injure the tender part of a horse's hoof. But if one went flying, it might land in the shadows, lost. He felt his way along one wall before his fingers found something hard and slender in the dust. His heart gave a single hard thump. A nail.

But it was larger than might be used for shoeing a horse—a tenpenny nail, too thick to fit into the keyhole. *I could kill the girl.* Tears gathered in his eyes, burning. His nose ran. He laid his head against the wood and closed his eyes as tears leaked slowly from his eyes and trickled through the dust on his face. *I could kill the girl. Hail Mary, full of grace,* he thought. *I could kill the girl. Hail Mary, full of grace . . .*

A measure of peace fell into the air with the words to rest across his shoulders and settle into his heart. The words of the Apostles' Creed came to him, as clear as if Sister Mary Thomas were standing over him in the barn, ruler in hand, tapping his skull each time he forgot a word. She had never hurt him, but that ruler was a constant threat. Eyes closed against the falling light, he whispered, "I believe in God, the Father Almighty,

Creator of heaven and earth. . . ." Murmuring the creed and starting the rest of the rosary, he searched the barn to the reaches of his bindings.

By the time he was done, he had found three more tenpenny nails and discovered the boards of a stall wall that had been replaced. The carpenter had dropped the nails during his repair job. Rick placed the nails with the rake head, a metal button, a buckle, part of a leather bridle with two rusted rings, a broken plastic spoon, and a dog collar. Nothing that would kill a vampire.

He was filthy, his sheet so full of dust that he looked as if he had been rolling around on the ground. Which he had. Sister Mary Thomas would have smacked him with her ruler if he'd come back in from recess looking like this. Nuns, especially the older ones, still believed in corporal punishment, although not to the black-and-blue state. And back when he was in school, he had figured they practiced punishment searching for perfection—though whether they hunted for the perfection of the method of chastisement or perfection of the souls of their charges, he had never decided. When he was a lot older and a little wiser, he figured he had been a pain in the nuns' collective butts and had brought the punishment on himself.

It was late afternoon when he thought to use the rake tines to pry and chop a stake from the old wood. And felt so stupid that he started laughing. "I'm an idiot," he said. "A damn fool idiot."

He chose a board low down on the wall that could be hidden in piled dust, and felt along it with his fingers, searching out a weak spot. He found one in the corner, damp from long contact with the ground. Rick pried into the grain with the tines and started to chop.

Rick stopped chopping before dark and hid his tools, tucking the rake head into the shadows of the stall wall across from his work site and covering it with a natural-looking pile of stall dust. He stepped back and, seeing his footprints, knelt and brushed them away. When it still didn't look totally natural, he picked up handfuls of dirt and tossed them into the air. They made a convincingly haphazard pattern when they fell, and he repeated the dirt-tossing everywhere. It left him sneezing but feeling safer.

He had decided during the slow course of his labor that he couldn't kill the little witch. She might deserve it, but she was as trapped as he was.

And maybe he didn't have premeditated murder in him. When it came to humans. But if push came to shove, he'd find a way to kill himself before he'd let Isleen bind him with black magic. And he had the weapon, nicely hidden, that would do the deed easily. If he couldn't get away in twenty-four hours, then . . . then he'd find the pulse point on the inside of his elbow and puncture his artery with a sharp tine. Or he'd fall on the tines. Something. He'd be dead meat when Isleen came for him, which brought grim satisfaction.

Just having a plan was enough to raise his spirits and help him to face another night bound to the stone. Well, a plan and the first of his weapons. If he'd had half a brain, he would have been ready to put the plan into action tonight, but he'd moped away half the day and had only part of the tools he needed.

He had excised two stakes from the bottom board of the stall wall; he hefted them in his hands, feeling for weight and balance. They were short, maybe too short at only eight inches, give or take.

A good stake needed to be wide enough at the base to provide stability in one's grip and strength in a thrust but narrow enough to slide between ribs. Vamp hunters each had their own preferences as to length and circumference, based on hand and grip size and upper-body strength. For most, fourteen inches was way too long and increased the chance that the vampire might bat the weapon away before it hit home or twist his body and cause the tip to miss the heart. Anything smaller than ten inches was considered too short. Rick's stakes were only around eight inches long, shorter than most, which put him at a disadvantage. Not that he'd planned it. He had been trying to pry out a single long stake with the objective of making two twelve-inch stakes from the one. It had broken, teaching him patience he hadn't wanted to learn.

The effect of the day's labor on his infected wounds was obvious. They were bigger and more painful, and his arm from fingertips to elbow was now a constant throb of infection. But he'd worry about the arm later. If he survived.

He tested the heft of the stakes, making sure he could grip with his swollen hand. The stakes were as big around on the blunt end as his thumb, and nicely pointed. Stakes needed to be about the circumference of a drumstick to pierce through skin, pass between ribs, and puncture a heart without snagging on muscle, cartilage, or bone, and without breaking. His were rough and full of splinters, which might catch on tissue instead of sliding through and between. Tomorrow he would smooth them as much as possible with the few metal scraps he had uncovered.

Rick had never killed a vampire. He'd never killed anything but deer and a few turkeys. He'd never forgotten his first kill—a buck that got hung on a downed limb in a bayou near his house and was being attacked by gators. He couldn't save the deer. So he'd stolen his daddy's shotgun and put it out of its misery. It had taken four rounds, and he'd cried for days.

But killing a vampire, killing Isleen, he figured he could do. And he wouldn't cry a single tear. He'd probably be laughing his head off when he buried his stake in her black heart.

He studied the final stake, now only half-removed from the wall. It was longer, a bit wider, and the wood was paler, with a tighter grain. Tomorrow night Isleen would have a problem when she showed up. Tonight . . . tonight he was going to be in a spot of discomfort. As the sun set and golden rays poured through the slats of the barn, he shook as much of the filth out of the sheet as he could, then used a stake to stretch to the hose and turn on the water Loriann had showered him with. Lastly he hid the stakes in different spots and covered his tracks. When the little witch showed up at his barn door, he was clean and dry and waiting.

That night was worse than the previous one, as much because of his psyche as the fact that the injured skin was being worked on again. And, of course, the throbbing of infection. He bled more, he had to work harder to control his breathing, and Loriann didn't drug him this time, so he felt everything. Including a whole lot more pissed off.

Somehow it had been easier to accept being tattooed against his will when he'd woken up chained. Having to lie down like a willing sacrifice and be shackled to the black stone sucked, especially when he'd sworn he'd never do it again. The only break the witch gave him was when she transferred her tools to the other side and started work on his other arm. It was some kind of circular design. He'd thought at first that she was tattooing Christ's crown of thorns on him, but when he asked, she shook her head and said, "Shut up. I'm working."

So much for casual conversation. There was no more getting-to-know-you conversation either. In fact the only sound was his breathing like a bellows, his occasional gasp, and Loriann mumbling under her breath. Spell casting, he figured.

But at least he knew what the big tat was. Cats. Which made some sense from her original question—cats, horses, or wolves? In her oblique way, she had had been asking him to pick his tat. He could make out a mountain lion and what looked like a house cat.

His mom would be royally ticked off. His parents had long ago proclaimed that no child of theirs would come home with a tattoo. But if he had to have a tattoo, Loriann did good work.

Two hours before dawn, Loriann packed up her torture implements and allowed him to wash off and eat a meal. Near dawn Isleen appeared in a whoosh of air, creating her own wind, and stood there bent over him, fully vamped-out, fangs exposed and fresh blood on her mouth and chin. Her fingers were almost warm—though still cooler than a human's—where she traced the tattoos, and they grew warmer when she slid her fingertips up to touch the pulse point in his throat.

Her body was bent weirdly, as if her spine was more articulated, snake-like. Her fingers were spread, and bloody claws were out, held wide, fingers curved as if to catch prey. Rick couldn't help the hard thump of his heart or the way it raced when she bent lower, folding herself in two, and licked the trace of his blood from his skin with a dead, cold tongue. A shiver raced over his skin, and Isleen laughed, her vamped-out eyes blacker than the doorway into hell.

"You have done well, little witch," she whispered, her chilled, fetid breath blowing across Rick's face. "He tastes . . . lovely."

"Thank you, mistress," Loriann whispered, her face averted from the vampire.

"You will be finished tomorrow?"

"Before the moon rises, mistress."

"Good. I shall be here. The ceremony will go forward."

"And Jason?" Loriann whispered even more softly, as if the words strangled in her throat.

"Who? Oh." Isleen stood and flicked her fingers as if brushing something inconsequential from her. "The child. You may have him when the work is completed."

"Will you bring him when you come?"

Isleen tilted her head to the side, that lizard-movement thing again that vampires never did in front of humans because they knew it creeped out their dinner. "I suppose I can bring him. Perhaps seeing him will convince you to work well and finish the project on time."

"Yes, mistress." But the witch was watching Rick through her dyed tresses, some meaning in her expression.

"Before midnight, then, witch, for the ceremony." And Isleen was gone. Loriann unlocked three of his shackles, gathered up her belongings, and walked to the door just as the sun rose over the horizon. Framed in golden light in the doorway, she stopped. "You'll have only a moment," she whispered. And then she, too, was gone.

Rick rose and wrapped himself in the clean sheet she had left folded on the black stone. Pressed into the dirt by the rectangular shape of the kit that carried her needles was a knife, its sturdy blade about four inches long, and a rasp, a kind of sanding implement used by farriers when they needed to reshape a horse's hooves. It was perfect for smoothing rough wood implements. The kind one might make with a knife, from boards in a barn, to kill vampires.

Rick laughed, the sound low and vicious and victorious. She had decided to trust him. She had arranged for the dangerous, insane vampire to bring Jason here tomorrow night. And at some point in the proceedings Loriann was going to make sure he got the chance to stake Isleen.

The knife and rasp made the work of chipping and shaping stakes much easier, and by noon Rick had six good stakes, two short ones and four well-shaped, well-balanced ones that hefted nicely in his hand. And he had the knife, which he had carefully honed with the rasp, though the edge wasn't particularly sharp; the rasp wasn't manufactured with the goal of smoothing steel, and his efforts had been laughable at best. It also wasn't plated with silver to kill a vampire. But it was a bladed weapon, and having the weapons improved his chances of saving his hide. Rick knew that fighting a pissed-off vamp while naked, weakened, hungry, and sick as he was wasn't likely a survivable endeavor, but he had decided that going down fighting was better than submitting.

Midafternoon he showered in the cold water, ate the small plate of food left by Loriann, and took a nap on the dusty floor, curled on the folded sheet, hoping to garner some strength for the night.

And he woke with a vampire's jaws at his throat. Drinking.

His body reacted instantly, sexually, to the attack. One of Isleen's hands was holding his nape, the other playing him. He couldn't scream; he couldn't fight. He couldn't stop her. And with the vampire saliva entering his bloodstream, he didn't want to. He was aroused, chained by the ankle, and drunk on vamp. Her hunger was insatiable. Her body corpse-cold. But resisting was all he had left.

One hand wound into her hair, holding her. His head fell back and his spine arched up, closer to her. His other hand found a stake under the edge of the sheet. He curled his fingers around it.

Isleen pulled away, her body moving so fast that he couldn't follow, seeing only a wisp of movement and the vampire standing in the shadows at his feet. The stake was in his hand, still hidden beneath the sheet. He'd missed his chance. Rick laughed, a biting bark of sound; he could almost see the laughter float around the barn, bitter as the taste of weeds and ash. Cold as the vampire's lips on his throat. Colder than the feel of her dead fingers on his flesh.

She held his eyes with hers, which glowed like a deer's in headlights; her blond hair fell around her face like a veil. He heard a *click* to the side, and a lamp lit the barn. Isleen was revealed out of the dusky shadows, dressed in a white lace gown. It was stained with blood, crusty brown overlaid with fresh blood, scarlet and damp. The fresh blood was his, he figured. The old stuff was probably from some other poor bastard she had trapped and chained up.

Isleen's eyes seemed to fix him in place, holding him as surely as her hand and fangs had only moments before.

He heard the roar of a generator in the distance. The sound of wind in the foliage outside. The twitter of birds nesting in the rafters overhead. He'd missed his chance. And he laughed again once, the sound crazy, harsh as graveyard sobs.

Loriann handed Isleen a small cup. Isleen spat into it. *My blood. She's spitting out my blood.* With one sharp canine tooth, the vampire pierced her finger and held it over the cup, allowing her cold, dead blood to drip down into his own blood, mixing them. The drops seemed to echo into the barn, distinct and ominous, flying like bats' wings, darting into the shadows.

Isleen handed Loriann the cup, then licked her finger and her lips, still holding his eyes. With a *poof* of sound, the vamp was gone. His arousal drained away. Tears he hadn't known had fallen dried on his face.

Loriann turned on more lights, and he could see clearly. He should have been embarrassed about the little witch watching while Isleen . . . But he wasn't. He couldn't seem to care about much tonight except his failure to stake the vamp. He turned his head, watching the witch as she moved around the small space, setting out her tools. She knelt at his side and handed him a plastic bottle of water. He drank. His throat ached with the movement. Isleen hadn't been gentle with him. When the bottle was empty, he said, "Is she gone?"

"Yes. She'll be back at midnight for me to finish the spell. And she'll bring Jason. It'll be your only chance."

He sat up slowly, belly muscles protesting, bringing the stake with him. "You didn't mean for me to stake her just now?"

Her eyes widened. "No. No, not until Jason is here."

"Mighta been nice to know that."

"I didn't think— Oh my God." She turned away, holding herself around the waist, her hair sliding forward, hiding her face. "Okay," she said after a moment. "Okay. Never mind." Her tone said that she was forgiving herself and him for the near miss. She stood straight and went back to work. "We don't have much time. Do I have to chain you to the stone tonight?"

"No. I'll be a good little human vamp snack." He could hear the bitterness and anger in his tone, but the hopelessness that had settled on him like a grave shroud had lightened. He had another chance. "Speaking of which, I smell food."

"I brought you some Popeyes chicken, biscuits, and sides. A gallon of tea. Hope you like it sweet."

"Yes. I'm starving. Can I eat while you work?"

"No. So eat fast. And we have to talk. I need to tell you how the spell works so you can pick the right time to . . . to kill her." Loriann placed a bucket of chicken at his side, and he dug in, listening, wondering at himself and at the way he could plan the death of an insane, undead monster with such enthusiasm.

Loriann was almost done with the tats. Around his right bicep was a circlet of something that looked like barbed wire but was really twisted vines in a dark green ink. Interspersed throughout the vines were claws and talons, recurved big-cat claws and raptor talons, some with small drops of blood on the tips—blood from Isleen and from his own body, mixed with some cat blood and scarlet dye, the mixture meant to bind his body to the vampire once the spell was complete. On his left shoulder, following the line of his collarbone, down across his left pec, down from his shoulder to his upper arm, and almost to his spine in back, was a mountain lion. He was a tawny beast, with darker markings on his face, body, and tail, his amber eyes staring. He was crouched as if to watch for unwary prey, the clublike tail curved up around his shoulder blade. Behind his predator's face peeked a smaller cat with pointed ears and curious, almost amused eyes, lips pulled up in a snarl to reveal predator teeth—a bobcat, snuggled up to the larger cat. It was beautiful work. But it was a spell woven into Rick's body.

"The gold in the eyes is pure gold foil, mixed with my grandmother's inks. It shouldn't infect or cause you trouble. And as long as you kill Isleen before the spell is finished, the eyes won't glow. If the binding is completed, you'll know it, because the eyes, all four of them, will catch the light and glimmer just like gold jewelry. Either way the tattoos won't fade, not ever. And you probably can't get them lasered off. Not with the dyes my grandmother used . . ." Loriann stopped and stood unmoving, her body almost vibrating with fear, exhaustion, and excitement. She met his eyes, hers dark ringed with fatigue and blood loss from feeding the vampire. "You'll save Jason?"

"We don't know where he'll be. In a stall. Hanging from the rafters in a cage. I'll kill Isleen. Whoever is closest will save Jason."

"Okay." Loriann licked her lips. "One last thing. I called Katie. A guy answered. I told him about you. About Isleen and Jason. He was pretty pissed."

Hope shot through Rick. He could feel his heart thud in his chest. His uncle Tom answered the phone at Katie's Ladies. "And?"

"I told him to expect a text message with directions. And I programmed the message with directions on how to get here." She pulled out a cell phone and snapped it open. "It's in my phone, waiting. As soon as Isleen arrives, and I see that my brother is still alive, I'll hit Send. If I can. I don't know—"

With a *pop* of displaced air, Isleen appeared. She held a small boy in the crook of her arm, his long legs dangling. The boy was asleep or unconscious but breathing. Isleen had fed again, and the front of her dress was soaked with blood. Rick had no idea how much of it was the boy's.

Loriann made a helpless moan of fear and longing and horror, one hand outstretched to the child. With her other hand, she pressed a button on the phone and sent the text message. Rick closed his eyes for a moment, hiding his relief. Help was coming. If he could keep them all alive until it arrived.

He focused on the vampire. Her hair was up in curls and waves, with a little hat and a scrap of netting perched on top, like something a woman from the eighteen hundreds might have worn. When she set the boy down, he saw that the lace dress had a bustle in back. And she wore pointed lace shoes. Strings of pearls were around her neck, crusty with dried blood. She looked like a parody of a horror movie, dressed for a wedding, covered in blood. She patted Jason on the head. The kid had pinprick holes in his neck. She had fed from him. Recently. It was all Rick could do to lie there and watch as Isleen positioned Jason on the dirt of the barn, curling him into the fetal position and covering him with a blanket she must have brought with her.

Rick was stretched out on the black stone, spread-eagled, his hands and feet appearing to be manacled but really free. The sheet was bunched at his side near his right hand, and beneath it were two stakes. Beneath his back were the knife and two more stakes. Hidden in the dust at the base of the black stone to his left and to his right were the two short stakes, his last-ditch-if-all-else-fails weapons. But help was coming. Help had to come.

"Begin," Isleen said to Loriann, standing above Jason like a threat from the grave. "If you do it right, your brother will live. If the man is not bound to me when you are done, the boy will die while you watch. Then you will die."

"Yes, mistress." Loriann sat by his side, above his shoulder so that his right arm would be unimpeded, her most delicate tattoo needle in her hand. On the stone near her was the pot of mixed blood. She had woven her spell into his flesh with the blood on the tips of the cat claws, leaving only parts of three to be filled in.

"Sit beside him on the stone there"—Loriann pointed with the needle—"in the crook of his left arm. I'll speak the ritual words while I fill in the last globules of blood on the cat's claws." Loriann met his eyes, telling him that she was ready.

All they needed was to put Isleen at a disadvantage, cause her to focus on something else just long enough for him to react. If the help came after the vampire was dead, he'd have a ride home. If the help came before, well, he'd have a weapon to protect the kid.

To Isleen, Loriann said, "When I say, 'For all time. For all time. For all time,' you have to bite him on his wrist and drink from him. One sip. And then you say, 'Blood to blood, flesh to flesh, soul to soul. I claim you as my own. For all time. For all time. For all time.' And it'll be done."

"How long?" Isleen asked, her fingers trailing down his face, cupping his cheek. He smelled old blood and something sweet and parched, like dried lilies. The smell of the vamp herself.

"The last globules will take about half an hour. I have to chant the whole time. If you talk, if you move, if you cause me to lose my concentration, it will break the spell."

"And the child will die." Isleen flashed her fangs. "Never forget that. Begin. Now."

Loriann closed her eyes and ducked her head as if to pray. Then she opened her eyes and placed the needle into the pot of blood. "Blood to blood, flesh to flesh, soul to soul. These two are one." She pierced Rick's flesh with the needle. "Blood to blood, flesh to flesh, soul to soul. These two are one. Blood to blood, flesh to flesh, soul to soul. These two are one."

The needle pierced him again and again as Isleen stared into his eyes, hunger in hers. He knew that she was trying to roll him, to do what vampires did to get free blood-meals and to bind blood-slaves and blood-servants. He could feel her compulsion tickling at the edges of his mind. If needles and fine blades hadn't been sticking into him, he might have succumbed. But the pain kept him alert. Ready. The minutes ticked by. His blood trickled around his bicep to pool on top of his dried blood on the black witch stone.

Loriann changed the chant when she started on the second globule. "Blood to blood, flesh to flesh, soul to soul. These two are one. Time and time and forever. Blood to blood, flesh to flesh, soul to soul. These two are one. Time and time and forever. Blood to blood, flesh to flesh, soul to soul. These two are one. Time and time and forever."

Rick regulated his breathing, keeping himself loose and relaxed. Letting Isleen believe that she was succeeding in rolling him. He slid his expression into a goofy smile. Let drunken love fill his face.

Loriann started on the last drop of blood on the last claw. Again her chant changed. "One blood, one flesh, one soul. Time and time and forever. One blood, one flesh, one soul. Time and time and forever. One blood, one flesh, one soul. Time and time and forever." The phrase was like a drum beating into his mind. His heart stuttered and found a new rhythm, meeting and following her words. "One blood, one flesh, one soul. Time and time and forever. One blood, one flesh, one soul. Time and time and forever. One blood, one flesh, one soul. Time and time and forever."

And then she said the words Isleen had been waiting for. "For all time. For all time. For all time." The tattoo was complete.

Isleen bit. The pain was instantaneous. An electric shock. Rick gripped the stake. And spun, pushing up and away. Fast. Faster than he had ever moved. He plunged the stake into Isleen's back. The point slammed through skin and muscle and cartilage.

Isleen screamed and ripped her teeth from his wrist. Twisted her body in a snakelike move no human could have duplicated. The stake missed her heart. Claws slashed down his abdomen. Struck at his throat. He scuttled away, taking the blade in his right hand. But his left hand had been injured by her teeth cutting their way out. He couldn't grip a stake. It rolled across the black stone.

Isleen attacked, moving so quickly that she was a blur. Her fangs slashed into his throat. Ripping. Tearing. Her claws pierced his chest. He threw back his head and screamed.

He missed what happened next. Missed it entirely. Loriann told him about it later, much later, in such vivid detail that it was almost as if he witnessed his rescue. His saviors.

Katie and Leo. The two master vampires blew the doors off the barn. And came inside. Katie staked Isleen. Leo cut off her head. Loriann cradled her brother. His uncle Tom lifted them both and carried them, curled up together, out of the barn. The last memory he had was a spray of his own blood. And the vamp-black eyes of the Master of the City, Leo Pellissier.

Rick woke up in his own bed, clean, sore, and sleepy, just after dawn. Sprawled in the chair at the foot of his bed was his mom, her eyes open, watching him. Tom sat in a kitchen chair beside her. When his uncle realized he had awakened, he said, "What do you want most? A rare steak or sex?"

Rick raised his head, surprised that there was no pain. No pain anywhere. He touched his throat, finding no scars, then smiled and stretched. "Neither. Breakfast would be good." He looked at his mother. "Blueberry pancakes?"

She blew out a breath so hard and deep it sounded like a mini-explosion. Uncle Tom grinned widely, a big toothy grin. "He's still himself. The binding didn't take."

"Pancakes it is," his mother whispered, blinking back tears. "But your father is going to have kittens at the idea of you with a tattoo."

Rick sat up on the edge of the bed and looked down at the tattoos on his shoulders, studying the eyes of the mountain lion. They didn't glow or sparkle like gold jewelry. They were just amber, the eyes of a mountain cat. "I can live with that," he said. "I can live with most anything now." He tilted his head to his uncle. "Thank you. I owe you. I owe you big-time."

"Yeah, you do. We'll talk."

"After the pancakes," Rick said. He looked at his mom. "With blueberry compote and whipped cream?"

She wiped a tear from her cheek and nodded. "Anything you want, son." She bustled out of the room, followed by his uncle, leaving him alone.

Rick shoved the pillows back against the headboard and propped himself up on them, listening to the chatter between Uncle Tom and his mother. He looked down again, studying the cats on his shoulder. Unsure what he would feel, he raised his hand and touched the amber eyes of the bobcat and then of the mountain lion. They felt like flesh—warm, resilient—and he could feel the pressure of his fingers as he traced the eyes. Nothing new in the tactile sensation. Just fingers. Just skin.

But the cats were part of the binding ceremony, part of his future that

Loriann had read, had seen, and maybe had changed. She had done something to him, to his future, when she'd made him choose an animal. He
knew it. He had felt it, like some tremor in the possible paths that life
would offer him. A new branch, darker, more shadowed.

Rick didn't know what it meant to have the cats on his body, beneath
his skin, part of him. But he figured the future would come whether he
wanted it to or not. He had no control over that. He never had. It was just
that, until now, he had never known how little power and influence over
life he really maintained.

With that unhappy thought, he got out of bed, feeling stronger than
he'd expected. He pulled on jeans and a long-sleeved white T-shirt, hiding
the tattoos, and looked at himself in the mirror over his bureau. He looked
unchanged. But only on the surface. Beneath, wildcats had entered his life.
And he would never be the same.

Kits

I wrapped the tools of my trade in padded cloth and secured them with Velcro. The bundle of stakes, knives, and my most important blade, a silver-plated main-gauche, was small enough to fit into the saddlebag of the old Yamaha bike and still leave room for a change of clothes and for odds and ends. The Yamaha wasn't my dream bike, but it would do for a while longer until I earned enough to buy the Harley I lusted after.

I tucked my money into the inside pocket of my jeans beside the red lipstick I favored. I French-braided my hip-length hair into a careless plait and tucked it into my leather jacket where it wouldn't be in the way or get windblown too badly. The jacket was used, purchased at a consignment store, and it still reeked of the last owner, at least to my sensitive nose. I'd tried spraying it with deodorizers, but nothing worked. If I took down the vamp I was gunning for and earned the bounty, I had promised myself a brand-new leather riding jacket. That and two real vamp-killers to replace the less than perfectly balanced main-gauche a local smith had modified with silver. Last, I adjusted my gold nugget on its double chain for riding. The necklace was my only jewelry.

I looked over the small efficiency apartment I had rented, making sure I was leaving nothing important behind, and locked the door after me. I helmeted up, keyed on the Yamaha, and headed out of town. I had a gig hunting down a suspected young rogue vamp that was terrorizing the inhabitants outside of Day Book, North Carolina. But first I was stopping off at a local restaurant to pick up a small tracking charm that would let me follow the whacked-out vamp through rough country, and to pay the balance of the cost to the earth witch who'd made it.

I parked the Yamaha in front of the herb shop and eatery, and entered. Seven Sassy Sisters' Herb Shop and Café, owned and run by the Everhart sisters, had a booming business, both locally and on the Internet, selling herbal mixtures and teas in bulk and by the ounce. The shop itself served high-quality brewed teas, specialty coffees, daily brunch and lunch, and dinner on weekends. It was mostly vegetarian fare, whipped up by the eldest sister, water witch, professor, and three-star chef, Evangelina Everhart. Carmen Miranda Everhart Newton, an air witch, newly married and pregnant, ran the register and took care of ordering supplies. Witch twins Boadacia and Elizabeth and two wholly human sisters, Regan and Amelia, ran the herb store and were waitstaff. I was looking for Molly Meagan Everhart Trueblood. Names with moxie seemed to run in the family.

I took a booth at the big window overlooking the city and ordered my usual. I had just discovered eggs Benedict, and a double order would just about keep up with my caloric requirements until lunch. Regan tilted her red head and said, "Honey, if I ate like you, I'd be bigger than a house. Hey, we got us a new Himalayan oolong. It's a semifermented Nepal tea; Evangelina says it combines the characteristics of a high-grown Darjeeling and a soulful oolong." She rolled her eyes and tapped her order pad with her pencil. "But you know Evangelina. She can wax poetic about tea better than most anybody."

I didn't really know Evangelina; the eldest witch sister wasn't exactly a warm and cuddly kinda gal, and since I lack a lot in the way of social skills, we hadn't hit it off. Though Evangelina hadn't yet come right out and said so, I could tell she had strong reservations about the friendship developing between Molly and motorcycle-mama me. I had stepped in between Mol and a group of ticked-off witch haters at the Ingles grocery store and we had become casual friends—a little closer than acquaintances, but not bosom buddies. Well, not yet. Maybe someday. I could hope. I liked Molly.

I ate the delectable eggs Benedict and drank the totally fabulous tea, sipping my third cup with my eyes closed so I could enjoy all the delicate flavors—the flowery, fruity aroma; the clean, smooth taste on my tongue. I wasn't a rich woman, but the quality of the tea was well worth the price, at four bucks per half an ounce of dry leaves. My appreciation of the tea went a long way to endearing me to Evangelina, who was watching me through the diner-style window between the kitchen and dining room.

Her mouth wasn't as pursed as it normally was, and her shoulders weren't quite as unyielding.

Over that last cup of tea, I asked Regan for Molly—who I figured was in the stockroom or the office doing accounts—so I could pick up and pay for the tracking charm. Regan slid into the seat opposite me and cupped her chin in her hand. Serious gray eyes met mine across the table. "Molly didn't come in to work today. And she didn't call. And she's not answering her phone. Evangelina's mad, but worried too, you know? Me and Amelia's going out to her place after work. You want I should take the money to her and bring back your charm?"

My Beast sat up inside my mind, kneading me with sharp mental claws. I'm not prescient. Not a lick. But a chilled finger of disquiet slid up my spine with the words. Molly was supposed to be here today. She was expecting me. And though I didn't know her well, I knew she was ethical from her toes to her eyeballs. I set the teacup on the saucer with a dull *clink*. "I think I'll ride out there and pick up the charm." At Regan's suddenly wary expression, I said, "I've known Molly for a while. Ever since she was cornered in the grocery store by the witch haters."

Most of the distrustful expression slid from her face. "That was you?" Witches were notoriously cautious and guarded of their privacy. They had been persecuted for thousands of years until the mid-twentieth century, when vamps and witches came out of the closet. They were currently negotiating for equal civil rights in the U.S., but Congress and the courts were having a tough time integrating the expanded life span of vamps and the power potential of witches into a code of law. And in many places the human population had a long way to go in accepting witches as anything other than the evil creatures portrayed in history, Scripture, and fiction.

"Yeah." I shrugged slightly and sipped my tea.

Regan looked me over in my biker jacket, jeans, and worn-out butt-stomper boots, and glanced back at the kitchen. I understood and sighed. "Go ask Evangelina. Though she'll probably tell you no way. Evangelina doesn't like me much."

Regan snorted though her tiny, pert nose. "My big sister doesn't like anyone much. You been to Molly's?"

I recited the address and said, "It's a double-wide mobile home with pale green trim and about two acres of grass for Big Evan to mow. He was mowing it last Saturday when I took the deposit by. He was riding a big yellow mower. Big Evan is redheaded like Molly; bearded, not like Molly; and built like a mountain." I thought a moment more and added, "And her kid is actually cute. You know. For a kid. Angie Baby has so many dolls, it's hard to find her bed under them all." Angie Baby was the nickname used by two-year-old Angelina's parents, which gave me another bona fide.

"And on the wall of Angelina's bedroom?"

I grinned. "Noah's ark with unicorns, griffins, and pixies on the gangplank." I couldn't help the softness I knew was taking over my smile when I said, "She climbed up in my lap and introduced her doll to me. Like it was alive." I shook my head and tucked my chin, looking at Regan under my brows. "I have never talked to a doll before."

Regan chuckled. "Not even when you were a kid?"

I remembered the children's home where I was raised from the time I was twelve, and the smile slid off my face. "No. Not even when I was a kid." Regan studied my face and the change of emotion there. After a moment she nodded. "Okay, so if you're such big friends, why ask me if you can go?"

That cold finger of unease brushed my spine again. "You think something doesn't feel right about Molly not coming in to work today and not calling." I shrugged slightly, lifting one shoulder. "I'm not a friend yet, but I like her. And I feel pretty worried too."

Regan stood, smoothing her waitress' apron down her jeans-clad legs. "Tell her to call us, okay?" Her face took on a mock-angry look. "And not to do this to us again."

I tossed a twenty onto the table. "I'll be appropriately irritated for you." Beast's claws gripped my mind in a steady pull, keeping me alert as I took the tunnel out of town, making good time to Molly's. But Beast's feeling of worry grew on me hard and fast, helped along by the odd dark gray cloud that seemed to hang over the crest of a hill in the general direction where I was headed. I had a feeling that the cloud wasn't natural. And that it was perched above Mol's house.

Kit, Beast thought at me. *Kit in danger.*

The weather had turned chilly and dry early. It was usually still hot and muggy in late September, but an unexpected cool spell had rolled in from the northwest, and though the trees were still dressed in summer green, autumn already had teeth. As I rode, the wind picked up and shoved into me like a warning hand, pushing me back, holding me away as I climbed the hill to Molly's. And the cloud that had perched serenely on her hill from a distance swirled in angry grays as I got closer, bent over the bike, gunning the motor. Lightning flickered through the cloud, and it looked odd, like black light. No way was it natural. Something magical was going seriously wrong.

The wind had torn down power lines, and they lay drooping in the fields and hanging on tree limbs. Higher up the road, they swirled like snakes on the wind, spitting sparks. Branches flew through the air. Rain pelted in irregular spits, as if the cloud couldn't quite make up its mind to storm.

When I was still a quarter mile from her house, I stopped the bike to call Seven Sassy Sisters' for backup, but I had no signal bars. Uncertain, I looked into the sky. I had no business heading into witch problems. *I should leave,* I thought. But above me the air was heavy and dense with moisture. The cloud thickened and divided and coalesced back into one densely packed dark thunderhead; it sparked with that odd purple-black lightning as energy built inside. The cloud began to roil. It darkened and spread out fingers like claws, as if it drew in energy from the calmer air around it.

Kit, Beast said. *Kit now!*

But when I turned the key to ride the rest of the way, the bike motor was silent. Dead. And from the hilltop I heard a scream. Tinny and thin with the distance. But a scream. It was Molly.

Kit! Beast screamed. *Run!*

I dropped the bike and dug in with my booted toes, racing uphill. Even in human form I'm faster than a human, thanks to the years I spent in Beast form, and with Beast flooding my system with adrenaline, I reached the yard in less than a minute. Just as the lightning stabbed at the ground. Purple-blue lighting, like nothing out of nature. And the wind swirled into a mini-tornado, a black funnel sparked with blue lights like mutant fireflies caught in a maelstrom.

I almost stopped. I did not want to do this. But Beast reached into me and forced me on, her scream rising into my throat.

The mobile home rocked in the wind on its foundation. Lightning struck, a severe blue flash, throwing me down, sizzling through me. I somersaulted through the air. My heart shuddered with pain as if I'd taken a blade to the chest. I hit the dry ground. What breath I still had in my lungs huffed out. I groaned and rolled to my side, nauseated. Small blue flames licked at the grass. A half-frozen blast of rain hit beside me and put out the fire. Molly screamed again. Big Evan's voice shouted. They were in trouble. *Big* trouble. I rolled to my knees and then to my feet and raced to the house.

Blue sparkles and a gray mist flowed down from the cloud. I recognized magic, both icy and scorching, undirected, dangerous. Malevolent. Searching. Almost sentient. Growing more powerful as I raced.

I was almost to the mobile home when the swirling tornado spiraled down, speeding, threatening. And touched down on the mobile home.

The wind ripped at the roof. Tearing. *Questing.* And it peeled back a corner of the roof. Directly over Angie Baby's room. Purplish lightning flickered down and struck the damaged home. The boom was deafening. Its flash was blinding. My hair rose, pulling itself from my braid. Sleet slashed at the earth like claws. The wind tried to lift me away, and I hunched low to the ground. The air was so full of magic that I couldn't take a breath.

Beast screamed. Flooded my body with strength. I leaped to the small porch and tore the door from its hinges. The wind gathered it up and yanked it away into the storm. Overhead the roof rolled back like an old-fashioned tin can. The ceiling went with it. I was inside. But so was the storm.

The wind roared in, brutal and sadistic. Rapacious. Sucking out blankets, clothing, a doll with its arms flailing. *Please, God, let it only be a doll. Not Angie Baby.* A dark blue-black mist swirled in, filling the front room with power. Uncontrolled.

Over the sound of the wind, I heard Molly and Big Evan chanting what sounded like a prayer. Angie screamed.

Kit! Beast screamed in return. I dove into the mist.

Magic poured over me. Fangs of power bit into me like angry snakes. Magical energy shot into my bloodstream like venom. And my body began to shift.

I fought the pull of the change, holding on to my own shape. Screaming with frustration, "No! Not now!" My own magic thrummed through me, feeding on the witch magic. Black motes of darkness. Gray mist against the blue.

Pain, pain, pain. Knives of power sliced into me, separating muscle from bone. Flaying skin away. Setting fire to nerves. Choosing the only shape I could take without planning, tools, and trappings to guide me.

My Beast screamed.

I screamed.

Pelt erupted through skin. Joints slid and twisted. Claws pierced my fingertips. Killing teeth filled my mouth.

I was Beast. I screamed anger against the storm. Clawed off Jane clothes. Leaped across room. Wind plucked at me. Tore at me. I raced down hall. Into girl kit's room. Witch man was sitting with eyes closed, back to wall, singing to wind. Air witch chant. Witch woman was standing against other wall. Smell of fear and desperation leaked from pores. Panic. Storm was awake. Angry. Not theirs to control.

Wind snaked into room. Grew in strength, like fist with claws. Bashed out windows. Picked up human things and carried them away. Fear smell grew. Woman's, man's, kit's.

Kit was on bed. Afraid. Screaming. Fear like human knives cut inside her. Power was coming from her fear—feeding storm. I—Beast—understood fear.

I leaped to bed, standing over kit. Screamed to wind. Kit safe. Safe with me. I am Beast!

Woman opened eyes. Her fear smell swirled thick into room. Fear of Beast. Woman's mouth moved in soundless cry. Woman was working magic with her hands. Rain poured in, heavy and hard.

I sat on bed. Curled around kit. Holding her with paw so wind with claws would not steal her. I licked her face. Human tears salty. Human skin milky. Smooth. Soft. She made funny sound. Hiccup. Swallowed hard. Crying stopped. Witch kit reached up and took my ears in her hands. Pulled Beast face to her. Stared for long moment, eye to eye. And closed eyes. Not afraid. Not anymore.

I curled legs and body around her. Protected her from rain and wind. Looked at woman. Not human. Powerful witch, like man. Like kit. I purred. Licked kit face.

Witch woman walked to witch man. Took hands. Chanting steadied like calm heartbeat. Power in storm shifted and eased. Rain softened. Warmed. I purred. Panted.

Man and woman worked magic like net, binding power in girl kit. Felt it curl under belly and paws, around small kit body. Time passed. Kit fell asleep.

Storm fell apart. Thunderhead darkening the sky thinned and wisped. Clear sky showed through. Magic disappeared like mist. Floating away.

Man fell over. Dead? No, breathing. Asleep. Empty of magic.

I purred and rested head on kit head. Keeping kit safe.

Storm was gone. Sunlight fell through where roof had been. Woman witch studied me. Fear tainted air, but confused fear. Not run-from-predator fear. I purred. Licked kit face. Moved kit off my leg with paw. Licked face again. Slowly stood. Slowly, slowly, not to frighten woman.

I looked at woman. She looked at me. At necklace on my neck. Jane's necklace.

"Jane?" she whispered. "Oh my God. *Jane.*"

I hacked. *Not God. Not Jane. Beast.*

I leaped from bed to land on wet, squishy cloth floor. Padded from room, rain puddles splashing. And out door. Kit safe.

I woke beside my bike, naked and cold, my bones aching. A half-moon and several million stars dusted light to the earth, enough for me to see with my night vision intact. I knew better than to change form in daylight, but I'd had no choice when I shifted into Beast. Now I hurt. I hurt badly.

In an emergency, like today, I could shift into Beast in daylight, but I couldn't change back to human in daylight. Or at least I'd never figured out the mechanism. And it wasn't as if I had anyone to teach me. I was the only skinwalker I had ever heard of. Hence the hours that had passed and the moonlight above me. And me naked and cold and starving.

Shivers gripped me and shook me hard. Teeth chattering, I opened the bike's saddlebags and pulled out my one change of clothes. Dressed but barefoot, I started the bike and rode up the hill into Molly's yard. The trailer was dark but for a candle guttering in a window. I killed the engine. Bare feet on cool earth, I waited. If Molly heard me, if she wanted to talk, she'd come out. If not, then I could ride on. But it would be a lot easier with my boots. Jacket. Helmet. Did she know what I had done? What I was? Crap. I didn't want her to find out this way. I didn't want her to find out at all.

The front door opened. Molly stood on the front porch, her white nightgown fluttering in the hilltop breeze. I couldn't have said why, but a trembling ran through me, part fear, part . . . something I couldn't name. I kicked the stand down and walked across the lawn, watching Molly's face in the light of the candle. She was smiling. And tears trickled slowly down her face.

I stopped at the bottom of the three steps leading to the tiny porch. And couldn't think of a solitary thing to say. My boots and jeans and torn clothes were folded in a neat stack by her feet. Yeah. She knew. *Crap. She knew.* I hunched my shoulders and tucked each hand under the opposite armpit. And waited for her judgment.

"You—" She stopped and caught a breath. I gathered that she had been crying for a while. "Thank you. You saved my baby." When I didn't reply, she went on, voice rough through her tears. "We were losing her. She was out of control. Too powerful. Neither of us was ready to deal with that much power. And not so early." I still didn't speak, and Molly said, "Her power wasn't due until her first menses. Not for years and years. We weren't ready." She heaved a breath, and it shuddered through her. "We almost lost her."

I nodded. And still couldn't think of a thing to say.

Suddenly Molly giggled. "What? Cat got your tongue?"

I jerked. An answering laugh tittered in my throat. I stuck my hands in my jeans pockets, shoulders still hunched. "Cute. You're okay with it? With me? Me being Beast?"

"I have no idea what you are, except a big-cat. But you saved my baby, and for that you have my undying thanks, my undying friendship, and any help you may need for as long I can give it."

Molly had given me three things, and I knew that witches did important things in threes. The cold that had settled in my bones, the ache of the shift that the magic had forced through me, warmed a bit, began to ease. "Well, I'll settle for my socks and boots. My feet are cold."

"I found them on the lawn," she said, laughter still in the tone, "and I've let them air-dry, though they're still pretty wet. Would you like some tea? Power is out, but I have a kettle on the camp stove."

I didn't have time for tea. I had to be on the road, had to get to the job. But that wasn't what came out of my mouth. "I'd love a cup. And, Molly? I'm a skinwalker. And I never told anyone that before tonight. Not anyone."

"So we can share secrets, is that what you're saying? You're a skinwalker, whatever that is, and my baby is an early-blooming, powerful witch? Come on in. Let's talk. And I'll get you that charm."

I pulled on my socks and carried my boots into what was left of Molly's house. We had tea. We shared secrets. Weirdly, Molly held my hand while we talked, as if protecting something fragile or sealing something precious. Even more weirdly, I let her. I think that, for the first time in my life, I had a real friend.

Haint(s)

Author's note: This story takes place after the short story "Kits" and before the short story "Signatures of the Dead." Molly Everhart Trueblood is the narrator.

"Nothing unusual here, Molly," she said.

I watched Jane Yellowrock as she crawled across the floor of the old house on all fours. Most adults looked foolish or ungainly when crawling, but Jane was graceful, her arms lifting and moving forward with feline balance, her legs raising and lowering, toes pointed like a dancer, even in her Western boots. My friend moved silently in the hot, sweaty room, easily avoiding the bird and mouse droppings, the holes in the old linoleum, and the signs of recent reconstruction—the broken plaster walls, large holes in the floor, and the shattered remains of the toilet, tub, and kitchen sink in the corner. Her shoulder blades, visible beneath her thin T-shirt, lifted up high with each crawling step, her head lowered on the thin stem of her neck, moving catlike. I envied her the grace and the slenderness, but little else. Jane was more alone than anyone I had ever known.

Now she breathed in with a strange sucking hiss. Flehmen behavior, she called it, using her hypersensitive senses to smell things the way a cat would, the way a mountain lion would, sucking air in over her tongue and the roof of her mouth, her lips pulled back and mouth open. Mostly, she did it only when she was alone, because it sounded weird and looked weirder—not a human action at all. But because I had asked her for help, and because no one but me would see her, she did it now, scenting for the smell of . . . of whatever.

As I watched, Jane crawled out of the half-renovated kitchen and into the dining room beyond. We were both dressed in old jeans and T-shirts, clothes that could get filthy and be tossed into the washer, and already Jane looked like something the cat dragged in, which was funny in all sorts of ways. Jane Yellowrock was a Cherokee skinwalker, and her favorite animal form was a mountain lion. She called it her inner beast, which I still didn't understand, but I figured she'd tell me someday.

I'd met Jane in the Ingles grocery store, when a group of witch haters caught me in the frozen foods section and harassed me. None of us Everharts were officially out of the closet then, but most townspeople were okay with my family maybe carrying the witch gene. It was the out-of-towners who had the problem—a group that wasn't from the religious right, but was just as rabid. I still don't know what Jane did—she stepped in front of me so all I saw was her back—but the haters departed. Fast. I gave her my thanks and a card to my family café and we parted ways.

The next morning Jane came into the Seven Sassy Sisters' Herb Shop and Café, and nearly cleaned us out of bacon, sausage, and pancakes. The appetite of that morning was because she had just changed back from an animal form and needed calories to make up for the shift, but I didn't know that then. I just thought it was a crying shame that a woman who was so skinny could eat like that. If I tried to shovel in that much food, even half that much food, I'd weigh four hundred pounds. I think I gained three pounds just watching her eat, that first day.

And then the group of witch haters from the day before started picketing out front. I guess they were in town and figured they should make the most of it. They were carrying signs about not suffering a witch to live—the usual crapola—and chanting, "Save our children! Save our children!" Two cars pulled by and slowed, as if to turn in, and then pulled on away. Such attention was going to be damaging to business.

Jane paid her bill, went outside, and revved up her bike. And revved up her bike. And revved up her bike again. At which point I realized she was doing it on purpose. Then she did something to the engine, and revved it up again. And black smoke came out. So Jane rode in circles around the parking lot, shouting to the witch haters, "So sorry about the noise! I have engine problems!" After about ten minutes of noise, the witch haters left. It was so cool. I thought the twins, Boadacia and Elizabeth, were going to have twin cows.

That's Jane. A loner with a cause. Any cause, as long as it's protecting someone.

She sneezed, bringing me back from my daydreams to my friend crawling around on the floor of a deserted, possibly haunted house.

The dining room had little floor left, and I could see the ground and the foundation beneath the house, between the struts. Still on her hands and knees, Jane moved into the foyer, circled its perimeter once, ignored the stairs leading to the second story, and crawled into the parlor beyond. I followed, watching from the foyer, which had been exposed when the construction crew pulled off the old boards covering the entrance. Oddly enough, though every other room in the house showed the results of men with mallets and hammers and crowbars, the parlor had still not been touched. The finish of the original handmade woodwork below the chair railing and the moldings at the ceiling was dark and filthy, the plaster between was cracked and split with water damage, and the last bits of old, red wallpaper curled, hanging loose, covered with spiderwebs and the dust of decades.

I stood in the six-foot-wide opening, watching my best friend track through the dust. The flooring beneath the accumulated filth was wood parquet, probably cut from the land the house stood on, milled by the lumber baron who'd built the house in the previous century. He had died a gruesome death, killed by a bear beside his train car, or so the old story went. His son had married a witch, and their daughter had inherited, and so had her daughter. However, the old house hadn't been occupied in decades, not since Monique Ravencroft, the most powerful witch in the Appalachians, had disappeared without a trace.

The family had died out except for a son who no longer wanted the property, and the old house had been sold to a local lawyer for his business offices. Construction had begun quickly thereafter. The workers, however, had abandoned the project two days ago, after a flying mallet attacked a plumber standing in an empty room. The construction company owner had asked the local coven in the little township of Hainbridge to investigate, but the women had had no luck identifying the spiritual miscreant. They had called me in to discover if the troublemaker was a ghost, demon, or haint—*haint* being a term applied, in this part of the woods, to a form of poltergeist, or supernatural energy that usually manifests around a person instead of around a place. Whatever had attacked the plumber, it needed to be identified so the coven could coerce or force it to vacate the premises. Unfortunately, all I'd found was a sense of something dead in the house, and I'd had no luck calling to or talking to any noncorporeal would-be-killer. I hoped Jane, with her hyper senses, might discover something I had missed.

Jane sniffed around the fireplace on the far side of the room, the interior walls black with wood or coal smoke, the old grate rusted through and coated with spiderwebs. She seemed to find the opening uninteresting, and moved on to the corner. She paused there, repeating the openmouthed sniffing, and looked up, puzzled. "Molly, are you sure there's something dead here?"

I nodded. I'm from a long family of witches, all of us pretty much in the witch closet, and while I'm an earth witch, with the gift of growing plants, healing bodies, and restoring balance to nature, I'm a little unusual for an earth witch, in that I can sense dead things. And there was definitely something dead in this house somewhere.

"I smell witch and vamp," Jane said.

The little hairs on the back of my neck stood up in alarm. "Vampire? There shouldn't be a vampire here."

"It's been years, but I think . . ." She put her nose back to the dust-covered floor, sniffed delicately, and started sneezing. She rolled to her feet and crossed the room, sneezing all the way, her nose buried in the crook of her elbow to keep her filthy hands away from her face. I counted twelve sneezes before she stopped and her face was red from the sneeze effort. "I think I smell vamp and witch together," she said, the back of a wrist to her nose, pressing against more sneezes, "and both of them were bleeding." She stood beside me and turned to face the room. The evidence of her crawling progression was a clear trail through the layers of dust.

"Mol," she said, "I dropped a stake." She pointed to the fourteen-inch-long stake in the corner. "Would you go get it, please?"

"No," I said instantly.

"Why not? You chicken?"

Anger shot through me. "I'm not going—" I stopped, and the anger filtered out of me. Around me the house seemed to wait, expectant, and I turned in a slow circle, standing in the doorway, letting my senses flow out, seeing the hand-carved woodwork, the once-elegant stairs leading up to the second floor, the carpenter's ladder against the wall. Smelling the dust, the fresh wood, the dirt under the house, and the sweat of the workers from two days past. Hearing the small sounds an old house makes, the *pops* and quiet groans. Feeling the breath of the house as air moved through it, cool and moist from the open floor and up the stairs, a faint trickle of breeze. I opened my mouth, as Jane did, and breathed, almost tasting the house, its age, elegance, and history.

Midway around, I closed my eyes and took a cleansing breath. The magic I hadn't noted pricked against my skin, cool and light, old, old, old magic, a spell frayed around the edges, one that hadn't been renewed in decades. "A ward," I muttered, "combined with something else. Maybe a keep-away spell. Yeah. I can feel it, feel them both, combined. It was a really good one to have lasted this long." I opened my eyes and studied Jane. "How'd you sense it when I didn't?"

"Dust," she said succinctly. At my puzzled expression, she said, "Every room in this place has been walked over, beaten on, knocked down, and partially renovated except this one. The footsteps all go right up to the entrance"—she pointed down to the floor at our feet—"where they removed whatever had been covering the room. And here they stop. I was the first person to so much as step into the room."

A small smile pulled at her lips, half-proud, half-embarrassed. "I'm guessing the spell treated me like a big-cat. And since hanging around you and Big Evan so much, I've realized that sometimes I can feel witch magics. Cool and sparkly on my skin."

That was a surprise. Humans can only feel magics when the spell is directed at them, as in a keep-away spell that shocks anyone who touches the spelled item. But then, Jane Yellowrock isn't human. I can do magic—it's in my very genes, passed along on the X chromosome from parent to child—but Jane *is* magic. And scary sometimes.

"Okay." I sat on the floor in the foyer, outside the opening to the parlor, and reached out with my magics. Immediately I *saw* the spell. It was mostly green, smelling of pine and hemlock and holly, marking the caster as an earth witch, like me. I held out my hands and touched the edges of the conjure; it flashed against my fingertips painfully, hot and cold together, with minute darker green flashes of deeper pain. Once I concentrated, I could see the parameters of the incantation and the place it was protecting, the far corner of the room where the dust was deepest. A bit of cloth was in the corner, like a man's old-fashioned handkerchief, and an old newspaper, the rubber band disintegrated into blue goo from the heat and moisture of the long-sealed room. A curl of wallpaper had fallen across it too. I guessed that the spell was tied to an amulet, probably hidden beneath the trash. I stood and brushed the dirt off my jeans.

"So," I said, "I guess I need to push through the spell and get a feel for what is causing the problem." The instant I said the words, a sense of dread fell on me. I *knew*, completely and totally, that if I went into the room, *I was going to die*. Worse, *my child would die*. I sucked in a breath, and it burned my throat. *My husband would die*. Tears started in the corners of my eyes. And *the deaths would be horrible, painful, tortured deaths*. It was illogical and stupid and clearly the result of the spell. But it was also *real*. I backed away, three unsteady steps. And the spell faded.

"Son of a witch on a switch," I cursed.

Jane was leaning against the molding in the opening, arms crossed, watching me. "Bad?"

"Totally and completely sucky." I described what I had been made to feel by the spell. "Whoever created that spell was good. Really, *really* good. And frighteningly inventive."

Jane nodded, only her head and the tip of her long braid moving. "The worker who nearly got brained by the magical flying hammer, was he getting ready to go in here?" she asked.

"Yes. Why?" I asked.

"Because that ladder"—she tilted her head to the metal stepladder—"wiggled when you decided to go in. I figured it was going to fly across the room and hit you if you didn't back off." Her lips pulled again in that half smile that was uniquely hers. "I was going to catch it before it hit you, of course."

"Thanks," I said, eyeing the ladder. "Like I said. That is a really good spell." I pointed to the corner. "I have a feeling that the original incantation is tied to something in that corner. Maybe an amulet hidden under the trash."

Jane nodded and uncrossed her arms. Stepping close, she pushed me farther away from the parlor opening and into the dining room opening on the other side of the foyer. Out of the way of flying carpenter tools, I realized. It was an odd dance step of a move, and Jane grinned down at me. She was a dancer, and I had three left feet and couldn't follow her; I nearly fell. "Careful," she said, holding me steady.

"Don't get hurt," I blurted.

Jane chuckled softly. "My reflexes are fast."

"Yeah," I said hesitantly. "Still . . ."

Jane shook her head in amusement and dropped to her knees again. She crawled into and around the parlor, one shoulder and hip brushing against the walls, just the way a cat would explore a room, around the outer edges first. When she reached the wallpaper and cloth on the far side, she batted the paper away in a move so catlike I covered my face to stifle a giggle. Then Jane grabbed up the cloth in two hands, held like paws, and rolled over with it, sending up clouds of dust. When her sneezing fit subsided, she batted the cloth away too, revealing a snake.

I lifted my hand to warn Jane, which was stupid as she had already lifted the snake to expose it as dry, cracked rubber tubing and small pieces of corroded metal. Jane said, "It looks like some weird kind of stethoscope. And this is the amulet, for sure. My hand is stinging, and some kind of green magic is running all over my skin." She crawled across the room on three limbs, the stethoscope in her left hand.

It was a weird design, with two earpieces and two flat chest pieces. Near where a doctor's chin might go, the two pieces were connected with a metal tube that had been wrapped in a circle, like a trumpet's body, and, like a trumpet, the connecting part was clearly designed to increase and maybe modulate sound waves. The dangling pieces seemed longer than most stethoscopes, and the little circular chest pieces were decidedly old-fashioned.

Green magics emanated from them and were climbing Jane's arm and wrapping around her body. Before she reached the doorway, and before the magic reached her head, she dropped the device and swatted it, just like an irritated cat. The spell instantly went still, into stasis, and Jane crawled out of the room, shaking her head, muttering, "I know. I know. I don't like it either." She crossed the entry to the room and stood, brushing off her clothes, scowling. But with Jane a scowl meant nothing; an expressionless face meant even less. At her best, Jane was inscrutable, and I'd always put that down to her being found in the mountains by park rangers, with no memory of anything, no language, no people, no nothing, and then being raised in a children's home and learning how to socialize—or not socialize—in an artificial "family."

Now that the amulet was closer, I knelt and studied it. From upstairs the creaks of the old house increased, but when I looked up, nothing had changed. Outside the windows, the wind picked up and buffeted the house. I shrugged and went back to studying. The chest pieces were made of some kind of plastic, maybe like that Bakelite stuff that was so popular in the early nineteen hundreds. If so, then that dated the device to that era. My grandmother had Bakelite jewelry, and it was quite collectible. The stethoscope was in fairly good repair, even the rubber parts, which one might have expected to disintegrate.

I heard clicks to my side and looked up to see that Jane had pulled a small digital camera out of her boot and was taking pictures of the house and the amulet. I made a small *mmm* of approval, but the photos might be blurred. Magics did that to photos sometimes.

From upstairs the creaks of the old house increased again, and developed a distinct rhythm. "Molly!" Jane shouted. Suddenly she was standing over me, her arms lifting high. She caught a wooden headboard as it roared down the stairs and slammed at me. "Out!" she shouted again, as she tossed the headboard and caught the flying footboard, using it to deflect a flying drawer or three from a bedroom upstairs.

Crouching to make a smaller target of myself, I raced for the front door, which flung itself open to allow me passage. Jane followed and the door slammed behind her. She pulled me to the street fast, the winds I had noted only moments before dying when we reached the curb.

"Is that the spell or is the house alive?" she demanded.

It might be a dumb or bizarre question to most people, but not to me, and clearly not to Jane. "I don't know," I said. I needed to ask Evangelina, my older sister and our new coven mistress since Mama retired and moved two towns over to take care of Grandma.

"Great. Just ducky." Jane scowled as she brushed more dust off her clothes. "Fine. One thing I can tell you. A vamp owned that stethoscope. I could smell him all over it."

Back in Asheville, I picked up my daughter, Angelina, from the family café, where my younger sisters were watching her, and arrived home, to our new house, before Big Evan did. My girl was worn-out after playing with my wholly human sisters, Regan and Amelia, which meant she went down for a nap while I fixed supper. I put Angie Baby in her bed and covered her with the blankie that Evangelina had crocheted while Angie was still kicking my insides out in the last horrible month of pregnancy.

When we painted the new house—after we lost the mobile home—I had chosen the soft sage green color for Angie's room based on the blankie, which my daughter loved. Darker green leprechauns and earth brown brownies sat on huge calla lily leaves beneath a magical spreading oak tree. Unicorns pranced in the background and rainbows crossed the horizon beyond the tree, all painted by Regan and Amelia. What they hadn't gotten in magical abilities they had made up for in artistic ability and talent. It was a room of love.

In the kitchen, I turned up the AGA, stirred the stew I had left bubbling on the stove, and put a loaf of bread in the oven. I also started a pot of brown rice, to stretch the stew so that Jane could join us. I couldn't pay her for the work this afternoon, so the least I could do was feed her supper.

I knew Evan was home before he even turned into the drive. The wards we had put up around the house warned me, identifying his signature. He came in, work boots clomping, and put his arms around me. Evan is a huge bear of a man, easily six feet six, with red hair and beard, lightly streaked with gray. He is older than I am, but with witches' expanded life spans, that matters less to us than to humans. When we met it was love at first sight. Lust at first sight too, but that was definitely the lesser of our earth-shattering reactions to one another. Evan was a witch, one of the rare male witches to survive to adulthood, and we were pretty certain that was why Angie Baby's gift had awakened so early—she had a witch gene from each of her parents, making her the most powerful witch on earth at this time, so far as we had been able to determine.

"Whose magics you been playing around with?" he mumbled into my hair, which tumbled over my eyes and tangled with his beard. Mine was not nearly as bright red as his. "Do I need to worry that another witch caught your eye?"

"Absolutely." I turned in his arms and wrapped mine around him. They didn't quite reach around his shoulders, but the fit was perfect around his chest, and I clasped my hands together in the middle of his back. "I think you need to remind me that I have the perfect man at home and shouldn't be playing the field anymore."

"Is Angie in her room?" His voice turned up hopefully on the end.

I buried my face in the crook of his shoulder. "Napping very deeply. She's making those little puffs of breath that she does when we just can't wake her."

"There is a God." Big Evan picked me up and carried me to the bathroom instead of the bed, which worked out quite well to remove the sweat of the day from him and the construction dust and stink of vamp and unfamiliar magics off of me.

When Jane got to the house my hair was still damp, but I was clean—very, very clean—and I was dressed in a T-shirt and a fitted denim shift with full skirt and deep, tucked pockets. I don't think Big Evan and I fooled her any, because she shook her head and smiled that small smile while looking back and forth between us. I had the feeling she thought we were cute, but at least she wasn't the teasing type.

She woke Angie Baby and kept her busy in her room while I finished up the evening meal, and then carried my girl to the table. Angie usually fought being put into the high chair, wanting to sit in a regular chair like a big girl, though the table came only to her nose that way and I didn't trust a stack of catalogs the way my own mother had. But tonight Jane surprised us all with a bright pink booster seat with Angie's name painted on the back. It had little suction cups on the bottom and a strap that attached it to the chair; another strap attached around Angie's waist, with an additional strap that looked special-made for Angie's current baby doll. Angie squealed and chattered and was enchanted with her big-girl chair. And Jane's face softened at Angie's obvious delight.

Over stew—heavy on the veggies, light on the beef—Jane told us what she had discovered about the strange stethoscope. "It's called a Kerr Symballophone, and it was designed in 1940 with two diaphragm chest pieces to allow doctors to hear different parts of the chest in both ears so they could differentiate the sounds from either lung, or from the top and bottom of a single lung, or from the heart and a lung. Kinda neat, really."

I leaned into my husband and said, "She's showing off her brand-new emergency medical training."

"You took an EMT course?" he said, surprised.

Jane gave a minuscule shrug and tore off a hunk of bread. "Finished last month. I figured it might come in handy," she said, her eyes on the bread and a smile tugging at her mouth, "for the day you finally give in to temptation and shoot Evangelina."

Evan coughed and turned red. I laughed. I guess it was possible that he didn't think his feelings about my eldest sister were quite so obvious. "You can't choose your family," I said sweetly. "More stew?" Evan nodded and Jane went on as I dipped up another humongous portion for my hubby. The man had to burn ten thousand calories a day.

"Anyway, I went to the Hainbridge Historical Society and did some research."

"I didn't even know Hainbridge *had* a history," I said.

Evan chuckled, shoveled in a mouthful, and gestured for Jane to go on.

"There was a doctor by the name of Hainbridge living in the city in 1840." She went back to the bread and dipped it into her stew, watching as the bread soaked up the thick broth. "And in 1870. And in 1910. And in 1940."

"A family of doctors?" Evan asked.

I remembered the smell of vamp and said, "No way. He wasn't—"

"Way," Jane said. "I've seen two small portraits, hand-painted, seventy years apart, and except for the beard, it's the same guy."

"I'll be," I said. "I know we have a lair in Asheville. Word is that the head vampire wants to start a barbecue joint in town." When Evan paused with his spoon in midair, I said, "Down, boy. So far, it's just a rumor." To Jane I said, "Barbecued ribs are his favorite. So. We had a lair here, way back when."

She nodded and glanced at Angelina, her look saying there was more to tell but not in front of tender ears. So I had to wait for details, and waiting never sat well with me. I have red hair. Some form of impatience is surely bred into me.

When Angie Baby was finally down again for the night, and Jane and Evan and I were all stretched out in the tiny living room, Jane finally dished. "Hainbridge was a vamp with a human son. The kid came down with what sounds like leukemia, when he was a child in 1845."

"Vamps can have kids? I mean, human kids?" Evan said.

"Sounds like it, but it must be really rare," Jane said. "According to the records, the doctor tried everything to cure the kid, and instead of being cured, the kid went crazy. The local newspaper called him a lunatic. He was seven."

"The father tried to turn his son to cure him of the leukemia," I whispered.

"Yeah. That's what I got out of it. And from what I've read, that's not permissible, to turn a child. And just as bad, Hainbridge didn't chain his child up."

I looked across the room to Angie's door. It was half-closed and I suddenly couldn't stand it. I stood and crossed to the opening and looked in. Angie was curled on her side, her thumb in her mouth. She didn't sleep with her thumb in her mouth often, only when she needed comfort, and I had to wonder if she had heard us talking, even in her sleep, and become distressed. I studied the wards on the room and tightened them here and there where they had grown a bit frayed. And I prayed too. I wasn't much of a prayer, not like Jane. She was a true believer and she prayed religiously—a small joke we shared. I was less . . . confident, less sanguine, about who and what God was, and about why He would give a rat's behind about any of us. But I prayed anyway—*God, keep my baby safe*. Just in case. And oddly, when I finished, Angie pulled her thumb out of her mouth, sighed, and rolled over. Coincidence was a strange mistress. When I settled in my chair and picked up my tea, Jane went on.

"He was accused of having rabies. The kid was," she clarified. "He bit several people, tried to chew off the arm of a little girl in town. No one got turned, but the kid disappeared and the doctor stopped practicing and went into seclusion. He wasn't seen by the townspeople often, but when the war started in 1861, he totally disappeared."

"The Civil War?" Evan asked.

"Yeah. And when he reappeared in Hainbridge in 1870, several years after the war ended, there weren't enough people there to remember him. Sherman did a number on the town."

"Is it true that Sherman was a werewolf?" I asked.

"No such thing as werewolves," Evan said firmly, raising up the foot of his oversized recliner and pushing back. "No such thing as weres at all."

Jane and I looked at each other and said nothing. There were witches and vampires and at least one skinwalker. Who could say about werewolves? "Anyway," Jane said, "when he came back to town, he was all into treatments for lunatics and research."

"His son was still alive," I guessed.

Jane shrugged and curled her legs under her. She was long and lean, dressed in a T-shirt and worn-out, skintight jeans, her boots left at the door and striped socks on her feet in shades of fuchsia and emerald; the socks were a gift from me. I doubted that she ever wore them unless she came here. Jane Yellowrock didn't have the most jocular of natures, but she was desperately appreciative of any small gift, which made my heart ache for her.

I shook my head as I remembered the storm that destroyed the mobile home we had lived in until a few months past when Angie's power awakened *way* too early and ripped the place apart. Jane had saved us all that night by turning into a mountain lion and calming Angie long enough for Evan and me to bind Angie's powers tightly to her. As if she knew what I was thinking, Jane met my eyes, glanced at Angie's room, and shrugged as if it had been nothing. It hadn't been nothing. If I believed in miracles, I'd say that was one.

"So, then he involved some witches who had come over from Ireland—a woman by the name of Ester Wilkins, her daughter Lauran, and her sister Ruth. They'd started a coven, under the covers, so to speak, out of sight, but they provided the doctor with herbal tinctures, decoctions, and concoctions." She tilted her head. "There's a difference between decoctions and concoctions?"

"Big difference," Evan said. I had thought he was asleep, sitting in his big chair, fingers laced over his middle, ankles crossed, and eyes closed. I laughed and he smiled, opened an eye, and blew me a kiss.

"Yeah, okay," Jane said. "You two need me to leave?"

"Nah," Evan said, his belly moving with silent laughter. "We took care of that before you got here."

"Ewwww," Jane said, shuddering with a breathy laugh.

I threw a couch pillow and hit him squarely in his beard—which just made him laugh harder. "Back to the vamp and witches," I said, trying to sound prim, but likely not succeeding.

"I don't know what happened next, but I do have hypotheses," Jane said. "I think the doctor kept on with his research for decades, coming and going to protect his identity. And then he involved the witches in a more personal way. I think he either tried to get witches to create a conjure to cure his son's lunatic-ism, or tried to get witches to let the kid drink witch blood to cure it, *or* he was trying to cure the leukemia that had made his son sick in the first place. Or something along those lines. I think he went to a witch one night and tried to force her to help. And of course the witch had warded her house. I think the ward transferred to the stethoscope when she tried to stake the vamp or he tried to drain her."

"Lots of unknowns in any of those situations," Evan rumbled.

"True, but any of those scenarios explains what I remember about the smells. . . ." She stopped dead, still not sure what Evan remembered of the mountain lion who saved the day when Angelina had her awakening. "I have a really good nose. I can smell some magics and some vampires."

Big Evan nodded, his expression unchanged, and Jane went on. "Any of those scenarios explains what I remember about the smells in the house, and the odd way the stethoscope protects the house. But, really, none of the specifics matter," Jane said. Evan widened his eyes in surprise. Jane leaned forward, turning her body directly to his, her elbows on her knees, her clasped hands hanging between her legs, partially mirroring his posture. "All we need to know for sure are the following." She held up a closed fist and one finger went up. "Did the stethoscope get the ward by accidental—or even by deliberate—transference?" Another finger went up. "Is the witch's ghost still in the house, which I don't think, but is important to know?" Followed quickly by a third finger. "Is the vamp still living or did she kill him true-dead with her spell? If she killed him, then that makes it blood magic, and much stronger and more unpredictable, right? And blood magic changes how you guys get rid of the spell."

Big Evan was staring at Jane intently now. Jane's lips went up slightly. "What? You didn't think I was smart enough to figure all that out?" When Evan didn't reply, Jane said, "The most important thing to figure out, though, is how you guys get paid."

"We don't," I said automatically.

"Why not?" Jane asked, still holding Evan's gaze. "You get rid of the ward and the apparent poltergeist effect, or the house can't be used. If the house can't be used, then somebody is out a lot of money spent on renovations so far. Getting rid of the scary stuff sounds like part of the renovations to me."

Evan smiled, showing teeth between mustache and beard. "You think the Hainbridge coven is getting paid, but knew that Molly was an easy mark. They planned to let her do the work and they get to pocket the money."

Jane sat back, her tiny smile in place.

"I am not an easy mark," I said.

Jane made a snorting sound. Big Evan said, "Sweetheart, you are the biggest mark alive. And that's why I love you so much. If you weren't so easy to fool, you'd never have married a big galumph like me."

"You're not a galumph," I said.

"See?" To Jane, Evan said, "What's the name of the construction company and what's the house going to be used for now?"

"Hainbridge General Construction. And it's owned by and is going to become a lawyer's office." My husband started to laugh.

The next morning Big Evan called Shadow Blackwell, the Hainbridge coven mistress, and suggested that I take over the job, informing Shadow that her coven could get a finder's fee, *if* one could be properly negotiated. Shadow Blackwell was not pleased, but it wasn't like she had much to fume about. She had tried to get the job done in an underhanded way, and had been caught.

Once the local coven was out of way, Evan contacted the owner of the construction company, speaking in my name. The contractor had an iron-clad agreement with the owner of the property that he would *not* be responsible for "acts of God" above and beyond what his company's insurance covered, and that insurance did not cover what amounted to an exorcism. Unfortunately he had not told the client that his office was haunted.

Last, my wonderful husband called the lawyer, one Chauncey L. Markwhite II, who was not a very cheery-natured man and refused to pay one red cent to me for my services. When it was explained to him that all construction had ceased on his property, and would not be starting again until the little matter of magical flying mallets was resolved, he accused Evan of extortion. Which totally ticked off my hot-tempered husband. Evan suggested that it was possible to prove the problem to Chauncey and a meeting was set up for the next morning before the start of business—meaning we were to meet him at his haunted house promptly at eight a.m. *Promptly* was the lawyer's term, and he expected Evan to abide by that. He clearly did not know my husband, who was not one to take orders.

I had kept out of the picture while all phone conversations took place, but I needed to be present during this one, as I would be speaking as the "witch expert," to keep Evan hidden in the witch closet. Jane wanted to be present too, as an outside witness, but I privately thought it might be more along the lines of wanting to watch Evan play with a lawyer the way a big-cat often plays with its dinner before killing and eating it.

By prearrangement, Jane was the first to arrive at the haunted house, watching for the lawyer, her cell phone ready. The moment the lawyer's car got there, she hit SEND and Evan started our car. We were ten minutes out, making Chauncey wait. As Jane had said, "Witches one, Chauncey zip."

When we got to the house, the front door was hanging open and neither Jane nor Chauncey was to be seen. We both were out of the car while it was still rocking on its suspension, Evan saying, "Good Golly, Miss Molly. You don't think she mistook him for a bloodsucker of a different sort and staked him, do you?"

I sputtered with laughter and was still laughing when we reached the front porch, which I am certain Evan had intended. Inside, Jane was leaning against the stairs, her arms crossed in her own particular stance, and a grin on her face. It was, by far, the ugliest grin I'd ever seen her wear, and she was making little huffing sounds of laughter under her breath, like a cat. The lawyer was six inches inside the parlor, standing as if frozen. His face was white, his eyes were at half-mast, and his skin stood up all over in goose bumps. Jane looked at us in the doorway. "The spell made you afraid that you or your family was going to die. I wonder what fears Lil' Chucky is experiencing."

"If we sit and watch until he dies, we don't make any money," Big Evan said, sounding totally rational, if unconcerned.

"Spoilsport," Jane said. But she leaned in and grabbed Chauncey by his collar and yanked him back into the foyer. He took a breath and started gasping; his lips were blue. I had a bad feeling that he had not taken a single breath while he stood, frozen, inside the parlor. His knees gave out and Jane pivoted him to her, holding him off the floor by collar and belt. She gave him a little shake. "That's the first part of the spell, Lil' Chucky. You wanna work in this room?" she asked him. "You wanna maybe make clients wait in this room for their appointments?"

"No," he wheezed. "No, I . . . Jesus—"

Jane dropped his belt, slapped his face, and had his pants again, the motion so fast I wasn't sure what I had seen. "No blasphemy, no swearing, no dirty language. Got it?"

Chauncey nodded. His color was looking better, and Jane set him on the steps to the upstairs. "So it's a haint, not a demon?" he asked when he'd caught his breath. Jane nodded. "What's part two of the spell?" he asked her.

Jane. Not me.

I stifled a small smile, watching my friend at work. I had never seen this part of her.

"You spend too much time in the room, Lil' Chucky," she said, "and things start flying around. Hammers, ladders, broken furniture from upstairs. And I'd say the flying debris is aimed at anything human, and with fatal intent. Now"—she pointed to me—"this nice woman put her life in danger yesterday to figure out what was wrong with the house. She thinks she can undo the spell and free the property for development, but it's dangerous. So here's the deal. You pay her a flat fee for her efforts. And you pay her another fee, plus expenses, when she's successful. You draw up the contract today, and as soon as her husband and I are satisfied, she goes to work. You get left with a usable building with a great history and a haunted house tale to delight your clients. Maybe hang a plaque on the wall to tell about it."

"How much?" he asked.

Evan named a price that made me wince.

"I spoke to the contractor," Chauncey said. "He had a deal with the Hainbridge coven for a lot less."

"They can't do the work. It's a complicated spell," Evan said. "They called in my wife, and she can. So you work with her or you can think about it for a few days, while the contractor starts another job somewhere and you get left with an unfinished building."

"I have a contract with Hainbridge General Construction," Chauncey said.

"With an 'act of God' clause in it. Haints fall under that category."

"And you can't negotiate with a haint," Jane said, amused.

"Will she do the job for what I was paying the coven?" he hedged.

"No. And it isn't extortion," Evan said, eyes narrowing. "Haints are dangerous. What my wife will give you is a solution to a bigger problem than you knew you had. Let us know when you make a decision." With that, Evan hustled me out of the house and Jane followed, her boots pattering down the front steps.

Before we reached the bottom step, Chauncey raced from the house, squealing like a child. A metal bucket barely missed his head. Jane must have been expecting it, because she caught it out of the air and handed it to him, shaking her head. "Bet you had to touch the stove to see if it was hot when you were a kid. Idiot." But it sounded like good-natured ribbing more than insult. To me she said, "Later, Molly."

Big Evan said, "See you around, Jane," and opened my car door for me. I got in. Evan came around to his side and got in, his bulk making the old rattletrap rock. Jane keyed on her used Yamaha motorcycle. And Chauncey caved. "Wait," he yelled. Jane turned off her bike. We got out of the car. To Evan, he said, "I can't afford the fee you named. I can go . . . maybe half that."

Evan and he dickered for a few minutes over price, and I had to turn away. My services were going to cost a lot more money than I thought they were worth, but they finally settled on a four-figure sum that meant I could get a new refrigerator and put something toward that new car we'd been saving for.

"I'll draw up the contract," Chauncey said. "I can fax or e-mail it over in two hours." He looked at me and said, "Can you get rid of the haint today?"

I almost said yes, but Jane shook her head, very slightly. *Right. Negotiation.* "By Wednesday," I said. "Sooner, if possible, but I can make no promises."

"Okay." He stuck his hand out at Jane. "Deal."

Jane pointed at me. "Your deal is with the lady and her oversized galumph."

We spent the rest of the morning flying spells. I write incantations, conjures, spells—which are pretty much, but not always, the same thing—out in longhand on legal pads. When I reach a point where the spell stops working, I fold it into a paper airplane and fly it across the room. Big Evan balls his up and plays trash can basketball. What we wanted was a spell that would keep us safe in the house, and a totally separate but overlapping conjure that would allow us to see the moment in time when the warding/

keep-away spell transferred to the stethoscope. That transference had caused all the house's problems. A spell that should have died had instead mutated and found a way to persist long after its creator was gone. It was going to be tricky, and that was even before we tried to dismantle the spell and free the house.

We spent lunchtime in the Hainbridge Historical Society, looking at photos of the people who had lived in the house, and photos of the towns-people, so if we happened to see one or two of them when we went search-ing for the pivotal, instigating event, we could call them by name. Then Evan and I went home for dinner and explained to Angelina that we'd be going out. She wasn't happy at being left behind, but when Regan and Amelia showed up carrying an armload of old movies on DVDs, a bag of popcorn big enough to feed an entire family for a month, hair color to add blond streaks to their reddish hair, a dozen shades of nail polish, and a bottle of wine, she perked right up. I was jealous of the girls' night I'd miss, but I was smart enough not to say so. We left the three watching the opening credits of an old black-and-white version of *Cinderella*, the scent of popcorn filling the house and the volume on the TV turned up high enough to rattle the walls.

At dusk, Evan and I entered the house, Jane behind us. I knew she had other things to do—tonight was belly dance class—but here she was, curi-ous as any cat. And she had brought a cooler with colas, iced tea, and sandwiches, two battery-operated lights, a first aid kit, and a bedroll. She was dressed for business in heavyweight denim jeans with stakes and blades strapped on her waist and thighs. When she saw me staring at the pile of supplies and at her silver-plated knives she shrugged. "Insurance, not that I expect to need any of it."

Evan, who was carrying a basket filled with candles, a batch of dried herbs, and a small camp stove for heating water, just nodded. "Good think-ing. Glad to have you watching our backs."

It was the first time Evan had shown open approval of Jane, and she ducked her head to hide a pleased smile. I decided they were going to play nice, letting me concentrate on the seeing spell Evan and I had settled on. The math of any spell was hard—altering physical laws by will and intent was a job fraught with danger and the likelihood of mistakes. A loss of concentration, a stray worry, and everything could fall apart—or blow up, which was rare, but a lot more scary.

First thing I did was to damp mop the foyer, concentrating on the area of floor directly in front of the parlor. Then, while the floor dried, I cleansed the house with a stick of burning dried sage. Once the house was cleansed I asked Jane, "Did you remember to bring your shirt?"

She lifted her brows and handed me a Ziploc bag with her filthy T-shirt from the day before. "You gonna tell me why you need my dirty laundry?"

"I'm going to shake the dust into a bowl and give it back."

"Least you could do is wash it first," she grumbled. At my expression she lifted a shoulder and added, "Just sayin'."

I shook my head and drew a circle about five feet across on the wood floor with white chalk and set a cut-crystal bowl in the center. I filled it with bottled water and put the empty in my bag. Using a compass, Evan set new, white pillar candles inside the circle at the cardinal points, and draped a silver cross around each. Outside, it was getting dark, making it very hard to see in the foyer. No electricity would be used tonight. Jane sat on the bottom step, out of the way, her knees drawn up and her arms around her ankles, as Evan lit the candles. I stepped into the circle and closed it with the piece of chalk. Evan backed away toward Jane and set the candle at magnetic north, which was to my left side and back a bit, the parlor opening facing east.

This was to be my ritual tonight, because as an earth witch, my magics were closest to the green magics of the spell we were trying to get a good look at. Evan, an air witch, could only offer support. I gathered my white dress close and sat behind the bowl, cross-legged, the bowl of water between my knees. I opened the plastic bag and held Jane's shirt over the bowl, shaking it gently, steadily. Dust from the parlor sprinkled onto the still surface of the water. I balled the shirt back up and sealed it into the bag, tucking it under my knee.

Satisfied, I nodded to Evan. From the bag he had carried, he lifted a silver bell with no clapper and the silver mallet that was used to ring it. He also brought out his father's old, leather-bound Bible—the book Old Man Trueblood had been holding when he was accepted into the church and baptized, when he married, when each of his children were born, and when he died. I wasn't much of a religious person—nowhere near as spiritual as Jane—but even I knew this book had power.

I took a deep breath and exhaled, repeating the clarifying exercise twice more to settle myself. Everything I did tonight would be in threes. I closed my eyes and nodded to Evan. As I opened my mouth he rang the bell, the clear, pure tone and my words overlapping each time I said the word *bell*. "Bell, book, and candle. Bell, book, and candle. Bell, book, and candle." The three tones seemed to ring on, echoing through the empty house, and continued, three times more with the first word of the next three lines. "Dust to dust, through time to now. Dust to dust, through time to now. Dust to dust, through time to now."

I opened my eyes, and without pausing went on into the next three lines, knowing that Evan had the cadence now and would keep up with me, ringing the bell with each first word, even though the method of lines was changing.

"Time of warding. Time of blood. Time of attack.

"Time of betrayal. Time of undead. Time of change.

"Time of vampire. Time of transference. Time of death."

I fell silent, the bell chimes shimmering through the empty house. As the last tone faded, the water between my knees seemed to brighten. And so did the floor of the parlor. In the far corner where the stethoscope had rested for so long, a soft green glow spiraled up, a mist full of light. Close to the opening of the foyer where the stethoscope rested now, a twin green, featherlike luminosity rose, twining and twisting. The mist rose from the floor like smoke, meeting the stained ceiling, pooling against the high corners before spreading and reaching slowly toward the center of the room, overhead. Both tendrils reached the center at the same instant and touched, tentative, like delicate green fingers of budding desire.

A single fixture appeared in the center of the ceiling, an old-fashioned electric ceiling light, bright in the dimness. The magical light of the spell merged with the old light and with its other half and curled back on itself, undulating across the ceiling, to brighten the room, revealing furnishings as they had once been. Where the milky light fell down, back to the floor, tendrils twirled and danced and revealed a moment out of time.

But this scene was not like any time spell I had ever seen. It wasn't misty or uncertain, no dreamlike underpinnings or unfinished supports. It was crisp and clear and certain, full of sharp edges. This was not the result of a seeing spell. This was something different, something I had never seen before.

I had been wrong. The spell tied to the stethoscope wasn't finished. The spell had, instead, created some kind of bizarre bubble universe, a pocket universe, a part of real time, sectioned off, sealed away from the world the rest of us knew, or maybe looping around and around over and over again.

Light blossomed out, opening like a flower in a segment of high-speed photography, to display the room as it had once been. The walls were wallpapered a deep blood rose shade. The furniture was from the late nineteen thirties or forties, with a velvet upholstered couch in a vibrant wine shade against the far wall, a wheeled tea tray before it, a teapot wrapped in a quilted cozy. Wing chairs were aligned to catch the heat from the fire burning merrily in the fireplace. A card table stood in one corner and a bookshelf across from it. An old-fashioned phonograph, the windup kind with an ornate brass horn, was on a side table, and a squeaky song came from it, a man's voice sounding hollow yet inordinately cheery.

A woman sat in a wing chair, a basket of yarn at her feet, a steaming teacup on a side table. She was small, with dark auburn hair, and dressed in a robe in a deep shade of navy, over a white nightgown. She was knitting with blue yarn that trailed up from a basket with large skeins, the pile of finished garment on her far side. She seemed to hear a noise and looked up, turning. Her eyes widened, mouth opened. A form fell upon her, the *pop* of vampiric speed sounding in the room like a gunshot. It was a child, dressed in dark pants and nothing else, his skin the dead white of the three-day dead. The vampire child, small but unnaturally strong, leaped, grabbed up the woman, and spun her in her chair. She screamed, fear and pain in the harsh note.

My mouth opened to murmur a rejection, but I stopped before it left my mouth. It might affect the efficacy of . . . of everything. They whirled, caught in the remnants of the vampire child's attacking speed. His fangs latched upon her neck, tearing. Her scream stopped, even as the two of them fell back. There was none of the tenderness of the vampire wooing his dinner, none of the pleasure I had heard could come from a feeding. A single strong sucking sounded, and he started to drink, even as they fell into the far corner.

The woman lifted her knitting needles. She stabbed the child.

He screamed, the awful keening note of the undead brought to true death.

I shuddered, knowing I could do nothing to stop this violence. Terrible, horrible violence. A woman and undead child in mortal combat. No wonder the warding spell had gone horribly wrong. It had never been intended to protect against a child, no matter how feral.

Tears started in my eyes and trailed down my cheeks. I caught a breath that ached deep inside. But it wasn't over.

Another *pop* sounded. Louder than the first. A man wearing an old-fashioned gray suit and carrying a black medical bag appeared in the room. He dropped the bag and pulled the woman and child apart. Blood pumped from a deep tear in her throat. Scarlet stained her white gown and splattered across the room. The child fell, a wooden knitting needle in his right side, the other in his chest, just to the left of center, a stake, positioned and angled in what looked like a deadly strike.

The woman's blood pumped over the man's chest. A stethoscope hung there—the Kerr Symballophone that now rested in the room. The child's blood splattered as well, a few small drops hitting the man, his face looking fully human and full of agony.

The three fell against the far wall, knocking over a small table. The man roared a single word, *"No!"* vamping-out so fast I couldn't follow the action. He fell to the floor beneath the two, cradling the woman and pulling the stakes from the child. He tore his own wrist and dribbled his blood into the child's mouth. The vampire scooped the woman's blood into the mouth of the child as well.

But it was clear the undead child was true-dead. And the woman died as I watched, her pupils growing wide, her face going slack.

The vampire screamed, his fangs nearly two inches long, lifting to the light. His bellow was powerful. As he sat there, the two bodies embraced on his lap, the stethoscope slid to the floor. And he seemed to look right at me.

The vision of the spell faded.

From behind me, Jane said, "Well, that sucked."

"The only thing that makes sense," I said, "is for it to be a bubble universe. That's the only way he could see me looking at him."

Evan finished chewing before answering. We were sitting in an all-night Taco Bell, and between them, Jane and Evan had devoured a table full of tacos, burritos, gorditas, and chalupas. Crumbs and wadded papers were everywhere. It looked as if a platoon of four-year-olds had had a food fight. "If it's a bubble universe, then what's powering it?" Evan asked when he'd swallowed. "Bubble universes—pocket universes—are theoretical in physics and unheard-of in magic since Tomás de Torquemada's time. And even then they were hearsay as much as heresy. No one's ever claimed to have made one, or been freed from one, or even found one." He picked up the last taco. "Bubble universes usually have their own time span, linear but not exactly like ours, like in the fairy tales, where time runs differently in Fairy from human Earth. This is more like a time loop, where things happen over and over again, in which case he wouldn't have seen you unless your viewing the loop disrupted it somehow." Evan shrugged. "Of course, the vampire could have been looking at something on the floor in his time, not seeing you."

"He saw me," I said. "Totally, *totally* saw me. That electric-eye-contact thing."

Jane was sitting across from us, lounging back, one jeans-clad leg up on the seat beside her, her weapons stowed in our trunk. "He saw Molly," she said. "No doubt. I was sitting behind her and I felt it too. Vamp zingers. When they vamp-out, you can feel their gazes." She sucked Pepsi through a straw and made a face. Jane liked Coke; Evan liked Pepsi better. The two had spent a friendly ten minutes arguing about the brands before the first part of the meal came. There had followed the silence of carnivores eating—the chomp of strong teeth and the crunch of bones—I mean tacos.

"So if we figure out how to break the spell," I said, "and reintegrate the bubble of time with our universe . . . can we save the witch?"

"Molly," Jane said gently. "She's dead. She's been dead since the little vamp tore her carotids out and the big vamp tried to save *him* instead of the witch." When I looked confused, she explained, "The bigger vamp's blood might have saved the witch, if he'd been fast enough. He made the wrong choice, and by not saving her, and by adding her blood and his son's blood into the mix while the spell was trying to save her, he warped the spell and trapped himself in the bubble universe."

"Holy crap. That makes sense," Evan said through a mouthful of taco.

Jane and Evan shared a look that had volumes in it. "What?" I demanded. "No, don't look at each other. Look at *me*. I do not need protecting. Tell me. What makes sense?"

"The vamp isn't dead," Jane said, her brows drawing down as she thought it through.

"Yeah," Evan said, gesturing with the last bite of taco. "What she said. I'm guessing that his undead life is keeping the looped spell going, and if you break the spell, he'll attack."

"And because his undead life force has been powering the spell, he'll be hungry," Jane said. "Like hungry for seventy years. That kinda hungry. He'll be *insane* with hunger. He'll have to be put down." She shrugged by making a tossing gesture with the Pepsi cup. "I'll do it, if needed. Gratis. Consider it my way of saying thanks for all the dinners."

"You bring the food half the time," I said, putting asperity into my tone, feeling guilt worm under my skin. I knew how much Jane got paid to kill a vampire. I understood, logically, how dangerous it was. But unless we went back to Chauncey for money—which might look like a shakedown—that kind of money was not in the budget. Jane had to know that. And I really wanted to put the extra into savings for the new car. Hence the guilt.

"Whatever. Gratis," she said. "That's my deal. Take it or leave it. And if you leave it, you can either find another vampire hunter or appeal to the vamp clan up in Asheville. I hear sane vamps are real sweeties."

"We'll take it, Jane," Evan said. "Thanks. So who was the witch?"

"Beats me," Jane said. "Molly?"

I knew they were working together to protect me, and if I hadn't been feeling like a thief, I'd have been gratified that they were working together on something. On *anything*. "Monique Ravencroft," I said. "She disappeared in the early nineteen forties. No one has seen or heard of her since."

"Ahhh," Jane said. "Her, yeah. Makes sense. Her house was treated as a crime scene, with signs of a struggle and blood at the scene. But there was no body, and no one was ever charged for her murder," Jane said. When I raised my brows at her, she shrugged with the cup again and said, "I did a little research on the house. Found a cold case, a suspended investigation, at that address. No leads, and the principal investigator has been dead nearly fifty years."

Evan and she locked gazes again and I said, "So?"

"Up to you, galumph," Jane said.

Evan heaved a breath and said, "If it's a bubble universe, and if we release the vampire, and if Jane kills him, and if we leave a woman's dead body from forty years ago, and a dead child vampire—"

Jane interrupted, "If we close this, it could leave a mess. Unless we film it, it'll be our word against, well, nothing. And whether we film it or not, I'll have to report the killing of a supposedly sane vamp to the MOC of Asheville. And you'll be called in to give witness." Jane looked at Evan. "And you'll be out of the closet. He'll smell that you're a witch."

"And if we don't close it, we don't get paid," I said, grumpily, finally understanding. "Which makes me sound all kinds of mercenary, but we really, *really* need a new fridge."

"Suggestion?" Jane offered. When Evan nodded, Jane said, "Ask a cop to come sit in on the undoing spell. I'll provide him with a stake and some silver ammo. I'll make sure he takes the kill shot. He takes down the vamp. You are each other's unimpeachable witnesses, he gets any reward from the Asheville MOC, and said vamp won't smell Evan. By the time vamps get on scene, Evan and I will be gone and the house aired out." Jane drained her Pepsi cup with an air rattle of cola through straw. "And if you're up for another suggestion, also in the paper, there's a new cop in town, out of New York, name of Paul Braxton. He'll be used to dealing with vamps and working with witches," she said. "My bet is that he'll let Molly stay in the closet to have her as an informant and"—she twirled a hand, looking for a word—"occult specialist. Sorta."

Evan gave Jane a small salute and she grinned at him, one of the rare, full-on grins I'd seen maybe ten times in our relationship. But her plan did have a certain allure. I looked at it from every side. It wasn't perfect, but it might work.

At eleven a.m. the next morning, Evan—who was missing another day of work—and I met with Detective Paul Braxton, out of New York. He had retired to the Appalachian Mountains, gotten bored fast, and gone to work for the local sheriff. We had found all this out on the Internet before we met at McDonald's, where we introduced ourselves, bought the detective a cup of coffee, and sat.

Braxton was a beefy guy—not as big as Evan, of course, no one is except
a few professional NFL linebackers. He had brown hair and eyes, and wore
a brown suit from the last decade. "So," he said, "how can I help you folks?"
He put both lower arms on the table and rested his weight forward, his
hands cradling the cup of steaming coffee.

"I'm a witch," I said, starting at the most important part. "But I'm not
in any police database."

"Seven Sassy Sisters' Herb Shop and Café," Paul said, his voice gravelly.
"It's not confirmed, but most locals think your mother was a witch. They
also think your older sister, Evangeline, also called Evangelina, is a witch.
The rest of you are above reproach, or were until today. Your friend over
there, hidden behind the newspaper she isn't reading, is Jane Yellowrock,
a vampire hunter." He tilted his head at Jane, who I hadn't even noticed,
and turned his attention back to us. Jane's hands clenched tight, crinkling
the paper. "So why call me in and ruin that spotless rep?"

"Jane," I said softly. "You're busted. You may as well get on over here."
Jane stood and moved across the room, graceful and nonchalant as any
pampered house cat. She slid into the empty seat at the table and passed
the detective her card. "We did not need protection," I said. "And curiosity killed the cat." Jane chuckled at the not-so-veiled reference to her supernatural nature, but kept her attention on the cop.

"'Have Stakes, Will Travel,'" he read from the card. "Cute." He tucked
the card into his inner jacket pocket, including us all when he added, "Talk
to me, people."

"I was hired to get rid of a ghost, demon, or haint—that's a poltergeist,
to you. Instead, I found what might be a bubble universe—my husband
says it's also called a pocket universe—with an unsolved murder hidden
in it." I now had Braxton's full attention. "To get rid of the problem, as I
was hired to, I have to release the universe, which will bring the murder,
the murdered, and the accidently killed back to our time. And that will
release a vampire who has been without blood since the 1940s."

"You know," the cop said, pulling a small electronic tablet out of a pocket
and starting to take notes, "I usually spend an hour getting this much information out of an informant. Succinct. I appreciate it, lady. Go on."

I explained it all to him, and his part in the solution if he was willing.
He was. He also agreed to keep my name out of his report if at all possible.

And we all agreed to meet at dusk back at the Hainbridge house for an exorcism. His last words to us were, "This will be different. I was afraid I'd be bored in this little town. Here's my card. Call me if you think of anything else. And I'm Brax, to my friends." Which sounded like a good way to start.

At dusk, Brax drove up to Monique Ravencroft's house in his unmarked police car, parked, and joined us in the foyer. I had already cleansed the house by burning some dried sage, the acerbic smoke strong on the air. The chalk circle, the lit candles, cut-crystal bowl, bell, and Bible were in place again, and, with the cop staring at the house and my equipment, I explained what I was going to do.

When I was done, he looked at Evan and said, "I get why you're here—to protect your wife." He looked at Jane and said, "What's your part in this?"

She shook her head. "The vamp I saw was sane, and I don't have a contract. You, however, can kill a sane vamp if one attacks. Think of me as your helpful witness." She held out a silver-tipped stake. "Just in case."

I knew that she had a half dozen identical stakes in her boot. If Brax missed, Jane would not let the vampire go free. She would take care of . . . well, everything and everyone around her. It was what she did.

"And this"—Jane handed him a silvered blade—"is for cutting off his head. You know, if needed."

"Helpful, huh?" Brax shook his head, turning the blade so the candle-light caught and reflected off the silver. "You do know that this is longer than the legal limit on concealed carry for bladed weapons, right?"

"I wasn't carrying it. It was in my saddlebag on my bike," she said with her humorless half smile.

"Uh-huh. You Southerners are even more polite and obliging than I was led to believe."

"That's us. Just itching to help out the New York Yankee cop." Jane handed him a sheath for the blade, one that strapped at waist and thigh.

Brax chuckled. "I've never used my vamp-fighting techniques, but I've kept certified and in practice." He strapped on the blade and accepted the stake. "I've never had to kill a vampire. The Master of the City of New York keeps a firm hand on his underlings. So this is a first for me."

"We hope you won't have to kill one tonight," I said. "We hope he'll be saner than he looked last."

"But we won't bet our lives on it," Evan said. "If he attacks and you need backup, you can deputize Jane."

"I'm not the sheriff," Brax said, "but consider Jane deputized if it'll keep my butt alive." He looked at Evan. "Okay, Mr. Trueblood, Mrs. Trueblood. Ready when you are."

It didn't take us long to prepare. I was wearing the same white dress, slightly grimy from the last time I'd worn it here. I gathered it close and sat behind the bowl, cross-legged, the bowl of water between my knees. Just like last night, I opened the Ziploc bag and held Jane's shirt over the bowl, shaking it with a snapping motion this time. There wasn't much dust from the parlor left, but what there was sprinkled onto the still surface of the water. I took my three deep breaths to settle myself and nodded to Evan, who lifted the silver bell. As I spoke the words he rang the bell with the silver mallet. "Bell, book, and candle. Bell, book, and candle. Bell, book, and candle." The tones were rich and true, echoing through the house. "Dust to dust, through time to now. Dust to dust, through time to now. Dust to dust, through time to now. Time of warding. Time of blood. Time of attack. Time of betrayal. Time of undead. Time of change. Time of vampire. Time of transference. Time of death."

As before, the bell chimes shivered through the empty house, leaving the air expectant. As the last tone faded, the water between my knees brightened, and so did the floor of the parlor. Twin green, luminous feathers of light rose, twining and twisting like smoke, up to the ceiling overhead, pooling against the high corners, spreading toward the center of the room.

The old-fashioned electric ceiling light appeared, adding light to the falling dark, revealing the furnishings of the past: the blood rose walls, the velvet upholstered couch and wheeled tea tray, the wing chairs and card table. The man's squeaky song came from the old-fashioned phonograph, hollow and cheery. The small, auburn-haired woman once again sat in the wing chair, the basket of yarn at her feet. I heard Brax take a slow, shocked breath.

The woman looked up, turned. Her eyes widened, mouth opened. The small form fell upon her, the *pop* of vampiric speed making Brax flinch. The child attacked, grabbing up the woman. She screamed. His fangs latched on and her scream stopped, to be replaced by a single strong sucking sound.

The woman lifted her knitting needles. She stabbed the child.

He screamed, the horrible note of true death.

The second *pop* sounded and the taller, adult vampire appeared. He pulled the woman and child apart. Blood pumped scarlet from her throat, all over her white gown and out into the room. The child dangled, the wooden knitting needles in his body.

The woman's blood pumped over the man's chest and the Kerr Symballophone. The child's blood splattered it again. The man roared the single word *"No!"* vamping-out and falling to the floor beneath the two, cradling the woman, pulling the stakes from the child. He tore his own wrist and dribbled his blood into the child's mouth, scooping the woman's blood in as well. Letting the woman die, the woman he might have saved. Everything was just like the last time I had seen it.

The vampire screamed, his fangs nearly two inches long, lifting to the light. His bellow was powerful. And as he sat there, the two bodies embraced on his lap, he looked right at me. He saw Jane behind me. Saw the cop and Evan.

Evan rang the bell again, one strong tone for each word of *freedom* and *free*, as I released my intent and purpose, saying, "Freedom be and freedom bought, freedom from the dead past sought. Free the house and end this spell. Free the dead to heaven and to hell."

As I spoke, the vampire raced at us. With each tone, he aged and shrank, his tissues draining and flesh caving in. His bloody eyes going feral, rabid, insane. He roared again, this time for blood.

The green light exploded out, the candles snuffed all at once. Dark fell on us. I was yanked back, Jane's hands shockingly like steel, bruising me. I was shoved into Evan's chest so hard my breath whuffed out of me. I heard the battle around me as Evan shuffled me out of the house into the night.

But I saw, in the moonlight through the open door, Jane Yellowrock, as she raced toward the vampire, her body moving far faster than human, her eyes glowing golden, her face frozen in a rictus of action, lips pulled back, showing her teeth. And the cop, staking the vampire, but clearly too low, a belly stab. Instantly Jane staked the vampire, one hard thrust in the heart. Brax mirrored her move, stabbing up with the knife, roaring with a battle scream. And then I was outside. In the cool night air, the breeze raising gooseflesh on my arms. And silence descended on the dark.

The sounds of battle had gone on for only seconds, but it seemed much longer. The scream of the vampire, the grunts of the people, the sound of blows hitting the night. Into the silence, I heard Jane say, "Not bad. You got your first vamp kill. But you have to take the vampires' heads. Both of them." And Brax cussed, long and hard, while Jane laughed.

Evan wrapped me in his arms, murmuring to me, "It's okay. It's done. It's okay now, sweetheart." And I could smell the stink of bowels on the air from the witch who had died so long ago, and only moments in the past.

Jane had told me about her inner beast, and I hadn't understood, not at all. I was pretty sure I had seen it tonight, however, in the golden glow of her eyes, in the way her lips pulled back like an attacking cat's. In the pure violence of her body flowing forward, supple and svelte and . . . and violence personified.

I had thought of her as human, as softer than she really was. While Jane Yellowrock had a soft side—the side I saw when she was with Angie Baby, or when she went into "protect mode" around the abused, or when she prayed—she was not human. And she was anything but soft.

I buried my head in Evan's chest and closed my eyes, blocking out that image of Jane—warrior Jane—attacking. Moments later, she came out of the house and down the stairs, her eyes on me, evaluating, questioning, conjecturing. As if she could smell my new awareness of her on the air. For all I knew, she could.

Behind her, Brax called out to Evan to come help him. He didn't say why, but my husband patted my arms and left me. The night air was cool on my flesh where he had held me, and I shivered.

Jane lilted up her lips at my shiver, the smile cynical and defensive. "I'm not a big, bad ugly," she said, her voice stiff. "I won't hurt you. And I'd never hurt your daughter."

I realized I had hurt her, though I had no idea how. "What?" I asked, perplexed. And then it occurred to me that tonight she had allowed me to see a part of her kept hidden until now. I had to wonder if anyone had ever seen her in killing mode. Well, anyone who was still alive. I wrapped my arms around myself and shivered again, thinking about warrior Jane near

Angie. She was right. Jane would never hurt my daughter. And Angelina would never be safer than when she was with Jane Yellowrock. "You're an idiot," I said, putting all the asperity I could into my voice. "I'm not scared of you. I'm *cold*."

Jane blinked, opened her mouth, and closed it, thinking. "You're not scared of me?"

I shook my head no.

Jane walked away a few paces and came back with her jacket, which she wrapped around my shoulders. "Thanks," she said, which I figured was my line, but I understood what she meant.

"You are welcome," I said. And she smiled at me, a real smile, soft and full and lovely.

The police investigation lasted for three weeks, with a complementary media hue and cry over the "unexplained appearance of people from seventy years in the past, all looking unchanged, yet all freshly killed," and the "witch paraphernalia found at the scene." The media attention went on until something more interesting happened and the news vans disappeared.

And, of course, even when the crime scene tape came down, I still didn't get paid. The lawyer didn't answer or return my calls. The morning my old fridge finally wore out, shutting off with a small cough of what sounded like apology, Jane called Brax. I didn't want her to, but Jane had a mind of her own and pretty much did what she wanted.

A wire transfer for the full amount appeared in my bank account that afternoon, only minutes after the newly transplanted local cop paid a visit to the lawyer, off the record, and suggested that he pay his bill. Evan and Jane delivered my spanking new fridge that evening, just in time to save my frozen food.

I fixed steaks that night, and the four of us—Jane, Evan, Angelina, and I—sat on the back porch, under the moonlight, eating and drinking and talking like old friends. It was a perfect night. Or almost. Until Angelina turned to me and said, "Mama. You gonna have a baby!"

In the shocked silence, Jane leaned in too and sniffed me, delicately, like a kitten exploring the world. "Huh. Angie Baby's right. And ten bucks says it's a boy."

Signatures of the Dead

It was nap time, and it wasn't often that I could get both children to sleep a full hour—the same full hour, that is. I stepped back and ran my hands over the healing and protection spells that enveloped my babies, Angelina and Evan Jr., also known as Little Evan. The complex incantations were getting a bit frayed around the edges, and I drew on Mother Earth and the forest on the mountainside out back to restore them. Not much power, not enough to endanger the ecosystem that was still being restored there. Just a bit. Just enough.

Few witches or sorcerers survive into puberty, and so I spend a lot of time making sure my babies are okay. I come from a long line of witches. Not the kind in pointy black hats with a cauldron in the front yard, and not the kind like the *Bewitched* television show that once tried to capitalize on our reclusive species. Witches aren't human, though we can breed true with humans, making little witches about fifty percent of the time. Unfortunately, witch babies have a poor survival rate, especially the males, most dying before they reach the age of twenty from various cancers. The ones who live through puberty, however, tend to live into their early hundreds.

The day each of my babies was conceived, I prayed and worked the same incantations Mama had used on her children, power weavings, to make sure my babies were protected. Mama had a better than average survival rate on her witches. For me, so far, so good. I said a little prayer over them and left the room.

Back in the kitchen, Paul Braxton—"Brax" to his friends, "Detective" or "Sir" to the bad guys he chased—Jane Yellowrock, and Evan were still sitting at the table, the photographs scattered all around. Crime scene photos of the McCarley house. And the McCarleys . . . It wasn't pretty.

The photos didn't belong in my warm, safe home. They didn't belong anywhere.

Evan and I were having trouble with them, with the blood and the butchery. Of course, nothing fazed Jane. And, after years of dealing with crime in New York City, little fazed Brax.

I met Evan's eyes, seeing the steely anger there. My husband was easygoing, slow to anger, and full of peace, but the photos of the five McCarleys had triggered something in him, a slow-burning, pitiless rage. He was feeling impotent, useless, and he wanted to smash things. The boxing bag in the garage would get a pummeling tonight, after the kids went to bed for the last time. I offered him a wan smile and went to the AGA stove; I poured fresh coffee for the men and tea for Jane and me. She had brought a new variety, a first-flush Darjeeling, and it was wonderful with my homemade bread and peach butter.

"Kids okay?" Brax asked, amusement in his tone.

I retook my seat and used the tip of a finger to push the photos away. I was pretty transparent, I guess, having to check on the babies after seeing the dead McCarleys. "They're fine. Still sleeping. Still . . . safe." Which made me feel all kinds of guilty to have my babies safe, while the entire McCarley family had been butchered. Drunk dry. Partly eaten.

"You finished thinking about it?" he asked. "Because I need an answer. If I'm going after them, I need to know, for sure, what they are. And if they're vamps, then I need to know how many there are and where they're sleeping in the daytime. And I'll need protection. I can pay."

I sighed and sipped my tea, added a spoonful of raw sugar, stirred, and sipped again. He was trying to yank my chain, make my natural guilt and our friendship work to his favor, and making him wait was my only reverse power play. Having to use it ticked me off. I put the cup down with a soft china *clink*. "You know I won't charge you for the protection spells, Brax."

"I don't want Molly going into that house," Evan said. He brushed crumbs from his reddish, graying beard and leaned across the table, holding my eyes. "You know it'll hurt you."

I'm an earth witch, from a long family of witches, and our gifts are herbs and growing things, healing bodies, restoring balance to nature. I'm a little unusual for earth witches, in that I can sense dead things, which is why Brax was urging me to go to the McCarley house. To tell him for sure if dead things, like vamps, had killed the family. How they'd died. He could wait for forensics, but that might take weeks. I was faster. And I could give him numbers to go on too: how many vamps were in the blood family, if they were healthy, or as healthy as dead things ever got. And, maybe, which direction they had gone at dawn, so he could guess where the vamps slept by day.

But once there, I would sense the horror, the fear that the violent deaths had left imprinted on the walls, floor, ceilings, furniture of the house. I took a breath to say no. "I'll go," I said instead. Evan pressed his lips together tight, holding in whatever he would say to me later, privately. "If I don't go, and another family is killed, I'll be a lot worse," I said to him. "And that *would* be partly my fault. Besides, some of that reward money would buy us a new car."

"You don't have to carry the weight of the world on your shoulders, Mol," he said, his voice a deep, rumbling bass. "And we can get the money in other ways." Not many people knew that Evan is a sorcerer, not even Brax. We wanted it that way, as protection for our family. If it was known that Evan carried the rare gene on his X chromosome, the gene that made witches, and that we had produced children who both carried the gene, we'd likely disappear into some government-controlled testing program. "Mol. Think about this," he begged. But I could see in his gentle brown eyes that he knew my mind was already made up.

"I'll go." I looked at Jane. "Will you go with me?" She nodded once, the beads in her many black braids clicking with the motion. To Brax, I said, "When do you want us there?"

The McCarley house was on Dogwood, up the hill overlooking the town of Spruce Pine, North Carolina, not that far, as the crow flies, from my house, which is outside the city limits, on the other side of the hill. The McCarley home was older, with a nineteen fifties feel to it, and from the outside it would have been hard to tell that anything bad had happened. The tiny brick house itself, with its elvish, high-peaked roof, green trim, and well-kept lawn, looked fine. But the crime scene tape was a dead giveaway.

I was still sitting in the car, staring at the house, trying to center myself for what I was about to do. It took time to become settled, to pull the energies of my gift around me, to create a skein of power that would heighten my senses.

Brax, dressed in a white plastic coat and shoe covers, was standing on the front porch, his hands in the coat pockets, his body at an angle, head down, not looking at anything. The set of his shoulders said he didn't want to go back inside, but he would, over and over again, until he found the killers.

Jane was standing by the car, patient, bike helmet in her hands, riding leathers unzipped, copper-skinned face turned to the sun for its meager warmth on this early fall day. Jane Yellowrock was full Cherokee, and was much more than she seemed. Like most witches, like Evan, who was still in the witch-closet, Jane had secrets that she guarded closely. I was pretty sure that I was the only one who knew any of them, and I didn't flatter myself that I knew them all. Yet, even though she kept things hidden, I needed her special abilities and gifts to augment my own on this death search.

I closed my eyes and concentrated on my breathing, huffing in and out, my lips in an O. My body and my gift came alive, tingling in hands and feet as my oxygen level rose. I pulled the gift of power around me like a cloak, protection and sensing at my fingertips.

When I was ready, I opened the door of the unmarked car and stepped out onto the drive, my eyes slightly slit. At times like this, when I'm about to read the dead, I experience everything so clearly: the sun on my shoulders, the breeze like a wisp of pressure on my face, the feel of the earth beneath my feet, grounding me, the smell of late-blooming flowers. The scent of old blood. But I don't like to open my eyes. The physical world is too intense. Too distracting.

Jane took my hand in her gloved one and placed it on her leather-covered wrist. My fingers wrapped around it for guidance and we walked to the house, the plastic shoe covers and plastic coat given to me by Brax making little *shush*ing sounds as I walked. I ducked under the crime scene tape Jane held for me. Her cowboy boots and plastic shoe covers crunched/ shushed on the gravel drive beside me. We climbed the concrete steps, four of them, to the small front porch. I heard Brax turn the key in the lock. The smells of old blood, feces, and pain whooshed out with the heated air trapped in the closed-up home.

Immediately I could sense the dead humans. Five of them had lived in this house: two parents, three children, a dog, and a cat. All dead. My earth gift, so much a thing of life, recoiled, closed up within me, like a flower gathering its petals back into an unopened bloom. Eyes still closed, I stepped inside.

The horror that was saturated into the walls, into the carpet, stung me, pricked me, like a swarm of bees, seeking my death. The air reeked when I sucked in a breath. Dizziness overtook me, and I put out my other hand. Jane caught and steadied me, her leather gloves protecting me from skin-to-skin contact that would have pulled me back, away from the death in the house. After a moment, I nodded that I was okay and she released me, though I still didn't open my eyes. I didn't want to see. A buzz of fear and horror filled my head.

I stood in the center of a small room, the walls pressing in on me. Eyes still closed, I saw the death energies, pointed, and said, "They came in through this door. One, two, three, four, five, six, seven of them. Fast."

I felt the urgency of their movements, faster than any human. Pain gripped my belly and I pressed my arms into it, trying to assuage an ache of hunger deeper than I had ever known. "So hungry," I murmured. The pain grew, swelling inside me. The imperative to *eat*. *Drink*. The craving for blood.

I turned to my left before I was overcome. "Two females took the man. He was surprised, startled, trying to stand. They attacked his throat. Started drinking. He died there."

I turned more to my right, still pointing, and said, "A child died there. Older. Maybe ten. A boy."

I touched my throat. It wanted to close up, to constrict at the feel of teeth, long canines, biting into me. The boy's fear and shock were so intense they robbed me of any kind of action. When I spoke, the words were harsh, whispered. "One, a female, took the boy. The other four, all males, moved into the house." The hunger grew, and with it the anger. And terror. Mind-numbing, thought-stealing terror. The boy's death struggles increased. The smell of blood and death and fear choked. "Both died within minutes."

I pointed again and Jane led me. The carpet squished under my feet. I knew it was blood, even with my eyes closed. I gagged and Jane stopped, letting me breathe, as well as I could in this death house, letting me find my balance, my sense of place on the earth. When I nodded again, she led me forward. I could tell I was in a kitchen by the cooking smells that underlay the blood. I pointed into a shadowy place. "A woman was brought down there. Two of them . . ." I flinched at what I saw. Pulled my hand from Jane's and crossed my arms over me, hugging myself. Rocking back and forth.

"They took her together. One drank while the other . . . the other . . . And then they switched places. They laughed. I can hear her crying. It took . . . a long . . . long time," I blundered away, bumping into Jane. She led me out, helping me to get away. But it only got worse.

I pointed in the direction I needed to go. My footsteps echoed on a wood floor. Then carpets. "Two little girls. Little . . . Oh, God in heaven. They . . ." I took a breath that shuddered painfully in my throat. Tears leaked down my cheeks, burning. "They raped them too. Two males. And they drank them dry." I opened my eyes, seeing twin beds, bare frames, the mattresses and sheets gone, surely taken by the crime scene crew. Blood had spattered up one wall in the shape of a small body. To the sides, the wall was smeared, like the figure of angel wings a child might make in the snow, but made of blood.

Gorge rose in my throat. "Get me out of here," I whispered. I turned away, my arms windmilling for the door. I tripped over something. Fell forward, into Brax. His face inches from mine. I was shaking, quivering like a seizure. Out of control. "Now! Get me out of here! NOW!" I shouted. But it was only a whisper.

Jane picked me up and hoisted me over her shoulder. Outside. Into the sun.

I came to myself, came awake, lying in the yard, the warm smells of leather and Jane all around. I touched her jacket and opened my eyes. She was sitting on the ground beside me, one knee up, the other stretched out, one arm on bent knee, the other bracing her. She was wearing a short-sleeved T-shirt in the cool air. She smiled her strange, humorless smile, one side of her mouth curling.

"You feeling better?" She was a woman of few words.

"I think so. Thank you for carrying me out."

"You might want to wait on the thanks. I dropped you, putting you down. Not far, but you might have a bruise or two."

I chuckled, feeling stiffness in my ribs. "I forgive you. Where's Brax? I need to tell him what I found."

Jane slanted her eyes to the side, and I swiveled my head to see the cop walking from his car. He wasn't a big man, standing five feet, nine inches, but he was solid and beefy. I liked Brax. He was a good cop, even if he did take me into some awful places to read the dead. To repay me, he did what he could to protect my family from the witch haters in the area. There were always a few in any town, even in the easygoing Appalachian Mountains. He dropped a knee on the ground beside me and grunted. It might have been the word, "Well?"

"Seven of them," I said, "four men, three women, all young rogues. One family, one bloodline. The sire is male. He's maybe a decade old. Maybe to the point where he would have been sane, had he been in the care of a master vamp. The others are younger. All crazy."

For the first years of their lives, vampires are little more than beasts. According to the gossip mags, a good sire kept his newbie rogues chained in the basement during the first decade or so of undead life, until they gained some sanity. Most experts thought that young rogues were likely the source of werewolf legends and the folklore of vampires as bloody killers. Rogues were mindless, carnal, blood-drinking machines, whether they were brand-new vampires or very old ones who had succumbed to the vampire version of dementia.

If a rogue had escaped his master and survived for a decade on his own, and had regained some of his mental functions, then he would be a very dangerous adversary. A vampire with the moral compass of a rogue, the cunning of a predator, and the reasoning abilities of a psychotic killer. I huddled under Jane's jacket at the thought.

"Are you up to walking around the house?" Brax asked. "Outside? I need an idea of which way they went." He looked at his watch. I looked at the sun. We were about four hours from sundown. Four hours before the blood family would rise again and go looking for food and fun.

I sat up and Jane stood, extending her hand. She pulled me up, and I offered her jacket back. "Keep it," she said, so I snuggled it around my shoulders, the scent of Jane rising around me like a warm animal. She followed as I circled the house, keeping between Brax and me, and I wondered what had come between the two while I was unconscious. Whatever it was, it crackled in the air, hostile, antagonistic. Jane didn't like most cops, and she tended to say whatever was on her mind, no matter how insulting, offensive, rude, or blunt it might be.

I stopped suddenly, feeling the chill of death under my feet. I was on the side of the house, and I had just crossed over the rogues' trail. They had come and gone this way. I looked at the front door. It was undamaged, so that meant they had been invited in or that the door had been unlocked. I didn't know if the old myth about vamps not being able to enter a house uninvited was true or not, but the door hadn't been knocked down.

I followed the path around the house and to the back of the grassy lot. There was a play set with a slide, swings, a teeter-totter, and monkey bars. I walked to it and stood there, seeing what the dead had done. They had played here. After they killed the children and parents, they had come by here, in the gray predawn, and played on the swings. "Have your crime people dusted this?"

"The swing set?" Brax said, surprised.

I nodded and moved on, into the edge of the woods. There was no trail. Just woods, deep and thick with rhododendrons, green leaves and sinuous limbs and straighter tree trunks blocking the way, a canopy of oak and maple arching overhead. I looked up, into the trees, still green, untouched as yet by the fresh chill in the air. I bent down and spotted an animal trail, the ground faintly marked with a narrow, bare path about three inches wide. There was a mostly clear area about two feet high, branches to the side. Some were broken off. A bit of cloth hung on one broken branch. "They came through here," I said. Brax knelt beside me. I pointed. "See that? I think it's from the shirt the blood-master was wearing."

"I'll bring the dogs. Get them started on the trail," he said, standing. "Thank you, Molly. I know this was hard on you."

I looked at Jane. She inclined her head slightly, agreeing. The dogs might get through the brush and brambles, but no dog handler was going to make it. Jane, however . . . Jane might be able to do something with this. But she would need a blood scent to follow. I thought about the house. No way could I go back in there, not even to hunt for a smear of vampire blood or other body fluid. But the bit of cloth stuck in the underbrush might have blood on it. If Jane could get to it before Brax did . . . I looked from Jane to the scrap of cloth and back again, a question in my eyes. She smiled that humorless half smile and inclined her head again. Message sent and received.

I stood and faced the house. "I want to walk around the house," I said to Brax. "And you might want to call the crime scene back. When the vampires played on the swings, they had the family pets. The dog was still alive for part of it." I registered Brax's grimace as I walked away. He followed. Jane didn't. I began to describe the crime scene to him, little things he could use to track the vamps. Things he could use in court, not that the vamps would ever make it to a courtroom. They would have to be staked and beheaded where he found them. But it kept Brax occupied, entering notes into his wireless notebook, so Jane could retrieve the scrap of cloth, and, hopefully the vampire's scent.

Jane was waiting in the drive when I finished describing what I had sensed and "seen" in the house to Brax, her long legs straddling her small, used Yamaha. I had never seen her drive a car. She was a motorbike girl, and lusted after a classic Harley, which she had promised to buy for herself when she got the money. She tilted her head to me, and I knew she had the cloth and the scent. Brax, who caught the exchange, looked quizzically between us, but when neither of us explained he shrugged and opened the car door for me.

The vampire attack made the regional news, and I spent the rest of the day hiding from the TV. I played with the kids, fed them supper, made a few batches of dried herbal mixtures to sell in my sisters' herb shop in town, and counted my blessings, trying to get the images of the McCarleys' horror and pain out of my mind. I knew I'd not sleep well tonight. Sometimes not even an earth witch can defeat the power of evil over dreams.

Just after dusk, with a cold front blowing through and the temperatures dropping, Jane rode up on her bike and parked it. Carrying my digital video camera, I met her in the front garden, and, without speaking, we walked together to the backyard and the boulder-piled herb garden beside my gardening house and the playhouse. Jane dropped ten pounds of raw steak on the ground while I set up my camera and tripod. She handed me the scrap of cloth retrieved from the woods. It was stiff with blood, and I was sure it wasn't all the vampires'.

Unashamedly, Jane stripped, while I looked away, giving her the privacy I would have wanted had it been me taking off my clothes. Anyone who happened to look this way with a telescope, as I had no neighbors close by, would surely think the witch and friend were going sky-clad for a ceremony, but I wasn't a Wiccan or a goddess worshipper, and I didn't dance around naked. Especially in the unseasonable cold.

When she was ready, her travel pack strapped around her neck, along with the gold nugget necklace she never removed, Jane climbed to the top of the rock garden, avoiding my herbs with careful footsteps, and sat. She was holding a fetish necklace in her hands, made from teeth, claws, and bones.

She looked at me, standing shivering in the falling light. "Can your camera record this dark?" When I nodded, my teeth chattering, she said, "Okay. I'll do my thing. You try to get it on film, and then you can drive me over. You got a blanket in the backseat in case we get stopped?" I nodded again and she grinned, not the half smile I usually got from her, but a real grin, full of happiness. We had talked about me filming her, so she could see what happened from the outside, but this was the first time we had actually tried. I was intensely curious about the procedure.

"It'll take about ten minutes," she said, "for me to get mentally ready. When I finish, don't be standing between me and the steaks, okay?" When I nodded again, she laughed, a low, smooth sound that made me think of whiskey and wood smoke. "What's the matter?" she said. "Cat got your tongue?"

I laughed with her then, for several reasons, only one of which was that Jane's rare laugh was contagious. I said, "Good luck." She inclined her head, blew out a breath, and went silent. Nearly ten minutes later, even in the night that had fallen around us, I could tell that something odd was happening. I hit the RECORD button on the camera and watched as gray light gathered around my friend.

If clouds were made of light instead of water vapor, they would look like this, all sparkly silver, thrust through with motes of blackness that danced and whirled. It coalesced, thickened, and eddied around her. Beautiful. And then Jane . . . shifted. Changed. Her body seemed to bend and flow like water, or like hot wax, a viscous, glutinous liquid, full of gray light. The bones beneath her flesh popped and cracked. She grunted, as if with pain. Her breathing changed. The light grew brighter, the dark motes darker.

Both began to dissipate.

On the top of the boulders where Jane had been sat a mountain lion, its eyes golden, with human-shaped pupils. *Puma concolor*, the big-cat of the Western Hemisphere, sat in my garden looking me over, Jane's travel pack around her neck making a strange lump on her back. The cat was darker than I remembered, tawny on back, shoulders, and hips, pelt darkening down her legs, around her face and ears. The tail, long and stubby, was dark at the tip. She huffed a breath. I saw teeth.

My shivers worsened, even though I knew this was Jane. Or had been Jane. She had assured me, not long ago, that she still had vestiges of her own personality even in cat form and wouldn't eat me. Easy to say when the big-cat isn't around. Then she yawned, snorted, and stood to her four feet. Incredibly graceful, long sinews and muscles pulling, she leaped to the ground and approached the raw steaks she had dumped earlier. She sniffed and made a distinctly disgusted sound.

I tittered and the cat looked at me. I mean, she *looked* at me. I froze. A moment later, she lay down on the ground and started to eat the cold, dead meat. Even in the dark, I could see her teeth biting, tearing.

I had missed some footage and rotated the camera to the eating cat. I also grabbed her fetish necklace and her clothes, stuffing them in a tote for later.

Thirty minutes later, after she had cleaned the blood off her paws and jaws with her tongue, I dismantled the tripod and drove to the McCarley home. Jane—or her cat—lay under a blanket on the backseat. Once there, I opened the doors and shut them behind us.

There was more crime scene tape up at the murder scene, but the place was once again deserted. Silent, my flashlight lighting the way for me with Jane in front, in the dark, we walked around the house to the woods' edge.

I cut off the flash to save her night vision, and held out the scrap of bloody cloth to the cat. She sniffed. Opened her mouth and sucked air in with a coughing, gagging *scree* of sound. I jumped back and I could have sworn Jane laughed, an amused hack. I broke out into a fear sweat that instantly chilled in the cold breeze. "Not funny," I said. "What the heck was that?"

Jane padded over and sat in front of me, her front paws crossed like a

Southern belle, ears pricked high, mouth closed, nostrils fluttering in the dark, waiting. Patient as ever. When I figured out that she wasn't going to eat me, feeling distinctly dense, I held out the bit of cloth. Again, she opened her mouth and sucked air, and I realized she was scenting through her mouth. Learning it. When she was done, which felt like forever, she looked up at me and hacked again. Her laugh, for certain. She turned and padded into the woods. I switched on my flash and hurried back to my car. It was the kids' bedtime. I needed to be home.

It was four a.m. when the phone rang. Evan grunted, a bear snort. I swear, the man could sleep through a train wreck or a tornado. I rolled and picked up the phone. Before I could say hello, Jane said, "I got it. Come get me. I'm freezing and starving. Don't forget the food."

"Where are you?" I asked. She told me and I said, "Okay. Half an hour."

Jane swore and hung up. She had warned me about her mouth when she was hungry. I poked my hubby and when he swore too, I said, "I'm heading out to the old Partman place to pick up Jane. I'll be back by dawn." He grunted again and I slid from the bed, dressed, and grabbed the huge bowl of oatmeal, sugar, and milk from the fridge. Jane had assured me she needed food after she shifted back, and didn't care what it was or what temp it was. I hoped she'd remember that when I gave it to her. Cold oatmeal was nasty.

Half an hour later, I reached the old Partman place, a turn-of-the-nineteenth-century homestead and later a mine, the homestead sold and deserted when the gemstones were discovered and the mine closed down in the 1950s when the gems ran out. It was grown over by fifty-year-old trees, and the drive was gravel, Jane standing hunched in the middle. Human, wearing the lightweight clothes she carried in the travel pouch, along with the cell phone and a few vamp-killing supplies.

I popped the doors and she climbed in, her long black hair like a veil around her, her thin clothes covering a shivering body, pimpled with cold. "Food," she said, her voice hoarse. I passed the bowl of oatmeal and a serving spoon to her. She tossed the top of the bowl onto the floor and dug in. I watched her eat from the corner of my eye as I drove. She didn't bother to chew, just shoveled the cold oatmeal in like she was starving. She looked thinner than usual, though Jane was never much more than skin, bone, and muscle—like her big-cat form, I thought. Criminy. Witches I could handle. But what Jane was? Maybe not so much. I hadn't known shape changers or skinwalkers even existed. No one did.

Bowl empty, she pulled her leather coat from the tote I had brought, snuggled under it, and lay back in her seat, cradling the empty bowl. She closed her eyes, looking exhausted. "That was not fun," she said, the words so soft I had to strain to hear. "Those vamps are fast. Faster than Beast."

"Beast?"

"My cat," she said. She laughed, the sound forlorn, lost, almost sad. "My big hunting cat. Who had to chase the scent back to their lair. Up and down mountains and through creeks and across the river. I had to soak in the river to throw off the heat. Beast isn't built for long-distance running." She sighed and adjusted the heating vents to blow onto her. "The vamps covered five miles from the McCarleys' place in less than an hour yesterday morning. It took me more than four hours to follow them back through the underbrush and another two to isolate the opening. I should have shifted into a faster cat, though Beast would have been ticked off."

"You found their lair?" I couldn't keep the excitement out of my voice. "At the Partman place?"

"Yeah. Sort of." She rolled her head to face me in the dark, her golden eyes glowing and forbidding. "They're living in the mine. They've been there for a long time. They were gone by the time I found it. They were famished when they left the lair. I could smell their hunger. I think they'll kill again tonight. Probably *have* killed again tonight."

I tightened my hands on the steering wheel and had to force myself to relax.

"Molly? The lair is only a mile from your house as the vamp runs. And witches smell different from humans."

A spike of fear raced through me. Followed by a mental image of a vampire leaning over Angelina's bed. I tightened my hands on the wheel so tight it made a soft sound of protest.

"You need to mount a defensive perimeter around your house," Jane said. "You and Evan. You hear? Something magical that'll scare off anything that moves, or freeze the blood of anything dead. Something like that. You make sure the kids are safe." She turned her head aside, to look out at the night. Jane loved my kids. She had never said so, but I could see

it in her eyes when she watched them. I drove on. Chilled to the bone by
fear and the early winter.

Jane was too tired to make it back to her apartment, and so she spent the
day sleeping on the cot in the back room of the shop. Seven Sassy Sisters'
Herb Shop and Café, owned and run by my family, had a booming business, both locally and on the Internet, selling herbal mixtures and teas by
bulk and by the ounce, the shop itself serving teas, specialty coffees, brunch
and lunch daily, and dinner on weekends. It was mostly vegetarian fare,
whipped up by my older sister, water witch, professor, and three-star chef,
Evangelina Everhart. My sister Carmen Miranda Everhart Newton, an air
witch, newly married and pregnant, ran the register and took care of ordering supplies. Two other witch sisters, twins Boadacia and Elizabeth, ran
the herb store, while our wholly human sisters, Regan and Amelia, were
waitstaff. I'm really Molly Meagan Everhart Trueblood. Names with moxie
run in my family. Without a single question about why this supposed
human needed a place to crash, my sisters let Jane sleep off the night run.

While my sisters worked around the cot and ran the business without
me, I went driving. To the Partman place. With Brax.

"You found this how?" he asked, sitting in the passenger seat. I was
driving so I could pretend that I was in control, not that Brax cared who
was in charge as long as the rogue vampires were brought down. "The dogs
got squirrelly twenty feet into the underbrush and refused to go on. It
doesn't make any sense, Molly. I never saw dogs go so nuts. They freaked
out. So I gotta ask how you know where they sleep." Detective Paul Braxton
was antsy. Worried. Scared. There had been no new reported deaths in the
area, yet I had just told him that the vamps had gone hunting last night.

There were some benefits to being a witch out of the closet. I let my
lips curl up knowingly. "I had a feeling at the McCarleys' yesterday, but I
didn't think it would work. I devised a spell to track the rogue vampires.
At dusk, I went to the McCarleys' and set it free. And it worked. I was able
to pinpoint their lair."

"How? I never heard of such a thing. No one has. I asked on NCIC this
morning after you called." At my raised brows he said, "NCIC is the
National Crime Information Center, run by the FBI, a computerized index
and database of criminal justice information."

"A database?" *Crap.* I hit the brakes, hard. Throwing us both against the seat belts. The wheels squealed, popped, and groaned as the antilock braking system went into play. Brax cussed as we came to a rocking halt. I spun in the seat to face him. "If you made me part of that system, then you've used me for the last time, you no good piece of—"

"Molly!" He held both hands palms out, still rocking in the seat. "No! I did *not* enter you into the system. We have an agreement. I wouldn't breach it."

"Then tell me what you did," I said, my voice low and threatening. "Because if you took away the privacy of my family and babies, I'll curse you to hell and back, and damn the consequences." I gathered my power to me, pulling from the earth and the forest and even the fish living in the nearby river, ecosystems be hanged. This *man* was endangering my babies.

Brax swallowed in the sudden silence of the old Volvo, as if he could feel the power I was drawing in. I could smell his fear, hear it in his fast breath, over the sounds of nearby traffic. "NCIC is just a database," he said. "I just input a series of questions. About witches. And how they work. And—"

"Witches are in the FBI's databank?" I hit the steering wheel with both fists as the thought sank in. "Why?"

"Because there are witch criminals in the U.S. Sorcerers who do blood magic. Witches who do dark magic. Witches are part of the database, now and forever."

"Son of a witch on a switch," I swore, cursing long and viciously, helpless anger in the tones, the syllables flowing and rich. Switching to the old language for impact, not that it had helped. Curses had a way of falling back on the curser rather than hurting the cursed.

I beat the steering wheel in impotent fury. I was a witch, for pity's sake. And I couldn't protect my own kind. Rage banging around me like a wrecking ball, I hit the steering wheel one last time and threw my old Volvo into drive. Fuming, silent, I drove to the Partman place.

The entrance, once meant for mining machinery and trucks, was still drivable, though the asphalt was crazed and broken, grass growing in the cracks. The drive wound around a hillock and was lost from view. Beyond it, signs of mining that were hidden from the road became more obvious. Trees were young and scraggly, the ground was scraped to bedrock, and rusted iron junk littered the site. An old car sat on busted tires, windows, hood, and doors long gone. The office of the mining site was an old WWII Quonset hut, the door hanging free to reveal the dark interior.

Though strip mining had been the primary means of getting to the gems, tunnels had gone into the side of the mountain. The entry to the mine was boarded over with two-by-tens, but some were missing, and it was clear that the opening had been well used.

Brax rubbed his mouth, looking over the place, not meeting my eyes. Finally he said, "I would never cause you or yours trouble, Molly Trueblood. I do my best to protect you from problems, harassment, or unwanted attention from law enforcement, federal NCIC or otherwise."

"Except you," I accused, annoyed that he had apologized before I blew off my mad.

He smiled behind his hand. "Except me. And maybe one day you'll trust me enough to tell me the truth about this so-called tracking spell you used to find this place. I'm going to check out the area. Stay here. If I don't come back, that disproves the myth that vamps sleep in the daylight. You get your pal Jane to stake my ass if I come back undead."

"Your heart," I said grumpily. "If you actually have one. Heart, not your ass."

He made a little chortling laugh and picked up the flashlight he had brought. "Ten minutes. Half an hour max. I'll be back."

"Better be fangless."

Forty-two minutes later Brax reappeared, dust all over his hair and suit. He clicked the flash off and strode to the car, got in with a wave of death-tainted air, and said, "Drive." I drove.

His shoulders slumped and he seemed to relax as we turned off on the secondary road and headed back to town, rubbing his hand over his head in a habitual gesture. Dust filtered off him into the air of the car, making motes that caught the late-afternoon sun. I rolled the windows down to let out the stink on him. We were nearly back to my house when he spoke again.

"I survived. They either didn't hear me or they were asleep. No myths busted today." When I didn't reply he went on. "They've been bringing people back to the mine for a while. Indigents, transients. Truant kids. There were remains scattered everywhere. Like the McCarleys, most were partially eaten." He stared out the windshield, seeing the scene he had left behind, not the bright, sunny day. "I'll have to get the city and county to compile a list of missing people."

A long moment later he said, "We have to go after them. Today. Before they need to feed again."

"Why not just seal them up in the mine till tomorrow after dawn?" I said, turning into my driveway, steering carefully around the tricycle and set of child-sized bongos left there. "Go in fresh, with enough weaponry and men to overpower them. The vamps would be weak, hungry, and apt to make mistakes."

"Good golly, Miss Molly," he said, his face transforming with a grin at the chance to use the old lyrics. "We could, couldn't we? Where was my brain?"

"Thinking about dead kids," I said softly, as I pulled to a stop. "I, on the other hand, had forty-two minutes to do nothing but think. All you need is a set of plans for the mine to make sure you seal over all the entrances. Set a guard with crosses and stakes at each one. That way you go in on your terms, not theirs."

"I think I love you."

"Stop with the lyrics. Go make police plans."

Unfortunately the vamps got out that night, through an entrance not on the owner's maps. They killed four of the police guarding other entrances. And then they went hunting. This time they struck close to home. Just after dawn, Brax woke me, standing at the front door, his face full of misery. Carmen Miranda Everhart Newton and her husband had been attacked in their home. Tommy Newton was dead. My little sister was missing and presumed dead.

The attention of the national media had been snared and news vans rolled into town, one setting up in the parking lot of the shop. Paralyzed by fear, my sisters closed everything down and gathered at my house to discuss options, to grieve, and to make halfhearted funeral plans.

I spent the day and the early evening hugging my children, watching TV news about the "vampire crisis," and devising offensive and defensive charms, making paper airplanes out of spells that didn't work, and flying them across the room to the delight of my babies and my four human nieces and nephews. I had to come up with something. Something that would offer protection to the person who went underground to revenge my sister.

Jane sat to the side, her cowboy boots, jeans, and T-shirt contrasting with the peasant tops, patchwork skirts, and hemp sandals worn by my sisters and me. She didn't say much, just drank tea and ate whatever was offered. Near dusk, she came to me and said softly, "I need a ride. To the mine."

I looked at her, grief holding my mouth shut, making it hard to breathe.

"I need some steak or a roast. You have one frozen in the freezer in the garage. I looked. You thaw it in the microwave, leave your car door open. I shift out back, get in, and hunker down. You make an excuse, drive me to the mine, and get back with a gallon of milk or something."

"Why?" I asked. "I don't understand."

Her eyes glowing a tawny yellow, Jane looked like a predator, ready to hunt. Excited by the thought. "I don't smell like a human. The older one won't be expecting me. I can go in, find where they're hiding, see if your sister is alive, and get back. Then we can make a plan."

Hope spiked in me like heated steel. "Why would the vampires keep her alive?" I asked. "And why would you go in there?"

"I told you. Witches smell different from humans. You smell, I don't know, powerful. If he's trying to build a blood family, and if he has some ability to reason, the new blood-master might hold on to her. To try to turn her. It's worth a shot." Jane grinned grimly, her beast rising in her. Bits of gray light hovered, dancing on her skin. "Besides. The governor and the vamp council of North Carolina just upped the bounty on the rogues to forty thou a head. I can use a quarter mil. And if you come up with a way to keep me safe down there, when I go in to hunt them down, I'll share. You said you need to replace that rattletrap you drive."

I put a hand to my mouth, holding in the sob that accompanied my sudden, hopeful tears. Unable to speak, I nodded. Jane went to get the roast.

I slept uneasily, waiting, hearing every creak, crack, and bump in the night. If we smelled differently from humans, would the vampires come after my family? My other sisters? Just after dawn, the phone rang. "Come and get me," Jane said, her voice both excited and exhausted. "Carmen's still alive."

I called my sisters on my cell as I drove and told them to get over to my house fast. We had work to do. When I got back with Jane, my kitchen had three witch sisters in it, each trying to brew coffee and tea, fry eggs, and cook grits and oatmeal. Evan was glowering in the corner, his hair standing up in tousles, reading the newspaper online and feeding Little Evan.

Jane pushed her way in, ignoring the babble of questions, and took the pot of oatmeal right off the stove, dumping in sugar and milk and digging in. She ate ten cups of hot oatmeal, two cups of sugar, and a quart of milk. It was the most oatmeal I had ever seen anyone eat in my life. Her belly bulged like a basketball. Then she took paper and pen and drew a map of the mine, talking. "No one'll be going into the mine today. Count on it. The vamps killed four of the men watching the entrances and the governor won't justify sending anyone in until the national guard gets here. Carmen is alive, here." She drew an X. "Along with two teenage girls. The rogue master's name is Adam and he has his faculties, enough to see to the feeding and care of his family, enough to make more scions. But if he dies, then the girls in his captivity are just another dinner to the rogues. So I have to take him down last. I need something like an immobility spell, or glue spell. But first, I need something to get me in close."

"Obfuscation spell," I said.

"No one's succeeded with that one in over five hundred years," Evangelina said, ever the skeptic.

"Maybe that's because *we* never tried," Boadacia said.

Elizabeth looked at her twin, challenge sparkling in her eyes. "Let's."

"But according to the histories, a witch has to be present to initialize it and to keep it running. No human can do it," Evangelina said.

"I'll go in with her," Evan said.

My sisters turned to him. The sudden silence was deafening. Little Evan took that moment to bang on his high chair and shout, "Milk, milk, milk, milk!" Which came out, *Mea, mea, mea, mea!*

"It would have to be an earth witch," Evangelina said slowly. "You're an air sorcerer. You can't make it work either." As one, they all turned to look at me. I was the only earth witch in the group.

"No," Evan said. "No way."

"Yes," I said. "It's the only way."

At four in the afternoon, My sisters and Evan and I were standing in front of the mine. Jane was geared up in her vamp hunting gear, a chain mail collar, leather pants, metal-studded leather coat over a chain vest, and a huge gun with an open stock, like a *Star Wars* shotgun. Silvered knives were strapped to her thighs, in her boots, along her forearms; studs were built into in her gloves; two handguns were holstered at her waist, under her coat; her long hair was braided and tied down. A dozen crosses hung around her neck. Stakes were twisted in her hair like hair sticks.

I was wearing jeans, sweaters, and Evangelina's faux-leather coat. As vegetarians, my sisters didn't own leather, and I couldn't afford it. I carried twelve stakes, an extra flashlight, medical supplies, ammunition, and five charms: two healing charms, one walking-away charm, one empowerment, and one obfuscation.

Evan was similarly dressed, refusing to be left behind, loaded down with talismans, charms, battery-powered lights, a machete, and a twenty-pound mallet suitable for bashing in heads. It wouldn't kill a vampire, but it would incapacitate one long enough to stake it and take its head. We were ready to go in when Brax drove up, got out, and sauntered over. He was dressed in SWAT team gear and guns. "What? You think I'd let civilians go after the rogues alone? Not gonna happen, people."

We hadn't told Brax. I glared at Evan, who shrugged, unapologetic.

"What are you carrying?" Jane asked. When he told her, she shook her head and handed him a box of ammunition. "Hand-packed silver-fléchette rounds, loaded for vamp. They can't heal from it. A direct heart shot will take them out."

The cop paused, maybe remembering the last time he went up against a vamp with Jane. "Sweet," Brax said, removing his ammunition from a shotgun and reloading as he looked us over. "So we got an earth witch, her husband, a vamp hunter, and me. Lock and load, people." Satisfied, he pushed in front and led the way. Once inside, we walked four abreast as my sisters set up a command center at the entrance. Behind us I could hear the three witches chanting protective incantations while Regan and Amelia began to pray.

We passed parts of several bodies. My earth gift recoiled, closing up. There were too many dead. I had hoped to be able to sense the presence of the rogue vampires, but with my gift so overloaded, I doubted I'd be of much help at all. The smell of rancid meat and rotting blood was beyond horrible. Charnel house effluvia. I stopped looking after the first limb—part of a young woman's leg.

Except for the stench and the body parts, the first hundred yards were easy. After that, things went to hell in a handbasket.

We heard singing, a childhood melody. "Starlight, star fright, first star . . . No. Starlight, blood fight . . . No. I don' 'member. I don' 'member—" The voice stopped, the cutoff sharp as a knife. "People," she whispered, the word echoing in the mine. "Blood . . ."

And she was on us. Face caught in the flashlight. A ravening animal. Flashing fangs. Bloodred eyes centered with blacker-than-night pupils. Nails like black claws. She took down Evan with one swipe. I screamed. Blood splattered. His flashlight fell. Its beam rocking in shadows. One glimpse of a body. Leaping. Flying. Landed on Jane. Inhumanly fast. Jane rolled into the dark.

I lost sight in the swinging light. Found Evan by falling on him. Hot blood pulsed into my hand. I pressed on the wound, guided by earth magic. I called on Mother Earth for healing. Moments later, Jane knelt beside me, breathing hard, smelling foul. She steadied the light. Evan was still alive, fighting to breathe, my hands covered with his blood. His skin was pasty. The wound was across his right shoulder, had sliced his jugular, and he had lost a lot of blood, though my healing had clotted over the wound.

I pressed one of the healing amulets my sisters had made over the wound, chanting in the old tongue, *"Cneasaigh, cneasaigh a bháis báite in fhuil,"* over and over. Gaelic for "Heal, heal, blood-soaked death."

Minutes later, I felt Evan take a full breath. Felt his heartbeat steady under my hands. In the uncertain light, my tears splashed on his face. He opened his eyes and looked up at me. His beard was brighter than usual, tangled with his blood. He held my gaze, telling me so much in that one look. He loved me. Trusted me. Knew I was going on without him. Promised to live. Promised to take care of our children if I didn't make it back. Demanded I live and come back to him. I sobbed with relief. Buried my face in his healing neck and cried.

We carried Evan back to the entrance, where my sisters called for an ambulance. As soon as he was stable, the three of us redistributed the supplies and headed back into the mine. I saw the severed head of the rogue in the shadows. Jane's first forty-thousand-dollar trophy.

We had done one useful thing. We had rewritten the history books. We had proven that vampires could move around in the daylight as long as they were in complete absence of the sun. That meant we would have to fight rather than just stake and run. Lucky us.

There were six vampires left and three of us. By now, the remaining ones were surely alerted to our presence. Not good odds.

We were deep underground when the next attack took place. Jane must have smelled them coming because she shouted, "Ten o'clock! Two of them." Her gun boomed. Brax's spat flames as it fired. Two vampires fell. Jane dispatched them with a knife shaped like a small sword. While she sawed, and I looked away, she murmured, "Three down, four to go," over and over, like a rich miser counting his gold.

We moved on. Down a level, deeper into the mountain. Jane led the way now, ignoring some branching tunnels, taking others, assuring us she knew where we were and where Carmen was. Like me, she ignored Brax's questions about how.

Just after we passed a cross-tunnel, two vampires came at us from behind, a flanking maneuver. I never heard them. In front of me, Jane whirled. I dropped to the tunnel floor, cowering. She fired. The muzzle flash blinded me. More gunshots sounded, echoing. Brax yelled, the sound full of pain.

Jane stepped over me, straddling me in the dark, her boots lit by a wildly tottering light. I snatched it and turned it on Brax. He knelt nearby, blood at his throat. A vampire lay at his knees, a stake through her chest. My ears were ringing, blasted by the concussion of firepower. In the light, I saw Jane hand a bandage to Brax and pull one of her knives. Her shadow on the mine wall raised up the knife and brought it down, beheading the rogues; my hearing began to come back; the chopping sounded soggy.

She left the heads. "For pickup on the way out. The odds just turned in our favor."

I couldn't look at the heads. I had been no help at all. I was the weak link in the trio. I squared my shoulders and fingered the charms I carried. I was supposed to hold them until Jane said to activate them. It would be soon.

We moved on down the widening tunnel. Jane touched my arm in the dark. I jumped. She tapped my hand and mouthed, *Charm one. Now,* her lips barely visible in the shadows.

Clumsily I pulled the charm, activated it, and tossed it to the left. The sound of footsteps echoed, as if we were still moving, but down a side tunnel. Then I activated the second charm, the one my sisters and I had worked on all day. The obfuscation charm. It was the closest thing in all of our histories to an invisibility spell, and no witch had perfected it in hundreds of years.

Following the directions I had memorized, I drew in the image of the rock floor and walls, and cloaked it around us. I nodded to Jane. She cut off the light. Moments later, she moved forward slowly, Brax at her side. I followed, one hand on each shoulder. The one on Brax's shoulder was sticky with blood. He was still bleeding. Vampires can smell blood. The obfuscation spell wasn't intended to block scents.

A faint light appeared ahead, growing brighter as we moved and the tunnel opened out. We stopped. The space before us was a juncture from which five tunnels branched. Centered was a table with a lantern, several chairs, and cots. Carmen was lying on one, cradling her belly, her eyes open and darting. Two teenage girls were on another cot, huddling together, eyes wide and fearful. No vampires were in the room.

We moved quietly to Carmen and I bent over her. I slammed my hand over her mouth. She bucked, squealing. "Carmen. It's Molly," I whispered. She stopped fighting. Raised a hand and touched mine. She nodded. I removed my hand.

She whispered, "They went that way."

"Come on. Tell the others to come. But be quiet."

Moving awkwardly, Carmen rolled off the cot and stood. She motioned to the two girls. "Come on. Come with me." When both girls refused, my baby sister waddled over, slapped them both resoundingly, gripped each by an arm, and hauled them up. "I said *come with me.* It wasn't a damn invitation."

The girls followed her, holding their jaws and watching Carmen fearfully. Pride blossomed in me. I adjusted the obfuscation spell, drawing in more of the cave walls and floor. Wrapped the spell around the three new bodies. The girls suddenly could see us. One screamed.

"So much for stealth," Jane said. "Move it!" She shoved the two girls and me toward the tunnel out. Stumbling, we raced to the dark. I switched on the flashlight, put it in Carmen's hands. Pulled the last two charms. The empowerment charm was meant to take strength from a winning opponent and give it to a losing, dying one. It could only be used in clear life-and-death situations. The other was my last healing charm.

We made the first turn, feet slapping the stone, gasping. Something crashed into us. A girl and Jane went down with the vampire. Tangled limbs. The vampire somersaulted. Taking Jane with him. Crouching. He held her in front of him. Jane's head in one hand. Twisting it up and back. His fangs extended fully. He sank fangs and claws into Jane's throat, above her mail collar. Ripping. The collar hit the ground.

Brax shouted, "Run!" He picked up the fallen girl and shoved her down the tunnel. The last vamp landed on his back. Brax went down. Rolling. Blood spurting. Shadows like monsters on the far wall.

In the wavering light, Jane's throat gushed blood. Pumping bright.

Carmen and I backed against the mine wall. I was frozen, indecisive. *Who to save?* I didn't know for sure who was winning or losing. I didn't know what would happen if I activated the empowerment charm. I pulled the extra flashlight and switched it on.

Brax rolled. Into the light. Eyes wild. The vampire rolled with him. Eating his throat. Brax was dying. I activated the empowerment charm. Tossed it.

It landed. Brax's breath gargled. The vampire fell. Brax rose over him, stake in hand. Brought the stake down. Missed his heart.

I pointed. "Run. That way." Carmen ran, her flashlight bouncing. I set down the last light, pulled stakes from my pockets. Rushed the vampire. Stabbed down with all my might. One sharpened stake ripped through his clothes. Into his flesh. I stabbed again. Blood splashed up, crimson and slick. I fumbled two more stakes.

Brax, beside me, took them. Rolled the vampire into the light. Raised his arms high. Rammed them into the rogue's chest.

Blood gushed. Brax fell over it. Silent. So silent. Neither moved.

I activated the healing amulet. Looked over my shoulder. At Jane.

The vampire was behind her. Her throat was mostly gone. Blood was everywhere. Spine bones were visible in the raw meat of her throat.

Yet, even without a trachea, she was growling. Face shifting. Gray light dancing. Her hands, clawed and tawny, reached back. Dug into the skull of the vampire. Whipped him forward. Over her. He slammed into the rock floor. Bounced limply.

Sobbing, I grabbed Brax's shoulder. Pulled him over. Dropped the charm on his chest.

Jane leaped onto the vampire. Ripped out his throat. Tore into his stomach. Slashed clothes and flesh. Blood spurted. She shifted. Gray light. Black motes. And her cat screamed.

I watched as her beast tore the vampire apart. Screaming with rage.

We made it to the mine entrance, Carmen and the girls running ahead, into the arms of my sisters. Evangelina raised a hand to me, framed by pale light, and pulled the girls outside, leaving the entrance empty, dawn pouring in. I didn't know how the night had passed, where the time had disappeared. But I stopped there, inside the mine with Jane, looking out into the day. In the urgency of finding the girls and getting them all back to safety, we hadn't spoken about the fight.

Now she touched her throat. Hitched Brax higher. He hadn't made it. Jane had carried him out, his blood seeping all over her, through the rents in her clothes made by fighting vampires and by Jane herself, as she shifted inside them. "Is he," she asked, her damaged voice raspy as stone, "dead because you used the last healing charm on me?" She swallowed, the movement of poorly healed muscles audible. "Is that why you're crying?"

Guilt lanced through me. Tears, falling for the last hour, burned my face. "No," I whispered. "I used it on Brax. But he was too far gone for a healing charm."

"And me?" The sound was pained, the words hurting her throat.

"I trusted in your beast to heal you."

She nodded, staring into the dawn. "You did the right thing." Again she hitched Brax higher. Whispery-voiced, she continued. "I got seven heads to pick up and turn in"—she slanted her eyes at me—"and we got a cool quarter mil waiting. Come on. Day's wasting." Jane Yellowrock walked into the sunlight, her tawny eyes still glowing.

And I walked beside her.

First Sight

Author's note: I love seeing Jane from the point of view of other characters. It is refreshing and often eye-opening. Bruiser is a huge fan favorite, and about half of the romance readers want Jane to end up with him and about half want her to end up with Leo. While I've written stories from Rick's POV before, I've never written one from Bruiser's, and I decided to try my hand at it in a scene stolen and reworked from *Skinwalker*. I discovered a lot about Bruiser. And I like him a lot better than I expected. I hope you enjoy.

I wasn't fond of doors without peepholes, which was surely quite telling about my age. I also found it difficult to remember security cameras were everywhere, even over the door to Katie's Ladies. I resisted the urge to look up and wink at the camera, as Katie herself was unlikely to be watching the security display screens and I had no desire to flirt with Tom, her muscle.

The door opened and . . . everything changed. A woman—an Amazon—stood there, needle thin, muscled, balanced, and ready, dressed in jeans and leather, a waterfall of black braids to her bum, a gun held low at her side, and a glowing cross in her other hand. I was inhaling when the door opened and I caught her scent. All I could think was *predator*. Without thought, training and muscle memory pulling me forward into the moves, I drew a knife and attacked.

She sidestepped fast—faster than human—and stuck out a foot. I tripped over it. Felt myself falling forward, prey to the oldest trick in the book. I cursed under my breath as she landed on me, riding me down. We hit and I could hear her heart pounding. She growled. We bounced, me on bottom, her knee landing against my spine just as Leo's weight fell onto us.

We had practiced this move hundreds of times, and I knew his hands would already be at her throat, but her braids tangled around them. Leo sucked in a breath, his fangs extending with a soft *snap*. They brushed the side of her neck, his killing bite coming down.

But she rammed back her head and connected, her skull hitting something softer. I heard his *oof* of expelled breath, followed by a faint sound of movement as of cloth on cloth. And I smelled the scent of burning flesh, remembering only then the cross in her hand. Silver. Glowing.

Leo howled and his weight fell away. The woman rolled, pulling me with her in a move that was both balletic and vicious, until we lay on the floor, her gun at my neck, my body on top of, and protecting, her. The reek of my sweat and hers and vamp pheromones bathed the air. She smelled of blood and exhaust and sex and—

"I'll shoot your blood-servant if you move again," she said to Leo, her voice low and cold. My master paused and went quiet, that undead shift from combat to utter stillness that had once been so startling and was now so telling. He believed her, and after centuries of human and nonhuman responses, he would know if she was speaking the truth. "If you listen, I'll let him live," she bargained.

Leo's stillness went deeper. Without giving myself away, I tried to gather myself, but her clawed hand dug into my windpipe. The woman shoved the muzzle hard under my ear, and I realized that if she had wanted us dead, we'd already be dead.

I should have beaten her, no matter the surprise, and I swore hard, under my breath. I'd gotten lazy sparring with humans and other bloodservants. I needed to fight for real, and fight Mithrans, not slower beings.

"If you resist," she said to me, "I'll rip out your throat, then behead your master. Pick and choose." A shocked silence filled the foyer. Slowly I went limp. "Wise move," she said.

"Leonard Pellissier, I'm Katie's out-of-town talent," she said, in an indefinable Southern accent. "I'm the tracker and hired gun the council contracted to take out the rogue. I don't want to kill either of you, but I will if I have to. The blood you smell was not spilled by me. I am not your enemy. Back. Off."

Leo backed, making a deliberate boot scuff so I would know. She tightened her grip on my throat, and I was having trouble getting a breath. "You gonna play nice?" she asked me.

I tried to swallow under the pressure of her hand, and when I spoke, the sound came out in a whistle from the pressure on my windpipe. "Yes." She sniffed at my ear, an action that was quite suddenly, unexpectedly erotic. Her scent filled my nose, smelling of sex and need and desire. I felt her breasts against my body, and I hardened. She released her hold. Damn woman. Laughter, a reaction neither of lust nor of combat, rolled up in my chest, and I forced it back. The woman I now knew was Jane Yellowrock had terrible timing.

I rolled to my feet and she followed me upright, her movements as sleek and as fast as a primo, keeping me between Leo and her own body, another clue that she wasn't after my master. I glanced at Leo and he tilted his head a fraction, telling me to stand down. There was humor in his eyes, letting me know he had detected my scent change and my interest in our attacker. I reached around and shut the outer door. When I moved to face her, I positioned myself in front of and slightly to the side of Leo. Oddly, weirdly, she switched the safety on the gun.

We were sodding lucky it hadn't gone off while we rolled around on the floor. It was stupid to wrestle while holding a gun, even while facing down a vampire and his security. Not that I could see a better way. If she hadn't done what she had, I'd have killed her and asked questions later. That was my job.

"You don't smell human," Leo said, his voice dropping into the smooth, honeyed, seductive tones he used when he spotted something or someone he wanted.

Irrationally, foolishly, I wanted to tell him to back off. The woman was mine. Which was stupid in every way I might care to think. I squelched the moment of possessiveness that had taken me.

"What are you?" Leo asked. And only then did I realize that I had no idea what the woman was, only that she wasn't human. No. Not human at all.

"Stop that," she said. "It doesn't work on me."

"She growled, boss," I said. "When she took me down."

"I heard her. What are you?"

"None of your business," she said.

"Whose blood do I smell?" Leo asked.

"Katie . . ." The woman stopped, as if not knowing what to say. The silence stretched, and Leo's humor improved—something I could feel through the blood-servant bond.

"I was forced to reprimand a member of my staff." Katie stood in the hallway, wearing a dressing gown that shimmered like silk. She was clearly naked beneath it, the thin fabric blood-free and molding to her thighs. I'd seen Katie in that robe. I'd helped her out of it numerous times before a feeding and what she called *blood pleasure*. "May I ask that your blood-servant assist with the transfusion?" Katie asked. "It is not my intent to lose him."

Leo glanced at me and I looked reluctantly from him to the stranger before I nodded to Katie that I was willing. But I stabbed the rogue-vampire hunter with a look, making it clear that I didn't like the idea of leaving her alone with my boss, promising to kill her slowly if she injured Leo. I rolled my head on my shoulders, and heard two cracks as my spine realigned itself, and I went down the hallway, my booted feet silent on the wood and carpets. Predator silent.

Blood, Fangs, and Going Furry

He didn't remember much about that first full moon except the pain, the burning, scalding, skin-crawling pain when his pelt wanted to thrust through his skin, when his bones begged—demanded—to shift. When his eyes went green gold, and the night came alive in rich blues and greens and silvers, and the detail of the world was so intense that it was like nothing he had ever seen before. When the scents on the air became acute, almost brutal in their concentration.

The sensory overload was like being tossed off a high bridge to land at the bottom of a rock-strewn crevasse and find himself broken, bloodied, but miraculously alive. Only to have a Mack truck run him down and crush out whatever life had been left. At the same time it was like having a live current rushing though his body, icy and burning, his brain on fire, his skin roasting, and no evidence of it except the funky green gold of his eyes.

He couldn't stop it, couldn't make it go away, couldn't shift into his cat to ease his pain. Kemnebi, the only other black were-leopard on the continent and arguably the highest alpha black were-leopard on the planet, had refused him aid, standing back and laughing at his torment. Even when Leo Pellissier, the Master of the City, had threatened to kill Kem if he didn't help, he had refused, saying that Rick had brought it on himself. Which he had. Totally.

He'd FUBARed it all the way, losing his humanity, the girl he had flipped over—Jane Yellowrock—and probably his job too.

Gee DiMercy, Leo Pellissier's Mercy Blade, had told him Jane could help. Which made no sense. Jane worked for the vamps as a security expert and rogue-vamp killer. Jane wasn't a were. But something in Gee's voice had been convincing, and Rick had found himself on his bike, blasting down the roads and across the Mississippi, into the Big Easy, believing Jane could—and maybe would, even after he'd betrayed her—help him.

Pain raging in him like a rabid cat clawing the inside of his skin, Rick had bent over the bike and roared away from the MOC's Clan Home. Later, when he was on the edge of dreams, still-shot moments of that ride came to him: taking the bridge east, flying in at nearly a hundred miles per hour, threading the needle between two eighteen-wheelers, hearing his own voice screaming with rage. Taking a curve, one boot on the pavement, the sole actually smoking. Dodging a car as it ran a red light, his reflexes like lightning on meth.

One thing stayed in the forefront of his mind—he had to get to Jane. She would know how to help. Help him to shift or help him to resist or maybe put a bullet through his brain if nothing better presented itself. He knew, because they'd had something once and because there had been no closure yet, and because Jane Yellowrock had saved his life.

He ended up on her street. She was half a block down, standing beside her bike in the middle of the street, her helmet off, her hair streaming back in the heated breeze, as if she had heard him coming and was waiting for him. He downshifted the red Kow-bike—the Kawasaki—and puttered to a stop. Put his feet down, bracing himself. His head and face were hidden by his helmet and face shield, and for a long moment, feeling anonymous yet knowing he wasn't, knowing that she had to know who he was, he watched her.

As the breeze that carried his scent reached her, her eyes did a feral shift and glowed golden. A lot like his tonight, except her eyes were always amber and his had been Frenchy black until this full moon. His first full moon with the taint of were-cat blood rushing through his veins, making him half-crazy with the pain.

Jane stalked toward him, her booted steps muffled beneath the sound of his bike, her body moving slowly, a liquid, feline heat in her walk. He keyed off the bike and slung his leg over it. Threw back the face mask and pulled off the helmet. Dropped it, knowing he'd scarred it, not caring. He took a breath.

The night was alive with smells, so rich and intense that it was like being hit with a bat at full swing and being stroked along his entire body all at once. His eyes closed in something akin to holy rapture. He smelled fish and coffee and hot grease and tar from the streets and water everywhere. The slow-moving bayous that wend through New Orleans, smelling of grasses and heated mud and rain-washed animal offal, nutria and deer and old blood. Lake Pontchartrain with the reek of old pollution and oil and the warmth of the sun on its waters. And the Mississippi River. He had never thought that water might smell of power, but it did, a heady mixture of mountain and snow and rain and animal, of the scents of tugboats and fish and water treatment plants. Of every source of its water all along its course through the nation. And riding over it all he smelled the Gulf of Mexico, fresh and salty and . . . amazing. The odors twined with the pain racing under his skin, becoming one with it. And he could smell his pain, like old meat and rancid butter. He never knew that pain had a smell.

Jane's boots drew closer, the leather soles abrading on the asphalt. The wind shifted, capricious, and he smelled her before she reached him, and he knew instantly that she wasn't human. How could he have missed that scent before? She was redolent of big-cat but not leopard, not Kenyan jungle nights and African tribal drums. She smelled of wild rushing streams and craggy passes clogged by snow; her scent sang of wildfire, of the cold taint of iron in the water trickling from cracks in the stone faces of mountains. Heat and blood pooled deep in his groin with an ache that wanted release. "I can't ssshift. It hurtsss," he said, his voice a growling hiss.

"I know," she whispered.

His eyes still closed, he felt her hand lift. The warmth and texture of her energy were like spiky vines, thorny and sharp, as her palm came close to his face. Her skin was like silk as it slid across his cheek. Tears burned beneath his lids, hot as acid. He had betrayed her.

"I can't ssshift. Kemnebi ssshays . . ." The words growled to a stop. He couldn't shift into his were-cat, but his vocal cords weren't working right either. With the rise of the full moon, his body had leaped toward the change and slammed to a halt, like a motorcycle hitting a rock cliff wall at a hundred twenty. His sense of smell was acute, his eyes were funky, and his voice was gone. His teeth felt weird against his tongue. Pain rode him like he was a bitch in a prison cell—no way out. None.

Her hand was hot, smelling of cat and clean sheets and the remembered smell of sex. He leaned his face into her palm, breathing deeply. She stroked his cheek, and her skin smelled better than anything he had ever smelled, better than Safia. And far, far better than the werewolves who had tortured him.

"Kem says what?" she whispered.

"Kem shasss shometing isss w'ong wi' me."

"And he let you go free? Into the night?"

Her question was weird. He knew that from the part of his brain that was still human. "Not Kem. Jzeee."

"Gee? Girrard DiMercy?" Jane's words came softly, gentle on the night air.

He rubbed his head against her palm, feeling her fingers thread into his hair. Massaging. Some of the pain in his scalp eased, and he heard his own sigh of pleasure. He wanted her to touch him everywhere like that, to relieve his need, release his pain, set him free from this agony. He raised his hands and curled them around hers, his fingers trailing up her wrists as far as her leathers allowed. Her skin was like silk, if silk could be electrified, if silk moved over muscle like rich oil over the bayou water, but sweet as honey.

"Leo's Mercy Blade?" she asked again. "He let you go?"

"Yesh."

"And Leo? Did he—"

Rick laughed, remembering only then the flashing image, the single snapshot vision of Leo Pellissier, Blood-Master of the City, his mouth open in shock. The sound of his voice roaring. The barbed, spiked texture of his power as he drew something electric and molten-smelling out of the air. And the stink of vamp blood, like pepper and green leaves. "I hit him. I sthink I . . . hurt him."

"Oh, Ricky Bo." Her sigh was like the first breath of spring on the air. "I'm so sorry."

The punch was faster, harder, deeper than he expected. Air exploded out of him like a balloon run over by an earthmover. She'd hit him before but never like this. Who knew Jane Yellowrock had been holding back all this time?

He woke in a cage. Raving and furious. He threw himself at the bars even though he knew—with that tiny human part of him—that he was hurting only himself and that there was no way out.

Someone turned a hose on him, hitting him with icy spray, the water like needles. He rammed the bars again, and the cage shook with the strike. And again and again. With each blow his body came away more bruised. He heard/felt/smelled the bone in his right arm break, and the added pain sent him to the corner of his cage to whimper and lick his wounds.

He smelled vamp and age and bricks weeping with the Mississippi. Mold and sickness and blood rode the other scents like the top note of a really expensive but foul perfume. It was the smell of blood that brought him back. Beef blood. Steak so rare it would grunt if you kicked it was piled on a plate, steaming hot, thin blood pooling on white china.

He caught himself. Found himself. Remembered who he was and what he was. And he saw the red fletching on the dart sticking out of his butt. They had drugged him, tranqed him. With an old-fashioned tranquilizer dart. Like a wild animal.

Forcing his fingers to bend in ways that paws would not have, he reached back and gripped the dart. Slid it from his flesh. Tossed it out of the cage. The drug was running through his veins like good bourbon, pushing back the pain, pushing back reality. He blinked, shook the wet hair out of his eyes, and focused on the room.

He was underground with no way out. The windows were small, arched on the top, set high and barred; the door was barred; the cage they had put him in was eight feet by eight feet, with bars for walls and a barred ceiling. And all those steel bars were set into stone. The stone smelled of old water and mold and had been in place for centuries. At the far end of the room, watching him, was Jane.

She was sitting on a tall, backless stool, her leather-clad legs loose and relaxed, one booted foot on a rung, the other on the floor. Her arms were back, elbows resting on a tall table pushed against the wall behind her, and her leather jacket hung open, revealing a thin, skintight knit Lycra T, the lines of the black bra under it barely visible. She smelled like sex and craving, and his body responded, growing hard and ready.

She tilted her head, her long, straight black hair falling in a slide that *shush*ed as it slithered to the side as if alive. "Do you know where you are?" she asked, sounding lazy.

He thought about that for a moment. Or an hour. Time was doing crazy shit, and he wasn't sure. He finally forced the words out. "Ware-house? In the Warehoush Dishtrick? The Nunnery?"

She nodded once, a single dip and lift of her chin. "In a temporary holding cell for young rogues. They'll let me keep you here for the three nights of the full moon. I couldn't take the chance that you might lose control and infect someone. I'm sorry."

He touched his jaw. "You hit like a guy."

She chuckled. "Thanks."

The three nights of the full moon. Yeah, right. He was less than a third of the way through this torture. But with the drugs circulating through him, holding the pain at bay, he at least remembered that he had once been human. He worked his jaw, and it felt normal. This time when he spoke, the words came out properly. "*They* let you keep me here?"

"Leo."

"Mmm." He thought about that for a while as water dripped and ran across the stone. He'd hurt Leo. Raising his hand, he curled his fingers into a fist. Already he was healing, his bruises fading. And the arm bone he had broken on the cell attack was little more than a bump that ached when he touched it. His skin felt hot, and the water was drying on his body more quickly than normal. Part of the benefits of the furry life: quick healing and a higher-than-human body temp. If not for the moon-change pain that fought the drugs in his system, he might have laughed. "What'd you have to promise Leo to get him to let you use this cage?"

"Nothing. Oddly. He called me on my cell just after I took you down, and offered. He's upstairs, and he's not his usual unruffled public self. His shirt is bloody." Her lips tilted up on one side. "Your work?"

"Probably."

"*You* took down a *vamp*," she deadpanned.

"I got the drop on him. Even vamps can be sucker punched." He shrugged. "And you took *me* down." He was suddenly conscious of being naked and aroused, sitting on a cool stone floor. And he was thirsty and more hungry than he'd ever been. He nodded to the food. "That mine?"

Jane uncoiled from her perch and sauntered to the plate. With the toe of her boot, she pushed it through a small space between the lower bar and the floor. She hooked a finger around a tall, narrow thermos with a built-in straw, like a kid's sippy cup, and passed it through too.

"No utensils?"

"Not until after the moon." She walked back to her perch and sat, her back to him this time, giving him privacy. He dug into the beef, stuffing it into his mouth, and the taste exploded through him like a bomb going off. When he had licked the plate clean, he drank the water. Tap water—chlorine and dankness and something slightly salty. He licked the half-cooked, watery blood from his fingers.

Jane seemed to know he was done and swiveled around on the stool seat, the leathers squeaking slightly. He pushed the plate and cup back through the bars, waiting, reading her body language better than he ever had before, and he knew that she had a lot to tell him. But first she took a satchel and threw it at the bars. It hit with a quiet *thud* and slid to the floor. "Clothes," she said. "Get dressed. You'll have visitors at eleven thirty."

He pulled the satchel through the bars and zipped it open. Inside were jeans, a T-shirt, and a package of new boxers, his size. They were made of some filmy material that seemed kind of girly, but he didn't complain. The T-shirt hid his scars and the mangled tattoos that were all he had left of the art on his shoulder and arm. As he pulled the shirt on, he caught a flash of gold from the eyes of the mountain lion tattooed there, but when he pulled up the sleeve to inspect it, the glow was gone.

"Visitors?" he asked as he stepped into the jeans.

"Local witches. Leo called them, and they said they might have a way to spell you through the shift, force you into your cat."

He stilled. Fear crawled up his spine like a snake up a tree. He'd been in the power of witches before. It hadn't been pretty or easy. He zipped up the jeans, feeling her interest, her gaze on him. Without looking at her, he asked, "You'll be here?"

"If you want me to."

"Yeah. I do. And if they try something hinky, you stop whatever it is they're doing."

"I'm supposed to know what's hinky with witches?"

He looked at her from under the too-long black hair that curled into his eyes. "I trust you to make an educated guess." She nodded again, that little chin-drop thing. He used to love that. Still did. But the wary look in her eyes held him off from saying anything about *them*, about their relationship or current lack of one. They had unresolved business, but it had to take a backseat. He understood that. Jane was always all about business and let nothing stand in the way of that, except sometimes dancing. He had a memory of her dancing once as he played the sax, her body writhing like a cobra on ecstasy, like sex on a stick, hot and sweaty. He went hard again just thinking about it. Jane laughed low, and he could smell his own arousal.

The heavy wooden door opened, and Leonard Pellissier, the Master of the City, walked in, followed by three others, but Rick kept his gaze on the MOC. The stink of vamp, peppery and minty, and blood, thick and slightly chilled, filled the room. Rick's arousal faded quickly, and he stepped back against the far bars, feeling the damp of the iron through his T.

Leo wasn't vamped-out like the last time Rick had seen him, but Leo was still wearing the bloody shirt, which said something about his state of mind. Rick crossed his arms and tucked his hands under his armpits, knowing that made him look defensive, but looking defensive was marginally better than looking aggressive. He got in the first salvo. "I apologize to the Master of the City of New Orleans for hitting you. Him." Rick wasn't good at the royal third-person speech, and *thees* and *thous* had always just confused him. Of course, Jane talked to Leo like she would to any other person, but he had a feeling that Leo allowed a lot of smack talk from Jane that he wouldn't from anyone else.

Leo, his chest not moving with breath, his eyes so black it was hard to read anything in them, studied Rick. Leo was dead. Or undead. Yeah. Standing there like a dead man, no sense of life left in him at all. Nothing in the room moved. No one coughed or sighed or shifted on the stone floor. It was so silent that Rick could hear his heartbeat and the sound of air breathing in and out of his lungs. A good two minutes too long later, Leo took a breath, and the movement startled Rick. He blinked, and that quickly, Leo was smiling.

"You have my blood. I have fed you more than once at the brink of death."

Rick nodded once, unconsciously mimicking Jane's little chin-drop nod. "The first time, I was on a slab of black stone, being spelled by a witch and drained by a vampire." He saw Jane start. He had never told her the story. He needed to remedy that. He had a lot of things to tell her, if she chose to listen. Later. Much later.

"I feel the pain that crawls under your skin like acid, burning like flames, like silver through your blood. One of my blood-servants prepared the medicine"—Leo flicked a finger at the tranq dart—"but he did not know what dosage would be required. It helped?"

"Yes. Thank you."

"I tried to bring our priestess to assist you, but she refused, saying she might be injured. I cannot force her, and my own blood was not enough to prevent your contagion, nor were the services of my Mercy Blade. Neither of us can cure you now that the taint has taken firm root."

Rick looked away, discomfort squirming though him. He remembered— in bits and snatches—the first days after Jane brought him, more dead than alive, to the MOC's Clan Home. Gee DiMercy and Leo had carried Rick to a bed and climbed in with him, healing him as best they could. It had been way more intimate than he was comfortable with, but they had kept him alive, so he couldn't bitch about their methods.

When it was obvious that Rick wasn't going to respond, Leo said, "The local witches wish to assist you. If you will permit." Rick looked back at him quickly. "The female who spelled you originally is no longer with the coven. You will be safe."

"Can you keep me drugged through it?"

"Of course." Leo moved closer, inhaling. "I smell your pain. It grows. I shall send in the witches." He turned to the man beside him. "Keep him comfortable." Moving human slow, he walked from the room.

"Yes, boss," George Dumas said, the words sounding odd when flavored with his faint British accent.

Rick dropped his arms and nodded to the blood-servant. The man was holding an oversized handgun, a tranquilizer gun. Rick had never liked the MOC's primo blood-servant and especially didn't like knowing that the overage half-human blood-sipper had shot him in the butt, but there were better times than now to complain about it. That gun was loaded with his sanity for the next three days. "Dumas."

"You'll be in charge of the dosing. Ask and I'll shoot. I understand the pain will likely be more intense whenever the moon is up and easier to bear when the moon is below the horizon. Of course, if they get you to shift, you'll be fine."

Rick's mouth twisted up. "Furry."

"That too." There was compassion in the blood-servant's eyes.

Hell. George Dumas was probably more human than Rick was now. He sighed. "Okay."

Moments later, five witches entered the room. A tiny blonde approached the bars, getting closer than anyone had since he'd woken up in the cell.

"We've met. You might remember me? Butterfly Lily?" She pointed at an older woman. "And my mom, Feather Storm?"

"I remember." He also remembered that they had claimed to be *"not real powerful. Mostly we're used as routing for group workings."* He'd rather have the most powerful witch in the city here, but beggars couldn't be choosers. "Thank you for coming."

She introduced the others as Rowan Rose, Running Doe Poppy, and Orchid Sunrise. Rick nodded, not smiling at the silly monikers. If they could help, they could call themselves Catwoman, Batwoman, and Hercules-etta for all he cared. Rowan Rose looked around the room, checked her watch, and shook her head. "We have eighteen minutes to get the circle drawn and the ritual started. This is not going to be fun, girls."

It wasn't. And that was an understatement.

By one a.m., Jane had left the room. By two a.m., Rick was on the floor of his cell, writhing in his own vomit, gagging like the worst case of dry heaves any drunk had ever had, shrieking, panting, screaming like a banshee, and begging for the next dose of medication. He got it. And he didn't wake until the moon fell below the horizon near dawn.

The sound of mocking laughter woke him. His eyes fluttered open, and he blinked, trying to focus on the floor of his cell, his left cheek on the cool, wet stone. His eyes were working but independently; his brain wasn't able to make the dual images into one. Water ran along the floor and trickled into a drain, running off him in fresh rivulets. He remembered where he was. And what he wasn't. And his stomach did somersaults until he gagged. His abdominal muscles cramped hard with the retching, and he wondered how bad his sickness had been to make him hurt this badly afterward despite the healing properties of were-taint in his system. He had a bad feeling that this hell-on-waking sensation was going to become overly familiar for the rest of his life.

He had been hosed off again and was wet to the skin in the clothes Jane had brought him, but at least he wasn't lying in his own filth anymore.

His stomach churned, but he shoved an arm under himself and rested on his elbow as the world whirled around him.

Kemnebi was standing outside the bars, his hands on his hips, a feral smile on his face. He was wearing loose white cotton pants and a button-down shirt, the set woven of cotton and many times washed into a softness that Rick could see. The African smelled of black leopard and jungle nights and freshly killed prey. And cruelty. And anger.

"You survived your first night," he said. "Good. Now I can watch you suffer again. And again. And eventually you will die in agony on the floor of that cell or by my fangs, my claws, and my killing teeth buried in your throa—"

The blur was faster than Rick could see. Faster than Kemnebi could react. It was less than sight, almost a sound, as of air being displaced. A snarl that echoed off the stone. Followed by the twin thuds of two bodies hitting the wall. The growls, hisses, and snarls of combat. A flash of a silvered blade. A shadow of black and yellow and scarlet. The smell of blood. Movement Rick couldn't follow except as smears on his retinas. Somehow, he was standing.

He knew by the smell that it was Jane fighting. Defending him. But his eyes wouldn't focus. He fell toward the bars, hitting face-first, breaking his fall with his cheek. Pain shattered through him like lightning through a lightning rod, bright as the beginning of the universe, tinted with stars and blood. "Fuck," he said of the pain, of the fight, of his helplessness. "Fuckfuck*fuck*. Jane? *Jane!*" he screamed.

An instant later George Dumas was in the room, moving almost as quickly as the other two, pulling Jane off the black were-leopard. But she didn't let go, and lifted Kemnebi with her, holding him off the stone. She held a knife at Kemnebi's throat.

Red blood ran into the man's white shirt, staining it scarlet. Rick growled, more vibration than actual sound. The blood smelled so . . . good. Kemnebi slanted a gaze at the cage, his eyes going wide. His irises were green gold. And they were afraid. Rick hissed. He hadn't seen Kemnebi since the first night of the full-moon cycle, and the man had changed. Or Rick had. He just hoped he'd remember that when the drugs wore off. "Being stoned can be a bitch sometimes." Only when the others all looked his way did he realize he had spoken aloud.

Jane pressed the blade into Kemnebi's neck and snarled, the sound so unlike her that Rick jerked in surprise, his skin moving over his muscles as if he had a pelt. Her growl echoed off the walls, and she said, "Bruiser, I swear by all that is holy in the highest realms of heaven, if you don't let me go, I'll kill him while you hold him. And I'll smear his blood onto your clothes so the other weres will think that you, and by extension Leo, are responsible for his death."

"You won't cause an international incident," George said. But Rick could smell the uncertainty in his sweat. When Jane didn't reply he said, more softly, "Kemnebi is here under the auspices of the International Association of Weres and of the Party of African Weres. He has diplomatic immunity."

"Won't stop him from dying."

"No. I suppose it won't." George relaxed his arms and slowly set both Jane and Kemnebi on the floor. Jane sprawled over the dark-skinned man, her knee pressed hard into Kemnebi's crotch, one hand holding back his head. Her silvered blade was at his throat, and his blood trickled down his neck into his collar and around to the back, where it gathered and plopped to the floor in soft splats of sound. Jane's eyes were golden and glowing. "I am alpha. Say it."

Kemnebi curled his lips back as if to show fangs. He growled low, the vibration a thrum passing through the stone beneath them and into the soles of Rick's feet.

"Say it. Or die."

"You are alpha. For now. But you will die beneath my claws, and no one will ever know that—"

"Forever. I am your alpha forever." She pressed the blade into the cut in his throat and her knee into his testicles. Kemnebi grunted with pain and shock. "What?" She chuckled, actually sounding happy. "You think I didn't take precautions? Look over my shoulder. The other one. See that small round thing in the corner of the wall and ceiling? That's a camera, Kemmy-boy. And I just got you declaring me alpha. So in this country, you are subject to me until you find sufficient reason to challenge me. I can do anything I want to you under were-law."

Kemnebi's eyes flashed green fire. His teeth were bared, gnashing; but his body language disagreed; he was pinned to the floor by his alpha. Rick smelled his capitulation.

"Yeah. I thought you'd say that," Jane said. "Leo has very good lawyers. I paid them a small fortune last night to research all this crap, and we both know I'm right. So say it again. I like the way it sounds."

"You are my *alpha*." The words were spitting, hissing anger.

"Good. You will take Rick under your kind and loving tutelage and teach him how to be a good were. You will teach him to shift. You will care for him. For now, he is my kit and under my protection. You are his guard. He dies, and you die. For every wound he suffers, you will suffer two. Got it?" When Kem nodded, the motion jerky, she said, "Repeat it. For the camera. For posterity. For the leader of the International Association of Weres. Just so we're all clear."

As if fighting himself, Kem repeated the words, sputtering as his eyes spat sparks. Rick could smell his humiliation and his subjugation. Satisfied, Jane rose and stepped back until the beta cat Kem, George, and Rick were all visible in her field of vision, but she didn't put the blade away. "We have plans to make. Bruiser, Rick's hurting again. Tranq him."

Rick saw George lift an arm, heard the soft spat of sound as the shot was fired. Felt the pain in his upper thigh. Without looking, he reached down and gripped the metal dart, pulled it from his leg, and tossed it at the blood-servant. It clattered to the floor. That was the last sound Rick heard as he toppled and the stone came at him, slowly filling his vision until gray, wet rock was all that there was in the world.

The floor hit and he bounced slightly, but the drugs were racing through him and he didn't feel the landing. He lay there, the earth itself wavering, swimming, the stone beneath him leaching out his body heat.

He had been a cop until the weres got him. He had been Jane's boyfriend and lover until the weres got him. Now he was in a cage, trying to go furry and still keep his sanity, hoping to survive the pain, while the primo blood-servant of the Master of the City of New Orleans shot him full of drugs.

The drugs lifted and carried him like a small limb on the mighty waters of the Mississippi. Down and down and down. And now . . . he was nothing.

Rick woke to the sight of daylight through tall trees and the scent of mountains. Jane's mountains. He was lying on a sleeping bag in a tent staked on a bed of leaves, its sides unzipped to allow air and light in through the mesh walls. He was out of pain, drug free, and alive.

Rolling to his back, he stared out, seeing mountain on one side, rising high, and a path on the other, leading down. He smelled people, strangers, though not close by; Kemnebi, beer, and food were very close. Fainter, he smelled Jane, the scent telling him she had gone. She had gotten him out of New Orleans and away from vamps and witches and a barred cell. Once again she had saved his life. He owed her. Especially he owed her an explanation, but it might be a while before he got that chance.

The still shots of the past three days raced through his mind, images of people, of Leo, of George, of witches with coven names that hid their identities. He vaguely remembered Leo telling him that he had an extended leave of absence from the NOPD—New Orleans Police Department— negotiated by a lawyer Leo kept as dinner.

And Rick was mostly sane, though he could still feel the moon. He had three weeks to learn whatever he needed to be able to shift. The wolves had done it. So could he. And then he was going after Jane. They had some talking to do.

Dance Master

This short story is dedicated to the Beast Claws.
You know why!

Author's note: This short is from Bruiser's point of view, and takes place after *Mercy Blade*, and before *Raven Cursed*, when Leo has been restored to sanity by the presence and blood of his Mercy Blade, Gee DiMercy, and when Jane and Rick are separated by his were-taint. Rick has disappeared to live in the Appalachian Mountains with Kemnebi. Jane is alone in New Orleans.

He heard the Harley's distinctive roar as it cruised down the street, slowed, and parked almost beneath him. He could feel her eyes on him from the street, but he didn't look down or allow himself to react. He snapped his fingers and placed his fork on the plate; the waiter took it immediately and freshened his coffee. The young man also poured Irish Breakfast tea, freshly brewed, into the cup across from him. George listened for her booted feet on the stairs as the man placed a perfectly turned Western omelet on her plate and withdrew. The breakfast service at DeJa Vu was always good, but he knew it was always better because of who he was.

George watched as she crossed the room to the balcony, moving from shadows into morning's light, long and lean and feline, dangerous. He could feel the tug of his master's mind and knew that Leo was watching as well, wanting her. Claiming her. Silently George resisted. He had given up many women to the Master of the City, but he had discovered that he couldn't give up this one.

You will leave her for me, Leo whispered into his mind. *The woman is mine.*

"The woman belongs to no one." George bowed his head as Leo lashed out at him. But he didn't give up. "She is free, my master. And you will not be able to take her."

You defy me, Leo thought at him, surprised.

George closed his eyes, knowing that pain might come but unable to hide anything from Leo. "Yes. She is not human, my master. She will fight you."

You have not defied me for many years. I will think on this. Leo left his mind, freeing George to smile at her.

"Jane." His voice was a caress, and he knew she heard the tenderness in the word; her color went higher and she glanced away, only a brief moment, to compose herself. He wanted Jane Yellowrock, even more than Leo did, because he wanted her with her own free will intact, unchanged and unchained. He wanted her to want him, to need him as badly.

Of course there was the small matter of the former undercover policeman, the black were-leopard, recently turned, and Jane's attachment to him. George knew the man, had studied his dossier quite well. Unless Rick LaFleur had changed drastically since he'd acquired the were-taint, he would not stand between them for long. His history suggested that he was incapable of maintaining a romantic relationship with only one woman for any length of time. And it was even more unlikely that he would survive his next full moon, though George wouldn't wish such pain and madness on anyone, even a faithless, charismatic rival. He would wait, bide his time. One thing that he had learned over the decades as the primo to the Master of the City was infinite patience.

Jane sat in the chair and looked at the steaming breakfast, a small smile on her lips. Her head gave a faint shake as if surprised at the food waiting for her, but she didn't comment. She sipped her tea, added two teaspoons of sugar and a dollop of fresh cream, and sipped again, making him wait. Little games she played as naturally as she breathed. "Hiya, Bruiser," she said as she picked up her fork and tasted the eggs. Chewing, she stared back at him, her face impassive, her amber eyes steely, as cold as the steel and silver in her braids and hidden on her body. "So. I'm here." She ate another bite and drank down half of her tea. The waiter refilled her cup. He'd been well tipped in the past and knew to stay close but out of earshot. "Your suckhead boss needs my help again?"

He smiled slowly, watching her face. "He allows you freedom and leeway that he allows no others." When her expression didn't change, he added, "I think perhaps he cares for you."

Jane leaned in slowly, her scent wild and untamed, feral as a hungry predator. She smelled of deep woods, and danger, and long hunts beneath a full moon. He didn't know what she was, and he wanted to. He wanted to know everything. Jane said, "Leo Pellissier cares for nobody and no one except those he drinks from . . . and owns," she added carefully, watching his reaction to her insult. George smiled, amused at the words. He had heard much worse over the decades. She said, "Leo doesn't own me. He has no control over me. None at all. And I could give a rat's hairy backside what he wants. I am a free agent, not one of his dinners."

George chuckled and curled his fingers under to keep from reaching out and caressing her face. "Then I pray he never drinks from you, Jane Yellowrock. I like this freedom of yours. This splendid, wonderful freedom."

"Yeah. Whatever. I got your e-mail with the request from His Royal Fanghead about the disturbance at the club. You got any more details than a rogue, but sane, vamp trying to drain the lead singer?"

"Yes. We've had two different attacks this week, incidents when we've found employees passed out, blood-drunk, but who claimed they had no memory of a Mithran accosting them. Such complete compulsion suggests an older, masterful Mithran, and none have come forward."

"And no one smelled a new vamp? I mean, I know the odors in the Royal Mojo Blues Company can be overwhelming, but vamps can smell other predators."

"Leo would like for you to inspect the premises and give us your opinion."

Her eyes narrowed, the amber irises constricting with her thoughts. "So he knows or guesses who it is, but he's playing politics. He can't move against the person himself, but I can."

"You are learning how Mithrans operate," he said with approval in his voice.

"Yeah. Back to that rat's hairy—"

"And you don't care about Mithran politics," he interrupted. "I know. Would you like to ride with me or follow on your bike?"

"I'll meet you there," she said. She finished the omelet with quick, economical bites and drank down the tea. Standing, she left the restaurant and he followed, watching her legs move beneath the jeans. Her legs were, arguably, the most incredible part of her. Her long braid bounced against her marvelous bottom, begging to differ with his assessment.

Behind him, the waiter cleaned the table. He would add the bill to Leo's account along with his customary thirty percent tip. Bruiser knew how hard most people worked to make a living, and he wasn't miserly.

He pulled his car in behind Jane and parked next to the bike she called Bitsa. He'd learned when she explained that the Harley was made from bitsa this and bitsa that, by a Harley Zen master, mostly from two old rusted bikes. He'd been a motorcycle man in his day. Someday he would show her his collection, and perhaps offer her one of the older pan heads. But not until she was already his.

With the key, he unlocked the restaurant and held the door for her. She lifted her eyebrows at the gallantry and he smiled, waiting for a comment about her being strong enough to open her own doors. But this time she said nothing as she moved into the dark of the club. She stood in the shadows, sniffing in long bursts, breathing in that odd way she had, so like a wild animal. Upon their first meeting, she had growled at him. He smiled to himself as he turned on the lights. She had taken both him and Leo down fast. It was one of his best memories of her—and he had many.

Lights on, the bar was revealed for what it was. An old building renovated to current standards for bathrooms, sprinkler systems, and wheelchair access, with a long bar, food service and kitchen, storeroom, and bandstand stage in front of a dance floor. He had watched Jane dance there several times, her body lissome and supple and exceedingly flexible. His smile widened as he remembered.

Jane moved across the room, smelling everything, going into bathrooms, checking out every part of the empty building. She ended up at the back door, and when she called he met her there. "Open this?"

He hadn't checked this entrance himself. It was a fire escape, and was unlocked from the inside during business hours. There was no way for anyone to use it without an alarm going off. But Jane didn't know that, and so she'd found something he had missed. *Fresh eyes and better-than-human nose. What is she?*

Using another key, he turned off the alarm and unlocked the door, which opened onto a narrow alley, no more than three feet wide.

When the door was open, Jane dropped to one knee and studied the filthy ground, sniffing, studying the alleyway. "Female vamp. Old. She stood in the alley for a while, then came in through here," she said. "Someone turned off the alarm for her and opened the door, so she has an accomplice. Human, I'd say, male, healthy, possibly a new blood-servant, blood-drunk, complaisant enough to do anything she wants." She pointed at the paved alley and George knelt beside her. "See these marks? Heels. Stilettos. Tiny feet, maybe a size five."

George saw what she was pointing to. He'd studied tracking with an old Arapaho Indian many years ago, but learning gained from a moccasin-wearing teacher was difficult to apply to modern footwear in a paved alley. He made a soft *hmmm* as he followed the footprints with his eyes, losing the print about ten feet down. Jane stood and moved along the alley, avoiding piles of trash and feces and wet spots that indicated vagrants had used the alley as a public toilet. He grimaced. He'd see it was hosed down after this was over.

She stopped in front of a recessed area in the brick of the building beside her. Like RMBC it had been many things over years, once a dress shop, once an art gallery, once even a strip club, back when this part of the French Quarter had catered mostly to the flesh.

Jane bent and studied the door, and once again he thought she was smelling it. Satisfied, she said, "I'll be right back. I'm going to walk around it." She moved into the daylight at the front of the building. Shortly she appeared at the back of the building, navigating the narrow space. Her jeans were dirty. Her T-shirt was dusty. Her boots were caked with something he didn't want to inspect too closely.

"She lairs here"—she thumbed at the building—"coming and going through this door most of the time, though she accessed the front door a few times too. The human who lets her in lives with her. And I believe she's there now. Do you want me to take her?"

"No. Not now. I'll pass the information to Leo. He'll make the final decision."

Jane shrugged. "We're done here, then." She looked at her boots. "Is there an outside spigot in back?"

"Yes. I'll let you back in from there and out through the front, to your bike."

"Ducky." She turned on her filthy heel and moved, catlike, back into the shadows.

When she came in the back door, she smelled fine, and he looked the question at her.

"It wasn't anything too nasty. Just an old, squishy hamburger."

She had washed her hands and brushed off her jeans and T-shirt, and looked . . . wonderful. Acutely aware of her, George locked the door and led her through the kitchens to the main room, where he had left an old seventies rock-and-roll LP on the record player in back. The music coming through the speakers was smooth and rich with a full-bodied sound, as only old vinyl and an excellent speaker system can make it.

Jane walked to the center of the dance floor and stopped, her head back, her braid dangling free. She seemed to inhale the music, her chest rising and falling. "Good sound. Allman Brothers?"

"From their *Decade of Hits* album."

"I like," she said. "Hey, Bruiser. Dance?" She held out her arm, her head still back, her eyes still closed.

His heart did a small thump, and he moved across the floor to take her in his arms, thinking about the beat, the sort of dance that might work with the music. He pulled her into a slow, easy number, part waltz, part something else that his feet seemed to find as he held her in a close embrace, the closed position of dance, which forced her to follow more intimately. With a subtle transfer of weight, he turned her beneath his arm, her body brushing his suggestively. Eyes still closed, she smiled, relaxed into his arms, and let him lead her through the dance. He thought she didn't relax often, and perhaps never with her eyes closed while another held her. There was a sensation of trust in the way her body moved. Of . . . giving in.

The music changed. He didn't listen to the music, though it was one of his favorite LPs; he adjusted the rhythm of the dance, slowing, and pulled her even closer, releasing her hand and sliding both arms around her, one hand flat on her back, between her shoulder blades, the other rising to rest against the back of her neck, under her braid. He could feel her breathing against his chest, her ribs moving slowly, her breasts pressing against him. She was hard and muscular, all angles and solid planes, but she was also all woman. He dropped his head to her neck and breathed in, controlling his arousal for fear of frightening her away. He'd lived many years with Mithrans, and had learned how to control his body, his reactions to fear and desire and delight and hunger. Jane brought out all of these in him. He *wanted* her.

And then the record ended, far too soon.

Jane slid a hand from his waist and up, between their bodies, and pressed him away.

George almost complied, but . . . he could not. He stilled his steps, sliding his hand around to cup her jaw, his thumb on her chin, and tilted her head up. Her eyes came open and she met his. So close. Dropped his mouth. Closer. Her lips opened. Her irises grew wide and black. He breathed her breath and gave it back to her. Lips nearly touching. *So close.*

She tilted her head, bringing her mouth to his. Lips to his. And she laughed softly, a sound that was pure desire, a purr of need and want, vibrating through him.

He felt it to his core. An electric flame sped through him, hot as a flash fire. He pulled her to him and kissed her as she laughed, rising on her toes, pressing hard to him. Her laughter softened as his tongue touched hers. Standing in the silent, empty bar, he danced a different kind of dance, pouring everything he knew about love and need and desire into the kiss. His body responded, growing hard. Demanding.

He dropped his hand and cupped her bottom, lifting her closer, pressing himself into the heat of her.

And her cell phone rang. It was a simple chime but insistent. She sighed into his mouth, a soft moan of longing and frustration. Without breaking the kiss, she pressed his chest away while reaching back and removing the cell from her back pocket. And she broke the kiss. Her eyes held his as the cell chimed, and she smiled, her lips full and slightly bruised. She answered the call.

"Jane Yellowrock." And she turned away, moving to the front door of the Royal Mojo Blues Company and out into the sunlight.

Yes. He'd have her. Of her own free will and her own need and her own trust. And this one he would share with no one. No one at all.

Golden Delicious

Rick's face was still tender, though the bruising was already yellow and the scabs had fallen off, revealing pink, healed skin. When he was human, it would have taken days to reach this stage of healing, but it had been less than twenty-four hours since he was sucker punched. There were very few good things about being infected with were-taint, but fast healing was on that short list.

"He was trying to hurt you, yet you held back." Soul glanced at him from the corners of her eyes. "It didn't go unnoticed."

He pushed on his teeth. They were no longer loose. "I'm betting he was a bully in high school," he said. "Not used to a guy forty pounds lighter and three inches shorter taking him down."

Soul's full lips lifted slowly. "Without breaking his jaw, his knees, or dislocating his shoulder, all of which you could have done." She made a left, turning onto a side road. Shadows covered them in the dim confines of the company car. "You taught him a valuable lesson. There are things out there that are bigger, faster, and won't care if he carries a PsyLED badge.

"Speaking of things bigger and faster than human, walk me through it again," she said, shifting their discussion as easily as she shifted gears.

"Human sense evaluation, initial technology, followed by enhanced senses," Rick said. "Then the pets and more tech as needed."

From the back, Pea twittered and Brute growled. Pea was a juvenile grindylow, Rick's pet and death sentence rolled up in one neon green–furred, steel-clawed, kitten-like cutie. The werewolf taking up the backseat was stuck in wolf form, thanks to contact with an angel, and he didn't like being called a pet, which meant that Rick did so every chance he got. The wolf hated leashes, his traveling cage, and eating from a bowl on the floor, but it wasn't like he had a choice. Since Brute couldn't shift back to human and had no thumbs, he had two choices: accept the leash and being treated like a dangerous dog, or sit in a cage all day. He'd gone for the partial freedom route, which meant partnering Rick LaFleur. Rick, who hadn't been human in two months himself, was at the training facility for the Psychometry Law Enforcement Division of Homeland Security—called PsyLED Spook School by the trainees.

The three composed a ready-made unit, a triumvirate of nonhuman specialists. If they could learn to work together. So far that didn't look likely. The werewolf might not be responsible for Rick's loss of humanity, job, and girlfriend, nor for the total FUBARed mess his life had become, but Brute had been part of the pack that kidnapped and tortured him. Rick didn't like the wolf or want him around, but like Brute, he had no choice right now. PsyLED had specifically requested them together, and had refused to accept Rick as a solo trainee. It was a package deal or no deal.

Soul said, "Treat this as if it's a paranormal crime and you're the first investigator on-site. If you spot something out of the accepted order, hold it for the proper time. You'll find that by training your investigative skills to work to a specific but fluid formula, you'll actually gain a freedom of thought processes that will work well in the field." Soul pulled into a driveway.

"This training site is the most difficult you will encounter during your time here. In the last two months, three students signed their quit forms and left the program after seeing the site." Her eyes narrowed, the skin around them crinkling. "And I can't explain why this particular crime scene has been so difficult on them." She turned off the car.

The small ranch house was dark, crime scene tape over the sealed doors, plywood over the windows. The grass was six inches high, the flower beds needed weeding. "Assuming that the grass was cut in the week prior," Rick said, "we're looking at maybe eight weeks since the crime."

Soul looked at him strangely. "You're the only one who even looked at the outside of the house."

"I was a cop," he said, feeling the loss in his bones. "We look at every-thing."

Soul grinned, losing years and making him wonder again about her. She could have been thirty or fifty, tribal American, gypsy, mixed African and European, or a combo. "I knew getting an undercover cop in this program was going to work. That's why I asked to be your mentor."

That was news. Soul was one of the top three mentors at Spook School, and Rick hadn't known how he'd been paired with her.

Soul opened her door, using the interior lights to twist a scrunchie around her platinum hair to keep it out of the way. "The neighbors called nine-one-one when they heard screaming and a dog howling. It was the second night of the full moon, nearly eight weeks ago. The first officers on the scene secured the area, called medics, made arrests based on the evidence, and then called PsyLED."

Rick stepped to the driveway and opened the back door for the pets. Brute leaped out—leash-free this time because there were no humans around—his white fur bright in the nearly full moon. Pea clung to his back, smiling, showing fangs as big as Brute's. Most people saw a green-dyed kitten when they saw her. It. Whatever. Pea was playful as a kitten and could get lost chasing a ball of twine for hours, but if he or Brute stepped out of line and risked passing along the were-taint to a human, she'd kill them without hesitation. That was her job.

"You stay by the door until I'm ready," Rick instructed. Brute scowled and emitted a low growl. This wasn't the first time they'd been over this. The last time Rick had brought it up, Brute had walked over to his instruction manual and lifted a leg. Rick had just barely saved the manual from a nasty drenching. Now, he held the wolf's eyes as the growl began to build.

Eventually, they'd have to deal with the question of who was in charge, and the wolf would have to accept beta status, acquiesce to Rick as alpha. Soul looked down at the wolf. "You're part of Rick's investigative team," she said, her tone cold. "I will not have silliness." Brute dropped his ears and whined, submissive, and Rick shook his head, wishing he knew her trick. Soul lifted her long skirts above the dew-damp grass and led the way to the door. She unlocked it and stood back, her fingers laced together.

Rick pulled on a pair of black nitrile gloves and flipped on the inside light. There was no furniture in the room, but it was far from empty. "It's a witch working, salt circle, internal pentagram composed of feathers, river-worn rocks, tiny moonstones, and dead plants. Two pools of blood in the pentagram suggest a blood rite, but it's an odd combo for one. Blood rites usually require full, five-element mixed covens." He stepped away from the front door, moving sun-wise, or clockwise, a foot outside the circle, to avoid activating any latent spells. "We have five practitioners, from four of the elements—air, water, two moon witches, and oddly, the death-magic branch of earth witches." Blood magic was rare, little known, and almost never practiced. Adepts were considered dangerous by other witches, because they used dying things to power workings, and when nothing around was dying, they would steal the life force of the living. In Spook School, he had learned how they worked. They were not nice people.

In the corner, standing with Soul, Brute was growling again, the basso so deep it was more a vibration on the air than actual sound. His mentor put a hand to the wolf's head, and Brute hunched, his shoulder blades high. Pea was staring at the circle, her eyes wide, one paw finger at her mouth. It was the animals' first crime scene, and Rick could imagine how awful the sights and smells must be to them.

"The composition of practitioners made for a lopsided but feasible working," Rick said. "The death witch was coven leader, sitting at the north, with a moon witch to either side, and air and water at the base, which made for the best balance the coven could get in during the full moon.

"The scorch mark in the center of the circle suggests they called up a demon, likely one that was moon-bound. If they called up a demon, it was for something bad, and I haven't heard of anything happening that might be demon-born."

Soul tilted her head, acknowledging his analysis but not giving him more information.

"The salt ring is broken in three places, which suggests that the working was completed or was interrupted in such a way that there's no residual power remaining. If this was a fresh crime scene and no one had been into the room, the first thing I'd do is verify with the psy-meter that the working is not active. Do you want me to go ahead and do that?"

Soul said, "Not now. Proceed."

Rick studied the circle. "Because of the blood magic, I'd call in Psy-CSI to take trace matter and blood samples to be held for possible DNA in the event that we have humans to compare, and in the event that this was a fatal crime."

Soul nodded, expressionless. "The investigators did so."

"Photographs, samples of each of the elements used, fingerprints, blood splatter workup . . ." Rick stopped. He was standing at the air point, studying the blood pattern. It was smeared and splattered over a large area, maybe four feet, but not puddled, as it would have been had the witch collected the blood in a bowl and then spilled or poured it. He bent closer and saw hairs in the blood. There were three, with more in the blood in the center of the circle, a lot more, some in small clumps. Stress caused some animals to lose hair. ". . . and speciation of the hairs," he finished after a brief pause. "Then I'd search the rest of the house. Shall I bother? It smells empty." Spook School knew everything about his situation, had tested his sensory perceptions extensively during his interview phase. Soul knew he had much better senses than a human, even in his current state.

Soul shook her head.

"End of human eval." Rick dropped to one knee in a tripod position, weight on knee, feet, and one hand. He sniffed in short, quick inhalations. An electric shock slammed through him, triggering the memories. Werewolf. He gasped, the jolt of pain and terror whipping through him. He managed a breath, then another, breathing deeper, forcing the fear and panic away with each breath. The witches had sacrificed a werewolf on the full moon. Rick opened an evidence packet. With a pair of tweezers, he picked up the hair closest. "Each hair is three inches long, pale at the root, fading to gray, and black at the tip."

Soul watched, assessing his reaction. She had known. Of course she had known. Except for Brute, this was the first were he had scented since the attack, the kidnapping, and the subsequent torture by the Lupus Pack in New Orleans. And his reaction to it was part of what would make or break his qualification and acceptance into PsyLED.

Slowly he lowered the hair into the evidence bag, fighting down the panic attack. He had thought he'd conquered the PTSD. Not so. The scars and the mangled tattoos on his shoulder and upper arm ached, feeling blistering hot, though they weren't. He forcibly relaxed, breathing slowly to decrease the fight-or-flight response brought on by the scent. The words clean and concise, his brain actually still functioning, Rick said, "Presumption: speciation of blood in the center of the circle was revealed to be werewolf blood. Second presumption: it bit the air witch, badly enough to transmit the were-taint."

At the words, Pea launched herself from Brute's shoulders and scampered across the room, leaping, crabbing sideways; she disturbed nothing. Brute followed slowly, but outside the circle, the overhead light throwing odd shadows, the darkest ones pooling under the werewolf. His growl, until now only a vibration, grew in volume. Rick realized that Brute had already detected the other werewolf, had known what had happened here from the moment they entered the room, and had been kept calm only by Soul's hand on his head. Rick would have to learn to read Brute in the field—assuming they passed the training.

Pea stopped at the center of the circle and scraped at the dried blood with one scalpel-sharp claw. She brought it to her nose and sniffed. She sneezed hard, covering her tiny mouth with a paw, then raced to the dried blood at Rick's feet. Brute and Pea stood nose-to-nose, sniffing.

Slowly Brute moved to the center of the circle and sniffed again. His ears went back and the vibration of his werewolf growl filled the room, seeming to bounce off the walls into Rick's chest. Brute's pale, crystalline eyes stared up at the former cop, his growl increasing in volume before falling away into a whine. If Rick hadn't known better, he would have thought the wolf was feeling worried, concerned. But three seconds spent with an Angel of the Light could have been no cure for Brute's cruelty.

Pea stepped over the salt circle and put her forelegs on Rick's jeans-clad shin, staring up at him. Her tail twitched, her face mournful. "Yeah," he said to her, stroking her once in comfort. "We're too late. Maybe weeks too late." He looked at Soul. "Did the witch turn?" Soul pressed her lips together and didn't answer. Rick figured that info was need-to-know, and trainees were the lowest on the information ladder.

On his knees, Rick circled the room, sniffing, letting the scent signatures settle into his brain, new memories, new associations. Rick turned to Brute. "You're up." The werewolf held Rick's eyes with a predator's intensity. This was something they had worked out the first day of school, a Q and A to keep them from having any Timmy-fell-down-the-well moments of attempted communication. "Take scent signatures of the subjects." Brute snarled at him but walked slowly around the circle, sniffing at each spot where a witch had knelt during the working. When he was finished, the wolf sat down again, waiting for the confirmatory questions.

"All the witches were female," Rick said.

"You can tell that by scent?" Soul interrupted, surprised.

Rick held up a finger, watching the wolf. There weren't many male witches because they tended to die at puberty, but it was always wise to confirm. The wolf nodded, which was a strange gesture on the animal.

"Were all the witches related?" Rick asked.

Brute shook his head.

"Two were related," Rick said.

Brute nodded once.

"This witch"—Rick indicated a point on the pentagram—"and that one."

Brute nodded again. Most covens were related by blood, even if widely spaced on the family tree.

Soul's eyes gleamed and her nostrils widened. Rick could hear her heart rate increase. "Very good," she murmured.

Pea stood on her hind feet, asking to be held. Rick boosted her up and Pea balanced across one shoulder, her tail curling around his neck, her furry cheek next to his. She didn't purr exactly. It was more part purr and part croon, rhythmical, musical, and harmonic.

Soul crossed the room, walking widdershins, or counterclockwise. When she reached him, she buried her hand in Brute's ruff, scratching his ears. The werewolf sighed in happiness. "None of the other trainees did half as well, not even the witches, and they had a better handle into magic working than you will ever have. Starting a week late, you are better at this than any of the others." A half smile curled her lips. "Don't tell them I said so."

"Psy-meter," he said, not responding to the compliment. Rick knew that, in his case, being the best was not a guarantee that his triumvirate would graduate and go on to be PsyLED agents. They had other issues. Lots of other issues.

Soul lifted the strap of the bulky device from around her head. The training units were older models, having been pulled from field use when the agency got lighter-weight, more compact ones, but the older models still worked. Rick stepped outside, clipped the box to his belt, and turned the unit on. He calibrated it according to the outside magical ambience, which should have been close to zero. The meter needle fluctuated and settled safely in the green zone. This particular device had been calibrated just for his unit, taking into account their magical energies, which had higher-than-human readings.

He deliberately did not look up at the sky. Tomorrow night was the first night of the full moon and he got weird close to the full moon, wanting to sit and stare up at it. For hours. Yeah. Weird.

Rick stepped back inside and instantly the meter spiked. Rick stopped and looked at Soul. The meter wasn't reacting to her—Soul showed up as human, though she definitely was not—but to something else in the room. "It's redlining. This far out time-wise from a working, it should be a low yellow, max."

"What might that signify?"

"Several possibilities. The working was interrupted. The working is still active, which means they transferred the working to an amulet. Or it had a delayed result yet to be released. But I don't see signs of anything magically active, so which was it?"

Soul shook her head. "We don't know yet." Rick handed Soul the psy-meter and she touched Brute's shoulder, which came to her waist. The gesture was part scratch and part something metaphysically calming, which made Rick once again wonder what Soul was. Fairy? Elf? The wolf started panting and closed his eyes.

Rick said, "I want to see the crime scene photos, the mug shots, and the notes of the OIC and the IO."

"Why?" She sounded sincerely curious, not if-I-ask-a-question-he'll-learn-something curious. "What do you think that the officer in charge and the investigating officer might have missed?"

"I don't know. But the meter's still redlining. I might see something that the rest of you missed, or something in the photos might hit on what I smelled or saw. I might draw a different conclusion or ask a different question. I want to see all that because tomorrow night is the start of the full moon. And we might have a werewolf out there."

Soul stared at him, her black eyes speculative. They were even blacker than his own Frenchy-black eyes, and usually they sparkled, throwing back the light like faceted black onyx. But tonight they were somber. Soul pulled a cell phone from a pocket in her gauzy skirt and punched in a number. "Have the on-call administrator call me back ASAP." She closed the cell.

Rick studied the circle once more. "Did our people make the three openings in the salt?"

That enigmatic half smile lit her features again. "No. It was that way when we found it." Soul's platinum ponytail slid to one shoulder and stayed there when she raised her head. She was graceful, small, and curvy in all the right places. He wanted to know more about her, but he also understood that the relationship between trainee and mentor was one of strictly enforced professionalism. There weren't a lot of law enforcement jobs open to someone who carried the were-taint. He wasn't going to blow his chance to work for PsyLED by giving the wrong signals. He'd made too many mistakes where women were concerned. He'd lost his humanity because of that. He turned and went outside.

The light inside the house went out behind him and he heard Soul lock the door. He could count the tumblers if he wanted to. Cat hearing was part of the enhanced senses he'd gained when he was bitten by a black wereleopard.

Soul's cell tinkled, new age musical chimes. She walked away, opened it, and instead of saying hello, said, "Mariella. Thank you for returning my call."

"How did your wonder boy do?" Mariella Russo, the instructional administrator, asked.

Though Rick had never met the IA, he'd remember that voice. It sounded as rough as splintered wood, as if she smoked four packs of cigarettes and drank a pint of rotgut whiskey every day. Soul knew he had acute senses, but she never acted accordingly and he'd learned a lot of interesting things by listening. He turned away so Soul couldn't read his face. Pea nuzzled his cheek and he stroked her, absently. Brute was a white shadow off to the side, glowering at him.

"Our best PsyLED investigators took two weeks to determine what his unit deduced in only twenty minutes," Soul said. "And, thanks to his law enforcement training, he added observations that the other trainee units missed. It will be in my report. He wants the crime scene photos, the mug shots, and the notes of the OIC and the IO. I am recommending he be given access."

"This situation is far too delicate and volatile for a trainee to have that sort of entrée," Russo said. "So the answer is no, Soul."

"Rick LaFleur didn't turn or go insane at the last full moon," Soul said. "He survived it. Intact. He may see something we missed. Or he may know something he doesn't realize he knows until the memory is triggered or the association falls into place."

"What Chief Smythe needs from him is the name of the witch who created his counterspell music. Get that and we'll reconsider."

Rick went cold. Was that why he had been invited to train at PsyLED? Because the department wanted access to his friend, an unknown witch, one not in the databases? Or access to a charm no one had ever heard of before—one that controlled the pain brought on by the full moon? And most important, why would Liz Smythe want it?

Pea made a twitter of concern and he stroked her gently. "It's okay, Pea." But it wasn't. Not by a long shot.

"The chief administrator can ask for her own information," Soul said. "Come on. Let Rick see the crime scene photos."

Russo sighed. "Why do you always try to get the protocols changed, Soul?"

Soul's laughter floated on the night air. "Because I'm the best. Because of what I am. Agree, Rus'. You know I'm right."

"Fine. An intern will deliver the file to LaFleur's private chamber before you get back to base."

Rick smiled tightly, his eyes on the house across the street. The private-chamber comment said a lot about his entire stay at Spook School.

"She agreed," Soul said. Brute flinched. Rick held his own recoil in. She had appeared right next to them without a sound, even with his and Brute's keen hearing. He remembered what she had said to Russo: *"Because of what I am."* And he wondered, not for the first time, what Soul was.

When he let himself into his quarters, the file was on his desk beside his MP3 player, which was loaded with the counterspell melodies he played during the full moon. The private chamber was a twelve-by-twelve space in the back of the Quonset hut that held Spook School's paranormal supplies. He slept away from the trainees' barracks for a lot of reasons: because of Brute and Pea, who were deemed too dangerous to sleep near humans, and who refused to sleep in cages—not that he blamed them. And because he was too dangerous to be around humans at the full moon; Rick refused to be caged too. Because PsyLED was afraid that he might snap some full moon and bite his partner, he would never be a solo investigator, never be paired with a human or witch. His nonhuman unit was already established—a de facto triumvirate—if he didn't kill Brute first.

Brute went to his bed—a cedar-chip-filled mattress on the floor in the corner—walked in a circle three times, lay down, and closed his eyes, Pea curled against his side. Rick showered and took the file to his own bed— a two-inch-thick mattress that had seen better days on a corroded, metal, folding bed frame. He hadn't complained. He'd take what he could get, hoping to salvage something of the law enforcement career he'd lost when he contracted the were-taint.

He opened the file and started through it. The first thing he noticed was that there were only four mug shots, not five. There had been five witches at the crime scene, he knew that by the scent patterns. He flipped through the arrest reports and discovered that the coven leader had gotten away and the other coven members had refused to name her. Rick closed the file. Delicate and volatile . . . That could mean most anything.

He flipped through the arrest interviews and quickly discovered that one of the witches was Laura McKormic, the wife of Senator McKormic, a hard-line Republican from the state of Georgia, and an avowed witch hater. Now Rick knew why Russo claimed that the situation was delicate. Politics.

Laura McKormic rang a bell different from politics, however, and Rick booted up his old laptop to Google her. According to news reports, Laura had been killed in a one-car accident forty-eight hours after the arrest, but Rick could find no coroner's report and no accident report. That meant she was likely the woman bitten at the scene and was hidden away in a private asylum—a werewolf, a danger to herself, her family, the public, and mostly, her husband's career. Female werewolves who survived the initial bite went into immediate and permanent heat, and insanity was never very far behind. Rick closed the laptop. He had personal knowledge of just how bad that could be for the bitches themselves, and for the humans who came into contact with them. He reached up and scratched the scars on his shoulder. That had to be why Smythe wanted the name of his friend, the witch who had provided the counterspell for his own were-shifting problem. To help Laura find a measure of peace from the binding of the were-taint.

From his pallet, Brute whined and thumped his tail. Slowly Rick turned his head to Brute and met the wolf's eyes. Brute was watching his hand on the scars. The wolf dropped his head to his paws and whined again. Rick frowned. He recalled little of his time with the Lupus Pack, under their control, but it had all been bad. Beatings. And worse. Stuff Rick chose not to remember. Some of it at Brute's hands back when the were had been able to shift to human. But Rick had been there when Brute came into contact with the angel Hayyel. Maybe the angel's presence had affected both of them, because having Brute in the corner of his bedroom didn't seem as awful as maybe it should have. Rick slid his hand away from the scars, ridged and numb and yet somehow burning. Brute's eyes followed.

"Full moon is coming," he said, and Brute whined again. Rick closed the folder, dropped it to the floor, and turned off the lamp. Rolled over and pulled up the blanket. "Go to sleep."

Morning was back to basics, which meant breakfast in the farmhouse kitchen. From the yard, as he climbed the steps, Rick could hear dishes clatter and classmates chatter. He wondered who would try to cause trouble this time. The cook frowned on weres and had tried to keep his entire unit out of the kitchen, saying that "animals should eat outside." Some of Rick's fellow trainees weren't much better. Brute and Pea beside him, wearing red-and-blue PsyLED K9 harnesses, Rick entered the big room and moved to the left of the doorway, out of silhouette—instinct, to get a wall at his back.

Mary, three tables down, looked over the rim of her coffee cup and nudged Walker. "Our were-animals are here," she murmured. "I had hoped they'd be out of the program by now."

Walker pursed his lips. "I tried."

Rick reached up and touched his face. The fading bruises were no longer painful, but they had been a virulent yellow in his shaving mirror this morning. "Not animals," he said, loudly enough to be heard by the other trainees. The room went silent and Mary blushed scarlet, the telltale of pale-skinned redheads. The other trainees swiveled their heads toward him, then to the couple. Rick stared Walker down and said, "A PsyLED unit. My unit." He pretended not to see Brute's ears prick up, and kept his eyes on Walker. He dropped his voice to a low growl and lied through his teeth, "And the next time you try to kick Brute, I'll either let him eat you, or I'll take you down. No chance to sucker punch me again." Brute chuffed and smiled at Walker, showing way too many teeth. "You may have me by forty pounds, but you won't get back up."

The other trainees looked from the guilty couple to the table holding the instructors and mentors, and then back to Rick. From the corner of his eye, he saw Soul put her hand on the arm of his jujitsu teacher, holding the man still. Rick winked at her, and her brows went up in surprise. "It's okay. He's lying," she murmured, her words audible to Rick only because of his enhanced hearing. "And the wolf is perfectly in control."

Two tables down, a blonde named Polly stood to see Walker. Into the uneasy silence, she said, "You tried to kick his partner? If LaFleur doesn't take you down, I will."

Brute chuffed quietly at the term *partner*. Pea chittered and sat up on the wolf's back to see better, sounding pleased.

The girl beside Polly leaned back in her chair and said, "And I'll help." She looked at Rick. "I knew he was hassling you. Sorry I didn't step in." She raised her voice so the instructors couldn't pretend not to hear. "I don't tolerate bullies."

Some of the tension Rick carried melted away as both girls patted an empty place at their table. "Come on, gorgeous," Polly said. "You can eat with us." She flicked a look up at Rick. "And your ugly, bruised handler too."

Rick shook his head at the ribbing. "Go sit with the nice ladies, Brute. Be charming. I'll bring you a plate." The wolf rolled his eyes up and Rick said, "Yeah, I know. Six eggs over easy, half a chicken, raw, and apples, quartered. Come on, Pea. Let's go through the line."

Rick tossed the grindylow to his shoulder and turned his back on the wolf, going to the buffet. While loading up three plates, he watched in the mirrors over the serving table as Brute padded to the table and sat beside Polly, who was a dead ringer for a young Gwyneth Paltrow. Brute rested his head on her thigh and looked up at her with puppy-dog eyes. Both girls went all mushy and started petting him.

It was ridiculous. Brute got more female attention than he did. And it wasn't like Rick was ugly, despite the bruises. At six feet even, with black eyes and black curling hair, he'd been known as a ladies' man, a player. Of course, that was part of the reason he'd been bitten by a female black were-leopard, tortured by werewolves, and had lost his humanity, his job with the NOPD, and his girlfriend, but that was another story.

Rick set Brute's plate on the floor, Pea's beside his on the table, and slid into the proffered seat, digging in. The eggs were perfect, and the pancakes,

while not as good as his mom's, weren't bad, especially when he poured
warm blueberry syrup over them.

"Is he really a werewolf?" Polly asked, her fingers in Brute's fur.

"Yep. The only tame werewolf in the world."

"You tamed him?" she said, her tone going skeptical.

"Nope. An angel named Hayyel did."

"No shit?"

"No shit at all. I was there. Saw the whole thing. Pass the coffee?" The
girls exchanged a pointed look and Polly poured him a cup. Rick glanced
at the wolf's pale eyes. Brute looked . . . ashamed. Rick narrowed his eyes.
The wolf was not feeling shame for what he had done in his life. No amount
of penance assigned by an angel could make that happen.

The schedule was a twelve-hour day: three hours of physical training and
combat sparring, six hours in class, with a break for lunch, then shooting,
at which Rick excelled. He grew up on a farm in the South and had practically been born with a gun in his hand. Dinner was at seven, with library
study time after. The library was a computer room with no books, but with
electronic links to everything: the National Crime Information Center,
the National Law Enforcement Telecommunication System, the FBI's Inte-
grated Automated Fingerprint Identification System, the U.S. Department
of State's database of biometric facial recognition and iris scans, and databases the CIA had been compiling since 9/11. They also had access to every
state's motor vehicle records, criminal warrant and parole records, and
wanted information. The computers allowed access to Interpol and most
of the law enforcement agencies in treaty nations, not to mention advanced
GPS and satellite photo programs that made Google Earth look like a high
school science project.

Everything was encrypted and was monitored by advanced artificial
intelligence counterterrorism software, just in case someone was running
unauthorized searches or a sleeper terrorist was compiling a database for
use against the U.S. It was a cop's wet dream. The library alone was reason
enough to join PsyLED, and that didn't count all the cool toys stored in
the other half of his Quonset hut quarters.

Polly joined Rick there for study. He could tell she was interested, but
for lots of reasons there would be no big love scene to end the evening: it

was against the rules for trainees to hook up, Polly had a night-training session, and the biggest reason—Rick could transmit were-taint to a human through sex. The proscription against sex—for the rest of his life—was something he hadn't been able to make himself think about yet. At all. Instead of encouraging Polly, he kept it casual.

Together they researched a bungled crime scene from the seventies and talked shop, while Brute and Pea lay curled in the corner. Later they all went to the farmhouse kitchen for snacks and beer. The nearly full moon was just rising over the trees when they said good night, Polly heading to the admin building to meet her mentor, and Rick to the Quonset hut to get out of the moon glow.

He nodded to the security guards he passed, his night vision so acute that he could pick them out in their night-black camo. Ernest lifted two fingers from the stock of his weapon and Rick waved back. Ernest was a former PsyLED operative, now fifty-seven and retired, working part-time to keep his hand in. Rick understood that; most cops had problems quitting full-time work, going from service and adrenaline to sitting in front of the TV or playing golf.

As he reached for the door handle, Brute came out of nowhere and slammed into his legs, sending Rick stumbling to the side. The wolf started that horrible, low-pitched growl, the one that made the hair stand up on Rick's arms. Rick stared at the handle. There was nothing there, nothing visual anyway. He bent and sniffed, but smelled nothing except his own scent. He looked at the wolf, who was staring at the door, head down, slightly hunched, as if he was going to pounce.

"Someone went into my quarters?"

Brute nodded, dropping his head once.

Rick ran through the scenarios. He wasn't allowed to carry his sidearm on campus. None of them were—they weren't on duty, they were in school—so going in alone would be stupid. But if he called for help and no one was in there, he'd look like an idiot. So . . . He took a slow breath and let it out. "Let's be stupid and see what this is." Rick stood to the side of his door, his back against the wall, and turned the knob slowly. Opened it an inch and sniffed. Brute stuffed his snout inside and sniffed too. After a moment, his ruff settled and he looked up at Rick. "I agree," Rick said. "Whoever it was, is gone." He reached in and turned on the switch, flooding the small space with light. No one was there. There weren't any hiding places. And witches didn't have invisibility spells. Or at least that was what he'd been taught. Of course, if they were invisible, how would you know?

They entered slowly, Brute at Rick's side, alert, quiet, intense. "We'll quarter the room. When you smell something, give me the signal." Rick moved around the room, his jeans brushing the wolf's side. Brute kept his nose to the floor, his ears pricked sharply. He sat in front of the small dresser, and again at the closet, which was the signal they had worked out for having found something. Rick opened both dresser and closet, but the wolf showed no particular change in attitude. The intruder hadn't done anything with his clothes, so why come in here? The wolf stopped at the old bed, the small laptop lying on top. Brute sniffed and sat.

Rick studied his computer. Pea leaped to the bed and raced around the laptop, twittering, almost as if she were scolding it. Rick still had a pair of gloves on his desk from the crime scene and he pulled them on before carefully lifting the screen. He didn't see it at first, and he never would have noticed it all except for Brute's nose and Pea's verbalizations. A tiny black dot was on the black keyboard where he would rest his palms when not typing.

He had to get someone in here to check it out, but if he was going back into the moonlight, he'd need his MP3 player and the counterspell music. He reached to the desk.

It was gone.

Shock swept through him, electric, hot. In an instant he was back at his first full moon, three days in a New Orleans cell, drugged to the gills, as his body tried to turn itself inside out, fighting to shift, struggling to change into the black were-leopard that was his beast. Tried and failed over and over again, held to his human shape by the mangled tattoo spell on his shoulder and upper chest. The artwork bound him to his human form and stopped every attempt to shift. The full moon meant pain like being struck by lightning, pain like being flayed alive. Mind-breaking pain. He didn't want to shift, didn't want to be a were, but even that would be better than the three days of hell.

His heart thundered. He broke into a hot sweat. The world telescoped down to the desktop, empty of the MP3 player. Rick reached out and touched the surface of his desk. Gone.

He blew out a breath, heated and hard. He had uploaded the music to a cloud backup system. He could easily download it to his computer for instant listening.

He dialed Soul on his cell. "Someone's been in my room and stole my MP3 player. They also left something on my laptop. Brute found it." He described the tiny dot and added, "I'm in my quarters. And no, I didn't touch anything except the light switch and my laptop, and I was wearing gloves."

"I'm on my way," she said.

Rick closed his cell. An hour later, his room had been swept for listening devices and video recorders, and the black dot had been confiscated. His room was clean, and Rick finally got to bed. He needed sleep, but he was edgy, restless, and couldn't keep his eyes closed. The full moon sucked. Each one could be the last night of his life, or leave him permanently furry like Brute. That was enough to make anyone jumpy. Finally, Rick opened the laptop, downloaded the counterspell, and hit PLAY, the laptop volume so low no human could pick it up. With the music playing in the background, he fell asleep.

At three twenty-two a.m., his cell rang, and Rick fumbled for it in the dark. "Yeah," he mumbled.

"Rick. Are you all right? Say something logical," Soul demanded.

"E equals MC squared. Isosceles"—he yawned in the middle of the words and swiveled his legs up, sitting—"triangle. 'Four score and seven years ago our fathers brought forth on this continent, a new nation, conceived in liberty,' and so on. Will that do?"

"I just heard back from the lab. The black dot recovered from your laptop was LSD on absorbent blotter paper with a sticky back. Someone wanted you incapacitated or out of control."

Rick grunted, thinking. "The list of people who might want me to become dangerous, and who know where I am, is confined to the people on campus." He heard Soul's long, drawn-out breath at the accusation. "Mary and Walk—" He stopped, remembering that Chief Smythe wanted the name of the witch who'd recorded his counterspell. Thinking about Polly's sudden interest in him—keeping him out late so someone could get into his room? "Mary and Walker. Maybe Polly. And whoever wanted my counterspell music."

After long moments, Soul said, "We need to talk."

"About Chief Smythe, who wants the name of the witch who made the counterspell?" Rick let the harsh tone cops use on suspects grate into his voice. "Wants it enough to enroll me here, even though I'm *dangerous*?"

"We need to talk," she repeated, her voice steely. "I'll be there shortly. Meet me in the kitchen."

"Yeah, yeah, sure." He closed his cell and got up, dressed, and headed out. Brute and Pea were there first, Brute blocking the door, Pea riding on his shoulder. Rick reached for the leash, but Brute growled and shook his head slowly, the human motion utterly un-wolf-like. Rick sighed. "Fine. But keep close."

Outside Rick leaned against the wall in the shadows and waited. Brute, however, went scent searching. He started right at the door, his nose to the ground, and began a circular pattern, walking and sniffing in an ever-widening spiral. He was about twenty feet out when he stopped, his nose buried in a clump of grass. Even in the moonlight, Rick could see his ruff stand on end.

"Brute?"

The wolf chuffed and breathed in and out in short, sharp bursts. Rick had seen the wolf get scent lost before, his wolf brain taking over, leaving the human part of him behind, disoriented and confused. Dog people called it *nose suck*, which might be humorous in a toy poodle, Chihuahua, or Shih Tzu, but not so much in a Rottweiler, pit bull, or werewolf.

Pea scrambled down from Brute's shoulder and inspected the tuft of grass with her nose as well. She scampered to Rick, mewling and chittering.

"Brute, are you scenting the person who put the LSD on my keyboard?" Brute didn't react or respond, and Rick knew better than to touch him. Wolves had violent physical reactions to being brought off a scent binding, and he wasn't in the mood to be mauled. "Brute?" He whistled softly and finally the wolf raised his head. His pale eyes were wholly wolf, feral. Rick went still, vamp still, not even daring to breathe. The wolf growled so low Rick felt it vibrate in his chest. "Brute? Stand down. Stand down." Pea launched herself across the two yards and landed on the wolf's head with a catlike yowl. Brute yelped. In a moment, they were rolling around on the ground, roughhousing, the scent forgotten.

Rick blew out, letting the adrenaline rush melt away. "Brute," he said, his voice a command. The animals' heads came up fast. They stopped playing, and Rick could see the intellect again in Brute's eyes. "Were you scenting the person who put the LSD on my keyboard?"

Brute dropped his head and raised it. Yes.

"Okay. Can you follow it? And not get scent lost again?" Rick asked. Brute nodded. A small, grim smile pulled at Rick's lips. "Then let's see where it goes."

With Pea riding his shoulder, Brute turned, sniffed, and started running to the back of the Quonset hut, his nose to the ground. Rick followed through the bright moonlight at a trot. He was halfway around the building when he ran out of the shadows into the moonlight. The moon call hit him. His breath stopped in his lungs, his muscles cramped in an electric spasm. He hit the ground face-first. The night vanished.

Rick woke slowly, the dark night full of scents. He knew where he was and who was with him by the scent patterns alone—the Quonset hut. Brute, Pea, and Soul were there. Soul was sitting on the edge of his bed, he was lying on the floor. His music was playing, the musical notes of the flute driving back the pain.

Even with the music, his skin burned as if he'd been flayed with stone blades, drenched in gasoline, and set on fire. All he wanted was to go back to sleep, find that dark and pain-free place he'd left upon waking, and stay there until the misery ended. Instead he said, "That was really stupid." The words were mumbled, but he knew he'd been understood when Soul laughed softly and Brute snorted.

"I do hope that is the last time you forget to carry your music when you go out under the full moon," she said. "I brought my old MP3 player and downloaded your music. Here." She leaned down and draped the cord over his head to rest on his neck, the speaker close by his ear. "Are you up to trying again, or shall the werewolf and I do this alone?"

Rick pushed up with his palms, groaning. His abdominals felt like he'd been stomped on by a herd of rampaging elephants. The rest of his muscles had a fine quiver through them, like his body was carrying an electric current. "Sure." Kneeling, he caught the desk as the room spun. "I feel just peachy. Just let me puke my guts out for an hour and I'll be ready to go."

Soul rested her hands on his shoulders. "See if this helps." The skin below her palms stopped aching. Instantly. From there it spread down his body, soothing and cool. Somehow the sensation made him think of the color green, green water, green grass in a green meadow. In two minutes he was mostly pain free.

Raising his head, he looked up at Soul. "You're not a witch. Not a were. You measure on the psy-meter as a human, but you're not. What kind of creature are you?"

"Creature." Soul *tsk*ed. "Such rude, personal questions. Surely your mother taught you better. Let's find the person who stole your music and wanted to drug you."

Rick cursed but managed to roll to his feet. All he wanted to do was curl up and sleep, but making the grade at Spook School would be an effort of perseverance, and the three days of the month when he was moon-called were the days the PTBs would watch him most closely. The world lurched and he nearly fell, but Brute came and sat at his side.

After a moment, Rick rested his hand on Brute's head. He had never touched the wolf before, and the long hair was coarse, but the shorter hair near the wolf's skin was softer, and warm. Far warmer than human skin. The heat felt good on Rick's chilled skin. Brute didn't react, didn't look up at him, or snap, or move away. Pea raced up the wolf's back then up Rick's arm to his shoulder. She nuzzled his cheek and crooned softly. Rick chuckled, his voice hoarse, and adjusted the player's strap.

"Brute. Follow . . ." He stopped. Soul had said something about his mama and manners. "Brute, would you please follow the scent you discovered outside?"

The werewolf huffed softly and went to the door, taking his warmth with him, leaving Rick's hand cold. He followed the wolf slowly, feeling the moon call's ache in his bones. But if he wanted to be a PsyLED agent, he had to make it through this full moon sane and functioning. And the next moon. And the next after that.

He paused at the threshold and took a slow breath, fear skittering up his spine on chitinous legs, sweat trickling in its wake. Stepping into the moonlight took an effort of will. But he followed the wolf back to the scent-marked grass in the moonlight. This time, Brute took a single sniff and started walking, nose to the ground, glancing back only once to make certain Rick was there. Soul close behind them, they moved across the compound, past the farmhouse kitchen. Toward the business offices, the library, and the communication building.

One of the security guards stepped from the shadows and looked them over. It was Ernest, and Soul paused, asking the guard to follow them. They wound through the compound, Brute's nose to the earth, and they reached the administration building. At the foot of the stairs, the werewolf paused, burying his nose in the grass again, breathing in and out with no rhythm, fast, short, long. Soul and Ernest stood silently behind them. Rick could hear the crackling of the guard's radio.

Finally Brute blew out and turned his head to Rick. The wolf's head was down, his shoulders high, ruff high, ears flat. Whatever he was smelling, it wasn't good. Brute started up the steps to the admin building, setting his paws carefully, slowly, his nose moving back and forth over each step. When he reached the narrow porch, that low-pitched, rumbling growl started, and Rick automatically reached for his weapon. He was unarmed and his hands closed on empty air. Brute snarled, showing fangs. Behind him, he heard the soft whisper of leather on steel as Earnest drew his sidearm and positioned to the left. Soul moved quickly to Rick's right, her feet silent on the wood.

Brute stared at Rick, his eyes almost glowing, trying to communicate . . . something.

"Are you still tracking the same scent from my quarters?" Rick asked.

Brute nodded once, then shook his head.

"Yes and no?"

Brute nodded, showing a gleam of teeth in the night.

Rick asked, "Have you smelled this scent before?"

Brute nodded, his eyes so intense that Rick felt, for a moment, like prey. He had no idea what to ask next. Brute huffed, put out a paw, and traced a jagged shape.

Rick asked, "The full moon?"

Brute shook his head.

Rick said, "It's just a circle."

Brute huffed, his head jutting forward.

"A witch circle," Rick said. "The witch circle at the crime scene. You found the coven leader. Here."

Brute nodded once, slowly.

"She's been here all along?"

Brute nodded and turned back to the door, his eyes, nose, and ears focused on the wood.

"Someone I've never had contact with."

Soul said, "Call backup, Ernest. Now."

The guard didn't bother to reply, but murmured into his mike, "Backup to admin. Silent, armed approach." To Soul, he said, "I'm carrying only standard ammo."

Soul pulled up her skirt to reveal a thigh holster. She handed Rick a Smith and Wesson .22, still warm from contact with her body.

Holding a weapon, Rick instantly felt better. He released the magazine and checked the ammo. "Silver shot," he said. He slammed the magazine back into place, pulled back on the slide, injecting a round into the chamber. Rick stepped into the shadows beside the door and slowly turned the knob. It wasn't locked.

He pointed to the wolf and held up one finger, then to himself and held up two fingers, then to Ernest with three fingers. The guard nodded, pointed left. Rick nodded and pointed right. He turned off his music and opened the door. Brute flowed in like a white cloud, hunched down, silent. Rick followed to the right, and felt, as much as heard, Ernest and Soul move left.

Inside the entry was dark, lit only by the green glow of computer battery backups. Brute didn't need more light; neither did he. They moved through the entry, around the counter, to the doorway in back. It opened to a hallway, offices on either side. Music flowed through the air, the mellow sounds of wood flutes, familiar and calming. His music, stolen from his quarters, the music that Chief Smythe had been so interested in.

The frame around one doorway was bright, and Brute padded down the hallway, nose down, to that door. Rick followed, and the music grew louder. He expected the office to be Chief Administrator Liz Smythe's. Instead, it was Mariella Russo's office, her name in gold leaf on the wood. Mariella Russo, who was on call the night he went to the crime scene.

He stood back and let Ernest take his place. The man reached out and took the knob in hand, turning it slowly. The door didn't creak as it swung open. Light flooded into the dark hall along with his music, amplified, and a stench like rotten cabbage, rotten eggs, and burned matches. Rick covered his nose. Brute padded inside two paces and halted.

The office furniture had been pushed back, exposing the wood floor, painted with a witch's circle and pentagram. In the circle was a dark cloud and a body, human, Caucasian, female. Blond. Rick felt the shock of recognition. Polly. He didn't have to wonder if she was dead. Her abdominal cavity had been ripped open, and the cloud was feeding on her. A demon. Mariella Russo was sitting at her desk, staring into the witch circle, her cupped hands in front of her, holding something that glowed yellow green.

Soul leaped for the desk, her body leaving the floor in one smooth, sleek movement. Agile. Inhuman. Both Ernest and Rick lifted their weapons in two-hand stances. Fired. Two taps. Ernest's slammed Russo midcenter of her body mass. Rick's shot hit her forehead.

A half second later, the concussion of the shots still echoing, Soul was standing behind the desk, holding Mariella's hands in hers. She eased the thing, whatever it was, from the dead administrator's hands. "Call for a containment vessel," she ordered. But Ernest was already doing so, his voice soft and in control.

Brute woofed and growled and ended on a faint whine, his eyes on Soul. *Yeah*, Rick thought, remembering her speed, like a time jump of movement. She wasn't human. No way, no how. Not with that leap. He walked to the circle and stood beside Brute, one hand on the wolf's head, scratching gently at the base of the upright ears.

The demon raised up out of Polly's naked body and hissed at them, showing a mouth full of sharp, pointed teeth. Ernest turned up the volume of the music and the demon closed its eyes, settling back to the corpse, as mellow as Rick felt when the music protected him from the moon call. He thought back to the spell at the crime scene. They had called up a moon demon. Soul lifted her eyes to Rick. "Please go back to your quarters."

Rick ejected the magazine of Soul's .22 and put the safety on before setting the gun on the desktop. He and his unit backed out just as four men rushed into the room, one carrying a cylindrical canister with a rounded top.

The next morning, Rick and his triumvirate were called to the chief administrator's office. Since he hadn't started with the other trainees, Rick hadn't met the CA, Dr. Smythe, but now, the chief was sitting at her desk, her face grave, her salt-and-pepper hair in a short bob, her face set in the no-nonsense expression of a drill instructor. Soul was standing against the window, her arms crossed, her shoulders hunched, her stance protective and uncertain, maybe just a bit defiant.

The former cop, the wolf, and the grindylow stood inside the office, Rick's eyes drawn to the pile of things on the CA's desk. It was his nine mil and holster, his backup ankle weapon, stakes, three silvered vamp-killers, his money, ID, credit cards, and the little black velvet jewelry box he'd purchased on his last leave.

He hadn't seen his stuff since that last leave, two weeks ago.

His next leave was days away.

It was two weeks until graduation.

They were booting him out.

Rick's heart dropped. Brute looked up at him and whined. Nudged his hip with his damp nose. Rick put his hand to the wolf's ears and scratched.

"It has been brought to my attention," the CA said, "that you were part of the reason—"

"The only reason," Soul interrupted.

The CA nodded serenely. "The only reason why Mariella Russo's crimes were discovered. We now believe the three students who supposedly signed quit forms in the last few weeks did not terminate their schooling, but may have been fed to her demon." The CA leaned back in her chair and templed her fingers at her chin. "We have launched a full investigation. We also understand that you witnessed"—she looked at Soul over her fingers—"something that is classified, and must remain so."

Did she mean the sight of Soul flowing/leaping/gliding over the desk to catch the thing in Mariella's hands before she dropped it? Or the containment cylinder? Or—

"But that isn't why I called you here," the CA said. "We have a problem in New Orleans. You are from there, yes?"

Rick straightened. This didn't sound like a "you're fired" speech. "Yes, ma'am."

"And you are familiar with Leo Pellissier, the Master of the City."

"I am." He was related to Leo's heir too, but he didn't offer that, not now, not ever.

"We would like you to travel there and deal with the situation." Rick's breath exploded out of him, and he sucked in another. He hadn't been aware that he'd been holding his breath. Smythe looked at Soul and her lips lifted into a faint smile. "Just so you know, Soul is against this. She feels you need more time here. Which is why, if you accept, she will be going with you."

Soul's mouth opened for a moment, then closed. "You could have told me," she said.

The CA chuckled. "If you agree to the assignment, Soul will accompany you into the field and provide both a temporary partnership and the last weeks of your training. You may return for graduation, of course. Soul, please explain the assignment to your in-field trainee. If he accepts, collect the necessary gear from the Quonset hut, and credit cards for your expenses from financial." Smythe stood and held out a wood box. "I am assuming you will accept. Your temporary badge."

Rick took the box and shook Smythe's hand. He wasn't being booted. He was being given an assignment. Before graduation. "Thank you, ma'am." The CA placed his gear in a paper bag, and had him sign for his personal belongings. Holding the bag and badge, Rick left the admin building with his unit and Soul. They stopped in the sunlight and Soul studied him, shading her eyes.

"They didn't kick my ass out." A smile pulled at his face. He wasn't sure how long since he'd grinned that widely. Probably since he'd lost his humanity. "I have a present for you," he said. Rick reached in the paper bag and held out the velvet box. "It was supposed to be a thank-you gift, for after graduation. But you should take it now. Sorry it isn't wrapped."

Soul raised her eyes to his and started to speak, but stopped and took the box instead. She opened it. Inside was a golden apple on a thin gold chain. "A golden delicious apple for the . . . creature." He laughed as sparks flew from her eyes when he brought up the fact that she wasn't human. "Tell me about the operation."

Cajun with Fangs

Author's note: This story takes place after *Raven Cursed*, but before the start of *Death's Rival*.

Bitsa's atypical roar and black smoke from her exhaust flowed down the bayou in a noxious, rough-sounding echo as I crossed the rickety, picturesque bridge into town. The bike's shudder had me worried. The Harley had undergone an engine and full system rehab as well as a touch-up paint job recently in Charlotte, North Carolina, and she should be running like a top. But the misfire was getting worse, and I knew I'd never make it over the Atchafalaya River Basin and into New Orleans before nightfall without a mishap. The idea of a breakdown after dark on the stretch of I-10 in southwestern Louisiana's mostly bayou/swamp/wetland or acres of farmland was not appealing. I hadn't seen a nice hotel in miles, and the mom-and-pop joints I *had* seen in the last five miles looked like bedbug-infested roach motels.

The little town I'd pulled into was called Bayou Oiseau, on the banks of the bayou of the same name. The weatherworn sign back on 10 had advertised TASSIN BROS AUTO FIX, OPEN SIX DAYS A WEEK, EXCEPT IN GATOR-HUNTING AND FISHING SEASON, which sounded better than nothing. There was no telling if the Tassin brothers could work on a Harley or not, and I had no idea if it was gator-hunting or fishing season; but I had a few tools with me, and the shade of a nice live oak, an ice-cold Coke, and a chocolate bar would hit the spot, either way. I could always call someone from New Orleans for a lift, but I was miles out, and owing a favor of that magnitude was not something I really wanted. I had a few hundred in cash on me, enough to grease the oil-stained palms of most motor mechanics—under the table, of course—for a bit of advice, supplies, and maybe some actual help. Though that last part was unlikely.

The town itself was quaint in an unlikely way. Bayou Oiseau, which I thought meant "bird bayou," looked like the love child spawned by the producer of a spaghetti Western and a mad Frenchwoman. At the crossroads of Broad Street and Oiseau Avenue (neither name appropriate for the narrow main street and its ugly, single-lane cousin), the architectural focal points were a mishmash of styles. As I thought that, Bitsa died. I spent a moment trying to kick-start her to no avail and finally sat, as the single traffic signal turned from red to green, balancing the bike and taking in the town in greater detail.

At my left, to the south, there was a huge brick Catholic church, the bell tower revealing a tarnished, patinated bell mostly hidden with decades of spiderwebs and home to dozens of pigeons. The large churchyard was enclosed by a brick wall with ornate bronze crosses set into the brick every two feet. On top of the wall were iron spikes, also shaped like sharp, pointed crosses. To the east of the church, across the road, was a bank made of beige brick and concrete, with the date 1824 on the lintel and green verdigris bars shaped like crosses on the windows and door. To my right was a strip mall that had seen better days, made of brick and glass, featuring a nail salon, hair salon, tanning salon, consignment shop, secondhand bookstore, bakery, Chinese fast-food joint, Mexican fast-food joint, and a Cajun butcher advertising andouille sausage, boudin, pork, chicken, locally caught fish, and a lunch special for $4.99. It smelled heavenly. Every single window and door in the strip mall was adorned with a decal cross. The Chinese place also had a picture of nunchuks and a pair of bloody stakes crossed beneath.

"Well," I muttered. "Wouldja look at this."

Inside, my Beast purred with delight and peered out at the world through my eyes. My Beast was the soul of a mountain lion, one I'd pulled inside me in a case of accidental black magic when I was about five years old. She had an opinion about most everything, and ever since she came into contact with a fighting angel and demon, she's been . . . different. More quiet. Less snarky. And though I'd never admit it to her, I missed her.

Directly ahead of me, catercornered from the church, was a saloon like something out of the French Quarter—two stories, white-painted wood with fancy black wrought iron on the balconies, narrow windows with working shutters, aged wood, double front doors carved to look like massive, weather-stained orchids. From it, I could smell beer and liquor and sex and blood—

common enough in any bar, but even more common in vamp bars. The name of the place was LeCompte Spirits and Pleasure, the words spelled out in bloodred letters on a white sign hanging from the second-floor balcony. Whoever had painted it had deliberately let the red paint drip so it looked like blood, a not-so-subtle promise of vampire ownership and clientele.

I pushed Bitsa to the side of the road against the sidewalk and paid the parking meter two quarters. There were cars parked here and there up and down the main intersection, and movement inside the strip mall's windows. Two hours before sunset, the town's pace was lazy and relaxed, and the place smelled great. Mostly the Cajun place smelled great; the blood, liquor, and herbal vamp smell, not so much.

I checked to make sure my weapons were hidden but easy to hand. I was licensed to carry concealed in Louisiana, and there was nothing illegal in my having three handguns and three vamp-killers on my person and under my riding leathers. But advertising it, walking around as if I was ready for a small war, sometimes actually caused trouble. Go figure. I placed my open hand directly over the center of the cross on the front door of Boudreaux's Meats and pushed.

The man inside moved like I'd thrown a knife at him, ducking fast and sprinting to the left, and when he stood straight, he was holding a shotgun. I stopped dead, elbows bending, hands raising slowly toward my chest in what looked like a gesture of peace but was really just bringing my hands closer to my weapons. "Easy there. I'm not here to rob, kill, or steal."

"Stranger, you is," he said in a strong Cajun accent.

"Yeah. My bike died out front. I was looking for the Tassin Bros Auto Fix."

"Bike?" His face showed honest confusion, clearing thinking bicycle.

"Motorbike. Harley. I just wanted directions and maybe some of that delicious food I'm smelling." His eyes lost some of the wariness, so I kept talking. "And maybe directions to a place to spend the night if I have to. Someplace clean and quiet. I have a card. Okay if I reach two fingers into the zippered pocket?" I pointed at my chest. The zipper was narrow, maybe two inches, way too small for most guns. He nodded, and I slowly lifted my left hand, zipping open the pocket. I dropped two fingers inside and pulled out a business card. When he gestured with the shotgun, I tossed the card to the glass-topped meat cabinet. He caught it one-handed, and the shotgun never wavered. He held it like he'd been born with one in his hand. Probably had.

He glanced at the card and back to me, and back to the card and back to me. "I hear a' you before. Dat rogue-vampire killer woman what took to work with Leo Pellissier. You her for real?"

"Yeah. I'm her. How about you put down the shotgun? A girl gets nervous with one pointed at her."

"How 'bout you open you jacket, reeeeal slow-like. You dat Jane Yellowrock for real, you have lotsa guns and tings, you do." He gestured again with the gun, firmed it into his shoulder, and waited.

I lifted my hand slowly and pulled the zipper, the ratchets loud in the silent room, and me not knowing if he wanted me to be Jane so he could kill me for a bounty—there had been a few put on my head by unhappy vamps in the last weeks—or wanted me to be Jane so he could befriend me. And there was nowhere to go in the narrow shop, with walls to either side and glass at my back. I was fast, but not faster than shotgun pellets.

The zipper open, I eased aside the left jacket lapel to reveal the special-made holster and the grip of a nine-mil H&K under my left arm. Still moving slowly, I pushed aside the other lapel to display the matching H&K at my waist on the right. The butcher grinned widely, revealing white teeth that would have looked good sitting in a glass, perfect in every way, though I was betting his were real, not dentures. "You is her, you is," he said. He broke open the shotgun and set it out of sight, moving around the meat counters with an outstretched hand. "I'm Lucky Landry. I a big fan of you."

I took his hand and we shook, and I felt all kinds of weird about it all and didn't know what to say. Me? With fans? I opened my mouth, closed it, and figured I had to say something. I settled on "Lucky *Landry*. What about Boudreaux?" I asked, indicating the sign reading BOUDREAUX'S MEATS on the back wall.

"My father-in-law." Lucky crossed his arms over his chest and I saw the full-sleeve tat down his left arm. It was of weird creatures—combos of snake and human, with fangs and scales, mouths open in what looked like agony—as red and yellow flames climbed up from his wrist to burn them. It was like some bizarre version of hell. He was maybe late forties, early fifties, Caucasian, with black hair and dark eyes—what the locals call *Frenchy*. "I married the daughter, and when her daddy done died dead, I took over dey business, I did. It a right fine pleasure t' meet you, it is, Miz Yellowrock."

"Ummm. Yeah. Pleasure and all. Call me Jane."

He moved behind the counter, beaming at me. "You hongry, Miz Jane? What I can get you for? I got some fried-up gator, fried-up catfish, fried-up boudin balls bigger'n my fist." He made one to show me. "I got me fried onion, fried squash, and fried mushroom. My own batter, secret recipe it is, and dat oil is fresh and hot for cooking."

Beast perked up at the description of the food. *Gator. Human killed gator? Human man is good hunter! Hungry for gator.* And the picture she sent me was a whole gator, snout, teeth, feet, claws, tail, skin, and all, crusty with batter. I chuckled and sent her a more likely mental picture. Inside she huffed with disappointment.

"Fried gator sounds good. Boudin balls and onion rings too. Got beer?"

"I can't sell you no beer, but I give you one. All my customers, I give one to, I do." He nudged the tip jar at me, and I understood. He had no license to sell beer, but he could give it away, and his customers could tip him to make it worth his while. I dropped a five into the tip jar, and he grinned widely. "Beer in dat cooler. He'p youself." I heard the hiss of gas being turned up, and smelled the gas scent and hot oil followed by the smell of raw meat.

There wasn't a statewide mandate on selling alcohol, and the voters of each parish could decide the issue. Seemed the voters of this parish had decided to keep it dry. At least officially. I wondered about the saloon across the street, and figured that vamps didn't have to follow the law around here—which might account for all the crosses everywhere.

I shoved a hand into the ice, grabbed a cold bottle from the bottom, pulled a Wynona's Big Brown Ale out of the cooler, and made a soft cooing sound. I like the taste of beer, from time to time, and Voodoo Brewery made some of the best microbrews in the South. I popped the top and took an exploratory sip. Though the alcohol did nothing for one of my kind—the metabolism of skinwalkers is simply too fast and burns alcohol off in minutes—the taste exploded in my mouth and the icy beer traced a trail down my esophagus. "Oh yeah," I murmured and took another.

By the time the beer was half-gone, I had a paper plate full of boudin balls and fried onion rings in front of me, grease spreading through the paper with a dull brown stain. My stomach growled and I popped a ring in my mouth while breaking open a boudin ball. I made an *ohhh* of sound and sucked air over my scalded tongue before I forked in a mouthful of fried boudin. Boudin is miscellaneous pork (though you can get it specially made with special cuts of pork) and white rice and spices, most of which are unique to each butcher or cook, and Lucky's boudin was excellent. "Dish ish goo'," I said, and I groaned.

Lucky laughed and brought a second plate with the promised fried gator meat. It was flaky and fishy and just as wonderful as the boudin, so perfect I didn't need seasoning salt from the big carved stone bowl on the table. Inside Beast let out a satisfied chuff. I tossed a ten on the table and it disappeared into Lucky's pocket. Ten minutes later I put down the fork and said, "You are a genius with this stuff. Do you ship your boudin?"

"Everywhere dey a post office, for sure."

"I'll be placing an order. Now, about the Tassin Bros?"

"Dis gator-huntin' season. Dey close dat shop for thirty day. Open back on first day nex' month."

"Well, crap." I had really hoped to make it back to New Orleans and my own bed tonight. "Guess I'll be making do with the tools I have on hand. Anyplace I can work in the shade?"

"You bes' be getting youself to Miz Onie's bed-and-breakfast before dark, and work on dat motorbike in da morning. We gots trouble in dis town after dark." He frowned. "Suckhead trouble wid dey witches, we always have, but dis time dey suckheads gone done too much."

I flashed on the crosses everywhere in the middle of town, on every window and door, crosses that had been there, in the open, for many more decades than vamps had been out of the coffin and a part of American life. I had a feeling this town had known about vamps for a lot longer than the rest of the world, and I had a moment to imagine—to remember— all the horrible things vamps could do to a town if they decided not to follow the Vampira Carta, the legal document that reined in the predatory and murderous instincts of all vamps.

Before I could ask, Lucky set another plate in front of me, opened and passed me another beer, straddled the chair across the table from me, and said, "Dis one on me." I had a feeling he didn't give beer away, and little hairs lifted on the back of my neck, like a warning.

"We had dey suckheads here since eighteen thirty," he said, "when de banker's son, dat Julius Chiasson, and he wife come back from Paris. Him a doctor now. Dey all change, dey was, dem and dey son. Dey be gone to Paris for twenty year and dey not aged. Look like same age as dey son, and dey not go out in de sun no more. Tings not too bad for few year, until dey son, Marcel Chiasson, go crazy. Townfolk figger he change to suckhead den and was set free.

"We learn only later dem suckhead supposed to be chain up for ten years befo' dey set free. Hard lesson dat was too, but dat another story.

"Wid dat Marcel Chiasson free, dey slaves, dey start to disappear, one by one. And more suckheads like Marcel appear. Crazy in dey head dey was, each and every one, crazy."

Despite myself I was drawn into the story. I ate onion rings and gator and drank the free beer, feeling the movement of the sun as it plummeted toward the horizon.

"De priest, Father Joseph, he made dem crosses to be everywhere, on every house and building, and most dey attacks in town stop. He teach dey townsfolk how to kill wid stakes and swords. Den de war come, and all de town boys go off to fight Yankees. Town was dying, it was." Lucky was turning the stone bowl full of spices in his hands, which were strong and knobby from years of handling heavy sides of meat. He stared into the spice-and-salt mixture as if it had the answers to all the secrets of the universe. "Father Joseph was turn one night. But he strong in de faith. He rise and he come to the church, holding his craziness inside all by hisself, and he tell dem townspeople to cut off he head. Dey did. But it nearly kill mos' dem all."

His voice softened. "Julius Chiasson and he older brother—human was old man Chaisson," he clarified, "old, *old* man by den. Dey know dey have to stop Marcel, 'cause he still crazy in de head. Dey set a trap. And dey kill dey own." Lucky shook his head. "Julius' wife, Victorie, her name was, she went crazy wid grief and attack and kill old man Chiasson, head of family, patriarch. Julius have to stake his wife." Lucky shook his head and opened his own beer. Took a swig. As he lifted his arm, I saw again the tats, and the flames seemed to ripple and flicker with the motion.

"But he not cut off her head. She rise from de grave, she did, and she kill and kill and kill. Church got itself a new priest, Father Matthieu, and he lead a hunt to kill her. Dey take her head and burn her body in center of de streets jus' befo' dawn, nex' morning." He pointed outside to the crossing of Broad Street and Oiseau Avenue.

"Dem Bordelon sisters, witches all, dey come gather up de ashes for to make hex. And Julius, when he hear of all dis, he make war on dey witches. Kill dem mostly. Dem witches, dey make de hex, and de suckheads cain't eat, cain't drink. Sick-like. Dey kidnap Dr. Leveroux, kill him when he cain't cure dem. Leave his body in middle of town, like warning."

Lucky pointed at my plate. "Fried gator not good cold. Eat, you." I shoveled food in my mouth, knowing I should get the heck out of Dodge—or out of Bayou Oiseau—but I was hooked. And I had no doubt that was what Lucky had intended.

"Dem witches join wid dem priests and fight dem suckheads. And war was everywhere, here, in de bayou"—he pronounced it *bi-oh*, which sounded odd to me—"in de swamp, in the north. In New Orleans, Flag Officer David Farragut was in charge; Louisiana territory was in control of de North. We had no help. Cut off from de rest of de world, we was." Lucky stood and reached to a phone on the wall, picked up and dialed. "Miz Onie," he said a moment later. "Dis Lucky Landry. Get you bes' room ready. Town got Jane Yellowrock here for de night. Yeah, dat so. Dat room on front of de house, one wid porch out front and green. Purty room it is," he added to me. "Yeah, I bring her over to you befo' de sun set. Yeah, sure." He hung up and sat back down. "Where I was?"

"Farragut in New Orleans, and war everywhere."

"Ah. Yeah." He picked up the bowl again, but this time sprinkled a little of the spice onto the table and set the bowl into the middle of the spices, so when the bowl turned on the surface, it made a soft scratching sound, as if grinding. "Amaury Pellissier hear of our trouble. He come on horseback, him and he nephew, Leo. He kill Julius for not runnin' he clan like he should, for not keepin de secret of de suckheads. And den he leave. But he leave behind de swamp suckheads, ones made and set free while dey still insane."

He raised his brows to make sure I understood, and I did. Vamps went into devoveo, the insanity that followed the change, for the first ten or twenty years after they were turned. He didn't seem to know the term, but he was aware of the insanity peculiar to vampires. I nodded that I understood and he continued, his voice as melodic as a song.

"Strongest suckhead, Clermont Doucette"—which came out *Cler-mon Doo-see*—"make hisself a new clan, become a blood-master. In 1865 dat war end and de slaves go free. Everythin' change, it did. Black folk take off for de north or into de swamp for freedom. Some join dem witches, some join dem suckheads, some leave, some stay, to make a free, human way here on land and swamp, in place dey know."

But they still had problems, which Lucky hadn't gotten to yet. "When did the first Cajuns get to Louisiana?" I asked.

"Moutons say dey get here in 1760, but my family, de Landrys, land in New Orleans in April 1764, but dey don' get here in dis town till 1769." He smiled his pretty teeth at me and waggled his brows, lifting and shifting the stone bowl from palm to palm like a magician with a nifty trick or a ballplayer half tossing his ball between innings. "My *gran'-mère* one dem Bordelon sisters, Cally Bordelon."

I began to see a glimmer here. Lucky Landry was way more than a butcher with a melodic quality to his voice. Here was a tattooed man from a witch family, a man with a rogue-vamp hunter suddenly stuck in his town, and in his power. And wouldn't you know it, Lucky's family had a Hatfields-versus-McCoys feud going on with vamps. I narrowed my eyes at him.

"Like my history, you do?" he asked.

"Yeah." I grinned back and set the empty beer bottle on the table with a soft *snap*. "I'm waiting for you to get to the part where you need me for something." Lucky's smile got wider, and he pointed a finger at me as if acknowledging a clever point in a debate. "But you're trying to keep me here until it's too late to leave town safely, even if I got my bike going again, which isn't likely."

"Smart lady, you."

"If I were smart, I'd have pushed my bike back to I-10 and slept under a tree, where only the mosquitoes would have sucked my blood and the nutria chewed on my bones."

Lucky laughed at that, his black eyes flashing.

And that was when it hit me. The history he knew so well, his nearly mesmeric storytelling. His witch family origins. The flames on his arm that had seemed to waver. The tats were a lot like a scenic tat I'd seen on another man's arm, chest, and shoulder. Spelled tats. "You're a male witch," I said, my voice cold as ice. "And you want *me* in this war."

I caught a hint of movement from the corner of my eye, and everything went dark.

Beast's claws flexed in my brain, waking me, yet holding me down. Through her memories, I knew instantly that I was in the best room of Miz Onie's bed-and-breakfast, lying on the edge of the bed, my hands and feet unbound and hanging over the side. Even without Beast's memories, I'd have guessed where I was, by the colors I could see through my tangled lashes: the emerald green bedspread, moss green walls, striped green drapery, and greenish fake flowers in a tall vase gave it away. That and the fact that Lucky Landry was sitting in a chair in a wide bay with tall windows and a door. That and the fact that I smelled his special peppers and spices in my hair. All that and the fact that my head was aching, yeah, that was a clue. "You sucker punched me," I growled, Beast in the tone. "With a spice bowl."

Lucky nodded. "Sorry 'bout dat, I am," though he didn't sound very sorry, and proved it when he added, "Ruin me a good batch of my special spice mixture."

Yeah. Funny guy. I grunted and sat up slowly, holding my head with one hand. It was pounding like a bass drum interspersed with clanging cymbals, sharp pain in every pulse. "What do you want?" I snarled when I could, though it came out more like a whisper.

"I tried to call Leo Pellissier. Him no take my calls. I want you to call him and ask him for help."

"No."

Lucky's eyebrows went up and he smiled. But this time the genial Cajun butcher was gone, and a powerful witch smiled in his place. I could feel the power crackle in the air. Male witches were very rare, most of them dying in their youth of childhood cancers. I thought about that for half a second until Beast informed me that Lucky had divested me of my weapons. My leather jacket was hanging open, and my holsters and blade sheaths were empty. Nary a gun nor a knife nor even a stake was still on me. Which really ticked me off.

I let a bit of Beast flow through me, and knew that my eyes were glowing gold. Beast was an ambush hunter herself, but that didn't mean she wanted to be ambushed. Lucky's body tightened at what he saw in my eyes, and he made a little swirling motion with one finger, not hiding that he was preparing a magical defense.

Tension stretched between us, pulling like a rubber band. The door in the bay was open, and the night poured in, smelling of night-blooming flowers, the stagnant water of swamp, the fresher scent of a recent rain, and the herbal tang of vamp. I heard a car passing by outside, the engine noise muted, the tires loudly splashing through a puddle.

I had met a few male witches in my life, way more than most people ever met. But as a traveling rogue-vamp hunter, I tended to end up with the supernats of any town I visited. My best pal was earth witch Molly, or had been until I killed her sister. Long story. Anyway, her husband was a witch, still in the closet, still hiding what he was. Her son was a witch, and I'd seen a third male witch die at the hand of a sabertooth lion. Another long story. My life was practically full of them. Now this dude with spell flames licking up his arm.

"No," I said again. "I'm not calling Leo. And if you hit me with a spell, I'll make you regret it."

"Make me?" He sounded mildly incredulous. Then his mouth pursed in thought. "Some spell you gots on you? To do combat wid me? Some witch spell like dat charm on you bike? Keep-away/don'-steal charm?" His finger stopped swirling, and the tension in the air seemed to float out the window into the night.

I had no spell, no real defense against magic, but I did have Beast, and I had seen her neutralize spells meant to harm me in the past. So I kept any trepidation I was feeling stowed deep inside, my eyes almost lazy, and I let my lips lift just a tiny bit on one side.

"Okay," Lucky said. "Why you not call Leo for me?"

"I'm not a deal broker."

"Mebbe you change you mind when I tell you rest o' my story."

"Skip a few centuries to the part where I rode into town."

Lucky nodded, lounged back in the chair, and pointed to my side. "Aspirin and water for you headache."

I didn't usually take drugs, but I did drink the water while Lucky got to his point.

"Suckhead coonass clan, Clan Doucette, in bayou, gots my daughter."

I nearly choked, then blinked, set down the glass, and shifted into a more comfortable position. "Okay. That I didn't expect." *Coonass* was an insulting word for Cajun, and it was interesting that Lucky, a Cajun himself, called another Cajun *coonass*. "Okay," I said again. "I'm listening."

"When Leo and Amaury Pellissier kill off de blood-master of Clan Chiasson, dey leave suckheads in swamp. No trainin' dey gots. No law. Some insane for decades. Suckheads and witches in dis town not get along, not never. Now dem suckheads got my girl, stole her dey did. Kidnap."

Beast shifted her claws in my brain and said, *Kit? We will save kit.* I nodded, as agreement to Beast and as a signal to the witch in the chair to continue.

"I want her back. Word in de street is Clermont Doucette boy gone turn my girl and run wild with her, or mebbe chain her up in he attic for ten year."

I blew out a sigh and felt part of the pain in my skull decrease. Skinwalkers healed a lot faster than humans, even after getting whapped over the head with a hunk of rock. I touched the sore place on my head, thinking. "Is your daughter a witch? Dumb question," I answered myself. "Daughters get one of their two X chromosomes from their father. The trait passes on his X chromosome, and so of course she's a witch. Got it. Witches don't take well to the turn. They sometimes stay in the devoveo for forever."

"She is witch, yes. Devoveo? Dis mean *insane*? Insane *forever*?" Lucky snarled. "Not my girl. No. I kill dem all firs'."

"Yeah, yeah. I get that you're ticked and wanting to stake every vamp in sight. You shoulda said all this in the first place, not coldcocked me. Understand that I am not happy and this is not over. But okay. I'll call Leo."

Lucky tossed me my throwaway cell, an unlisted one I had purchased at RadioShack. I'd had no calls on it in the last week, not one, because no one knew the number and I hadn't called anyone to share my new contact info. I hadn't even stopped at a library on the road to update my website and check for potential jobs, because I knew certain contract employees of Leo's could tell if I had done so, determine which town I had updated from, and come looking for me. The only way to be invisible these days was to stay totally and completely off the grid. And even then it was hard.

I had to call Leo anyway. My retainer had run out, and I needed to make sure the vamps had received my resignation papers and clarify that I was done working for and with the vamps of New Orleans. The last job in Asheville had done a number on me in lots of emotional ways, and I'd had enough. My retainer had run out two weeks past, and I had mailed back all the electronic devices that tied me to the MOC of New Orleans. In the packet, I had included a letter of resignation as well as an "intent to vacate" the premises to my landlady.

I had hit the road, sightseeing in the Deep, *Deep* South in preparation for heading back to Asheville. My belongings were packed in boxes back in my freebie house, ready to be shipped out. It was past time to make sure the chief fanghead understood that I was really going away. Getting him to man up and take over this vamp problem left by his power-crazy uncle back when he was the man in charge and Leo was only his heir would be a suitable and satisfying going-away present. I had been putting off this phone call for days.

"So?" Lucky said. "You gone call?"

"How old is your daughter?" I asked.

"Twenty-two. Firs' college graduate in our family ever, she is." His lips twisted into a lopsided smile, one with tears close to the surface. "Her my baby."

"Name?"

"Shauna Landry." The tears gathered. *Crap. I hate it when people cry.* "Black hair like mine, blue eyes from her mama. Beautiful from de day she born."

I opened the cell and dialed Leo's number at the Clan Home. The call was answered by an unknown voice, likely an upper-level blood-servant I hadn't met, and I said, "Jane Yellowrock for Leo or Bru—George Dumas."

"One moment, please. I'll see if Mr. Dumas is available."

I figured I'd sit on hold forever, but the line was picked up in less than five seconds. "Jane."

I couldn't help the way my heart lightened at the sound of my name in his voice. "Hiya, Bruiser."

"Where are you?"

"Little place called Bayou Oiseau. It's in—"

"I know where it is. Are you . . . well?"

"I'm just ducky. Except that I landed in the middle of a war between witches and vamps. One left in full swing by Amaury Pellissier back in the eighteen hundreds, and Leo needs to deal with it. Oh. And I may be a prisoner of the witches. I'm not sure."

Lucky chuckled softly at that, his power once again flowing through the air and up my arms and legs like either a promise or a threat. *Okay. Prisoner. Gotcha.*

Bruiser was silent for a moment, probably processing all that I'd said, and still he surprised me with his reply. "How can you not be certain whether you are a prisoner?"

"I'm not in a jail, I'm not handcuffed or chained to a radiator, and so far I've been only lightly beaten."

Lucky shrugged as if to say, *Some things are out of my control.*

"Lightly beaten." Bruiser's voice was low and cold, and I remembered that he grew up in a time when men didn't hit women. Not for anything. Bruiser had strong protective instincts, and his tone promised retribution to whoever had hurt me. Bruiser was also the primo blood-servant to the MOC, and he had power of his own.

"Yeah, but I'm fine. Ducky, remember?" Before he could reply, I quickly recapped the history of Bayou Oiseau, told him about the daughter being held by the vamps.

Bruiser listened silently, but at some point I heard a *click* and figured I'd been put on speakerphone, which meant Leo was listening. When I reached the end of my soliloquy, I said, "Hey, Leo. I just can't get away from you, can I?"

"No, my Enforcer. You cannot," Leo said.

Ooookay. I didn't like the sound of that at all.

"I remember this town and its people; they wanted only to fight. They refused our counsel and when more important political matters required our presence, we left." Leo paused and I could almost hear him thinking. Patience isn't my strong suit, and it was misery to wait, but I managed it. Go, me.

"As my Enforcer, you have my authority," Leo said.

I nearly cussed. That Enforcer thing had been nothing but problems, and it was all my own fault. Dang it. Me and my big mouth. I wished I had never heard the term. "I don't work for you, Leo."

The silence over the phone was electric, and I heard Leo take a breath that hissed. He said, "Consider it a new contract, a short-term extension of the services you provided under the retainer you have resigned."

Without waiting for me to reply, he went on. "You have the freedom to handle this situation any way you wish. If you must stake the leader of this so-called clan, one that has not sworn to me, yet exists inside my territory, then you may do so." My eyebrows went up, but I didn't say anything and Leo went on. "I will messenger over the necessary papers, and George will contact all legal authorities who might be involved or who might show an interest." Meaning the local town cops—if any—the parish sheriff and deputies, the FBI, the Louisiana State Police, probably out of the Lafayette office, and PsyLED, the Psychometry Law Enforcement Division of Homeland Security. Which reminded me of Rick LaFleur and all the unsettled, unsatisfied elements in our not-really-a-relationship. Bruiser was gonna be a busy boy.

At that thought, almost as if conjured, Bruiser came on the line. I heard Leo in the background again, issuing orders. He sounded pretty ticked off, which made me smile. There wasn't much I liked better than yanking a vamp's chain. When Leo's cultured French voice fell silent, Bruiser said to me, "We will attempt to smooth the way for you, Jane. But I will also send Derek and three of his best to assist."

"Yeah? What am I being paid?"

He named a sum that would let me laze around for six months if I wanted to splurge, ten if I wanted to scrimp a bit. "It's hazard pay," he said, which took the joy out of my reaction. Yeah. I was going into unknown territory against an unknown number of vamps on one side and witches on the other—witches who might not like the way I handled things. "Call me daily with an update," Bruiser said. "If I don't hear from you for twenty-four hours, I'll come myself. If you have been"—he paused as if trying to find the right word and settled on—"damaged, I will burn a path through the swamp wider than Sherman did during the war," he promised. "Tell them that. And be careful, Jane." The connection ended.

"He say you can stake Doucette?" Lucky asked, and his expression went fierce when I nodded. "Who gone burn a path tru' dis town?"

I closed the phone, knowing that Lucky had overheard a lot of the conversation. "Leo Pellissier's right-hand meal," I said. "If I get hurt, he'll make everyone pay, which means the witches too." At Lucky's shock I laughed, but there was nothing humorous in it at all. I had a feeling that Bruiser could be a very dangerous enemy, and it was nice to know he would revenge my death. Nice but cold. Being dead would see to that. So I just had to stay alive all by my lonesome. "Tell me everything you know about the Doucette vamps and everything about the witches. I need to know numbers, strengths, strongholds, and weaknesses. And make sure there are four more rooms available in this B and B. I have some men coming. Oh, and you pay for the accommodations. It's part of my fee."

"Dat Leo Pellissier pay you fee. You tink you get paid two times?"

I just stared at him and Lucky made a very French gesture, a tossing of one hand in agreement. He leaned forward, fingers interlaced, elbows on his knees, and dished about the vamps. I figured he was giving me everything he had on the vamps, and was holding back about ninety percent on the witches.

I started work the next morning just after nine a.m., when Derek and his guys motored into town in mud-spattered four-wheel-drive Humvees, vehicles last used in a war somewhere and decommissioned. Derek was a former marine, still tough as Uncle Sam can make a man, and he ran a group of former military mercenaries who had originally banded together to fight rogue vamps in their neighborhood in New Orleans. He was muscle and tech support too and had the toys and the know-how to do the job.

Miz Onie, an olive-skinned, dark-haired Frenchwoman, was agreeable to renting out her entire B and B, and laid out a huge breakfast for me, Derek, and his Vodka Boys: V. Martini, V. Chi Chi, and V. Angel Tit. Miz Onie might have been pushing sixty, but she appreciated the pretty vision of a man in a uniform, even a paramilitary uniform like Derek's men wore— camo pants and marine green Ts. She served up pancakes, several pounds of bacon, two dozen eggs, and a fruit bowl big enough to use as a hot tub.

We cleared the dishes of their edible burdens, then the table of the dishes, and laid out topo maps of the area, the guys using weapons to hold down the corners. "Our intel of the area sucks," Derek said. "This is all Angel could find on Google Maps, and the printed stuff is so pixeled out it's pretty much useless. Everything's flat, so we got only rooftops and treetops to go by, and no one has done a street cam drive-by."

"No streets," Lucky said. The former marine had guns on him in the echo of the first word. "Bayou only way. You want in, you go in by boat or gator back." He grinned at his own joke, standing in the door, seeming totally relaxed even with all the guns on him. His bare arms were upraised, holding on to the jambs of the door, the flames along one arm dancing with his power.

I rolled my eyes and said, "Meet the father of the kidnap victim."

The Vodka Boys made half the guns disappear. The rest went back on the table, holding down the maps. *Men and their toys.* Of course, I had a vamp-killer in a boot sheath and six stakes in my bun, so maybe I wasn't much better.

Lucky sauntered over, put a hand on the table, and rested his weight on it as the tattoos danced. "Dat right dere"—he tapped a page—"is Clermont Doucette place." The rooftop was reflective aluminum, making it hard to see anything except that there were lots of angles and offshoots, as if the Clan Home had been added onto by whim and caprice for years. The house sat on a narrow tongue of land, a bayou winding around the house on three sides and what looked like swamp on the other. Trash was everywhere, piles of unidentifiable things, but what we could see was not going to make any outright attack easy. Docks large and small were positioned around the house, sticking out into the water, and there were a half dozen outbuildings, animal pens, and even a rusted school bus under the trees. I almost asked how they got the bus out into the bayou, and then changed my mind. More important were the boats; at least six were pulled up to the dock and on shore, and I figured the tree canopy hid more. There were a lot of people at the house.

"I figure he keeping Shauna here." Lucky pointed to a room away from the moving water, next to the swampy side and sticking out all by itself.

Derek looked at me, his eyes saying what I had figured out. We had way too few men. I stifled a sigh but decided I had to address that now, right up front. "Lucky, we don't have enough men to launch an attack and get Shauna." The witch's eyes flashed fire and his power sparked painfully across my skin, like brushing against cacti. I added quickly, "So I'm going in to talk."

"Talk is nothin' to dese suckheads," he spat. The power in the room swirled like flames and wind, hot, and pulling all the moisture out of the air.

Derek sat back, his arms outstretched along the chair arms, and looked at me, ignoring the angry father. I took his cue and repositioned so Lucky was visible only in my peripheral vision. Sometimes ignoring people's anger made them calm down. Of course, sometimes it made them shoot everyone in sight. "We can go in just before dusk," Derek said to me, "when the vamps are waking up and eating breakfast and the blood-servants are busiest. Disable the boats, set up a perimeter. Then you can come in, making a lot of noise. Distract them from anything we might do." Meaning that if they saw the girl, they'd take her if it was possible, with me being the distraction.

I nodded. "How are you getting in?" I asked. "They'll hear motors for miles in the flat water and land."

Derek pointed to what looked like a trail on the map; it was marked with the designation Brown Fox Road. "We drive into there this afternoon and pole in on johnboats."

Lucky snorted, a very Gaelic and totally dismissive sound, but the burning sensation diminished again. "Polin' johnboat a skill, not somethin' you pick up and do."

Derek lifted a brow. "I poled my first boat when I was five, white boy. I think I still remember how. And my men will do fine," he added to me.

I nodded. "Okay. Lucky, we need johnboats and something motorized for me to show up in. And before you ask or demand, no. You can't go with us." Instantly I felt that spiky power skitter hotly along my skin. "And that's precisely why." I pointed at him. "You're too emotionally involved. You'll end up getting the men hurt, and maybe Shauna killed."

Lucky blinked, started to say or do something, then the magic twirled away and died. He dropped his head and stared at the floor for long seconds, his hands opening and closing in fists. "Yeah. Okay. My wife say de same. But I don' like it."

I felt it was much too fast a capitulation, but I didn't smell an outright lie. I said, "Instead I need you to get the equipment for us and find us two former military men who still hunt, who still use their skills, and get one to be Derek's guide and one to be my guide. If you can't do that and keep out of our way, then the gig is off. You understand?"

"I'm not stupid."

Which didn't answer my question, but I let it go. He gave me a time when he'd have the equipment ready, picked up Miz Onie's landline phone, and made two calls. When he hung up he said, "Auguste and Benoît twins, in army dey was. Dey hunt alligator, most years. Dis year dey mama broke hip. Dey not have time to get tags."

I understood. In Louisiana there was a lottery for the alligator harvest program, and tags to hunt on public swamp and land in gator country were issued only at certain times. If you missed that time, you didn't hunt, or you paid your hunting license fee and hunted on private lands. The twins didn't have access to private land, so this year they were sitting around. "Sober?" I asked.

"Mostly," Lucky said. I figured that was the best I was gonna get.

"Dey got a sister too. She a sharpshooter, she was. Tough as gator skin. She come along too. You put her in a tree with good line o' sight, and she provide cover. Her name Margaud."

After Lucky Landry left, Derek and his men and I created contingency plans for everything we could think of, giving each problem and plan a code name so we would be prepared to act on a moment's notice. *Silver* was the code to kill every vamp we could find. *Swim* was the code indicating that each combatant would have to get home the best way he could. *Bogus* was the code for our allies telling lies and setting us up. *Burn* was the code to set everything on fire with incendiaries. *FUBAR* meant anything and everything. *FUBAR* was the code I was most worried about. It meant we'd all most likely die.

The boat shuddered under my feet, the Chevy engine adding its own vibration as well as noise enough to wake the undead, and the propeller at my back sucked air through its cage as we flew over the water—not in a plane, but in an airboat. The boat had almost no draft, maybe six inches when it was sitting still, and it was eco-friendly except for the noise, which was so loud it could deafen a catfish, and which precluded any form of communication except hand signals. The prop, mounted in the cage at the back of the boat, was wood, handmade by Amish people, which felt all wrong somehow, but added an artistic element to a boat that was designed to skim over the bayou, swamp water, or marshy land. This boat was painted in red and yellow with flames along the sides, similar to the flames on Lucky's arms, and belonged to the twins. It had two bench seats with heavy-gauge steel arms and leather upholstery in the yellow of the flames. Built-in coolers, tackle boxes, and a shotgun rack completed the Cajun dream-boat.

Benoît had led Derek's men in two hours ago and they were in place on the Clan Home property. Auguste was my pilot, sitting in the bench seat above and behind me, working the controls. Margaud sat beside me, a sharpshooter's sniper rifle in a sling across her back and a heavy military gobag at her booted feet.

The brothers might have passed for ogres, each weighing in at an easy three hundred pounds, hirsute, sour with last night's beer, and both smelling of the fish they had caught and cleaned. Maybe days ago. The men wore T-shirts that might once have been white in another universe or decade, old-fashioned bib overalls, and work boots that looked like they had never seen oil, polish, or even laces.

Margaud was as beautiful as her brothers were ugly, with ash brown hair blonded by the sun, deep brown eyes, and skin tanned golden. She was petite and delicate and looked too small to transport or position the rifle for firing, but she was muscular and fit and carried herself with a capable, confident air. The sharpshooter wore a homemade one-piece camo uni that had been made out of strips of thin cotton cloth in green, brown, black, and tan, like a hand-pieced quilt. Irregular lengths of green yarn rippled from it in the hard wind created by the passage of the airboat, and I realized that it worked like a ghillie suit, but looked a lot more comfortable. I had to wonder what a girl needed a ghillie suit for, but I figured it was for hunting. And if it wasn't for hunting, then I wasn't sure I wanted to know.

The siblings were all human and all taciturn—expressionless faces and none talking much even by my standards. It felt weird going into battle with the silent Cajuns at my back, unknowns in a gig more full of unknowns than usual.

We spun through the bayou, whipping around clumps of trees and over long, swordlike grasses. I held on to the bench seat with one hand, watching the world fly by. The airboat hit something in the water with a hollow, solid *thump* under my feet, but Margaud didn't react and the boat neither slowed nor sprang a leak, so I just gripped the seat harder. If we came to a sudden and total stop, I didn't want to go flying into the dark water or up against a cypress tree.

I had on ear protectors, my fighting leathers, and all my weapons, including the Benelli M4. They had all been brought by Derek, lifted from my gun safe in the closet of my freebie house in New Orleans. Even in what amounted to autumn in the Deep South, I was sweating, and my hair had come free from the fighting queue, blown back by the wind. It was long enough that I was seriously concerned about getting it caught in the prop, and sat holding it twined around my arm and clasped in one hand, a pose that could have serious image consequences if we were attacked en route. Auguste had agreed to idle down a quarter mile out and motor in slowly, which would give me time to fix my hair.

It wasn't like I was trying for a stealth approach. There was no chance we'd surprise anyone, not in a boat that could be heard two or three miles away. So the slow entrance lost us nothing and might actually help, giving me time to look over the Doucette Clan Home, allowing Derek's men to carry out their part of the plan, and also giving the appearance of courage and strength. Of course, vamps could smell my sweat, so they'd know I was nervous once I was close enough for them to take my scent. And since they had never smelled me, and since they weren't Leo's people, my predator scent would really annoy them as well as make them more dangerous.

Hence, I was loaded for vamp with hand-packed silver-fléchette rounds in the M4 and the nine mils. I had my specially made holsters on and had a Heckler and Koch nine mil under my left arm, one at my right hip, a lovely little red-gripped .380 at my spine, and a .32 six-shooter on my ankle. Most of the weapons were loaded with silver shot. The .380s carried standard ammo; that was for annoying vamps and killing humans, though I didn't intend to kill any humans. Unless they tried to kill me.

I had six blades on me: four short-bladed throwing knives and two silver-plated vamp-killers. Ash stakes were sheathed in my right boot, for immobilizing vamps if I could manage that instead of killing them. Three silver stakes would go in my bun, three more in the left boot, should killing vamps be necessary. One had the blood-master's name on it. Clermont Doucette was a dead man. Which was funny in every way I could look at it.

I wore my silver-plated titanium throat protector and superhard plastic armor at elbows, groin, and knees—places where vamps liked to attack and drink. I looked deadly.

The airboat slowed and skewed to the side in an eddy move worthy of a powerboat. Margaud jutted her chin at my hair and climbed from the boat onto a tongue of land, and I started to rebraid my tousled locks.

Auguste handed us both bottles of chilled water. We were less than half a mile out, and I could see the yellow of the school bus in the distance.

It was only minutes later, but when Auguste keyed on the airboat motor and blasted out the night sounds, the sun was setting on the horizon, silhouetting the cypress trees and low-growing scrub on the small islets and islands between marsh and swamp and bayou. Night came fast in the bayou.

We left Margaud perched in the branches of a tree with a clear line of sight of the front door and most of the Doucette Clan Home. She had her rifle and a night-vision scope and several toys that were not civilian legal, and she handled them like a pro. Even so, I didn't like the idea of leaving anyone alone in the swamp, but the woman's fierce glare suggested that I should keep that thought to myself.

I went over her report as we made our slow way to the Clan Home. There were heat signatures for twenty humans, and no indications of vamps anywhere, which meant they were still in their lairs. Under the house were dozens of chickens and several large mammals, what looked like pigs. "Be careful of the pigs," she said, as her last warning. "They're mean and dangerous."

Great. Just ducky. Like vamps weren't bad enough. Now we had mad pigs to worry about.

Making enough racket to raise revenants, we motored up to the Doucette place, me sitting so a nine mil was partially hidden in my left hand, and my right was draped over the armrest. The lights ahead went dark, making the house hard to see, but giving an added advantage to the vamps, with their near-perfect night vision.

As we roared up, I looked lazy and unconcerned. But my heart was pounding and my Beast was staring out at the lengthening shadows with her predator's stare, my eyes showing that odd shade of gold peculiar to Beast. With her added night vision, the dark was all greens and silvers and shades of gray, and I could see with a preternatural clarity.

Security met us at the dock, buff male hunks dressed in jeans, muscle Ts, and multiple guns. They smelled human, or nearly so—blood-slaves who had all received recent, copious, but controlled drinks of blood from multiple vamps. The intake had to be carefully measured or the consequences were problematic. Too much blood would get a human blood-drunk and he'd be useless. Too little blood and a human would have less power to draw on. I wondered why the big bad vamps had sent blood-slaves to meet me instead of blood-servants, and it was just one more reminder that these backwoods—or maybe backwater—vamps would be unlike the vamps I'd met in other places. It was possible that these vamps had never even seen the Vampira Carta. These were like vamps from the Wild West, vamps with their own rules and laws and nasty habits and nastier accoutrements.

Like guns, trained on me.

I lounged back in my seat, keeping the Heckler and Koch nine mil out of sight, a round in the chamber, safety off, and my finger off the trigger and on the guard. I wanted to be ready, but I didn't want to accidently shoot off a round and punch a hole in the boat. Sinking just off the dock and wading wet and dripping to shore was not the way to make an impression of being strong and in command.

I smelled Derek upwind of me, and as soon as the vamps were up and outside, they would smell my guys too. Best to get inside quickly. Auguste gunned the engine and spun us up to the dock, cut the motor, and let us drift until we touched the rubberized edge.

I tossed away the ear protectors and pushed in the earbud the instant we stopped. The night closed in around me in muggy shadows, mist, and the buzz of mosquitoes. And the *chock-a-chock* sound of a shotgun being readied for firing. The timing was calculated, and I laughed softly.

"Copy that, Legs," Derek said into the com unit to the sound of my laughter. I was tied into the system.

With my free hand I tossed my card onto the dock. Muscles One and Muscles Two looked at each other in confusion. The laughter was unexpected, my relaxed posture (legs stretched out with one bent at the knee) was unexpected, my yellow glowing eyes were unexpected, and now they had to figure out how they were going to manage bending over and picking up my card.

After a long, undecided fidget, Muscles Two, who was holding two semiautomatic handguns, holstered one and knelt down, eyes on me, feeling along the wood boards until he had the card, and then stood. He stared down at it, his blood-slave enhanced vision making out the words and his lips moving with the effort. He said, "Dis here say, 'Jane Yellowrock. Have Stakes, Will Travel.'"

"Vampire hunter? You dat Jane Yellowrock?" Muscles One asked. "Leo Pellissier's cun—"

Without thinking, I slid my finger around the trigger, raised the Heckler and Koch and shot the guy, a quick, ticked-off two-tap. The first bullet caught him in the left thigh, high and outside, dead-on where I'd intended, in a location where one might do minimal damage but knock out an enemy combatant. The second shot took him in the left elbow. I'd been aiming at his left side, at the waist, where there were few major organs to hit. Muscles One started to fall and lost the shotgun, his breath sucking in for a scream.

Instantly, I moved the weapon to Muscles Two and caught him trying to redraw the weapon he'd holstered. Stupid. He had one still drawn. He shoulda shot me already. When he realized his error, he stopped, nearly as immobile as a vamp, one hand on the weapon in the holster, one with the gun pointed at the dock, his eyes on me, wide like a cat's. I let a lot more of Beast bleed into my eyes and chuckled again as I gathered my weapon into a two-handed grip, pulled my boots under me, and stood. The airboat wobbled under the weight change and I made sure of my balance before I stepped onto the dock. "I don't like that word," I said, over the ringing in my ears.

"Throw it into the water," I added, nodding to his gun. "Both of them." I wasn't leaving an armed bad guy behind me. When he had disposed of both guns, I jutted my chin at the shotgun. "That one too."

"Herbert kill me, he will," he said, pronouncing it *A-bear*, a common Cajun last name.

"And I'll kill you if you don't," I lied sweetly.

Muscles toed the shotgun off into the bayou, and Herbert moaned. I wasn't sure if he was upset over the gun being tossed, or the pain. Maybe both.

The last light went out at the house and I heard the soft *schnick* of a round being chambered from the front door. I grabbed Muscles and whirled him, stepping quickly behind him, placing the barrel of my weapon against his spine. Muscles went still as an oak board and it was clear that he knew he had a gun at his back and one ahead. "Think they'll kill you to get to me?" I whispered to him over the ringing in my ears.

I was six feet, two and a half inches tall in my teal Lucchese boots, and my eyes barely peeked over his shoulder. This close, even over the stink of fired weapons, I could identify the four vamps he had fed from by their herbal signatures—wilting funeral flowers, lemon mint, sage, parsley, and something sweet, like agave. I breathed them in, learning what I could of each: gender, race, relationships. In human form I didn't have the nose of my Beast, but my sense of smell was far better than any human's, maybe a by-product of the decades I had spent in her form, or perhaps the result of my natural skinwalker abilities. I didn't have another skinwalker around to tell me stuff like that.

Ahead of me, I heard more weapons *schnick* and *chock-a-chock* in firing readiness. Muscles swallowed so hard I felt it through his spine.

"Call out. Tell them who I am."

Without waiting for a second prompt, Muscles shouted, "Dis here Jane Yellowrock. She come for . . ." To me he whispered, "What you come for?"

I thought about that. Admitting that I was itching to stake his master would probably not be my smartest move. "As Leo Pellissier's envoy. He's heard about the witch girl and wants to talk," I said softly, knowing that we were possibly close enough for any vamps to hear.

"Leo send her," Muscles shouted. "She want to talk about Shauna Landry."

"Tell them we're walking up to the door. Tell them to stand down."

"We coming. Put you guns away."

I didn't hear any sounds of that, but I pushed at Muscles and we walked toward the front door and up a hill I hadn't noted from the satellite maps, keeping slightly to the right of the entrance, keeping what I hoped was a clear line of sight for Margaud.

The hill was a berm of built-up land, and the house was on stilts some ten feet higher. I figured the height was to protect against storm surge from the gulf or flood from upstream.

I stopped fifteen feet from the bottom step and called up, "I'm Jane Yellowrock, Leo Pellissier's Enforcer, here to talk parley with Clermont Doucette."

"Parley? What dat is?" A deep voice asked from the door.

Mentally I stopped for a long moment. *Right. I'm not in New Orleans anymore.* "The Vampira Carta has a special section for parley, meaning that one person asks for parley and hospitality and the other accepts the request and offers and guarantees safety. Both agree not to kill the other or act in violence except in self-defense."

"I don' believe in dat Latin paper. We gots our own code."

"Fine. You wanna talk or you wanna fight? 'Cause you will surely lose if you choose fighting."

He laughed, the sound one of silken delight that vamps employ when they want to cajole and charm. Or insult. I could hear the insolent amusement in this tone. From my right I heard the distinctive sound of a shotgun readied for firing. From my left, I heard the same distinctive sound. And I saw a small red laser appear on the forehead of a vamp lost in the shadows until then. The chuckle died away and the targeted vamp stepped back, behind the door and into safety. A silence filled the night where the Doucette Clan Home stood, the silence of the dead, broken only by the breathing of humans. I counted ten, three of them my guys, two of them Muscles and me, making five more on the porch high over my head.

"How you get your men onto my land?" the vamp asked. "Close to my home?" It was a real inquiry, touched with mild confusion, and it identified the speaker as Clermont Doucette himself.

I didn't answer his question. Instead I repeated my own. "Talk or fight?"

"Talk," Clermont said. Before the word died, his men had safetied and holstered their weapons, or broken open the shotguns. A match was struck and an oil lamp was lit inside, visible through an unshuttered window, though I was certain the light I had seen earlier had been electric. The men and women who had previously barred my way cleared a path across the front porch and left the head bloodsucker in the center. A woman carried the lamp from the doorway to a table on the porch and set it down before backing away.

"We talk," Clermont said. "My house de same as your house, my blood de same as your blood, your safety good as my safety. My word on dis."

It sounded like a formal saying, the giving of his word, and I knew that meant something to people as old as Clermont. I figured I was supposed to say something back, and I thrashed around in my skull for anything appropriate as a rejoinder. I settled on, "Yeah. I won't shoot you or stake you unless you attack me first." After a moment I added, "Or behead you."

Clermont chuckled, this time with real amusement. "Bring Pierre Herbert for healin'," he said to someone at his side, and a young human raced down the steps, passing me. I didn't like having anyone behind me, but I figured Derek had him covered. I gently pushed Muscles away and took a deep breath, trying to settle my heart rate and calm myself. It was never wise to go into a nest of vamps when one smelled worried. Muscles looked at me over his shoulder before moving up the stairs, his feet loud on the plain wooden treads. I followed more slowly, holstering my weapon as I climbed. At the top, Clermont and I looked each other over, taking in details and drawing impressions.

He was tall for a man of his time, nearly six feet, lean and gangly, with dark brown eyes and blondish hair, a combination that seemed common in this area. He was dressed in worn jeans, an ironed white dress shirt, a suit jacket in pale gray or dull blue, and a narrow, charcoal-colored tie. And boots, which somehow surprised me, though boots were ubiquitous in Louisiana. A pair of reading glasses perched on his head and reflected the light.

I don't know what he thought of me, but he indicated the chair closest and waited until I sat, the gesture of a man of his time for a woman, not the way a warrior would act with another warrior. But I wasn't in a position to gripe about his good manners. I was now in the nest of vipers, and no matter how good Derek or Margaud was, any Doucette could kill me way faster than my people could react to save me.

Clermont leaned in and sniffed delicately. "What kind of predator you is?"

"Not one that will hurt you or your people unless you try to hurt me first."

Clermont thought about that for a while, putting together the phrase *try to hurt me* with the thought that I obviously believed they would not be successful. He nodded slowly and studied me. "I like you boots."

Which was just weird. I said, "Thanks. Um. They're Lucchese. I like yours too. Tony Lamas?"

He grinned happily, showing only his human teeth, and pulled up his pant legs to display his boots. "You know boots? Dat a good ting. Tony made dese boot for me hisself in nineteen forty-two. Bes' boots I ever have, dey is." He dropped his pant legs and said, "I got wine, beer, cola, bottled water, coffee, tea. May I offer you some libation to wet you whistle?"

All I could think was, *Crap, I have no idea how to handle this.* I said, "Uh, thanks but no thanks. I'm fine."

He spread his fingers as if to say, *Fine. Down to business. State your piece*, which was a lot to gather from a single gesture, but there it was. Clermont crossed his ankles and laced his fingers in what looked like a posture personal to him, back when he had been human.

I wasn't good at diplomacy, blowing things up and shooting things being more my way, but I gave it a shot. "Leo Pellissier sent me to . . ." I paused and chose my words carefully. ". . . to inquire about Shauna Landry, who, he has heard, is here against her will, to be turned against her will."

"Why?" When I looked puzzled, Clermont said, "Why Leo, Blood-Master of New Orleans, show an interest in us now? Why not a hundred year ago, or when he take over for dat worthless king Amaury?"

To that I had no answer. After a seriously awkward pause, I said, "I think he thought it was your choice to swear to him, or him to conquer you in a Blood Challenge, and he . . . mmm, he, mmm, respected you too much to come after you." Which was a lot better than *he thought you weren't worth the effort.* Knowing Leo it was the latter.

"Blood Challenge? Like a duel?" Clermont asked.

I hadn't studied a Blood Challenge, but I'd run across the term and that definition seemed to fit the parameters. "Sorta, yeah."

Clermont seemed to study the night sky. When his head moved, I realized he was in a rocking chair, and it started to squeak as he rocked, a pleasant rhythm in the night. Almost as if he called them to sing, frogs started to croak. I'd heard them before while in Beast form, the deep, almost-aching, nearly demanding basso profundo melody. Crickets joined in the song. A barred owl gave its hoot, *hoo-hoo-hoo-hooooo.* Something large splashed in the bayou out front. A night breeze strengthened and the lamp flame wavered, casting shadows that moved and crawled.

The porch we sat on was maybe thirty feet wide and fifteen deep, the house and its entrance behind us and rooms on either end. This protected it from wind and rain on three sides and yet still provided a view of the bayou out front, the live oaks on the property, and the cypress standing in the water, knees pushed up above the surface anchoring the trees in the silty bottom. The last of the sunset was a pale pink line on the horizon, the sky quickly fading to a dark cerulean overhead.

I shouldn't have felt so suddenly peaceful, but I did. I let my body relax into the chair, and I realized that I didn't chill out very often. To take the opportunity in this perilous place was stupid and dangerous, but even knowing that, I let my muscles soften and my backside settle, just a hint, just a bit. "If the offer of tea is still open," I said, "I'd like a cup of hot."

"Black," Clermont said to the shadows. "That good China black what come de mail las' week. And bring out de girl. She can speak for herself to de famed vampire hunter."

"Thank you," I said.

Shauna arrived before the tea, holding the hand of a male vampire. She fit her father's description and the small graduation photo provided by Lucky. Her hair was pulled back and braided, leaving her face and narrow jaw fully exposed. She was prettier than her photo, or she had already been fed a lot of vamp blood, improving her skin and her vitality. The boy holding her hand was fully vamped-out, his two-inch fangs down, his pupils wide and black in bloodred sclera; he was close to losing control. If he had been aping human he would have been a pretty boy, with brown hair to his waist, some braided, some hanging free, an aquiline nose and almond-shaped eyes. Gently I asked, "You're Clermont's son?"

"And heir," he said, his words only slightly misshapen by his fangs. "Gabriel Doucette," he said, pronouncing it *Gab-rel Doo-see*. "I can give her everything. A home. A place. A long, full life. I love her."

While he spoke, the girl held his hand tighter and gazed at him with fierce adoration in her eyes.

Well, crap. So much for kidnap or vamp glamour. I hadn't studied Shakespeare in high school, but even I knew this was starting to look a little like it was more along the lines of *Romeo and Juliet* than a kidnap plot. Unlike *Romeo and Juliet*, however, this story left one family holding all the cards. Lucky Landry had lied to me. Surprise, surprise.

Because he was so close to the edge, I turned my gaze to the girl for a moment, indicating I was speaking to her, before looking off into the night. I said, "Your father thinks you were kidnapped. You're here of your own free will?"

At the word *kidnapped*, power spiked along my arms and settled in my fingertips, an electric pain that promised more if I wasn't careful. It was an attack spell, something prepared beforehand and waiting, a defensive measure worthy of my friends the Everharts. And I had a feeling if she let loose with it, I'd get hurt. Shauna's voice, when she spoke, was calm, determined. "I love Gabriel."

I thought about that for a moment before turning to Clermont. "How many witches have you turned in the last hundred or so years?"

His brows went up. He opened his mouth and closed it, pursed his lips, thinking. "Four," he said, his voice quiet, almost buried in the night noises. I could see him thinking, putting two and two together—his history with witches, my question, my being here at all, which, considering the danger I was in, must be important.

Keeping my tone soft and gentle, I asked, "Have you ever seen a witch make the change into vampire?" When he said nothing, I added, "Witches don't accept the change as well as humans. Witches seldom come out of the devoveo—what you may call the insanity—at all."

Gabriel growled and his lips pulled back. Beast flooded me with adrenaline. *Kit shows killing teeth,* she thought at me.

"Gabe!" Clermont barked. But Gabriel didn't back down.

I kept my gaze in the distance and my voice soft, saying, "Shauna, did you know there's a strong possibility you could remain insane forever if you get turned?"

She didn't answer, but her eyes widened and her lips parted in alarm. And Gabriel let go of her hand. In the blink of an eye, everything went to hell in a handbasket.

Gabriel lunged at me.

A spot of red appeared on his shirtfront.

He yanked up my arm, his vampire claws piercing my wrist.

The *crack* of a rifle sounded in the night.

Clermont *moved*, his fist impacting his son's chin.

Gabe's body snapped back; his claws shredded my flesh.

Twin *booms* sounded off to either side.

Vamps all around me vamped-out.

The smell of blood and vampires filled the night.

I dropped back to the chair and stabbed upward with a vamp-killer, the twelve-inch blade sliding into the belly of a vamp who was reaching for me, fangs-first. My angle was wrong to pull the M4, but I managed to get a .380 out. Off safety. Fired. Hitting a vamp in the face. Another in the shoulder. Vamps screamed, the piercing, horrible wail of death I could hear even over the acoustic damage of the firearms.

Some small part of my brain knew I'd just sentenced a vamp to a slow, painful death by silver poisoning with the vamp-killer, but the gun's ammo was standard, and no vamps would die from that. Humans could, though. Collateral damage. I did not want to hurt the humans.

Derek and one of his men were on the porch. I saw Derek toss two hand grenades into the house, his movements seen as overlays of static images. I closed my eyes and threw an arm over them. The flashbangs took down every vamp inside with the blinding light and intense noise. More vamps were wailing, my ears vibrating painfully with the high tone.

I opened my eyes in time to see more forms flow up the stairs led by Lucky Landry. Magics spat down his arms from his tattoos and shot out his fingertips. Blue flames whipped among the vamps and humans on the porch.

"Bogus!" I screamed. Derek turned to the witch and hit him with the butt of his shotgun. It wasn't a weapon Lucky had prepared a defense against. The witch fell like he'd been poleaxed. The forms behind him stopped and stared at their leader. And the vamps turned on them.

Beast shoved her power into me and I threw myself back and up. Taking Clermont around the neck in a sleeper hold, I shoved the vamp-killer at his neck. "Hold!" I shouted.

Everyone on the porch and steps and inside the house went still and silent. My ears buzzed with complaint. Into Clermont's ear, I said, "Thanks for knocking your kid outta the way so I didn't have to kill him. And sorry about that hospitality thing and all, but if your suckheads don't back off, I'll kill you. Understand?"

Clermont nodded slightly, the silver scorching his skin where it touched. I caught the scent of burned, dead flesh and curled my lips back against the stink. And realized that a sleeper hold was likely useless to a vamp except for immobilizing him. Good thing I'd been holding the blade.

"Derek?" I asked.

He bent over Lucky and checked his pulse and pupils. "He'll live," Derek said, his tone unconcerned. "I mighta broke his jaw, though."

"Margaud. Report," I said. "Numbers?"

Slightly garbled by my earbud, I made out Margaud's words. "Vamps?

Ten I can count. Witches? Six standing. Dem was under de house, behind de pilings, and their sigs blended in widda pigs'. Sorry 'bout dat."

Sigs. Heat signatures. *Right.* I raised my voice. "Witches, sit on the ground. Vamps, sit on the porch. Now!" When no one moved, I said into Clermont's ear, "Tell them. This gets settled one way or another, and I don't really care how. Oh, and by the way. I have Leo Pellissier's *permission* to take him your head. *In writing.*"

"Sit," Clermont said. The vamps and their humans sat. When the witches didn't follow suit, Derek kicked one witch in the backs of the knees. He fell; the rest sat. Derek and his men went around gathering guns and blades. They made a nice pile at the base of the stairs.

When everyone was disarmed and sitting, I said to Clermont, "I stabbed one of your people with a silvered knife. If they get fed enough blood by a strong enough vamp or their master, there is a chance they'll live. Also, I fired standard ammo, but my sharpshooter used silver-plated. If it didn't pass clear through him, your idiot son might have a silver slug in his chest. Can anyone here dig that out?"

"Surgeon, I am," Clermont said, surprising the heck outta me, "or was, long time ago. I still know how to dig out a rifle round. And my blood is strong. I can treat my people."

"Well, good." Which sounded lame, but it was all I had.

"You gone call dat Leo? Take my head?"

"I'd rather not. You willing to make your son act like he has some sense?"

"I am. You willing to make Lucky Landry act like he have him a brain in he head?"

"I am. I guess that means I'm letting you go now."

"Dat be right nice. Pain in de neck, you is."

I couldn't help it. I laughed. And so did Clermont. As he did, his fangs—which I hadn't even noticed—clicked back into the roof of his mouth on their tiny little hinges. Vamps can't laugh—a human emotion—and be vamped-out at the same time. I let him go and he bent to the vamp lying on the porch boards. Blood was a dark pool beneath her, and she was breathing with the painful rasp of a human who had traumatic lung damage and whose lungs were filling up with blood. Clermont bent over her and held his wrist to her mouth. Her fangs bit into him, and her lips sucked like a starving baby's, a weak and desperate motion. A minute later, she reached up and grabbed his wrist, holding him to her, and her sucking increased in depth and intensity. A minute after that, Clermont peeled her away and a human man sat beside her, cradling her close so she could latch onto his neck. It was intimate and lover-like, and I turned away. Some things I just don't need to see.

The witches were sitting on the ground at the bottom of the stairs, three of them laying on hands, healing Lucky Landry. "Margaud?" I said. "We have anything or anyone else on the way or hidden with the pigs?"

"No, sir," she said, sounding like a soldier who had just been censured by her sergeant. "Clear."

"Derek, Clermont, Gabe, and Shauna. As soon as Lucky can think straight and Gabe has the silver out of his body, we're gonna have us a nice long talk. We have aaall night."

It took two hours to heal all the injured, and while I waited I drank the tea Clermont had promised. It was a delicious, stylish, pungent black from China, described on the package as a Super Fancy Tippy Golden Flowery Orange Pekoe. Having discovered that we were fellow tea lovers, he and I talked teas while he dug the slug out of his son. It was bizarre conversation, talking about attractive, chunky, golden-tipped first flushes from various provinces in China, India, Sri Lanka, Ceylon, and other places. To a non–tea lover it was silly talk, and I caught Derek rolling his eyes once as he drank coffee passed out by a beautiful, mixed-tribe, American Indian blood-slave, one who was over a hundred years old and not above teasing the much, much, *much* younger man with sly looks and come-hither stares. Not that Derek understood that she was a slave by choice and old enough to be his great-great-grandmother. Vamps and their humans are sneaky.

Derek called Auguste and Benoît in. The brothers had been waiting in the dark to remove us in retreat or victory, either one. And then Derek, Auguste, and a vamp went to get Margaud, who didn't want to abandon her position to sit with the enemy suckheads. She put up a good verbal resistance and fired off three warning shots before I pulled out my earbud. Eventually someone took her off the air. I didn't know how Derek finally convinced Margaud into the airboat, but Derek was good-looking and persuasive, or maybe the former military angle worked. Or maybe her brother just picked her up and tossed her on board. Don't ask, don't tell.

Near two a.m., I judged that everyone was healed and calm enough for discussion and called all the participants to the front porch. There weren't enough chairs, so Clermont made everyone but the main participants sit on the floor, equaling out one and all. There were vamps and humans and witches sitting side by side, close together, sharing floor space without bloodshed. It would have been inspiring had Clermont and I not promised utmost retribution to anyone who caused trouble.

I opened the meeting with a few vampire terms and their meanings, including the devoveo and the dolore, the insanity of freshly turned vamps and the insanity of vamps who suffered the loss of a close loved one. I explained that witches were seldom successfully turned vamp, remaining in the devoveo forever, and ended with a plea for both sides to find a way to end the rift between the races and find a way for the lovers to be together. It was a lot of words for me, with even more *mmm*s and *hmmm*s and *uh*s and *ah*s. I'm not a public speaker. Not at all. It's easier to shoot first and divide up the dead later, but maybe I was growing up.

When I was done, Clermont stood and spoke to Lucky Landry. Lucky was tied to a chair and to the porch railing, just in case, but he listened far better than I expected, maybe because Clermont opened with the words, "I tired o' this war between coonass and coonass."

Despite himself, Lucky chuckled and looked down. He took a deep breath and said, "I tired o' it too." He looked at his daughter, sitting on the floor, hand in hand with Gabe, love and determination in her eyes. "You want dis suck— You want dis vampire? You love him for real?"

"I do," Shauna said. Her chin came up defiantly. "And I'm carrying his baby."

Lucky pulled in a breath and the flames danced along his bound arms.

"I love him, Daddy. If you hurt him, I'll never forgive you. Not. Ever. And I'll spend the rest of my life keeping your grandchild away from you."

Lucky looked at me. "Suc— Vampires can have babies like human and witch do? Despite we different races? Dem babies not be mule?"

"So far as I know, vamps can have babies, though it's very, very rare. Whether the children are sterile I don't know."

Clermont said, "Dem babies not easy to have in de human way. Vampires treasure dem few. Dey can have babies of dere own, and dey special to us. Special power dey all has. Dis be first vampire-and-witch baby we have. Make him better and more special, I'm thinking."

Lucky studied his daughter. "He say *he*. You carrying my first grandson, for real?"

Shauna placed a hand on her belly. "I don't know how I know, but I know. All you other children has girls, so yes, dis boy be your first. And we already named him." She looked at Gabe and he lifted their fisted hands to his mouth and kissed her fingers gently. Everyone on the porch said, or had to restrain, a soft, "Awwww" of delight.

"We name our baby by family name and alphabet," Gabe said, which confused me until they went on.

"Hem be Clermont Jérôme Landry Doucette," Shauna said, "and we call him Clerjer." It came out *Clarshar*, and it sounded pretty on her tongue.

Laundry looked at Clermont and said, "Why not JerCler?"

"Dat not alphabet," the vampire said, deadpan.

Both men laughed softly, measuring one another.

"What we can do to stop killin' and killin'?" Lucky asked.

"Baptize dis baby in church," Clermont said. And everyone, even the vamps, took a deep, shocked breath. "Marry dem two in front o' de church first, o' course."

Lucky nodded slowly. "Vampire can go in de church?"

"Not so much. But in de yard, yeah, we can do dat. You talk to de priest first, make hem see reason."

"If he don' see reason, den dey can marry in my church," a voice said from the far reaches of the porch. "I marry dem. No need for no priest."

"Who dat is?" Lucky asked.

A skinny man stood at the back, his face resolute, if pale.

"Preacher Michael? You a blood-slave to dese suckheads?" Lucky said, horror in his voice.

"Dey heal me a cancer wid dey blood. It take a lot o' blood, and many month o' time," Preacher Michael said. "I give back to dem when dey need."

Lucky made a Gaelic-sounding snort. "Well, I be dam—uh, I be a monkey's uncle."

"And a grandfather," Shauna said.

A goofy smile lit Lucky's face. He looked at his erstwhile enemy again and pursed his lips to make the smile less obvious. "But how you keep my girl not crazy?"

Clermont said, "Blood-kin, we call dem. Gabe make her blood-kin. She live mebbe two hundred years. She have good long life, here wid my son and wid us, and in town wid you and yours." He held out his hand and said, "Dat a good enough start for me. Dat good start for you?"

Lucky Landry slapped his hand into Clermont's and the men shook. "Dat a start. But first ting is, dem two been living in sin. Dey gets marry tonight."

"Done, my brother. How about now and here? Brother Michael can marry dem in eyes of de church and God and dem get license later what for de state."

Lucky started to speak and stopped, his mouth open. After a long pause he said, "My wife kill me, she not here. . . . Shauna's sisters too. No. Dem two gets marry *tomorrow* night, in town at church. Yes?"

"I say yes," Clermont said, the men's hands still clasped.

"Don't I get a say?" Shauna demanded.

"No!" both men stated. And everyone on the porch laughed.

Twenty-four hours later, the first vampire–witch marriage in Bayou Oiseau took place in the yard of the Catholic church. A second ceremony followed in the churchyard of the Pentecostal Holiness, One God, King James Church. In both ceremonies, Shauna was wearing her mother's wedding dress, a creamy satin, full-skirted, hooped gown with puffy sleeves. With it she wore a hat shaped a bit like a satin cowboy hat with a pouf of veil on top. She looked stunning, glowing with happiness. Gabe wore a black tuxedo, his long hair in braids and love in his eyes. Just before the start of the first ceremony, he met his bride in the back of church with two dozen roses to carry down the aisle. As he gave them to her he said, "Dese here roses are twelve red and twelve white. Together dem symbol of union between vampire and witch. Every single rose I done clip off its thorn, to symbolize the way I protect you from all harm. Dis for my whole undead life." There wasn't a dry eye in the churchyard.

To finish the night off properly, Leo Pellissier, Master of the City of New Orleans and most of the Southeast, gave his blessing over my cell phone, in the yard of the Pentecostal church. Everyone in Bayou Oiseau heard it, and heard his invitation to Clermont to come to New Orleans and parley as equals once the baby was born.

Clermont looked at me when the phone call was done and said, "You do dis thing? Set up dis parley?"

I shrugged, smiled, and walked away. What I'd done was tell Leo he was an idiot and to get off his butt and fix this stupid situation with Clermont and the Doucette Clan or I would. What the heck. It seemed to work.

Once all the official stuff was done, the entire town turned out to eat, drink, and dance the night away. Not that it was perfect. There was a fistfight between a small group of humans and witches and an even smaller group of vampires, but the clan leaders broke it up and made an example of them to the rest. It wasn't deadly, but it wasn't pretty either. There was another moment of tension when a vampire asked a human woman to dance, but that too got smoothed over, and I didn't ask how. Most vamps can dance like nobody's business, and once the human women saw that vamps were willing partners, there wasn't an empty dance floor for the rest of the party.

I pulled Derek onto the dance floor and kept him there for two numbers. That man can *dance!*

It was a good night, a better party, with fantastic food and energetic dancing. A great solution to a problem that had been simmering in the Louisiana backwaters for decades. As the locals might say, "Dem coonass clans Doucette and Landry? Dem family now, yeah dey is." Heck of a lot better than any old *Romeo and Juliet*–style ending.

And best of all? I got paid.

The Devil's Left Boot

Liz tossed the rag into the dishpan and lifted it to take the dirty dishes to the kitchen. Seven Sassy Sisters' Herb Shop and Café used heavy country china and good-quality stainless flatware instead of the cheaper stuff. The customers liked the quality and the homey atmosphere, but being busboy—or -girl—was tough on her back.

"I've got it," Cia said, and scooped the heavy pan out of her arms. "Share and share alike," she added. Liz's once reticent and introverted twin had been doing a lot of that since Liz's injury. And it wasn't necessary. So, okay, Liz got short of breath. And her ribs hurt sometimes. She was still healing, and no one could expect complete and instantaneous recuperation after having a huge rock land on her chest in the middle of a magical attack. By their own coven leader . . . and elder sister.

Grief welled up again, and Liz blinked furiously against the tears. Evangelina's death had hit all the sisters hard, but the four witch sisters had felt her death most deeply because they had also lost a coven leader, and by the foulest means—addiction to demons. Although the actual cause of death had been a knife blade to the torso, the Evangelina they had grown up with and practiced their craft with for their whole lives had been dead for months before that.

Liz sighed, feeling the weakness in her ribs, a slow, low-level pain, and pulled out a clean rag to wipe down the next table. She was polishing the final booth, standing by the front door, when the flashy red Thunderbird wheeled up and parked. It wasn't a practical car for Asheville, but it was memorable, and that was what the driver wanted—to be known as an icon in her hometown. Liz huffed out a breath and called, "Cia! Company. And not the good kind."

Her twin was by her side in a heartbeat. "Is that *Layla*? Too bad we don't have access to Evie's demon. It could eat her."

"Not funny," Liz said. The demon *had* eaten a few humans before it was sent back into the dark. "Maybe she's changed since high school."

"Once a bitch, always a bitch," Cia said. "What's that she's carrying?"

"A baby goat? What the—"

The door opened, and their archenemy from their high school years stepped in, bringing with her a cold spring wind through the air lock doors. Layla's face was as beautiful as ever, which made Liz stiffen and Cia narrow her eyes. Layla was black haired and pale skinned and skinny and graceful and delicate and feminine and damn near perfect. In high school she'd been the leader of a cadre of girls who had all been gorgeous and popular, most of them cheerleaders. Unlike the Everharts, all of Layla's pals had been human. And most of them had been mean. Now, just like in high school, the twins stood side by side, facing their enemy.

The inner doors swished closed after Layla and she stopped, standing with the poise of a model, slender and lovely, wearing a Ralph Lauren leather jacket, tailored pants, and a pair of bling-studded Manolo Blahnik ankle boots that were drool-worthy. She stared at the twins across the small space and across the years. No one spoke. When the baby pygmy goat under Layla's arm started to struggle, she soothed it with a gentle hand, and Liz felt Cia stiffen. *Layla Shiffen should not be gentle.*

"Boadacia Everhart and Elizabeth Everhart," she said, the words sounding almost formulaic, her expression determined, "I require help."

Cia crossed her arms and made a huffing sound. Liz dropped her rag and mimicked her sister.

The resolve on Layla's face flickered. "I can pay. And I brought my own goat."

Liz laughed, the sound slightly wheezing from her damaged lungs.

Cia said, "Help? For what." It didn't sound like a question—more like an accusation. Or a challenge. "And what does our help have to do with a goat?"

Layla shifted, her composure faltering again before her lips firmed in determination. "I need you to find my mother. The goat is for the sacrifice."

"Sac—," Liz started, then stopped.

"We don't do blood magic," Cia spat. She pointed at the door. "Get out."

"But . . ." Layla's eyes filled with tears. "But I need you. I said the words right. I researched how to say it." She sobbed once. A real sob. Not like the fake sobs she'd used in the school play the year she had the lead in *Romeo and Juliet.* "I don't have anyone else. The police can't help. Or *won't.* They say there's no sign of foul play. They took a missing-persons report and that's all they'll do," she said, her words running together. "My mom's in trouble. I *know* it. And I don't know where to turn." Tears fell across her perfect cheeks and dripped onto the silk scarf around her neck. "P-please."

Neither twin reacted. They still stood side by side, staring and silent. Liz could feel the power building up under her twin's skin, prickly and cold, like winter moonlight. It was slow to rise, with the moon beneath the horizon, but it was powerful magic, especially when she was angry. Their human sisters must have felt it too. They stepped in through the archway opening from the herb shop, one with a shotgun held down by her leg. The other sister would be armed as well, nonmagical, but deadly in the face of danger. One robbery was all it had taken for their human sisters to find a way to protect themselves. Liz shook her head at them, a minuscule motion.

"Big whoop," Cia said. "I don't like you. I remember too much."

Layla's face went all blotchy and red under her porcelain makeup. Her nose started running, and she raised a wrist to wipe it, bringing the goat close to her. The goat butted her chin and made a soft bleating noise. She tucked the animal under her chin as if cuddling it and said, "Please. You have to help me." She looked back and forth between them, her expression growing frantic. She clutched the baby goat to her chest. "You *have* to. It's my *mother.*"

Liz felt Cia shudder faintly at the last word and knew that Layla had won, just like in high school. Nothing had changed since they were teens. "Son of a witch on a switch," Cia cursed.

Liz sighed and waved their sisters off. Regan and Amelia both frowned, recognizing the woman and knowing her history with the witch twins. But they went back to the herb shop side of Seven Sassy Sisters', moving reluctantly and keeping an eye on the café. Both crises averted—magical and weapons fire—Liz dropped into a booth at the front window and pointed to the bench seat across the newly cleaned table. Liz had good reason to keep Cia busy and off the TV and Internet. Maybe this would do that. "Sit," she said to Layla. "What's your mother's name and why do you think she's in trouble?"

Layla sat and settled the baby goat on her lap before reaching into her Bruno Magli Maddalena suede bag for a tissue and patting her face. Liz could almost feel Cia's covetousness as her twin slid onto the bench seat, reestablishing the arm-to-arm, skin-to-skin contact. Of course, even if an Everhart could afford a bag that went for more than two thousand dollars new, none of the sisters would buy it. Maybe a vintage one in need of TLC and a little magical cleanup. Everharts were notoriously cheap. Covetous but cheap. Liz nearly smiled.

"My mother is Evelyn Janice McMann. She called me the day before yesterday on her way home from work. We ended the call when she locked the door behind her, just like always. It's this"—Layla waved one hand in the air, as if searching for a word—"safety thing we do when Mom works late. She works for a developer, and late-night business meetings are common, as you might imagine."

Liz had no idea what hours developers kept, but she nodded, understanding security measures.

"Her boss called the house the next morning. Mom had missed an important meeting. Which she never does. *Never.*"

Liz had to wonder if that had been a problem for Layla growing up. Maybe growing up second to the job.

"So I went by there. Mom's house looked perfect, as always. Except her clothes, the ones she wore when we had lunch the day before, were scattered everywhere, like they'd been thrown. Carelessly. There is *nothing* careless about my mother. So I went to the police." She wiped her face again. "And they made me wait until this morning to file a missing-persons report. They think she was having a *fling* and took off with some *man,*" Layla said, her tone bitter. "My mother doesn't have *time* for a man in her life. *Trust* me. She works fourteen hours a day. *Every day.* Always has."

Cia nudged her, and Liz knew her twin was thinking along the same lines. Abandonment issues, much? It might explain a lot about Layla, growing up. Not that her having issues made them forgive her. Not gonna happen.

"Her keys? Purse? Cell?" Liz asked.

"All on the floor with her clothes." Fresh tears gathered in Layla's eyes and she bent over the goat. It nudged her jaw and licked her chin. "I don't know what to do. Can you help me? Can you find her?"

Cia and Liz shared looks that said, *No. Yes. No. Maybe. No.*

Layla eased the goat back into the crook of her arm, placed the expensive pocketbook on the table, and opened the flap. "I can pay." She pulled out a stack of hundred-dollar bills and pushed it across the table toward them. Neither twin looked at the money, but they both saw it. More money than they made in tips in a month. Maybe two.

Cia's magic rose again, like a wave at high tide, hard and powerful and angry. She leaned forward and said, "We can try. Trying is a flat fee of a thousand. Success is another two thousand. Nonnegotiable." When Liz started to debate the amount, Cia said, "That's Jane Yellowrock's fee for a PI job. And she doesn't have magic. And"—she looked hard at Layla—"if we get your mom back, the fee is required, no matter what shape your mom is in."

Liz sucked in a slow, painful breath. Layla gasped, her face paling. The comment was blunt enough to be worthy of Jane Yellowrock herself, and the rogue-vampire hunter was honest to the point of being brusque. Cia meant that Layla's mom could be dead. She was the gentler twin. Usually. Suddenly Liz remembered what it had felt like to bear the brunt of Layla's cruelty—the goading, the taunting. And that one time . . . In that single indrawn breath, the memory descended, full, complete, and awful.

"Boadecia," Layla had hissed. "Stupid name for a stupid girl. Some people think the twins have some kind of power. I just think they're ugly." A shove, hidden from the teachers by the group of girls surrounding them. "Stupid and ugly. Ugly red hair and ugly freckles. When Mother Nature messes up, she messes up bad. She made two of them." Another shove. A yank of hair.

The moon had been full that day, making Cia less stable, more reckless, like stormy waves on an icy ocean, pushed by a full-moon tide. Fear had grown up inside Liz, like frozen rocks hanging on a cliff face, ready to fall.

Not fear of the taunting girls, but fear of themselves, fear of losing control. Fear that one of them would erupt and pull the other into her magical reaction through the twin bond. Fear that they would misuse their gifts and pay the price. Then the bell had sounded. They had gotten away, barely, before one of them lost control and they hurt the girls.

Liz blew out her breath. *Yeah. Okay. Cia was right.* That girl who hurt them back in high school was the woman facing them. To an enemy, their services shouldn't be offered as a gift freely given, the way they were *supposed* to be for one in need. "What she said. That's our price."

"No matter what," Layla said. Her hands trembling, she counted out thirty hundred-dollar bills. "I pay up front. You do your best." She stood, tucking the goat into the crook of her arm and soothing it with an absent-minded caress.

"We need to see the house," Cia said, her tone still hard. "We'll need to take something your mother was wearing the day she disappeared. To do a working to find her."

Layla opened her pocketbook and removed an expensive-looking pen and planner. She wrote down her mother's address and tore off the sheet. Then she tossed down a business card, glossy and dark, with her contact info on it. "Call me."

She turned on the heel of the Manolo and left the café, the icy spring wind whipping inside.

"She wanted us to sacrifice a goat kid."

"She's an idiot. She called us by our full names, as if we're fae and can be commanded."

"Not our full names," Liz said.

"Nope. I'm not sure we ever told anyone our full names. But I'd kill for those boots," Cia said.

"I'd fight you for them."

Her twin gave her a hard slash of smile and said, "Good idea on Jane's prices, huh?"

Liz nodded and opened her mouth to tell Cia that Jane Yellowrock was in town for the hearing about the day their sister died. About the day Jane had killed her to save human lives. But she closed it on the words. Some things needed to die peacefully, things like the memory of their sister being put out of her insane, raving, psychotic, demon-drunk misery on live TV. So far she had been able to keep the news from her twin. Why spoil it?

Cia handed Liz the address and card and said, "Let's get set up for lunch. I have the kitchen, and while the soups aren't demanding, the salads and breads are." Cia sashayed toward the back. "As soon as we're done here for the afternoon," she added, "let's go by the mom's house and get this over with."

"Evangelina never had trouble handling the kitchen," Liz grumbled. "Why can't we get the knack? We need to hire a chef."

"On it," Cia said from behind the kitchen bar. "Résumés in a stack." She waved a sheaf of papers in the air. "Maybe we should have a cook-off."

Liz snorted and headed to the back to wash the breakfast dishes. A café didn't run by itself.

The Subaru idled at the curb as the twins studied the house. It was a small home in the Montford Historic District, two-story, traditional, steeply gabled, slate roofed, painted in shades of charcoal, pale gray, and white. The windows were new, triple-paned replacements, glinting in the cold sunlight. The winter plantings were tasteful, and a batch of early spring jonquils pushed up through the soil on the south side of the house. The white picket fence was newly painted. The bare branches of a small oak tree stretched over the Lexus parked in the short gravel drive.

"Looks okay," Liz said.

"Looks expensive."

"Is expensive. Probably goes for nearly seven fifty in today's market." Liz could see her sister adding the necessary zeros to her housing cost figure.

"We could buy a place," Cia said. "Not this nice, but we could buy a place somewhere else. We have the money from Evie's estate. If we combined it—"

"No way. When you marry that guitar-playing, long-haired hippie you're dating and start having all the six kids he wants, what happens to me?"

"You get to babysit, sis."

"Babysitting I can handle. It's life as a live-in nanny I'm not interested in."

"That long-haired hippie is rich as Midas. If Ray and I get married someday, we'll get our own place and you can have our house." Cia sounded part smug, part smitten, part unsure, the way she always did when she talked about Ray, the country singer who had fallen head over heels the first time he saw her and who had made a habit of sending flowers and candy and presents to get her attention.

A red car passed them slowly. "She's here." Liz couldn't hide the bitterness in her words.

The vintage T-bird rolled into the drive and nestled into the small space behind the Lexus. When their archenemy stepped from the car, she was once again holding the baby goat. And it was wearing a diaper. Cia breathed out a giggle, but oddly, Layla didn't look ridiculous. More like a socialite with a chic, pampered lapdog. *Lap goat.* Liz resisted a smile.

"Does it look to you like she's making a pet of the kid?" she asked.

"Yeah," Cia said. Unspoken but understood was the phrase *that's weird.* "Can you house-train them?"

"No. And they'll eat literally anything and everything. Shoes. Fancy pocketbooks."

Cia laughed softly and shared a glance, both of them imagining the scene of the goat eating the pricey bag. Layla screaming and stomping her feet.

"And their poop stinks. Like, really bad," Liz added.

"I see a rude awakening on the horizon," Cia said with barely restrained glee. "Hope it's today so I can watch."

They got out of their car and moved across the street to the house, Cia in front, as if to protect her weaker sister. Cia's dress blew back in the slow wind, the shifting shades of color mimicking the silver pinkish hues of moonlight on orchids. She wore a long vintage wool coat from the sixties, gray with tan lapel and cuffs, unbuttoned so the dress would show. Her red hair, dyed to a deep wine, was pulled into a chignon that looked smooth and chic. Her boots, never worn until today—never worn despite her boot fetish—struck the pavement with steady force. She looked classy and quirky and expensive, like the rich man's toy that Ray might want to make her.

Cia hadn't been wearing the Old Gringo boots, the coat, or the moonlight dress when they left the house this morning. The pricey buff-colored boots, hand-stitched with scarlet dragons climbing each side, had been Ray's gift, one she hadn't felt like she could wear, and she had kept them in the box, under her bed. Until today. She had put aside her uncertainty about accepting Ray's present to show off to Layla.

Liz looked down at her own well-worn hiking boots, old jeans, and warm sweater crocheted by Evangelina last winter, before she started consorting with demons. It wasn't often that the twins' clothing choices were so dissimilar.

She frowned, not liking the change in her sister but powerless to affect it. The fear reaction to the loss of Evangelina had been stimulating Cia's aggressive tendencies for months, and this close to the full moon, Liz was going to be able only to mitigate her twin's reaction, not stop it. Getting through the loss of their sister would take time, and though it might be helped along by Liz getting well and strong again, that wasn't going to happen overnight.

Liz followed in Cia's wake, walking more slowly, taking in the house the way she had seen their friend—if their sister's killer could be called that—Jane Yellowrock do. None of the perfectly placed rocks beside the drive had been moved out of position. No leaves had been allowed to catch in the nooks and crannies of roots and winter plants. The gravel beside the Lexus looked undisturbed, no signs of struggle anywhere.

The small front porch where Layla waited was freshly painted and the door was locked. Liz made sure to search for signs of problems, like, say, a size-twelve boot print and a busted door, or overturned flowerpots. There was nothing. "Wait," Liz said. She walked around the porch, tilting back the clay pots until she found the extra key. Brass, shiny, looking new, it sat on the painted boards, an invitation of sorts. It had taken her less than fifteen seconds to find it. If anyone had wanted inside, they could have unlocked the door and walked in with no trouble. Layla looked horrified, her eyes wide.

"I'm going to walk around the house," Liz said, planting the key in Layla's palm.

Cia stared hard at her for a moment and then nodded in understanding. "Yeah. Okay." Leaving Layla—who entered the house without them—Liz led the way and Cia followed, her boots drumming on the carefully placed stepping-stones that ringed the house. The yard to the left side of the house was shadowed, chilly, and narrow, and the gate in the picket fence at the back edge of the house was unlocked. There was no obvious damage. The backyard was deeper than it was wide, and not fenced. Deer tracks and scat indicated that wildlife was welcome out back. The back door was closed, locked, and looked undisturbed. There were no broken windows that a kidnapper or burglar might have used.

On the south side of the house there was a small greenhouse filled with bags of soil, fertilizer, and yard tools, and a gate, identical to the one on the other side. It too was unlocked, with only a tiny catch. Near the front corner of the house was the patch of green pushing up through the soil, the jonquils looking cheerful.

"Nothing," Cia said.

"Yeah." They went back up the short flight of steps to the door and it opened before they could knock, Layla watching through the door's leaded-glass window. She stepped aside and the twins entered, drawing together, as usual, in the unfamiliar place.

The air was warm inside, the heat at a comfortable level, not a lower setting. Most people might decrease the setting of the central heat when planning an extended out-of-town stay, and the comfortable temp seemed significant. Liz unbuttoned her sweater and tucked her hands into her jeans pockets, thinking about fingerprints. Even though she wasn't looking, Cia put her hands in her jacket pockets too. Twin stuff.

The house had wide-board hardwood floors, creamy painted walls hung with framed art, painted floor moldings and ceiling moldings. Ten-foot ceilings. Antique furniture juxtaposed with designer pieces. The living room boasted an Oriental rug in wine and blues to match the navy leather couch and burgundy upholstered chairs. The dining room sported navy-and-wine-striped fabric on the dining chairs and a floral rug under the antique table for ten. Perfect. The kitchen was clean, not a dish out of place on the granite-topped cabinets. The stovetop looked as if it had never been used.

Liz pointed up the stairs, a question on her face, and replaced her hands in her pockets. Layla shrugged. The twins went up alone and found two guest rooms with a Jack-and-Jill bath between, and a sewing room/craft room/extra-superneat junk room behind a closed door. Theirs were the only footprints on the neutral carpet. Having learned nothing, they went back downstairs.

The house was free of dust, piles of mail, and accumulated rubbish. There were no coats tossed over chair backs. No shoes in a corner or slippers by the front door or gloves on a side table. No clutter. The framed art consisted of impersonal prints that a decorator might have chosen. There were no photos or mementos anywhere. No plants to water. No dog or cat bowls. The house was something for a magazine shoot, not a place to relax, to live.

Until Layla, still silent and watching them with curious and sober eyes, led them into the master suite. Which was totally different.

The suite looked like it had been hit by a whirlwind. The king-sized bed was unmade, the covers and comforter in a heap on the floor. Clothes were everywhere. A bottle of wine was open on a side table near a sitting area, a single long-stemmed glass beside it. Wine ringed the glass, partially evaporated. One glass. Not two, as one might expect if she'd met a man, had a tryst, and taken off with him, as the police seemed to think. Jewelry was in a pile on the bureau, diamonds and gold. A lot of both. The marble bath en suite was clean and untouched, Evelyn's makeup in a white leather travel case, open but well organized, the contents in sizes accepted by airlines and strict travel security. Larger sizes of shampoos, conditioners, and lotions were arranged in a cabinet that Liz opened with her hand tucked around her sweater hem. Towels were perfectly folded, as were washcloths. Even the laundry basket's contents were already separated— colors in one side, whites in the other.

"Everything is neat. As close to perfect as it's possible to be and still be a real home. But the bedroom?" Liz said, making it a question as she walked back into that room.

"It's never looked like this before. *Ever*," Layla said grimly. "My mother is OCD about her stuff. *Impossibly* OCD."

Another reason to think that Layla had not had a cheery childhood.

Liz took in the room's disarray. The clothes on the floor seemed weird somehow, as if they had been dropped in a circle. As if Evelyn had stood in the middle of the room and turned slowly around, dropping her clothes as she undressed. Grabbing the bedcovers and pulling them with her, then dropping them too. The fabrics and clothing formed a spiral.

To get a better feel for the layout, Liz stepped inside the bare space on the floor and turned around. Yeah. A spiral. Facing one corner of the room, Evelyn had started disrobing while turning in a slow circle, releasing her clothes in a nearly circular, doughnut-shaped pile. Coat, then scarf, gloves, jacket, shirt, bra, boots, dress pants, leggings, and undies, dropped in that order. "Except . . . ," Liz said, studying the clothing, "there's only one boot."

Cia, who had been watching, walked slowly around the room, checking corners. Her hands still in her pockets, she opened the door beside the bath to reveal a huge walk-in closet. She flipped the light switch, illuminating the rows of designer clothes, arranged by color and season. "What kind of boot?" she asked.

Liz bent and studied it. "Christian Louboutin, a five-inch-spike-heeled black suede boot with fringe down the back seam. Size six and a half. A right boot." Liz almost smiled, feeling her sister's desire through the air and the twin bond. Cia loved boots. Like, really *loved* them. It was a miracle she hadn't worn her boyfriend's gift until today. She owned dozens of vintage boots, which took up most of the closet floor in their rental house. And they both wore size six and a half.

"No single left boot in here," Cia said, "by any designer." The light clicked off.

Liz tilted her head, studying the fringed boot and the floor beneath it. "There's something under it." Using only the fingernails of her forefinger and thumb, Liz lifted the boot and knelt to see the floor. Beneath the boot, there was a small spatter of . . . dried blood. The drops were so tiny she might have missed them had she not looked extra closely. But blood could mean either foul play or black magic used against the missing woman. And either one would mean that this was a police case—local human law enforcement or PsyLED, the Psychometry Law Enforcement Division.

They would have to give the money back. Liz drooped. She had, unconsciously, already made plans for that money.

Cia said, "Got something here."

Liz looked up and found her sister standing in front of a glass case that displayed collectibles, expensive stuff like bronze statues and porcelain figurines. Cia was holding a short black ribbon, and from it dangled a small lacquered figure about an inch high.

Even from where she knelt on the floor Liz could tell it was black magic. Blood magic. Liz looked back at the spatter. Softly, she said, "Damn."

"What?" Layla asked.

The twins looked at each other, communicating silently.

"*What?*" Layla demanded, a note of panic in her voice. The goat under her arm bleated in fright and pain; Layla relaxed the grip she had on it and set it on the floor. The baby goat thundered off on unsteady legs, its little hooves a tattoo of noise as it raced out of the room and down the hall. Probably scuffing the expensive wood. Evelyn would have a cow—to go along with her daughter's goat. If she lived to see it.

"Tell me," Layla said, calmer.

"You know how we said we don't do blood magic?" Cia asked.

Layla nodded, drawing the lapels of her leather coat closed over her chest.

"Well, this is blood magic," Cia said. To Liz she added, "Carved horn. It looks like a set of tiny carved elk horns, layered with blood from past workings."

Liz set the boot back where she had found it and stepped out of the circle, orienting herself to the north by feel and the position of the sun beyond the windows. The figurine case was on due north and matched the exact spot where Evelyn had started to disrobe. As if the figurine case were the number twelve on a clockface, Liz moved clockwise through the room. At about two o'clock, she found another of the little charms, this one tacked to the back of a dainty upholstered chair. She lifted the charm by its ribbon, just as Cia had done, and studied the carved figure. "This one's a tiny knife, carved from old bloodstained ivory."

"What does it mean?" Layla demanded, her voice cold.

Cia moved to the number five on the clockface and lifted another charm. "This one is an owl, some kind of stone."

"Bloodstone," Liz said with a glance, feeling the stone resonate with her own magic. She took the next point, between seven and eight. There she found and lifted a charm that looked like a tooth. She held it in the light at the window and said, "A wolf tooth. A real one."

Cia nodded and moved to the number ten. This charm, unlike the others, wasn't hanging from a thin black ribbon. It was nestled in the pile of expensive jewelry Evelyn had been wearing. "Ivory again," Cia said. "Probably walrus. It's scrimshaw, attached to her bracelet with a silver link."

It all fit. And it was all bad. "The boot's in the middle of the pentagram. There's a splatter of blood under it."

"Middle of *what*?" Layla asked. "How did you know where to find those things?" Inherent in her question was the accusation that the Everhart witches had put them there.

"They were on the points of a pentagram, the geometric shape that allows a witch coven to contain their power and safely do workings," Cia said. "Once you discover the north point of the five-pointed star, you can find the rest based on the angles and the size of the working space."

"High school geometry," Liz said softly, remembering that Layla had been in their geometry class. The twins had excelled at geometry. Layla, not so much.

"The charms have nothing in common," Cia said, "except the fact that they seem to have old blood on them. That lack of similarity of matrix—meaning that some are biological items that an earth witch might use, and some are stone—combined with the old blood, and the fresher blood in the middle, suggests that a blood witch set up a conjure in this room and triggered it."

"Your mother didn't run off," Liz said. "Or at least not of her own free will."

"Your mother was kidnapped by a practitioner of the black arts," Cia said grimly.

"With a spell," Liz said. "And if we're reading it right, she was taken from the middle of this room."

"*What?*" Layla said, pulling her coat tighter, the seams stretching, her face white. "Like, transported out? Like *Star Trek*?" Her voice rose. "You can *do* that?"

"*We* can't," Cia said.

"And we've never met a practitioner who can."

"The police won't believe it," Cia said.

"No. But Layla will need to tell them. Get them back here, get them working a kidnapping case with witchcraft elements. They'll call PsyLED and get someone in here to read the room with a psy-meter."

"PsyLED? How long will that *take*?" Layla asked, seeming to understand that it would take far too much time. That her mother might not survive long enough for law enforcement to find her.

"We could do a finding," Cia said with a faint shrug, holding Liz's gaze, "like we planned."

"It just won't be easy." Liz pointed to the clothes on the floor. "But only the left boot is missing. She was likely wearing them both when she was taken."

"We could find the left boot with the right one. Give the cops something to go on."

"Or figure it out before they even get started on the case." The twins turned to Layla as one and said, almost in unison, "It's up to you."

"What's up to me?" she demanded.

"If we take the boot and keep working to find your mom," Cia said, "or return your money and let the cops take over."

Layla looked back and forth between them, her breath coming too fast between perfectly parted lips. "I guess my mother stands the best chance of being found with both the police and you working to find her." On that happy note, the goat raced back down the hallway and skittered to a halt in front of Layla, her hooves dancing.

Her diaper filled the room with goat-poop stink.

Layla gagged softly.

Cia giggled.

The sisters couldn't do the finding inside the house, not without both contaminating any remaining magical energies left over from the blood-magic spell and also maybe having their own working skewed or corrupted by the black magic. More magic on the scene would tick off any PsyLED investigator. It might also alert the blood-magic witch. To be safe, the twins had to start somewhere else, which meant interviews, phone calls, and computer research. They had seen Jane Yellowrock track down a missing person. They had an idea of basic electronic investigative methodology, if not access to the specialized databases that the security professional used.

Rather than further contaminate a crime scene, the girls retired to Layla's exquisite three-bedroom Weirbridge Village apartment. It was one of the luxury corner units, and like Layla herself, the apartment was elegant and refined. Unlike her mother's place, Layla's home looked lived-in, yet was still spotless. Early training in perfection had paid off in a neat freak.

Though painfully worried about her mother—or maybe to keep occupied—Layla served them colas and pita chips and Brie with fresh grapes on the side. And gave them access to her electronic tablets and an older laptop and her phone while her stinky goat raced around the apartment on tap-tapping hooves that had to be driving the people on the floor below crazy.

Between talking to Layla, talking to Evelyn's office assistant (in a phone call placed by Layla when they asked), and doing a bit of Internet research, the Everhart sisters discovered quite a bit. In just ninety minutes, they had a good solid lead on where to cast their working.

The property development firm that Evelyn worked for—Mayhew

Developments—specialized in turning mountain properties into ski resorts, hotels, and vacation retreats. According to the county planning board, Evelyn was in the middle of helping her boss to develop some of his family's property north of Asheville into what was expected to be his signature project—upscale, exclusive, lavish.

According to the assistant, the property had been in the Mayhew family for nearly 120 years, and once actually boasted a town, Mayhew Downs. All that was left of the town today were a few foundation stones and a graveyard. And, most important, the property was the last stop Evelyn had made on her way home the evening she disappeared.

"That has *bingo* written all over it," Cia said.

"So you'll go to the property," Layla said, sounding uncertain.

"Yeah, and you'll call PsyLED," Liz said, eating the last grape, "and then the local cops again. Tell PsyLED that you've called the cops, and tell the cops that you called PsyLED. Competition will make them more likely to get in there fast."

"When?" Layla asked. At the twins' uncomprehending expressions, she said, "When do you go to the property? To do the working?"

"Dusk," Cia said.

Liz thought about the season and the moon cycle and realized that the moon would be over the horizon at dusk. Cia would be at her strongest then. "Yeah. We need to be on-site an hour before that." She pulled her cell, checked the time, and said to Cia, "Which means we need to leave now." To Layla she said, "We'll call when we know something. It might be just a directional thing or it might be a firm address. Or it might not work at all."

"Okay. I'd rather go with."

"No," the twins said in unison.

"No observers," Cia added. "Makes us nervous."

The mountain view was spectacular through the bare branches, but the cold wind barreling up the steep slope was cutting. They weren't wearing heavy clothes, but like with most mountain dwellers, their vehicle emergency supplies included small blankets, which they wrapped around their shoulders while they surveyed the site, and an extra pair of sneakers and sweatpants, which Cia pulled on under her dress. The dress, sneakers, coat, purple sweats, and green plaid blanket looked moderately ludicrous, especially with the hot pink backpack on her shoulders, strapped over it all. Not that Liz would say so.

There weren't many undeveloped places left around Asheville, especially not with so much open acreage. The nearly six hundred open, unforested acres were obviously perfect for a ski slope, and the old town would be rebuilt with classic rentals for boutiques, shopping, and restaurants. The small graveyard would be an attraction for people on romantic walks or more energetic hikes.

"Doesn't it strike you as strange that this hasn't been developed already?" Cia asked.

"Yeah. Kinda weird." Liz pulled her blanket close against the cold wind and eyed the foundation stones and mostly rotten boards peeking through the weeds. "This property has been in his family for over a hundred years. Mayhew could have been making good money on it all this time, and yet he let it sit here, unused." She pointed to an open area with a flat space between the young trees. "That looks like a good spot. Ground looks smooth and not very rocky. No trees, nothing to get in the way of making or holding a circle."

Cia checked the tree height and the position of the horizon. The moon was just starting to rise and the daylight was going. "Okay." She struggled out of the backpack and set it in the middle of the open space. Liz found a sturdy stick and jammed it in the ground in the center of the clearing. Tying a ten-foot length of string to the branch, Liz held the other end and walked a near-perfect circle, dragging one heel in the soft loam. Then she cut the string in half and walked a smaller circle. Building circles in the earth was second nature to a stone witch, but with Liz's ribs still healing, the twins had switched their jobs around. Liz could start a circle, but when they had to dig a trench into the earth, Cia now had to finish it. And Liz kept her dismay at no longer building the circles in their entirety to herself.

Half of being a witch was knowing the math. Half was practice. Half was gift. And half was instinct. At least that was the way it worked being twins and having four halves. When they had come into their gifts, at puberty, within two days of each other, the sisters were painfully surprised to discover that they had different gifts. Liz's gift had awakened two days before the full moon, and she was drawn instantly to the rock garden behind her sister's trailer home. Not for the plants but for the stones.

Granite from the skin of the mountain had formed a large nodule there, and Molly, an earth witch, had carried in soil and planted the rocky area with native plants and ferns. Liz walked out of her sister's small trailer and stretched out across the rock as if sucking power right out of the mountain.

Three nights later, at the height of the full moon, Cia had been taken by her own gift. Her transition was more difficult. She crawled out of bed and disappeared. The next morning, Molly called in Jane Yellowrock to find her. Jane discovered Cia sitting in the middle of a stream on a downed tree, staring up at the night sky, transfixed by the waning moon. She had been scratched, bruised, had two broken toes, and was badly dehydrated, still caught in moon madness. Over time Cia had gained more control over her attraction to the moon and the power that flooded her when it was high in the sky. Well, usually. Liz still sometimes found her outside, staring up at the sky, but she was more often wearing slippers and a warm robe.

It had taken the twins months to come to terms with their very different gifts, but now they worked together like the gears of a clock (even when their jobs changed because of health issues), meshing their powers seamlessly.

With a small foldable shovel that she kept in the backpack, Cia scored the circles deeper, cutting them into the earth, while Liz found true north and put a lantern there—once Cia's job. Any candles used outside would be extinguished, but the special hurricane lantern (with one mirrored side to increase and direct the light) was made to survive high winds. Liz lit the wick with a match, turned it so the flame was pointed toward the center of the circle, and placed cushions on the cold ground, then took the one that faced away from the horizon and the rim of moon. As she waited, she unbraided her hair and let it fall to her shoulders. Unlike Cia, Liz hadn't dyed her hair, going instead for blondish streaks. Identical twins didn't have to be totally identical.

Cia finished building the circles and sat across from Liz, facing the rising moon and letting her own hair down from the chignon. She closed her eyes and breathed as the moon's power refreshed and filled her. Liz took off her gloves and dug into the earth, placing her hands into the skin of the mountain, sending her gift penetrating deep, searching for great stones in the heart of the mountain, stones she could use to focus her gift.

There were many here, broken and fractured and split, and others whole, rounded, and solid, made of magma that had pushed up and cooled. They were rich with power, energies so strong that they seemed to reach up and sizzle into her bones. Liz took a deep breath and the power flowed into the healing spell that Cia had set in place. Instantly the residual pain in her ribs was . . . gone. "Whoa," Liz breathed.

When they were both settled, Cia opened the backpack and handed Liz her necklace—forty-two inches of large, polished nuggets strung on heavy-duty beading wire. Liz placed the necklace over her head and wrapped it around her neck, doubling it. Cia did the same thing with her own necklace, one made from moonstones that had been left out in the night air to charge with moon power. Both necklaces were new, and the twins were still getting used to them. Their old ones had been destroyed in the battle with Evangelina, when their elder sister had tried to kill them—and nearly succeeded with Liz, when the demon-smitten coven leader dropped a boulder on her chest.

Knowing her twin's thoughts, Cia said, *"Don't,"* her tone stern.

"Yeah," Liz said, shaking off the dark feelings. "I know. Sorry."

"Powering the outer circle." Cia touched her necklace and then touched the ground. This was a simple working, and when the moon was high, they could draw on Cia's power and muscle their way through it rather than do the math. Moon power was useless twelve hours a day and three full days a month, but anywhere near the full moon, outside, with the moon up, magic was so-o-o easy.

"Cuir tús le," Cia said, which, loosely translated, was Irish Gaelic for *begin.* Her moon gift raced from her hands around the outer circle. Power flowed across them both like mist in the moonlight, chill, thick, intense.

Far more intense than it should have been. Both twins gasped. "Come to mama," Cia murmured, delighted. "Oh . . . yes . . ."

Liz took a breath; the moon power flared against her lungs and out through her fingertips, into the ground and the stones below. The mountain seemed to sigh with satisfaction. "What was that?" she whispered, shivering with the might of it.

Cia didn't answer, just let her head fall back so the moon could bathe her face with its power. The circle was strong and heavy, more like what a full-moon circle had been back when they'd had Evangelina to center them and direct their gifts to a specific purpose. The power was so unexpected that Liz might have worried, but the circle was steady, with no indication of problems, like flares or weak spots. She shook off her momentary apprehension.

Night fell around them, gray with newness and soft with the coming spring. The air cooled and the updraft winds of nightfall blew across the clearing, lifting their red hair. It was peaceful, and if they hadn't needed to work, they could have stayed like this for hours.

"Feels good," Cia murmured.

"Yeah. I can tell. Just don't get moon-drunk. We have work to do."

"Mmm. I'm good. Put the boot in the inner circle."

Liz put the boot in place and Cia touched the inner circle. Her moon power flared and enclosed the boot. Liz put her hands into the soil and said, "Evelyn Janice McMann, *a lorg*." The words *a lorg* formed the name of a working that had been in their family for centuries, a working holding the power for a seeking spell in the simple syllables.

"Evelyn Janice McMann," Cia said, "taken by blood and darkness and death most foul, we seek you. *A lorg*."

"*A lorg*," Liz repeated. "We seek to know your place. Show us where you are."

In the center circle the boot slid to the side, up against the slightly piled earth and the ring of energy. Liz opened her mouth in warning. Before she could get the single word out, the boot slid out of the powered circle. *Which was not supposed to happen.* Liz reached into the earth, pulled might from the buried, stony heart of the mountain, and sent more power into the inner circle, firming it.

Cia's brows came together as she felt the imbalance and the resulting change of the power levels. "What's happening?" she whispered.

There was a *pop*, like the sound of displaced air. And the inner circle was suddenly crowded, two people lying in the small space. Liz blinked. And the figures were still there. "Oh. Oh. Ummm, Cia?"

Cia opened her eyes and looked at the circle. She made a little breath of surprise. "Well. Would you look at that."

That was a black-haired woman in a black nightgown, an older version of Layla—without a doubt her mother—and another woman, a copper-skinned woman wearing a dress from the previous century. Or maybe the one before that. They were curled up on a blanket like two puppies, asleep.

"She's wearing a bustle," Cia breathed. "And the left boot we just called for."

"And she has fangs. Big vampire fangs."

The bustled vampire opened her eyes. Looked lost for a moment. And then she screamed. Cia lifted her hands to the moon and shouted, *"Hedge of thorns!"* The inner circle glowed red with silver motes of power. The warding sank into the earth, deep as the mountain's heart, as Liz drew from the depths and pumped more power into it. The hedge drew in overhead, a long oval-shaped ellipse of power, as Cia wove it closed with moonlight.

The vamp dove at Liz, but struck the ward. She bounced off and screamed again, this time a high-pitched keening that hurt their ears. Then she saw the right boot—the Christian Louboutin, its five-inch spike heel angled away, its black suede toe not quite touching the hedge. She dropped to the ground, her hands pressing against the earth, and leaned forward until her nose nearly touched the hedge. "I want. Mine!" She tried to grab the boot and screamed when her hand came into contact with the hedge, its gray/silver sparks jumping out at her.

She looked at Cia and her fangs snicked back into the roof of her mouth. Her pupils stayed wide in scarlet sclera, however, and Liz thought she remembered that vamped-out eyes were a bad thing. Lack of control? A case of the crazies? A case of uncontrolled and unfulfilled hunger? Something bad, whatever it was.

"It bit me," the vampire said, pointing to the hedge. "Make it stop. Make it go away."

Cia moistened her dry lips with her tongue and swallowed. "Can't," she said softly.

The vampire pointed at the boot. *"My shoe.* Give it to me."

"Can't," Cia said again.

The vampire cocked her head at a weird angle, like something a bird could do but not a human. She spotted the human in the ring with her, and pointed to the woman. "She was wearing them when she came to steal my land. I took them and I took her, but . . ."—bloody tears welled in her eyes—"but I lost one." The vamp bent over Evelyn. Faster than Liz's eyes could follow, the vamp yanked the woman into her arms, shoved her head back, and bit down on her neck. And started sucking. On the vamp's feet were a pair of old, tattered, lace-up short boots from the nineteen hundreds. They had once been very fancy shoes. On the blanket beside her were other shoes, all expensive— made with lace, and woven with beads, satins, and tooled leathers.

Liz, still frozen in place, analyzed the vamp and their quarry. Evelyn was emaciated and paler than the moonlight, her skin a grayish hue. Black circles ringed her eyes. Her veins were dark blue in her pale skin, and her tendons stood out starkly in the dim light. She looked as if she'd had no food or drink in days, probably since she'd been abducted. Humans could live for forty-eight to seventy-two hours without fluid. That time period was based on their being healthy to start with, and not if they were being used as a juice box by a vamp. Evelyn moaned, a harsh sound full of desire and need. She was blood-drunk—the chemicals in vampire saliva and blood, and a vamp's ability to mesmerize victims, were working like a drug on her mind. She had no idea where she was or what was happening. She wouldn't be helping to save herself.

And she was caught in a magical trap with an insane vampire with a shoe fetish. In the circle, the vamp withdrew her fangs, curled around her prey, and closed her eyes.

Cia whispered softly, "If Evelyn dies, will she rise as an unwilling, insane vampire?" Liz didn't reply, and Cia said, "We have to *do* something."

Without thinking, Liz said, "Think she'd trade Evelyn for the other boot?"

Cia giggled, a slightly hysterical sound, cut off quickly. She pressed her hands to her mouth, as if to shut down the inappropriate laughter.

Liz shook her head, pushing away the horror and the realization that there was an important truth she had kept from her twin. Earlier it hadn't mattered. Now it did, and Cia would be pissed. Her mouth dry, Liz took the plunge, saying, "We could . . . call Jane."

"She's in New Orleans. She's too far away. We need to figure out who the vamp is and who to call to take care of this. Unwilling feeding, kidnap. It's got to be against vampire law."

"No. Jane's in town. She's here."

Cia's eyes found her across the circles, the sleeping vampire, and her victim. "What did you say?"

"I said, Jane's in town. For the inquiry into Evangelina's death."

Cia's hair rose in an unseen wind. At the sight of it, chills ran down Liz's arms and into the ground through her icy fingertips. "And you didn't think I needed to know this?" Cia asked, her words low, full of threat.

"Do you remember taking the heavy dishpan out of my arms this morning?"

"*What?* What does that have to do with anything? I took it because you're still weak."

"And right now the moon is full. And you're more powerful but less stable. So, just like you took the dishpan, I kept the news off and you busy so you wouldn't have to deal with it right now. I was trying to help." Cia didn't reply. Liz said, "We've got two problems here. One—a blood witch who helped to kidnap a human female. Two—a vampire snacking on that human female. It's our responsibility to take care of the witch. Jane takes care of vampires. It's her job, and as the Enforcer for the master of the southeastern U.S.A., it's her responsibility."

The power wind lifting Cia's hair settled slowly, the dark red strands falling around her shoulders, which slumped. Her eyes filled with tears as she came back to herself, found her center, and put it all together. "Ohhh . . . damn," she muttered. She took a ragged breath. "Evangelina was our responsibility, but we let Jane handle it. We were cowards. It was our job and we . . . let Jane . . ." Cia took a slow breath, Liz mirroring the action. Liz could almost see the moon power waver across the circle between them. "We let her kill our sister for us."

Cia lifted a hand and pointed at the *hedge of thorns* ward, saying, *"Ní mór fós i bhfeidhm,"* which was Irish Gaelic for *Must remain in place.*

Liz felt the power of the mountain shoot up through the ground and the moon power smash into the earth, securing the *hedge of thorns* ward in place. Her sister's casual use of power when working beneath the moon was a wonderful and frightening thing. But this time it felt wrong. Too potent.

"Something about this place," Cia said, rubbing her upper arms against the chill.

"Yeah. This was too easy."

"We actually transported a vampire and her victim out of her lair and into our circle with a simple *find* spell. I'm good and all," Cia said, looking up at the black sky, "but I'm not this good."

"Me neither." They had until sunrise to figure out what to do. At sunrise the vamp would burn to death. And from the look of her, by sunrise, Evelyn would be long dead.

Thoughtfully Cia closed the outer circle, and the twins walked to the car.

Back at the Subaru, they had a good signal and Liz dialed Jane on her cell. Cia went to work on her tablet, researching the property they were on to see if she could discover why the power levels were so strong.

"Yellowrock," she answered.

"It's Liz." Jane didn't say anything. Jane didn't say much of anything at the best of times, and this couldn't be one of them. "I know we need to talk about Evie, and about family and about . . . stuff, and all, but, well, Cia and I were hired to do a finding spell for a missing woman who turned out to have been kidnapped in the middle of a blood-magic spell, and now we have a psychotic vampire and her kidnapped dinner—that missing human woman—stuck in a *hedge of thorns* spell on the side of a mountain."

Jane chuckled. She actually laughed. "Why is this funny?" Liz demanded.

"You Everharts are . . . interesting." Which was marginally better than other things Jane might have said.

"Fine. You have any advice?"

"Yeah. Send your GPS to my cell. Stay put. Asheville's heir and I'll be there as fast as we can."

"Liz? Don't hang up," Cia said, holding her hand out for the phone. Liz passed it to her, and Cia said, "Jane, we're on a site that used to be called Mayhew Downs, about a hundred twenty years ago. That didn't seem important until our magic was a lot more powerful than it should have been. So I went back online to the history site and discovered that there was this big mystery about the town in the 1890s. The town was fine one day. By the next week, all the inhabitants had disappeared. Which is weird, right?"

Liz heard Jane grunt an affirmative.

"So I looked through all the daguerreotypes on the site and one shows the mayor and his wife—who is a dead ringer—pardon the pun—for the vampire trapped in our circle."

"Hold." The cell muted. When it came back on, the background noise had changed and they were clearly on speakerphone. Jane asked, "How did you get directed to that mountain?"

"By a Christian Louboutin boot, five-inch-spike-heeled black suede with fringe down the back seam. Size six and a half. It's a right boot, and it was left in the middle of the missing woman's bedroom," Liz said.

"Huh. And how do you know the spell that took her was a blood ceremony?"

"Blood-magic charms in her bedroom."

"Hold," she said again. A moment later Jane came back on and practically snarled, "Do not get out of the car. Do not go back to the circle. Send me the coordinates. We'll be there as fast as we can."

The connection ended, and Liz sent the directions before putting her phone away. Outside, the black of night was filled with shifting shadows and a pale gray fog. "Did the vamp empty the town?" Liz asked, as much to hold off the night as to communicate with her twin. "Where did all the people go? And why?"

"I don't know, but I have a feeling it has something to do with why our magic was so strong tonight." Cia reached over and took her sister's hand.

A little over ninety minutes later, Cia nudged her and Liz came awake with a start. "Lights." Three, no, four sets of headlights were winding up the mountain, a line of cars that—even in the dark—looked heavy and powerful. "Is that what I think it is?" Liz asked.

Cia said nothing, but her grip on Liz's hand tightened.

The cars pulled in and parked in a half circle around them; the engines went off and the headlights went dark. There was nothing sinister in the positioning of the vehicles, but Liz's palms grew itchy. Sitting in the Subaru felt vaguely like being at the end of a net that was about to close. Forms emerged from the cars, gliding forms that moved with a predatory grace. "Vampires," Cia whispered.

"And Jane."

The security specialist was dressed in black jeans, a black vest with a white shirt that gleamed in the moonlight, and a silver gray designer jacket. Black high-heeled boots made her even taller than her usual six feet, and her shoulders looked more powerful than Liz remembered. Jane had always been painfully slender, but she had packed on muscle. She looked good. And then Liz saw the holster on her chest and the knives on her thighs. And the silver stakes twisted in her long black hair, braided, upswept, shining in the moonlight.

She tapped on the window and Liz opened the door, letting in the chill night. The twins stepped out and closed the doors. The mountain was silent, except for the sough of the rising wind. The vampires were spread out around them, and Liz once again had the feeling of being prey.

"You Everharts discovered something the vamps want hushed up," Jane said without prelude. "They're willing to bargain for your silence."

The sisters shared a glance across the car. Cia looked frightened and Liz held out her hand. Cia fairly flew around the car to her and slid an arm around her. Instantly Liz felt better. They were witches. They were wearing their necklaces, and the stones were full of stored power. Together they were stronger than this line of vampires. "We'll bargain, but only if they can save the human woman."

Jane looked at the vampires, at two in particular. Liz clenched inside. She had lived in Asheville all her life, and she had never been in the presence of the blood-master or his heir. Now the two stood together, staring at them—Lincoln Shaddock, tall and spare, and his heir, Dacy Mooney, short and round and blond, both of them as old as the missing mountain town. . . .

"Ohhh," Liz said. "The vampire in the circle. She's an old rogue and she got free."

Cia added, "And they're responsible for what she's done."

"Yeah. Got it in one. Or two," Jane said, making a twin joke. "Her name is Romona, and she's deadly dangerous. She never came out of the devoveo, the insanity that vamps descend into after they're changed, and she was supposed to be put down a century ago. Unfortunately the mayor of Mayhew Downs, who was her husband and her maker, couldn't do it." Jane's tone sounded tired, as if she had dealt with this before. "The last time she got free, she killed the entire town. The vamps hushed it up."

The twins breathed in with shock.

As if she had shared their thoughts, Jane said, "But things are different now." She nodded at the line of vamps, unmoving in the night. "They know they can't let her go unpunished. They can't let her maker go unpunished." She nodded to another man standing silent and vamp still beside Dacy Mooney.

It was the mayor from the daguerreotype. It was also the man who was trying to develop Mayhew Downs. *Evelyn's boss is a vampire.* Everything fell into place with a little thump in Liz's mind. It was all tied together. Mayhew had made his wife into a vamp. It hadn't gone well, and he had kept her prisoner for over a hundred years. Mayhew was wearing silver chains at his wrists and neck. If the wind had been right, Liz was sure they would have smelled charring skin.

Jane finished with, "You need to know. Romona is a witch."

Something clicked in Liz's mind and she took a slow breath. Beside her, Cia put it all together as well. Her voice so low it was barely a caress on the night, Cia said, "Romona drained the whole town of Mayhew Downs. But she didn't do it just as a vampire, she did it as a vampire *witch*. She put their blood and their death energies, the power of their souls, into the earth."

"Yes," Dacy said. "Then Mayhew decided to develop the land that she had made her own with the blood of the townspeople. When Romona learned about it, she got free." Dacy shook the chain on Mayhew's neck. "But he didn't tell us. Romona couldn't find him, but she did find Evelyn, his right-hand gal, and she took her."

"The mountain is soaked with blood magic," Jane acknowledged unhappily.

Cia squeezed Liz's hand, communicating the message, *That's why our magic was so strong tonight. We mixed our magics in the working. We absorbed stored blood magic.*

Liz squeezed back, thinking, *It was like the mountain was . . . feeding us. And Jane knows.*

Cia's face went white, but her jaw hardened. "We'll get purified. We'll call a coven. . . ." She stopped. They didn't have a full coven anymore. Not with Evie gone. Not unless they brought in another witch on a permanent basis, someone they could trust with this knowledge. "We'll find a way."

Jane said, "The vamps have a request. By today's laws, now that Romona has attacked a human, she'll be brought to true death. By my hand. And they want you to agree not to talk about what you learned here tonight. They're willing to pay for your silence. Vamps are always willing to pay," she said, her tone grim and tired.

"Like we said," Cia said, drawing on her power. "If they save Evelyn, we'll agree to keep quiet. If they don't . . . well, we'll have to see."

Liz smiled in the night. "And if they think they can make us, remember that blood magic doesn't just go away. I've had my hands in the soil tonight."

"And I've had my face in the moonlight," Cia added.

As one, the line of vamps stepped back. Jane relaxed and laughed, her laughter flowing down the hillside, through the fog. "Good to hear."

Liz realized that the tension she had felt in Jane was gone, replaced by something that was nearly jovial. "You've been worried," Liz said, "that you were going to have to figure out a way to protect us if the vamps decided we might talk." Liz looked at the blond vamp, standing beside her maker and master in the moonlight. "We'd have fried you to a crisp, lady."

Both of the vampires looked nonplussed, and Jane laughed again. "Vamps and witches go back a long way. Vamps seem to have a . . . let's call it a fascination with witches. Sometimes that makes 'em stupid." Dacy frowned at that, but Jane indicated that the twins should lead the way. "Let's get this show on the road."

The vampires stood in an arc outside the unpowered outer circle, their faces white, still, pale as marble statues. The mayor was unchained and stood with them, Dacy's hand on his shoulder. He was holding a Neiman Marcus bag, and tears ran down his face. "Do it," Dacy said, applying pressure to his shoulder. "Do it or I will."

The vamp walked to the hedge, where Romona sat, watching them, her eyes vamped-out, blood on her face. Beside her, Evelyn lay in a boneless tangle of limbs. She was breathing fast—far too fast.

Mayhew opened the shopping bag and lifted out a shoe box. The vamp in the circle was suddenly standing, her hands behind her back, leaning forward in that odd birdlike, snakelike motion that just looked so wrong. Her face took on an expression of sharp avarice. "For me, my darling?"

"For you, my love." He opened the box and pulled out a pair of gorgeous shoes. Cia sucked in a breath of desire. "Those are ruby-toned Giuseppe Zanotti five-inch stilettos, encrusted with Swarovski crystals and beads. They sell for nineteen hundred dollars. Oh. My. God."

Mayhew went on. "I'll trade for them."

Romona tilted her head. "Trade?"

"Shoes for the human."

Romona glanced at the woman and said, "She's nearly gone anyway. Yes." She held out her hands. "Shoes. Mine." Then she pointed at the black boot on the ground. "Mine too."

"Yes," Mayhew said, bloody tears on both cheeks. "Yours too."

"Acceptable to me." And Romona smiled, a nearly human expression, full of delight and a winsome mischievousness.

Jane pulled two silver stakes from her hair and nodded at Liz. She and Cia sat on the cold ground just outside the *hedge of thorns*. They buried their hands in the chilled soil and Cia said, "From blood and death and moon above, release." Everything happened so fast, like photos that overlaid one another, shuffled in a strong hand. The hedge fell.

Romona leaped. Jane whirled the stakes out in dual backswings. Cia and Liz rolled out of the way. Romona landed on Mayhew, thrusting him back. Jane stepped across the falling bodies, her hands coming together and down, like a scissors closing. The stakes slammed through Romona. A shriek sounded, so piercing it was deafening. A death keening. Cia and Liz covered their ears in shock. Blood fountained up over Jane's hands.

The keening shut off. Jane pulled the dead vampire away from her husband. He was sobbing, his anguish human and pitiable. Two other vamps reattached his shackles as Jane hefted the dead vampire to her shoulder and carried the body into the dark. Mayhew raised his face to the night sky and screamed his grief. The sound of a blade chopping echoed. Once. Twice.

Dacy knelt over the limp body of Evelyn McMann, a small knife in her hand. With an economical motion and no flinching at all, she sliced her own wrist and placed it at Evelyn's mouth. The blood trickled in, and Dacy held Evelyn's jaw until the human woman swallowed. Liz and Cia stood in the cold wind, arms around each other for warmth and comfort, watching the second-most-powerful vampire in Asheville healing their enemy's mother. Evelyn reached up with two skeletal hands and gripped Dacy's wrist. The vampire looked at them and said, "She will live. Your word, if you please."

"We'll never speak of this to anyone without your permission," Cia said.

"We'll never speak of this to anyone unless it means the life of another," Liz amended.

"Acceptable," Lincoln Shaddock said. Dacy picked Evelyn up like she was a baby and started for the cars.

Moments later Jane came back, from a different direction. There was blood on her white shirt. "We're done," she said. "The policing of Lincoln Shaddock for his clan is acceptable to Leo Pellissier, the Master of the City of New Orleans and most of the southeastern United States, including the Appalachian Mountains, where we stand. Pay the Everharts." She pointed to Cia and Liz.

Lincoln Shaddock removed an envelope from his pocket and extended it. Cia accepted it. The twins gathered up their belongings and raced to their car to find Evelyn asleep in the backseat. They were halfway down the mountain before they caught their breath. "That was wicked weird," Cia said.

"Yeah. Let's get Evelyn back to Layla and start studying up on how to get purified before the blood magics sink too deep."

"Yeah. Good plan." Cia tore open Lincoln Shaddock's envelope and drew in a slow breath.

"How much?"

"A hundred thousand dollars. Combined with Evie's estate, I think we just made enough money to put a huge down payment on a house, sister mine." They started to giggle. Neither of them said anything about the hysterical edge to their laughter, or what it hid. Not yet.

When the twins left the elegant house in the Montford Historic District, Layla—sans makeup and wearing old jeans—was crying and hugging her mother, having wrapped her in a blanket in the middle of her bed. She was force-feeding her water and Gatorade and cucumber sandwiches.

"Like, who keeps cucumber sandwiches on hand?" Cia said as they walked out of the house.

"People who don't know the value of leftover homemade soup and yeast bread from Seven Sassy Sisters'."

Cia said, "Oh yeah. We eat, and then we figure out how to get the blood magics off us."

"Done." Liz took a slow breath. Her lungs and ribs didn't hurt, not at all. She didn't want to say the words, but couldn't keep them in. "Jane Yellowrock might have saved our lives. If Romona had gotten free and drawn on the blood magic of the mountain . . ."

"Yeah." Cia's tone was grudging. "We'd have been her dinner."

The silence after her words stretched as the sisters got in the car and drove away. Cia finally said, "When you had the rock on you, the rock Evangelina threw at you when she was trying to kill us all? I tried to push it off. I couldn't. It was too heavy. You weren't breathing. Like, at all. Jane—in her cat form—pushed it off. She saved you. I think she saved Carmen that day too. And she did what we couldn't when she . . ." Cia heaved a breath that seemed to hurt. "When she *took care of* Evie too."

Liz knew that *took care of* meant *killed*.

"Not because we didn't have the power or the skills to handle Evangelina, but because Jane *thinks*, instead of being frozen by fear."

Liz blinked away tears and said, "Why didn't you tell me? Now we *have* to forgive her for killing Evangelina."

"Which is why I didn't tell you. I'm not . . . I *wasn't* ready to forgive." Cia turned away, looking out into the night. "Maybe I'm ready now."

"Yeah. Well." Liz took a deeper breath than any she had been able to manage in months. "The blood magic? I think it healed me." She took another breath. "No pain."

"Crap. We used blood magic, just like Evie did." Cia's mouth pulled down. "And it felt good."

"*Addictive* good," Liz whispered. "I can feel the pull of the mountain even now. We are in so much trouble."

"Yeah. But there is a silver lining. The totally cool Christian Louboutins Layla gave me—once I get the blood off them."

Liz erupted with laughter, which was what her twin intended. "*Us*. She gave them to *us*."

"Fine," Cia said. "And the cash. Share and share alike."

"Yeah. Like always. Even a blood curse we don't know how to get rid of."

"We'll figure it out. We always do."

Beneath a Bloody Moon

Author's note: This novella takes place (in the Jane Yellowrock timeline) after *Blood Trade*, after the short "The Devil's Left Boot," and before *Black Arts*. It takes place over two days in February, before Mardi Gras.

"Jane."

I turned to the side and pulled the cell closer to my ear so my partners couldn't see the stupid smile on my face. Deep inside, my Beast rolled to her paws, gathered them tight beneath her, and started to purr. I could hear her response in the tone of my voice when I drawled, "Ricky Bo LaFleur, as I live and breathe."

He chuckled. "You've been in New Orleans too long if you're picking up the lingo and the accent."

Too long without you. But I didn't say it. I was getting smarter. Finally. Our jobs and his *little problem* meant stealing moments when we could, and none of them were particularly satisfying. Rick is a special agent with PsyLED, the Psychometry Law Enforcement Division of Homeland Security, and so some things he can't share. His job takes him all over the Southeast. My job means traveling too, hunting and killing rogue vampires or keeping the secrets of the sane ones, so ditto on the not sharing. It puts a barrier between us.

The relationship—if I could call it that—with Rick was still wobbly: bruised by miscommunication, stupid accusations, big-cat pheromones, and worse, the tattoo spells that kept my were-cat sorta-boyfriend in human form. Oh. And the were-taint that was said to be communicable by, um, *having fun*. Okay, maybe *relationship* was too strong a word nowadays. I pulled my hip-length hair across my shoulder as I walked out the side door and onto the porch. "So, where are you?"

"Too far for a meet and greet. I hope to get your way soon and make up for lost time, if you still have room for me with all the new men in your life."

"New men?" Incredulity laced the word.

"The Younger brothers?"

I'm not the most man-savvy gal in town, but even I detected the hint of jealousy in his tone. "Partners, Ricky Bo. Not hanky-panky."

"Good." His voice dropped into the big-cat-purr register, more vibration than note. "I was kinda hoping you'd save all the hanky and the panky for me."

"I was leaning that way. But for that to work, we need to cross paths sometime. You suck at the boyfriend stuff almost as much as I suck at the girlfriend stuff."

"Soon," he promised, "we'll remedy that. But meanwhile, would you be interested in a side job for Uncle Sam?"

I sat on the edge of the porch, my legs in the weak March sun, feet in the lemon thyme ground cover. The smell wafted up from my feet and tickled my nose. "PsyLED?" The arm of the government that employed Rick seemed more likely to want me on a dissection table than on their payroll. Of course, maybe not. They *had* hired Rick. "Do they know . . ." *About me?* Not said aloud.

"That I'm dating a *statuesque Cherokee*? I told them all about us. They're good with it."

The subtle emphasis on *statuesque Cherokee* told me that he was keeping my secret. Not that my being a skinwalker would be secret for long. Not now that I had been outed to the paranormal world in such a spectacular way—by changing to one of my animal forms in the back of a car—in front of numerous people, including the vampire Master of the City of New Orleans, Leo Pellissier. It was the only thing that had saved my life. But yeah. My anonymity wouldn't last long. "Why don't you do it, what's the job, how dangerous, and how much?"

"You don't have to sound so suspicious," he chuckled, "because this one is boring and the pay sucks."

"Oh, well, as long it's all that."

"And more, Jane. Seriously, though, there have been a number of wild dog attacks west and south of you." His tone changed and I couldn't tell

at first why. "They've been going on for four months with increasing sever-
ity. All on the full moon. All the victims died. Eaten."

Werewolf, I thought, feeling all the joy leach out of me. I had helped
decimate the pack of werewolves that had invaded Louisiana, killing
almost the entire pack to save Rick from them. Instantly I remembered
the sound of gunfire, the sight of wolves falling and dying, their howls
and screams of fury and pain.

My team and I had saved Rick, but he'd nearly died. And saving him
had left him scars, not the least of which were the spelled tattoos the alpha
wolf-bitch had tried to eat from his arm and shoulder. She had mangled
the tattoos badly, and messed up the magic spelled into them, which now
kept him from turning into his were-cat black leopard form on the full
moon. He had been tortured. Raped. Abused beyond sanity, yet he had
survived. Rick was tougher than nails, which was not something I had
expected when I met the pretty boy on my first day in New Orleans.

His tone in the safety zone of cop-speak, he went on. "The attacks
started in Alexandria, and at first seemed to follow a trail leading south,
along I-49." The location and trail indicated that there could be a connection between the decimated werewolf pack and the pack of so-called wild
dogs. Wild dogs didn't follow highways. Werewolves might. "Recently the
attacks have been centered near Chauvin, which is two hours from New
Orleans and south of Houma. And I'm stuck farther north for the next few
days."

I thought about that. Centering in one location meant that they had
chosen hunting ground and claimed territory. However many there were
now, they were likely getting ready to expand their numbers—build a big
pack. And two hours was within the distance I could safely travel from
New Orleans. Long story, but I was bound to the MOC, the chief fanghead.
Only he didn't know it. The job Rick offered was doable. And I was bored. . . .

Carefully, trying to keep from hurting him, I said, "So. Okay. I'm to
rule out . . . um . . . werewolves. That's the job, and you're too far away, and
that's why you aren't doing it. So what about the danger and the pay? I'm
still listening."

"We need you to ride around, talk to the sheriff and the local law, see
what you can sniff out." He meant in animal form but wasn't saying that
over a phone. He added more slowly, "Inspect both the crime scene pic-

tures and the scenes themselves. I've seen the pics, but you might see things I missed."

Gruesome. The pics would be gruesome. But my other half, my Beast, wouldn't be bothered by them. She liked to hunt, kill, and eat her dinner raw and still kicking. And she knew something about pack hunters and how they ate. *Pack,* she murmured deep inside. *Hate pack hunters.*

"Yeah," I said to both of them. "So what else?" With cops there was always more.

"The sheriff asked me personally to look into this." It took a second to make sense of the sheriff calling a special agent with PsyLED.

"And the sheriff is . . ."

He had the grace to sound embarrassed, even if only mildly. "Related. I have family there."

"Reeeeeally?" I said, trying for droll but probably just managing sarcasm. "Old home week?" Rick ignored the tone and plowed on. "Uncles and aunts, my first cousin Nadine, the sheriff of the parish, a good number of other first, second, and third cousins. One second cousin who has a single-engine plane if you need to scout. LaFleur kids in the local schools. Some in diapers and day care. A few in nursing homes up in Houma and Terrebonne. A first cousin who has a hotel south of Chauvin who'll donate rooms." In other words a large extended family, people he cared for. "If you take the job, I'll let them know you're coming. They'll help any way they can."

"Uh-huh." This sounded too easy. Had to be a catch. "How many people are whispering the word *werewolf*?" When Rick didn't reply, I said, "And heading into the swamps and woods with torches and shotguns. And forming mobs with pitchforks and priests."

Rick chuckled, but it didn't sound amused. "It isn't that bad. Yet."

I put it together and shook my head. My words wry, I said, "Your cuz the sheriff called you and pleaded her case, and you pushed all the paperwork through to keep the family populace happy."

"To keep Mama happy, actually."

"Ouch." Southern women were tough as nails. New Orleans women were that and more. Rick's mama was a charming New Orleans woman, graceful, gentle, and delicate. She was also determined, strong-willed, and manipulative—scary good at getting her way. The whole barbed-wire fist in a velvet glove, or maybe pearls, pink pumps, and a horsewhip, or, worse, crinolines, debutants, and shotguns. Take your pick, that was his mother. I'd spent a week or so getting to know his family when Rick and I first started hanging out. His mama scared me.

"How many do we think there are?" I hedged. "Werewolves." Not mamas. Fortunately there was only one of those.

"Maybe three. From the pictures and paw prints. One or two small, and one . . . big. Real big. I don't want to say more because I want you to draw your own conclusions.

"You're not to take them on," he said. "That's not the job. All we want is for you to rule out or confirm weres. Then, if you have time, see if you can determine a general direction or location. I'm thinking a day. Two, max. And PsyLED will pick up expenses and pay a stipend and—"

"I have a contract for this stuff," I interrupted. "I'll fax it to you. We can dicker. But there *will* be a contract, and liability *will* be covered by Uncle Sam. Flat fee and all expenses. And Leo has to vet it." Leo was my boss, but he didn't really *have* to approve the job. It was entirely up to me. But I wanted all my bases covered if I was going to accept a contract with PsyLED.

I could hear the smile in Rick's voice when he gave me a fax number. "I'll push it up the hierarchy and get back to you ASAP. Thanks, darlin'." The call ended.

Darlin'? Where had that come from?

I walked back into the house. In the living room, Alex was bent over a bunch of screens, incorporating all of them into one huge touch-screen computer that would eventually cover an entire wall, his straggly hair hanging in tight curls, hiding his face. Alex was the tech guy for our security company, also known as the Kid for various reasons.

His brother Eli was standing in front of the wide-screen TV, a forty-five-pound hunk of iron disguised as a hand weight in his left hand. He was watching the news—CNN, NBC, and Fox in three corners of the screen, and a local station on the fourth, as he did reps. Ten reps with each arm, his dark skin glistening with a thin sheen of sweat, his muscles bunching and relaxing, his workout clothes sweaty and sticking to him. He'd been at it awhile and he looked good. Eli was a totally buff former Ranger who ate only healthy food in healthy portions, and who exercised and trained daily. Like all day. As if Uncle Sam's army might call him back any minute to fight a war, and he wanted to be ready. Eli didn't have a nickname. Yet. Or maybe never. Some people just didn't need one.

"You looking at my butt, babe?" Eli asked, without turning around.

"I'm not your babe. But it's a nice butt," I said. Without raising his eyes, Alex made a gagging sound. Eli tilted his head to me, giving me his version of a wide grin—lips moving a fraction of an inch, a hint of his pearly whites. Expression-wise, Eli was a minimalist all the way. "It is," I said.

"Babe, I *know* my butt is good. Real good. But I'm taken. Keep the eyes off my butt."

I grinned at him and cocked out a hip, waggling the cell at him. "Yeah, I know. No poaching on Syl's territory. But I could take her, you know. I could." Sylvia Turpin was his hunny-bunny, and also the sheriff of Adams County, out of Natchez, Mississippi.

"Chick fight," the Kid muttered, and I could hear the laughter in his voice. I decided to stop the teasing before we all started trying to outsnark each other.

"YS might have a job," I said. YS came out *Wiseass*, which was our current nickname for our security company, more formally known as Yellowrock Securities. I let my grin widen. "With PsyLED."

"No sh—way," the Kid said, lifting his head, his eyes bugging out. Eli went still, his left arm frozen midcurl.

I raised my eyebrows. "You lost count, didn't you?"

Eli frowned. "That was just cruel, babe. Cruel."

I laughed. "Yeah, now your arms will be all lopsided. When you finish pumping up and showering, we can talk about the job. Meanwhile, Kid, e-mail Rick LaFleur our standard short-term, hunting-only, no-termination contract, and the liability one and"—I waved my empty hand in the air to suggest my uncertainty—"something to cover us having to kill supernats to protect the human populace in any life-threatening, emergency, crisis, legal-mumbo-jumbo situation. And whatever else you think we need." The Kid had taken over the company paperwork and instituted files' and files' worth—various contracts, disclaimers, exclusions, standard expenses, and even a rider list (things the customer had to provide for us to do a job), all in legalese. Reams of the stuff. Ten times what I used to have as a one-woman company. He was a teenage mutant ninja geek, and he was worth his weight in gold, even at today's rates. I rattled off the fax number. Eli headed upstairs to shower, muttering under his breath about cruel women.

I got my old laptop and did a sat-map search for Chauvin, Louisiana. It was an odd little place by mountain standards, mostly a lot of water, a lot of swampy ground, a lot of weird canals going everywhere and nowhere, and most of them looking unused, some flatland along Highway 56, and less lining Highway 55. The city stretched out along the two parallel roads, hugging them like lifelines, which they probably were during hurricane season.

Chauvin was in Terrebonne Parish, the sheriff's office in Houma, north of Chauvin. So far as I could tell, Chauvin had no independent police and depended on the sheriff for law enforcement. There was no public airport closer than New Orleans, no hospital in Chauvin, and most of the parish social life seemed to take place in Houma. So I'd start out there. Assuming I took the job.

Eli trundled down the steps, the scent of vanilla preceding him. The shampoo had been a prezzie from his girlfriend, and Alex had razzed him unmercifully about how sweet he smelled and how his old Ranger buddies would think he was pretty. Neither man was homophobic, and Eli took the teasing well, which all was a sign of how important his relationship with Syl was. He rounded the corner wearing only jeans and a T-shirt slung over one shoulder. *Sweet mama, he looks good.* And he knew it, flaunting it. *And I have been too long without Ricky Bo.* I just shook my head as he opened the fridge and pulled out a container of boiled, peeled eggs.

"Details," Eli said. He stuffed a whole egg in his mouth and dropped into a chair, chomping with exaggerated jaw motions.

I told him all I knew about our job and said, "I'll stick a bag in the SUV and head out. I'll text you with the hotel and where to meet up."

Eli had eaten three eggs while I talked, and stuffed a fourth one in his mouth as I walked off. Over my shoulder, I said, "One thing. If those eggs give you gas, I will *not* pay to have the hotel room fumigated."

Alex groaned and snorted with laughter behind me. "His egg farts are enough to gag a goat."

"Yeah, you should worry about that, Kid," I said. "You'll be sharing a room with your brother."

"Aw man. No private rooms? Gimme that box of eggs. Give it to me." There were sounds of scuffles, muted screams, and laughter behind me, and I was pretty sure Eli gave me an obscene hand gesture, but I didn't look back to be sure if the guys were really killing each other or not. It took effort to live with two men, and part of that effort meant treating them like brothers, crudities and all. And besides, Eli did get awful eggy flatulence, and he had been on an egg protein kick for weeks.

Weapons locked into the special compartment and a satchel of work clothes tossed in the back of the SUV along with all the special equipment I might need in a were-hunt, I helmeted up and zipped up my winter riding leathers. No one who had lived in the Appalachian Mountains would call the temps cold, but the air was always wet. What some locals called humid in summer was just damp and miserable in winter. Unpleasant most anytime.

Eli—who was truly a jack of all trades—had become a pretty good Harley mechanic. Just last week we had taken the carb apart and cleaned it, replaced the plugs and checked the points and spacings, made sure the battery was working well and that the fuel lines were flowing. I had noticed it took more general maintenance to keep a bike running smoothly in the humidity of the Deep South. Dense, wet air is hard on engines, and thanks to Eli's expertise, Bitsa was in excellent working condition as I took off on her, the engine a dark snarling purr between my thighs.

But even with a smoothly running bike, riding a hog in Louisiana is a challenge. The roads are ribbed because their surfaces expand and shrink, and because the ground beneath them is marshy, with a high water table. By the time I got to Houma, I was vibrating all over and my hands were swollen like the hands of a jackhammer operator, so I stopped for a late lunch just outside town. After a fried soft-shell-crab po'boy and a huge vanilla shake, I cleaned up in the restaurant bathroom before I went to visit the sheriff. She was Rick's first cousin, and I wanted to be presentable. I even put on lipstick, the bloodred I preferred, and rebraided my hair.

Like a lot of places in the South, everything important to a town—except for grocery stores—is within walking distance, having been built back when walking was the poor man's transportation method of necessity, if not of choice. Churches, graveyards, lawyers' offices, restaurants, specialty shops, businesses, hair and nail salons, antiques shops were cheek by jowl with parish offices, farm bureau offices, and corporate offices. There were Porta-Potties on street corners and men in construction clothes, most of the workers looking Latino—part of life in this part of the world, so close to the gulf and Mexico. The place smelled of water, but different from New Orleans. There, the scent hinted of power and sometimes I thought I could almost *feel* the force of the Mississippi moving so close by. Here I still smelled the salt of the gulf and the brine of the swamps, but I also got the lazy, sunbaked, rotting-vegetation scent of marsh, and the smell of slow-flowing water. *Languid* was the word that came to mind.

And the food scents filling the air from deep-fat fryers and ovens and stovetops smelled equally of Mexican and fish, different from New Orleans. And here there was no overreaching stink of urine and vomit, scents I had come to ignore most of the time in the party city of the South. The air smelled cleaner. Slower. Easier.

The sheriff's office and the tax collector were in the same white, two-story building where I parked Bitsa under a tree and entered the front doors. I was stopped by a guard, a big-bellied man of about sixty, with a gun and an attitude. He hooked one hand over the butt of his gun and the other into his belt and stepped in front of me as I entered. "Hold on there, little lady," he said to me. "How can I help you?" He smelled of chewing tobacco and his teeth were stained dark brown. He was going bald on top and trying to disguise that fact with a futile comb-over from just above his left ear.

I chuckled and said, "Little lady? Really?"

He squinted at me as if checking to make sure he had gotten my gender right. "What else I'm supposed to call you?" he asked, his eyebrows coming together. I looked like a motorcycle mama in my leathers, and my skin was dark, like a *furriner*, so I knew why people didn't want to let me in. But really. *Little lady?*

I didn't bother to enlighten him on the modern forms of address. When I was growing up in the children's home, it was called throwing pearls before swine to try to explain manners or etiquette and simple basic pleasantness to people who simply had no clue. "I'm looking for Sheriff LaFleur. She's expecting me."

"You don't say. Lemme check on that. Name? ID?"

"Jane Yellowrock."

He grunted, looked at my driver's license, and told me to have a seat. Instead I stood, staring at him until he began to sweat. Then pulled my cell and dialed Rick. I didn't give him time to even say hello. "Special Agent Rick LaFleur. I am trying to get into the sheriff's office, and Officer"—I peeked at the man's badge—"Officer Delorme won't let me in."

"I'll call the office. Sit tight."

"I'd rather stand and stare at Delorme."

"Be nice to the locals, Yellowrock."

I laughed and disconnected. About two and a half minutes later a woman rounded the corner. "Dellie, this is the woman I was expecting."

"You sure, Nadine?"

"I'm sure."

I followed Nadine LaFleur to her utilitarian office, admiring the building but fighting off a case of the sneezes. The building was old enough to have a faint, nose-wrinkling stink of mold and dust and age. The sheriff's perfume was strong enough to take the edge off, but was also an additional odor for my sinuses to fight.

I stepped into Nadine's office and took my first good look at Rick's first cousin. She was Frenchy—dark-eyed, black-haired—and stout, maybe five feet four inches of shrewd, narrow-eyed political acumen. She looked meticulous, tough, and competent, giving off a far different impression from Rick's pretty-boy, come-hither personality. Not that Rick wasn't smart and tough, but he hid it well. Nadine didn't try to hide it. Underneath her perfume were pheromones of aggression, anger, frustration, and territoriality.

Nadine was glad I was here but equally wanted me to be gone. She settled on a grudging but determined welcome. Closing the office door with a firm *snap*, she stuck out a hand and gave mine a firm shake before indicating one of the chairs in front of her no-nonsense desk. "Rick says you can help me with the dog attacks," she said.

"Uh—"

"Except I don't think it's dogs. I think it's werewolves." She slapped a stack of files on the desk in front of me, opened the top one, and spread the photographs inside across the desktop. I had been right in my first estimation of what I would see here. It was gruesome. And Nadine was watching me like a hawk for any reaction that was squeamish or girlie. I hadn't taken a seat yet, and so I inhaled slowly as I leaned over the desk, palm flat on the desktop, letting my weight fall onto my left arm and using my right hand to reposition the photos in order of interest: overall crime scene photos together, heads together, torsos together, limbs together.

My Beast pushed into the forefront of my brain and looked with me, though she still had some trouble accepting two-dimensional photographic representations of anything. *No scent,* she thought at me. *No dead meat smell.*

No scent, I agreed. Paper pictures.

Stupid paper pictures. Need scent.

I have a feeling we'll get all the scent we want, I thought back. *Sadly.*

A quick scan of the first crime scene showed me body parts scattered over a small clearing, blood soaked into the ground, clothes bloodied and shredded, a backpack, contents spread to the side. The body had been dismembered and eaten. The age and gender of the victim were impossible to discern: no face, eyes, nose, or lips over the gory skull, no flesh or viscera over the chest and abdomen, hands too swollen by decomposition to guess at a gender. Long brown hair on a chewed scalp. And maggots. Lots of maggots. I *hate* maggots.

Oh, yeah, Nadine was watching me like a hawk.

I lined the photos up the way I wanted and opened the file beneath. This one had sat in the sun for a while before it was discovered. Scavengers had been on the scene longer. There was less to see. The third crime scene, however, was fresher and had taken place after a rain. The black mud had dried, protecting the tracks and physical evidence better than the other scenes. I checked the time stamp. Yesterday. These pics were the ones I needed.

I had studied up on wolves, wild dogs, and other predators after I fought the werewolves, research that would have come in handy ahead of time, though that wasn't something I could have planned on needing. But it was handy now, and I dredged up the facts from my memory.

"Measurements differ on how and who you ask, but researchers with digital bite meters have done testing and discovered that adult humans have a narrow range of bite force between one twenty to two hundred twenty pounds per square inch, or PSI, of bite force." My voice sounded dispassionate, reasoned, and almost pedantic. Maybe even bored. And not at all nauseated. *Go, me.* Keeping my eyes on the photos, I continued. "Wild dogs, German shepherds, pit bulls, and Rottweilers can have a bite force from three twenty to five hundred PSI. Hyenas, by contrast, have a PSI of a thousand, and wild male crocodiles have been measured at around six thousand, by far the highest bite force on the planet. Wolves at play measured in at four hundred. Wolves *eating* have, rarely, measured in at fifteen hundred and can snap their way through an elk femur in less than eight bites."

I turned the shot of the shattered femur to Nadine. "I'm guessing this wolf bite was upward of twelve hundred PSI, maybe even higher than fifteen hundred, because I'm not seeing but two bite marks, which means he snapped it like a twig."

I pushed the skull pictures to her. "The orbital bones are cracked, the jaw was forcibly removed in what looks like a massive wrenching motion, and the skull itself was cracked open." I turned to another shot. "Brain removed." I pushed a photo of the torso toward her. "All internal organs eaten." I pointed to what looked like two puncture marks. "Wolves and dogs share a similar canine tooth length and have the same number of teeth—forty-two—but this one bite mark"—I indicated a set of score marks on a meatless bone—"looks deeper than dog canines. What did the medical examiner say?"

Grudgingly Nadine said, "He suggested the canines of the predator were longer and sharper than a dog's. Maybe two and a quarter inches long."

That was big even for a werewolf. "And?"

"He says there's no animal in the state that has teeth that long except the Florida panther."

She was testing me. Nadine smelled of challenge. Which meant she was holding back on something and was wondering if I'd catch it. I paged through the photos and realized what was missing. Inside me, Beast huffed with amusement. *Alpha woman is playing cat games. Hiding paw prints in mud.* Inside me, she yawned to show her canines. *Beast killing teeth are longer than small cousin called Flo-ree-da.*

Still mostly toneless, I asked, "Where are the photos of the footprints?"

Nadine relaxed suddenly and blew out a breath. "Okay. You know your way around. I wasn't sure Rick—never mind. Here." She handed me another folder, this one much thinner.

I chuckled drily and opened the file to expose pics of prints in the mud, cracked and desiccated, several full of dried blood. Without looking up, I said, "You weren't sure if he sent you some ditzy woman he was sleeping with or a real expert."

"Yeah," she said, her tone as dry as mine. "Women seem attracted to my cuz."

I separated out and placed three different paw prints on the desk. "He is a pretty boy, not saying he isn't." I pointed from print to print. "All these photos have claws in the prints. *Puma concolor coryi*, like all pumas, have retractable claws and most prints display clawless, meaning claws retracted. Yours?"

"All with claws exposed. So. Not a lion."

"And Florida panthers have been extinct in this state for a century or more," I said. "It would be astounding to have three in one place." I tapped the smallest print and spread my hand over it. According to the ruler beside the print, the paw pad was more than four inches across. "This wolf or dog is the smallest of the three, and while the density and water content of the substrate makes a difference in the size of the paw prints, I'd estimate this one weighed in at one twenty. Big for a gray wolf." I pointed to the larger print, which was more than five inches long and more than four inches across. "Maybe three hundred pounds. Gray wolves in this country are big, very big, at one fifty. That medical examiner?"

Nadine shook her head. "He said something about a dire wolf." She shrugged. "An extinct wolf. He's an amateur paleontologist and archeologist."

I went back to the photos and handed her shots as I explained them to her.

"The limbs were disjointed by wrenching, pulling, and biting, the tendons twisted and snapped. The femurs were well gnawed but also cracked open for access to the marrow, indicating that strong bite I mentioned. The pelvic cavity was wrenched apart. I need to see the site to be sure, but I'm inclined to say werewolves, at least three, and one of them a freaking monster."

Nadine shook her head and rubbed the back of her neck as if to massage away tension. Her face and forearms were tanned, but above her sleeve line her skin was pale olive and very much like Rick's. She gathered up all the photos and shuffled them into the order she liked and set them in the proper folders. Then she sat in one chair on the supplicant side of her desk and pointed again at the other chair. It put us sitting side by side. She crossed her legs to reveal a pair of fancy cowboy boots, which I wanted to inspect, but I figured it might be rude for me to grab her foot and haul it up. She tapped the folders on her knee, staring off into the distance.

"Ricky said you have a contract with PsyLED to identify the animals and/or perpetrators and attempt a general location."

I guessed where this was going. "And kill it or them only if necessity or emergency or exigent situation requires it. At which point I get paid a flat kill fee per head. All liability to be covered by the federal government."

"How about if I get the governor to one-up that?"

Ah. Negotiation. I was getting good at negotiation. Innocently I asked, "Meaning?"

"What if the state government and the governor agree to pay for any liability over and above what the feds pay, but you agree to per-head cost for kills?" She met my eyes, hers cold and hard and mean. "Those things killed Mason Walker. He was a harmless, homeless war vet with enough medals to decorate a good-sized Christmas tree. He lived under one of the overpasses in town that cross over the canal. There was no reason for him to be down in Chauvin, or none that I could see. He didn't have transportation, he didn't have money, he didn't have anything to offer anyone."

Except sport, I thought. And didn't say it aloud because sometimes the truth is unnecessary and cruel. Instead I said, "So someone picked him up. Drove him south. Into the woods or the marsh."

"And chased him. And killed him. *And. Ate. Him.*" Her words were harsh, her tone vicious. Okay, so she got the sport part.

"And you liked him," I said gently.

"He was nice. Would give you the shirt off his back. Nice people are few and far between in this world." She slapped the folders onto her desk with a sound like a gunshot. "I want them dead. Not in a jail where I can't keep them. Not in a court system that would just as likely let them loose because they *can't help it if they are this way.* I want them dead."

"And the way to get the governor to do this?" Because in my experience the governor of a state had a dearth of both money and compassion.

But Nadine smiled, and it would have looked good on an alligator, all teeth and killing intent. "Because I used to be married to him. And because I asked. And because he owes me more than money can ever repay and he knows it."

Ah. Blackmail of sorts. Nadine had something on her ex and wasn't above using it. I gave her a figure and her eyes didn't bug out, which I thought was a good start. "Per head." Still unbugged. "Not including all expenses, hotels, ammo, food, lost or damaged weapons to be replaced, all medical costs or burial costs in the event one of my men is injured or dies, all liability costs, and a nice fancy piece of paper that waives any chance of litigation should someone innocent or collateral get injured or killed before, during, or after the takedown. Your ex will be expected to sign a contract and get it witnessed."

"I'll send you the fax number at the governor's office."

"Ricky Bo might get riled at you taking this away from PsyLED."

Nadine suggested that Rick could do something anatomically impossible with himself. I left the sheriff's office laughing, with a promise of a call about the governor's agreement. And the promise of the contracts to be faxed once that agreement was reached. I could probably have gotten the promise of her firstborn if the kid was a big enough pain in the butt, but I had the Kid. I didn't need another. I promised her nothing, except to read any contract the governor marked up and sent back to me. I didn't expect it to happen, but it would be interesting if it did.

Twenty miles later I checked the time and the GPS Rick had sent me. The crime scenes and two wolf sightings were south of the small burb of Chauvin. I made the ride through the small town—mostly a fishing and sports enthusiast locale—and continued down Highway 56 another few miles. By then it was getting close to sundown and I had things I needed to do, like check out the hotel that had been donated and see if it was someplace I was willing to stay.

I checked in at the Sandlapper Guesthouse, the mom-and-pop hotel owned by Rick's family, which usually catered to fishermen—if the fish-cleaning stations and the fenced gear lockers on the grounds were anything to go by. Clara and Harold were nice people and welcomed me like family. I was pretty sure they'd been contacted by Nadine before my arrival, because they didn't even look surprised when I walked in, though it was the off-season and the place was deserted.

The rooms were up on stilts and offered a view of the marsh and open water across the street. It was a lot better than a box hotel. It had ambience. And oddly, a small granite boulder near the front steps. It was painted white with the word WELCOME on it in red, but it was granite and it was possible that I might need some mass, if I had to go after a giant werewolf.

I got adjoining rooms, hoping Eli's eggy gas problem would be over by the time they arrived. I really didn't want to have to apologize to Clara and Harold for the stench.

After checking e-mail, I took a catnap for half an hour as a stray storm blew through, the rain like a mad drummer at my window. When it passed, there was an odd stillness in the room and outside, as if the world were waiting for something to happen. I shook off the thought and dressed for dinner, which mostly meant a fast shower, rebraiding my hair, and clean undies and T-shirt. I was sliding into my Lucchese boots when I heard the SUV pulling up next to Bitsa. And it was weird how just hearing the engine lightened my heart. I wasn't sure when the Younger brothers had become family, but it had happened pretty fast. I wasn't sure how I felt about people having ties on my feelings. It was weird. And maybe kinda scary. The last time that happened was with my best friend, Molly. And she had broken off the friendship. I was hard on relationships and I hated having a broken heart.

I stuck my head out the door and shouted to the Younger boys, "I figure the seafood in this town should be spectacular." I wasn't wrong.

The boys and I still reeked of the wonderful stink of fried fish and shrimp, and fried veggies—onion rings and squash and okra—and hush puppies as we gathered around the small table in their room. The Kid had his tablets set up and my old laptop, and we were studying Google Maps and some sat maps from a source known only to the Kid. I had a terrible fear they were classified U.S. government maps, but I didn't ask and neither did his brother. We were viewing from about a thousand feet aboveground, with the crime scenes and wolf sightings tagged in bright red droplets.

"If this was the work of real wolves," Eli said, "we could trace out a hunting ground from the sites, but since our wolves can drive around . . ." He let the sentence trail off.

"Put dates to all the sites," I said, "and see if they form a time-stamp pattern."

They didn't. The Kid shook his head, his scraggly hair swinging, and mumbled, "We're missing something. What what what?" He opened the takeout container and nibbled on a cooling hush puppy. "Got it!"

Leaving the maps in place, he opened another program and drew lines from place to place, some curving, some straight. And when I saw what he was doing, I laughed.

Only one thing connected the kill sites, and that was the canals. The werewolves were traveling to places most easily reached by boat and water. Canals were everywhere along the Gulf of Mexico, some long and straight as rulers for miles and miles, some curved in massive semicircles, some with a rare zigzag like something out of a geometry book. "What's with that?" Eli asked.

"I had always thought slaves built the canals in the Deep South," I said. "But that looks like something . . . humans couldn't do."

The Kid opened another program and traced one canal, a double canal with a raised area between the waterways like the center line on a road. It entered the gulf to reappear, still in a straight line, on an island out in the deep water. "It's over a hundred miles long," he said, his voice low as if he were sharing a secret or revealing a sacred mystery. "Holy freaking ancient aliens, Batman."

"Do a search on ancient canals," Eli said.

And when the Kid did, dozens of sites popped up, most related to a single site about the canals. He opened six of the sites simultaneously and arranged his tablets so we could see them all at once. There were prehistoric canals all over the world. And the greatest majority of them were right here, in southern Louisiana, Mississippi, and Florida. I got the willies just looking at the numbers of canals and their locations.

The Kid read from one site and paraphrased for us. "Some of them are from the early twentieth-century oil exploration. Probably ones like this and this." He pointed at some canals that seemed to be of the same width. "But some were there when the Spanish came, and they were old even then. Duuude," he said softly, using the word almost as an expletive. "These other, older canals have been estimated at seven thousand years old, from before the end of the last ice age. The civilization that built them was considered to be a worldwide, water-going civilization, back when the oceans were five to seven feet lower than now."

My eyes darted from screen to screen, from miles-long canals in straight lines to what looked like building sites in the marsh, as seen from the air, if the canals had been roads. Like water-going neighborhoods. Eli said, "Huh."

A few screens later the Kid said, "The civilization—assuming it existed—was either destroyed when a massive ice dam in Canada broke and a wall of water twenty feet high flooded the entire U.S., or when the second Storegga"—he stumbled over the word—"methane gas eruption in Denmark and Iceland caused a subsurface landslide six hundred miles long and forty miles wide. That's been estimated to have created a mega-supertsunami that swept west and buried the entire East Coast of the U.S. under thirty to a hundred feet of water. Like . . . duuude."

"So basically, archeologists don't want to consider a geometry-loving, water-going, water-based, monolith-building, higher civilization, prior to the Egyptians, even though there's evidence all over the world," Eli said. He snorted softly. "Worse than bureaucrats." For Eli that was a major insult.

The Kid said, "In their defense, archeologists are academics. They have to publish papers to keep their jobs and funding, and no one is going to reconsider new evidence or old evidence that contradicts what they already put in print and got paid for."

"Bureaucrats."

"Scientists with an agenda. And speaking of which, I got accepted into MIT. I'm looking at a new doctorate. I can start when my parole is up."

The room went deathly silent. No one moved. I forgot to breathe. I had just been thinking about how great it was to have family. Stupid other shoe had just dropped. My eyes went hot and dry. Where was MIT? Up north someplace.

The Kid went on, his voice casual. "I also have an offer from Tulane. They just opened a brand-new computer science doctorate program and they stole three of MIT's top professors to do it." I could hear the smile in his voice, when he added, offhand, "I get a free ride at TU. That's all expenses paid, for you Neanderthals. And I can start at TU this coming fall, even with the parole in place. Just something to think about."

I remembered to breathe.

Eli said, "You little shit."

I didn't comment about language. This time I fully agreed. "What he said." And I swatted the Kid on the back of the head.

Alex laughed without looking up. "You don't think I'd leave you two alone, do you? You'd end up dead without me in, like, three days. Two if we had a job going.

"So. Tomorrow," he went on, "I think we need to take that plane ride Rick told us about and get a feel for logistics. And see about renting a boat. Maybe an airboat, so we can go over marsh."

"Sounds like a plan," Eli said.

"Okay," I said, letting the feeling of relief flutter through me like butterfly wings. "I'm for bed. Let's start early. Like four a.m."

The Kid groaned. Eli just thumbed his phone on and threw himself on the queen bed he'd chosen. "Hey, gorgeous. Guess where I am? Nope. Way farther south."

I left for my room, closing the door between the guys and me. Eli was talking to Syl, his girlfriend of sorts, and the Kid was downloading a *World of Warcraft* game on his tablet. I stripped and fell onto my bed, and was asleep instantly.

Rick's family was freaking everywhere this far south. The pilot, Rick's second cousin on his mother's side, was a Vietnam vet named Sarge Walker, a grizzled guy about sixty-five years old, who met us at his front door just before dawn, wearing camo pants and a beat-up flight jacket that looked old enough to have been to war with the man, and carrying a satchel that smelled of coffee and snacks. He grunted as we introduced ourselves, and grunted again when he pointed around the house, to the backyard. We turned away and I caught the faint scent of magic, as if someone in the house was a practitioner. I was betting that Sarge's wife was an earth witch, a conclusion I drew from the look of the lush gardens. Without magic, it was impossible to keep a garden so green, even in southern Louisiana. And Sarge didn't smell of magic. Just coffee.

And then his copilot trotted up.

The two-hundred-pound tan monster was named Pity Party, PP for short. The mastiff–bison mix (had to be, because she was too big to be anything else) had no manners, and sniffed us each in proper doggy style. No one objected. Though I wanted to swat her nose away, I held very still as the dog took her time with me. I could feel her low-pitched growl at my confusing, mixed human-predator scent, and waited until she decided I wasn't going to attack and eat her master. PP was still wary of me, and I made certain to put plenty of room between Sarge and his protection and me, with Eli and the Kid between us. It was often true that dogs and cats don't get along well, especially a dog bred for war, one who was big enough to give Beast a run for her money in a fight, and a big-cat. And for once, Beast kept her snark to herself and didn't disagree. PP was huge, menacing, and . . . huge.

The airstrip actually wasn't. An airstrip, that is. It was a canal, out in back of Sarge's house, the water a straight stretch, blacker than night, the only sounds the drone of insects and the rare splash of fish. The plane appeared out of the gloom like a white swan illuminated by the rising sun; it looked too delicate to survive a takeoff, let alone a flight.

I didn't like flying in planes. Wings and feathers were different, and I was almost used to the way that flight worked as a bird, the shift of wing and body, the spreading of flight feathers, the angling of wing into the wind, the way my body would plummet when I folded my wings and dove. This was no bird.

The plane was a single-engine Cessna with amphibian landing gear, and the inside stank like PP and fish, a combo that made me want to laugh when I thought about it. The cabin was cramped and tight for four plus Sarge's dog and the pile of stuff in back. Some of it looked like fishing gear, and some of it looked like plastic wrapped up in twine. One seat was fitted with a seat belt harness for PP, and she seemed as at ease in the plane as Sarge was himself, and even more taciturn.

I had never made a water-to-air flight, and it felt all wrong, so I closed my eyes, gripped the arms of the seats, and swallowed my breakfast back. It had been tasty going down. Not so great coming back up. Once we left the drag of the water, Sarge spent several minutes talking into his headset about his flight path and altitude and flying stuff, all of which I ignored, just glad he actually spoke airplane-speak.

But the sight that met my eyes once we were airborne and leveled out gave me chills. This was the way the world had to have looked back at the dawn of life on Earth. The sun was a golden ball at the horizon, the clouds a dozen shades of pink and plum and purple, with feathery fringes of gray and charcoal. We were low enough to see the black fingers of trees reaching for the plane, low enough to see fishing boats leaving the canals for the open gulf, their wakes rolling with the reflected sun. The water below us was black as sin except where it reflected back the sky's pink light and the falling, nearly full moon. It looked bloody—bloody moon, bloody water, blood, blood everywhere, and I couldn't repress a shudder at the sight. It felt like an omen. It was glorious and frightening, and it meant nothing, nothing at all, my brain assured me. It was only the sun rising. But my heart felt different.

The moment we leveled out, Sarge started drinking his coffee and talking to us over the roar of the engine. We got a geology lesson, with an emphasis on why Louisiana had so much oil and natural gas, a geography lesson with the central tenet being the rivers: the Mississippi, the Atchafalaya, the Red, the Sabine, the Calcasieu, and a dozen others, most with Indian tribal names. So much for taciturn, but the chatter did help settle my nerves—along with the sun rising and turning the world golden instead of bloody. I listened with half an ear until the Kid got a question in.

"We mostly want to see the sites of the coordinates of the dog attacks."

"Werewolf attacks," Sarge said.

"Why would you think that?" Alex asked.

"You'll think I'm crazy, I know, but there's stuff out here in these marshes and canals and bayous, stuff no one's ever seen before. Stuff the U.S. government won't let no one near. Places they won't let no one go to no more."

"Like what?" The Kid suddenly looked younger than his nineteen years. Like a puppy, all agog with the world. Like a kid looking up to an idol. I wasn't sure it was real fascination or just a way to get the older man to talk, but it worked.

"We got people who don't appear on no census, got no footprint on any information grid, and who live off the land and the water. We also got people who are there one day and disappear the next. Just gone, like that." He snapped his fingers. PP wagged her tail. "We got animals that scream in the night and leave eviscerated carcasses on the banks of bayous—carcasses that have been surgically dissected and drained of blood."

I perked up. That was sounding like the possibility of rogue vamps eating whatever they could once their favorite food source was killed off. Before I took up working for Leo, I'd made my living killing rogue vamps, and the old pocketbook could always use a positive attitude adjustment. Leo Pellissier paid better than Uncle Sam any old day.

"What else?" Alex asked.

Sarge looked at him out of the corner of his eye, as if to measure Alex's interest, or maybe his level of gullibility. "We got magic. Real magic. The magic of the earth and the sky and the slow-moving water. There's power here, buried deep. And the government is trying to cover it up."

"You mean like ley lines?"

Sarge tucked his chin in surprise. "You know about magic?"

"I know a witch or two," Alex said. "Or maybe five or six."

Sarge made a huffing sound. "I ain't talking about no witches. I'm talking about the rainbow people. The sirens. And the people of the straight ways."

The Kid looked back at me, his expression saying, *Can you believe this guy?* But actually I could. I'd seen a person-shaped being leap through the air once, forming a rainbow of light and shadow, a here-not-here stream of energy and motion that covered the distance in a flowing surge of light-motion-force-time. *Rainbow people* was a good description. Sirens I didn't know about, except for the mythical creatures that sang sailors off their ships and into the sea. Maybe they were the same thing. But the straight ways—they seemed to slide off into ancient geometry and ancient mystical practices, like the Freemasons, but even older. Maybe as old as the ruler-straight canals below us.

I took a shot. "Were the canals built along the ley lines?"

"Not so's we can tell, at this time," Sarge said. "Ley lines are straight lines that connect certain, specific ancient sites, and the lines have to connect three or more sites in a single straight line to count as powerful." Sarge looked over and back at me as he banked the plane. "Only five major lines run through Chauvin, though I expect we'll find more as archeologists discover more ancient sites in Mexico and South America."

"They aren't, like, magical power lines?" I asked.

"Sure they are. But ley lines are not something humans can use. Only witches can use 'em, and the last witches disappeared from here in the early nineteen hundreds."

"Disappeared how?" Eli asked.

"Disappeared as in vanished from their beds overnight. Signs of struggle, some blood in the house, and they were never seen or heard from again."

"Oh." I had seen a house like that. The witches had been taken by vamps and were nearly dead by the time I had found them.

"What about liminal thresholds?" the Kid asked. Beside me, Eli's eyebrows twitched slightly in what might have been surprise at his brother's question.

"Liminal thresholds are different buggers entirely, son. They run in three curving lines across the earth," Sarge said, "but only one matters here. It starts in southwestern Mexico, curves across the Gulf of Mexico to Chauvin. Then it follows the Appalachians east and north." His hand made a curving shape up and down, like what the trade winds might make, but bigger and smoother. "It curves up through New York and Nova Scotia, across the North Atlantic, and back down toward the U.K. There it intersects some ancient sites including Stonehenge, follows the map through middle Europe and down Greece into the Mediterranean, through Saudi Arabia and into the Indian Ocean."

I didn't know what liminal thresholds were, and I no longer had a witch best friend to ask. Fortunately the taciturn man who hadn't even spoken on land was voluble and verbose in the air. "Liminal thresholds are sites and places where the fabric of reality is thin, where one reality can bleed into another. Like physicists tell us, the universes are likely piled one atop another like a stack of coins. You ever hear of that?"

Alex nodded.

"Well, at certain places along the liminal thresholds, some beings can push through from one reality to another, and sometimes they end up here. Near Chauvin. And then there's the vertices," he added, and I figured he was now pulling our collective legs.

"Okay, fine," I said. "But we're interested in the crime scenes and the dog sightings."

"Werewolves," Sarge spat.

He said it with such certainty that I didn't bother to disagree. I'd seen the photos. He was right. "Fine. Show us those." The plane banked again and took us along Highway 56, back south to Chauvin.

The sites were all over the place, one close to 56, one near the end of 55, one off a canal on a spit of land that could be reached only by boat or plane. One was in downtown Chauvin. The others were scattered here and there, with no apparent relation to one another. Nine deaths in three months, here, and more, older ones, scattered along roads heading north. If this had been a mystery story, we would have been able to draw lines from site to site and determine the murderer's home at the site where the lines intersected, but that didn't work. Not here. The only thing the sites had in common was that there was always water nearby, but in Chauvin, there literally was water, water everywhere, on all sides as far as the eye could see.

And then I began to notice another similar feature of the earth and water below us. "Can you graph the sites," I asked the Kid, "and tie them to the biggest ancient canal? The one with two lanes that goes so many miles? And then maybe put them in order along access from that one canal, with little numbers beside each one, so we can get a timeline based on the canal? I know the ones in town—"

"The two closest to town were the first and second ones," the Kid interrupted, seeing where I was going. "Like they were hungry when they got to Chauvin. All the following ones were on the water. And yeah. All on the smaller canals that look like neighborhoods." He traced them with his fingers. "And all related to and accessible from the big canal."

I stared down and down, trying to memorize the world from above and hoping that I'd be able to put this view together with the Kid's tablets and then the actual, ground-and-water-level sites.

"You want to see the sites?" Sarge asked. His tone was without inflection, and he didn't take his eyes from the sky and the horizon line, but I could detect a scent from his pores that said he was disturbed, and far too interested in the answer to his unruffled question.

"How close can you get us?" Eli asked into the silence.

Sarge took the tablet from Alex and studied it for a moment. "I can land near some of 'em. Get you to within a few feet of shore. I keep a self-inflating, two-person raft packed in back." He jabbed a thumb to the back of the cabin, and I figured that the twine-wrapped plastic was the raft.

"Let's do it," Eli said. "Which site first?"

I sat, thinking, as the men discussed landings and locations. It didn't really matter which one we saw. I'd seen the pics both before and after the cops finished with them. And scavengers would have dealt with anything the cops left behind. We wouldn't see much.

More quickly than I had expected, we were dropping altitude and I got queasy again. Not because of the flight. But because of the smells I'd expect to find on the ground. My Beast was used to the smells of rot and decay; she even ate things that were farther along in decomposition than were strictly smart, at least from a human perspective. But . . . there could be maggots hatching from blood-dried ground or from small bits of tissue missed by the cops. I hate maggots. I just do.

We made the Kid stay in the cockpit with Sarge and PP, which he pouted about, but we wanted to see as many sites as possible before sundown. And a two-person raft meant time spent ferrying back and forth over the water if he came. "I promise pizza suppers once a week for four weeks when we get home," I said to cheer him up. His brother harrumphed softly, and Sarge chuckled, but Alex grumbled to silence at the promised treat.

The raft was easy to use but had a musty smell, as if PP had slept here one night. And as if Sarge fished from the raft from time to time. But it was functional, if a little black-moldy.

There wasn't much left at the first crime scene site we visited, which had taken place on the second full moon after the wolves arrived. Even most of the smell of rot had been washed away by wind and rain and the movement of tides, and now there was little more than the stink of distant death, snakes, rats, nutria—humongous rats—and maybe armadillos, which would have been attracted to the insects feeding on the leftovers. And I caught the old wet-dog-that-rolled-in-something-dead smell of a werewolf, only one—a male, of course, since females went into permanent heat and went insane very quickly after being changed.

The second site was much the same, differing only by the smell of alligator. But the third site, which had taken place on the most recent full moon, only four weeks past, was very different. The paw prints and indentations in the mud were gone, thanks to the weather, and the body had been very carefully removed. But here I could still pick up not only the stink of rot but the gender of the victim. She had been young. And terrified.

I moved across the clearing made by death and wolves and many human law enforcement officers and crime scene people, using my nose, and sometimes my eyes, to tell me what had happened here. And by what I saw and scented, we had a bigger problem than I'd expected.

"Eli?" I said. "Those three wolves? Two were males and the other one was in heat."

Eli grunted. He'd heard the stories about werewolves. He understood what I meant. We had a crazy female on our hands, and the bitches were always smart, wily, and inevitably in charge, thanks to the mating, rutting madness that drove a pack with a female in it.

And then I smelled something else. I bent and let my nose guide me into the edge of the rough land, the low trees and brush of the wet world. I found where a boat had come ashore, a scar on the mud, one that extended up into the brush as if it had been pulled high. And from the scents scattered all around, he had changed into his wolf, in the boat, before leaping into the brush.

I said, "The wolf—*a* wolf, maybe not one of *the* wolves—came to the site, maybe back to the site, recently, like maybe yesterday, which is odd. Why would he do that?" I moved to the edge of the killing ground and found his scent stronger there. He had marked his territory only once, against a short, broken tree, as if leaving a calling card. And it was definitely not one of the three wolves who had done this killing. "Eli, we have three wolves killing. And one, maybe, investigating. Or something. And this one was smart. Not a single good track left anywhere."

I found one poor, dried-out paw print, mostly just leaves pushed into the soil, but there was enough to compare against the tracks of the crime scene photos. *Not* one of the killer wolves. It didn't make sense. But yeah. "We have four wolves, three in a pack and one a lone wolf," I repeated. Which, for reasons I didn't examine, scared me more than anything else.

We landed back at Sarge's place for lunch and to gas up, eating sandwiches on the dock, watching him work. The sun was high in the sky, and temps were cool, so there were few mosquitoes and gnats and there was enough wind to keep the no-see-ums away. If the full moon hadn't been near, it would have been pleasant lying back on the dock, sleeping in the sun. Or it would have been if PP hadn't lumbered over and stuck her slobbery face into mine. I had felt her heavy paws landing on the board of the dock, and I didn't react. Just lay still while she snuffled my neck. She didn't bite or growl and I figured it was a form of acceptance, so I slowly reached up and scratched her belly. She flopped down beside me, exposing her underside to me. "You'll never be finished with her now," Sarge said. I figured out what he meant when she head-butted me to keep scratching. Lunch was a nice break from the noise and vibration of the small plane.

In the early afternoon, we saw two other sites before heading back to Sarge's place. One of them had been visited by the fourth werewolf, after Crime Scene Investigations had finished with it, and he had landed on the same side of the small bit of land where the crime scene people had come ashore. He had stayed a long time at that one. He had tracked the other wolves back to their landing site on the other side of the spit of land, where the pack's boat had come ashore. He had marked this site only once too, which just felt wrong for wolves of any kind. I bent over the site and sniffed, pulling in air over my tongue and the roof of my mouth. Eli looked away as I did it, and I couldn't tell if he was fighting laughter at the expression I made or some other emotion.

When I stopped and stood upright he said, "Babe, just a suggestion. Don't do that in front of a date. It's . . . not pretty." When I grinned at him, Eli flipped a hand to show he was *just sayin'*, and I chuckled.

Either way, the lone wolf smelled . . . worried.

Oddly this one had smelled as if he'd been a wolf for some time. He smelled in control, and even when he lingered over a place where the bitch had relieved herself, he hadn't gone into the male werewolf version of mating frenzy. He had kept it in control. And what was even odder, this guy— like the rogue weres—hadn't been traveling with a grindylow. He had nothing to keep him in line, to keep him from killing and eating humans, or turning humans into pack. Our lone wolf was in control of himself and really, really alone.

Over a dinner of fresh seafood at a place called Joe's Got Crabs (this time mine was broiled, with fried soft-shell crabs on the side, with a house-made, Cajun-style rémoulade sauce that was to die for) I explained to the guys what I'd deduced. "This last guy, the lone wolf, has lived here long enough to have bayou skills. He knows the area."

Eli nodded and gestured with his fork as he chewed. "He knows how to approach, how to move along the edges of the kill sites. Even in broad daylight, he'd move almost unseen."

"And he's worried about the other werewolves."

"Worried how?" the Kid asked. I shrugged, and he went on. "Like he's afraid they'll track him? Attack him? Hurt him?"

"Interfere with his standard of living?" Eli asked.

I thought about that one. "Weres used to live in Lousiana. Then they had a run-in with Leo Pellissier and he kicked them out of the state. What if one—I don't know—stayed? Took up residence? Lived among humans without turning anyone?"

"And now his lifestyle is in danger," Eli said, having allowed us to provide potential confirmation toward his own point. He ordered beer for us both and bowls of ice cream all around. When Alex looked dumbfounded, Eli said, "You were a good sport today, staying in the cabin with the dog and the old guy. Figured you deserved a treat."

"I'd rather have a Ferrari, but ice cream isn't bad."

I spent an hour texting Rick, because his carrier didn't offer good cell coverage this far south. Sometimes the government's predilection to pick the cheapest bid on a job caused problems later on. Go figure. Rick made plans to join us, but it would be another day before that could happen, which left me many hours before he could get here. And few hours before the first day of the full moon.

Just after the texting ended, I heard back from the sheriff and the governor. The gov felt that PsyLED would take too long to find and kill the "wild dogs" and offered me a contract. But the wild-dog clause was a problem, legally speaking. With the tentative exception of vamps, supernats and their legal standing had not yet been addressed by Congress. Vamps were already in a legal limbo, with Leo having asked for a status like American tribal Indians had—called tribal sovereignty, making vamps a dependent sovereign nation within the federal government. It would give them a position that was similar to a state in some situations, and similar to a nation in others, with certain amounts of recognition, self-government, and sovereignty. It was a huge legal jumble of problems, which would take decades to sort out, and even longer to implement, all of which made the Master of the City of the Southwestern states happy, because it left him in charge of his people and free to act in any way that led to the safety of the human public. However, no such legal interference had been instituted or started for weres or witches, making their legal limbo even worse than the vamps'. And calling a were a wild dog was . . . wrong. Werewolves were sentient beings.

Yet people were dying. And I was stuck in the middle of the problems.

I copied Leo, my partners, and Rick on the offer and got a single-word text reply from my sorta-boyfriend.

Sigh . . . , it read.

"Yeah," I said to my empty room. Our "wild dog" were had suddenly become a pack of three led by a sex-starved female. Add a lone wolf into the picture, and a state government that wanted in on the kill action, and this was suddenly FUBAR territory. I was not touching this with a ten-foot pole, not until Rick's bosses at PsyLED decided on a course of action. Which might mean we were headed home in the morning. Yet the next night was the full moon, which would mean death for someone unless I acted. Which the legal situation could prevent. This sucked. I wanted to hit something, but Eli was asleep. Which sounded all wrong too. I rolled over in bed and commanded myself to sleep. I felt Beast sling out a claw and instantly I went under. My last conscious thought was of Beast as a sleeping pill.

It rained all night, sometimes so hard it beat against the windows, with lightning and thunder all around, the noise enough to rouse me several times. Mostly, thanks to Beast, I slept through it, knowing that the next three days could be sleepless and dangerous and deadly. Or not.

Sometime during the night, I got an official e-mail from PsyLED, but with the noise outside, I missed it. An hour before dawn, the storm broke, Beast slapped me awake, and I found my cell blinking. I rolled up to a sitting position and discovered that I had an official offer from the U.S. government, one worked out with Leo's lawyers and two congressional committees, approved by the Louisiana governor, and vetted by the president himself, all in just under seven hours.

I had a kill order to take down the pack. And I was gonna get paid big bucks. "How cool is that?" I asked my dark, silent room. And best? No one said anything about the lone wolf, who hadn't been in on the carnage and feasting.

As I sat there, I got a second text from Nadine, the sheriff, with a new sighting location. During the storm the night before, four local fishermen had taken refuge on land in the swamp over near Lake Boudreaux. They had seen two huge dogs and a bear as the storm cleared. Nadine sent both a map and a GPS, saved by the men. I pulled up a sat map and studied it. The sighting had been inland, if you can call the swampy area north of Lake Boudreaux inland, up through an old canal, on actual land.

I studied the site on sat maps and determined that we could get there via boat. I loved modern detecting methods. I got up, stretched hard and slow, and walked to the connecting door.

Banging on the Younger brothers' door, I shouted, "Wake up, sleepy-heads! We got a job with a GPS to start the day. Big enough bucks to buy the Kid a pony for his birthday!" I started to turn away but banged once again, my fist flat on the door. "And I'll need my special equipment, pronto." I sent the proposal and the GPS to them and got dressed, glad I'd gotten some sleep. I was gonna need it.

I was packing my boots and other supplies into a bag when my cell chimed. On the screen were the words Darlin'. PsyL authorized me to area. Officially. Flight landing at NOLA at two. See you at 4p.

"Again with the *darlin'*?" But something like longing or hunger flowed through me and I dropped onto the bed, grinning foolishly into the dark. Rick was coming. Maybe I should have gotten nonconnecting rooms. Not that there would be any actual sex—not with the possibility of me getting the were-taint as a really bad, incurable, untreatable STD—but maybe I should have gotten nonconnecting rooms anyway. Just in case.

I texted back, I may not be me. Fair warning. Rick was a were. He'd figure it out.

Several minutes later he texted to me. Noted. Which made me happy all over for reasons I didn't understand.

Eli knocked on my door, one tap. That was all. One. Mr. Minimalist. "Come." Who says I can't do terse?

Eli entered, geared up for the day, a bulge under his arm visible as he entered, another in the back of his shirt, both of which were nine-millimeter semiautomatics. I knew he'd have more weapons on—a silver-plated knife or two and a few stakes. All that just to greet the dawn. Eli, a minimalist in all other ways, was not into austerity where weapons were concerned. In his hand was my fetish box. He put it on the bed beside me, and for once was unable to keep his curiosity off his face.

Feeling a little uncertain, because I'd never done this in front of him before, I opened the box and rummaged around inside, finally pulling out a short necklace strung with glass beads and wired with canine teeth and three largish bones. I knew what almost all my necklaces were, animal-wise, but some I didn't use often, and this one I had never used.

Trying to sound offhand, Eli said, "You're gonna track in animal form?"

My eyes on the bones, I nodded, letting a small smile form. I said, "Think you can find the most recent sighting place?"

"Does a mountain lion scream in the woods?"

I smiled wider without looking at him. "Loud. Even if no one is there. And yeah. Animal form. One with a good nose and who can swim."

"In gator-infested waters?" He sounded half-teasing, half-appalled.

I chuckled softly. "Most gators are hibernating. Water's still too cold for them to feed." I looked up under my eyebrows. "Sarge told me. Anyway, swimming is only important if I really need it."

"And?" The word was phrased the way he must have spoken in the Rangers, sharp and cutting and demanding of more than just an answer.

"Newfoundland," I said. "I have the bones of a huge black Newfound-land, two years old, who was in training to work with an SAR team because of her swimming ability and because she had an air nose."

Eli grunted. "Change in here or the Kid will want to watch. I'll go get some protein." He left, closing the door behind him. He hadn't asked about the air nose comment, because he knew what it meant.

Some dogs track on the ground. Others over water. Yet others—some very special few others—can track through the air, sometimes for miles. They were the wunderkinds of tracking dogs as far as I was concerned.

I stripped and put the folded clothes into the bag. It was bright pink with big flowers in hot pink, red, and fuchsia, with green leaves on it. Peonies maybe. The zippered duffel had been a gag gift from the Kid, who expected me to retch and throw it away. Instead I'd brought it on two other jobs. And Eli made him carry it while we both cooed about how cute he looked. Mean? Yeah. Probably. But *turnabout's fair play* had been fun.

Naked, sitting guru-style, I adjusted the length of my doubled gold chain around my neck. On it was wired a gold nugget from the first place I'd changed after I left Bethel Nondenominational Christian Children's Home when I was eighteen, and a tooth from the biggest mountain lion I'd ever seen. It was a sort of safety tool, a last-ditch survivor device. If I got killed, and if I had time between my last heartbeat and death, I could change into my Beast form and maybe live. It had saved me a couple of times already, and I went nowhere without it.

I propped a pillow behind me, got comfy on the bed, and dropped into the place of the change. Once upon a time, and not that far in the past, changing into a different shape had been much more difficult. I'd had to calm my heart rate and breathing, meditate, really work at it. Now—maybe because of the times I'd changed in extremis, which could also be called near-death experiences—I could drop into the place of gray energies much faster.

My magic was some active form of quantum mechanics, but I wasn't smart enough to understand it. I just knew how to use it in the same way I could turn a light on without knowing how electricity worked. I held the fetish necklace in both hands as my breathing evened out; I again dropped into the gray place of the change.

I sank deep into the bones and teeth and marrow of the Newfoundland, finding the snake that lives in the heart of all animal cells, the double helix of DNA that skinwalkers knew about and knew how to use long before the human medical research community discovered it.

I let myself flow into the genetic makeup of the dog that had died saving its trainer from an attacker, shot before she could ever use the training she was getting to save more lives. My skinwalker energies rose. Pain shocked through me, sharp as a knife blade slicing along my bones. I sucked in a final breath and . . . changed.

Smells and smells and smells. Snuffled in scents and blew out, dewlaps fluttering. Snorted. Scented in again. I was Beast, but not Beast. Something was wrong. I smelled female human, scent strong and powerful. Layered beneath her were smells of many other humans. Strong, vital, sick, old, young. Many humans. Much smell of fish. Rain. Female human scent was familiar.

Oh. Jane's scent.

Jane woke slowly in brain of dog, stunned, as always, by overwhelming power of scents around me/us. I chuffed, Beast's sound different from New-found-land-dog's mouth. More . . . doggy. *Do not like dogs.*

Beast? Jane murmured into the deeps of mind.

Beast is here. Ugly dog. Tilted big dog head. *Not as ugly as last dog. Good smells. Good fish smells. Feed us? Am hungry.*

Eli said he'd have food, Jane thought back, trying to remember why I/ we were in this form. The smells nauseating to her, too strong, disorienting.

As Jane struggled to get her bearings, Beast stood on the covers of the bed, stepped to the floor, and went to the doorway, where I/we rose on my/our back legs to make me/us taller.

What are you—? Stop!

I snuffled with laughter and tapped on door with claws. Ugly black claws, hard and short and not made for hooking prey.

Door opened. Kid smell swept out.

Lunged inside. Knocked Kid down. Stood over him huffing into his face, drooling on his jaw.

"Holy crap. How can you have dog breath?" Head tucked, he rubbed his head on the floor back and forth as if to protect his throat and get away at the same time. *Stupid prey move. Should attack instead.* Alex Kid shoved with his hands into our belly, making us *oof* out a breath. "Ugh. Get off me!" he shouted. Loud in dog ears.

Stepped to side and chuffed up at Eli. He was leaning against wall, shoulder taking his weight, smelling of laughter, small smile on his face. He looked to us. "Did you sign a no-pets clause on this room?"

Jane took over for us and snorted with laughter. Shook head, like human shakes head. Eli held out a leash. Again Jane shook head. I trotted back to deeps of mind and let Jane take over.

I wanted to say the ambush wasn't my fault, it was a big-cat move, but I was laughing too hard. The Kid's body odor was strong enough to choke a goat—or a Newfoundland—this morning. No more snack foods for him. He stank of the house-made, Cajun-style rémoulade sauce and fried fish and obviously hadn't showered today. Or last night. Ewwww. And then I smelled eggs cooking.

Eli bent and put a plate of microwaved eggs on the floor beneath my head. Like maybe two dozen eggs. And they must have been delicious because I inhaled them—probably nearly literally because dogs don't have a great sense of taste to complement their great noses.

While I changed, Eli had been loading up the SUV and we were ready to go. Rather than stay near the Kid, I licked the egg plate clean, trotted out the door and down the stairs to ground level, and leaped into the backseat. From the seat, I jumped over onto the gear in the very back. And we were off.

The rented airboat was loud. Like really, *really* loud, when Eli cranked it over. There was no ear protection for dogs as part of the rental, so I'd just have to stand it. The craft was a wide, flat-bottomed johnboat, powered by a gasoline engine and a wooden, aircraft-type propeller in a massive cage. It had two bench-style seats, the back one mounted higher than the front one, with the accelerator and the steering mechanism—a long handle that operated rudders—located up at the backseat.

I leaped onto the front seat and shoved Alex off it, forcing him to sit up behind me with his brother on the backseat. Eli clearly had a massive sinus infection because he was able to ignore Stinky beside him. I let Eli strap me into the seat belt, figuring that a sideways spin might slide me right into the water without it. As we took off from the dock, I stretched out on the seat I had claimed, closed my eyes, let my tongue loll out, and took in the wind. It buffeted my facial hair, flopped my ears back, caressed my face, and filled my nose with goodgoodgood smells, and I was in doggy heaven.

Even Beast seemed okay with this form. Inside me she rolled over and lay on her side, eyes closed in enjoyment.

Time is different when I'm in animal form. Minutes and hours seldom matter. There is only now, this moment, this set of smells, all finding places in my doggy brain. A scent dog's brain is wired vastly differently from a human's brain. It's like a huge card catalog, each smell, with its breakdown, root smells, tucked in a different niche or drawer, each interconnected and attuned to memories. But I had no dog memories in this form, so each smell had to find its place. I'd done this before, in bloodhound form, and the experience was totally befuddling, disorienting, and weird. And wonderful.

The other times I'd been in dog form were before I met Eli and Alex, working alone, usually for a single fast bit of reconnoitering. This would be something very different. I'd be working with humans. *My* humans. Like *my* brothers, or *my* family. Possessive, personal, intense. That was the way the dog instincts made it feel. As if the Younger brothers were *my* humans.

In this form, with them present, I wanted to *work*. Despite how great I felt as the sun rose around us, heating the air and warming my coat, no matter how great the world smelled, I felt excitement rushing through me at the thought of getting to land and starting a search for big bad uglies.

Maybe this feeling was why humans had begun to domesticate wolves and breed dogs into today's breeds, because some wolves had wanted to work with humans, had liked the challenge, and because wolves could breed down into something manageable. Maybe. Or maybe humans bred wolves to have something around that fleas liked better than they did humans.

Flea catcher, Beast murmured into my hind brain, chuffing with laughter. *Stupid dogs.*

There was no awareness or measurement of time, except the sun lifting from the watery horizon, until the stench hit me, I sat up on the seat, my nostrils widening and fluttering. *Werewolves.* A pong on the air like rotten flesh, wet-dog stink, a reek like nothing else, especially in this form. I stayed upright, taking in the wind, snuffling and shaking my head when the odors of dead fish and dead carrion—turtle, I thought—buzzards, armadillos, rotting vegetation, were too strong. Seeking the were-scent. I could get used to being a dog.

Beast chuffed, her ear tabs lying flat in disapproval. *Ugly dog,* she thought at me.

The airboat ran up on the ground with a slight lift and change of its center of gravity. I rocked back and forth on the seat, digging in with my claws, and huffed. Without opening my eyes, I took in the site, smelling human males. They had urinated everywhere, used one particular area as a toilet for other functions, another as a fish-cleaning station, pitched tents in the lee of some kind of aromatic tree. They had done a little fishing, a little target practice. I smelled guns and nitrocellulose, beer. Lots of beer. No weres had been here. The wide-bottomed boat shifted again and I barked.

Okay. That felt weird. Sounded weird too. I opened my eyes to see the brothers looking at me. Musta sounded weird to them too. I focused on Eli, who had one foot up in the air, about to get off the boat, and shook my head slowly. He stopped his weight transition, thinking, and put the foot back into the boat. "No one here?" When I didn't respond he asked, "No were-smell here?"

I huffed again, agreeing with his statement.

"Can you smell them?"

I huffed, broke our gaze, and turned my head. We were on a long, straight canal that ran, unwavering, for several miles through the swamp. The stink of werewolves floated down the wind from that way. Eli returned to his seat, started the rented airboat, and backed us off the flat expanse of muddy land. I kept my gaze in the direction that I wanted us to go.

It wasn't far. It was actually within visual distance of the drunken fishermen, just as they had said. I stared hard at the small outcropping of land and—despite the seat belt—wagged my tail at the site. Eli, following my visual cues, pulled up to the shore, and beached the boat. Saw grass grew in bunches here, some taller than my dog form's shoulder, and stunted, weather-twisted trees, with a number of buzzards sitting in the branches. It was hard to estimate in a dog brain, but Beast whispered to me, *More than five birds of the dead. Something large dead here.* It was jungle, reeking with the overpowering stink of . . . *Ahhhh . . . dead alligator and stink of werewolf.* Eli released me from the seat belt and I leaped out to the muddy bank, paws sinking into mud. There was no smell of human, just were—

The attack came from my left. It bowled me over, into the mud, and rolled me into the water. Teeth, fangs like razors, came at me from above. Beast ripped me away and slung me to the back of my mind.

Rolled away from attacker, deeper into canal. Feet found log beneath, not deep. Pushed off. Leaping, rising, slinging self out of water. Screaming with dog roar. Leaping, stretching, *leaping*, hard, muscles pulling. Seeing two attackers. Werewolves. Sick. Male. Smell of were-taint on air. They lunged. Heard gunshot.

Landed on smaller werewolf. Bowled him over. Saw hairless belly. Sank teeth into ab-do-men. Foul, stinky blood, awful taste in mouth. Ripped into belly. Shook head, tearing flesh free. Heard yelps. Dog screams. More gunshots. More than five. Swung head hard. Tore out chunk of werewolf flesh. Spat it out. Bad taste.

Wolf scrambled onshore, wolf claws sinking into mud. Insides of wolf trailing on ground. Prey-enemy-pack-hunter was wounded. *Beast is good hunter!*

Lunged for wolf.

Was hit in side. Lifted. Batted away by paw. Big paw. *Bigger wolf attacking.* Was slammed up. Into air. Beast side rammed into sharpness of airboat. Screamed, yelped. Fell. Wolf-killing teeth/fangs sank into Beast neck. Tore into flesh. Smelled/felt hot dog blood. Was yanked to side. *Painpainpain. No breath. More gunshots. Too many to count.* Bigger wolf staggered. Stumbled. Jaws opened and Beast/New-found-land fell free. Rolled into water.

Beast tried to swim. Could not move. Pain arched across ribs. Sank deep. Water covered head. *Painpainpain. Cannot breathe.* Looked up. Saw through water. Big wolf had gray coat, hairs with black tips. White under-belly. Black claws and muzzle. Big teeth. Biggest wolf ever. Short back legs. Sloping back. *Big. Bigbigbig.*

Dire wolf, Jane murmured into brain. *Holy crap. A dire werewolf.*

Wolf backed away. Carrying injured, smaller wolf in jaws, like pup.

World began to go black around edges of eyes. Beast—I/we—was dam-aged. Was wounded. Blood poured into dark brown water, staining it with blood. Death striking deep.

Oh crap, Jane thought. *We're bleeding. Holy crap. We're dying. Too late to shift! Again.*

Saw Alex dive into water, spindly arms and knobby legs. Water moved in ripples of cold. Felt Kid grab ruff of neck. Darkness fell over Beast.

"You will *not* die, damn you."

Eli voice. Saying words Jane did not like.

But breath did not come. Only blood bubbling from mouth. Ribs cracked and moving out of order. Broken. Piercing lungs. Throat shredded. *Am dying.*

Light began to go. Darkness flickered around edges of vision.

"Damn you! You will *not* die! I will *not* lose another one!"

"Bro. Stop." The Kid's voice, full of pain. "She's gone, bro. Stop. Jane's dead."

Eli grabbed head and swung it around. Stared hard into eyes. Fierce. Lips pulled back to show blunt human teeth. "If you die, I'll fucking kill you myself. *Again.* So shift or I'll shoot you, I swear to God, I'll shoot your dead body full of silver."

We had never done this—shift from another, lesser animal into Beast.

Inside, Jane laughed, sound broken and far away. *We got nothing left to lose. So. Try it. Shift already,* she said.

I reached down into self, and . . . *shifted.*

Eli scrambled away. Shaking his hands in pain. Cussing.

Jane laughed, laughter half-wild and feral. *Yes!* she shouted into mind.

I fell into self. Into Beast. Energies like lightning and fire, and loud, like thunder. Rumbled through gray place of change. Screamed with pain. *Am Beast!*

I died.

And lived.

I lay in water, half-in, half-out. Took breath. Filled lungs. Vomited water out of lungs, onto shore. Gagged with misery and agony. Spluttered water onto land. And breathed. I lay on Beast paws and closed eyes, body half in water of canal. Deep in brain, Jane cussed. I breathed.

Clawed onto land, out of water. Pulled self onto shore. Claws extended. Body, mud-caked. Stinking of mud and rotten flesh. Dead alligator loomed at eye level, thick skin torn open, flesh spilled onto mud. In rushes saw dire werewolf, small dead werewolf in jaws. It watched and growled low. Smelled of anger and confusion, watching big dog that was now big-cat.

I clawed to feet and stood. Screamed into sky. *Am Beast. Have killed pack hunter. Have killed enemy. Have killed werewolf.* Screamed into sky. *Have won!*

Yeah. Go, us, Jane thought into mind, thoughts tasting of sadness. *Attack it.*

I lunged. But bigger werewolf dragged smaller one away. Deep into saw grass. Into shadows of trees. It ran.

I chuffed. *Jane and Beast live.*

I was in Beast form. *Puma concolor.* I looked to Eli and the Kid. They smelled of fear. I chuffed. *Do not be afraid. I am Beast. Will not eat you.*

"Jane?" Eli asked. "Are you there?"

I chuffed in laughter. And I smelled the were-magic of the change. Wolves changing, one still alive. Then smelled second one, smaller one change. Heal. In distance, I heard sound of boat starting, high-pitched, mechanical, electrical. Human sound. Boat moving off small area of land, and into water. Humans did not hear—too far away.

Well, crap, Jane murmured, *we lost them.*

Smelled smell that was familiar. Will find them again.

Well, maybe. Maybe not. We just got bitten by a werewolf again. Jane took over thoughts and padded to airboat. Sniffed blood on boat sides. Stepped over low side and up onto seat. Lay down. Closed eyes.

Woke to hear the Kid, voice on cell phone—metal thing with ears and mouth, alive and not alive. Heard voice on other ear of cell, then another voice. Then heard voice of Gee DiMercy, Mercy Blade of Leo. "Tell me exactly what happened," Gee said. Alex told him about wonderful fight with werewolves. Told how Beast killed one. *Beast is good hunter.* Told how werewolf bit Beast in dog form.

I opened eyes. Sat up on the seat of airboat. Mercy Blade killed rogue things. Would kill werewolf Jane. Deep inside, Jane woke. *What?* she asked. I/we stared at the Kid.

"How soon can you be here?"

Eli took cell and said, "Take the helo." Handed cell back to Alex.

Mercy Blade and killer of devoveo vampires said, "Yes. That I can do. I'll be there soon." Call ended.

I growled low, pulling back lips, showing killing teeth. The Kid backed away, moving slow. Frightened prey.

Eli laughed. Showed white teeth in dark-skinned face. "Not coming to kill you, Janie girl. Coming to heal you of the were-taint. Meanwhile, let's get you into the SUV and back to the hotel for a bath." He unhooked seat belts.

I/we stopped growling. Looked around. Had not noticed where we were. Were back at boat landing near hotel. Saw ess-u-vee near. Thought about humans. Thought about humans with guns, afraid of big-cat. I chuffed. Stepped from airboat and into water. Lay down and rolled in water over rock called cement. Mud and blood came loose from coat. Rolled into water and rolled. Rolled. Stood and walked to shore. Walked to the Kid. And shook water from pelt.

The Kid yelped. I chuffed with laughter, walked to Eli. He raised hair over eyes and pulled steel claw. "Try it," he said. Eli had hungry look on face, as if would try to hurt Beast with puny steel claw. As if he wanted to fight big-cat. Jane watched deep in brain, saying nothing. Waiting. I blew deep breath like sigh. Walked over to ess-u-vee. Climbed into back onto blanket Eli had spread there. Blanket was green and smelled of man chemicals for cleaning. Stinky. Stuck nose into middle. Smelled old blood. Much old blood, Eli blood hidden beneath smell of chemicals. Looked at Eli, reaching up to close door of ess-u-vee. Saw scar on Eli collarbone.

Eli had died on this blanket. Was blanket of warrior. Of hero.

Curled up on blanket, laid head on paws. Closed eyes.

Metal and glass bird with noisy wings settled onto road, in wide broken pavement of old parking lot. *Helicopter,* Jane thought.

Stupid bird. Too loud to catch prey. More like a buzzing bee, but with no stinger. And vomits out live people. I chuffed with laughter, watching as Mercy Blade climbed from bubble stomach of noisy, stinky helo. Narrowed Beast eyes. *Will not ride in bird again. Do not think you can force me.*

I don't. I won't try.

Mercy Blade was pretty human by Jane thinking, small, with long, lean muscles, long hair in tight braid, narrow pelvis, and wide shoulders. Moved like dancer or hunter. Like swan on water. Wore denim jeans and boots and long-sleeved shirt that glimmered in sunlight. Wore magics like cloth layered over body; hard to see real body under magics, but maybe bird form. Blue and green and silver magics in Jane's vision; green and silver in Beast-vision. Gee carried sword on belt, on side, in green leather sheath.

Muscles tensed to leap out of ess-u-vee, but Eli put hand on head. Scratched behind ears.

"Easy, there. I won't let him pull that sword."

Looked up at Eli, sitting on back of ess-u-vee. Smelled gun oil and bullets. Eli had pulled gun, hidden by side in edge of blanket where Eli died one time. Chuffed with laughter.

Mercy Blade stepped to ess-u-vee. "Jane?" he asked.

I chuffed. Kept narrow eyes on him. Pulled back lips to show killing teeth.

"Hello, little goddess. It has been many years since I dealt with a shape changer in animal form."

Jane sat up tall inside mind. *How long? What kind of shape changer?*

Mercy Blade did not hear. Did not answer. I closed lips over killing teeth. Leaned into Eli's hand. His fingers started scratching head again, and up under jaw. Yawned to show teeth and happiness with Eli.

"Well. Let's get on with it, then," Gee said. He moved slowly in presence of big-cat, and reached toward head.

I growled.

Eli swatted ears. "Stop that."

I showed killing teeth to Eli. Growled louder.

"I'm not impressed, Jane. Not even a little."

Inside Jane laughed. I huffed and stopped growl. Laid head on paws. Glared/stared at Gee, sniffing air, delicate nose membranes fluttering. Last time when he healed me/us, it was a one-day moon and we were in Jane form. He smelled then of jasmine and pine. Today he smelled of pink flowers and green grass and pine needles. And a little of catnip. *Catnip is good. Like to roll in catnip.*

Gee touched face. I/we flinched. Then lay still. Fingers of Gee's hands cupped face and curled into bristly hair. Pressing over scent sacs in jaw and over eyes. His magics flowed down his arms and across his hands. Toward Beast.

Hot and cold, green and silver. A net of many magics that crawled over Beast and into Beast. Stinging. Hurting. I/we spat. Hissed. Snarled. Pulled away from Eli and Mercy Blade.

Gee DiMercy released head and stepped back. He smelled confused. Face looked strange, lips drawn up and pointing like bird's beak. "I don't understand. There is no were-contagion."

Jane looked through Beast eyes at Gee DiMercy. Heart was beating hard. Was thinking of Rick. Of mating Rick. Of not getting were-taint through mating.

"Was she in human form when she was bitten? And then changed into the puma form?" he asked.

"No," Eli said, his voice without emotion. But his body smelled of fear and worry. "She was in dog form, a Newfoundland. She was injured, the werewolf took out her throat—carotids, jugulars, trachea. She was dying."

"And when she shifted, she became"—he made a sweeping movement with arm and hand like swan's wing over water, but over *Puma concolor* body—"this? Not her human form first, then into this?"

"No," Eli said, smelling now of protection. Inside Beast, Jane crouched, listening, not sure what was wrong but certain that *something* was wrong. Eli's fingers clenched in Beast pelt, at neck. Holding on, like kit in den to mother cat. He pulled we/us to his side. He smelled of den and home, of kits and littermates. "From dog to this."

"You are certain?"

Eli looked at Mercy Blade with thin eyelids. "Yes. Why does it matter?"

Gee DiMercy stepped away from ess-u-vee. "When she died, she should have resolved into her natural birth form. Jane is not a were-cat to be born in her cat form and then later to find a human shape. She is a—" He stopped, tilted head, looking Beast over. "I thought she was a little goddess, but perhaps I was wrong." He looked back at helo-bird and whipped arm in circle. Helo-bird made whirring noise that rang in ears. Strange winds began to turn. Beast bent ear tabs down to protect ears. "I don't know what she is, but whatever she is, or whatever bit her, she is free of were-taint. Without my services."

Changing from dog to me would have left me with the taint? But changing from a dog to Beast means I don't have it? So being with Rick would . . . what? What? I'd have to have sex in dog form and then change into a cat? Ewww. Not gonna . . . Just ewww.

But Gee DiMercy was in helo and the clumsy bird was lifting away. Jane cursed inside mind. Beast stayed silent and still, remembering presence of angel Hayyel and . . . things he did to me/us. Things Beast could not tell Jane.

"You okay, Janie?" Eli whispered.

Beast pressed head into Eli side, demanding scratches. But Beast did not purr.

"I like your hair down," Rick said.

I was in human form, sitting at the top of the hotel steps, watching the day end, waiting for him to arrive. He'd ridden up in a small red car, a rental, and had gotten out, walking straight to me in the dying light, his car door left open.

My body reacted to the heat in his voice and I shifted on the cold step, orienting to face him. He stood below me on the staircase landing, halfway up. The light was mostly gone and he looked like a black silhouette against the dusk, lean and feral, dangerous. He smelled of cat and human and lust. Earbuds hung on his neck, playing magic music, the musical spell that kept him from going insane from the pain of being a were-cat who couldn't change form.

I turned from my sorta-boyfriend to the last glimmer of sunset and moonrise. The moon was full and huge and bright, resting in the clouds on the horizon—a pumpkin orange ball nested into bloodred bright clouds. The moon's reflection spread across the water like blood and flower petals, like the promise of spring and the curse of death. I looked back at him, moving just my eyes. "You okay?"

He shrugged, the movement uncannily catlike. "As well as can be expected."

I shook my head, my hair sliding across one shoulder to pool on the steps. He watched it move. Like a cat intent upon a toy. I knew without asking that he wanted to gather up my hair and run his claws through it. I almost asked if he knew about the pronouncement made by Gee, and then I closed my mouth on it. Eli and the Kid wouldn't tell him. Nor would Gee or Leo.

And I didn't know if I wanted him to know or not, that there was some small possibility that we could be together and me not get the were-taint. Before I could tell him that, before we could explore that remote possibility, I had to ask some tough questions, and even asking them was . . . probably stupid. Frustration zinged through me like a pinball, alarms sounding. I took a breath, knowing I had to ask. Knowing as I did that it might break us. "I gotta know, Ricky Bo. Did you know you were sending me into a life-or-death situation? One where a werewolf was trying to start a pack? *And had a female?*"

I watched Rick's face fall as he remembered his own past as a hostage, kidnapped by a werewolf pack. "No," he murmured. One hand reached up to massage his shoulder where the werewolf bitch had tried to chew off his tattoos. "No. No females. Not possible."

"Yes. And not only possible. *Fact.* Two males, one huge, big enough to be a dire werewolf, coat color gray. The other male was smaller, more familiar in size, reddish, like the pack that attacked me once before. Attacked you. And died, the whole sick lot of them. Or so we thought.

"One of the males must have survived, and he made a female. She survived her first turn and now lives, if you can call it that, as a crazy bitch in heat. I know. I smelled her."

Rick climbed the steps slowly, his boots slipping out and up. He stopped two steps below me and sat, his scent surrounding me, hot and rich, with just a hint of Old Spice. An odd choice for a young man, but maybe his cat liked it. My Beast did.

He shook his head, looking up at me as the yellowish lights of the hotel stairwell came on. "Are you sure?" I hadn't noticed, but he had a blade in one hand, the center plated with sterling silver. He turned it, the sterling catching the light.

"Yeah. I'm sure," I said. "The small one smelled like the bitch who tortured you. He smelled like her pack. The bigger one smelled like . . . like something else."

The white form of Rick's partner—the white werewolf stuck in wolf form—climbed the steps behind Rick. The irony of a were-cat stuck in human form and a werewolf stuck in wolf form being partners for the Psychometry Law Enforcement Division wasn't lost on me, but that didn't mean I'd cut him any slack. "Hey, Brute. What's kicking? Anyone broken your nose lately?" He snarled at me, fangs white in the darkness, and I chuckled. "Try it, big boy. How many times do I have to break your ugly snout to make you understand that you're *only a wolf*?" I made the last three words an insult, and I heard a chittering in the night, though I didn't see the source. Staring the wolf down, I said, "Sorry, Pea," though I knew she could smell the lie on me.

I heard a scrape in the hallway behind me as Eli decided to reveal himself. He knew he needed to be downwind if he wanted to spy on crea-tures with better-than-human noses, so clearly he had wanted his presence known. "LaFleur," he said.

"Younger," Rick said back, measuring the former Ranger.

It was like a testosterone factory out here. I sighed and stood, pivoting on a boot heel and walking down the hallway to my room. Hand on the knob, I pointed three rooms down. "Room fourteen."

Rick looked at the door of room fourteen and back to me, his face suddenly playful. "Is that a challenge? Because if it is, consider it taken, darlin'."

Heat sang through me. Pea, Rick's supernatural grindylow, the mythical creature charged with keeping were-animals from spreading the were-taint, chittered angrily and stood up from her perch in Brute's fur. Eli, instead of taking my side, laughed. "She needs to get laid, man, can't say she don't, but my room's right next door, so keep it quiet."

"Good grief," I muttered, and went into my room, closing the door with finality. To the empty room I said, "Men." And not in a nice way. Then I turned to my weapons, laying them out on the bed. These I under-stood. Men, not so much.

Moments later I heard a tap on the door and soft music from outside. I opened the door a crack. Rick stood in the hallway's yellow light, that same expression on his face—laughter, playfulness, teasing. Dear God in heaven, I'd missed that look. The heat that had started in the stairwell bloomed and spread through me. He leaned in, smelling totally delicious. "You're really gonna make me stay all the way down there?"

"I really am." The words were more whisper than I wanted, and I cleared my voice.

Rick's smile widened, and I knew he could smell my need on the air. "You gonna join me?"

"I'm really not."

Rick nodded, his lips drawing into a thoughtful frown. "Well, then. We should take advantage of the moonlight. Let's hunt."

My Beast reared up in me, staring through my eyes at a man she had claimed as her mate. *Mine*, she purred. I didn't bother to push her down but opened the door to reveal my room with my weapons spread on every surface. "Was kinda hoping you'd wanna hunt," I said.

Rick whistled and Brute trotted up. I looked at the wolf. "He willing to chase down a wolf who might have been his hunting buddy once upon a time?"

"He's good with it." Rick nodded to the adjoining room. "Your pals up for a night hunt?"

The adjoining door opened. "Thought you'd never ask," Eli said. "Where do we start?"

"That restaurant we ate at last. The werewolves have eaten there. I smelled the house-made, Cajun-style rémoulade sauce on them when they changed back to human. By the stink, I'd say they're regulars at Joe's Got Crabs."

The waitress at the restaurant wasn't interested in talking to me about the threesome who ate there every night. But when Rick walked in, things changed fast. He turned that million-dollar smile on her and I thought she'd toss off her clothes right then and there and take him on the floor.

I sat at the bar and watched, nursing a beer so they wouldn't toss us out, Eli with a Coke standing behind me. The waitress bent over Rick and let him get a good look at her cleavage while they chatted. I couldn't decide if I was jealous or if she was pathetic. Both probably.

Eli leaned over me and said, "So. You want to rip her head off or tear her a new one lower down?"

"Both. Neither. She stinks of mango, jasmine, and rose perfume with a dash of fried fish and horseradish. He can act interested all he wants, but I can see his nostrils. To him? She reeks."

"Even with those boobs?"

I looked down at my own chest and back to the waitress. "There are the boobs," I acknowledged. "And the long blond hair." And the fact that Rick was a pretty boy and generally unfaithful. Minutes later Rick walked back to us, a strip of paper in his fingers.

"Her number?" I asked, hearing the snark in my voice, which—hopefully—disguised the hurt.

"A license number, a credit card number, a name, and an address," he said with pride and not a little swagger. He handed me the strip of paper.

"And you didn't get her number?" Eli asked, disbelieving.

"Oh, I got her number." Rick pulled out another strip of paper and extended it to Eli. "For you." Eli's eyes went wide as he looked from Rick's hand to the waitress. She gave him a little wave. "My good-looking friend who is smitten with her down-home Southern looks and charm, but who is too shy to get her number."

"You didn't." There was a Beast-worthy growl in the words.

Rick tucked the paper into Eli's shirt pocket and patted it down. "Oh, but I did."

Chortling with laughter and more relieved than I wanted to admit to myself, I waved to the waitress as I followed the men out the door. "Be sure to burn that," I advised Eli, "before Sylvia sees it. She wouldn't bother with ripping off your head. She'd let Smith and Wesson do the talking."

The water sped by us in the rented airboat, the moon now cold and icy, bright on the black water. We had given the Kid the information that the waitress had provided, matched it with newcomers to the area and missing-persons reports in the parish—information provided by the police—three prime addresses to work with, all easiest to find by boat. Eli drove, Brute sitting beside him, Rick and me on the lower, front seat, his arm around my shoulders, seat belts holding us in place. You really needed the nylon flex straps in an airboat at *any* speed.

The first place was a vacant mobile home that had been used for target practice by the locals for so long that it was mostly a hole. Neither Brute nor I got a whiff of werewolf. And it felt weird to be working with the wolf, asking him if he smelled our prey. Beast growled low in the back of my mind, and I had to soothe her raised ruff. *It's just for now,* I thought at her. *Want to fight wolf. Scratched his nose one time.*

You did? I didn't remember that, but I thought it might be prudent not to continue the conversation. And when Eli whirled the airboat in a tight arc to take us to the next place on our list, I used the centrifugal force as an excuse to hold on to Rick and not respond.

The second place was more likely. I smelled werewolf stink from yards away. The airboat roared up onto land in front of a house; the engine cut off.

Brute stepped over the back of the seat and shoved his snout between Rick and me, pushing us apart, sniffing, getting dog drool on my shirt. I was sure it wasn't an accident. I shoved his nose away. "I smell it," I said.

I stepped onto the land, boot heels sinking into the mud. Brute landed beside me, shaking his head, the human gesture looking all wrong on him.

"What?" Rick asked. "Is this the right place?"

Brute nodded.

"Are the weres here?"

Brute lifted his snout and sniffed as the airboat went silent and shook his head.

"They're hunting," I said softly.

Brute snuffled agreement. Pea crawled up his back, holding his ruff in her tiny little fists. She sat astride his neck, holding on, and sniffed the air. She chittered, the sound menacing and deadly, strange coming from the green-coated, kitten-sized grindy. She closed her eyes and sniffed, tiny explosions of air. She opened her eyes and looked at Rick. There was an intensity in her gaze that belied her cuteness.

"I haven't touched Jane. Oh. Wait. You know where the werewolves went?"

Pea sniffed again and pointed with a tiny paw/hand, one finger extended, the two-inch steel claw at the tip. Deep inside, Beast hissed at the sight. *I know,* I thought at her. *I don't know where she keeps them either, but when she pulls them out, they are* scary.

Behind us, silent, Eli started the engine again, the prop deafening in the night. Brute and I leaped back inside, and we followed Pea's nose and steel claw down the canal.

Pea directed us to shore along a stretch of water that was black as sin. Eli pulled up and beached the boat, cutting the engine. Another airboat was beached beside ours, and it stank of were. And wolf in heat. And terrified human. Female. They had captured a woman. When she was in the boat, she was unharmed, no blood smell. But she had been so filled with fear that her sweat stank of it. And she had urinated on herself. Recently.

Eli turned a bright flash on the boat, where we could see clothing, shoes, beer cans, and jewelry in piles. He moved the light and studied the muddy bank. Close to the boat it was hard to tell what was what; there were human prints and wolf prints. But farther out, one pair of bare human feet led off into the brush. And three wolves followed.

Eli leaned over the seats and started passing out weapons. The rest of us took them, checking their readiness by feel, holstering them, checking the slide of blades and the position of, well, everything. My M4 Benelli was in its spine holster, the grip above my ear, loaded with hand-packed rounds containing silver fléchettes. They had been designed to kill vamps, but most supernats could be poisoned by silver, weres among them. I retied my bootlaces. Made sure water bottles were easy to hand. Eli carried a U.S. Army med kit, mostly for him and any hurt victim, because the rest of us would be likely to heal fast. He had walked me through everything in it, and their uses. I had managed not to laugh at his description of the uses of tampons—"Great bandages to insert into gunshot wounds. They have their own tail to locate the injury later." Uh-huh. Kinda knew that.

When we were all ready, we stepped to the bank, and mud sucked at our feet, each step a slurping sound, each foot an effort to lift. With a whiff of satisfaction in his pheromones, Eli pocketed the keys of both boats. The wolves had left theirs. He turned off the flash and we stood to let our eyes acclimate.

There were no lights anywhere. There was only the stink of rotting vegetation, scat, the rot of a dead animal in the distance, and the smell of fear, aggression, violence. No sounds but the rare splash of a water animal, the trickle of slow-moving bayou and tide. In summer there would be frogs croaking, insects buzzing, night birds hooting and calling. Gators roaring. The smell of animals nesting and sleeping and hunting everywhere. From time to time, there would be boats and campsites with lights and fire pits, and the sounds of drunken humans would echo through the dark. But the weather had turned cold in what passed for winter here, and tonight it was just us and the smells and the small round moon on the black water and the silence that was left after the roar of the boat. Until the scream rent the air.

Everyone but Eli jumped. Eli settled his low-light gear over one eye and, with the other one, looked at the tiny kitten and the white wolf. "You take point. Move slow and steady. No matter what you hear." To us, he added, "Stay together. Jane, you got our six." It wasn't a request, and I fell in at the back. When it came to paramilitary operations I was the novice, he was the expert. And he was the one with the fully automatic weapon. I had learned that current Louisiana gun laws didn't prohibit magazine capacity, and that was why Eli felt so safe carrying them everywhere we went. I hadn't asked, and he had seen no reason to enlighten me.

I had also learned that no wet place in Louisiana is similar to any other. Walking through land bordering a saline marsh meant mud, shrubs, mud, stunted trees, mud, broken limbs (some sharp as stakes), mud, saw grass and regular grasses (lots of them taller than we were), and more mud. It clung to our boots and sucked at each footstep. The white wolf was two-toned, his bottom half black with muck, his upper half bright in the moon-light. Pea chittered softly, directing the wolf, using his hair like reins, pulling him where she wanted. It was a weird hunt, to be at the back of a pack, and I pulled on every sense Beast could lend me, from power in my leg muscles, to her night vision, which was much better than mine. Beast didn't like this hunt. Neither did I. Not with the snarls and yips and screams that came from ahead, in the dark.

The snarls and yips were excited and vicious; the screams were full of terror and agony, and we were taking too long—*too long!*— to get there. But the muddy terrain set the pace, not the victim, who, by her screams, was being torn apart, eaten alive, so damaged she would die, no matter how fast we got there. I bared my teeth in a killing rage. Forcing my feet to lift high, to run faster. Ahead, Eli did the same, and I could smell his desperation and fury.

The screams ended with a panting, pained moan, over and over with each fast breath, moans that seemed to roll out over the water and the low land, seeming to come from everywhere. "Jesus. Jesus. Jesus. Jesus. Jesus. Je . . . ssssuusss." And then there was nothing but the sounds of tearing and growls and the crack of bone. Just ahead.

We slogged out of the low trees into a clearing, Eli firing a burst from his automatic weapon, the sound and the muzzle fire ripping through the night. Yelps, howls, and shrieks followed. Beast flooded me with strength and I raced for the body on the ground. I took it in with a fast glance and didn't need to check for a pulse. She was dead—very dead, with nothing left inside her abdomen and a pool of blood on the wet ground an inch deep. It trickled off in tiny rivulets, toward the water.

If we had gotten here sooner . . .

I screamed and whirled and dove into the fight, a vamp-killer in one hand and a nine mil loaded with silver shot in the other.

Brute was battling a reddish wolf, the coat color visible in the moon-light. Rick was side by side with Eli, taking on a . . . a monster. I fired into the monster's side, aiming for his heart, emptying my weapon into him. I slapped the blade flat under my arm and changed mags.

I caught a hint of motion out of the corner of my eye and dropped to one knee, lifting the vamp-killer. The bitch was in midair, midleap. Her body lancing through the space where I had stood. My blade took the bitch along the side of the belly, the point penetrating deepest beneath the back left leg. She screamed with rage and ducked her head, tumbling in midjump. Her fangs snapped close to my face with a *click* I heard over the deafness of the nine mil firing. I fell back. Into the mud. Rolled to my knees.

The bitch landed two feet away, spun on three legs, and rammed me. Lifting me high.

I slammed into something. Took a broken branch to my lower ribs. Right side.

I fired at the bitch point-blank. She yelped and raced away, into the saw grass. The monster whirled and followed her, limping. The third wolf was hanging in Brute's jaws, dangling and broken.

I was injured. I knew it was bad because I was hung on the broken tree as if I'd been skewered for cooking, bleeding like a stuck pig. I was having trouble getting a breath. Rick and Eli dropped to either side of me. Both turned flashes on me, so bright I closed my eyes. Or maybe it was the sight of the wound, vivid and slick with blood. I smelled bowel. Saw what might have been a strip of liver. Inside me, Beast hissed, and I hissed with her.

"If she were human, we'd cut the limb and take it with us to an ER," Eli said to Rick. "But maybe she'll—"

"Pull her off it, fast, before the pain sets in," Rick said.

Before? I thought. *Too late.*

"Under her arms," Rick said. "On three." They grabbed me under my arms, braced their bodies, and Rick counted. On three they lifted and jerked me off the branch. I didn't even scream. I couldn't. I had no breath. My chest ached, heart suddenly beating unevenly and with pain in each contraction. Lung collapsing maybe.

They let me down gently into the mud. I was under the branch I'd been impaled on. It was covered in gore for the first five inches. And yes, there was a piece of tissue hanging on the wood that looked suspiciously like part of my liver.

"Idiot damn woman!" Eli spat. "Just because you can heal is no reason to keep dying." His voice was gruff, not even trying to hide his worry/ anger/fear. "You could *try* to be more careful."

"What's the fun in that?" I whispered. *Huh.* My lips were numb.

"Someday you're gonna wait too long," he warned.

I managed a chuff of laughter as he turned my body to the side. I was facing the water. It was closer than I had thought. Just beyond where the girl's body lay, her blood trickling into the canal. At the edge of the water something glimmered, an arc of bright light, all the colors of the rainbow, swimming through the water, moving with the up-and-down sweeps of a dolphin or porpoise. It was beautiful. Cool and bright and muted all at once, like a rainbow come to life and shot through with silver. I tried to point, but my hands weren't working.

The light being, so much like Rick's partner, Soul, but not, most certainly not, cavorted in the cold water, leaping in and out of the canal without a splash. When it came close to the shore, it halted, the light of its spirit body coruscating. It slithered closer, like a water snake, and seemed to dip part of its energies into a trail of the dead girl's blood. It wrenched itself back, leaped into the air, and was gone. Something indefinable inside me mourned. And the light, what little there was of it, began to go.

"Shift," Rick said as he cut through my clothing and loosened my holsters and my Kevlar vest. "*Shift*, Jane. *Now!*" He unbelted leather and zipped my pants down. Eli unlaced my boots, their flashlights dancing pools of light on the scrub around us. If the wolves came back they'd never know in time. I tried to tell them, but my mouth wasn't working. I shivered in the cold air. Or in the cold of death. It's hard to tell sometimes.

I sought the gray place of the change, the place of my skinwalker energies. But it eluded me, like phosphorescent water slipping through my fingers.

Beast? Can you help?

Jane is stupid human. But deep in my mind, I felt her bend and pick me up by the scruff of my neck. Holding me in her killing teeth as tenderly as though I were one of her kits.

And together we dropped into the gray place of the change.

The energies of what I had determined might be quantum mechanics, of the movement of electrons and neutrons and all the trons, were a nimbus of light, arcing and racing and waving and dancing in a silver cloud of light. The energies were struck through with darker sparks of black light and blue-white sparks of brilliance.

The pain increased, but a different kind of pain, sharper, cutting. As if my flesh were being stripped from my bones.

Beast leaped away from men, shaking free of boots and clothing and racing up a stunted tree. Screamed into the night, big-cat scream. Claiming life and hunting grounds and calling to spirit being that had fled the dead.

"Jane?"

I hissed. *Am Beast. Not Jane. Jane is asleep inside.* Then smelled blood. Not Jane blood. Not dead-girl blood. Not werewolf blood. *Rick* blood. I dropped to ground, sniffing. Opened mouth and pulled air in over scent sacs in roof of mouth. Tasting/smelling mate. He was injured.

I walked to him and stuck snout to arm. Rick held still, not even breathing. Smelled Rick and smelled werewolf. Rick was bitten. Backed away. Hissed, snarled. Turned to Brute and snarled again. Brute and Pea were Rick's pack. His den-mates. *Should have protected Rick like kit against predator,* I thought at them. I growled and walked toward them. Angry. *Should have protected mate.*

Wolf backed away. Lowered head. Dropped dead werewolf. Like offering. Pea chittered from Brute back. Sounded sorry. Beast looked at Pea. *Will mate become werewolf? Werewolf and were-cat too? Will mate die?*

Pea jumped from Brute and raced to Rick. Climbed up his leg. Studied bite mark. Rick lifted Pea to shoulder and bent over Jane clothes.

"You're hit," Eli said, opening box with bandages. Voice was toneless, but Eli body's smell changed, unhappy. Thinking many things. He put flashlight in mouth, held it with blunt human teeth. Ripped open large bandage. Cussed at sight of wound. "It bit you?" Placed sheet of white over Rick's arm.

"Yeah." Rick wrapped wounded arm and bandage in Jane T-shirt. Pea chittered softly. Sad. "Tie it off," Rick said. Eli swathed T-shirt bandage in stinky stuff that changed shape to bind arm. Pressed on wound. Rick hissed with pain. "He tried to rip off a hunk of muscle, but he got distracted when Jane shot him full of silver."

"Bad?"

"Hurts like a mother. But I'll heal."

"But . . ." Eli stopped. Bent and gathered up Jane clothes and weapons. "Let's book. We got a hike to make. And two pissed off wolves between us and it."

"And you with their keys," Rick said, laughter in tone. Rick said, "Brute. That thing dead?" Brute nodded head up and down, human gesture. *Looks stupid.* Pea chittered in triumph, claiming kill.

"Okay," Rick said. Slung weapons over shoulder. Rick stood, wavering on two feet. Should be on four feet. Would not waver.

Brute looked at girl, dead on ground. She smelled of meat. Of food. Beast was hungry. Needed meat after change. Did not look at girl meat. Growled at Brute. Wolf dropped own head and turned away from prey meat.

"Jane?" Rick said. "Let's get back to the . . . back to the . . . boat." But Rick dropped to knees. And fell to ground, face in mud.

Pea leaped clear. Landed on Beast. Made soft mewling sound in ear, like kit. Beast chuffed with laughter.

Eli rearranged weapons and Jane gear. "Brute, get over here." Wolf growled, knowing what Eli wanted. "You'll carry him or I'll shoot you myself," Eli said. Not mad. Not angry. Speaking truth. Brute walked to Rick, growling.

Making grunting sound, Eli lifted Rick and laid him on Brute back. With more stinky stuff, tied Rick to Brute. I laughed. Went to Rick. Smelled wound. It stank. Stank of were-taint.

Pea mewled in ear. Not death sound. But sound like Rick was sick again. Sick with wolf. Beast swiveled head to see Pea. Thinking. Thinking like Jane. Was hard. Pea should have chased werewolves when they ran. Was Pea's job. But Pea stayed with Rick. Knew Rick was sick. Knew Eli and Jane and Beast would kill wolves. Beast walked upwind. Sniffing. No werewolf scent ahead. But they might circle in back. Hunters. Pack hunters. Sneaky pack hunters. But big wolf was full of silver. Could not change back to human form with silver inside. Would have to get female wolf to cut out silver bullets. Did not know what werewolves would do, attack or run away and try to heal.

"Okay. Let's go," Eli said to Beast. Beast turned and faced water and scrub and bushes. Walked into dark. "So what? You taking our six?"

Beast chuffed with agreement.

"Good by me."

Trip back to boat was long. Beast was hungry. Was muddy, dirty. *Do not like mud. Do not like mud at all. Belly aches with hunger. Body is weak. Want to eat. Want to eat deer and cow and rabbit.* Looked at Eli. Looked at Brute. *Would even eat Brute.*

Eli untied Rick from Brute back while Beast stood watching trees and scrub. Did not smell wolves. Eli lifted Rick to lay on long seat of airboat. Was noisy—feet on hollow boat bottom. Rick groaned. Was sick. Retching.

Brute jumped into canal and swam. Blood and mud washed away.

"You too, Jane," Eli said. "Make it quick."

Beast snarled. *Am not Jane. Am Beast.* But stepped into water. Swam out from shore and back. Looked for spirit being of rainbow colors but did not see it. Followed Brute from water. Brute shook, pelt showering water and mud all over Beast. Shook with laughter.

Beast snarled. Leaped on Brute. Sank in claws. Bit hard on nose. Holding. Brute yelped/whined. Quivered. Did not know what to do. Froze like prey.

Beast let go and walked back to water. Washed again. Shook water from pelt. Climbed into airboat and sat beside mate. Kept back to wolf, but eyes turned to see. In wolf pack, Beast would be alpha. Wolf would be beta. Saw him lick his snout. Could smell his blood on air.

Was near dawn when we got to hotel. Jane was awake, watching through Beast eyes. Eli carried mate upstairs to room. Wolf and Beast followed. Eli turned on shower in Rick room, washed Rick. Cut off his clothes. Opened wound and saw healing. Carried Rick to bed and laid him, naked, on bed.

Beast went to mate and sniffed. Rick was sick. Sick with were-taint. Pea jumped from Beast back to bed with Rick and curled up in space at shoulder, neck, ear. "Is he gonna turn wolf?" Eli asked. Jane was shocked at question. Felt her pull away. Fear action.

Pea made sound, "Uuuuu," and shook head.

"Is he gonna die?"

Pea made same sound and shook head again.

"So he's just gonna be sick as a dog and then get better?"

Pea made "Sssss" sound and nodded head.

Jane made choking laughter sound deep inside Beast.

"Janie? You want to wait till dark to go after the wolves?"

Beast nodded head. Padded from room and went to door of Jane room. Eli opened door and Beast went inside. The Kid rushed out of room talking too much, too loud. Was prey action when werewolves were hunting. Stupid human. Beast pawed door shut and lay down on floor. Entered gray place of change.

"Oh crap. That hurt." It still hurt. And I had a wide, white scar to show me how close I'd come to dying. I made it to the shower, turned the water on hot, and rested against the wall as the water beat against me. I was starving. I could tell from the way my ribs stuck out that I'd lost at least ten pounds from shifting twice with no caloric intake. I needed food and a lot of it if I was going on a hunt. *Beast? You there?*

Beast is here.

What happened?

Beast showed me. Showed me everything. When I saw Rick fall, I ached inside. When I saw the spirit being, the thing like Rick's Soul, I was taken off guard. But there wasn't time to whine or grieve or worry. Dawn had broken. We needed food, guns, and planning, and we needed to get back in the swamp. I half crawled from the shower and dried off, using the blow-dryer on my hair. Tossed my wet, muddy, bloody clothes into the shower and washed them off, wrung them out, and left them hanging over the shower door. I fell on the bed and closed my eyes, desperately needing rest, maybe even more than I needed food.

After my forty winks, I dressed in clean clothes and weaponed up, the leathers wet and slick even after I dried them with a towel. They needed oiling and a lot of attention, but they weren't going to get that until the wolves were dead.

I knocked on the connecting room door. Eli opened it and stood aside to let me enter. He had showered with scentless soap and dressed in clean clothes, not wearing the smelly stuff his girlfriend gave him. Brute was on the floor near his bed. Eating. Before I could accuse him of feeding the wolf before he fed me, Eli shoved a fork and a plate of microwaved scrambled eggs at me. I sank to the floor and shoveled the eggs in. Before I was done, he dropped four pancakes on my eggy plate and drenched them with syrup.

Then more eggs. And then he handed me a twenty-ounce protein shake that tasted like chalk and artificial blueberries, but I downed it too.

Then he handed me my M4 harness and helped me strap it on. All without a word spoken. When I was weaponed up, and he had checked the readiness of my slimy, wet leather gear, he said, "I called the death in to Rick's partner. They'll handle the crime scene, rather than calling in the state boys, since we fu—messed it up so bad. I heard the call go out forty minutes ago." I nodded and he pointed at me. "You, the wolf, and me. Back on the water. Now. We need to hit them while the big wolf is weak, while the female is still cutting rounds out of his body and he's injured and stuck in wolf form. Our best bet is the crime scene, since they can't get off the water while wounded and without their boat. Okay?"

I nodded. And accepted the bag of candy bars, energy bars, prepackaged high-protein energy drinks, and chips packed by the Kid. On top was a sugary, icing-coated, cream-stuffed snack cake. It looked totally bad for me and totally delicious. It had to have come from his secret stash, the one he hid from his brother, the health-food nut. I tucked the cellophane package deeper in the treats with a smile, and he shrugged. "Enjoy. Be safe. And keep him safe." He thumbed at Eli. "He's hard enough to live with now, without him adding raw meat to his diet and howling at the moon three nights a month."

Eli ruffled his brother's hair as if he were a child and loped down the stairs, Brute on his heels. I followed more slowly, not because I felt bad, but because my stomach was so full I could hardly move. And I was already thinking about eating the snack cake.

The sun was high overhead when we hit the water. The airboat trip back into the canal took too long, and we were too late anyway. The wolves' airboat was gone. Eli killed the engine, leaving us floating with the meager current, thinking. "They had another key," he said.

"Looks like," I agreed.

"I hate when the bad guys are smart enough to plan ahead."

I opened an electronic tablet and pulled up the crime scene GPS locations, and compared them to the current crime scene, then layered them on a satellite map and showed it to Eli. He nodded and spun the airboat in a three-quarter turn before heading to the closest house, which was the house we had started out at the night before. No one was home. There was no scent of werewolf, no scent of blood. I figured they had smelled us on the beach and found another place to lair up, so we took a deeper turn into the swamp. That GPS location turned out to be a burned-out hulk. The next place we got to was a falling-in mess of wind-damaged, water-damaged timbers, maybe the result of a hurricane—Katrina or Rita. Three places later, we were stumped, but we had no cell signal at all, to call the Kid for advice. So Eli texted his genius of a brother and we ate a late lunch: Brute wolfed down a three-pound roast that smelled a little rank, I ate most of the goodies in the pack Alex had made for me, and Eli ate a veggie-and–pulled pork sub sandwich he had hidden in a cooler in the bow. I thought he was sneaky to keep the sandwich for himself. He thought I was stupid for eating the "crap food" his brother packed for me. And we got Cokes all around.

You haven't lived until you've seen a white werewolf drinking Coke from a bowl and then having a sneezing fit when the carbonation got up his nose. The laugh did me good, even if it did make Brute mad. Fortunately, before he could decide to fight me over the offense, we got a text from Alex accusing us of sitting on our butts. Dang cell phones were nothing more than tracking devices. We went back to searching. And the day went back to getting shorter and shorter. We were running out of time.

An hour before dusk, I said, "Let's check back at the house that they used. The one we were at before Pea sent us off after the wolves. Maybe they circled back to it, thinking we wouldn't."

Eli didn't reply, but moments later we were heading back along Lake Boudreaux and into the canals.

We raced by the house once, as if we were fishermen on the way elsewhere, studying the grounds. By daylight it was bigger than I had thought, with a long, two-story screened porch starting on ground level and the rest of the house up on stilts to protect it from hurricane surge. It stank of werewolves and blood and pain, which made my face contort in what might have been considered by some to be a really ugly smile.

Brute gave a low chuff, a darkly gratified sound I'd heard during the fight with the werewolves in the night. It was the sound he made when he got to kill something that needed killing. My eyes met the wolf's icy ones and something exchanged between us. We might not like each other, but we understood each other. We were both killers of a sort. And I absolutely did not like that about myself.

Eli pulled the airboat to a halt far downwind and turned off the engine. "Tromp back and attack by stealth or race back and execute a Normandy?" he asked. When I looked confused, he said, "The One Sixteenth hit the beach by daylight. World War Two."

I narrowed my eyes at him. "Yeah. I remember my history lesson. They died like flies."

"Beach the boat for a frontal attack, versus time and energy to muck it back overland, time when they might heal and be stronger." He looked up at the sky and the sun that was already below the tree line. It would be dark soon. The moment the moon rose, they'd be stronger, healing the damage the silver bullets had caused, and helping to extrude the bullets. Always assuming they were still alive, of course.

Brute chuffed and stared back down the canal. An immediate beach landing was his vote. But I tilted my head, thinking about the low ground, the house's floor plan, and even the foliage I'd seen as we raced by. "How about we point the airboat at the beach, but we all jump off before we get there? The boat makes a lot of noise from the beach side, gets their attention, draws them toward the water, and we take them from the rear."

Brute yipped and grinned, his tongue hanging out to one side.

"Could work," Eli said, turning my suggestion over in his mind.

Half joking, half provoking, I added to the wolf, "Keep out of the line of fire, dog face. No one here likes you well enough to cut silver out of your hide."

Brute narrowed his eyes at me, as if telling me that payback would be painful. But there was something different in his gaze this time. To call it friendlier was an overstatement, but maybe less animosity after the fights in the swamp and a day in a roaring airboat.

"Enough," Eli said. "Jane, you drive. Angle in close to shore on the first pass. When you swerve to angle back out, the wolf and I'll jump. Brute will head for the far side of the house; I'll be in the trees for a clear shot. Take the boat down the canal a ways and then head back at speed for the Normandy. Make sure we get at least three minutes to get in place before you hit the beach."

BENEATH A BLOODY MOON

"Maybe I was stunned and not hearing right. Do I remember you telling me not to take so many chances? To be more careful?"

"If they're in wolf form, you'll have the advantage. They'll have to charge you across open ground, giving Brute plenty of time to hamstring them, and you and me plenty of time to fill them full of silver. And the shooting angles should keep us out of the line of fire."

"And," I said, "if they're in human form, all bets are off. They'll shoot me, then Brute, then hunt you down and shoot you. This is Louisiana in the middle of nowhere with werewolves who hunt and take down humans like it's a game. And eat them for supper, by moonlight. They'll have *guns*."

"Yeah." Eli grinned, showing teeth. "That's the most important part of the plan. Don't get shot." I didn't roll my eyes, but it was a near thing. He turned on the airboat, put me in the driver's seat, and gave me a quick tutorial. Once I was satisfied, I made sure my weapons were easy to hand and gunned it down the canal. I'd be glad if I never heard the sound again.

Eli's plan would have worked except the wolves were on the beach when I roared up. They were in wolf form, waiting for the moon to rise. Or maybe they had smelled me as I roared past and decided to meet me head-on. Whatever.

It was too late to abort. I had still-shot visions of what might/could/ would happen, no matter what decision I made. In half a second I saw what would happen if I tried to whirl the airboat back into the canal. The big wolf would jump on board and eat me. In the next half second, I saw what would happen if I raced along the water and tried to draw them after me. The big wolf would jump on board and eat me. In the final half second, I saw what would happen if I rammed the shore, hoping to break a few legs—hopefully not my own. And that seemed like my best shot. I yanked my seat belt tighter, braced my booted feel on the bench seat in front of me, and rammed the accelerator forward.

I'm pretty sure I was screaming the whole way.

The airboat hit the shore at full speed. I remembered to let off the acceleration only after I hit land. The boat dragged/slowed/stalled. Going from fast to a slewing, out-of-control crawl. The seat belt caught my weight and momentum, trying to cut me in two. My feet slid and flew forward. I reached to catch myself on the seat in front, and bumped wrong. My blade sailed out of my hand. And the dire werewolf leaped. I had another still-shot moment of his massive body, stretched out in the air. Fangs white and fierce.

He landed on me. It was like being hit by a . . . by a four-hundred-pound werewolf. But the boat and I were still in motion. His weight skewed the boat up on its side, around, and back into the water. His claws scrabbled into my hair and scalp, drawing blood. Across my side, abdomen, and hip. Digging deep. The boat kept tilting. Except for the seat belt, I'd have been over and into the water, held down by a monster. Instead the boat rolled over, into the shallow water.

The prop cage went deeper, the still-moving prop showering us hard with tiny, cutting water droplets. The engine whined and stopped. We rolled upside down, into the mud, and began to sink. The only thing holding us out of the water was the seat belt and the quickly sinking cage.

The wolf released his body-hugging embrace and fell into the water at an angle, his mouth an inch from my face. Snarling, snapping. His body was twisted and pinned by the seat back in front of me. I struggled to both pull a nine mil and get the seat belt loose at the same time. Neither was working, with my body imprisoned by the coiled safety straps.

I yanked a boot free and kicked the wolf's jaw. His head whipped back. The boat sank farther, pulling his body under the surface of the water. Only his teeth and nostrils showed. My head was closer to the high end of the angled boat, but it was only seconds before I'd go under too.

I stopped trying to get the gun free and used that hand and my feet to lift my weight off the seat belt. The narrow strap finally popped free. I caught my body on the seat bracing and pushed off into the water. The wolf's head vanished under the surface in the same heartbeat. Bubbles came up from the muddy canal. "Yeah," I huffed for breath as I swam, my weapons weighing me down into the mud. "Drown," I said to him. "Please."

The mud was sticky and deeper than my arms, and the canal seemed to have no actual bottom, just mud and mud and more mud, and *things* were buried in it that I didn't want to touch but had no choice as I crawled toward shore.

As I crawled I heard growling and snarling and I saw Brute and two other werewolves fighting, the bitch and a small black male. The bitch had Brute by the ear and jaw, and he slung her hard, slamming her against a dock pillar while the black werewolf attacked Brute's hindquarters, trying to hamstring him. The bitch held on, though I smelled blood.

Eli, his rifle to his shoulder, moved at a crouch from the low trees, watching for a shot, watching the house, and keeping an eye out for more wolves. I was still kneeling in about six inches of water when the three snarling, growling wolves rolled toward me in a mass of snapping teeth, claws, blood, and fur.

I pulled the nine mil and took two shots into the black wolf's side. He squealed and broke free, rolling from the fight, making an awful *arrarrarr* sound of doggy pain and surprise.

I aimed at the bitch. Eli raced into the line of fire, shouting my name. Just as something snared my boot and hauled me back into the water. And under.

The dire wolf had my ankle in his jaws and was backing through the mud. His coat and eyes were the color of the muddy water, and all I could see were his teeth. And my combat boot in his jaws. My heart hit like a jackhammer.

I didn't have nightmares of drowning. Or suffocation. Until he yanked me hard and my head went under. The mud and water was a thick, slimy consistency and if I gave in and took a breath, I'd be full of mud. And I'd die.

I could shift, but Beast would be underwater too. And would die.

The wolf pulled me deeper, placed a paw on my belly, pushing me down. I fought. Struggling to get away.

I needed to breathe. I needed to *breathe. Breathe. Breathe. Breathebreathebreathe.* There was no air. The water was deep and dark and sluggish. I had mud in my eyes and ears, and my butt was buried in it, dragging a trail deeper. There was no light. Werewolf claws pierced my belly.

Give in. Stop fighting, Beast thought at me. *Pull body to paws and fire.*

It was not an intuitive action. And I had no idea if the gun would work in muddy water. But I did it. I stopped fighting to get away and drew my body tight, crunching down toward my feet. I couldn't see him, but I could feel him. I shoved the muzzle of the nine-millimeter semiautomatic into the first hard thing I found that wasn't me. And fired. The wolf let go.

It was too dark to see, and I wasn't sure which way was up or sideways, disoriented by the cloying mud. Once again I had to let go and stop fighting. Hardest thing in the world. Hardest thing ever. Harder than fighting.

Harder than dying. To not move and not breathe. Panic clutched at me with suffocating fingers.

But I let my body relax. And I started to float. I was ready to breathe mud long before my butt broke the surface. I was facing bottom and had to writhe upright. The breath I sucked in then was part slime, part air, and part water. It was glorious. I coughed, sputtered, coughed some more. Spat mud that left a grainy coarse film in my mouth and nostrils. My teeth ground on it like on fine sandpaper. And it tasted like rotten leaves and clay and dead fish. I wiped my eyes, blinking against the filth that coated them and scraped my corneas.

Eli was standing ankle-deep in mud onshore, and he tossed me a rope. Mr. Prepared.

I wrapped it around my left wrist, because I was still holding the nine mil in the right, and I let him haul me ashore, which mostly meant him dragging me through a trough of mud until I was far enough on what passed for dry land to crawl out of the watery furrow and struggle to my knees. Again. Eli started laughing, and I looked down at myself in the dusky light. In the sunset and moonrise, I was covered in a slick, slimy layer of dark brown mud. I coughed and sputtered some more.

Brute trotted up, laughing at me, tongue lolling. Behind him lay two dead wolves, one reddish and one black. They had died in wolf form and showed no signs of morphing back to human, which was a good way to keep Eli out of jail for murder and Brute off an animal control officer's death list.

I made it to my feet, Eli not offering a hand up, holding on to his rifle, which was a good thing.

I was standing in six inches of mud and water, trying to find my balance, when the werewolf lunged out of the canal straight at me. Eli screamed, *"Down!"* bringing his weapon up toward me. I dropped, rolled, and brought up my handgun. Eli fired. I fired. My weapon didn't. Misfire. The werewolf was directly over me. Jaws reaching.

Brute collided with him. Midair. I heard the *thud* of bodies over the gun blast. They fell, jaws locked around each other. And landed with me in the middle. Paws shoved me down, deep into the mud. Claws slicing me, them dancing on hind legs. One paw landed on my solar plexus and the last of my air *oof*ed out.

The water was a frothy, muddy mess all around me. I rolled, pushing deeper into the slick slime. Pushed away from the fighting weres. I came up within arm's reach of the combatants, my lungs full of mud. I threw up muddy water. Breathing between each retch with a frantic, rubbery, tearing sound. I tasted blood, gagged, and vomited again.

Eli held his weapon, ready to fire, the night-vision scope doing nothing to help him differentiate the two mud-covered werewolves. I caught my breath, staying low to the surface of the water, and crawled through the canal, back to shore, again, still, miraculously, holding my useless, mud-caked weapon. I fell, gasping, on the beach. The roar of the wolves made my eardrums shudder.

They fought in hip-deep mud and water, two enormous wolves. Wrestling like grizzlies, biting, fangs raking, claws trying to keep purchase on wet fur, jostling in the water with supernatural speed as the sun set behind them. I smelled wolf blood and heard their harsh breathing, like broken bellows. I was shivering, hard shudders bashing through me. It was still winter. And I'd been in the winter-cold water too long. And I'd nearly drowned in mud. Twice. My body was reacting to the stress with a case of shock.

The werewolves fought onto shore, Eli backing slowly, not daring to take a shot, unable to tell the two wolves apart. Then one broke away. Rushing toward me. Jaws wide. Eli fired, the concussion echoing across the still water. The wolf stumbled. And Brute landed on top of him. Sinking his fangs deep into the back of the other wolf's neck. With a wrenching motion, he snapped the enemy wolf's spine with a *crack* that rebounded across the black water.

Together, the wolves fell, slowly, to the beach. Brute didn't let go, but worried the wolf's spine, tugging, tearing, until there was no way that even the accelerated healing of a were could recuperate from the damage. Eli came closer, moving with the careful step and determined stance of the warrior. He placed his weapon against the skull of the dire wolf and said, "Now."

Brute leaped back.

Eli fired. And fired. And fired.

When there was nothing but pulp left of the dire werewolf's head, he stepped back. The wolf's blood flowed into the canal water. Brute lifted his snout and howled, long and lonely. Again and again. No one answered. No wolf replied.

But across the canal I saw a silhouette framed in the sunset, the bloody, setting sun on one side of him, the bloody, rising moon on the other. It was another werewolf. Silent. Controlled. Watching. He met my eyes across the water, letting me see him, letting me know him. It was the lone wolf, sitting in the shadows of the trees, downwind, absolutely still. Beside him was a dog I recognized, her gaze as intense as the wolf's. I thought about telling Eli, about getting him to shoot the wolf. But . . . the wolf wasn't a threat. I knew that. He was a lone wolf, watching, living among humans in perfect harmony and control. I lifted a hand to acknowledge the gaze, and his place in the swamps. He dipped his head to me and turned slowly, trotting into the quickly falling night, PP at his side.

Half an hour later, I heard the whine of the airplane engine, and the coughing *thump* as the propeller turned over. Moments later, from a mile away, a plane skimmed over the trees, rising into the air, flying beneath a bloody moon. I had no idea how he had masked his scent, but I figured Sarge was a wily old wolf and knew a trick or two.

It took the equivalent of a fire hose to clean us both off, Brute and me. The mud was caked to us, thick and dry, by the time we got to the hotel, and we were colder than a winter death, even huddled together on the floor of the pilfered wolves' airboat. Which we stole with impunity. But finally Brute was white in the moonlight and I was . . . at least clean, though shivering so hard I couldn't talk, even with Beast heating my blood. I managed to climb to my room and stand, fully clothed, under the scalding shower until I was warm again.

It was only then, as the memories of the battle recurred again and again, that I realized that Brute had saved my life. If the werewolf had landed on me, in his leaping attack, jaws open, he'd have caught my throat in his fangs and ripped my head off.

I owed the werewolf my life.

"Well, c-c-c-c-c-crap," I said to the shower walls.

I was asleep beneath a mound of covers when I heard my door open. "Don't shoot. It's me," Rick said, his voice a croak. He sounded worn to the bone, and when he crawled beside me into the bed, he was feverish hot, barely strong enough pull the covers over himself after he fell against me. Pea scampered between us, nestling into the angle of hip and thigh.

"Your virtue is safe," Rick murmured, "this time. I honestly just want to . . . cuddle."

He curled in beside me and fell asleep against my shoulder. I curled my body around him, breathing in his cat scent, absorbing the heat of his cat. Together, we three fell asleep.

Note from Faith: I hope you liked *Beneath a Bloody Moon*. I fell in love with the gulf years ago, and have wondered for years about the canals. For research on this subject, I talked with John Jensen, and was given privy to some of his groundbreaking research on the area. If you are interested, search for *Earth Epochs*.

Black Water

Author's note: This novella takes place (in the JY timeline) after *Blood Trade* and before *Black Arts*.

I took the long, bumpy roads south of New Orleans to the backwaters of Louisiana, in Terrebonne Parish. I had been there recently with my business partners in Yellowrock Securities, Eli and Alex Younger. With us had been PsyLED special agent Rick LaFleur and his supernat team, Brute and Pea. We had been hired to track and kill a werewolf pack, which we had done. We left the place better off than when we found it.

Or so I'd thought.

Until I'd received a text from Harold, who owned the Sandlapper Guesthouse with his wife, Clara. We'd stayed with them partly because Harold was the uncle of my sorta-boyfriend, Rick. Harold's text was to the point: Man w gun looking for you. Come quick. On the heels of the text had been the news coming from Chauvin, Louisiana, today—video of cops at a crime scene, near the Sandlapper.

The press hadn't said much except that a rampage had occurred in Chauvin and news vans were on the way with more to follow soon in this "breaking news report." Harold didn't respond to my texts back. And Rick hadn't replied to my texts asking for details. Harold and Clara were part of Rick's extended family. He would know what had happened. And he wasn't saying.

So here I was, riding Bitsa (built with bitsa this and bitsa that, from two rotted, rusted Harley bikes) down the horrible Louisiana roads and into danger—a man with a gun looking for me. Lately my enemies all had fangs, and most weres and vamps didn't use guns. Humans used guns. I had no idea what human I had ticked off in Chauvin, but I was gifted that way—ticking off people. I had cleaned house, and someone wasn't happy about it.

I pulled into the parking lot of the Sandlapper Guesthouse, on 56, south of Chauvin, and wheeled between sheriff deputy cars, a CSI van, and video news vans. The deputies looked relaxed and at ease, so they had been there awhile and had everything under control, but the news teams were still active. *Crap.* I was gonna get filmed, appear on TV news, and then I'd have to explain to my business partners why I'd come back here, alone, without the team. They needed time off. They were human; I wasn't. And the last job, here in Chauvin, had been draining. But that argument wasn't going to fly, and I knew it. I'd deal with that later. For now, I needed to get to Harold and Clara.

I cut off Bitsa, set the kick, bungeed my helmet to the back of the seat, stuck my hands in my pockets to appear nonthreatening to the sheriff's deputies, and headed closer, wearing a friendly smile. I kept my face turned away from the news cameras, but if the media wanted to know who I was, they'd figure it out. There weren't that many six-foot-tall, long-black-haired Cherokee females anywhere.

The county LEOs—law enforcement officers—studying me wore distinctly hostile faces, hands near gun butts, and I paused at the youngest cop, a redhead with freckles and bright eyes. Trying for innocent, I said, "Hey. What's going on here?"

"You need to move along, miss," the older one said, his hand sliding over his gun. The small strap that kept the weapon seated came unsnapped with a tiny *click* of sound. Somebody was in a mood. But I was smart enough not to say it.

Before I could reply, the wind shifted, and I smelled the sickly stench of old blood. Human. I came to a stop, mouth open, breathing in air over my tongue and the roof of my mouth, scenting as my Beast did, with a soft *scree* of sound. I took the place in more carefully, smelling the old blood, the fresher stink of injured humans, and the nitrocellulose of fired weapons. By the smells, Harold and Clara were on the premises, wounded. I wasn't sure how that was possible. Cops usually made sure any injured people were taken to a hospital right away.

I couldn't shake the feeling this was connected to my last job somehow.

The cops were looking at me strangely and I attempted a smile while I took another breath. A hint of magic tingled on my tongue, an old and weary magic. *Crap.* Where were Harold and Clara?

The mom-and-pop hotel was built on stilts to protect it from high tides and storm surge. The extra height gave every room fabulous water views, with fish-cleaning stations, parking, and rentable, fenced gear lockers/storage units underneath the hotel proper. Fishermen loved it. So had I. Harold and Clara lived on the far side. And there were other ways in, instead of through the cops.

Not waiting to get permission to enter—which I wasn't going to get in any case—I lifted a hand in what might have been interpreted as a farewell gesture and headed back to Bitsa. I pushed the bike farther into the shadows under the hotel. And slid into the darkness. I pulled my cell. The unit was top-of-the-line, a communication device built for the military, to deflect bullets and work off anything—Internet towers, satellite, Wi-Fi, *anything*. It also let the Master of the City of New Orleans, Leo Pellissier, keep tabs on my whereabouts. Which reminded me that I hadn't called to tell him I was coming here. My bad. Currently I had text messages waiting, most from the Kid. I sent back a quick K, not bothering to read them. Alex was wordy and I could digest them later. Unzipping my motorcycle jacket, I drew the nine-millimeter semiautomatic, slid the safety off, and chambered a round without looking. Muscle memory. Handy thing, that. It was an automatic reaction, probably a stupid one, since I'd just been seen by the cops, but I couldn't make myself put the weapon away. Instead I added to it. With my left hand, I palmed a blade, a silver-plated, steel-edged throwing knife. Silver was poisonous to most supernatural creatures, and everything that might hurt me could bleed. The TV cameras hadn't followed me. The deputies were shooting the breeze with a medic crew. I'd been forgotten. Good.

As I ascended the back stairs, I evaluated scents. Except for human blood, the acrid residue from fired weapons, and the salty taste of the Gulf of Mexico, nothing I smelled was familiar. Not were, not witch, not vamp, not anything I remembered smelling before, and my repertoire of scents was vast, compared to humans'.

I made my way up the last step, as silent as the squeaky, weather-worn wood allowed. The smell got stronger, but oddly it made me relax. The gunfire had happened much earlier, and someone was cleaning up. I smelled bleach. Heard water sloshing. Heard soft cursing and softer laughter. It wasn't happy laughter, but rather the kind of laughter humans made when they could either laugh or bust out crying. I recognized the voices of Clara and Harold. I chuffed out a relieved breath.

Inside my Beast relaxed. *Humans not dead,* she thought at me. *I/we knew this.*

I slid the small blade out of sight, into its thigh sheath, but thought better of holstering my sidearm. I didn't want to be unarmed if the couple was under compulsion or had uninvited guests that the cops had missed. I followed the smells to their corner rooms and stopped just outside in the covered walkway. The light was against me. If I bobbed my head to peer in the windows, anyone inside would see me silhouetted against the bright afternoon sky. If there were still cops inside, they wouldn't like the fact that I'd bypassed their crime scene tape. Weapon by my thigh in one hand, index finger along the slide, off the trigger, I made my way to the door, passing right in front of the windows. The glare obscured everything inside, but no one shot me. That was always a good thing. I tapped on the door and it opened almost instantly.

Harold's welcoming gaze changed to surprise as it shifted from my face and down to my gun. I shrugged with what I hoped was a good-natured smile, sniffed to make sure there was no magical residue or compulsion on him—just in case—removed the round from the chamber, and holstered the weapon. The extra round went into a pocket.

"Flying carpet?" Harold asked, holding the door open.

"Um." Which seemed like a perfectly acceptable response to the odd question.

"Thanks for getting here so fast," he added.

"Oh. Yeah. Sure," I said, entering the second-floor apartment. I was such a smooth talker.

Except for muscular arms, Harold was a round kinda guy. Round belly, round, bald head, round eyes, and round face, which now had horizontal lines across the forehead and vertical lines along the sides of his mouth. His face reminded me of a pop quiz in a geometry class in school.

The entry was divided by a counter with apparatus and paperwork for guests to sign in. Behind it was the couple's living quarters. I breathed in the room's smells and took in dainty, delicate Clara on her knees just inside the door, a bucket beside her giving off the stink of chlorine bleach and soap. She had a sponge in one hand, a small brush in the other, and relief on her face.

"Thank God you're here," Clara said.

Before we could get farther, my cell rang, an unknown number on it. I answered and said, "Yellowrock Securities."

"Jane."

Inside my Beast sat up and purred. "Ricky Bo, as I live and breathe. You must be calling from your office number."

"Got it in one, darlin'."

Instantly, inexplicably, I was irritated, mostly at the *darlin'* but also because this couldn't be good news. I was standing at a crime scene in his relatives' home. Rick had to be wanting me to do him a favor. *Again.* Even though I had yet to be paid by Uncle Sam for the last one. I snarled, "What's with the *darlin'* stuff?"

"I . . . uh." He stopped talking and then seemed to change, as if he put my mood in a box, sealed it up, and tossed it in the basement. If he had a basement. He turned on his business voice. *Cop* business. "I need a favor in Chauvin. A big favor."

I blew out a breath and most of my irritation. He was a cop to his bones and a man loyal to his family, traits I liked. I couldn't—*shouldn't*—get upset when the behaviors resulting from his natural inclinations and his job worked against me. A wordless apology in my tone, I said, "I'm standing in front of Harold now."

"Yeah? Why?" he asked, voice cautious.

"Because Harold texted me that a man with a gun wanted to see me. I figured that whatever happened could be related to my last job here, and if not, then I'd see what I could do to help your uncle. I'm nice that way."

I could hear the smile back in his voice when he said, "Yes, you are. And what do you think about the crime?"

"No werewolf stink. No one dead." I shrugged and punched the screen. "You're on speakerphone. Local LEOs are gone. Press is still out front. Clara is cleaning up human blood." I meandered as I talked and placed my finger over one of many holes in the front door, measuring. "There's evidence of a shotgun being fired into the door." I sniffed the hole and smelled fresh gunpowder and fresh wood. An interesting combo. "Shot came from inside; door was open at the time. Blood on the wall and floor inside. Crime scene tape, but no CSI around, which tells me there was a crime but it was unimportant, or the cops were too lazy to work it up, which doesn't sound like your cousin, the sheriff." I looked at Harold. "What happened?"

Harold said, "Let's back up. The real crime took place up Highway 56. An inmate escaped Angola two days ago. John-Roy Wayne's family was in Alexandria, and that's where everyone figured he was heading. Instead he came here. From what the po-lice said, he had no reason to be in Chauvin, so the sheriff's department wasn't expecting any kind of trouble. Last night he took two young mothers hostage."

I had heard about the prison break two days before, and about the massive manhunt that had followed. Angola State Prison was up near the top of the instep of the boot-shaped state, near the Mississippi border. The hellhole was for the hard-timers, the most violent prisoners in the state. Alexandria, Louisiana, was in the middle of the state, almost due north of Chauvin. Chauvin was the wrong corner of a triangle. I was doing lots of geometry today, but I was still confused and let that show on my face.

Harold walked to the sitting area and turned off the muted TV. He flopped on the couch and put his feet on the shabby-chic coffee table, with a small groan of relief. He looked exhausted, dark rings under his eyes. I hadn't known about the kidnapping, which had probably happened just prior to my leaving New Orleans. But even if I'd known about it, I wouldn't have put those events together with Chauvin and Harold and Clara. "They came here," Harold said.

"We were checking in two fishermen," Clara said, standing, holding one hand out to the side, indicating that I should join Harold in the sitting area. She moved to the sink, where she washed her hands, saying, "John-Roy Wayne busted in the door."

"I was in back"—Harold thumbed at a doorless opening in the shadows of a hallway—"getting extra pillows and blankets. I heard Clara scream. Not a scream," he corrected. "More a startled, scared yelp."

"The man had a gun. He wanted money," Clara said. I could hear the underlying fear in her voice, and smell the fear stink from her pores. She had been terrified. Still was, though her hands, drying on a towel, were steady and sure. "And he wanted to know where you were."

"Me?" I had never even heard of John-Roy Wayne.

"Yeah, you," Harold said. "He said, 'Where's the Cherokee bitch?'" He looked at his wife. "Sorry for the profanity, honey. Anyways, I grabbed my gun and came out here. Moved so fast that I hit the doorway." Harold held up his right arm to reveal a bandage on the back, just below the elbow. "That's my blood all over. Took us a while to get it to stop bleeding. The doc at the emergency room said I hit a small artery. At the time, I didn't even notice. Anyways, Clara, she's a smart one. She hit the deck when I came charging out. *Everyone* hit the floor, and I fired at John-Roy. He ran. My rounds hit the door, but I think I missed John-Roy. Anyways, he took off with wheels screeching."

"In a stolen car." Clara brought me a glass of iced tea with a wedge of lemon and indicated I should take a seat on the love seat, across from Harold, in the tiny sitting area, and I centered the cell on the table between us. It was all very domestic, considering the circumstances. I took the tea, sat, and sipped. Clara said, "The sheriff thinks he probably stole an airboat off the wharf a mile or so north. One's been reported missing, and the stolen car was found there."

Over the cell, Rick said, "CSI is on-site. There's evidence the women were in the car."

I didn't want to ask what kind of evidence. I had a bad feeling about what they were going through. A real bad feeling.

"Anyways," Harold said, which he said a lot, "the fishermen bailed. Haven't seen them since. But their room is ready anytime they want to come back. Extra pillows and blankets waiting." From the satisfied way he smiled, I assumed that the men had already paid for the room. Whether they used it or not was up to them.

"The police think he'll head north along the waterways." Clara handed me a linen tea napkin, like a cocktail napkin but classier. "They think he'll likely end up back in Alexandria."

Rick said, "I'd agree, except for the tiny mention of a Cherokee female. I did some checking. This hasn't been released to the press, but the female werewolf you killed, Jane, was the prisoner's little sister, Victoria Wayne."

My heart fell. I had already begun to consider that, somehow, the crimes were related to me. I'd just gotten the *why*s of it all backward. Of course, *I* hadn't killed the were-bitch, but I was the visible face of Yellowrock Securities. YS's previous hunt for the "wild dogs" in the area had hit the news about three days after we left Chauvin. My photo, taken directly from the pages of YellowrockSecurities.com, had stared back at me for all of fifteen seconds on the news that night. No one had mentioned the presence of Rick and PsyLED, or the Younger brothers. Just me and the fact that I had stayed at the Sandlapper. Apparently I looked good on the small screen. My partners had made fun of me for days for being a movie star. I had figured that was the end of it. I'd figured wrong.

My fifteen seconds of fame was all it took for John-Roy to decide I'd killed his sister.

Rick went on, relentless in his cop voice, that toneless expression they use when they tell bad news. "The facts, ma'am. Just the facts," courtesy of Joe Friday on *Dragnet*. "We had thought that the law enforcement roadblocks out of Angola forced him to steer south, but with Uncle Harold's statement, I've revised that scenario. It's only been a few days since John-Roy's sister died, and it isn't like he had Internet access in the state facility. He's looking for you, and because of the media, he thinks you're still in Chauvin."

That made sense of a sort. "Go on."

"According to the timeline we've developed, he took the women to make travel easier. Their families didn't notice they were gone until night came and they didn't come home. No one put two and two together for hours. No one was searching for an armed man traveling south with two females. And by then they were gone."

"That's not the only reason why he took the women," I said softly.

"No. Probably not." The cop tone was stronger now, harder, colder.

"And he's got them down here in the swamps somewhere. Because he thinks, what?" I tried to think like an angry human. "His sister died in the area and the media posted it all over that I'd stayed here. So therefore Harold and Clara would know where I was?"

"That's what we think."

We. The cops. "Does he have survival skills? Weapons? Friends who might help?"

"Yeah. Also not released to the public. A pawnshop was broken into in Thibodaux," Rick said. "Guns, ammo, and camping supplies were stolen. Some dehydrated meals. A first aid kit. And John-Roy has a former cell mate living in Galliano. Goes by the moniker Snake. Snake didn't show up for work this morning. Lastly we just discovered two DBs in a gas station bathroom. We think it might be the work of our missing felon."

DBs. Dead bodies. I said, "So we have two missing women, probably already traumatized. Two cons, maybe together, maybe not. All four human. And a lot of swamp. Why are you calling me?" I figured I knew, but I believed in laying my cards on the table, and I wanted that from my sorta-boyfriend.

"John-Roy and Snake are hunting for you. I think once John-Roy regroups and gains access to the Internet and other media, he'll figure out that you live in New Orleans and he'll head there. That needs not to happen."

I realized what he meant. It was hunt for them out there, where there were fewer possibilities of collateral damage—meaning dead humans—or have them hunt me in the city, where someone unrelated to the case might get hurt. It was a no-brainer.

"The sheriff's department might be willing for you to help track the guys." He didn't say it, but with his cousin Nadine being the sheriff, it was likely he had already broached the possibility. More of those tangled familial ties. "I'd send Brute to help you track, but I need him here."

I snorted a laugh. That one I hadn't expected. Rick's werewolf partner and I mighta worked together okay for a while, and I was grateful that he saved my life and all, but he was a pain in the butt. "I got another idea who I can get to help." Not that I'd tell Rick who. Some secrets should go to the grave. "You want to notify Nadine and tell her to keep her men from shooting me and my team?"

Sarge was related to Rick and Harold and Clara. He was also a lone wolf, a werewolf who ran and hunted alone beneath the full moon, and had done so for decades—sane—all of which was unheard of for were-wolves. He was a grizzled war vet and pilot, and at the time I had felt pretty good about not telling the world about him. About not filling him full of silver rounds. I felt even smarter about it now. *If* he would help me.

"Yeah. Thanks, Jane," Rick said, his voice softening.

"Why is this so important to you?" I asked. "Your job is hunting super-naturals. This isn't your sister kidnapped. Your family wasn't harmed except for a self-inflicted flesh wound. The culprits and victims are human. What's PsyLED's interest?"

"PsyLED could give a rat's ass for this case," Rick growled, his black big-cat sounding in his voice. "But all this came from our job down there. It's unfinished business."

That I understood perfectly. I nodded. "Okay. I'll stay. I'll track the escaped prisoner. And I'll let the sheriff's office handle hostage negotiation and taking prisoners unless I see a reason to do otherwise. And this one's on me," I added. "Like you said. It's unfinished business. Get Nadine to send all pertinent info to my cell and e-mail."

I ended the call and dialed the Kid, the electronic genius member of the firm. The Kid—given name Alex, and sometimes still called Stinky because of his occasional lack of personal hygiene—answered, "Jane. Where are you? Eli said we're doing pizza tonight."

I took a breath and prepared to accept the consequences of going off on my own. "You guys go ahead. I'm in Chauvin."

I heard a faint click, a change in the ambient noise on the other end, and Eli, the weapons and tactics guy of the firm, said, "Why?" Never one to waste words, my partner.

"Unfinished business. The escaped Angola prisoner was brother to the were-bitch we took down. John-Roy Wayne picked up an old cell mate and they have two women, young mothers, hostage."

"We'll be there in four hours." The connection ended.

"Well, crap," I said, staring at the phone.

"They're your brothers, dear," Clara said, assuming. "Brothers are like that. They have to protect their sisters."

I started to say that we weren't family, but we were all three orphans. We lived together. We did sorta physically resemble each other: Eli and Alex were mixed race, and I was Cherokee, giving us all dark skin and hair. We were more than friends. *Family.* "Yes," I said. "My brothers are pains in the neck. Okay if we take our old rooms?"

"I'll get them aired out, dear," Clara said.

I carried my empty tea glass to the sink and headed to the door. "I'll be back. I'm heading out to talk to a pilot and borrow a dog."

Without turning from the sink, where she was washing my glass, Clara said, "Tell Sarge and Chris and their great monster dog that we said hi."

"Will do," I said. And took off down the stairs, to wade through the newsies who were waiting for me, blocking both exits, microphones extended. I thought about ignoring them but realized that this might be the best way of keeping the escaped con in the area. I slowed and said, "I have a statement." The cameras and reporters gathered around me like flies to beer. "I'm Jane Yellowrock. I'm in Chauvin. And I'm hunting John-Roy Wayne. You want me, Johnnie boy? Come and get me." I climbed on Bitsa and took off, helmet still on the bike, my braid streaming in the wind.

One thing about riding a Harley. You can outpace a news van in no time flat.

Beyond a quick glance at the lush greenery, the kind only an earth witch can coax to grow in wintertime, I hadn't paid much attention to Sarge's place when Yellowrock Securities hired him to fly us to the kill sites of werewolf attacks. The house was an old tidewater, built on low stilts, with lattice covering the open space beneath. Sarge had been expecting us last time we came. Not so much now. The Vietnam War vet didn't like most people, and he had the guns to make sure they stayed away.

I pulled into his drive, up to the house, and walked to the door. Knocking was superfluous after the noise of Bitsa, but it was also polite, and good manners had been part of the curriculum in the Christian children's home where I was raised. I knocked. Sarge opened the door before I dropped my hand. He was holding a shotgun. At his side was PP, short for Pity Party. The part mastiff, part buffalo, part elephant growled at me, showing teeth. Freaking *big* teeth.

Beast padded to the front of my brain and glowered out at her. Beast chuffed, wanting to take the challenge PP offered. PP growled low, as if she detected a change in my scent, morphing into something dangerous. Most dogs could sense the big-cat of my Beast, my mountain lion, hiding deep inside. Or maybe Pity Party just didn't like me.

I shoved Beast down and raised both hands in the universal gesture of peace, or maybe the universal gesture of *I am not holding a gun. See? Don't shoot.* "Sarge," I said, "I'm not here to cause you trouble. Or to tell anyone about your secret."

"Then why *are* you here?"

"Partly because I need answers to a couple of questions."

"I've never turned anyone. Not once. Ain't interested in making a pack. Never was. I got what I want. And I'll defend it to my last dying breath. That about cover it?"

I chuckled and said, "That covers the questions part of why I'm here."

"What's the other part? I got lunch waiting." PP growled again, this time deeper. And Sarge still had the gun leveled at my chest.

"I need a partner and the necessary equipment to help me track down an escaped inmate and another ex-con who took two women prisoner. They took off into the countryside. Waterside. Whatever you call this swamp. The men are violent, armed, have survival equipment and skills. And they'll kill us as soon as look at us."

"Long as it ain't something dangerous, then," he said, laconic, a twinkle in his eyes. Sarge broke open his shotgun and draped it across an arm, pushing open the door. "Come on in. I reckon we got a lot to talk about. Let her in, PP. And go get Christabel. Tell her we got company."

The dog was gonna tell someone they had company? Huh.

PP padded away, her claws clicking on the floor. Inside, the house was decorated in French country, with lots of wood and crockery and copper pots hanging near the AGA stove. There were white quartz countertops and dark green walls with weathered gray cabinets. And flowers every-where, in vases, in pitchers, stemless blooms floating in shallow bowls. Over the floral fragrances, I could smell Italian sausage simmering on the AGA and pasta and fresh bread and aromatic cheeses. My mouth watered. And it made me feel guilty, to think of my stomach while two young women were being . . . I shook my head to make the images go away.

"Sit a spell," Sarge said as we entered a great room with matching leather couch, love seat, and recliner, upholstered ottomans, and a beautiful wall-hanging over the fireplace, made of different lengths and colors of horsehair, an image suggestive of the black water swamp and the sky under moonlight. "Hope you're hungry. My wife will insist you join us." He didn't sound too happy about it, and placed the shotgun on a small side table instead of putting it away. I took that as a sign to be *very* careful. Sarge dropped into the recliner in the corner, house wall at his back, windows and doors in his line of sight, and shotgun about a quarter second from his hand.

"I don't have time to eat," I said. "I don't have time to visit. I just need to know if you'll help me."

"Sit," he said again, this time pointing to the chair that put my back to everything important. I wanted to sock him to make him listen to me, but I took a seat catercorner to him, not the one he'd wanted me to take.

It wasn't the best seat in the house from a defensive standpoint, but it *was* second-best. Somehow my chair choice made a point for me; Sarge chuckled. "So, what do you want me to do for you?" he asked.

"I was hoping you and PP might join me." He didn't appear to be opposed to the idea, so I took a quick breath and added, "Both on leashes."

Sarge didn't shoot me. He didn't move at all. I heard ticking, slow and sonorous, and saw the pendulum of a grandfather clock swaying off to my right. The ticking seemed to echo through the house. My palms started to sweat. I didn't want to fight a werewolf in any form, especially not one with a shotgun close to hand. Weres are fast.

Then Sarge started to chuckle and I unclenched my fists. "You hear that, Christabel? This skinny little thing wants to put a leash on me."

"It worked for me," a breathy voice said.

I turned my head, only slightly, and took in the woman standing next to the clock. She was slight, model-thin, like a size zero, with waist-length hair in calico-cat patterns, patches of white and silver, black and brown, blond and reds. I envied her dye job. If it was a dye job. I sniffed. She smelled of trees. Oak, pine, sycamore, sourwood, and sweet gum. She wasn't human. I wasn't even sure she was mammalian. I didn't know how long she'd been there, and that bothered me. I didn't smell witchy magics on the air, but then, the trees, garlic, and spices were strong enough to mask most any other scent. "Come," she said to both of us. "Let us break bread."

Sarge came up out of the recliner like a bullet and I jerked. He laughed again, and I knew the wolf leap had been to push my buttons. I rose from the chair, coming to my feet closer than was polite in human terms. He didn't back down. I didn't either. And this close, I could smell the were-stink on him. A low growl came from my other side, reminding me that PP would love to join in a fight.

"Do not toy with the *u'tlun'ta*, my love," Christabel chided. "Even if you tree her, she may bite."

"I'm not a liver eater," I said, stung.

Christabel shrugged, hands folded at her waist, her hair moving in the air current of the heating vent as she replied, "It is only a matter of time."

This woman knew what I was. And knew of the curse that clung to my kind, to eventually go insane and start eating people. I forced my breathing to remain steady, calmed my heart rate. I was too close to them to win any kind of fight with the werewolf/husband/protector, his part-mammoth dog, and his wife, the nonhuman whatever-she-was. And Christabel might have some answers to questions about my magic and heritage.

Sarge extended an arm like a refined waiter and said, "After you, my ladies."

I followed Christabel to the kitchen, Sarge and PP on my heels. I tried real hard not to sweat or let my breathing speed at the thought of them behind me. I didn't succeed. I heard Sarge pant once, in delight or hunger or both.

They indicated a chair, and since it had a decent wall behind it, I took it. "There are women in trouble. *Mothers*," I repeated as I sat, to shove my urgency deeper into them, like a needle under a fingernail. Sarge sat at the table and toasted first his wife, then PP, sitting on the floor, her head at Sarge's elbow, then me, and sipped his wine. "You'd only need to be leashed in front of cops," I said.

"After lunch," Sarge said again.

I barely contained a growl and picked up my fork. I stopped before I shoved it into the pasta. Neither of them had started eating. This was a test? Holding my fork in the air, I sniffed, searching for what was wrong. And then it hit me. They were waiting for grace. I wanted to stab Sarge with the fork, but I laid it on the table and lowered my head. But I didn't close my eyes.

Christabel closed hers and said, "May the all-knowing and all-seeing, the creator gods of the first Word, bless our repasts and our day. We give thanks for life and all that is green, for all water and all rain, for all fish in the seas, for all plants that grow. For sun and moon and earth and sky. We pray for peace among all beings."

Sarge said, "Father, bless this day, this food, this house, this wife, and this hunt. May the blood of my enemies stain my teeth this day."

He was going on the hunt. And he wanted to eat people. *All righty, then,* I thought.

A beat too late, I realized they were waiting for me to pray aloud, round-robin-style. Which I hadn't done since I'd left the children's home. In fact, I hadn't prayed in, well . . . a while. More guilt wormed beneath my skin and sucked out my spirit, like a leech, attached to my soul. "Ah maaaan," I sighed, knowing this was another test. I was gonna have to pray. Aloud. In front of people who didn't believe anything I did.

Thinking how I might contribute, aware that prayers revealed more about the pray-er than the deity prayed to. Looking back and forth between them, I dredged up the memory of a childhood course about the names of God, and mentally added to it, the way The People, the Cherokee, spoke when they talked to God.

I said, "Um. To El Roi, the God Who Sees Me, I pray. See this food. I am grateful. See this house. Bless it and keep it safe. See this couple. Bless this union. And see the men I hunt. May they be found and given over to the mercies of"—I stumbled my way through—"Elohei-Mishpat, the God of Justice. May Jehovah Sabaoth, the Lord of Armies, give them into my hand in battle. El Roi, see the women the evil ones have stolen. El Rechem, God the Merciful, keep them safe."

"Jewish?" Sarge asked, open curiosity on his face as he stuffed a forkful of sausage into his mouth.

"Christian."

"I don't like Christians."

"Most of us aren't likable. But then most people aren't very likable either, and Christians are people."

"Huh. You hear that, Christabel? This *u'tlun'ta* is a philosopher."

"Not an *u'tlun'ta*, and not a philosopher," I said, following Sarge's lead and taking a bite of the sausage, which burst into flavor so intense I thought my head might explode. "As a child, I was trained as a War Woman of The People."

"It is a worthy calling for an *u'tlun'ta*. These women the prisoner took," Christabel said, not waiting for me to deny it. "They are your family?"

"Wouldn't know them from Eve's house cat," I said.

"Eve kept several house cats." Christabel sipped her wine and ate a piece of pasta as I watched. Her teeth were not the blunt teeth of a primate or an herbivore, but the pointed teeth of a predator. "Her favorite was a tawny Abyssinian named Lilith."

"Uh-huh." I shoved in a bite, chewed, swallowed, sipped, swallowed, shoved in another bite. It was delicious. It was decadent. It was also taking too long. I shoved in another bite, watching them.

"If you do not have . . . relation to them . . ." Christabel stopped and started over. "If you do not have a *relationship* with them, why do you wish to hunt for them and kill their enemies? Humans die often in this place.

The digested meat and gnawed bones of many humans lie in the muck at the bottom of the bayous, channels, ditches, and lakes. This is a place of death." She swirled pasta on her fork, stabbed a sausage, and inserted it into her mouth—which opened wider than it should have. I tamped down on the urge to shudder, but she smiled as if she saw it anyway.

"The young of humans are important to the sane among us," I said, which said a lot and nothing, so I added, "And the females are as well."

Christabel laughed, a sound more akin to hollow wood wind chimes than true laughter. "You speak lies, u'tlun'ta. I have watched human males rape and kill their young and their women for longer than you can imagine."

"Yeah?" I put down my fork. It landed with a small *clink* on the china plate. "My grandmother and I hunted down and killed the men who raped my mother. It was slow and painful and it took a long, long time."

Christabel laughed again, this time clapping her hands. Her hair floated around her like gossamer strands of silk, fine as spiderweb, fine as the fluffy down of baby birds. "I like this one," she said to Sarge. "Hunt with her. And bring me the scalps of the ones you kill."

"Fine," Sarge said, "I can do that," as if it was Christabel's decision that counted. As if, had she said, offhand, *Kill this woman,* he would have stood up and strangled me. "Lemme get my guns and change. We can meet at the dock and take my airboat. You'll need to move that hog. I don't want anyone to think Christabel's here with company." While he was gone, I helped Christabel clear the table. She prattled the whole time about recipes. I made noises of agreement and didn't tell her I don't cook.

It was on my way out that I got a closer look at the wall hanging, the one I'd thought was made of horsehair. It wasn't horse. It was human hair. And Christabel had told her pet werewolf to bring her scalps. Something told me the command wasn't metaphorical. *Holy crap.* One of the nonhuman beings I'd eaten dinner with was an artist with death. I closed the door, mounted Bitsa, and tightened the bungees that held my helmet in place on the back wheel fender. Looking at the sky, I muttered, "I'll bargain most anything you want to not have to go back in there again. Just sayin'."

No one answered. I didn't really expect him to.

PP left the house, strapped into an overcoat-sized harness like a service dog, but this harness didn't have pockets filled with the TV remote, phone, pencils, paper, and things a disabled person might need. This harness was strapped with weapons.

PP was wearing several handguns and what looked like a Mossberg shotgun on her far side, a Sterlingworth twelve gauge on the side closest. And knives. Lots of them. Her pockets were full of gear. Nothing fancy, nothing Eli would bring along, just guns to hunt with. I liked.

The harness was a good design. I heard no clanking when she trotted up, and PP carried her leash in her mouth. When she reached my bike, she sat and looked at me, waiting, then turned and looked to the back of the house, at the black water, trying to tell me where I was supposed to be.

I gunned Bitsa and followed PP around back, aware that if the bizarre couple wanted to kill me and hide the evidence, I was giving them ample opportunity. And my hair was really long. Christabel could probably do wonders with it.

I wheeled Bitsa beneath the extended overhang of an outbuilding, in the shade and out of any possible rain, checked my weapons, holstered up, added a few extra mags of ammo and a bag of turkey jerky, and joined PP at the shoreline. Sarge's plane was . . . moored, I guessed, at the dock, and on the other side of it, an airboat had been pulled up onshore. I hadn't noticed the boat the last time we were here, but then, my attention had been on the thought of flying. Which I hated.

PP's head turned back to the house at the same instant that I smelled werewolf. I managed not to draw on my host, and also to pivot slowly instead of whirling, but it was a near thing. I had thought Sarge had meant he was going to change clothes to start this hunt, but he had taken me literally when I said he'd be leashed. A big gray wolf sat on the back deck staring at me with eyes the color of rainbow moonstone. Christabel's hand was on his head, petting his ears as if he were a dog. Whatever magic had hidden his scent, it was gone now, with him in wolf form.

Previously I had seen Sarge in his wolf form only at a distance, in poor lighting. Seen closer, his coat was silver, each hair black-tipped, black legs and tail, a silver brow with a black stop and a black stripe that ran down his nose. He nudged Christabel, who knelt and strapped him into a harness like PP's, but his was looser and had a strap up the tail, which would keep the harness in place while in dog form but allow him to change to human form while wearing it.

Once he was harnessed, Sarge picked a leash up in his mouth and carried it to me. As he left her, Christabel caught my gaze and held it with hers. She grinned, her mouth full of sharp, pointed teeth. I nodded once. I understood. If I didn't bring her family back unharmed, she'd find me, kill me, eat me, and take my scalp for her trophy wall. Though maybe not in that order.

Sarge stopped at my feet and moved his eyes from me to the airboat. I untied the rope and put my back into getting the boat offshore, into the water. When the bow was still on sand, Sarge whuffed and I stood straight, arching my back to loosen the muscles. Sarge and PP leaped into the boat and I followed. There were seat belt–like harnesses suitable for big dogs on the front bench seat, and seat belts for humans on the upper seat. The key was in the ignition. A storage trunk ran the width of the johnboat, just in front of the prop. There was plenty of gasoline in the tanks, and the steering mechanism was the same as another I'd driven, a stick that controlled the rudders. In moments, I had the canines belted in, and we were practically flying toward the last known location of the escaped prisoner and his two hostages, the roar of the airboat deafening. There would be no sneaking up on anyone in an airboat.

Sheriff Nadine LaFleur was onshore, with haphazardly parked cruisers, a crime scene van, and local law enforcement behind her. Lots of cops and deputies, male, female, all races, dressed in a mélange of uniform styles, street clothes, and business attire designating their branches of law enforcement. *The gang's all here,* I thought. Media vans were in the distance with telephoto lenses, trying to see what was going on.

I beached the boat near the small pier off Highway 56, known to the locals as Little Caillou Road, Nadine's eyes checking out the canines. She ignored PP, as if she'd seen the dog before, but the wolf was a different matter. Nadine wasn't happy to see him.

As the noise of the airboat abated, law enforcement types spread out, all armed, most carrying shotguns in addition to their sidearms, two with sniper rifles. Every single one of them turned a weapon in our direction.

I did my best to look innocent, but the black leather jacket, vamp-killers strapped to my thighs, and bulges of more weapons beneath my clothes didn't help. Sarge made a barking sound and grinned at the humans like a frisky pup. PP took her cues from him and sat up, barking, looking as pretty as a buffalo dog can.

"Don't tease the humans, Fido," I said. Sarge's mouth snapped shut and the look he gave me was not playful. "What?" I murmured, for his ears only. "You want me to call you Sarge?" I could see all sorts of things flicker through the wolf's eyes before he vocalized softly and ducked his head. I'd made my point. I smoothed my wind-tangled hair, keeping my hands visible, tucking the ends into my braid as Nadine approached. The stocky, dark-haired woman was frowning, the stink of hatred and fear in her wake. The cops didn't like werewolves. Which was okay by me. I didn't like them either.

I studied the group as they advanced on the airboat. There were dogs and multijurisdictional vehicles and boats and gear. The LEOs were preparing to start a search and rescue, an SAR, for John-Roy and the kidnapped women, but they hadn't left yet, which was good. Their passage would mess up the air currents and any scents the wind might carry. We were just in time. *Ducky.*

"What is *that*?" Nadine jerked her chin at Sarge.

"Sarge loaned me PP, and the wolf came by boat." Which was not a lie. Go, me.

"Sarge is always willing to loan his dog. That wasn't my question. Where did you get the werewolf and why don't I just shoot him where he sits?" One of the snipers raised his rifle and took a bead on Sarge.

"Fido's people-friendly, won't bite, and has the best nose in the business. He knows what and who we're looking for, and because he has a human intelligence coupled with the nose of a hunting predator, and because it isn't the full moon, he's our best bet for success. Between the two canines, we hope to find the bad guys, call you to come take them in, and rescue the women." I looked at the snipers and said, "And if you have standard ammo, not silver, nothing short of an elephant gun will kill him. And then you'll have a fast-healing, pissed-off werewolf on your hands."

"Stand down," Nadine said to her men. To me she said, "Why? What do you get out of it? You think you're responsible because you killed John-

Roy Wayne's werewolf sister Victoria?" Nadine was brutally direct. I liked that in a woman.

"Not me. But yeah. My team. A job for which I have yet to be paid," I added. Nadine responded with a frown, so I finished in a soft voice meant just for her and not the men behind her. "This is a freebie. Now, you gonna let my friends here sniff the stolen car you got cordoned off over there and let us get on the water, or are you just gonna stand here wasting my time?"

Nadine's eyebrows shot up, she snorted, and she stepped away from the boat. "Let the trackers at the vehicle, y'all," she called out. "Let's see what the werewolf and PP can do."

I released the canines from their seat belt harnesses and snapped on the leashes, made of strong, durable, nylon flex, and jumped from the bow to the hard-packed ground. The cops opened a wedge of space, like a gauntlet, for us to pass through. The huge critters at my sides, we walked through the cops to the car. It was sitting at an angle across the faded parking lines, all four doors open. Inside it was a mess, paper food wrappers, a stuffed animal that looked as if it had spent a year in a city dump, clothes, pillows, and blankets. My sense of smell was much better than a human's, and I leaned in with the canines, pulling the air over my tongue with a *scree* of sound. The car smelled of fast food, fear, blood, and semen.

Fury lit in my gut, flashing through me like a wildfire. Sarge swiveled his head to me and growled at the stink and what it might mean. "Yeah," I said softly to him. Since Crime Scene was finished with the vehicle, I crawled inside and followed my nose until I found the place where the stink came from. It was on the back of the front seat, and beside it was a smear of blood.

"Fido, smell this. See if the blood belongs to the same man." Sarge wriggled up beside me, far closer than I really wanted the werewolf, and placed his nose near the blood. He gave two quick sniffs and backed away, a canine grin on his face. "She hurt him, didn't she?"

Sarge chuffed and growled, dipping his head in agreement. The women had been hurt too, though, and the stink of fear and pain was strong in the car.

Louder, without turning my head, I said, "Somebody was beaten in the car. Fido can smell it." Nadine cursed. I was aware that her men had gathered in a tight circle around us, but their commingled scent was less antagonistic than it had been.

"Was everyone alive when they left the car?" I asked Sarge. He nodded once. "Two women?" He nodded. "How many men?" He dipped his head twice. I looked around, wondering how the other guy got here.

"You got any more vehicles unaccounted for here?" I asked Nadine. "Because John-Roy Wayne probably already had male company when he took off." Nadine cursed again and sent her men to check vehicle tags. I said softly, "You got the scent?" Sarge whuffed. "Let's go, then. We're gonna move real casual, back toward the boat, and soon as we get settled, we're gonna blow outta here. We're not gonna be slowed down by cops trying to keep up. We're not waiting for them to get the SAR team ready and give out little radios and coordinate a plan. Understood?"

Sarge tilted his head at me and licked his chops.

Fifteen minutes later my cell buzzed in my pocket. We were far enough away that I couldn't see the shore, and there had been no pursuit, so I killed the motor, leaving the airboat gliding across the water. I popped the cell and ignored the files on John-Roy, sent to me by Nadine, because I recognized the number from earlier. I said, "Ricky Bo. Yes. No. Yes. And I will."

"What?" he asked, thoroughly confused, which was what I'd intended.

"Yes, I left your cousin on the shore with the slow, disorganized cops. No, I won't go back. Yes, we have a scent. And I'll be careful."

There was a short silence on the other end and then Rick said, "Good. But you left one question unanswered. Where'd you get a werewolf to hunt with?"

"Yeah, that was the only curious part of the plan, wasn't it? You do know that Leo had some weres prisoner once. And you do know that there are werewolf packs in the U.S. And you do know that some wolves are sane. I happened to find me one, and he was willing to help. He came to Chauvin, changed into his wolf, and let me leash him. Now, if you don't mind, I have things to do." I ended the call, scanned John-Roy's criminal history file sent to me by Nadine, sent my partners a text, turned off the cell, and removed the battery.

"You still got the scent?" I asked Sarge. He nodded and faced in the direction he wanted me to go, nose into the wind. "Okay. Let's do this."

It took hours. It took numerous times starting and stopping, backtracking, weaving through glade, swamp, muck, and mud as the air currents wove, splintered, and dissipated. It took Sarge and PP getting off the boat and padding across marshy land, through head-high scrub. It took an hour sitting on a wet bank as the temperature dropped and a lightning storm raged over us, the metal boat pulled up and tied to a stunted tree. It took hours in the unexpected cold and rain for us to get an idea of where the stolen airboat had gone. The law enforcement helicopter that had buzzed us several times early on was a distraction, but the storm chased it away.

We made it far north of Lake Boudreaux before Sarge bumped my knee with his nose and stared hard at shore. I pulled in, beaching the airboat on a muddy bank, tangled with roots. On the still air I smelled fire and beef cooking over coals. The sun was going, and a mist was rising off the water as icy air moved in. We were running out of time.

"I take it this is as far as we can go in the boat?" I asked. Sarge nodded once and nosed my cell phone. "You want me to make a call for you?" He looked away, indicating I was stupid. Staring at the fancy, bulletproof device, I said, "If I turn it on, they can find us." Sarge dropped his head to his chest in agreement, lay down, and put his head on his paws. "Fine. Whatever you want." I inserted the battery and booted it up. "*Now* what?"

He just stared at me, then tapped the floor of the airboat twice. I tried to remember all the stuff that the device could do, and combined with the tapped paw, I asked if he wanted our GPS. When he looked interested, I pulled up our current location. It took a few questions and more than a few interpretative decisions on my part, but eventually I pulled up a satellite map of our location.

Not far from us, according to the sat map, was a small island with a fancy house on stilts. Except for a narrow beach and a boat dock, the island was surrounded by water like a moat, with a narrow ring of an islet circling protectively outside the moat. The house could be reached by boat or helo; both methods would give advance notice of our arrival. Parachute landing might go unnoticed. Or wings, if I wanted to go in as a bird and then change back to human—to fight weaponless and naked. *Not.*

I studied the sat photos. The water between the island and the circling islet was gated on two sides, with only the one area of the island open to the surrounding water, where we could manage a frontal attack. "Now, why would an escaped con head to a house in the middle of nowhere? Unless he was killing two birds with one stone?" I hadn't really studied the file sent to me by Nadine. I opened and skimmed it again, finally finding a summary of John-Roy Wayne's arrest history. The guy had been going for a world record in violence.

The info from my partners was more helpful. It contained a list of people who might assist John-Roy, and another list of people he might want to kill just for funsies. "Go, Alex," I said to myself. "You get pizza for all this." I thought about the info and about the house not far ahead, on stilts.

"Sarge? Do you know who lives in that well-secured house?" He nodded, his eyes suddenly tight on me. It was unnerving to be looked at with such intensity by any predator, but a werewolf was in a category by himself. I stifled my shudder and assured myself it was only the cold and the damp that lent me a chill. I was lying, but it made me feel better. I said, "If I read a list of names, can you tell me if any of them live here?"

Sarge nodded slowly, his eyes never leaving me. I started with the people John-Roy might want to kill. The wolf made no reaction to any of the names, but when I started on the list of people John-Roy would like to hang with, I got a response. Elvis Clyde McPhatter Lamont. I texted the name to Alex, along with the location of the island house. Moments later, Eli texted back, Kid says Elvis is bad news. Get close. Pick landing site. Keep cell on. I drop in 1900. Eli had already figured out he needed to parachute. He was close. *Go, Rangers!*

Alex sent me an arrest photograph of Elvis Lamont and a list of his priors, which included kidnapping and running a forced sex-slave ring. The tat on his neck would make him easy to recognize. It was an oversized penis. I shared all this with Sarge, showing him the sat maps, and finished with, "My partner will be here at seven o'clock. We need to be on that island by then. He'll use my cell as a homing beacon to jump in.

"It's gonna be miserable by seven," I continued. "I suggest we move close to the island, and then hunker. Which sounds like a cold winter swim." Sarge tilted his head, whuffed with laughter, and tugged on the seat harness. When I released him, Sarge picked up a paddle in his teeth and dropped it at my feet, then leaped over the seats to the storage chest at the base of the propeller cage. Inside was an inflatable two-person raft.

"Oh," I said. "Soooo much better." We'd be crowded, but we wouldn't have to swim. PP, who had closed her eyes for a nap, whuffed at me. I texted our plan to the guys and spread open the tiny raft, plugged it into the airboat's battery, and hit the AUTOINFLATE button. I had paddled an inflatable raft before, and in short order, we were on board, though sitting low in the water with so many bodies. It took a bit of practice to remember how to navigate with a single paddle, but I managed, and we moved through the sluggish mist and the remains of the storm.

Water plinked onto water between drenchings—when water drummed onto water. It was cold and miserable. And it was helpful. No one would see us unless they had low-light or infrared-light devices, and even then they wouldn't be able to tell what the odd-shaped bundle was. But it was slow going, and even with my Beast to warm me, it was cold.

Rain running down my neck worsened my chill. Rain wasn't good for riding leathers, unless I got a chance to dry and clean my jacket right away, and that wasn't happening. Stupid thoughts to keep the ones that mattered at bay. The island, isolated, secure, was a perfect location to break in new women to the forced sex trade. The two kidnapped women, already brutalized, were probably going to be sold for cash.

My mother had been raped by two men, the same ones who killed my father. I had evened the score. The heat of vengeance spread through me at the memories, and while I tamped down on them, I also let them warm me. I could use this anger.

After nearly two hours we got close to the house. The light of day had dulled down to mostly nothing, the sunset smothered by clouds, the water hidden by fog. I wished I had Eli's cool tech devices to see through the fog if there were people patrolling with guns, but I'd have to go on canine noses and skinwalker senses. The house windows blazed with light, haloing the mist. Something bumped the bottom of the boat. Sarge growled, low and full of menace. "Gators?" I whispered. Sarge's eyes swept the water around us, but eventually he went silent. And I paddled on. It was too cold for gators. I hoped.

My cell buzzed. I opened the titanium case to see the text. Airborne. Where land?

Hoping I was right, I texted back, 170 ft due N my position. Which, if he timed it perfectly, would put him in back of the house. If he missed, he'd be *on* the house.

Long minutes later my cell buzzed. The text said, Ten minutes. Hit shore. Take front door. Careful. Gators in water around house.

"Well, that's just ducky," I said.

Eight minutes later, we had maneuvered between slivers of islands, past a dock where three boats had been moored—boats now floating free, thanks to a sharp knife severing the mooring lines, moving slowly into the water of the channel. No one was getting off the island tonight. In the pitch dark, we beached on the one small muddy shore not protected by gators fenced into a moat. Two airboats were moored there. Smoke and voices filtered through the mist, the fog making it hard to tell where they came from. The canines were staring at one airboat and the shore, nostrils flaring. Even in human form, I could smell the prisoners, the kidnapped women. We had the right place. I slipped from the raft and removed the keys from the other airboats and, after a moment's hesitation, unhooked the gas lines from the motors.

"Sarge?" I whispered. "They might have nighttime vision equipment. They might have guns. Or we could be wrong and our target's not here." Sarge snorted, telling me the women were here, and so was John-Roy. "You and PP be careful."

Sarge grunted and he and PP, still laden with weapons, leaped off the boat and moved into fog-filled shadows. I felt a tingle of magic on my skin that told me Sarge had started to change back into human form. I just hoped he'd brought clothes with him, and grinned at the thought of the war vet attacking naked. It was my only grin of the day, and it faded fast.

I checked my cell. My time was up. I drew a vamp-killer and a nine mil, the metal dry and warm from contact with my body. Weapons to my sides, the blade held back against my forearm, steel handle in a steady grip, I walked toward the house. For the first time in my career, for the first time since I'd killed my father's murderers, I was deliberately hunting humans.

My nose was little use in the fog, but I pulled on Beast's better vision, and the night smoothed out into grays and silvers and greens. The form of a man appeared in front of me, my nose telling me he wasn't one of mine, though he was facing the house. I walked up to him and bonked him on the head. He fell silently. I searched him quick and came up with a small subgun and a walkie-talkie. They made nice splashes in the water.

I met no one else outside. The house was a two-story mansion on pylons. This close, I could smell people. Humans, lots of them, came and went all the time, but for now, the numbers were few. The night went silent, the voices I had been hearing stopped. I tried the door. I texted Eli: Unlocked.

Instantly I got back Go.

I opened the door and stepped inside, into the shadow of a fake ficus tree. Warmth and sensory overload hit me simultaneously, and I looked around, first for people—none—and then for cameras. None also. Which was smart in a way. If you were doing something illegal, you needed to make sure nothing was filmed or recorded. Of course, if you were under attack, the lack of cameras was stupid.

I took a breath. The air reeked of cigars, expensive liquor, pain, fear, sex, and blood. And young females. Beast slammed into me. *Kits!* she thought at me. *Hurting.*

She wanted to run straight for the scent, but I clamped down on her. *Stealth,* I thought at her. Beast snarled but held still. I stepped to the side and took in the foyer. Cypress-wood floors, rugs, smoking lounge to my right, bar to my left. Large-screen TVs in each room. A game room was ahead, with pool tables, dartboard, comfy chairs. I moved cautiously into it. And found a stage with a brass pole. No people. Stairs going up and the stink of fear coming down.

A moment later, Eli appeared from the shadows at the back of the house, wearing night camo and loaded for war. He was carrying a pistol with a suppressor screwed on the end, legal in Louisiana. He could fire and the sound, while still loud, was unlikely to carry far. He held up three fingers to indicate how many he had taken down outside, then one finger to show how many he had taken down inside. There was no stink of gunfire or blood, suggesting that he had used nonlethal methods, just as I had. I extended one finger, then used it to point up the stairs. I mouthed, *Prison.*

My partner's mouth turned down. He mouthed what I thought might have been *No mercy*, and he moved up the stairs. I followed. I was halfway up when I heard a woman scream.

Eli ducked right, toward the sound, moving fast in a bent-kneed run. I covered him, seeing a wide hallway running left and right, doors along it, and floor-to-ceiling windows at each, two recliners in front of each window. Which was odd. Until I looked in the closest one and saw a man curled up on a large, four-poster bed, facing away from the glass. Asleep. There were chains on the bedposts and bruises on the young man's back.

Movement caught my eye and a human-shaped Sarge appeared, coming from the end of the hallway. He carried a shotgun and wore black cotton pants and a T-shirt, his hairy feet bare. PP trotted by his side. There was blood on her muzzle. Sarge began to check all the rooms on the far end of the hall, the scent of his anger strong.

Satisfied that he had my back, I slipped from room to room up to Eli. The recliners in front of the window on the end room both held incapacitated bodies, their heads at odd angles. Not breathing. Very dead. One of them was John-Roy's cell pal. The other I didn't know. Sarge had been at work.

Inside the room were two men and two women. The show the men had been watching was ugly. Real ugly. Eli opened the door and said softly, "John-Roy." When the man rose, a gun in his meaty hand, the barrel moving toward the door, Eli fired, the sound not much louder than a dictionary dropped flat from shoulder height. John-Roy fell, screaming, a hole in his abdomen. Eli's next two shots hit the back wall; suppressors made hitting a target at any distance problematic. The second man grabbed a woman and backed from the bed, holding her as a shield.

Eli raced inside. Fast as a big-cat, I followed and centered the sight of my nine mil on the standing man's forehead. I didn't recognize him except for the tattoo of the penis. This was Elvis Clyde McPhatter Lamont, king of the forced sex trade. He wore gold on his wrists and hanging around his neck, but otherwise he was naked, holding a woman, also naked, bleeding, and bruised. But not broken. She looked enraged, her eyes telling me she was ready for anything. Elvis pulled her to the wall.

On the floor, one hand pressing on his belly wound, John-Roy was looking at me. He yelled, "You!" and turned the gun toward me. TV shows where the bad guy always drops his gun are stupid. In real life, it doesn't happen all that often. Eli shot him, again in the abdomen, off center. Not a miss, a deliberate target. Eli wanted him alive.

I laughed, the sound a register lower than my human voice. It carried menace, fury, and delight, and it was all Beast. From behind me, PP leaped into the room, straight to the woman still on the bed. The huge dog lay down next to her, protecting. Ignoring the man and his hostage, Eli secured the room.

Behind me, Sarge walked in, the grizzled man taking in everything. He closed the door behind him, the sound soft and final. "Son," Sarge said to Elvis, "I can't allow you to get away with this. You let the lady go and I'll let you die easy. You keep her, and I'll make sure you die slow." Which sounded pretty generous to me.

But Elvis disagreed. A door I hadn't noticed opened behind him and before I could react, he was gone. Sarge leaped across the room, a distance a human couldn't have covered. Sarge rammed into the door as it closed, splintering wood and revealing a steel core. He bellowed.

I ran out of the room and down the stairs, catching a glimpse of Eli dragging John-Roy by the hair. There was no way off the island tonight, in the fog, except by boat. There hadn't been a land-based boathouse on the sat map—which could have been sadly out-of-date—but I was trusting that it was up-to-date and that the men had arrived in the boats that had been tied to the docks. I raced that way, out of the house, into the black fog of night. Beast, still close to the front of my mind, guided me, her balance assisting mine, her vision lighting the night world. I let her take over.

Can smell nothing new, no female-prisoner smell, no man-predator stink, she thought.

As I reached shore, the lights in the house went out. All of them. "That's because we got out in front of him," I murmured, certain. "We're between him and his getaway boat." I dropped to a crouch and faced the house.

He came from my right, the woman silent, stumbling, her breath shaking. I heard her take a breath and start to scream, the faint hiss followed by a *thump* and the sound of a falling body. The reek of fresh blood was strong on the air. One pair of running footsteps came toward me. He'd hurt her to keep her quiet, and then had to leave her when he'd been too harsh. Which just made my job easier. When he appeared out of the fog, I rose fast. And let him rush onto my blade. It caught him low in the abdomen, and I yanked the blade up, severing everything in its path. Hot blood gushed over my hand, and still I lifted the blade, tilting it to the right so it would miss his aorta and his heart. He went limp, and I let him fall, taking my blade with him.

Around me the heavens opened and a deluge fell. The lights came back on in the house, showing me not much of anything but shadows and a dying man at my feet. Sarge strode up, picked up my prisoner, and flipped the body into his own airboat. PP jumped up beside him, tongue lolling. "Keys," Sarge demanded.

I tossed them to him and moments later, the airboat vanished into the mist, the powerful prop roaring. Eli came from my left, through the rain, carrying the woman Elvis had dropped. "I need to get her inside, into a safe place. She doesn't need to wake up with a man near her," he said. "Call this in. Get medic and the law."

"Yeah," I said, trudging back to the hell house. "Sarge took Elvis. What happened to John-Roy?"

"He ran off into the night," Eli said. "I heard a splash. I think he fell into the moat."

I thought about that for a moment. A gut-shot man *accidently* falling into a moat full of gators. Maybe they'd eat him. Maybe he'd drown first. Maybe not. "Good," I said.

The rest of the night was chaos. Nadine and a sheriff from the parish to the north vied for jurisdictional control of the scene, and the FBI showed, kicking them both out because of the human trafficking. Eli and I were allowed to leave at ten the next morning, free to go after long interrogations. Sarge met us at the shore in his airboat. Together we went back to Chauvin. The media circus onshore was unimaginable, but they ignored us, looking like locals with nothing to say, the reporters too busy trying to hire, bribe, or buy a way to the island in the middle of the black water.

A month later, I got a package in the mail. It was my vamp-killer, smelling of cleansers and oil, the blade freshly honed. There was no note. No explanation. I didn't need one. The blade was explanation enough.

Off the Grid

Author's note: This story takes place just before *Broken Soul*. In it, you'll meet Nell, who will be getting her own series! The first book, *Blood of the Earth*, will be published in August 2016.

I'd stayed in Charlotte for two days, overseeing the latest repairs on my bike, Bitsa. She was pretty well trashed, and she'd be a different bike when I got her back, very slightly chopped, with wider wheel fenders, and this time, no teal in the paint job. Jacob—the semiretired Harley restoration mechanic/Zen Harley priest living along the Catawba River, the guy who had created Bitsa in the first place using parts from two busted, rusted bikes I'd found in a junkyard—had shaken his head when I asked when the bike would be ready to ride to New Orleans. Bitsa had been crashed by a being made of light, and the damage was extensive. It sounded weird when I said it like that—*a being of light*—but my life had gotten pretty weird since I went to work for the Master of the City of New Orleans and the Greater Southeast, Leo Pellissier. Jacob had taken my money but refused to discuss the paint job, saying only that I'd love it. And then he'd plopped me on a loaner bike and shooed me out of his shop as if I were twelve.

I'd ridden the loaner before, a chopped bike named Fang, and though the balance on a chopper-style bike was different from the easy, familiar comfort of Bitsa, it hadn't taken long to settle in for the ride to Asheville, where I'd hugged my godchildren, eaten at their mother's café, and then hit the road for Knoxville, Tennessee. My visit north had been occasioned by a request from Knoxville's top vamp, the Glass Clan blood-master, to try to solve some little problem she had reported to her up-line boss, Leo. Nothing urgent, but Leo was stroking his clan blood-masters' egos a lot, now that the European Council vampires were planning a visit.

The ride had been great, the weather not too hot for spring, not rainy or cross-windy, but my cell phone battery hadn't survived the trip across the mountains, roaming the whole way. I had no communications when I hit the town, and no way to find out contact info.

Without my map app, I had to ask directions, which was kinda old-school, and my badass-motorcycle-mama façade made the Starbucks clerk's eyebrows rise in concern, but she knew her city, and I made it to the Glass Clan Home just after dusk. Not *at* dusk, which might be construed as an offer to be a breakfast snack for the fangy Glass vamps, but just after dusk, which in early summer meant nine p.m. I was entering the Clan Home without backup and without coms, with no one in New Orleans knowing I had arrived safely. I was acting in the capacity of the Enforcer of the NOLA MOC, which meant I'd arrive at the Glass Clan Home fully weaponed out, and I wouldn't be giving up my guns, blades, or stakes to security guards at the door. I wasn't expecting trouble, but I try to always be prepared. It was kinda the modus operandi of a rogue-vamp hunter turned vamp Enforcer for said MOC.

The house was off U.S. 70, not far from the Confederate Memorial Hall, and overlooking the Tennessee River. I'd Googled the house and seen it from above; it was maybe ten thousand square feet, with a six-car attached garage, a slate roof, a swimming pool, a tennis court, and what might have been a putting green. There was an outbuilding, probably a barn, a deduction made from the jump rings set up on the sculpted lawn. Lots of spreading oak trees shaded the heavily landscaped grounds.

The entrance to the address was gated, and I pulled off my helmet, presented ID, and tried to look both unthreatening and as though I could kill without a thought—a difficult combo—to the camera, before the gate rolled back on small, squeaky wheels. It was the perfect ambience for a visit to a bloodsucker. But the midlevel-grade security gate quickly became wood fencing and trailed off into the night, turning into barbed wire only yards out. No cameras followed the fencing, no motion monitors, nada, nothing. The security sucked unless there were armed human guards patrolling, working with dogs. I'd started out in security and I knew an antiquated system when I saw it.

My Beast liked the low-hanging limbs of the old oaks and sent me an image of her sprawled over one, waiting for deer, followed by another one of her swimming in the river, which I could smell close by. "Maybe later," I muttered to her. "Business first." Beast chuffed at me in disgust.

The drive was long and winding, concrete made to look like cobbles, and I could smell horses, a chlorinated pool, clay (maybe for the tennis courts), and the west-flowing river. It was a distinct scent, different from the raw power of the Mississippi by the time it reached New Orleans, different from the North Carolina rivers that flowed east. The Tennessee flowed west, toward the upper Mississippi, a snaky and slow flow, deceptive in its sluggish nature and far more powerful than it looked or smelled. The house the drive led to was an old renovated historical home, the original house made of dull brown river rock, added onto over the years with brick of a similar color.

I left my helmet on the bike seat, adjusted my weapons to be visible but not insulting, and climbed the steps to the front entrance. The door opened before I knocked, and the butler—an honest-to-God butler, wearing a dove gray tuxedo—showed me into the parlor, asked after my ride in, and offered me iced black tea with lemon or mint, which sounded great. I accepted the minty tea, and it appeared in about ten seconds, carried in on a silver tray by a maid, also in gray livery. The butler pointed to the guest restroom with the offer that I might freshen up, which I accepted. I carried the tea glass—draining it—into the powder room and washed up, put on bloodred lipstick, and smoothed my hip-length braid with spigot water. I also plugged in my cell to charge.

My summer riding clothes—jeans and a denim jacket—were sweaty from the day in the sun, and I would rather have showered, eaten, and taken a nap, or shifted to my Beast form and taken that swim in the river, than carry out all the posing and proper etiquette that the older vamps expected, but I didn't have that choice. Leo's primo had made the appointment, and I liked my paycheck. Back in the parlor, I settled on a comfy leather chair, in a room with as much square footage as the entire first floor in my house. It had high ceilings, attic fans, modern furniture—all leather, of course. Vamps had a thing for dead skin. I rolled my empty glass between my palms, patient as my stalking big-cat.

Blood-Master Glass didn't keep me waiting, but her entrance was calculated. I caught movement from the corner of my eye as she walked slowly into the room, with a black-suited human and the butler behind her, the servant carrying another tray with more tea glasses, a pitcher, and tiny sandwiches that smelled like cucumber. Taking them all in with a sweeping look, I set the glass down on the coaster that had been provided and stood.

My Beast moved into the front of my brain and peeked out of my eyes, evaluating the blood-master by sight and smell.

The blood-master was elegant, petite, and of Asian descent, with almond-shaped eyes of a peculiar dark honey hue, black hair worn long but up on the sides in a fancy 'do that probably took a personal servant or two to create, and pale, smooth skin the color of ivory. She was wearing a silk gown of gold and black brocade with touches of crimson embroidery—golden dragons cavorting on a black background that suggested rugged hills, the dragons spitting red fire. Vamps were partial to that particular shade of bloodred. And they liked rubies. Glass was wearing one the size of a robin's egg on a gold chain around her neck.

The butler set the tray on the table in front of me and said, "The Glass Clan blood-master, Ming Zhane." Technically, Ming should have changed her last name to Glass when she defeated the clan founder about a hundred years ago, but Ming wasn't one for abiding by the rules unless they suited her, according to her dossier. Yeah. I had dossiers on most of the vamps in Leo's hunting territories. My team stayed busy.

The butler withdrew after pouring tea into two glasses and refilling my own. The other human stood to the side and I figured that meant it was time for the fancy chitchat. I nodded, a sort of half bow, and introduced myself. "The Enforcer of Leonard Pellissier, Master of the City of New Orleans and the Greater Southeast, Jane Yellowrock, at your command, ma'am."

She smiled, looking pretty much human, except for the paleness, and the thin lines along her eyes contributed to the human appearance. They looked like stress lines, which was odd. Vamps didn't feel or show stress. Mindless insanity, blood thirst, and a tendency to kill anything that moved, yes. Stress, no.

Ming moved closer and breathed in my scent. Her nose wrinkled as she smelled the predator in me. I had discovered that all vamps could smell the danger that I presented, and until the blood-master of a clan or a city approved of me, they all had a tendency to react with violence. Leo was Ming's up-line boss, but he was far away, and that meant she was top dog here. It was hard not to pull away with her so close, but I held still as she sniffed again. "Your scent is not unpleasing, and the photos in your dossier and on your Internet page do not do you justice," Ming said. "You are most lovely."

"I'm just the Enforcer, ma'am. I'm not paid to be pretty." Her eyes darkened and instantly I knew I'd miscalculated, so I said quickly, "But you're thoughtful and . . . uh . . . courteous to say so. Your kind of beauty is something I'll never achieve." Which was all true. She was a stunner. Ming looked a little mollified, so I revised a line Alex had written into her dossier, and piled it on a little more thick. "Your photos show elegance and loveliness, and your personal presence suggests a powerful magic." Yeah. I was getting pretty good at blowing smoke up vamps' backsides, what they called gracious conversation, and I called a load of bull hockey. But not to their faces.

She tilted her head, one of those minuscule, wrong-angled-move gestures vamps can do, and I figured I was out of the woods as to protocol. She indicated with a wave of her hand that I should sit, and weirdly, her fingers trembled just a hint. Vamps didn't tremble either. Ming took the wingback chair beside mine and folded her hands in her lap. The human stood beside her, watching my every move. Ming said, "The master of New Orleans is kind to send assistance in this, our time of need."

"Yes, ma'am. Blood-Master Pellissier is eager to assist all those loyal to him." As I said, smoke up her backside, though my words were still true. Leo was a good master, as far as a bloodsucking-ruler-over-all-he-surveyed type of loyalty went. "How can the Enforcer assist the Glass blood-master and her Mithrans?"

The human in the black suit reached into his jacket at chest level, and I tensed. He stopped the action instantly and then continued, much more slowly. This was Ming's primo, Asian, slender, and deadly. Very, very deadly in a martial arts kinda way. As if he could break me into tiny little pieces with his fingertips, a hard look, and a toothpick before I could blink. "A Mithran has gone missing," he said. "She was last seen with this person." The man—Cai, no last name, or maybe no first name, I wasn't sure—pulled out two sheaves of papers, not a weapon, and placed them on the small table between Ming and me.

I lifted one batch of pages and saw the photo of an old man, maybe in his seventies, with sun-lined skin, sun spots, raised and rough age spots, kinda brown and freckled all over. Faded blue eyes. He was mostly bald. A narrow-eyed, mean-looking man, the kind who was raised on whuppin's, hardtack, and moonshine, and who hated the world. I flipped through the three attached pages. The info said his name was Colonel Ernest Jackson, but there was no mention of military service in the scant record.

The second file showed a digital photo of the vamp in question, Heyda Cohen. She was tiny and very beautiful. Vamps offered people the change for lots of reasons, and personal beauty was high on the list. But Heyda's intelligent, piercing eyes suggested that she was special in other ways as well.

"Heyda was in charge of my personal security and she was contacted by that human man"—Ming pointed at his photo—"a communication that carried a threat to me. She tracked him." Ming's speech, accented by her native Asian language, sped up and her syntax grew more fractured. "Then she met with that human and three of his followers. In a park. In the city. Then she went away with him. Without contacting us or alerting her support team, who were waiting in the park, watching. They allowed her to leave, as she did not appear distressed. We do not know why she left with him. She did not come home afterward." Suddenly Ming was all but wringing her hands, leaning toward me in her chair, shoulders tense. "The man refuses to see us. Refuses to allow us to see her. He hides in his compound and . . ." She glanced up at her primo, and her face crumpled. Her shoulders went up high, and Cai placed a hand on one in tender concern.

I had to wonder why this had been reported as a minor problem, and not the urgent one that a kidnapping represented. Especially the kidnapping of a head of clan security. When I asked that question, Cai said, "Heyda gave us no signal that she was in danger. She often worked with the human community to forge ties. We assumed that was what she was doing. But she didn't return. She didn't contact us. That is not like her."

"In this day and age," Ming said, "one with cameras and detection devices, there are many places we dare not enter. We are not allowed to protect our own." Ming's eyes bled slowly black, her sclera going scarlet, but her fangs remained up in her mouth on their little bone hinges. It was a demonstration of intent and control. "Heyda must be returned to us. Or avenged. If they have made her true-dead, I will drink them all down. Humans go too far in this modern time."

All righty, then. "Did Heyda's team video the meet? Do you have an idea where she might have been taken?"

"Yes," Cai said. "We have gathered all video and intelligence related to this situation. The compound's security is tight, using cameras, guards, and patrolling dogs. And we smell silver in their weapons. We could raid the compound, but my people smell explosives in addition to the other weapons and measures. My master is disturbed."

I focused on the word making the most impact. "Compound?"

"That human male has land," Ming said. "It has been in his family for longer than I have been blood-master. He calls his holdings a church, but it is not. It is something else."

I looked my question at the primo. Cai was standing with his hands loose at his sides, and he shrugged slightly. "They claim the right of religious freedom, but their women are not free to choose."

"Ah. A cult," I said, cold starting to seep into my bones as I began putting this together. It had *FUBAR* written all over it.

"Yes," Cai said.

A powerful vamp in the hands of a cult likely meant they'd drain her, starve her, torture her, and eventually stake her. And until they finished her off, they would have access to her blood to make them stronger, healthier, and longer-lived, blood that would heal any of their sick. They also would become addicted to the effect of vamp blood on their systems, but people are inherently stupid about addictive substances. The kidnappers— if that was what they were—had to know that the vamps would come after her. So someone in the compound had a reason to drink vamp blood—an important human was sick or dying. Or it was a trap. Either one was a problem. *Oh goody.*

"I'll need everything you have on the cult—the grounds, any legal problems, legal names and AKAs, everything. All electronic info. Anything in paper form needs to be scanned and sent." I handed Cai a card. "This is my electronic specialist's contact info. He'll be collaborating with us on intel. For now, I'll let him work with you and anyone else we need to talk to. And I'd like to see Heyda's rooms."

"Of course," Ming said. "When will you attack? It must be before dawn."

"Not tonight."

"*Tonight!*" Ming shouted, her fangs dropping down with little *snicks* of sound, her hands clenched on the chair arms, her talons shining in the lamplight and piercing the expensive leather. She was completely vamped-out, that fast. Ming looked fragile, but vamps are freaky strong. I didn't want to have to stake her to save my life only to have Cai kill me later. And probably a lot slower. So I sat still, unmoving, my eyes on Cai, not running like prey, or fighting like a contender for territory. Not focusing on Ming; keeping my eyes averted. But the hand by my thigh was holding a silver stake. I'm not stupid.

Moving slowly, as if he were reaching out to a wild animal, Cai placed a hand on Ming's shoulder again, the gesture a soothing caress. He said something in Chinese. Mandarin was their first language, according to Ming's dossier. Ming turned away, hunching in on herself. It looked as though she fought for control.

Her primo said softly, "Heyda has been in their hands for four days and four nights. We fear for her."

"I understand. But I have to know where to place troops, where all the entrances are, and where they might be hiding explosives. The situation was never expressed to me as urgent or an imminent danger, and I don't have my tactics guy here. Alex is the next best bet. He's good at finding out things others can't, so I need his intel or the rescue team might trigger an explosion that will kill them or the hostage."

"Her name is Heyda. Not *hostage*," Ming said, her back still turned.

"I know. I'm trying to get Heyda back to you in one piece. I'll get back to you before dawn with an update."

"Quarters have been arranged here for you," Ming said.

"Thank you for that consideration, but the Master of the City of New Orleans has booked rooms for me uptown." No way was I staying under a vamp roof, where there might be collaborators in the kidnapping, or vamps wanting to try skinwalker blood. Or a blood-master on edge. No freaking way.

"As you wish." Ming, again looking mostly human, turned her face to me and stood. I stood just as fast. Protocol and all that. The butler appeared at the entrance to the parlor like some kind of magic trick—gone one moment, present the next. "I expect a report before dawn. You are dismissed."

Yeah. Right. I gathered up the papers and followed the butler to Heyda's rooms, which I searched as well as I was able, getting Cai to take photos of everything and send them to Alex with a text telling him I had arrived and was okay. Before I left, I removed Heyda's pillowcase from her pillow and took it with me. I might need a scent item to track her and wanted to be ready. I grabbed my cell on the way out, happy to be back in communication with my team.

With the cell battery at least partially charged, I called the Kid back home. The Younger brothers were frantic, and I spent the ride to my hotel updating them.

By the time I got checked into the suite—one of those corner rooms with windows on both outer walls, all with a view, a sitting area, a king-sized bed, a desk with computer access, and a fridge—it was two a.m. and I was exhausted. To wake up enough to function, I took a fast, frigid shower, dressed in the clean jeans and T-shirt I had carried up from Fang's saddlebags, and made my way to the business lounge. Access to that department was quickly facilitated by the hotel night manager, who let me into the computer room for a number of twenties. In the short elapsed time, Alex had gathered more info to add to what we knew. A lot more.

A cup of double-strong black tea on the desk beside me, I opened up the file compiled by Alex and read the summary he had prepared. Colonel Ernest Jackson was a third-generation cult member, grandson of the founder of God's Cloud of Glory Church, a backwoods religious cult of polygamists who lived on three hundred acres of hillside property not far from Beaver Ridge, which sounded appropriate for the cult in so many ways.

God's Cloud had a recent batch of problems, however, with papers filed against them by the Tennessee Department of Children's Services and the Department of Human Services for human trafficking and child endangerment. Reports suggested that they married off their female children long before they were women. Two days prior to Heyda's being abducted, there had been an attempted raid on the complex, but the church had clearly been alerted to the law enforcement plans, because by the time the

LEOs got there, the access roads to the compound had been barricaded with recently felled trees and booby-trapped with nails, scrap iron, and rolls of rusted barbed wire. The social services types and the cops hadn't exactly gone home with their tails between their legs, but they were stymied at the front gates of the church compound. It was looking like a combo of Ruby Ridge and the Nevada Showdown.

I had to wonder how the colonel and his pals had gotten off the property to kidnap Heyda and then gotten back in without a law enforcement incident. I made a note to look for hidden entries. Cave passages, maybe? There were lots of caves in the hills of Knoxville. Maybe an undocumented cave accessed the property.

Satellite maps and topographical maps of the area showed ridges of hills running through Knox County vaguely north and south and making a long curve, like a fishhook. It looked like a fault line, but nothing in the maps said so. The rivers ran between the folds of hills with large flatlands between. Tax records indicated that some areas of the hills were affluent, some much less so. I pored over the topo maps, water table maps, survey maps, and photocopied maps from the 1950s and '60s that still revealed logging roads, farm roads, and other access points not on current maps. The satellite maps of the church lands showed buildings, outbuildings, barns, places where large earth-moving projects had been initiated and later finished, and foundations where new buildings were being started. But the most recent sat maps were six months old and there was no telling what was happening there now.

While Beast slept in the back of my mind, bored, I sent texts to Eli, Alex's former Army Ranger brother, the tactics and strategy part of our three-person team. I needed him to give me an opinion on the best way into the compound, the most likely location of the missing vamp—anything that looked like a prison or holding cell—and then the best way out.

I got back a single sentence from Eli. *This intel sucks.*

"Yeah," I muttered to the empty, quiet room. "It does."

Still with no plan, I started in on the current legal charges filed by the state of Tennessee. That part of the research was mind-numbing, and meant more extra-strong tea. Lots more. The charges were scary, and if true, meant that the so-called Christians treated their womenfolk no better than the Taliban treated theirs.

Close to dawn, I spotted two names that could mean assistance in my quest. John Ingram and his wife, Nell, had left the church and moved to the other side of the ridge some years past. Outcast or reformed, I didn't know, but people who had former ties with cults could provide helpful suggestions. So could access to their property, one hundred fifty acres that shared a narrow border with God's Cloud's church property. "Oh yeah," I said to the silent room. "Oooooh yeah." I sent the couple's names to Alex for a full workup, and a text to Eli to look at the boundary of the two properties as possible access points.

I was back at the Clan Home half an hour before dawn, made my report, and then rode Fang into the rising sun and back to the hotel, where I sacked out for four hours of desperately needed sleep.

Unfortunately, when I woke, it was to learn that John Ingram had died several years before, and that his young widow had no high school diploma, no GED, no telephone, no cell phone recorded under her name, no computer, and a dozen guns registered to her. She used wood, solar, and wind to power her meager needs, and her house had a well and a septic tank. She had a driver's license, and paid insurance on an old Chevy truck. Nell lived off the grid. In other words, Nell was a recluse. The only thing she did have was a very active library card. She might be a hermit, but Nell was an eclectically self-educated hermit who had library books checked out on varied subjects, and the books were checked out every Monday, Wednesday, and Friday. Every week. For the last five years.

Nell studied herbs, plants, farming, carpentry, electric wiring, remodeling, world and U.S. history, business mathematics, banking, religious history, and philosophy. Currently she had five books checked out: *Philosophy for Beginners*, written by Osborne and illustrated by Edney; *Solar Power for Your Home*, by David Findley; *A History of the Church in the Middle Ages*, by Donald Logan; *Witches, Midwives, and Nurses: A History of Women Healers*, by Barbara Ehrenreich and Deirdre English; and a trilogy of contemporary romances by Nora Roberts. There were a dozen different music CDs and two DVDs checked out, one a chick flick and the other a techno-disaster thriller. Yeah. Eclectic. But it was Wednesday. And according to the library checkout timetable, which Alex had easily hacked, Nell Ingram always left the library at two p.m.

I packed up and took off on Fang, most of my weapons left in the hotel room so I didn't scare anyone. My cell was fully charged, and I felt as though I was part of the world again. Being so cut off had been creepy. I had no idea when a cell phone had become part of my security blanket, along with the blades, stakes, and guns, but it had.

Knox County's main library was called the Lawson-McGhee Public Library, located on the corner of West Church Avenue and Walnut Street, with a little public park behind it, and public parking close by, where I left Fang, two spaces down from Nell's beat-up but scrupulously clean pickup truck, which I confirmed by her license plate number. Security was so much easier in the modern day, with access to so many public records protected by such poor security.

I wandered around the block, scoping out the neighborhood, which had churches, public buildings, trees, and clean streets, and decided the location was pretty, even if the library itself wasn't. The building looked like something out of the seventies, bulky and blocky. It was built of nondescript brown brick, had few windows, a few emergency exits that sounded an alarm when opened, and no security cameras on the exterior.

As I approached the front entrance, I saw two homeless, bearded guys sitting on the front steps, being rousted by a cop. They needed showers and access to washing machines, but looked as though they preferred to sleep out under the night sky, weather permitting, or in a tent, rather than in a house. One of the guys had dozens of military patches on his old jacket, and the other had only one arm, no prosthesis, and stood with a hard lean to one side, as if he lived with pain.

Just on the off chance that the men were really U.S. veterans, I gave them each a twenty to get a decent meal. Maybe they'd spend it on cheap wine, but how they used my gift wasn't something I could control. Mostly I just wanted to say thank you for their service, and say it loud enough to remind the cop of that gift. When the homeless men took off, they were happy, the cop was thoughtful, and I was, well, I was still me, a two-souled Cherokee skinwalker who—at least now—had constant Internet access. But I was in a city I barely knew from previous security jobs, not well enough to rescue a kidnapped vamp. I had no backup, a thought that once would never have crossed my mind but now seemed acutely important. I liked working with the Youngers. I *missed* working with them, and hated that they were so far away.

I felt the magic the moment I walked inside the library. It wasn't powerful or deadly like the magic of Molly, my best friend and the mother of the aforementioned godchildren, or cold like most vamps' magic. At first, this energy had no taste, no smell, and there was nothing I could see, unlike the glowing motes of witch power and the gray place of the change of my own magic. Yet I could sense it on the air, as if it danced across my skin, testing me, trying to get an impression of what I was. I stepped to the side of the entry and worked to exude calm as I studied the place, searching out the person who emitted the odd sensation, and trying to discern what I was really feeling.

I drew on my Beast's senses. She was awake, deep inside me, alert from the joy of riding Fang through the city. She loved riding a motorcycle, the wind in my/our face, the sights flashing by, the smells that reminded her of home, of the mountain world that we had left behind for the contract in NOLA. It had been supposed to be a short gig, but it had blossomed into a lot more. I opened my lips and drew in the air, the synesthesia-like feeling I rarely experienced reaching up and taking hold of me.

The magic was faint but not weak, a green gold with an edge of smoky charcoal gray. It smelled like sunlight on leaves in old-forest woods, and like the fire that would raze it to the ground, the scent indistinct and dampened, as if reined in. No human alive could have followed such a scent, but I had Beast's senses to draw on, and I had also been a bloodhound a time or two. When I had shifted back to human, I was pretty sure that my Beast had hung on to some of the olfactory senses bred into the tracking dog's DNA. I located the scent trail and walked along it.

Knox County's main public library had books, a video department, an audio department, and, like any modern library, it also had a room of loaner PCs, which was where the scent originated. I followed it through the library to the computer room, where old-fashioned PCs were kept for public use. The magic was coming from the far corner, from a girl hunched over the screen, her fingers flying over the keyboard as she searched the Internet. I settled into a chair within line of sight of her but from behind, and not close enough so that she'd see me unless she was hunting me. I logged on, watching her from a safe distance. I had only an old driver's license photo to go by, but I thought that this, this mousy little thing, this unregistered magic user, could possibly be Nell Nicholson Ingram. How 'bout that?

Something about her scent was teasing forward in my memory, my ancient, less-than-half-recalled Cherokee memory from a childhood so far in the past that no one alive today could remember. Well, except for the undead, who lived forever if they weren't staked or beheaded. But there was something I couldn't place in that scent memory. At least not yet.

The girl had brown hair, straight and long, tanned skin, slight rings of dirt deep under her fingernails, though she smelled and looked clean. She wore a long-sleeved T-shirt, bibbed overalls (what they once called hog washers), and lace-up work boots. But the clothes weren't a fashion state-ment. More as if they were what she wore because she had to, as if she was too poor to afford anything else. She could be a farmer. Or work in a green-house, or for a landscape company, off the books, as there was no record of that on her meager tax forms. She was a woman who put her hands in the soil.

Her magic almost had an earth-witch smell to it, but it *felt* different. Very different. It wasn't something I could put into words, but the differ-ence pricked my skin. She was slight but wiry, muscular but not in a bodybuilder way, more as though she did hard physical labor. And she looked hyperalert, as if she stayed on edge, as though she was always in jeopardy. There was a slight scent of adrenaline in the air, tinged with worry. But she didn't seem afraid, not exactly. Just tense and vigilant. I managed to snap a photo with my cell.

She whipped up her head and looked around the room, eyes narrow, mouth firm. It was indeed Nell Ingram—older, harder, but her. I bent to the screen, typing in my e-mail addy and sending notification to the Youngers that I'd found Nell. Bent over, I looked involved and unaware of anything around me, while I kept her in my peripheral vision, smelling, knowing that fight-or-flight impulse she was feeling.

After several minutes of indecision, Nell went back to her screen, and I was cautious about centering my attention on her again. Her magic was peculiar, but it clearly had a sensory net of spatial awareness, an ability to tell when she was being studied or hunted. My Beast had the same aware-ness. Most wild things did.

As I keyed in my e-mail, I kept half an eye on the girl, my mind working on the scent memory. The word came to me slowly, the Tsalagi syllables sounding in my mind, whispery and slow. *Yi-ne hi.* Or maybe *yv-wi tsv-di.* Or *a-ma-yi-ne-hi.* Fairies, dwarves, the little people, or in her case, maybe wood nymphs would be closer. Mixed with human. Mostly human. Fairies in Cherokee folklore weren't evil, just private and elusive, and sometimes tricksters, but this girl didn't look tricky. Just wary. But the magic was woodsy, like the fey, the little folk. In American tribal lore, only the Cherokee had fairies and little people, possibly from the British who intermarried among them for so many centuries.

When it looked as though she'd be there awhile, I did a quick search for places to buy personal things I hadn't brought, like ammo, new underwear, and combat boots. I also found several barbecue restaurants. I had eaten on the run since my lunch in Asheville at Seven Sassy Sisters' Café, and I needed a good, meaty meal.

Just before two p.m. the girl finished with her research. I closed down my browser and watched her leave the room, then quickly took my place at her computer and looked into the Internet search history. It was an invasion of privacy, but I was intrigued. Nell had spent a lot of time on just four sites, one on a legal case against a polygamist cult out West, one on a site where unusual herbs could be ordered in dried or seed form, one on herbal antibiotics, and one on Greek history, specifically the god Apollo and how similar stories were prevalent in many ancient people's mythology. I logged off and left the library, following Nell's scent trail.

She had lingered at the checkout desk and left through the main doors, turning onto Walnut, crossing the street to walk on the far side, away from the unattended police unit parked on the street in designated parking. Then she had crossed back over the street and into the tiny parklike area, where she stood with her back against a tree. Watching for me.

"Busted," I murmured, pulling my cell. I hit a button, then set it in my T-shirt pocket, where it stuck up above the fabric, videoing everything as I cautiously approached her.

Nell gave me half a smile and slid her hand from behind her. She was holding a small snub-nosed .32. "So busted," she said back. She had heard me, which was really strange. Even witches didn't have preternatural hearing. "I don't want to shoot you, but I will," she said, a faint eastern Tennessee twang in her words. "Then toss you in the back of my truck, cover you with a tarp, drive slowly out of the city and into the woods, and bury you."

"You do that a lot?" I asked.

She smiled, and I had the uncanny feeling that she had, indeed, disposed of bodies before. This girl—this woman—was way more than she seemed. Way more than her scant records had indicated. "Who are you?" she asked, sliding the weapon back beside her leg.

"Jane Yellowrock. I'm—"

"The vampire hunter whore who has sex with the vampire Leo Pellissier in New Orleans." She pronounced it *Pely-ser*, but I wasn't going to correct her pronunciation.

"I don't sleep with fangheads," I said, unexpectedly stung by the *whore* accusation. "I do take their money when the hunt is justified, and I do provide security when they pay for it."

"So. Just a whore of a different kind."

And that made me mad. I took a step closer and she lifted the weapon again, a hard twist to her lips. "Remember that burial in a remote place."

"I remember. So let's talk about the philosophy of whoredom. All people provide services for money. You look like a farmer. You sell jelly and honey and preserves and fresh tomatoes and eggs and veggies to the tourists?" She gave me a scant nod, her long hair moving beside her narrow face. "What does that make you?" I asked. "A vegetable whore?"

She giggled through her nose. The sound was so unexpected that she stopped midgiggle, her eyes going wide. It looked as though Nell Ingram had forgotten how her laugh sounded. Which had to suck.

"I'm here to find a missing Mithran," I said. "What you call a vampire. She disappeared with the leader of God's Cloud of Glory Church, a man who calls himself Colonel Ernest Jackson. He walked her to his car and drove off with her. This was four, no, five, nights ago. No one has heard from her since."

Nell's face paled beneath her tan in what looked like shock. "Then she's dead," she said baldly. "Or been passed around so much she wants to be dead."

I lifted my head. "I'm going in after her. I need your help."

Nell lifted the .32 again and backed slowly to her truck, opened the door, checked the interior with a swift rake of her eyes, and climbed in. She switched the gun to a left-hand grip, which looked rock solid, the weapon still aimed at my midsection, as though she practiced with both hands, for, well, for moments like now. She started the truck and backed slowly out of the parking spot and pulled down the road. I smelled fear on the air. Nell Ingram was terrified.

I didn't move, just watched her go. Then I pulled my cell and asked, "You got that?"

"I got it," Alex said. "I want to marry her. There's nothing so sexy as a woman who knows how to use a gun, and can hold off a skinwalker with a hard look and a, what was that? A thirty-eight?"

My mouth twisted in grim humor. "Worse. A thirty-two."

"She took you with a thirty-two?" he said, appalled and laughing all at once. "I am totally in love."

"Shut up, Alex. I'm going to follow her home."

"Copy that. Restore the cell to video when you get there so we have a record."

"Yeah, yeah, yeah." I closed the cell's Kevlar-protected cover and strad-dled Fang. I turned the key that started the bike, which was one reason why I wouldn't buy it. Key starts were totally wussy. I rode a Harley, and a real Harley had that kick start. That's all there was to it. Not that my opinion was shared by many, but it was mine and I was sticking to it.

Long miles of city driving and then country roads followed. I stayed out of her rearview, following by scent patterns and dead reckoning. All the way to Nell Ingram's farm.

I turned off the curving road that switchbacked up the low mountain, or high hill, into the one-lane entrance of a dirt drive, and over a narrow bridge spanning a deep ditch sculpted to carry runoff. The mailbox had no name, only a number, 196, Nell's address on her tax records. I keyed off the bike, rolling Fang behind a tree, where it would be hard to see from the road. The driveway angled back down and curved out of sight through trees that looked as though they had somehow escaped the mass deforestation of the late eighteen hundreds and early nineteen hundreds. The trees were colossal. Healthy. Some trees were bigger than three people could have wrapped their arms around. Farther down the drive and up the hill were even bigger trees. The leaf canopies merged high overhead, blocking out the sunlight and creating deep shadows that seemed to crawl across the ground as sunlight tried to filter through, just enough to make a bower for ferns and mosses and shade-loving plants. High overhead, the leaves rustled in a breeze I didn't feel, standing so far below.

I had no idea why, but goose bumps rose on my arms and traveled down my legs, in a sensation like someone walking over my grave, a saying used by one of my housemothers at the Christian children's home where I was raised. Creepy but not for any obvious reason. Standing behind the tree, I turned slowly around, taking in the hillside with all my senses. On the breeze I smelled rabbit, deer, turkey, dozens of bird varieties, black bear, early berries, late spring flowers, green tomatoes, herbs, okra buds, and bean plants, plants I remembered from the farm at the children's home and from Molly's garden. But there was that slightly different something on the breeze that made my unease increase. The hair on the back of my neck stood up. For no reason at all.

I had no cell signal, but I texted Alex to look at every sat map he could find and study the land and the mountain, a message that might get to him now but would certainly reach him the next time I was near a tower. I had a feeling that there was something hidden here, like a place of power, a terminal line, or some place that was holy to the tribal Americans. Some place I should see while I was here, though that was outside of my job.

In the distance, the sound of Nell's truck went silent, leaving the air still and . . . and empty. No motors, no traffic, nothing sounded as the roar of the truck faded. I could have been transported back a hundred years or more. No cars, tractors, no airplanes overhead. As the silence deepened, birds began to call, a turkey buzzard soared on rising thermals. Dogs barked somewhere close, the happy welcoming sound of well-loved pets. I liked this place. My Beast liked this place.

Want to shift and hunt, she thought at me. *Many deer are here, big and strong and fast.*

When the vamp is safe, I thought back.

She sniffed, and I was pretty sure it was meant to be sarcastic. *Vampires are good hunters.*

I thought about that for a moment. They were, weren't they? So what was Heyda hunting for when she let herself be taken prisoner without a fight? Or . . . what was she protecting? Or whom? I texted that question to Alex too.

The wind changed, and I smelled a human. Male. Wearing cologne to cover up the day's sweat. He wasn't close, and so I closed my eyes, letting the wind tell me where he was.

The topo maps of Nell's property showed a ridge of rock on the other side of the road, just beyond her land. A likely hiding place for a deer hunter, except the season was wrong and only an idiot hunter would wear cologne that his prey could smell. Unless his prey was Nell.

Slipping into the trees, I moved into the deep shadows. It felt stupid, but the woods seemed to welcome me, until, as I moved away from Nell's property, the trees became smaller, younger, maybe thirty or forty years old, and the feeling disappeared.

I'm not as silent when walking in human form as I am when walking in my four-footed Beast form, but I got close enough for my phone to manage a few photos. A man in camo was sitting in a deer stand, but he wasn't holding a rifle. He was holding binoculars, and he was aiming them down Nell's drive. Watching Nell's house. The deer stand was off Nell's property, near the juncture where her land met the church's property and two other parcels of land. Was he protecting her? I had a feeling not, but I'd been wrong before. Weird stuff happened all the time. I moved closer through the brush, placing my feet silently among the leaves left from the previous autumn. I got a better scent, a head and lung full of the man and his feelings, emotions that emanated from his pores. Beneath the cologne, he smelled sweaty, angry, and something else, something I couldn't quite name. I drew in the air again and this time the pheromones and scent chemicals found their way into my brain. If vicious had an odor, this was it. And possessive. That too.

I sent a third text to the Kid asking who owned the adjoining parcels of land, and to see if he could get driver's license photos of the owners and their kids. Satisfied that I had done all I could for now, short of assaulting and then interrogating the spy, I eased away, back to Nell's driveway and down the two-rut gravel lane, keeping to the shadows and angling in on the tree line.

As I walked, I felt the faintest of tingles through my boot soles, a magic permeating the ground. It came in waves, like the ocean onto the shore at low tide, a surge, rising and falling away. I figured only a witch or someone like me could sense it, but it was there, a low thrum of power and scent. It got stronger as I neared the opening in the trees ahead, a low rolling yard of maybe three acres.

The house was in the center of the acreage, set at an angle to the drive, showing the front and one side, and providing a glimpse of the rear corner. It was a ranch-style post-and-beam construction with wide-plank siding painted a fading green, white trim on the window and door frames, and dormers in the high-pitched front roof. It had a long front porch with rockers and a swing, the chain rusted. The house had been situated to take advantage of the view, the undulating hills and the distant vista of city buildings. The back porch was screened and narrow.

The acre-sized garden at the side of the house was fenced with chicken wire to keep out the rabbits and the deer. Even this early in the growing season, there were plants standing tall, flowering, and promising bounty. The lawn had been recently cut, the grass thick and green. I turned on my cell to record video again.

Three dogs announced me, barking like fools, according to Beast, but I had a feeling that Nell had known I was on her land anyway. I was still fifty feet from the house when she stepped from the front door, a shotgun aimed my way. "If it ain't Miss Busted." She sounded a lot more poised than most twenty-two-year-old women.

Her dogs caught my scent. As one, their tails dropped and they spread out from her feet, a semicircle of intent and threat. I could hear them growling, that low throaty sound that said I was about to be attacked.

"Yeah," I said, holding my hands out to the side to show I wasn't holding weapons. "Sorry to intrude."

"Liar."

I thought about that. She was right. I wasn't sorry to intrude. I'd done it on purpose. "You know you got a guy in a deer stand up the hill"—I thumbed the direction—"watching your place?"

"He ain't on my land, so I don't care. If he comes onto my land, I'll shoot him. You *are* on my land. Give me one reason I shouldn't shoot you and give you to my dogs."

Her aim looked rock steady, and I believed her. But I wondered how such a tiny thing was going to handle the kick of the shotgun. I had tried polite words, information relating to her security, both usually effective in dealing with humans, and Nell Ingram wasn't interested, but all I had was honesty.

"I told you. Four nights ago, Colonel Ernest Jackson and his so-called church kidnapped a female vampire named Heyda Cohen. You think she's being raped. I think she's being drained of her blood too. I intend to get her back."

Nell's fear increased, a ripple of unease so strong I could see it prickle over her skin. I'd have been able to smell her reaction if the breeze had permitted. But other than that, Nell didn't move, didn't speak. Birds called. The dogs circled closer to me, showing teeth, snarling. I didn't want to hurt the dogs, two of them old beagle mixes and the other an old bird dog, but I would if attacked. Nell whistled softly and the dogs instantly stopped moving, but they didn't take their eyes off me.

I wondered what the man in the deer stand was thinking about the standoff. I felt an itch between my shoulder blades, as if he had a scope on me even now. After the silence had stretched out far too long, Nell said, "Going onto the church property is a stupid move, but you don't look stupid. You also don't look easy to kill." She frowned, thinking things through. "What do you want from me?"

"Everything. I want to know everything you know and remember about the compound, the people in it, and their habits. I want to know how they got off the property when the cops had the accesses guarded. I want to know if there are caves leading onto the church land. Then I want access to the compound through your property for my men. And I want to be able to retreat through your property when we're done. And anything else you might have to offer or suggest."

Nell laughed, the sound as stuttered and clogged as before. "Don't want much, do you?"

Honesty seemed to be working, so I pushed ahead with it. "I want lots of stuff. Most of which will put you in danger from the church."

"Woman, I been in trouble from God's Cloud of Glory and the colonel ever since I turned twelve and he tried to marry me. Anything you can do to piss him off will just make my day."

She dropped the weapon as her words penetrated my brain. *"Marry you? At twelve?"*

"Yeah. He's an old pervert. Come on in. I got coffee going and food in the slow cooker. Hope you like chicken and dumplings. I missed lunch and I'm starving."

"I'm always hungry. But *twelve*?" Nell didn't smile, but she did call off her dogs. That and an offer to feed me was a start.

Nell knew stuff. Nell was like a font of knowledge and wisdom, strength and power, innocence and hard-won independence. I liked her instantly, which didn't happen to me often. I sat at her antique kitchen table, the boards smooth from long use, the finish mostly gone and the grain of the wood satiny beneath my fingertips. She had an old boom box loaded up with CDs: jazz and blues and even some forty-year-old hard rock, which started while we set the table. And her chicken and dumplings smelled so good I wanted to cry. Trusting her for reasons that had everything to do with her magic and her calm self-assuredness, I turned off the video; I had no desire to record Nell Ingram. She was a private woman and I wanted to honor that.

Nell didn't offer grace, and when I commented on that, considering her ultra-right-wing background, she said, "I believe in God. I just don't know if I like him much. I sure don't like the colonel's God, but then Ernest Jackson's going to hell someday. If I get lucky, I'll be the one to send him there."

She was fierce for such a tiny little thing. Sharp-faced, delicate, and lean, with long, slender, strong fingers and hair she had never cut, worn parted down the middle and hanging to her hips. She'd have been almost pretty, if she had tried to be. But Nell didn't put on airs for anyone. Nell was just purely Nell. Pale-skinned where she wasn't tanned, farmer-John-style clothes, work boots. Capable-looking. And, man, could she cook! The odors were enough to make Beast want to come out and chow down, the music selection was funky enough to make me want to dance, and Nell had cooked enough to feed herself for a week, which meant that there was plenty for me without the guilt of taking someone else's food.

As I ate my second helping of flaky biscuitlike dumplings in thick chicken gravy, served up in green, hand-thrown pottery bowls big enough to double as horse troughs, Nell sketched what she remembered of the compound. I was able to overlay her sketch with the sat-map photos of the current compound, and quite a few of the buildings were unchanged, which helped a lot in the planning stage of a raid. She knew which building the colonel lived in and where the jail was. And best of all, she knew where the armaments were stored. "They keep 'em here"—she tapped the uneven rectangle that represented a building—"which is right next to the nursery. They know no one's gonna blow up the weapons and risk killing all the children."

"Yeah. That's"—I thought through possibilities and discarded *cruel*, *insane*, and *evil*, to choose—"not unexpected."

Nell snorted, and it wasn't a ladylike snort; it was a hard, ferocious sound. "It's the way cowards work."

I didn't disagree.

"You asked about caves," she said. "They got several, but they're used for storage. So far as I ever heard, they weren't the kind that went anywhere. But there's a long crevasse here." She pointed at my sat map to a darker green area. I had thought it was just a different kind of tree growing close together so the leaves overlapped, but according to the topo map, she was right: it was a narrow ravine. "That's how they get in and out. A crick runs along the bottom, then goes underground for a ways. It comes back out on the Philemons' property, and the entrance can be seen from their house. There's no way past. Trust me. The Philemon family are church-related, and they let the colonel use their vehicles in return for concessions."

"Money?" I asked.

"Access to the womenfolk." Her eyes went harder, a flint green. "Young womenfolk, the ones who don't agree with the plans made for them by their men."

"Oh," I said softly. I had no idea what this woman had been through in her short life, but it sounded as though it might have been pretty horrible. Somehow she had escaped. She had survived. I was curious, but the expression on her face warned me not to intrude. I kept my questions and my sympathy to myself.

Nell knew the history of all the families who were members of the church, and showed me her family's house on the church grounds. She also posited one reason why Heyda had gone with the colonel. "There's a family named Cohen in the compound. If one of them was sick or in danger, or was confined to the punishment house, and if they were related, she mighta gone with the men willingly, thinking she could do something to help."

"Punishment house?"

She tapped the drawing she had made, and when she spoke her voice was colder than any winter wind. "Here. Where the women are kept until they achieve the proper *Scriptural* attitude of obedience and *do what they're told*."

I took a chance and asked, "Did you do what you were told?"

Nell shot me a look of pure venom. "My life is none of your business."

"Okay." I sent another text to Alex to check out the Cohens, but so far, he hadn't responded. When Nell realized that I wouldn't bring up her former life again, she quickly became talkative and helpful, but all her reticence did was make me want to know more—a history I knew she wouldn't share.

The very best thing Nell told me was about the old logging road that twisted through the woods from her property right into the heart of the church grounds. It curved around and under a ledge of rock and hadn't been visible from cameras in the sky. "Last time I looked, which was this past winter, when we had a couple of feet of snow on the ground, they didn't have the road blocked or booby-trapped, but it's grown up pretty bad. You'll havta hoof it in."

"This may make all the difference in saving the v—Mithran the colonel took prisoner."

"Sure. One thing," she said, tucking a strand of hair behind her ear. "Vampires. Are they spawn of Satan? That's what we were taught at the church. And if they're devils, why help them? Why work for them?"

I gave her a halfhearted shrug. "I was taught the same thing. But I've met humans who are surely Satan's children. And I've met vamps who are no worse than the best of us. Except for that whole needing-to-drink-human-blood thing."

She grinned and slid her hands into the bib of her overalls. "I reckon that could be a mite off-puttin'."

I expected her to ask if I'd ever been bitten, but she didn't. Private to her core, was Nell. I walked to the door, where she shook my hand, hers feeling tiny but with a grip like a mule skinner's. I said, "Thank you so much. I have no way of letting you know when we'll get back here, what with no cell signal, but either tonight or tomorrow night."

"I'm good for whenever, but you better take out my observer if you want this to go off in secret. I got no idea who it is, but it's a good guess he reports to the church. Most folk hereabouts do." She stuffed a plastic grocery bag into my hands, one filled with Ball jars of raw honey and preserves. "If he's still there, he'll think you got my name from someone in town and came for remedies or jelly." She smiled shyly. "I make pretty good jellies, and my antioxidant tea is great for colds."

I smothered my surprise at her use of the word *antioxidant*. Nell might talk like a country hick and wear clothes that swathed her in shapelessness, but she wasn't stupid. Not at all. "In that case, I'll pay my way," I said, and placed two twenties on the table. Before she could object, I said, "The hospitality was free. I know that. But my partners will love the treats, so I'm paying for them. Period." She smiled, and her face was transformed from merely almost pretty to downright lovely.

I left Nell washing dishes and walked back up the drive, this time not keeping to the shadows and tree line, but walking out as if I had a right to be there. Fang was sitting just as I'd left it, behind the tree. I started the bike and draped the grocery bag around the handlebars where it could be seen. I dawdled my way down the mountain and back to Knoxville. On the way I ascertained that the deer stand was still manned, and this time I got a good look at him. White male, brown, greasy hair, scruffy beard, pasty-skinned and wearing camo. I could pick him out of a lineup if needed, but I intended to make sure that he never got a chance to be in one. One way or another, I'd see that Nell Nicholson Ingram's spy was sent packing or was left to crawl away and lick his wounds.

When I got close enough to civilization to get a cell signal, I found multiple texts from Alex. One of them was excellent news. Leo had made arrangements to fly the Younger brothers in on his private plane, and they were waiting at my hotel. I had been dreading working with unknown vamps and blood-servants when we went into the compound. Eli's presence raised my expectation of success considerably, and I stopped at a barbecue place, bringing in enough food to feed my small army.

The rest of the day was busy, kept that way by a long meeting with Eli, Cai, and Glass Clan's secundo blood-servant, who was also Heyda's second-in-command of security and Heyda's best blood-meal. Her name was Chessy, and she was a local gal, one who looked a lot like Nell—sharp-faced and lean. And if Heyda had been driven insane—a common problem with vamps who had been starved, bled dry, and tortured—Chessy was the most likely person to bring the vamp out alive. Undead. Whatever.

Based on the intel we had received from Nell, we decided not to wait. The longer we put off a raid, the greater the likelihood that we'd tip off the colonel to our plans. We'd go in tonight. And we'd go in without alerting local law enforcement ahead of time, just in case the leaker who had warned the church about the local LEO's child services raid was also a police officer.

We met at the Glass Clan Home two hours before dusk, and Eli and Chessy laid out the plans to Chessy's handpicked team. The insertion team was composed of fifteen: Chessy; six vamps, all over the age of one hundred, all with military experience; and five humans, ditto on the military backgrounds. Eli and I made fourteen pairs of boots on the ground. Alex would be stationed with access to a satellite phone and talkies at Nell's place. And we'd have a driver. If we were lucky (if the sat phone worked the way it should), we'd have coms between us, as well as access to the outside world.

We used a beat-up panel van to get across town, one with a logo on it that said, TRUCK BROKE? WE CAN FIX IT! The number painted under the logo rang back to the Glass Clan Home, where a human was ready to answer and take queries, as part of our cover. The van's exterior was a crummy rust bucket, but the interior was sealed from light and quite cushy—good for vamps to travel across town anonymously. I'd have to see about getting Leo to consider adding a couple of vans like this to his fleet of vehicles. Remaining unidentified was healthy sometimes.

We parked down the hill and Eli went in alone just before dusk. Silent, using the skills Uncle Sam had taught him in the Rangers, he took out the watcher in the deer stand and carried the man a mile down the mountain to dump him at my feet outside the panel van. The guy was older than I had first assumed, maybe twenty-eight, with a ratty beard, and a body odor that proclaimed he had missed his weekly bath, but believed that cologne made up for good old soap and water. Holy moly, he stank. While he was still unconscious, I secured him with multiple zip strips and Eli and I hefted the human into the van, where he rolled at the feet of the insertion team. We jumped in, slammed the side door, and the van proceed uphill, toward Nell's place.

One of the vamps wrinkled his nose and said, "Human men are idiots. Present company excepted, and no offense." He toed the limp form. "This one stinks."

Eli, not even winded from the exertion, said, "Offense accepted anyway, suckhead."

The vamp narrowed his eyes at Eli and I turned to the vamp. "Back down. Your comment was insulting and your apology was lacking in both grace and sincerity. Try again. Now." And I let a bit of Beast into my gaze, seeing the golden glow in the dark of the van.

The vamp ignored me and said, "You let a *woman* fight your battles for you?"

"Two things," Eli said, his voice without inflection. "One: I'm not letting you goad me into ruining this mission. Two: the Enforcer is not just a woman, just a human, or just an anything," Eli added, his masculinity not the least injured. "Once this is over, I'll beat your ass. But for now, the Enforcer needs your cold undead body to rescue your head of security. Either you are in or you are out. And if you're out, I'll happily secure you with silver tape and leave you to burn while we complete this mission."

The vamp seemed to consider that for a moment. Then he said, "Challenge accepted."

"Knives," Eli said. "Numbers limited to two, each no larger than a six-inch blade."

"First blood," I said, hoping to keep Eli uninjured, and the vamp alive. "And if the human is injured, he will be healed."

"Done," both males said.

"You're both idiots," Alex said, grumpy as only a nineteen-year-old, younger Younger could be. "And an apology still hasn't been issued."

"Noted," the vamp said.

Alex started to continue the argument, but I held up a hand and he subsided. A working frenemy was the best I'd get and I sat back while the van took the narrow, twisting road up as night fell.

We halted the panel van in Nell's drive and I went to her door. She opened it before I knocked, her eyes wide and skin pale. She was breathing fast, and with Beast so close to the surface, I could hear her heart beating too fast, and smell her reaction to . . . what? "What's wrong?" I asked.

"Something dead," she whispered, staring at the truck repair van. "Something wrong."

"Vampires," I said. "They won't hurt you. I promise."

"Will they hurt the colonel?"

"Planning on it."

Nell nodded, the movement jerky. "Good. But they still feel wrong." She closed the door in my face.

To save Nell more discomfort, the vamps and the blood-servants exited the van and raced into the woods, their night vision allowing them to see the narrow opening in the trees where a trail had once woven. They scattered through and along the old farm road, ducking into hiding places. Eli followed, his low-light and infrared headgear allowing him to see as well as the vamps.

I stayed with the driver and Alex as the van rolled across the back of Nell's three-acre lawn and into the trees, following the trail as far as the vehicle's city-street undercarriage could manage before making a twelve-point turn to face back down the mountain. I made sure the van had a working sat signal before slipping out and taking off after the insertion team. As I ran, I pulled on Beast, who flooded my system with adrenaline and shared her night vision, turning the world silver and gray with tints of green.

I caught up with and passed the two vamps who were staying on the road to make sure we all got out, placed to maintain coms with Alex. Both lifted a hand to acknowledge me. I left them in my dust.

Beast chuffed inside me. *Hunt. Ready to hunt. Want to kill and eat.*

Let's try not to kill anyone, and the idea of eating humans and vamps is not appealing in the least.

Hunt deer. Soon.

Yeah. Deal, I thought at her, spotting sprinting human-shaped forms just ahead.

The race through the woods revealed no barricades, no downed trees, and no booby traps. The colonel hadn't expected attack from this direction, and the topo maps had shown why—a long vertical drop of nearly fifty feet into the compound. No human law enforcement agency would have been able to manage the descent with any kind of order or speed. And the little slip of a girl who looked like something you could break in two with one hand tied behind your back was clearly no menace, not with a spy in the trees.

We ducked beneath the rock ledge that hid the old road from the eyes in the sky and sprinted through the deeper dark, around the heart of the ancient mountain, and out the far side. The trees were smaller on this side of the mountain. The underbrush was thick and dense. The land smelled different from Nell's property. Stressed and sleeping and unhappy. Weird thoughts for another time.

We crested the hill and the compound appeared below us. The hill fell away, a sheer drop seen on the topo maps but not realized until now. Nearly fifty feet of vertical fall. There was no fence. No barrier. Just the drop. My heart stuttered and sped. The terrain must have seemed like the perfect protection to the church's security crew.

The vamps didn't even slow. They raced out and leaped. Down. The humans hardly slowed, slapping lines around tree trunks and leaping off for a fast rappel. At the back of the crew, I was undecided but still moving fast. Beast slammed into me, the pain so sudden and intense that I tripped over my own feet and rolled off the ledge. The world tumbled around me.

Beast reached up and grabbed a root, swinging me out over the cliff. "Holy crap," I grunted. The ground was way, way down there. I let her have us. Jumping down cliffs was a *Puma concolor* thing. The steeper and more impossible, the better. I was just glad my chicken and dumplings had digested. I didn't want to lose that delicious meal when I landed, broke my legs, and threw up all over the place. But Beast wasn't planning on any of that.

A tiny rock stuck out about twenty-five feet down. She pushed off with my free hand, accelerating the momentum of our swing, and let go of the root. I/we landed with the left toes of my boot on the rock and pushed off. The rock gave way, tumbling straight down to the vamp who had baited Eli. He caught the rock just as I/we landed in a crouch at his feet, perfectly balanced on my/our toes and fingertips.

I looked up and growled at the vamp. He took a quick step back, dropping the rock. I/we hacked in challenge. He stabilized his balance and nodded slightly at me/us, one of the regal nods that old vamps, especially old royalty who had been turned, used to acknowledge one another, or sometimes gave to someone they thought their equal. I had a feeling that someday this vamp and I might tussle and I'd hurt him. Just enough to let him know he shouldn't have dissed the Enforcer of the MOC of New Orleans. Not even if he *was* a prince of vamps. Maybe he'd bleed a bit. But for now we had a vamp to rescue. And a bunch of kids too.

I gave him a regal nod back and pressed the button on my mic, a signal that would be relayed to Alex, who, unbeknownst to the vamps, would be calling the local LEOs (currently at a standoff on the blockaded road) in on an emergency raid, up through the secret entrance at the Philemon family farm. No way was I rescuing a suckhead and leaving women and children in the hands of cultists who would consider marrying off a twelve-year-old girl. And who had a "punishment house" for *disobedient* women and girls. No way.

Electric lights lit the compound grounds. The buildings were all painted a blinding white that threw back the security lights and created darker shadows. Path borders were neatly marked with rounded river rocks. The smells of many people and many dogs were strong on the night air. I oriented myself and waited. Four of our vamps had orders to neutralize the dogs and guards on the grounds, and then take down the armed guards keeping out the LEOs. There would be no killed humans to give the LEOs reason to charge vamps with a crime; instead the orders were to deliver a heavy-handed thump on the head to make the humans and canines woozy and then more zip strips to keep both dogs and humans out of the way. A little duct tape to keep them quiet, if needed. But no DBs— dead bodies. None.

The vamps, like my Beast, could spot the dogs by smell alone. More important, we could smell the humans. And vamp blood. It hung thick on the air. The vampires vamped-out and slid into the shadows.

I heard thumps and a growl close by, mostly hidden by raucous music from a building on the far side of the compound. It sounded like a bluegrass band, with banjos and guitars and drums. Playing a rollicking . . . hymn. "Battle Hymn of the Republic," men's voices rolling into the night along with the scent of sweat and testosterone. They were in the church, and they smelled and sounded as though they were celebrating. Maybe they were. They had the state of Tennessee's finest stymied at the front gate.

Following our plan, Chessy and another human and the vampire prince tore off, chasing the smell of Heyda's blood. A third human followed, covering them from the rear with a nasty-looking fully automatic weapon that bore a strong resemblance to an M4A1 carbine, a semiautomatic rifle that fired a 5.56-millimeter NATO round. U.S. military issue. It would chew up anything it hit. Instant hamburger. I *so* didn't want it to be used. If a human died on this raid, Leo and Ming would do all they could to protect the vamps, but the humans could possibly be hung out to dry—which meant that I might spend a long time in jail.

Once the guards were taken care of, Eli took the humans and vamps with the most recent military boots-on-the-ground experience, and divided them into two groups. Eli's group vanished into the shadows of the ammo building while the other group stood guard. When exploding ammo was no longer a threat, Eli would make sure there was no footage of tonight's raid for the cops to find. Eli was good.

The rest of us—those with little or no military experience—headed for the nursery. The door was locked from the inside, but the two vamps with me took the door down. It wasn't quiet, but it wasn't as loud as I might have expected either. Vamp reflexes were so fast that when they busted in the door, they caught it before it hit the wall behind. Between that and the loud music, no one heard us except an older woman who was reading the Bible by the light of a flashlight just inside the door. She looked up with her mouth in an O of surprise. The vamp nearest grabbed the human up by the scruff of the neck and set her down gently beside me. While I secured the human and shoved a sock into her mouth to keep her quiet, the vamp disabled an alarm button under the desk by the most simple and efficient method. She broke it with her fist. I liked her style.

Together, we checked on the children, hoping they were all safe and asleep and that there were no more adults who might give a warning. Unfortunately two of the children had been beaten recently. Their scents told us they were bruised and had cried themselves to sleep. The scents also told us who had done the beating—the nurse. Her knuckles still showed the damage. The vamp who had disabled the alarm made sure that she didn't get a chance to wash her hands and maybe rinse away trace evidence. She knocked the nurse out with a swift and well-delivered left jab. "Nice," I said.

"Yeah. Bet she'd be tasty."

"I bet she would," I said mildly.

The vamp studied her face, and I had to wonder if the human nurse would get a visit one night from a vampire vigilante. Satisfied that the kids were bruised but okay, and that the older woman was the only guard, I left the nursery in the care of our humans and took my two vamps to raid the punishment house. The men were still singing, and anger had begun to heat my blood.

The punishment house was a small, nondescript building of white siding, post-and-beam construction, with thick walls. No windows. It looked like a nicely kept storage building. But I could smell the pain and fear inside it. So could the vamps. The female vamp who had busted the alarm had attached herself to me, and she took down this door the same way she had the nursery door—a swift kick—though this door took three kicks, and they weren't quiet. When the door splintered open, we were met with the business end of a shotgun. Which my personal vamp took away in a move that was faster than I could follow in the shadows. It was a single, fluid move of kick, grab the barrel, whip up the gunstock to hit the guard in the jaw, and catch both guard and gun before they hit the floor. It was pretty. It was the last pretty thing I saw in the punishment house. There were four beds in a single room, a bathroom running along the back wall. No privacy curtains. Two women were shackled on the beds, and by the time I found light, they were crying and whimpering.

The vamp looked at them and cursed under her breath. Still moving fast, she broke the wrist cuffs with her bare hands and gathered the women up in the sheets and blankets from the beds. Drawing on her vamp strength, she pulled them close to her on the edge of one bed, murmuring endearments as she gave off a vamp compulsion, the energies cold and icy on my skin. I almost told her to stop, until I realized she was exuding calm, a gentle relaxing vibe that encouraged the women to accept help. I had never seen vamp compulsion powers being used for something good, not like this, and my respect for the vamp went up another notch. She needed a nickname, something better than "the female vamp with a great left fist."

I stood to the side, weapon ready, watching the darkness outside and the vamp inside, until the women prisoners were sleepy and content, their heads lolling on the vamp's shoulders. Gently she laid them down and stood, looking up at me, her hands patting the women into deeper sleep. Softly she said, "I recognize them. This is why Heyda let herself be taken. These are her grandchildren, Berta and Wilhelmina. Berta is in her twenties. Willie is in her forties. They've been . . . abused."

I knew what she meant. I had known by the smells from the moment the door had slammed open and all the scents hit my nose. They had been beaten by several people while secured to the beds and unable to defend themselves. They had then been taught a different kind of lesson by a man. I didn't realize the extent of my own anger—mine and Beast's—until I spoke to the two vamps under my command. My voice was a deeper register than my normal human voice. "I smell the stink of sexual predators who hide behind religion. What say we find the man in charge?"

"His blood will be yummy," the woman said. And she vamped-out. Fast.

"Not to kill," I amended, to the vamp, who I nicknamed Yummy. "But let's scare the bejesus outta him."

"He won't have any Jesus in him," Yummy said around her fangs, "but scared blood is the best kind."

For once I didn't disagree.

We found the colonel's house and entered, to the accompaniment of a new hymn from the church, "A Mighty Fortress Is Our God," and I had to wonder if the colonel was singing with the men, bragging to God that his people had defeated the government types at the gates. But he wasn't singing. He was in bed with three naked girls, one who looked about twenty and two others who looked much, much younger.

The colonel rose to his knees on the mattress and shouted, "Guards! Guards!" I switched on a lamp to see the shriveled, wasted man, his skin hanging in long folds on his lanky, pasty body. His tanned hands were fisted in the hair of a child. She wasn't crying. She didn't even seem to be afraid. She was staring out the window into the night, vacant-eyed, empty-souled.

His was the scent on the women in the punishment house. His scent was on the child he held. The anger that was simmering in my blood began to boil. I felt Beast's claws press against the tips of my fingers. *Kill one who hurt kits,* she thought.

"Your guards, they're not gonna help you," Yummy said between her fangs.

"Vampire! I call upon the Holy Ghost to smite thee, demon of hell!"

he roared, shaking the child by her hair. Her body juddered and quivered. But she didn't make a sound.

"Me and the big guy up there are close, personal pals," Yummy said. "He's too busy at the moment to answer. You're all mine, baby."

I reached across Yummy, stopping her forward movement, and took the colonel's wrist in mine. The girl couldn't see what I was doing. What I was going to do. Silently, watching his face, I broke his index finger. The colonel cursed and let the girl go. I dropped the colonel's maimed hand and covered the girl with the blankets. Sometime in the last few moments, the other girls had disappeared out the front door into the night.

Yummy laughed, her eyes on me, and said, "Yeah. Just like that." To the colonel, she said, "The Holy Ghost wants to have a word of prayer with you, old man." Faster than I could see, she gripped the man around the throat and yanked him to her.

Yummy's power raced over me like a burst of static electricity, lifting the hairs on the back of my arms. "This one is mine," she said, her words measured and low. It was a challenge I wasn't going to argue. I gave her a slow, steady nod. Yummy took the old man out the front door, carrying him by the throat.

It was against the law for vamps to kill humans. My morals and the law were at odds, but . . . I looked at the silent girl, huddling on the sheets, still staring into the dark. I didn't feel the least bit bad about the colonel. He had been alive when I last saw him. As far as the law was concerned, that was enough to protect me.

Sirens sounded in the distance. We were out of time. Local law enforcement and the state cops had made the trek through the crevasse and were on the premises, somehow with a cop car. I tapped my mic on and whispered, "Time's up. You got her?"

"We have her," Prince said. "We are taking her up the cliff now."

"Let's go home, boys and girls," I said into the mic. "See you back at the van." As I left, I checked the Cohen house out, the one marked on Nell's map. It looked secure. I smelled women and children. No blood. I hoped their safety was worth whatever Heyda had been through.

The drive back was silent except for the sounds of Heyda feeding. She had been out of her mind with anguish and blood loss when found, and it had been all the vamps could do to get her back to the van. Once off the mountain and heading home, all the humans from her clan fed her, followed by all the vamps. It took a lot of blood to feed a drained and tortured vampire back to sanity. I'd seen a vamp drained into madness before. It was pretty awful.

Heyda's skin was the blue white of death, except where she was bruised from beatings. Her head had been shaved. There were dozens of half-healed cuts on her. Her wrists and ankles had been shackled with silver and were blistered, the skin torn and blackened in places. I didn't know what Yummy had done with the colonel, but no matter what she had done, it wasn't enough. It just wasn't.

When we got back to the Clan Home, Ming met us in the drive. Heyda fell out of the back of the van, into her maker's arms. Instantly Ming pulled the injured vamp to her and leaned back her neck in one of those not-human movements. Heyda, already vamped-out, bit down into Ming's carotid and started drinking. The other vamps gathered around, the mixed power of vamps rising on the night air in a ceremony that I had seen once, but never completely understood. The prince was part of the mix, his arms around both vamps. I guessed the little challenge between him and Eli was off for the time being, which was fine by me.

The driver closed the side doors and got back in the cab, gunning the motor of the old van and heading away from the Clan Home, back to our hotel. I closed my eyes and leaned my head against the leather headrest.

Yummy hadn't been with us on the ride home. I figured that was a good thing. It might be good if I never saw the vamp again. But there's something about the universe that forces us to face our fears and our pasts and our weaknesses. I had a feeling that Yummy and I would cross paths again someday.

On the drive through Knoxville, Alex hacked into the police coms and informed us that the local and state law enforcement officers were taking a number of children and women into protective custody and had arrested several men and women for various and sundry crimes, with more arrests and charges pending. It wasn't enough, not with what I'd seen and smelled at the compound, but like a lot of things in my life, it would have to do.

The next afternoon, I rode Fang up the hillside to see Nell, to thank her for the help and for the intel. To determine a few things about her. To suggest a few things to her about her security and, maybe, a few things about her future. This time when she met me on the front porch, she wasn't carrying a gun. She was wearing a long skirt and flip-flops, her brown hair pulled back in a braid, much like the way I wore mine. She was sitting on the swing, whose chain supports had been replaced with new steel that creaked pleasantly when she pushed off with a toe. I hoped the money Alex had left on the front porch last night had gone toward the dress and the chains.

I rode Fang all the way up to the end of the drive and left the bike in the sun, the metal pinging and ticking as it cooled. "Afternoon, Nell," I said.

"Jane Yellowrock. You 'uns come set a spell," she said in the local vernacular. "I got you some good strong iced tea with honey and ginger in it."

I never drank tea that way, but it seemed impolite to make a face. I climbed the steps and accepted a sweating tea glass. The green glass was old, bubbled with air like old, handblown glass. It probably was an antique; there were treasures in these hills. I sat, sipped, and was pleasantly surprised by the taste. After a comfortable moment, I said, "You act like you were expecting me."

"I was, sorta. Don't know why."

"Is it because of the magic I feel every time I put a foot on the ground here?"

Nell's face paled to nearly vamp white. She whispered, "I'm not a witch."

"Thou shalt not suffer a witch to live. Right? That's the way you were taught."

Nell just stared and I felt the land around me rise, as if aware, as if to protect her, the current of intent passing through the foundation of the house, into the porch chair where I sat, and into me. And I caught again the scent of Nell Nicholson Ingram. "My people would have called you *yi-ne-hi*. Or maybe *yv-wi tsv-di*. Or even *a-ma-yi-ne-hi*. You would have been respected and maybe a little feared, but not burned or tortured or beaten."

Nell frowned, not knowing that her body language was telling me so much about her. About her life in another time, another place, but still so close. Just over the ridge.

"I'm not a witch," she whispered again, as if saying it so tonelessly, so repetitively over the years, had kept her safe.

"No. Your gift isn't witch magic."

Nell blinked. "It's not?"

I let my mouth curl up slightly. "I'm not even a hundred percent sure it would properly be called magic. More a paranormal gift of some sort, but then, I'm not a specialist."

"You're not human either."

My smile went wider and I sipped the tea, letting her put things together.

"Are you like me?"

I heard the plaintive tone in her words. I knew what it was to be so very alone in the world. I knew that my answer would cause her pain and leave her feeling even more alone. "No." My smile slid away. "I only ever met one other like me before. He tried to kill me. I had to kill him to save my life. Now I'm alone. Maybe forever."

Nell looked away from my eyes, holding her green glass in both hands. "Forever is a long time to be alone."

Nell had been alone since her husband died, according to what Alex had been able to dig up on her—which was next to nothing. Just Nell and her dogs, on this mountain land, for years. "It's all good," I said. "Life is good. I do good for humans and for others, outcasts, people in need. I protect the innocent when I can. There may not be others like me, but I found a place for myself. Found friends. People who came to me and we made a family. I have a job. A purpose."

"You think *I* need a purpose. You think that living here, making my way, reading my books, and growing things isn't good enough." Her chin lifted. "Proust said, 'The real voyage of discovery consists not in seeking new landscapes, but in having new eyes.' I got new eyes aplenty. I don't want to leave. I'm not a hundred percent sure I even can."

I thought about that for a while, as the old bird dog climbed the short steps and curled under Nell's swing, his tail thumping on the smooth boards. I had been chained to Leo Pellissier once upon a time. I hadn't been able to leave his side for long without getting terribly sick. Maybe Nell was chained to the land in much the same way. "You never know how far you can travel until you start walking."

"Who said that?"

"I did. And no one said you'd have to leave the land forever."

"You already told people about me, didn't you?"

"I did. I'm sorry. But the vampires who ran across your mountain felt your magic in the land. Felt it thrum up through their feet. They knew you were something special. To keep them from coming after you, maybe changing you whether you want it or not, I told a friend about you. He'll be coming to talk to you soon. To offer his protection. To try to get you to work with him. Working with him offers you safety from all the others. Working with him will keep the vamps from sniffing around. Working with him will keep you safer from the church, from whoever takes over for the colonel."

"You made the colonel disappear, didn't you?"

"Not me. But I didn't stop the one who did."

Nell looked out over her land, the lawn rolling down the sloping hill into the trees, something odd on her face. Something I couldn't read. "The colonel's heir is Jackson Jr.," she said, without looking at me. "He's evil through and through. Jackie hates me with a hatred like a forge, burning hot. Hatred like that shapes a man, and never in a good way. Jackie will kill me if he gets half a chance. Kill me and take my land." She sighed, the sound wistful. "Life is like train tracks, parallel rails—one side blessings, the other side troubles. I've been blessed for years. Now I guess I might have to ride the other rail for a while, again."

"And that other rail, it might prove to be a blessing too."

Nell shook her head sadly. "Go away, Jane Yellowrock. Go back to your vampires and your witches and your search for whatever you are. Get off my land. Leave me in peace. Please."

I stood and set the green iced tea glass on a small table. Beside it I placed a card. "This belongs to the friend I mentioned. He's a cop in PsyLED. He's a pretty boy, black hair and black eyes. Up here, he'd be called Indian-looking, Cherokee, like me. But he's mostly Frenchy. He'll take care of you. Get you introduced to his people. Just don't fall in love with him. He'll break your heart."

"You already done that, Jane. You already done that."

Knowing I had changed this girl's life forever, I walked down the steps and swung my leg over Fang. "I can't say I'm sorry," I said. "I'd do it again. You losing your peaceful life meant getting one hundred thirty-eight physically and mentally abused children out of the clutches of God's Cloud of Glory Church. And you might not want to admit it yet, but you'd let me do it again too."

I had done the best I could, despite shoving Nell out of the shadows and into the limelight. She was no longer off the grid. No longer hidden away. The rest was up to Nell. I keyed the bike on and rode off Nell's mountain and back into Knoxville. I had a private jet waiting on me, a flight back to New Orleans and the problems that awaited me there. There were always problems with fangheads.

Usually I had buyer's remorse about taking a job with the vamps. Usually I spent a lot of time in self-recrimination and guilt and second-guessing myself and my choices and my decisions. But just this once, I felt good about a job for the bloodsuckers. A job well done. One hundred thirty-eight children set free. And a pedophile and sexual predator gone missing.

I wondered where Yummy had buried the old man.

I wondered if he had died on Nell's land.

I wonder a lot of things. But I seldom have answers. Rogue-vamp hunters and Enforcers act in a vacuum, flying by the seat of our pants. And now, flying back to New Orleans in the Master of the City's private jet, I knew I was flying back into trouble. But I was flying with the Youngers. A girl could do a lot worse.

Not All Is as It Seems

This story was previously published in the anthology Temporally Out of Order, *released by the small press Zombies Need Brains LLC, and is still in print. Used by permission.*

Author's note: This short story takes place (in the JY timeline) after *Broken Soul* and before *Dark Heir*.

I didn't like moonless nights. Even with the protective ward up over the house and grounds, I felt isolated and vulnerable, not that I'd ever tell Big Evan. After years of struggling, his business had recently taken off, the result of an offer from the rich son of a sultan to create astounding and extravagant lighting for his string of casinos and clubs around the world. It required travel, this time back to Brazil for a week, which we all hated, but the gïg was profitable enough for us to finally put money aside for the children's educations. And Evan was making a name for himself and his fantastic lighting creations. He was fulfilled and excited. I could live with a little disquiet.

I finished washing dishes, listening to the kids play in their rooms, Angie talking to an imaginary friend or a doll or toy soldier and Little Evan making growling noises as he played with his newest toy bear. He'd picked it out himself, a pink bear with purple nose, paw pads, and eyes. Probably a girl's toy, but no one cared in this household. Our children were being raised to express themselves and their imaginations as every proper, nascent witch should—

The *ding* on the wards interrupted my woolgathering. I dried my hands, spotting two figures standing on the street, side by side, slender males by their body shapes, possibly human, but they could be anything. There was no car by the road, so they had walked, or flown, or run. Or teleported. I studied them, and they didn't move, though they could surely see me outlined in the lighted window. There was no movement, no small shifts of posture or weight distribution, no change in body position at all. I smiled grimly. It was one hour after dusk, the perfect time for vamps to come calling. Not that I ever had vamps come calling. But these two didn't move, exactly the way vampires didn't move, in that whole undead thing. With the Mithran/Witch Accords being planned, there was no way to ignore them or send them on their way.

I picked up the landline phone and held it up for them to see, then pointed at it to indicate I was checking them out. One bowed, an old-fashioned and proper bow. The other waved, a modern gesture.

Son of a witch on a switch! I have vamp callers.

I dialed Jane Yellowrock at Yellowrock Securities and went through the electronic procedures to be put through to my best friend. While I waited, I put on a kettle for tea. Even though things had been strained between us, I knew she would take my call. Jane killed rogue vamps for a living and there was no one better to give me advice. When she answered I said, "Big-cat, I've got vamps in front of the wards and my hubs is out of town."

"Descriptions." That was my pal: economy of, well, of everything.

I gave her the descriptions and heard her make a call on another line, her voice growing clipped, pointed, and slightly snarly. When she came back on she said, "Lincoln Shaddock sent them on an errand. I wasn't able to find out what kinda errand. I don't like it, though I have no reason to tell you to turn them into fried toads. Your call whether to let them in." Jane sounded ticked off, letting me know that she was not happy that visitors had come calling without her prior approval. I had a feeling it wouldn't happen again. Ever.

Turn them into fried toads was my BFF's way of describing my new death magics, if used to defend myself. At the simple thought, I felt my powers rise, eager to be let loose, free and destructive. The only problem was that I might not be able to get them back under control. I could kill the ones I loved while trying to defend them. No. Not an option.

I breathed slowly, forcing the magics back down as I stared into the dark, watching the patient-looking vamps. With the accords so close, little moments like this might make a huge difference in vamp–witch relations for years to come. "I'm letting them in."

"Your call," she repeated. "I've sent a message to them that if they hurt you or yours, heads will roll." Jane was a rogue-vampire hunter and the on-again/off-again Enforcer to the biggest, baddest fanghead in the Southeast, so when she said heads would roll, she meant it literally.

"Thanks. Later, Big-cat." I ended the call and set the phone down. I held up one finger so the vamps would understand that I needed a moment, and went to my living room, where I prepared three defensive workings and one offensive working. The defensive ones would turn an attacker into fried vamp, which would take a long, painful time to heal, even with access to healing, master vamp blood. The offensive one would kill them true-dead.

I checked on the children, who were playing together now in Little Evan's room, bear and toy soldiers in some form of Godzilla bear versus the U.S. Army. I closed the door and opened the front door. Night air breezed through, still warm from the day, but holding the bite of deepening night. I took another breath and let it out, thinking, *Bite. Ha-ha.* Nerves. I prepared the easiest defensive *wyrd* spell, dropped the ward with a thought, and waited.

The vamps walked slowly up the drive, not moving with vamp speed, but like humans, which should have put me at ease but didn't. Nothing a vamp could do could put me at ease, not with Big Evan gone and me with the kids to protect. The vamps stopped a polite three feet from the open doorway and I looked them over. One was wearing jeans, his red hair in a shaggy, mid-eighties style, his hands clasped behind his back. The other had dark brown hair cut short, wore a suit and tie, and looked like a lawyer at first glance. Until I looked down at his hands. They were callused (strange among vamps) and stained with dye or ink—a working man's hands, not the smooth hands of most dilettante vamps, letting humans do everything for them. Something about the man's hands set me at ease, and I nodded once.

The suited one bowed slightly again, something military in the action, and offered me his full titles, in the formal way of vampires who want to parley. "Jerel D. Heritage, at your services, ma'am. Of Clan Dufresnee, turned in 1785 by Charles Dufresnee, in Providence, and brought south when Dufresnee acquired the Raleigh/Durham area. Currently stationed with Clan Shaddock of Asheville."

The other vamp said, "Holly, turned by the love of my life in 1982, and now serving with my mistress, Amy, under Clan Shaddock." Unassuming history, no last name, making him very young as vampires went. More interesting, he was ordinary-looking, until he smiled, a fangless, human smile, but one that transformed him into a beautiful man. I knew why Amy, whoever she was, had turned him. It was that smile. He tilted his head in a less formal bow than Jerel's and yet somehow turned it into a graceful gesture. "We come in peace," he said, the smile of greeting morphing into true humor.

Jerel looked like a fighter and a gentleman from his own age, a bit stiff, too formal for modern custom, yet the kind of man who stood by his word. Holly looked like a dancer and a poet. Yet, possibly, Holly might be the more dangerous of the two because he looked so unvampily kind. Looks can be deceiving.

Reluctantly I said, "Molly Everhart Trueblood, earth witch of the Everhart witches. I grant safety in my home to guests who come in peace."

The two seemed to think about my words before they carefully stepped in. They took chairs in my great room, the space and furniture sized for Big Evan, oversized leather couches and recliners and lots of wood. The smaller vamps looked like Angie Baby's dolls in the chairs. The one in the suit—Jerel—said, "We come at the request of the Master of the City of Asheville, to ask if you recently came into possession of a teapot."

My brows went up, and I barely managed not to laugh. This visit by vampires was about a *teapot*? I said, "I drink black China tea when Jane Yellowrock, *my friend*," I enunciated carefully, to remind them that I had friends in high vamp places, "is here to visit. I prepare herbal teas as needed for health. I have *several* teapots. None recently acquired."

"We received a call from the Enforcer's partner Alex Younger, while we awaited your response to our visit," Jerel said. "No insult was intended in our unannounced arrival. Please allow me to explain.

"The Master of the City, Lincoln Shaddock, was turned in 1864. When he was freed from the devoveo—the madness that assaults our minds after we are turned—the first thing he did was visit his wife, though this was strongly opposed by his master. The year was 1874, and his wife had remarried. The meeting was . . . unfortunate."

"I'll bet," I said.

Holly smiled and Jerel frowned before going on. "The teapot we seek was his wife's. It is a redware, hand-thrown, English-styled piece, salt-glazed in the local tradition, and painted with a yellow daisy."

"I see," I said, not seeing at all. My powers, my death magics, had begun to roil as he spoke. I held on to them with effort, trying to balance my waning earth magic with my growing death magic. "Again. I have acquired no teapot in the last few months and certainly not one like you described."

"May we"—Jerel took a breath and his face twisted in what I might have assumed was human distaste, had I not known he drank blood for substance—"inspect your kitchen?" he asked.

I stood in surprise and said, "No. You may not."

Angie Baby burst from behind the door opening and down the two steps into the great room, shouting, "You can't have him! You can't!" Child fast, she whirled, strawberry blond hair streaming behind her, and ran through the house. The door to her room slammed.

My mouth slowly closed; I hadn't been aware that it hung open. Everything—every single thing—had just changed. "Will you do me the kindness of waiting here while I speak with my eldest?" I asked carefully. When they both nodded, as unsure as I was, I added, "There is a kettle of hot water on the stove. Tea is in the tin beside it. Please make yourselves at home in my kitchen. And if you take the opportunity to search for the teapot you desire, I assure you, it isn't there."

Jerel said, just as carefully, "As I recall, children are . . . difficult, at times."

"Yes. I'll return as soon as I know what's going on." They nodded and I followed my daughter to her room. When I was still several feet away, I heard the sound of furniture moving and realized that Angelina was bar-ricading her door. My eldest, possibly the only preadolescent witch with two witch genes on the face of the earth, was hiding something. Something important. Something dangerous. Something that could hurt her? Had bespelled her?

I didn't bother with simple responses. I unleashed the spell I had pre-pared for the vampires and blew her door off the hinges. It was a restricted spell, releasing and containing any debris, intended to toss vamps off my property but not injure them. Much. Angie's door shuddered, tilted in from the top, and fell forward to rest upright against my daughter's bed.

Big Evan would have some new things in his honey-do jar when he got home.

Angie was standing at the foot of the bed, fists on her hips, and shouted, "You broke my door!"

"Yes. I did," I said as I crawled over the mess of the door, the bed, and the toy box, and into the room. Except for tears and an outpoked bottom lip, Angie Baby looked all right—no streams of black magic wafting off her, no dark manacles. Standing with my hands on my hips I demanded, "Young lady, what is going on?"

"George is *mine*. He came to *me*," she shouted, arms out wide, her face red, tears streaking her cheeks. "They can't have him!" She was positively furious. I struggled not to smile at the picture she presented; she needed only a sword and blue paint to look like a Celtic warrior princess, and something about her stance made me feel inordinately proud. My baby was defending something, not bespelled.

I sat on the foot of the bed and laced my fingers together. From behind me, my familiar—not that I had a familiar; no witches have familiars—leaped into the room and stalked across the bed, purring. I said, "Tell me about George."

Angie's eyes narrowed with suspicion, but when I didn't do anything more frightening, she opened her toy box and removed a teapot. It was redware, made from local red-brown clay and glazed in red-brown, except for the yellow daisy on the front. Angie cuddled the teapot like a doll in both arms. And I had never seen it before, which pricked all my protective instincts again. "How did you get it?" I asked. "Did you buy it with your allowance? Did someone give it to you?"

"No," Angie said crossly. "It showed up in my toy box this morning. Like poof." *Like poof* meant like a spell. Like magic. "Its name is George. It loves me."

"May I hold it for a moment? Please?"

Angie scowled but passed the teapot to me. It tingled in my hands like an active working, a spell still strong. Worse, it felt . . . alive somehow. As if it quivered in terror. I handed it back to my daughter, who petted the teapot and said, "It's okay, Georgie. I got you now. It's okay."

"Angie Baby, do you remember the time KitKit disappeared? We looked and looked and then we found her at Mrs. Simpson's place, down the hill?" Angie's scowl was back and, if possible, was meaner. "She was lapping up milk from a bowl and Mrs. Simpson was mincing salmon for her. KitKit had no interest in coming home, but she belonged here, with us. Remember? Mrs. Simpson gave her back to us."

Angie looked down at the teapot, her hair falling forward over it, a tear splashing on the top handle. "But . . ." She stopped, sniffling. "Okay. But I wanna give George to them myself."

"Okay. Can you be nice?"

"I don't *wanna* be nice. But"—she sniffled—"I can be nice."

I stood and grabbed up KitKit in one hand and helped Angie over the mess of her broken door with the other. In the great room, Angie, with huge tears racing down her cheeks, walked slowly over to the two vampires. They watched her come with strange lights in their eyes, and I realized that human parents didn't allow their children anywhere near vamps. Human children, and especially witch children, were surely rarities in their lives. Angie stopped about six feet away, inspecting them. To Jerel, she said, "You're not wearing a sword. You got one?"

"Yes, little witch child. I have a sword."

"Can you use it good? Well?" she corrected before I could. "Can you use it well?"

"I can. I am a swords master as well as a master cabinetmaker."

"You get to protect George and fight off the bad guys." To Holly, she said. "Here. George is scared. It needs you to hold it close and pet it. Like this." Angie demonstrated, one hand stroking the pot.

Holly knelt on one knee and extended his hands. Grudgingly Angie placed the teapot in his hands. Holly gathered it close, holding it as Angie had, and petted it. Angie let out a sob and raced to me, burying her face against my capri-clad thighs.

I pointed to the door and the vampires both bowed, so vampy formal, and departed, closing the door quietly. I watched and as soon as they reached the end of the drive, I raised the protective wards and pulled Angie to me on the couch. At the door to the hallway, Little Evan was hugging the jamb, crying in sympathy with his big sister. I held out a hand to him too, and we all four snuggled on the couch, my children, my unfortunate not-familiar, and me.

An hour later, as I was tucking a sleeping Angie back into bed, I heard another ward *ding*. I had a very bad feeling when I looked out and saw the same two forms at the end of the drive, illuminated by the security light. With trepidation, I went to the toy box and looked inside. The teapot was nestled into a corner.

I knew my daughter was strongly gifted with power, and she was probably capable of calling the pot back to her, but I hadn't felt any kind of magical working in the house or on the grounds. Which meant the teapot had come back on its own or under another's working. It might be a danger to us all. As if it were made of dynamite instead of fired clay, I lifted it from the box and carried it out onto the front lawn, to within four feet of the ward and within six feet of the vamps. Who now looked like what they were—dangerous predators; unhappy, dangerous predators.

"Do you taunt us with the return of our master's teapot?" Jerel asked.

"No. It came back on its own." Both vamps blinked, the twin gestures too human for the bloodsuckers. "It's heavily spelled and seems to have a will of its own. I'd like to try an experiment. I'd like to drop the ward, hand you the teapot, and see what happens."

"You did not call the teapot back to you?" Jerel asked.

"No. My word is my bond."

Jerel nodded once, the gesture curt.

I dropped the ward, stepped to the vampires, placed the teapot in Jerel's hands this time, and stepped back. The ward snapped back into place. Within thirty seconds, the teapot disappeared. "Not me. Not my magic. Certainly not my daughter's magic." I let derision enter my tone, because no witch's gifts came upon them before they reached puberty. Except Angie's. And that was a secret. A dangerous secret, to be protected as much as my children themselves.

The vamps looked from me to each other, and back. "What do we do now?" Holly asked.

"You will break this spell," Jerel demanded.

"Tell me the tale of the teapot. And how the Master of the City knew it had appeared at my house. I'd be very interested in that one."

Holly's eyes went wide—human wide, not vamped-out. "That never occurred to me. Where did it come from and how did it get here, and how did our master know of it?"

"Right," I said. "You go back to the vamp master and ask him those questions, because if he wants his teapot—or whatever it really is—back, I'll need to know everything to break whatever spell is on it."

"We will be back by midnight," Holly said, excitement in the words.

"Wrong. I have a family and you two have intruded enough on family time tonight. You go back and chat with your master. I'll see you an hour after dusk at Seven Sassy Sisters' Herb Shop and Café."

"Your family business," Jerel said, letting me know that my entire extended family could be in danger because of the blasted teapot.

"Tomorrow," I said, and turned my back on the vamps. Secure behind the strongest wards that Big Evan and I could create, I walked slowly back to my house and shut the door on the bloodsuckers. And leaned against it, trembling. I was in so much trouble. I had less than twenty-four hours to break a spell on a weird teapot that was clearly far more than a teapot. No wonder Lincoln Shaddock wanted it, whatever it really was.

I got the children off to school in the morning, without letting Angie discover that the teapot had returned to her toy box, and texted my sisters: 911 my house. Hurry soonest after breakfast crowd. They'd all get here as fast as possible. The 911 call was used only for extreme emergencies. Meanwhile I set four loaves to rise and made salad enough for all of us, all my sisters. There were seven of us, or had been until our eldest had died after turning to the black arts. We were still grieving over that one. Four of us were witches, and the remaining two were human. Four of the youngest were taking classes at various universities and colleges in the area, but they'd get here any way they could after the 911 text. Family always came first.

Carmen Miranda Everhart Newton, my air witch sister, set her toddler Iseabeal Roisin—pronounced *Ish-bale Rosh-een*—down at the door. Ishy ran, shouting for the cat—"Kekekeke"—her arms raised. The witch twins, Boadacia and Elizabeth, had called in sick for their morning classes and closed the herb shop. Our wholly human sisters, Regan and Amelia, were the last to arrive, having cleaned up the café after the last of the breakfast crowd.

When we were all sitting in my kitchen, the toddlers happily talking to each other in incomprehensible kid language, I realized how long it had been since we'd sat like this, working on a magical problem. Since our eldest, Evangelina, had died as a result of consorting with demons. Well, at the hand of my BFF, but that was another story. We were all red-haired, some more blond, some more brown, some of us flaming scarlet. All of us with pale skin that simply couldn't tan. All of us rowdy and chattering and happy to be together again. We had to do this more often. Not the teapot part, just the playing-hooky-and-visiting part.

To capture their attention, I centered the teapot atop the old farmhouse table, then caught them up on the teapot problem, the vamp problem, and the time limit problem. I had been studying the teapot for hours, so I already had some new things to share. "It isn't, strictly speaking, just a teapot. It's both a teapot and not a teapot, the result of a spell, and is magical, in some way, on its own. I can't tell why it keeps coming back here and I can't make it stay away."

"Yeah," the human Regan said. "That whole not having a magic wand really sucks."

"Ha-ha," Liz said, sounding bored with the oft-used banter.

"What I want to do is to raise the wards on the house, make a magic circle, and study it together." I looked at the human sisters. "You two will have to babysit and keep watch. Pull us out if anything strange happens."

"We always get stuck with babysitting duty," Regan complained.

"Word," Amelia said, sighing her agreement. "Fine. I'll go play with the kiddies." To her sister she said, "If you need help hitting them with a broomstick to break a circle, lemme know. I want in on some of that."

I raised the house wards and my witch sisters made a protective circle around my kitchen table by joining hands. It wasn't as formal as the circle in my herb garden, but it was enough to study the current situation. The combined magical power of the Everhart sisters is weighty, intense, and deep. It tingles on the skin, it whispers in the air, and in this case, it made a teapot spill its secrets.

Half an hour after staring, we broke for tea and slices of fresh bread with my homemade peach hot, untraditional peach preserves with chili peppers. While I put the snack together, Liz said, "His name is George."

"Not *he*, as in a human *he*," Cia said, "but a male something."

"He stinks," Carmen said. "A bit like muskrat. Or squirrel. Something rodent-ish."

"I got wet dog out of the scent," I said.

"Whatever he is, he's alive," Liz said.

"And not evil," Cia added. "Trapped. The result of a hex."

"Only a witch could have done a spell that captured a soul with a hex, and a blood witch at that," Liz said, exasperated. Blood witches spilled blood to power spells. The bigger the spell, the more blood needed. Human sacrifice had been known to be involved in black-magic ceremonies.

As we talked, I passed out plates, butter, and the peach hot, and topped up our mugs. "It feels like wild magic. Something not planned, but the result of something else. As if the incantation is sparking off all over the place."

"Why did it come here?" Cia asked.

"Opposites attract?" Carmen asked. "Your house is free and happy and he isn't?"

"Maybe he thought you could free him?" Liz asked.

"Or the death magics pulled him in against his will," the human twins said, nearly synchronous, walking into the kitchen together.

"Somebody didn't call us for the eats. Bad sisters," Regan said.

Amelia added, "Right. Evil sisters. And anyway, you left out the death-magic possibility. Maybe it's here to get Molly to do something deadly to it." No one replied, and I sat frozen in my chair, my hands cupped around my heated mug.

"What?" Amelia asked, her tone belligerent. "Sis, the witches among us were there when your magic turned on the earth."

"The rest of us saw the garden of death afterward," Regan added.

"And we all know it's still dead," Amelia said. "Doesn't take a witch to know that nothing will ever grow in that soil again."

"And then there's the whole thing about your familiar keeping you in control," Regan said, the conversation ping-ponging as my world skidded around me.

"And about the music spell Big Evan made to keep your magics under control," Amelia said. "Not talking about this is stupid. Gives it power."

Regan said, "My twin is taking her second year of psychology. Pass the cream. Thanks. She's teacher's pet because she can add the witch perspective to the psycho stuff."

Amelia huffed with disgust. "Not *psycho stuff*. That's rude to people with emotional or mental disorders or illness." Regan rolled her eyes and buttered her bread, taking a big bite.

The time my human sisters argued allowed me to settle. "Okay." The Everharts went still as vamps themselves. Because Amelia was right. It wasn't something we talked about. Ever. And secrets, things hidden, buried, and left to molder in the dark of one's soul, did give evil the power to rule. "So," I said, taking a fortifying gulp of tea. "What do you think about the death magics? Did the teapot come to me to die?"

My sisters all broke into talking at once, suggesting things like meditation and prayer, singing chants, spells to disrupt my death magic, and hinting that we simply bust the teapot and see if that would work to free the trapped soul. At that one, the teapot vanished, and appeared instantly back in hiding in my daughter's toy box. Liz dubbed it the teleporting teapot. Then the human sisters cleared the table and started research into Lincoln Shaddock's history, trying to find out about his relationship to witches and the teapot. There was nothing in the standard online databases, but I had an ace in the hole with Jane Yellowrock. She had tons of data on vamps, including Lincoln Shaddock, and she sent it to us, no questions asked. The information she offered confirmed the vamps' story.

Shaddock had been turned after a battle in the Civil War. When he came through the devoveo, he traveled to find his family. His wife had remarried and moved south. She rejected him. According to the data, there was evidence that she was an untrained, unacknowledged witch, not uncommon in those witch-hating times. There was nothing about a teapot, not that it mattered.

By lunchtime, we had a plan. Of sorts.

We closed the café and the herb shop at dusk, and rearranged the tables so there was an open place in the middle of the café. All of us, children, witches, and humans, stood in the middle, circled around the toy box with its magical teleporting teapot, held hands, warded the space where we would work, and blessed our family line with the simple words, "Good health and happiness. Protection and safety. Wisdom and knowledge used well and for good. Everharts, ever hearts, together, always." Then we broke the circle and the human twins piled our children into my car and headed back to my house. We witches? We waited.

Seven Sassy Sisters' was decorated in mountain country chic, with scuffed hardwood floors, bundles of herbs hanging against the back brick wall, tables, and several tall-backed booths, seats upholstered with burgundy faux leather and the tables covered with burgundy and navy blue check cloths. The kitchen was visible through a serving window. It was comfortable, a place where families and friends could come and get good wholesome food, herbal teas, fresh bread, rolls, and a healing touch if they wanted it. We also served the best coffee and tea in the area. But it wasn't the sort of place that vampires, with their fancy-schmancy, hoity-toity attitudes, would ever come. Until they knocked on the door just after dusk.

This time there were four vamps: Holly, his red hair in a ponytail; Jerel; a blond female vamp wearing a fringed leather vest, jeans covered in bling, and cowboy boots; and Lincoln Shaddock. He bore a striking resemblance to the actor in *Abraham Lincoln: Vampire Hunter*, a beak-nosed frontiersman, but with a clean-shaven chin, tall, rawboned, and rough around the edges. Unlike most vamps, who dressed for effect, Shaddock was wearing dark brown jeans and a T-shirt with a light jacket. And an honest-to-God bolo tie with a gold nugget as the clasp.

I took a steadying breath and unlocked the door, stepping back as they filed in and stood in a semicircle on one side of the toy box. The witches stood ranged on the other side. Holly said, "May I present—"

The outer door slammed open and Angie Baby raced inside, strawberry blond curls streaming and tangled, face flushed and sweaty. She had run from . . . somewhere. She dashed between us, rammed the toy box open, grabbed the teapot, and screamed, "George is mine! He likes me, not you!" And . . . she stuck her tongue out at Lincoln Shaddock, the most important master vamp in the Appalachian Mountains.

We were all frozen, my sisters in horror, me in sudden, blinding fear for my child, Jerel with a sword half-drawn, Holly with a bemused smile on his face, and Shaddock in . . . fury. Utter, encompassing fury. His pale skin flushed with blood, his eyes vamping-out, the pupils widening, white sclera flaming scarlet as the capillaries dilated. And his fangs clicked down from the roof of his mouth, the *snap* the only sound in the dead-silent room. Then everything happened at once.

Lincoln pointed a long, bony finger at Angie and took a single step toward her.

Moving faster than I could follow, Jerel drew his sword with a soft hiss of steel on leather. Holly stepped toward Angie Baby. Both vamps put themselves between my daughter and the enraged vampire. Jerel pointed his sword at his master's throat. Holly maneuvered, bare-handed, his feet rooted and knees bent, clearly much more dangerous than he appeared— a martial art master of some form or other. Or several. Bladed. That was what Jane called it. His body was bladed. He was primed to attack his boss.

Lincoln slowed but shouted, "Witches deal falsely! We will have our property!"

"Children are sacrosanct, my lord," Jerel said softly.

"It would pain us to bring you harm," Holly said, his red ponytail swinging.

"I am not ready to become the MOC, just yet, honey, but if you hurt that young 'un, I'll let 'em take your head," the blonde said, which identified her as the heir apparent of the Shaddock Clan, Dacy Mooney. And she too stepped between the vamp and the rest of us. I remembered to breathe and reached for Angie, pulling her close enough for Carmen to activate the ward we had prepared. It closed us in and closed the vamps out. "Take a good cleansing breath, Link," Dacy said. "Relax. Or it will be the last time you lose your temper."

Outside, my van squealed into the lot and stopped hard. The twins bailed out before the vehicle even stopped rocking, one holding two handguns, the other with a shotgun. "Son of a witch on a switch," I cursed softly.

"I'm not here as the blood-master of my clan," Lincoln Shaddock said with a strong Tennessee/Kentucky accent. "I'm here to regain what I lost."

"We all want to regain what we lost when our humanity left us," Dacy said, "but we got rules and limits. And memories. That has to be enough," she finished, her tone telling how much she had lost and how painful memories could be.

"Children. Are. Sacrosanct," Jerel said, his tone adamant, light glinting off the steel of his long sword.

The twins moved into the room and positioned themselves so they could shoot Shaddock and not one of us. Holly shifted so he could get to Regan and Shaddock both. His face was intent, focused, and troubled. He would kill if he had to. But he clearly didn't want to.

Lincoln blinked and looked at my daughter, cradling a reddish and yellow teapot like a pet. His fangs clicked back into his mouth. His eyes paled and lightened, as did his skin. And he blew out a puff of breath as if he really needed to breathe for something other than talking. He looked up to me. "My apologies, ladies. I am . . . not myself tonight, I haven't been myself ever since I felt the burst of magic. I raced to see if . . ." He paused and shook his head as if changing what he had been about to say. "But it was only the teapot. But the teapot was better than nothing. Better than the nothing that I had. I ask your forgiveness."

And then he did the strangest thing. The fiercest fanghead in the hills dropped to one knee. The three defending vampires stepped slightly to the side so Lincoln could see us, but not so far that he could get to us if he still wanted. He said to Angie Baby, "I especially beg your forgiveness, little witch child. I was distraught and forgot how frightening my kind can be."

"George is scared of you," Angie said.

Lincoln smiled, a purely human smile, and said, "No. The dog was named George, not the teapot."

Angie narrowed her eyes fiercely. "What kind of dog?"

Lincoln's smile widened. "A basset hound. He was my best, my very best, dog. Ever. I gave him into my Dorothy's keeping before I went off to war. He was ancient and toothless and fierce in protecting her when I appeared that night. Until he caught my scent. There must have been something still of the human scent about me. For he came to me when my Dorothy would not."

"Bassets weren't imported to the U.S. until the late eighteen hundreds," Regan said, her shotgun broken open and resting on a table, her eyes on her tablet.

"Incorrect," Shaddock said, as if a discussion about basset hounds were the purpose of this gathering. As if he hadn't just threatened my baby. "George Washington himself received a pair of bassets from Lafayette."

"Huh. Yeah. You're right. Legend, unsupported."

"Truth," Lincoln said.

I asked, "What did you hope when you felt the magic last night?"

Shaddock shook his head slowly, in sorrow. "The foolish dreams of an old man. When my Dorothy rejected me, she threw out a . . . It was as if I was hit with a bolt of lightning. I never saw the like, not before, not after.

When I came to, my wife was gone, along with the teapot she had been holding, and the old dog. Gone and never returned, never seen again. Last evening, I felt the same jolt of power, of lightning, and I ran to the old log cabin, hoping . . . hoping foolishly." He shook his head. "Hoping that my Dorothy had come back to me. Somehow."

Dacy Mooney said, "By all that's holy. That's why you kept that old cabin? Hoping your wife would come back?"

"'Tis so, Dacy. Foolish. I know. Foolish," he shook his head. "She returned to her husband. She lived on until her natural death."

"Had you been bleeding when you woke from your wife's"—*temper tantrum* wouldn't work—"anger?" I asked.

"Yes. I had healed, but I could still smell my blood, going sweet and rancid on the air. How did you know?"

Because wild magic did this. And wild magic is even stronger with blood, I thought, though I didn't share this with Shaddock. Carefully, feeling my way, I said, "There is a spirit trapped in this teapot. It isn't human. It's possible, maybe, that the dog's soul is stuck in the teapot and it is tied to your blood."

"George doesn't like you," Angie Baby said. "Weeell, he likes you, but he's mad at you." Her eyes went wide. "He's pooping on your pillow!"

Lincoln dropped to the floor, sitting on a level with my baby, eye to eye, on the far side of the ward. He looked awestruck, if vamps could look struck with awe. "I went away for a week," he said, "to do business in town, to register to fight in a war I never wanted. George was but a few months old. When I returned he raced to our marriage bed and he . . ." Lincoln's smile went wide. "He defecated on my pillow." Lincoln's eyes rested on the teapot in Angie's arms. "Oh my God. It's George." He held out his hands, beseeching. "I never wanted to leave you. Never. War was never my desire."

Angie scowled so hard she looked like that Celtic warrior, fierce and unyielding. My baby was going to grow up . . . a warrior. A true warrior. Pride filled me. I said, "Angie? What do you think?"

Still scowling, Angie walked to the edge of the ward and I quickly dropped it. For all I knew, my powerful child could walk straight to them with no ill effect, but I didn't want that to get around, if so. Grudgingly she placed the teapot in Lincoln's outstretched hands and he gathered the reddish and yellow teapot close, stroking it, murmuring, "I am so sorry. I beg your forgiveness. And yours, little witch child. Most earnestly." To me he said, "I owe you and yours a boon, whatever you may want, at a time of your choosing. If it is within my power to provide, it shall be yours."

I wasn't holding my breath for that. "Angie, go to your aunt Regan." My daughter walked around Lincoln, sitting on the shop floor, cuddling a teapot, and took her aunt's hand, her face long and woebegone. I was pretty sure Regan hissed a threat to beat her black and blue if she ever jumped out of a moving car again. And then hugged her fiercely. I'd deal with my daughter later. For now, we still had vampires in my family business, and vamps still drank blood. Dangerous, even if they did look cute and defenseless sitting on the floor.

"Ummm," I said. "We may have a way to free George." If it really was the spirit of a dog stuck inside the stoneware teapot. "But we need the teapot back for a bit." Without hesitation, Shaddock placed it on the toy box and took a step back to the tables and chairs that we had placed along the wall. Holly pulled out a chair and Link sat, his eyes never leaving the teapot.

It was a wild magic spell, somehow tied to Shaddock, for him to have felt the reappearance after so many years. I didn't ask where the teapot had been, but I had a bad feeling that Dorothy's wild magic had knocked it out of its own timeline and into the future a century and a half or so. The four of us witches stood at the four cardinal points, circled around the toy box, hands clasped. As eldest, I took north, even with my magic so damaged and me having to rein in my death magics beneath fierce will.

Together we said the words to an old family spell, softly chanting. The *wyrd* spell was originally meant to heal that which had been wounded by black magic. *"Cneasaigh, cneasaigh a bháis ar maos in fhuil,"* we said together. The rough translation, from Irish Gaelic: "Heal, heal, that which is soaked in blood."

We chanted the words over and over as our power rose. And rose. I closed my eyes, feeling my sisters' magic flow through me and through the floor, into the earth. Fecund and rich and potent. Power. Life. And when our massed magics were meshed and full, we directed the working, like a pin, a pick, an awl, directly at the teapot.

It shattered.

Pieces flew through the air, and beyond the circle, breaking it. The power that we had been using blazed up and out in a *poof* of heated air and broken stoneware. We ducked. Shattered pottery crashed into the floor and walls. And into Lincoln Shaddock's bony knees.

The vamps reacted faster than I could see, racing at us, weapons to hand. Ready to kill.

"George!" Angie Baby shouted, and broke free from a dumbfounded Regan to throw herself at the multicolored, long-eared dog standing on the toy box. He licked her face and nuzzled her. And then he turned to stare at Lincoln. He sniffed, smelling, tasting the air, redolent with the ozone of burned power and vampire blood.

"Son of a witch," Carmen muttered. "It worked."

George slowly dropped his front paws off the box and waddled to his old master, to Lincoln, licking the trace of blood off Lincoln's bleeding knees.

"Son of a witch," Carmen muttered again. "It really worked."

Lincoln Shaddock dropped again to the floor and pulled George into his arms. He was crying, purely human tears, and the old dog licked them from his cheeks. Lincoln chuckled and rubbed the basset behind the ears. "You are a sight for sore eyes, you are, old boy. Good old boy. Good George."

It was the first major working we had done as a family since we'd lost our coven leader and big sister. Tears fell down my face in joy and delight and excitement. My earth magics weren't what they had been before. But they weren't dead. Not yet.

One week later to the day, there came a knock on the wards. Holly and Jerel stood there, in the dusky night, waiting patiently. Carrying KitKit, I went to the front door and dropped the wards. When the vamps reached the porch, Jerel bowed again, stiffly formal, and opened a folded note. Vamps have great night vision, and when he read, I had no doubt he could see the words.

"Lincoln Shaddock, Blood-Master of Clan Shaddock, does not forget his promise of a boon to Molly Everhart Trueblood and to Angelina, her daughter. But he offers this small token of thanks, for the memories and humanity gifted by the child and her tender care of his beloved dog, George."

Holly knelt and set a small bundle on the grass at the bottom of the low porch. "He is from a line of champions. And his name is George."

From behind me, Angie squealed and threw herself off the porch and directly at the basset puppy. The two tumbled across the night-damp grass and rolled, the puppy licking her face. In my arms, KitKit struggled and scratched and hissed, and made a twisting, leaping, flying movement out of my arms, over my shoulder and back inside. The puppy, seeing the movement, raced after, managing to trip over his huge paws and step on his own ear, sending him flying. Angie, to my horror, whirled and threw herself into Holly's arms for a hug that left him shocked and motionless on his knees, and then slammed into Jerel to hug his knees. And then she was gone, inside, chasing after the pets. *Oh dear.* I had a dog. Big Evan would be home tomorrow and . . . we had a basset.

Before he stood, Holly removed something from his pocket and handed it to me. "Final thanks," he said, backing away, "but not a boon."

I looked down at my hand and saw what looked like a diamond. Payment for an old dog was a diamond? A *diamond*? When I looked up, the vamps had gone, disappeared into the shadows. I closed the door and reset the wards. And went to check on my enlarged family.

Big Evan would have a cow.

Cat Fight

Author's note: This short story takes place (in the JY timeline) after *Dark Heir*.

"The Master of the City of New Orleans sends you greetings and a missive." The words had that old-fashioned ring, a sure sign of a powerful vamp's official notice—and the fact that the courier was a vamp himself, and not a human blood-servant—which indicated that this situation could only be trouble. I'd heard similar words once when the chief fanghead had told me to get out of his city or he'd eat me. And not in a good way.

I cocked a hip onto the doorjamb, crossed my arms, and stared at the envelope in the vamp's hand. "He sends his favorite slave as messenger boy? Can't be good news," I said. "Give me one good reason why I should accept the note."

Edmund Hartley smiled, an act that turned his nondescript face into something almost human, and certainly charming. "Because I have healed you and those you love several times, without asking for recompense, or requesting you in my bed or your blood in my fangs in return. Because I am fascinating and intriguing and you are curious about my history and my life." His smile twisted slightly on one side, indicating a mischievous side I hadn't seen before. "Because you like me and we have become friends of a sort?"

All of those things were true, but I wasn't going to give in so easily, not to a fancy note from Leo. I scowled at him. "Friends with a *vamp*?"

Like Edmund, Beast thought at me. *Would make good vampire mate.*

Down, Beast. We have a mate.

Beast chuffed with amusement.

"It is true that if we were locked in a dungeon together," he said, an innocent, practically winsome look on his face, "I would certainly drink you down. But other than situations resulting in starvation, you are safe from me, I assure you." He was teasing me. It was a novel conversation to have with a vamp.

I looked at the note. The previous note, delivered by Bruiser a long time ago, had been a scroll, tied with a ribbon. This one was inside a handmade envelope constructed from heavy cloth paper, and had my name written on it in Leo's own handwriting, with a real fountain pen, all the scrolls and twirls and dips and stuff, like they used to write way back when. And like the last one, it was closed with a bloodred drop of wax and Leo's seal.

I had been avoiding Leo and his messages and texts, which may be the reason he had sent a messenger. It was harder to ignore a human-shaped face than a beep or two or three dozen on my cell. I stared hard at the envelope, hoping it would disappear. It didn't.

I was pretty sure that the note was a request—make that a demand— that I take up my responsibilities as Leo's Enforcer, which I hadn't done since I tracked and captured the Son of Darkness. I'd been hurt in that job and so had my team. We deserved some time off. But Leo probably thought a week was long enough, hence the increased number of unanswered texts and voice mails and phone calls. And now the note. Which was surely some form of orders, and I had never been partial to getting ordered around.

Leo Pellissier was a . . . I couldn't think of a word bad enough to call him, even silently, except for corrupt CEO or debauched king. He was a high-handed, demanding, megalomaniacal, exacting, meticulous, fussy, taxing, body-part-of-your-choice fanghead. According to the contract we had signed, he was also my boss, or had been until the SoD incident less than a month ago.

"My master wishes you back in his employ."

"Uh-huh." I jutted out my jaw, thinking. I hadn't even closed the door on the messenger or opened the dang note, and I was already mad. I snapped out my hand and Edmund snapped the envelope into my palm, practically choreographed. I broke the seal and pulled out the note, which was written on equally fancy, heavy paper. The note said:

My Dearest Jane,

As per our agreement, there are duties awaiting your return. If you wish a longer holiday, that can be arranged, however, the Clan Blood-Master of Bayou Oiseau, Clermont Doucette, has requested your presence. If you are not available to assist him I will send another.

I am placing the Mercy Blade and Edmund Hartley at your disposal.

Leonard Pellissier,
Blood-Master of the
City of New Orleans

I grunted. Not too long ago, I had stopped over in Bayou Oiseau, a pretty little Cajun town on the banks of the bayou of the same name, and solved a problem that had been brewing between the witches and the vamps for a long time. After my visit, Leo and the chief suckhead of the town, Clermont Doucette, which was pronounced in the patois of the region as *Cler-mon Doo-see*, had been supposed to parley together and settle the long-standing difficulties between them, but I hadn't seen Clermont in New Orleans, and Leo hadn't gone south to Bayou Oiseau, so maybe any peace I had created between the two had evaporated after I left. That had been known to happen.

Both vamps had overly high opinions of themselves, and I could easily see where problems might arise. Leo was an even bigger predator than I am—and I'm half–mountain lion—and he could be a mite off-putting when he got into a snit. Clermont could too.

I held the note over my shoulder and it skated from my fingers, tugged away by one of my partners, Alex Younger, the younger Younger. The smart one of the team. The stinkiest too, when he hadn't showered in a while, and he had been playing *World of Warcraft* for the last couple of days. Edmund's nose wrinkled and he took a half step back before he caught himself. It was that nearly human reaction to the stench that made me chuckle and relax. I said, "I know, right?"

"How does he stand himself?" Edmund whispered.

"Beats me." I jerked my head to the interior of the house and pushed the door wide. "Come on in. You know what the note said?"

"I do. I am supposed to escort you to Bayou Oiseau as your personal protection and as Leo's personal delegate."

"Personal protection? I'm my own personal protection." I stared at Edmund as he entered, his hands clasped behind his back. He was shorter than my six feet, nondescript, with brown eyes and brown hair, and looked scholarly and bookish, like a schoolteacher, a librarian, or a slightly cynical professor. "Or my partners are," I added. "I don't need more personal protection."

"I hope you might think of me as your primo."

I closed the front door behind us and led the way through the dimly lit house and into the kitchen, thinking about what he was saying and what he might really be meaning. With vamps there is no simple truth, just layered, multipurposed, dual- or triple-intentioned half lies. "Only vampires have primos. And primos are human."

"Exactly. Having a primo would be a way to provide cachet, to raise your value, to suggest that you are something more than simply an Enforcer, a bully boy. And Leo having two Enforcers adds to that effect. All these changes will make the Mithran world, even the *European* Mithran world, sit up and take notice. It will give you power in our world. You would be one of the very few human Enforcers ever to have a *Mithran* primo. And I do believe that I would serve you best in that capacity." Edmund looked too pleased with this idea, as if maybe he had come up with it himself. Actually, knowing Edmund, he probably had.

"Hmmm." I topped off my mug and added the secret ingredient. "I'm having tea. Want a cup?"

Edmund looked at my mug and stuck his nose in the air. "Not if it has . . . Is that *Cool Whip* on top?"

I hid a grin. "That sounded like a tea snob's outrage."

"Good God, woman. It's a sacrilege."

I couldn't help it. I laughed. And then I said, "One of my favorite housemothers when I was growing up was a woman named Brenda. She always put Cool Whip on her tea."

While Edmund prepared a *proper cuppa*, expounding on the virtues of real cream and real sugar, I added more tea to my cup and another dollop of Cool Whip. Yanking vamps' chains always made my day brighter.

I got the essentials from Edmund, which were pretty simple but not terribly informative, not the kind of thing to require a Mithran mailman. "The witches and non-Mithrans in Bayou Oiseau are once again at war and the Blood-Master of New Orleans directs you to broker a peace agreement."

"Again."

"Yes." I could have sworn that Edmund was hiding laughter.

"In an area where vamps ran unchecked and unrestrained by the Vampira Carta"—which was the written law for all Mithran vampires—"for centuries. To a place where the witches who survived learned a lot of tricks to keep the bloodsuckers at bay. A place where blood ran in the streets and witches and vamps were burned at dawn. Back there."

"Yes. That is his request."

"Uh-huh. I got the broad picture," I said to my erstwhile primo. "Now I want the deets, the stuff you know, but that Leo told you not to tell me unless I asked. Consider this asking."

"Gladly, my mistress. According to Clermont Doucette, a valuable item was stolen by a witch from the Clan Home. It has made its way to the witch coven. It has not been returned."

So far as I knew, there was only one witch living at the Clan Home, and she was the witch daughter of Lucky Landry, a witch leader in the town. Shauna Landry Doucette had married the vamp heir, Gabriel, and this marriage was the sole reason for the peace agreement I had brokered in Bayou O. A kind of successful *Romeo and Juliet* story. At the time.

I grunted, which must have sounded like encouragement, because he went on.

"Clermont's daughter-in-law stole the item." Seems Juliet hadn't remained loyal for long.

"The Master of the City also desires me to bring back any magical item that you might discover."

That was an ongoing order, an order I never followed through on. "Ducky," I said.

"And I am to go with you."

"No." I refused Edmund's assistance and that of the Mercy Blade, and sent my messenger skipping into the night scenting of amusement and irritation in equal measure. Well, strolling languidly, though the mental image of the ultracool, elegant vamp skipping down the street left me with a smile. He had been gone exactly forty-seven seconds when my cell rang, displaying a studio pic of Captain America on the screen, which was my current image for Eli Younger. I accepted the call and stared at the Kid, who pretended to ignore me. "Eli. Yes, yes, yes." I paused and thought and added, "Yes, and what do you think?"

My partner, the former Army Ranger, chuckled. "Think you got me pegged, babe?"

"Yup. Yes, your brother is nosy, and yes, he is correct. Edmund Hartley did come visit with a letter from Leo. Yes, it offers us a gig as part of my Enforcer position southwest of New Orleans, in Bayou Oiseau. But I don't think Clermont would have told Leo everything. He's canny and sneaky and probably wants help on *his* terms. He probably kept back mucho info from Leo, hoping to salvage the situation in his favor. So we might be walking into a mess.

"And yes, there has been a suggestion, made by Edmund, that Edmund should be my primo. It sounds like something he'd come up with, all Machiavellian, and probably with an evil intention and outcome all planned out. You know. The usual vamp crap. And what do you think about it all?"

Eli chuckled, and I heard his sweetie pie in the background.

"Put her on speaker." Eli thumbed a button and I said, "Hey, Syl. It shouldn't be dangerous. But it *is* dealing with Cajun vamps and witches, so all redneck possibilities will apply."

Sylvia chuckled and said, "You have my blessing and an order for you to keep Eli's blood in his veins."

"I'll take all precautions."

"And, Eli, you keep her blood in her veins too."

"That's the plan, boss." He clicked the speaker off, and, a moment later, ended the call.

"Boss?" I asked.

"Syl and I don't do PDAs."

PDAs. Public displays of affection. Even verbal ones, it seemed. "So, you're in?"

"Syl's got a murder scene to take care of. Some big muckety-muck in Natchez took a three-tap, and had a kilo of cocaine in the trunk of his Mercedes. I'm heading home, because while I love the woman, watching her and her crime scene techs crawl around in some guy's guts and brains isn't what I call a romantic evening. We'll talk when I get there, about Edmund wanting to be your primo. That should be my job."

"No, you're my partner. If I accepted, Edmund would be our vampire servant."

"Come to think of it, that sounds all kinds-a classy. He could clean our toilets. See you soon, babe."

The call ended and I stood there, still staring at Alex, who hadn't yet looked up, ignoring me the way only a gamer in the middle of a *World of Warcraft* game could. I said, "Take a shower within one hour or I'll pull the plug."

He snorted, the sound remarkably like my own. "No, you won't."

I lifted my brows at the challenge and started toward the cord.

"I have battery backup," Alex said, his voice sly, his eyes still down.

"Shower. Or I'll stop all credit on all computer and all related purchases. And I'll tell Eli how bad you stink."

Alex lifted his arm and took a sniff. "Holy sh . . ." He did look up then. "I'll be in the shower before he gets to town. And I'll strip the bedsheets and put new ones on both the beds upstairs. And I'll put out fresh towels. And I'll wash a load of clothes."

Yeah. He stank that bad. "You could also call the cleaning service and they could clean the whole house while we're gone. Not the shower part. You're on your own for that."

"Spoilsport."

"True dat," I said, in the patois of Louisiana. I left the room to pack. I no longer had fighting leathers of any kind, thanks to the battle with the Son of Darkness, and I still didn't have Bitsa, so I wouldn't need bike riding clothes, which meant that it didn't take long to pack. Packing done—jeans and T-shirts, boots and undies, toiletries and one pair of summer jammies—I took the time to call my own . . . whatever he was, and schedule a few hours at his place for when I got back. We were seriously overdue for some "us time," but Bruiser was still out of town doing something Onorio-ish. We made plans for when I got back, which was likely two days away at best. Lately our trips were overlapping. Sometimes working for suckheads . . . well . . . sucked.

I-10 was a straight shot west, and rest stops, gas stations, and restaurants were few and far between, yet, even with a straight shot and no roadside distractions, the trip to Bayou Oiseau took longer than we expected because of the rain. A front had moseyed in and settled over the lower half of the state like it intended to sign a lease and stay. Beast slept as we drove, and I spent the drive time reading the case notes aloud to the boys so they would be up to speed on the small town and the events that took me over when Bitsa needed a mechanic on my only other trip there.

The inhabitants were mostly Cajun—vamp, witch, and human. The vamps had a bad history of abusing the populace for generations, and they knew (or had known) nothing about the Vampira Carta, which are the legal papers that govern all Mithrans. Worse, the vamps had not been aligned with Leo, and therefore had no oversight.

The witches were unaligned with the NOLA witches. Ditto on the lack of oversight.

In between were the humans who had either taken off for safer environs, joined forces with one faction or the other, or hunkered down to fight a war of attrition.

The Youngers both chuckled when I told them I had played matchmaker and peacemaker between the vamps and witches. I had no idea why they thought it was amusing. The wedding had been beautiful.

Edmund, who had appeared with a pop of air just as we were about to back out of our parking spot in front of my house, was unexpectedly romantic. "I am quite certain that it was the social event of the year," he said. I wondered if there had been a hint of irony in the statement. Eli grunted. Alex ignored us all, still playing his game.

None of us were particularly happy to have Edmund along, but the vamp had insisted and so had Leo. The MOC—Master of the City—had claimed that Edmund's attendance would be beneficial and give weight and clout to our presence. Whatever. The call was short and unsweet and to the point. "You will take Edmund." *Click.*

Not that he had the time, but Leo had said nothing about Edmund being a primo, which made me think even more that the primo idea was Edmund's alone. A primo would be around often, if Leo gave him to me, and if I accepted him as such, which wasn't likely. If I took Ed on and he turned out to be a pain in the butt, then I'd have to fire him, which would also be a pain in the butt. So far, the vamp had held his peace and kept quiet, not intruding on the comradery the Youngers and I had established, but no way would a vamp be able to maintain subservience to humans and a skinwalker. I was waiting for the other shoe to drop.

I finished my reading of the case notes with, "Mostly, BO is a back-water community of churches, a blood bar, a few shops, a grocery, a couple of restaurants, a B and B, a dozen wild game processors"—which was the polite term for *butchers for hunters' kills*—"alligator and boar hunting, fishing businesses for tourists, an airboat tour guide company, and a few thousand citizens spread over a wide area of bayou, swamp, and sinking land. It needs paint, repaved roads, an influx of tax money, and a general makeover."

"Looks like the town is finally getting that makeover," Eli said, as the SUV lurched over ruts in the road. He slowed, his headlights taking in the rain-wet dark.

The two-lane state road we turned onto from I-10 had been freshly graded in the last couple of days, judging by the coarse road surface, in preparation for new paving. The heavily armored SUV bounced over the ruts and splashed through standing pools as we rolled past road-paving machines parked on the sides. In the rain, in the momentary clarity provided by the windshield wipers, I thought that they looked like stalled dinosaurs, which made Beast perk up and look out through my eyes.

Want to hunt dino-saucers. Or cow!

Not on this trip. Just vampires and witches.

My Beast curled up inside, closed her eyes, and pouted. She hadn't been out a whole lot recently, and she was grumpy about not getting to hunt. *Could hunt cow from window of ess-u-vee,* she finished.

The SUV was part of my gear as Leo's Enforcer, and it had all the bells and whistles and onboard computer—as well as the bullet-resistant, multilayer, polycarbonate glass and Kevlar inserts around the cab—that Eli's personal SUV didn't have. I had been shot at recently and appreciated the protection that the heavy vehicle provided, but the extra weight made a jolting ride on the rough road.

We made it to the small town long after midnight, the few streetlights offering small globes of visual warmth in the downpour. There were dump trucks and construction vehicles and more of the road-grading machines parked everywhere, but in the darkness and the rain, no workers.

The town name meant *bird bayou*, and the first time I saw the quaint little place, I thought it looked like a love child spawned by the producer of a spaghetti Western and a mad Frenchwoman. The main crossroads were the intersection of Broad Street and Oiseau Avenue, which wasn't as pretty as it might have sounded. Broad Street was narrow, and the buildings lining its single-lane cousin were downright ugly. There was only one traffic signal in the entire town, and despite the crossroads being the main intersection, tonight there was no social life either. Everything was at a standstill, and not just because it was so late.

A circle of drenched women blocked the main crossing. Twelve women. The scent of magic was strong in the air, tickling along my skin and making me want to sneeze, despite the insulating rubber tires and the pouring rain, not that insulation worked against magic as well as it worked against electricity. Or at all, actually.

Eli pulled to a stop some twenty feet away from the witch circle, the soaking-wet women illuminated by his headlights. Witch circles can be composed of different numbers of practitioners, and I had seen circles with two, five, twelve, three, four, and nine witches, depending on the geometry and mathematics being used to rout the magical energies. Twelve witches made up the most potent kind of circle, and working with that kind of energy and potential could do scary things, including take over the witches and use their combined life force to power the working, leaving dead witches behind and their magic operational but out of control. These witches were bedraggled and dripping and so involved that they didn't seem to notice or care about the weather. Or us. And oddly, they were standing outside the circle they were working. Which meant that something inside had their full attention.

I tried to make out what it was, even pulling on Beast's vision, but all I saw were dull kaleidoscopic colors, all in the green and blue part of the color spectrum, with a hint of yellow. It looked locked down, well contained, whatever it was.

"Twelve, eh?" Eli sounded casual, but he had fought beside me when a full circle had changed the local vamps in Natchez into bizarro insectoid creepazoids. Wiping out the vamps had been the worst fight of my life, and I'd had some bad fights to compare it to. "Last time we ran into one of those," he murmured, "I met Syl. That was a good time in my life."

Alex made a gagging sound. "Ignore the lovestruck idiot in the driver's seat," he said. "Can you see what they're doing?"

"The circle looks like a form of Molly's *hedge of thorns* spell," I said, "but they're outside the hedge. I think I see some kind of circle outside the hedge, but it's weak as well water. There's something in the middle of the street and in the center of the circle." I squinted to see it better. Tried to look at it from the edges of my vision, focusing on a tree in the distance to make the blue-green fog of dullness. "Is it a . . . a hat?"

Beast rose from her nap and studied the scene through my eyes. *Witches are studying prey.* Which was as good an explanation as any I had.

"I can't imagine why you sound so shocked," Edmund murmured. "Not so many years ago, most women loved hats."

"Jane's not most women, dude," Alex said for me. "And it isn't a hat—it's one of those laurel wreath things that the Greeks and the Romans used to wear."

At the comment, Edmund sat up straight and leaned across the opening between the front seats to get a better look. As he studied the wreath, he slowly vamped-out, his pupils going wide, the sclera going scarlet, and his fangs slowly dropping with a soft *schnick* of sound on the hinges in the roof of his mouth. "Well, well, well," he said. "I do wonder what that can be."

I couldn't have said why, but I had a feeling that Edmund knew exactly what it was, and for whatever reason, he wasn't saying. I thought about calling him on it, but decided to hold my tongue, saying instead, "Down boy. That's a dangerous circle, so no matter what it is, we aren't getting near it."

I gave directions to the bed-and-breakfast where I stayed last time I was in town and Eli put the SUV in reverse and backed a few feet but didn't pull away. The headlights gave us a clear view of the town and the women, despite the rain, and I could see him taking in everything, the way Uncle Sam had trained him in the Rangers. If he had to, Eli could now draw an exact replica map of the town for house-to-house warfare. Hopefully we wouldn't need that map or that much bloodshed, but it was a handy skill set.

On the south corner of the intersection, there was a huge, brick Catholic church, the bell tower hiding a tarnished, patinated bell in its shadows. The large churchyard was enclosed by a brick wall, with ornate bronze crosses set into niches in the brick every two feet. On top of the wall were iron spikes, also shaped like sharp, pointed crosses. The sight made Edmund growl and sit back. I just smiled. The church in Bayou Oiseau had been fighting vamps for decades. It never hurt to remind a vampire that he had enemies and that there were ways to fight his power.

To the east of the church, across the road, was a bank, beige brick and concrete, with the date 1824 on the lintel and green verdigris bars shaped like crosses on the windows and door. To my right was a strip mall that had seen better days, brick and glass, with every single window and door in the strip adorned with a cross, either painted or decaled on. The mall featured a nail salon, hair salon, tanning salon, consignment shop, secondhand bookstore, bakery, a Chinese fast-food joint, a Mexican fast-food joint, and a Cajun butcher advertising andouille sausage, boudin, pork, chicken, locally caught fish, and a lunch special for $4.99.

"Is that Lucky Landry's place?" Alex asked.

"That's it," I said. "Best food in fifty miles."

Beast thought, *Good meat smell. Lucky is good hunter to hunt so much meat. Want to hunt with Lucky Landry.*

Directly ahead of the SUV, catercornered from the church, was a saloon, like something out of the French Quarter—two stories, white-painted wood with fancy black wrought iron on the gallery, long narrow window doors with working shutters, and aged double front doors, the wood carved to look like massive, weather-stained orchids. The building's name and purpose was spelled out in bloodred letters on a white sign hanging from the second-floor gallery, LECOMPTE SPIRITS AND PLEASURE. It was the town's blood bar, and the only building without built-in crosses at every access point. I rolled down the window and took a sniff. Unlike the last time I was here, I couldn't smell beer and liquor and sex and blood, only rain and magic. The bar was closed and someone had nailed a cross over the front doors. Somehow that felt like a bad omen.

Eli backed another few feet and his headlights fell on something that had been hidden in the shadows. A small group of people stood in the downpour, about ten feet away from the witches' circle's north point. People, standing, immobile, in the rain. Not breathing. Not doing anything. *Suckheads.* Watching the witches. Wet and undead and scary silent.

In the backseat, my babysitter vamp cocked his head and studied them. Softly he said, "Interesting." But his tone said it was more than just interesting—it was unexpected, disturbing, and dangerous. Wordless, Eli backed down the street and turned into a narrow alley to bypass the intersection and the . . . whatever was going on there.

Miz Onie's Bed and Breakfast was closed for the night, but the woman was a light sleeper and met us at the door before we could even knock, dressed in a fluffy purple housecoat with her graying hair up in twisty cloth curlers. She was not yet sixty, but was using a cane this time, and her gait looked pained.

"I see you come down de street," she said, her Cajun accent mellifluous. "Come in out de rain. You rooms ready. Wet clothes go hang on de rack," she pointed. Without waiting, she led the way up the steps and we followed her uneven, slow steps.

"Are you injured, Miz Onie?" I asked.

Woman is sick. Smells old. Cull her from herd?

No!

Beast chuffed, but I didn't really know if she was being funny or hiding a serious question.

"Broke my ankle back a month ago. Doctor say it a spiral fracture and take longer to heal. Got to wear dis boot, which make *clump-clump* noise, but I making good progress." She looked at the Youngers. "You not the same boys what come with Jane last time," she said as we dumped equipment and gear in the hallway upstairs. "Them boys be U.S. military. Who you is?"

I remembered that Miz Onie had liked men in uniform and had given special attention to the men, including huge breakfasts and food left out to munch on all day. "Former U.S. Army Ranger, Miz Onie," I said, "and his younger brother, Alex. And Edmund Hartley."

She looked them all over, nodding to herself at the sight of the Youngers. But her eyes squinted when she got to Ed. I couldn't tell from her body language or her scent how she felt about the vamp, but she didn't kick him out. She turned for the stairs and her room on the first floor, walking hunched over, gripping her robe tightly closed with her free hand. "Breakfast at seven. Towels in each bath. This wet weather has me out of sorts and strangely sleepy, so good night, all."

Once again she gave me the best room, on the front of the house, the green room, with emerald green bedspread, moss green walls, striped green drapery, and greenish fake flowers in a tall vase near a wide bay with soaring windows and a door out to a gallery. The boys were sent into the room Derek had used on the last visit, which had two twin beds and a view into the garden out back. Edmund was left standing in the hallway alone, until she pointed to a third room, a nook at the top of the stairs. He frowned as he took in the windows and the draperies—which could be opened to let in the light while he slept, if an enemy was so inclined to watch him burn to death in bed.

He raised his brows. "Doesn't like Mithrans, I take it?"

"Not fond of anyone one but military boys."

"I fought in the Civil War. Does that count?"

"Confederate?"

"No."

"I'd keep it to yourself, then," I said, tossing my sleepwear on the bed and my toiletries on the bathroom counter, and laying out my weapons with much greater care.

Patiently Edmund said, "Where am I to sleep, my master?"

Sleep with Beast!

I ignored her and stood straight, staring at him. "None of that 'my master' crap. Not now, not ever. In fact, you can take that primo idea and stuff it where the sun don't shine. As to your sleeping needs, I doubt the B and B has a vamp-sealed room, so I guess that, if the bedroom she assigned to you doesn't make you all jolly, you get to spend the day in my closet."

Edmund didn't sigh, as vamps don't have to breathe, but his body took on a long-suffering posture.

"Don't worry. I'll put a pallet in there with a nice comfy pillow from my bed. Meanwhile, why don't you go see what the vamps are up to and get the lowdown on their point of view. I'm going to catch a couple of hours of shut-eye and head back out at five a.m."

"Even when I was human that was an ungodly hour. And in case you haven't noticed, it's raining outside."

"You'll dry." I pushed him out of the room and shut the door in his face. "Nighty night, Edmund."

I texted Clermont Doucette that I was in town, put a nine mil on the bedside table along with a stake and a vamp-killer, kicked off my traveling boots, crawled between the covers, which smelled faintly of lavender and vanilla, and closed my eyes. I was instantly asleep. I woke when the single door to the gallery opened and wet air blew in. The nine mil was targeted on the dim outline before I got my eyes fully opened. "It's loaded with silver," I said, my voice gravelly with sleep.

"I would die, then, true-dead, if you shot me," Edmund said, sounding unconcerned.

"Why are you entering my room from a second-story window?" I asked, as the night breeze fluttered the pale curtains into the room. The curtains were new since my last visit, and they had ruffles. I hate ruffles. "All the novels say suckheads can turn into bats and fly around. I thought it was fiction."

Edmund made a *pfft* sound with his lips. "There is a tree outside your window with low branches. You need to put that toy away and come see this spectacle." The guy really did have big brass ones. At the thought, I couldn't help but grin, and Edmund's eyebrows went up a notch. I waved the inquiring look away and rolled to the edge of the bed, my aim not wavering, and hit the floor in my sock feet. The bay window was narrow, and I motioned Edmund back with the weapon. He stepped out into the dark of night, onto the gallery, and I followed. The main intersection of Broad Street and Oiseau Avenue was visible between the waxy leaves of a magnolia in the yard of the B and B.

The witches were still standing in a circle in the middle of the cross-roads. Standing behind them were two vamps for every one witch. They were positioned to attack and though the witches were outside the hedge circle—which was weird enough on its own—the vamps hadn't yet attacked. *Weird.*

"How long?" I asked.

"Since the rain stopped."

"How long until dawn?" I clarified.

"Perhaps fifteen minutes."

"I was supposed to be up before this."

"According to Clermont Doucette, the witches put a sleep spell on the entire town. Once humans go to sleep, they don't wake until after dawn."

I grunted. I wasn't human, so why was I affected? Miz Onie had still been up when we got here. Or had been woken. I had to wonder if Miz Onie was immune to sleep spells or wasn't human, to be able to be up and about. "What happens at dawn?"

"The Mithrans attack, moving at speed. The intent is to capture every witch and take back the wreath, which may be magical, though no one seems to know what its purpose is.

"When Shauna brought the wreath to her father, Landry decided that it was a religious artifact instead of a witch artifact and took it to the Catholic priest, who then called the bishop of Orleans Parish, St. Tammany Parish, St. Bernard Parish, Plaquemines Parish, and Jefferson Parish, who happens to be the same person, the preeminent religious figure in the southeast part of the state. The bishop sent a spokesperson, who kept it all of one day before deciding to send it Rome for exorcism."

He paused for my reaction, but I didn't have one to give, except to lower my weapon.

He inclined his head in recognition of his change in status from prisoner of a sort to gossip artist. "It has a great deal of power. I could smell it on the air. When the Mithrans heard that it was to be sent to Rome, they came en masse to the church. But it had been closed up behind the crosses on the walls and doused in holy water."

I looked back at the gathering on the street and sighed. "Leo sent me into a mess, didn't he?"

"To be fair to the Blood-Master of New Orleans, he did not know that things had become so dire."

"Uh-huh. Go on with your story of intrigue, love lost, and magic crap."

"Someone, not a Mithran, as he was undeterred by holy icons, stole over the wall to the church grounds, and pilfered the wreath from the priests."

I started laughing softly, though I wasn't sure it was from amusement or something more dismal. Watching the tableau in the street, the sodden witches and the hyperalert vamps, was like watching paint dry.

"That person took the wreath to the coven of witches, the female witches of the town, and the coven immediately recognized the power of the artifact."

"So we have the vamps, the Holy Roman Church, and the witches all after the same thing."

Edmund was definitely laughing now; his eyes were even twinkling. "The coven has been studying it for three nights, attempting different tests and spells to identify the magical signature—these are the words of Elodie and Gilbert, Mithrans who would speak to me, not my own. The wreath has been resistant to everything, even to being used as a power source for a spell of healing, the most simple and beneficial of all spells. While clearly powerful, the wreath is not assisting and is resistant to anyone spending its stored power."

"And they called it a wreath?"

Edmund paused, his lips pursing slightly as he thought back. "I called it so. They did not object or suggest another name or title."

"Go on."

"The Mithrans want the wreath back, but the witches are in place before dusk and remain in place until after dawn. They are safe from attack by use of a spell that I have never seen or heard of before—what they call an *electric dog collar*. If anyone touches the faint circle that encloses them, they are instantly zapped with a strong force, sufficient to set a Mithran attacker ablaze, or stop a human heart. Or to send a wood beam catapulting across the square," he added drily. "A human tried that one and received a broken arm for his troubles."

I laughed then and took a seat on the small chair inside the room, the gun hanging down between my knees.

"Neither the Mithrans nor their humans can get to the witches," Edmund said. There is evidence that the love match between the witch Shauna and her husband, Gabriel Doucette, is under strain."

"No kidding. Okay. You say that the coven has been studying the thing for three nights. What happens at dawn?"

"The Mithrans pop away, as you might say, to their lairs, safely away from the sun, and the witches drop their *dog collar* spell, pick up the wreath, and walk away."

"Go wake up the boys, will you? And be prepared for Eli to try to kill you. He'll be unhappy to have slept past four a.m."

"I'll toss a bucket of water on him from a safe distance. That often works for mad dogs."

Before he could move for the door, I heard a *pop* of sound and focused on the open gallery door. A form stood there, silhouetted in the faint gray light, his hands raised in a gesture of peace. It was Gabriel Doucette, heir of Clan Doucette, husband of Shauna Landry, the witch who had stolen the wreath. And a vamp.

I was glad I was still holding my weapon, because it was instantly settled on Gabriel's pretty face. Gabe wasn't the brightest bulb in the chandelier when I met him the last time, and time and marriage hadn't made him any smarter. He vamped-out—eyes, fangs, talons, the whole nine yards. Before I could squeeze the trigger and fill him full of silver-lead rounds, Edmund had my visitor's head in his claws and his body bent back over one knee, exposing Gabriel's belly and throat. It was clearly a position of forced submission.

"What do you want with my master?" Edmund asked, his power spiking so high it sizzled along my skin like the flare of sparklers, if the burning could be frozen into icicles taught to dance.

Gabriel made a sound like, "Gurk igh ugh eee."

Edmund eased his hold and said, "Speak the full truth or die," which was not what I'd come to do, but sounded pretty effective.

"I got to speak to the Enforcer before dawn."

"You're speaking to her," I said.

Gabe's eyeballs rolled around in his head until he could see me. "I have a . . . a petition for Enforcer of de Master of de City of New Orleans." Which was formal talk, taken directly from the Vampira Carta. The local suckheads had been studying, it seemed.

"Let him go, Edmund. But if he gets riled, you can take back up where you were." I frowned at the meek-looking vampire. "You *were* going to hurt him, right?"

"Yes, my master, his death, for entering your presence uninvited."

Yeah. That seemed a little strong to me, but I wasn't going to argue, not with Eli and the Kid still spelled asleep while flying vamps invaded. There might be others wanting to enter. I did glare at the use of "my master," a title I was *not* going to accept.

Edmund gave me his meek look in return. He wasn't bad at it, puppy-dog eyes and all, but I knew a fake when I saw it. Practicing that look in the presence of vamps might have given him extra acting skills, but having been a clan blood-master for so long had unbalanced it in favor of an underlayment of arrogance.

"Whatever," I muttered. I looked at our prisoner. I didn't have a real firm grasp on the proper response, except that it was equally formal. I sighed and pulled back the slide on my weapon, ejecting the round. I set it and the nine mil on the small bedside table and moved to the edge of the bed, where I sat again, empty hands dangling. I needed more downtime than I'd gotten. Vamp time was hard on a girl's beauty sleep. "The Enforcer of the Master of the City of New Orleans and the Greater Southeast United States, with the exception of Florida, will hear you." When he didn't say anything I added, "Talk, Gabe. Make it clear, concise, and fast."

"I the man who responsible for the troubles in this town, I am."

That was pretty concise. I hadn't paid much attention to Gabe's voice when I was here last, trying to keep my skin on my bones and my blood in my veins. But his Cajun syllables were clear and pleasant, a higher tone that contrasted markedly to his father's deeper voice. "Okay. Let's hear your side."

"A vampire man, a Mithran as the Vampira Carta say, he have certain needs."

My head went back. "If this is about sex, I'm not interested in suckhead infidelity."

"No, no, no. Not *sex*. *Blood*."

Edmund didn't bother to hide an amused grin. My prudishness was a source of cynical entertainment among the vamps. I frowned at him and caught a glimpse of my own reflection in the mirror over the vanity. My hair was everywhere, as if I'd fought a vamp in my dreams. I sighed and said, "Edmund, we're safe here. Go check on the boys. No buckets of water."

Edmund dropped Gabriel, saying, "As my master commands." With a pop of displaced air, he was gone.

"Get up and sit"—I pointed to the floral upholstered chair I had just deserted—"and tell me what you did that got all this started."

Gabriel rose from the floor with the fluid grace of the undead and took the small chair. He was dressed in rain-wet jeans and a camo shirt, work boots, and leather armbands worked in Celtic symbols with the logo of a rock-and-roll band. Around his neck he wore a leather thong with a tiny gold Celtic circle hanging from it. His brown hair fell to his waist, some braided, some hanging free, all of it wet and dripping, which might have made another man look like a soaked dog, but on Gabe, with his aquiline nose and almond-shaped eyes, it just made him prettier. When he bowed his head over his interlaced fingers, his hair touched the floor. It was a graceful gesture, and it was no wonder that the witch, Shauna, had fallen for the pretty boy. "Been a fool, I have," he said.

That was a good start. I pulled a vamp-killer, which I placed at my side. His eyes went wide and he swallowed, a totally vamp reaction to the presence of a fourteen-inch-long steel blade plated with silver. I reached around and began unplaiting my braid, going for casual and killer all at once. I nodded for him to continue.

His eyes on the weapon, he said, "All dis mess"—he jerked his head to the outside in a gesture that was particularly Cajun and Gaelic and Frenchy—"might . . . *pro'lly*, have start when Shauna found dat I done drank—one time only—from someone else." My eyebrows went up in surprise. "Shauna, she got baby blues after our lil' boy, Clerjer, born." It came out *Clarshar*, the name all pretty and flowing syllables of the expectation of peace.

The child had been the first vampire-witch baby born in the traditional human way, as opposed to a vamp turning, in ages. His name had been a hopeful blending of the names of the leaders of the witches and vamps in the small town, Clermont Jérôme Landry Doucette, the baby being the first and only thing bringing the two opposing groups together in, well, forever.

I nodded again, showing I understood.

"Shauna, her go anemic. Not have blood for me. I have to feed or I go"—his hand made a circle around his ear—"crazy in de head."

I thought about that. Two young people madly in love. Baby. Weakness. One not able to feed from the other. Postpartum depression. It made sense, on the face of it, for him to drink from someone else. It seemed right and proper, the gentlemanly thing to do, to get sustenance from elsewhere.

Except that for vamps, feeding and sex were usually synonymous. "Who'd you drink from?" I frowned at him. "I'm guessing that it wasn't from your sire or a brother?" Gabe shook his head, his eyes back down in shame. I blew out a breath, and if my sarcasm was a bit strong, I felt it was well placed. "I take it she was pretty?"

"Yeah," he said after a pause that went on too long. "She is dat."

"And you had sex with her?"

"No! I no cheat on my Shauna! Her blood-kin to Doucette clan. I no dishonor her like dat."

"Sooo . . . ," I said, thinking, my fingers combing through the mess of my hair. "No fun and games." And then it hit me. "She walked in on you?" Gabe nodded, the motion as jerky as a human. "And it *looked* like you were having a little too much fun?"

"Yeah. It did dat."

"Idiot."

"Yeah, I am dat too."

"Who was she?" I asked as I started rebraiding my hip-length hair at the base of my head, pulling and slinging each third through the rest.

"You know her," he said after a few quiet seconds. "Her be Margaud."

I stopped braiding and narrowed my eyes at him. He glanced up at my silence and the expression on his face said he knew how stupid he had been. Simply put, the three Mouton siblings hated vamps. The three adult children of the family were the former army twins, Auguste and Benoît— alligator hunters and vamp haters from way back—and their sister, who was as beautiful as they were ugly. A trained sniper, Margaud had seen some real-time action in some foreign battlefield. And she hated vamps maybe even more than her brothers did. "Just to clarify. You drank from Margaud?"

"I did."

"She *let* you drink from her?"

"I at de bar. All alone on Saturday night. *Hongry,* I was. She come in, sit beside me, order her a whiskey. We talk a bit. She buy me a whiskey. We talk some more. She say, 'How you doin', Gabe? You looking pale.' She smile. She ask, real sof'-like, 'You need some-a dis?' I stupid."

I don't cuss as a rule, except sometimes to yank people's chains, but this was a special case. "You're a dickhead."

"I dat too. Before she sit by me? I found later dat she done call Shauna and tell her to come to de blood bar. Dat why Shauna walk into back room when I feeding from Margaud."

I yanked on my hair, braiding fast, thinking. "You know she was trying to cause trouble, right?"

"I know." Gabriel sounded ashamed and devastated all at the same time. He looked at me, and his eyes, still human-looking, filled with pale pink tears. "I love my Shauna. I die now of heartbreak, I am. I die for sure, before I drink again."

Pinkish tears meant, well, not starvation, but certainly long-term hunger. His body looked thinner, as if lanky had been stretched to its limits. His physical control, under the hunger constraints, was pretty amazing. It left me with nothing to say. Margaud was a bitch and Gabe was an idiot. A starving idiot, but still an idiot. I finished braiding my hair and twisted an elastic band around the tip. "Anything else I need to know?"

Gabe's head dropped even lower, so I couldn't see his face. His voice a mutter, he said, "When Shauna come through the door and see us, she throw a vase at us, she did. Margaud, her run to Shauna and take her hand, like friend. Say she willing to . . . to *share me* with Shauna."

"Oh." *Yeah, That's a great way to make everything worse.*

"Fight, there was. Catfight. I stupid, and blood-drunk just a bit, so long since I drink my fill, and I laugh. Shauna left. Went back to Clan Home, took Clerjer, took the wreath, and disappear."

"The wreath outside in the witch circle?"

"De same."

"Margaud set up the whole thing to mess with the vamps and start trouble."

"Yeah. I tink dat so too."

Margaud was a beautiful, deadly woman, with ash brown hair, blonded by the sun, deep brown eyes, and skin tanned golden. She was petite and delicate and last I saw her, she had looked too small to transport or position the sniper rifle she had used to give us cover when my team approached the Doucette Clan Home. She was muscular and fit, and carried herself with a capable, confident air, the exact opposite of a woman who'd just had a baby, all full of baby fat and hormones. No matter how unearthly beautiful Shauna Landry Doucette was, the sight of her husband in the other woman's arms would have hurt. Bad.

The sharpshooter had played a hand and played it well, and now I had not only to try to fix things with the wreath and repair the damage to the marriage, but figure out Margaud's next move and stop it before it happened.

I frowned. People skills were not among my best talents; I was more a shoot-first-and-bang-heads-together-later kinda gal. "You talked to the witches? To Shauna's daddy?"

"I try. Him come at me with carving knife, he did. And then him throw spell at me from them fire tattoos on he arm. I get away alive, but barely."

Lucky Landry was one of the rare male witches, and he had full-sleeve tats down his left arm. They were of weird creatures, combos of snake and human, with fangs and scales, mouths open in what looked like agony, as red and yellow flames climbed up from his wrist to burn them. It was like some bizarre vision of hell.

It wasn't commonly known, but spells could be tattooed into the flesh of witches for use, and into the flesh of humans for binding them, all of which was strictly illegal according to witch law, but the supernatural inhabitants of Bayou Oiseau had been cut off from others of their own kind for a century, give or take. Things were different here. *Every*thing was different here.

I heard stirring in the boys' room, male voices, no screaming or shots fired, so Edmund must have been nice in his waking. From the lower part of the house, the smell of bacon rose on the air. Miz Onie was up early, starting one of her amazing breakfasts. I stood and, carrying my vamp-killer, went to the door of the gallery, turning my back on Gabe, which was a pure insult to the vamp, the way an alpha proves strength in the face of a weaker opponent, definitely an insult, almost a dare. One Gabe didn't take.

Dawn was coming, gray streaks across the dark sky, red clouds in the east. The vamps stood two and two behind each witch, vamped-out, claws and fangs and bloody vampy eyes, pupils like pits into hell that I could see even from here, with Beast so close to the surface, aiding my vision. One vamp spot was empty. "Better hurry," I said.

I felt the air move and swirl as Gabe leaped from the gallery, slower than most vamps. Blood starved. Stupid man. He appeared as if by magic beside his father, both vamps standing behind the witch at the north point of the circle, usually the leader of the coven. It was hard to make out much about the woman because she stood in a shadow cast by another magnolia tree, drenched and dripping as they all were. She was tall and strongly built, an Amazon fully six feet tall—my height, and she had me by fifty pounds at least, and from here, all of it looked like pure muscle. The vamps moved in, closer, so close that one jerked back as if shocked by electricity.

I don't catch scents as well in human form as I do in my Beast form, or in tracking dog form, but even from here I could smell the ozone tingle of witch magic, the herbal and blood scent of vamps, the overriding scent of rain. The smells were powerful and full of the vamp version of adrenaline. The vamps were getting ready to do something.

The shadows changed, shifting, as the sun tried to lift itself over the horizon. Just before the day lightened, the vamps rushed the witches. As one, they slammed into the *dog collar* circle. The ward sparked, flashed, power so bright I spun away, covering my face with my arm. I heard the awful screams of vamps dying—or thinking they were. A chorus of ululations so high that my eardrums vibrated in pain. I heard/smelled meat sizzle.

The first rays of the sun swept in and, with a small explosion of sound, the vamps disappeared, leaving behind the stink of burned vamp, and the echo of vamps in pain as they rushed into the blood bar and what were probably lairs beneath the ground.

I blinked down and saw humans rush to stand in front of the blood bar doorway. Big men in muscle shirts and carrying truncheons creating a barricade of muscled flesh and iron pipes. The protection of loyal blood-servants.

Behind me, I felt a draft of fast-moving air, and the closet door in my room opened and closed. A vamp, God help me, was climbing into his safe haven for the day. In my bedroom. My life was still getting weirder by the day.

Down below, the witches stood straight and stretched. With a gesture, the Amazon woman dropped the inner *hedge of thorns* and walked to the center of the inner circle. She picked up the wreath, holding it like a holy relic. In the dawn light it was clearly not a Christmas wreath, but just what we had thought—a laurel wreath or olive wreath, like the ancients used to indicate royalty. The haze of pale magics it contained were grayer, duller, less clear in the brighter light. And even from here, I could smell the magic wafting from it like ozone from a power plant or after a lightning strike. An internal shiver raced along my spine at the thought of lightning. I'd been struck by lightning and nearly died. Never again. *Never.*

The Amazon walked away carrying the wreath. *Just ducky.* A magical gadget in the hands of a witch who clearly was powerful all on her own, and who also had the power to draw on the magic of others. A town full of witches, protecting the magical thingamabob. One that my boss would want in his greedy, taloned hands.

This whole thing sucked.

We had a breakfast big enough to last all day, with a slab of thick-cut bacon that had to have come from Lucky Landry's butcher shop, Boudreaux's Meats. Best meat I had ever eaten—well, cooked, and me in human form. Beast had other thoughts about her preference of freshly brought down meat, raw and still kicking. Not my preference. There were also sausage links with the intense spicy flavor of Lucky's special spice and herb rub recipe, free-range scrambled eggs from a neighbor's hens, fresh-baked bread, three kinds of muffins, and a bowl of fruit big enough to take a bath in had the fruit not been in the way. The Kid ate huge servings of everything, even the fruit. He was suddenly putting on weight, the muscle kind, and I was sure he had grown another inch. He would be topping his older brother if this kept up, and I saw Eli glancing at his baby brother from time to time as Alex ate. Eli was no slouch in the eat-his-fill department, and neither was I. We managed to put a hurting on the food before Eli decided it was time to talk.

"Who the hell put a sleep spell on us?" he growled.

"Language," Alex said.

Eli's eyes narrowed, but he patted his lips with his napkin and placed it beside his plate before taking a tiny sip of coffee. The motions were tight and tense, and I knew he was holding himself in check with effort. Eli had control issues. Spells pushed his buttons. Oversleeping pushed his buttons. Edmund waking him up pushed his buttons. Especially if Edmund was tossing cold water on him or, worse as far as Eli was concerned, whispering sweet nothings in his ear. I managed not to smile at the thought, but it was a near thing.

"Who the *heck* put a sleep spell on us?" Eli's voice was ubercontrolled.

"The whole town was spelled," I said, "not just us. And I'm betting that Leo didn't know this part."

"Why?"

"Because he would have shared this with us. Being put to sleep could mean the difference between success and failure, so Clermont didn't tell him. They're back to playing vamp games." I told the boys about my visitor and the intel I had been given. At some point in the narrative, Eli calmed down. The fact that the spell had been a general one, and not particular to us, seemed to ease his anger. For me, that made it worse, as it spoke of a huge usage of magical power, but I kept that to myself. When I finished with my tale of love lost and male stupidity and female scorned and revenge, Eli sighed and poured himself another cup of coffee. The small porcelain cups were dainty and pretty, with little pink and yellow flowers on them, and they held about a third of what our mugs did at home, but Eli hadn't let that stop him getting caffeined up. He was steadily making his way through a second pot of Miz Onie's dark French roast brew. "Well, at least we got a good night's sleep." He gave me his patented grin—a slight twitch of his lips, which, on anyone else, could have passed for indigestion. "Except you."

"Yeah. Thanks for the sympathy. I also have a vamp sleeping in my closet. No sympathy for that either?"

"Not a hint."

"Fine. We have a good nine hours of daylight left before the vamps rise. Alex, I want you to find out the historical and/or current relationship between the Doucettes, the Moutons, the Landrys, and the Bordelons, four powerful families that I remember from my last trip here." Alex pulled out his electronic tablet and took down the names, but he looked at me curiously.

"I talked with Lucky Landry about the town, back on my first visit, and he told me when the first Cajuns got to Louisiana." Trying out a Cajun accent, I said, *"Dey Moutons say dey get here in 1760, but my family, de Landrys, land in New Orleans in April 1764, but dey don' get here in dis town till 1769."*

Alex pulled a face. "That was terrible."

Eli added, "It sounded like you were talking while chewing gum and eating hot mashed potatoes."

I decided further attempts weren't worth the trouble. I really needed to find time for French lessons. "His grandmother was one of two Bordelon witch sisters, Cally Bordelon. The Bordelons were the strongest witches in these parts when the vamp-witch-human wars started in Bayou Oiseau. Lucky Landry is related to all the witches in the area, and we might need to know the historical context of this situation. Or we might not. I'd rather have intel and not need it than need it and not have it. Anyway, the family tree between the Bordelons and the Landrys might be important, especially if we find a Doucette or a Mouton in there somewhere."

"Got it. On it," Alex said, already bent over his tablet.

To Eli I said, "I think I need to talk to Shauna's daddy and get the witch side of the story, then maybe see the Amazon witch in the street."

"Weapons?" Eli asked.

"Me, nothing. You got three-eighties and a vamp-killer?"

"No collateral damage. Got it. Fifteen," he said, meaning he'd be ready in fifteen minutes. He looked at his brother. "While we're gone, see what you can find about a magic wreath. Get us dossiers on the living and undead principals to fill out Jane's old ones. See if there's anything in Reach's database to update what we know. And get a shower. You stink."

"Again?"

"Garlic," I said. "You sweat garlic and testosterone."

"I'm da man?" he asked hopefully.

"No," Eli and I said together.

"You just need to shower more often," I added, trying for kindness.

"A lot more often," Eli said, going for honesty.

We started out at Boudreaux's Meats, which opened at eight a.m. according to the sign on the door, but actually opened closer to nine. Maybe so the proprietor could get a few winks in between dawn and opening. I hadn't seen Lucky in the circle, but I had no doubt that he was involved somehow, his daughter being the center of the whole situation.

Boudreaux's had been owned and run by Old Man Boudreaux, until Lucky married the man's daughter and Boudreaux took his son-in-law under his wing, teaching him everything he knew about carving up pig, cow, wild boar, squirrel, gator, and seafood. And cooking all of the afore-mentioned protein on a grill. And making various meat-based delights out of it. I'd been in the state of Louisiana for a long time now, and I'd never found another eatery as good as Boudreaux's Meats. The outside was dec-orated with signs advertising the meat and the day's meals, with the specials written in chalk on a blackboard. There were also crosses painted on each window in brilliant blue, which was new. Inside, the place was changed a bit too, with blue plastic tablecloths on the few tables, new backless benches, the floor painted blue and polished to a high shine, and the smell of bacon flavoring the air. The cooler was still in the same place, full of ice and beer. And just like last time, I was met with the bad end of a gun.

"Jane Yellowrock," Lucky said from behind the counter. "Raise your hands. Keep 'em high. You too, boy." Eli narrowed his eyes at Lucky, the word *boy* being pejorative in these parts, but he raised his arms. Lucky had a deep, heavy Cajun accent, hard to understand sometimes, but there was no mistaking the intent of a double-barreled shotgun. The witch was in his early fifties, Caucasian, with black hair and dark eyes—what the locals call Frenchy. A few strands of silver marked his hair, new since I was here last. "Why you here?"

"I was asked to come by the Master of the City of New Orleans."

"To stop de witches of dis town, here? To steal *le breloque* what Shauna found?"

I wasn't sure what a *breloque* was, so I ignored that part. "To find out what was going on and restore peace if possible."

Lucky snorted, a deep and resonant sound that belonged on the back-streets of Paris or in the deeps of the swamps.

"And no," I said, "I have no intention of trying to steal the wreath or whatever it is. I'd like to stop the bloodshed before it starts, though."

"*Le breloque.* Tell you what. You cut de head off Gabriel Doucette and I let you go way 'live."

"I'll tell *you* what. You put that shotgun down, I'll let you live. Deal?"

Lucky snorted again and I smelled the tingle of his magic on the air. No way was I letting him hit me with a spell.

Everything happened *fast*.

I drew on Beast. Leaped hard across the storefront. Pushed off with a foot and lunged left, then right, behind the counter. *Fast, fast, fast.*

My partner dove behind the cooler, pulling both guns.

He was still midmove when I knocked the shotgun to the side with one forearm and twisted it out of Lucky's hands. The spell he threw shot over my shoulder and slammed into the wall behind me. Something crashed. I didn't have time to look. I turned the shotgun on Lucky. And snarled. *Fun,* my Beast thought. *More!*

"Move and bleed," I growled.

Lucky wore a sheen of sweat that hadn't been there before, slicking his olive skin.

"What was that spell?" I demanded.

"A *get away from me* spell," he said, his mouth turning down. Sadness in his tone, he said, "Broke my wall, it did."

I glanced once, fast. The back wall of the meat shop looked like a cannonball had gone through it. There was a hole open to the shop next door and the sounds of screams came from it weakly, as if the ladies inside were running away. Smart women.

"You not so easy to stop dis time. Why dat is?" he asked.

"I was expecting the shotgun. You were expecting a human. I'm no longer aping human." Which still sounded weird when I said it, but secrets could no longer help me.

"What you is?"

I grinned and let more of Beast shine through me, seeing the golden reflection in Lucky's black eyes. "Not saying. Tell me what happened. Everything. Or my partner will put a hole through your forearm that will take some healing spells and physical therapy to get over."

From the side I heard a vamp-killer being drawn.

Lucky didn't spare my partner a glance. "*Le bâtard*, Gabriel Doucette, done cheat on my girl."

So far the stories were close, which was better than I feared. "And?"

"And she took my *gran'bébé*, my *petit-fils*, and *le breloque*, what called by de suckheads *la corona*, and she brung it to me, she did."

"And?"

Lucky's eyes narrowed.

"I'm looking for a timeline here, Lucky—everything you know or suspect. If you want to live by your nickname, talk. And if you want to live at all, you better call off the magic, because I have no problem knocking you out and carrying you to the Doucettes'."

"You not do dat."

"Try me."

Lucky snorted again, but this time with less force, as if he was rethinking my intentions. Odd what things you can pick up from a snort as melodious as Lucky's.

"I take *la corona* to de priest. Him call de bishop, who send us a scholar. De scholar decide *la corona* belong to dem. Pack to send it to Rome, they did. Shauna, her climb de fence and steal dat package back. *Le breloque*, it go to de strongest witch and coven leader."

I frowned, letting the events settle in my mind. Asking the same questions of different people was a standard investigative technique. One always learned something new, a different slant, a different sliver of intel. It was boring, but it was useful. This time I had learned that Shauna was not just reactionary, hormonal, ticked off, and a wronged spouse, she was also a thief. Of course, the priest and the bishop's henchman might be thieves too, if I included their taking the wreath and planning to send it away, as thievery. Which I did. Unless . . .

I thought about the laurel wreath and the Roman Catholic Church and, for a fraction of a second, wondered if it could be something other than a witch artifact. Maybe the reason that everyone was so interested was because the laurel wreath was something else entirely. Something glamoured to look like a witch icon. Maybe another circlet, maybe one made of thorns. Now, that would be a powerful talisman. Vamps were always looking for things related to Golgotha, to the place of the skull, from which they took their beginnings. So was the Church for similar and yet wildly opposing reasons. Both wanting the same things . . .

The wreath part of the crown of thorns was supposedly in Rome, while the thorn parts had supposedly been removed from the twisted vine and sent as gifts, bargaining chips, and items of priceless monetary and unimaginable spiritual value to various kings, cities, churches, and armies over the course of history. I had never heard of the crown of thorns being taken from Rome, never heard of it being stolen by vamps or used by witches.

And besides, a vine of thorns wouldn't have been a laurel. If it had gone missing, I surely would have heard about it—the whole world would have heard about it. So the wreath wasn't *that* crown. I shook off the thought and said, "I thought you were coven leader."

"No man can be leader of de coven. Man magic too strong, unpredictable, to lead full coven. Too what dey call *volatile* to do all de maths for a group."

Witch magics were dependent on mathematics, geometry, and physics. Lucky was indeed too volatile to run a coven, which took control, finesse, and good people skills as well as strength, but I knew another male witch who could have handled the positon well. "Okay. You did know that Margaud didn't have sex with Gabriel, right?"

Lucky frowned, a ferocious expression that went all the way to his toes as he tensed. "My girl walk in on dem, she did!"

"She walked in on Gabe feeding on Margaud, after Margaud got him drunk, called Shauna, and then offered him dinner."

"You lie."

"I don't. Margaud and her brothers hate vamps. She set the whole thing up, using Shauna's postpartum depression and anemia, and Gabe's starvation, as a way to start trouble."

Lucky's frown lessened. "What?"

"You didn't know Shauna was anemic? Depressed? Women do awful things at times like that, or so I hear."

Lucky scowled, an expression that suggested he was thinking back. "Her taking iron pills," he said reluctantly.

"Uh-huh. And Gabe was starving to death because he wasn't feeding. I'm not saying that drinking whiskey on an empty stomach was smart, and I'm not saying that Margaud wouldn't have slept with Gabe, or that she didn't spike his liquor with something even stronger. I'm not saying that Gabe isn't an idiot, because he is. What I *am* saying is that you didn't get the full story. Your daughter is"—I pulled a Cajun saying out of the air—"the pole around which this johnboat twirls."

"You say my Shauna causing trouble?"

"Yep. First off, it sounds like she also has postpartum depression. And that's on top of you raising her to think she could get anything she wanted out of life just on her looks." Lucky started to object. "Don't. I met her. I knew girls like her, growing up. I recognized the signs the first time I met her, and that was before the depression set in. You let Shauna wrap you around her little finger her whole life. You need to see all your people for who they really are. Shauna, Gabe, and Margaud too. And then you need to stop being flighty, emotional, and volatile, and be a leader. Don't tell me you can't just because you're a male witch. That excuse might have worked when you were fourteen and full of testosterone, but it stops working today. Right this minute."

I set the shotgun on the counter and let Lucky go. He didn't lunge for the gun, which kept him alive; Eli had a vamp-killer in one hand and his .380 in the other, aimed through the glass butcher counter. At this range, he could have hit Lucky—and a gorgeous ham—with his eyes closed.

He said, "You done come to dis town and you try teach me lesson?"

"Somebody needs to. Lucky, this town is this close"—I held my thumb and index finger a quarter inch apart—"to going up in flames or turning into a bloodbath. Or both."

"Okay. I hear dat." He squinted at me. "You too young to be my *gran'-mère*, but you sound just like her."

"I'll take that as a compliment." The rest of the convocation went much more smoothly.

The shop door closed behind us. Eli said mildly, "Grandmaw?"

"*Boy?*"

"Yeah, 'bout that." He scowled. "Coonass," he said, evaluating and passing judgment.

"Agreed."

"But . . . *Grandmaw?*"

"Cherokee chick," I corrected.

"Badass, motorcycle-mama, deadly Cherokee chick," he amended.

I nodded contemplatively, taking in everything about the small town as we walked, including the still-unused heavy equipment parked in the streets around the main intersection. "Badass, gun-toting, loyal, former military, take-no-prisoners-and-leave-no-one-behind"—I paused, thinking about Eli's milk-and-coffee skin tone and his possible ethnic background—"caramel candy man."

"Sylvia says my skin is sweet as sugar," he agreed, looking relaxed as a tourist, but his eyes taking in everything, glancing at me, making sure

I saw what he did. The unused equipment didn't have state or county license tags. Some private company had gotten a contract to repave the city streets, and then, for reasons unknown but probably having to do with bloodsuckers, the workers had disappeared. "She likes to lick me aaaall over." His twitch of a smile was half-teasing, half–evil swagger.

"Ick. TMI. Boy talk. Not what I needed to hear. If I weren't so badass I'd stick my fingers in my ears."

He laughed. Finished with the questions, insults, clarifications, and bragging rights, Eli slipped his sunglasses on against the glare. The day was heating up in what South Louisianans called fall weather: mid-nineties, dead air, with a blistering sun. Even with my healing abilities I had taken to wearing sunscreen. Sunburn was unpleasant, and it might be a while before I could shift into Beast and heal the minor hurts. "The only good thing we got out of our chat with Lucky was lunch plans." He shook his head as we sauntered toward the Catholic church on the far corner. Eli went on, "I ate until I was stuffed at breakfast, and I'm already hungry just from smelling Boudreaux's."

"I think it's a spell. A *make people hungry* spell."

Eli's stomach growled softly in reply.

"See?"

The Catholic church hadn't changed since my last visit. The bell tower was the tallest building in the town, built of thick brick walls that shadowed its tarnished, patinated bell, the openings high landing and nesting places for pigeons. The church itself was cross-shaped, brick and mortar. Brick fencing encased the expanse of close-cut lawn. The ornate bronze crosses in the niches of the fence had tarnished and leaked various shades of verdigris down the brick, like the stains of ancient tears. The top of the wall, with its pointed cross iron spikes, made the whole place look like a fortress of religion instead of a church.

The town had been at war for far too long, vamps and witches fighting, humans fighting both, the church stuck in the middle, taking sides as it could, and somehow surviving the bloodletting. At one point after the Civil War, the witches and humans had joined with the priests and taken the war to the vamps. There were beheadings and burnings and death in the streets everywhere. The Middle East today had nothing on Bayou Oiseau at the height of the vamp wars.

Eli stopped at the entrance to the gate and pulled his phone. He now had a bullet-resistant, Kevlar-protected official cell like mine, a leash to Leo, but handy in so many ways that he hadn't been able to leave it behind. He scrolled through his address book and tapped an icon on the screen. He put the cell against his ear and walked away, so I couldn't hear the person on the other end, even with Beast being nosy. A moment later Eli said, "Joe, my brother. Yeah. Okay. You? The arm? That's good, that's real good. Yeah, business. I'm in a little town called Bayou Oiseau, Louisiana. We've got a magical artifact here that the witches and suckheads are fighting over. The church had it for a while and then it was stolen back. According to some, the church sent a scholar to look it over. Would you take a look and see if there's anything I need to know? Text would be great. Yeah, this number. Thanks, dude. Yeah, yeah, I might make that one. You too." He closed his cell and gestured inside.

"You gonna tell me what that was all about?"

"I'd prefer not to. But if I have to, then yes."

We walked through the gate of the church, and instantly the flesh on the back of my neck started to crawl. Predator/prey response. "We being watched?" I murmured to Eli, my lips not moving, so my words couldn't be read by a lip-reader.

"Targeted," he said casually, his lips equally still. "Eyes in the bell tower. One rifle barrel."

"How did you see it?" I asked, curious.

"Birds shuffled."

"Ah. That or magic glasses."

Eli huffed out a soft laugh but didn't contradict me. And that got me thinking about what the government might be able to do if they had witches helping them. The national registration of the supernats could someday happen, and if it did, the possible results and repercussions for those with magical potential were dire. Like forcing witches to work for the government, creating new and harmful weapons, and, worse, at the risk of families and friends being hurt if witches didn't comply. I could see the Department of Defense chaining vamps to the wall and draining them for sips of blood before soldiers go into battle. I could see—

"You getting all the way from 'maybe' to 'stupid' with the conspiracy theories, yet?" Eli asked, an edge to his voice.

"Pretty close, after that phone call," I said.

"Don't. The glasses were five bucks at CVS on Decatur Street. Uncle Sam trained me well. That's it."

I smiled, using the excuse to tilt up my head. The rifle barrel was still following us, pointed down now. "I wasn't trying to push your buttons."

"Did it anyway."

I shoved open the heavy wood door, and cool air flowed out. Cool air was one reason for the thick walls when building back in the days before central air-conditioning. "I'm sorry," I said. And I was. I changed the subject. "Did Lucky mention the priest's name?"

"'Father' usually works."

"Hmmm. Is the bishop's scholar still here?"

"Didn't get that intel either. Flying by the seat of our pants, just like usual, ain't we, babe?"

"Except for your mysterious phone call." Eli didn't reply, and I sighed again. "I shoulda asked Lucky."

"Shoulda," Eli agreed.

"I forgot." Sometimes I wondered whether my adrenaline-addicted partner let me forget to find out stuff just so he could play commando games again. But . . . *nah. Surely not.*

The door closed behind us. We were standing in a darkened foyer sort of place, windowless, the interior walls constructed of wide planks of cypress wood, the finish darkened by time and damp. Ahead, I could see the sanctuary, which, if I remembered right, Roman Catholics called something else. Inside, it was obvious that the church was shaped like a cross, the thick brick walls pierced open with stained glass windows letting in the sunlight in colors of ocean blue and bloodred. The exposed beams of the roof system were far overhead, beams bigger around than my waist. Verdigris-stained brass chandeliers dangled on rusted iron chains. In niches were statues dressed in clothing from Roman times, all with halos, and some with wings. Saints and angels. At the front of the church was a cross, some twenty feet tall, with a plaster Jesus hanging there, all bloody and beaten, wearing a blue scarf over his privates and a crown of thorns. This crown looked nothing like the one in the street in the dark of a rainy night.

"Where do you think the priest is?" I asked.

"This time of day? The sacristy or his home. Or maybe he's the sharp-shooter in the belfry." Eli pulled his cell and checked a text message, frowning.

"Sacristy?"

Eli shot me a glance and removed his glasses, the gloom too much even for the loss of cool factor. With them he indicated the room we were in. "Narthex." He glasses-pointed ahead. "Nave. The center area is the crossing with the transcepts as the cross' arms. The head of the cross shape is the apse, with the chancel and the altar. Behind that wall is the sacristy. This church is built on the classic, historical, cruciform architecture."

I was pretty sure I was goggling. "Are you Catholic?"

He tapped his chest with the glasses. "Ranger. We know everything."

"What can I do for you, my children?"

The man who was speaking was standing in the crossing, half-hidden in a shadow cast by a plaster statue, bloody and clawed, with a lion rampant, about to bite him. The statue. Not the priest. Beast peered out from my eyes, amused at the statues. *Small teeth and claws. Beast's are bigger,* she thought. The priest was a middle-aged, pink-skinned, redheaded man, slight of build and serious-looking, his hands in the pockets of his long black robes.

Eli murmured, "The black robes make him an old-school Jesuit." He narrowed his eyes as if that was important somehow and spoke louder. "Father."

We started down the center aisle, our boots loud on the wood floor, echoing up into the rafters. The air inside was still, the way an empty house feels when its people have been on an extended vacation. It smelled of cleansers and lemon oil and ashes, and the stink of Silvadene. The silver-based cream was used for second- and third-degree burns on humans. On vamps, it would be a poison.

The priest repeated, "What can I do for you, my children?"

Before Eli could reply, I said, "The Mithran Master of the City of New Orleans, Leo Pellissier, sent us to see what was going on in Bayou Oiseau between the suc—the vampires and the witches."

He didn't change posture, but I smelled the priest's interest and the shot of pure adrenaline that pumped into his bloodstream. I had an instant certainty that the priest wasn't just a priest. At my side, I felt Eli shift a step to my left, his body slightly left-side-forward, right hand at his side. That was a fighting position, and I caught a whiff of gun oil. Eli had drawn a weapon. Not good. Now that we were closer to the priest, he stank of old fire and cooked meat and frustration tightly controlled. I studied the priest, his black robes and sash unrelieved by color except for the splotch of red above his waist on his left side and the white around his collar.

The priest said, "A vampire sent you to this town?"

"Yeah. At the request of the local Clan blood-master."

His voice soft a breeze, Eli said, "We understand that you had control of the wreath, what the Mithrans call *la corona* in Latin, or *le breloque*, in French."

I didn't react, but . . . how did my partner know that was Latin? No way could he blame that on being a Ranger.

The priest said, "The wreath is spelled, hiding what it is. Spells are of the devil."

"Not all of them," I said.

"Yes. All."

"Powers and principalities are not all from Satan."

"*You* wish to bandy Scripture and Church history with *me*?" Something in the emphasis suggested that I was out of my league in that department, that he could squash me under his metaphorical, verbal, scholarly boot. I decided on another tack.

I said, "Is the vine of the true crown still in the Vatican? Or did it go missing?" The priest removed his hands from his pockets, and Eli tensed, not that anyone else would have noted the minute changes in his body. It was more a scent change than motion, and it eased when the priest appeared to clasp his white-gloved hands behind his back. The stink of burned meat and Silvadene was instantly stronger on the air.

I knew my partner needed something, so I went on the offensive, drawing the priest's attention to me with a single step forward and what little I had gained from the Kid's info. "Or should I say, one of the *many* vines of the crown of thorns. Several are in France, one in Germany, one in Belgium. Spain and Italy have pieces of it, even the Ukraine. And the thorns are *every*where. For the Church to send an important guy like you, it must be possible that the real one has gone missing, and they thought it might be here, sealed into the *corona*.

"Or . . . worse," I said, thinking, "maybe an even more ancient *corona* showed up here. Something the Greeks would have attributed to a god or goddess or the witches could use to get back at the Church for a millennium of oppression, and . . ." I cocked my head and grinned at the man. His face was placid, but he stank of anger. ". . . the Church couldn't have that, could it?"

As I spoke, the Jesuit's nostrils flared with fury and then his skin paled with something like dread. I wasn't good at guessing games, but I was very good at flying by the seat of my pants, and I had a feeling that I'd just flown over the priest's home base. I thought about the smells and the white gloves. Or not just gloves. No.

"Idiot," I said scathingly. "You tried to burn it, didn't you? But it wouldn't burn. It burned you instead. That's what"—I almost said that was what *I smelled*, but I changed it to—"you're hiding with the gloves. They're bandages hiding the burned skin."

Eli said, softly, "I talked to Joseph Makris at the Vatican."

At the name, the priest's eyes went wide with despair and his shoulders dropped. At the same moment he capitulated, there was a soft *ding* and the priest answered the cell phone in his pocket. He carried on a soft-voiced conversation before putting the phone away. Afterward, he looked even more dejected. To Eli, he said, "That was Makris. But then, you knew that, yes?"

Eli gave one of his abbreviated nods.

"We tried everything we could in the small time we were allowed. Perhaps it wasn't for us to decipher. Perhaps we were full of hubris and foolishness."

The priest wavered on his feet, looking drunk or hurt or . . . spelled. Yeah. Spelled and hurt both. He went on, his speech slower, his words growing less clear, slightly slurred.

"It is not of the Church, nor of the place of the skull. The writing on its rim is archaic and unlike anything I have ever seen—if it really is writing and not some form of decorative work. Not cuneiform. More ancient. Like clay tokens or runes in their simplicity, mixed with squiggly, jagged lines, lightning bolts. If it is a witch artifact, it came from an ancient past so distant that history itself has swallowed it whole."

"Do you know what it does?" Eli asked. "What magic power it holds?"

"No. I was unable to determine anything before it . . ." He lifted both hands, and it was clear that they had been wrapped with something like medical sticky wrap and that the gloves were too large for his hands, holding the bandages in place. "I don't know what it is, but it . . . it makes people think things they shouldn't." He closed his eyes, squeezing them tightly. I smelled his tears, hot and toxic. "If I had to name it," he said, "I would call it the crown of temptation. Or the crown of despair. *Desperatio coronam*. It brings such grief, such anguish of the soul." He looked to Eli. "If you find it, bring the evil thing to me, my son. I will send it to Rome, where it can be destroyed."

"Question," I said. "Did you start feeling unhappy and miserable before or after you tried to hurt the thing? Before or after you got burned?"

The priest's eyes moved from Eli to his burned hands, and his lips parted.

Surprise, surprise. I shrugged. "Maybe despair and lack of clear thinking is part of a punishment for trying to hurt it. Burned hands. Grief. Maybe, like the hands, it'll heal. And maybe it would heal faster if you let a witch heal you. Or a vamp."

The man's eyes blazed with righteous fury and the stink of the burn grew on the air as he clenched his hands into bloated fists. Before he could speak, I said, "Never mind. Eli, let's get out of here before the man sets himself on fire with indignation." Eli backed away and I followed suit, though how the priest could shoot us with burned hands seemed impossible. To be on the safe side, I angled my body to the entrance as we moved back down the nave into the narthex. And out into the noon sun.

Instantly I started sweating. Eli holstered his weapon, looking cool and unaffected by the encounter or the heat. "You want to tell me what was going on in there?" I asked.

"Yeah. My pal Joe sent back a text about a certain emblem being worn by a small, renegade group of the clergy in the Western Hemisphere." He slipped on his sunglasses. "The emblem is a small red thing attached to their vestments. The group is composed of professor-type priests looking for magical things and magical people. A few things and a few people have gone missing."

"Missing as in kidnapped?"

Eli shrugged, not willing to speculate.

"Think they're working against the Mithrans?"

"Joe thinks they have an agenda that they haven't revealed yet. And he thinks someone in Rome is responsible."

The sun felt good on my back as we left the church grounds, but the knowledge of a sniper in the belfry didn't. "Think he'll shoot us?" I asked as casually as I could with sweat trickling down my spine and a target on my back.

"No. But I need to report everything to Joe."

"Fine," I said as we passed through the brick gates unscathed. "Question. You knew all this before we got here, didn't you?"

"I knew some. There's been some chatter about magical devices. Alex has been monitoring it and did some deeper searching in Reach's database. As soon as we heard about a magical device near us, I got in touch with people I know."

Reach had been the best researcher of all, ever, anywhere, when it came to the arcane, the weird, the woo-woo stuff. Then he'd been attacked by a human and two vamps and disappeared. Or so we thought. There wasn't any direct evidence either way. I still didn't know if Reach was alive.

I'd come into possession of his database in what, under any other circumstance, I'd call coincidence. But I no longer believed in that, not when it came to the vamps and the layers of history and death and conspiracy they so loved. Someone had wanted me to get the data. I just didn't know who yet.

Deep inside, my Beast chuffed with amusement. I didn't know why, but I'd learned that Beast would tell me stuff when she was good and ready and not one moment sooner. I said, "And you got in touch with your friend Joe. A former Ranger?"

Eli gave his patented nonsmile, a twitch of his lips that he probably thought was cool. It could also have been constipation. Someday I'd hit him with that one and see how he reacted.

"Someone in the Vatican, maybe? People who want the magical stuff I've collected?"

"They think they can heal the world's wounds with them," he said. "And they think they're the only ones who should have them."

"Which means they're the last people on earth who should have them."

"Correctomundo."

"Joe. Former military?"

"Current."

"I thought you were on the outs with the Army because of me."

Eli gave me a real smile, showing a hint of pearly whites. "Worth it, babe. Totally worth it." More seriously he said, "I have friends who know why I was blackballed and who still keep me in the loop."

I looked away. The guilt about Eli's being ostracized by the military always got me deep down, but I also knew he was speaking total truth when he said it was worth it. I could smell that on him. "Okay. Joe. What's he do?"

"Joe is the U.S. liaison in charge of overseeing the Pope's safety."

"Wait. The Pope as in the *Pope*? In Rome? That Pope?"

"Oh yeah. You have no idea how much the U.S. has invested in terms of time, intel, and equipment, keeping the Vatican's citizens safe and alive, all of them, for the last twenty or so years, since the jihad extremist movement got so big again."

"Okay. And Joe says?"

"That there was a blip in the Holy Vicar's security intel yesterday morning, and it necessitated sending a small group of God's warriors to the U.S. They landed at John F. Kennedy International this morning. They have a direct flight charter scheduled for New Orleans at four p.m. And then, unless they go the helo route, they'll have a drive in."

"Oh crap. We're gonna have to fight the Vatican, aren't we?"

"The Holy Roman See, to be specific, not the Vatican. And the See is considered a sovereign state. Which means all their men will be considered papal representatives and will be accorded all protections under law afforded to all international ambassadors on U.S. soil."

"Soooo they can do anything to anyone and get off scot-free. But . . ." I thought it through. "The vamps are currently under a temporary but similar legal protection."

"Until the U.S. government in all its wisdom and glory—"

I snorted derisively.

"—decides if they are citizens or not."

"So we have to involve Leo. Like, now."

Eli laughed evilly. "He's sooo gonna be pissed."

I'd have socked him, a good, solid thump, but it would have only made him laugh harder.

We didn't have long before the people from Rome arrived and made a bad situation worse. I was pretty sure that Lucky, despite being a witch whose ancestors were technically hunted by the Catholic Church since the witch hunts in the Middle Ages, and terrorized by the Church in the time of the Inquisition, was a Catholic. Pretty sure. Not totally. But his daughter, Shauna, and her vamp husband had been married in the yard of the Catholic church. . . . Would the priest be in trouble for his part of the ceremony? *Crap.* This was getting sticky. I decided to go back to Boudreaux's Meats, ostensibly for lunch. And after a good meal, Eli and I needed to get info. Any way we could. Even if it mean hurting Lucky. That bothered me. A lot.

Alex met us at Boudreaux's and we dined on the Cardiac Confidence, my name for the lunch that consisted of fried gator, fried smallmouth bass, fried soft-shell crabs, and fried boudin balls bigger than Lucky's fist. He made one to show us the truth of that statement. We also had beer-battered fried onion rings, fried squash, fried pickles, fried crab-stuffed hot peppers, and fried mushrooms in a basket so greasy it took a handful of paper towels to stop the drippage. Lucky said, exactly as he did the last time I ate here, "My own batter, secret recipe it is, and dat oil is fresh and hot for cooking." Certainly lard, but while we ate, imminent heart disease seemed worth it. After dinner, while we were disposing of the beer bottles that were illegal to sell in the dry parish but were totally legal to give away for "tips," I said casually, "Lucky. I remember you telling me that you had family who were killed in the vamp-witch wars here in BO."

He narrowed his eyes at me, and I thought I saw the flame tattoos on his arm flex in irritation before subsiding. "Priest in dem wars, Father Joseph, he was, before the war." Lucky was talking about the Civil War, I knew because I had heard the story. "He teach townsfolk how to kill wid stakes and swords. Him made dem crosses to be everywhere, on every house and building, and most dey attacks in town stop. Peoples, dey safe in town until Father Joseph was turn by de suckheads one night. But he strong in de faith. He rise and still in he right mind. Fight de blood/drink/ kill temptation. He come to de church and tell dem townspeople to cut off he head. Dey did. But it nearly kill most dem all to kill priest." His mouth turned down, and he crossed the room, taking a beer from the cooler before sitting at the table with us. When he started again, it was nearly word for word as he had said it last time, history by rote.

"Vamp turn on vamp. Kill each other, they did." He popped off the top of a LA 31 Boucanée with a shell-shaped bottle opener. The beer was made by Bayou Teche Brewing in Arnaudville, Louisiana, and it smelled of hops and smoked cherrywood. He drank a third of it, tossed back some of his own fried mushrooms, chewed, swallowed, and continued, his eyes faraway as if he saw the story he told.

"But they not always find suckhead to cut off head. One, they stake her. She rise from de grave, she did, and she kill and kill and kill. Church got itself a new priest, Father Matthieu, and he lead a hunt to kill her. Dey take her head and burn her body in center of de streets jus' befo' dawn, nex' morning." He jutted his jaw outside, to the crossing of Broad Street and Oiseau Avenue.

"Bordelon sisters, witches all, dey come gather up de ashes for to make hex. And Julius, blood-master, hem was, when he hear of all dis, he make war on dey witches. Kill dem mostly. Dem witches, dey make de hex, and de suckheads cain't eat, cain't drink. Sick-like. Dey kidnap local doctor, Dr. Leveroux, kill hem when he cain't cure dem. Leave his body in middle of town, like warning.

"Dem witches, some of my peoples, dey join wid priest and fight dem suckheads. War was everywhere, here, in de bayou"—he pronounced it *bi-oh*, which sounded odd to me—"in de swamp. My *gran-mère* be one dem Bordelon sisters, Cally Bordelon. She still alive when war was over. Most dem suckheads, most dem witches, dey dead."

"Would a priest today help you, join with you, to fight the vamps?" I asked.

Lucky snorted and finished off his beer, one that should be consumed slowly to appreciate all the goodness in the bottle. "Priest today not too interested in helping us no more. Turn he back, he did, when my Shauna marry . . ." He stopped.

"After Shauna married Gabe in the eyes of the Church."

"Yeah." Lucky picked up the bottle and dropped it with a *clink* on the table. "Dat priest sent away. New priest . . . hem witch hater, from new sect of priests. Call demselves Keepers of Truth. Got priests from all different orders and societies. Michaelites, what dey call dem Salesians. Augustinians. Dominicans. And some dem Jesuits. Black Robe what they brung in, hem witch hater even more than local boys.

"What I'm gone do?" he asked me. "My Shauna. You see her. Black hair what she got from me, blue eyes from her mama. Beautiful like angel from day she born, my baby, she is."

"But not acting like herself due to the hormones and the depression. The priest? We didn't see the local guy. Black Robe, that's a Jesuit scholar?" I glanced at Eli and received a scant nod. "They want the *corona* to be sent to Rome to be studied. Meaning destroyed."

Lucky lifted his eyes from his beer bottle and said, distinctly, "No. Not to Rome. I throw it in de swamp for de gator to eat first." I started to reply, but he spoke over me. "Dat Church in Rome hunt witches all through history. Torture them all. Burn them. Kill them. I a man of forgiveness, but they don't want no forgive. They still take war to my peoples."

"I need to talk to Shauna. And to Margaud," I said.

Lucky's tats blazed with his reaction. Anger flaming up his arms. Eli pressed a gun to his side and said, simply, "Don't."

Lucky cursed in French and his English patois, but his heat faded quickly. He looked down at the muzzle over his kidney. "You really shoot me wid that gun?"

Eli didn't respond and Lucky raised his gaze to Eli's eyes. "All dis. Dis because I call you *boy*?"

"I'm a man of forgiveness," Eli paraphrased Lucky's words, "but they don't want forgiveness. They still take war to my people."

Lucky snorted, full-nosed and half in his throat. "You right. Troublemaker in my nature. I am ass, I is." He stuck out his hand. "I ask you forgiveness. You accept? Then you put dat pop gun away?"

"Deal," Eli said. They shook, and Eli put the gun away. I noticed the safety was still on, and he had never injected a round into the chamber.

"You got Margaud's contact info?" I asked.

"I do. And You can see my Shauna now. No mo' customer come in today, not wid all trouble. I close up shop and we go my house." Lucky kicked his bench back and stood, disappearing into the back of the shop. "Leave all dat," he said, pointing over the counter to the messy table and greasy paper and plastic products. "I clean it up when I get back."

Lucky Landry's house was not what I was expecting. I hadn't been invited home on my last visit, but I had subconsciously created a vision of a redneck double-wide and cars on cement blocks in the yard. Maybe a toilet planted with petunias, positioned on the front porch. The white tidewater home with centipede lawn and tastefully planted flower beds was a shocker. I did manage to wipe my surprise off my face before I got out of the SUV.

Lucky parked his ancient blue pickup truck behind a half-shed carport, invisible from the road, and we all got out, Alex moving slowly as he gathered all his electronic equipment. Lucky led the way to the front door, speaking over his shoulder to us. "My wife, she make me park where my coonass huntin' truck can't be seen by de neighbors. Not for her, I be living in trash, I know."

The front door opened and the woman standing there was, well, also not what I had expected. Blue eyes, nearly black hair with just the slightest hint of red when the sun hit it, petite and curvy and pretty. And not dressed like a country singer at Mardi Gras, all bling and fringe, but in suit pants, a fitted shirt, and a business jacket. Except for her height, which was far too short for a successful model, she could have walked out of a fashion catalog.

"Lucky, bring your friends right on in. I got cold sweet tea with mint or lemon and some tasty lemon cookies. They're store-bought, but you'd never know it. You're that Jane Yellowrock woman, aren't you?"

"Who?" The word hammered at the air from inside. "If that bitch is here I'll kill her! This is all her fault!"

Shauna Landry Doucette raced around her mama and out the door, fast as a vamp. Her mama caught her in both arms and held her in place, magics sparking all around them both. Lucky snapped his fingers, and a portable protective ward went up around him. It was too small to hold us too, and I grabbed Eli, pulling him down behind the ward. "Get down!" I shouted to Alex. He hit the dirt behind the bole of an oak. Uncontrolled magics sparked in the air, burning on our skin. Eli jerked and whispered a curse.

"You hurt me," Mrs. Landry said, holding her daughter tightly, "and I'll be seriously unhappy with you, young lady. And if you turn your magics on me, I'll send you to your *grandmother* in a heartbeat."

The word *grandmother* must have been an awful threat because Shauna burst into tears. The painful magics faded.

Her mother shook her hard. "This is no one's fault but yours and that blood-drinking husband of yours. You don't think. You don't plan. Marriage isn't roses and chocolate and candles and great sex. Most of the time it's hard work and pain and forgiveness, on both sides. You marry a bloodsucker and you got to plan for a whole lot more forgiveness than most."

Shauna sobbed on her mother's shoulder. The girl was gorgeous, even with the twenty extra pounds of baby fat and her pale, anemic skin. Alex, rising from his undignified crouch behind the tree, took a sharp breath at the sight of her before retrieving his gear from the ground. Even Eli, with his dedication to Syl, couldn't help a spark of interest.

A trace of fatigue in his voice, Lucky said, "My wife, Bobbie. You know my girl, Shauna. Sorry 'bout dem fireworks. Shauna not herself."

"Shauna needs vamp blood," I said, "and not from her husband." And that got their attention. I stopped at the bottom of the steps, crossed my arms, and stared up at the women on the narrow front porch. "Her husband is starving. Do you know what happens to vamps when they starve? The pain is physical, a raging in their blood. The blood hunger is so intense that they often go insane. He needs human blood. You're anemic, Shauna. You need some blood to heal, and Gabe doesn't have enough to spare. Your blood isn't enough to keep *you* healthy, let alone a young vamp. They need more blood than older vamps. Didn't Gabe tell you that before you married?"

Shauna ducked her chin and averted her eyes from all of us.

"Shauna," Lucky barked. "Dis lady done come long way to help you. You answer her question." His expression darkened. "Or you *gran'-mère* be here for real. You mother and me, we give you to her. Together."

Shauna's mouth opened and I had the feeling that she had been playing one parent against the other. "I asked you a question, Shauna," Lucky all but growled. "Did Gabe warn you?"

Bobbie's hands tightened on Shauna's arms and Shauna nodded jerkily. "Yes. He told me. But I thought . . ." Her pale face flushed with embarrassment. "I thought the sex feeling was just for me. I didn't know it was for every feeding. I thought I was the only one who would be in that . . . position. . . . When I found out it was for everyone, I . . . I lost it. And I saw that bastard laying on top of Margaud. I should have . . ." She broke down again, without telling us what she should have done.

"Shauna, your husband can be taught to drink without sexual feeling. He probably never thought to ask if it was possible, and if Clermont Doucette is like most men of his generation, he probably never thought to tell his son." Shauna's face lifted, her mouth open again, like a pale pink rosebud. I'd never seen a mouth so small and perfect. My own was wide and straight and showed a lot of teeth. I frowned and went on. "Gabe isn't the brightest bulb in the chandelier, but he was starving himself to death to make you happy. Then Margaud spiked his drink, called you, and set up a feeding. I'm not saying that Gabe doesn't deserve some kind of punishment for his lack of control, but you can solve this. You need to get yourself help. And starting a vamp-and-witch war isn't going to help anyone, including your baby."

Shauna broke into a crying fit. From inside the house a baby started wailing too.

Eli chuckled softly. "Way to go, Yellowrock. You just made a sick woman *and* her baby cry. You gotta win points for that somewhere."

"Shut up," I said. To Lucky I added, "Can we go inside now and chat. It's hot and miserable and the air's wet and I need tea."

"Come on in. Her mama and me, we spoil her so when she a child, her so pretty and all."

I realized that was both confession and apology. "Uh-huh," I said, starting up the walk in Lucky's wake, Eli and Alex behind me.

Once we were in place in the spacious living room with iced tea in hand, Shauna in a rocking chair with her back turned, nursing her baby, I asked, "What can you tell me about the wreath?"

"My family be leaders of coven here in Bayou Oiseau, my mother and my sister, Solene. Solene can tell you what dem learn." Lucky punched a number on his cell and when the call was answered, he said, "Jane Yellowrock back in town, her sent by Leo Pellissier to fix things here. You talk to her? Tell her what you learn? Yeah. Dat fine. Come now is good."

Lucky ended the call and said, "Solene on de way. She talk to you."

"Just in case, I'm hiding behind you when she gets here."

Lucky laughed. But I was serious. Ticked-off witches were scary.

We drank tea, made uncomfortable small talk. Shauna made me hold her baby, and then laughed when I made a panicked squeak and the little boy screamed. I blushed and the Youngers laughed with her. It was mortifying, a word my housemother Brenda used to use instead of *embarrassing*. Previously, the usage was confusing, but for the first time ever, I totally understood the connotation. It came from a word that meant killing or putting to death, and I surely wanted to die with the baby in my arms. The last time I held a baby it was my godchild Little Evan, and that had been a long time past.

Beast, however, was totally at ease and she shoved me out of the way, purring over the child. *Kit. Human kit. Want kit.*

Yeah. No. Later.

Beast growled and milked my mind with her claws, long sharp claws that gave me a headache, while forcing me to lean down and sniff the little boy, who smelled of lotion, baby powder, urine, poo, milk, and witch, from his mother. I was still holding the baby when the witch magics shuddered through me. The sink of roiling energies filled the home even as the door opened and she walked soundlessly inside. It was the Amazon. And she was fully powered up, angry and expecting trouble. And me with my hands full of baby.

Behind her, just outside of her range, two ogres followed, Auguste and Benoît, Margaud's brothers, ugly as homemade sin and twice as big. Margaud's brothers each weighed in at an easy three hundred pounds, hirsute, sour with last night's beer, and both smelling of fish and gator. Their last showers were weeks ago. Maybe months. Maybe never and the men thought wading through a bayou was the same thing as a bath. The men wore matching T-shirts, this time in subtle shades of orange, or maybe that was just the expanded sweat rings under old-fashioned bib overalls; on their feet were unlaced work boots that might have been brown once upon a time. I set the baby on the couch and stood, motioning Eli to stay put. I stepped in front of him, allowing him opportunity to ready weapons. The brothers were human and taciturn, even by my standards, with expressionless faces. The only active thing about them was the stink, and it might have walked around the house all by itself. The silent Cajuns glowered as they crowded inside.

The witch was huge, six feet tall, and outweighed me by more than I had thought, all muscle and attitude. Dark hair and eyes, packed into T-shirt, jeans, and running shoes. Breasts like beach balls. I had a quick image of a blue-painted, tattooed, Celtic queen going into war buck naked, a knife and spear her only weapons, with the bones of her enemies tangled in her hair. She was surrounded by a haze of power that made my own bones ache. She extended a hand to activate a preprepared magical working.

Lucky grabbed his small family and snapped up a ward. Leaving the boys and me at the hands of the witch, me with access only to mundane weapons, which I'd never use in the confined space. So I went with my best talent, my smart mouth. "I know ogres eat human flesh. I have to warn you, I'm older and stringier and harder to kill than I look." I pointed at Eli. "Military." I pointed at the Kid. "Underage. *Be nice!*"

I pointed the same finger to the witch, and then dropped it when her eyes landed on the finger. It looked accusing instead of attention-getting. I folded all my fingers into loose fists. "I'm Jane Yellowrock, and I have no desire to fight. The vamps call it *parley*, and it's as good a word as any. I'm here to parley. Rules of parley include guarantee of safety to all involved and truce for the duration. So power down on the magical crap and let's chat."

The Amazon's eyebrows went up. "Magical *crap?*"

"Magical stuff. Magical boo stuff. Magical woo-woo stuff. Spells. Workings. Magical thunder and lightning. Call it what you want. You win. Now *power down and let's talk.*"

"Leo Pellissier would allow you to dodge a fight?"

"Leo is male and he thinks in terms of war, strategy, and one-upmanship. He also has testicles, which I've come to understand means he thinks with them as often as with his upper brain."

The Amazon's eyes crinkled, but if it was a smile it never reached her mouth. "You've come to parley about balls?"

Auguste, or maybe it was Benoît, laughed, displaying an impressive number of missing teeth. The other brother scratched his butt. Through his clothes, thank God.

I figured laughter, even laughter at my expense, was better than a magical war. "It seems to have worked as a conversational gambit."

The witch chuckled, dropped her ward and all the aggressive power she had gathered. She plopped onto the recliner nearest the door and motioned to the ogres. "Wait outside, boys. There's lemonade in the truck."

"Hard?" one grunted.

"No. Freshly squeezed," she said. "You can drink the hard stuff on your own time." The ogres shuffled out and the stink in the house lessened appreciably. "So. Jane Yellowrock. Parley away."

"First, who the heck are *you*?"

"I'm sorry." She inclined her head regally, the gesture somehow increasing the image I had of her with tattooed blue skin and the finger bones of her enemies tied into her hair, maybe also in a necklace around her neck, some warrior goddess leading a tribe into battle. "I'm Solene Landry Gaudet, Oiseau Coven leader, sister to our host, aunt to the hotheaded fool hiding her baby."

"You don't talk like him," I said, nodding to Lucky.

"Turn on dat coonass mojo, I can, if I need to," she said, then dropped the accent. "But I went away to college and learned to speak in a socially correct way, so far as the rest of the country is concerned. Are we gonna parley or not? Sundown isn't that far away, and I'm busy."

I told her everything I knew, had figured out, guessed at, and deduced. It didn't take long. "What we need here," I said in conclusion, "is a way to stop the war, repair a marriage, and open lines of communication between the vamps and the witches. And then get you both tied in with the regional councils so dumb stuff like this doesn't happen again."

"I'm not giving the *corona* back to the suckheads," Solene said. "It isn't theirs."

"It came from them," I said, going for reasonable. "Shauna stole it."

"*This* time. The *corona* is witch magic, old, and half-forgotten. Therefore, originally, it was witches who made it."

"That's one possibility. Another is that witch magic itself came from someone or somewhere else and that someone else made it and technically owns it. Or that the magic feels like witch magic but isn't. Maybe humans made it and witches added the magic later, under contract to a third party. Which would make it belong to that third party. Or maybe it's like a magic teapot, a spirit captured inside and needing to be set free."

"Like a genie? Rub my lamp and you get three wishes?" She made a sound of disgust. "Tell you what. That third party shows up, proves it belongs to them, and I'll give it to them."

"What kind of proof of ownership is necessary?" I asked "How about if they can unlock the thing's magic and use it? Would that do?"

Solene narrowed her eyes at me. It was clear that she hadn't planned on my accepting her suggestion or having a rejoinder to it. I put on my best innocent expression. I'd never been very good at fake innocence, and I didn't think Solene believed this face, but I kept it in place, hoping for the best. "All I'd need is to see it, take a pic of it with my cell, and we can start searching out its . . . provenance—isn't that the word?—to get it back to its legal owner, its creator, or at least the person who should be responsible for it."

"If it belongs to Satan, one of his emissaries, a demon, a Watcher, or any of the dark pantheon, the witches will keep it."

"As long as the phrase *dark pantheon* is not construed to include Mithrans or vampires, I'll agree to that. If the vamps actually own it, it goes to Leo Pellissier."

"If you can provide appropriate provenance that it belongs to the suckheads, I'll turn it over to them. I'll stipulate that I'll 'turn it over to the rightful owners.'"

That was too easy. I had a feeling that Solene *knew* the wreath had never really belonged to the vamps, and that maybe she had knowledge and proof that they had stolen it themselves. But, remembering the *corona* in the street, hazed by energies and the rain, I had another thought about the crown, one dealing with some of the squiggly lines on the base, the ones shaped like lightning bolts.

Before I could act on it, Solene said, "One other caveat. The suckheads never were able to crack the magics. If we crack the wreath's magics tonight, all bets are off. If we can use it, it's ours." She looked too self-satisfied, as if she knew she'd crack the magics and she had just been playing with me up until now. But realistically, if they cracked the spell on the thing and could use the energies contained in it, there was no way I'd get it back. They'd turn us into fried toads if we tried to take it away.

I scowled but said, "Agreed. When can I see it and take pictures of it?"

"Now. Auguste and Benoît have been guarding it in the truck." Solene grinned at what she saw on my face. "I'm not dumb enough to leave it anywhere unprotected. The suckheads might be bound by daylight and night, but their blood-slaves and -servants aren't."

I stood and motioned the Youngers up too. I saw Eli pocketing some-thing as he stood, and I figured he'd had a weapon ready the whole time. Knowing the elder Younger, he'd have more than one at hand. As if we'd all been pals forever, we made our way out of the tidewater house to the truck, Lucky and his family following at a safe distance. It was one of those *real* Humvees, the ones that had been used in wars, if I was any judge of such things, because it was still painted in desert camo, was scarred, scratched, dented, beat-up, had a less-than-minimalist interior—two seats and a flat metal bed behind them—and looked like a survivor. It had to sound like a herd of charging rhinos when it ran. And I hadn't heard anything until the door opened. *Solene has a spell that can dampen audio.* Now *that* would be cool to have. Maybe I could bargain for that later on.

The ogres got out of the Humvee and stood to the side as Solene opened the back door, lifted out a battered blue cooler, and set it on the ground. She raised the plastic top and took out the wreath. Up close, I saw pretty much what I'd seen the night before, but in more detail. It was a metal wreath, neither silver nor gold, but a hue that might have been a mixture of both, or maybe white and yellow gold mixed together. It was a dully gleaming metal circlet, carved or incised along the base with markings that could indeed have been decorative or early language, triangles and circles and squares in no particular order. The upper part was carved or shaped in ascending points in what could have been laurel leaves. Some kind of leaf, anyway. There were no stones or other ornamentation. But the haze of magics was much clearer at this distance, even with the sunlight.

I didn't ask to touch it. I simply pulled out my cell and started taking photos of it, walking around Solene to get the *corona* from every angle, taking the attention of the group with me, so Eli and Alex could do what-ever they wanted without anyone noticing. I asked to photograph the wreath in sunlight and in shadows under the trees. I didn't ask to touch it, which seemed to make Solene more agreeable. I also got a shot of it on the ground with a quarter and a dollar bill beside it for measurement purposes.

When I was done I said, "Thank you. If I can figure out how to call for a parley, I might like to request another meeting before the coven meets tonight."

Solene shrugged easily. "Fine. In the main intersection of town, a quarter hour before dusk. After that, the circles will be formed and we won't come out until dawn or until we figure out the magics in the wreath."

I nodded and turned to Lucky. "Thank you for your hospitality. Shake a knot in Shauna's chain so she can fix this thing with Gabe. Your daughter is a spoiled-rotten brat with delusions of what a mature relationship really is. She needs to understand how the different kinds of vamp relationships really work, how vamps feed, and how much blood they need. Gabe needs to be taught how to feed without a sexual component. I'd suggest you and Bobbie, Clermont Doucette, Shauna, and Gabe sit down together and explain the facts of life to them both. And I suggest it be done tonight, as soon after sunset as possible. I'll send a request to Clermont if you want and facilitate this particular discussion. Text me when you decide. But let me make this clear." I drew on Beast, lifted my head, and assumed all the power of the Enforcer position. Lucky stepped back at the glow in my eyes, and Solene did a double take. The leader of the BO witches stepped between me and her niece, as if her human flesh was a shield. That simple action made my heart melt with both tenderness and anguish, because no one in my entire childhood memories had stepped between me and possible danger. But a melting heart didn't stop me.

With the full force of my skinwalker energies pulled up around me, I said, "If I have to get in the middle of a lovers' spat, I'm not gonna be kind or gentle. I'll make sure things are fixed one way or another, but the happiness and safety of two stupid kids is not my primary goal. *You people will handle this.* Understood?" Lucky and Bobbie nodded. I turned my gaze to Solene. "Because as it turns out, relationship issues are the least important part of why I'm in BO. I'm here for the wreath, to find its rightful owner. And I won't leave without seeing that done. That's not a threat. It's a statement of intent."

Without letting the witch leader reply, I pivoted on one toe and walked to the SUV, giving her my back as if showing her there was no way to harm me. That was a lie, but it wasn't one I'd admit to, not after such a great parting shot. I climbed into the passenger side and closed my door, hearing two others shut in the same moment, as if we had choreographed it. Eli started the engine and the powerful motor hummed as we rolled sedately out of the drive and down the street. I twisted in my seat and smiled brightly between my partners. "That went well. What did you find out?"

Alex shook his head. "You are one scary woman, Jane Yellowrock."

"Yup. A big-cat. Which is *way* scary."

Eli's face was totally expressionless, even more so than normal. This was his battle face. "Two things. One. Never step between me and a target. Two. I brought the psy-meter. The wreath redlines."

Psy-meters had been developed by Uncle Sam and were used to measure paranormal energy. Eli should never have been able to get his hands on one, and I had never asked how he came to possess it, for fear it had "fallen off a truck" somewhere. Eli had sources I didn't want to know about. Every species and mystic device had a reading, one when at rest and another when actively using magic. Magic itself had a reading. Even I had readings. The wreath redlining when at rest meant one of two things. *La corona* contained massive power, or it was always in use.

"Okay," I said, processing that and adding it to the overall picture of the thing. "No stepping between you and a target, not even to allow you a chance to draw a weapon." I didn't add, *Fortunately she wasn't a target, and there wasn't room in the house to step the other way.* That would have been an excuse. Eli didn't accept excuses. There was always another way.

Eli gave me a stare before swiveling his eyes back to the road. He wasn't happy. Maybe he had heard my silent excuses?

Alex said, "I started a search online, which is still ongoing, for magical implements shaped like a circle or a wreath. I also ran it through Reach's database. Currently we have forty-seven magical and historical things that are shaped like circles, are made of metal, and are, at present, missing."

"Keep me in the loop." I took out my cell, the one with all the pics, and sent them to Alex and Eli for record-keeping. Then I sent three of the best to one of my contacts in PsyLED, the Psychometry Law Enforcement Division of Homeland Security. I figured I'd hear back fast if it was anything. I yawned hugely and said, "Sundown comes quick. I need some shut-eye. Unlike you two, I didn't sleep last night. Take me back to the B and B."

Eli sent me a sly expression that fell somewhere between a smile and a smirk. "Sharing a room with Edmund, are you?"

"Yeah. He's in my closet. Get over it." Eli slid his eyes back to the road, miffed that I didn't rise to the bait. But truth be told, I wasn't happy about the vamp sleeping in my closet, which sounded like the punch line to a very bad joke. Not happy at all.

I slept for four hours, about normal during an investigation, and Edmund behaved himself, maybe because I kept the blinds slit open and Eli woke me an hour before sunset. Not giving an opponent an opportunity to attack (or try to be snarky or try to seduce me) is the best offense. Being offensive to Edmund Hartley seemed the wisest course of action.

I showered and dressed in jeans, boots, and a T-shirt, and pulled a lightweight jacket on, black summer wool for a touch of formality that said I was taking everything seriously. I wished I had fighting leathers, but until I could afford more, I was out of luck. No way was I asking Leo to pay for them, no matter that some people seemed to think fighting leathers were part of my job expenses and therefore his financial responsibility. Just in case I had trouble, I pulled on a pair of cheap black sneakers—good for traction, easy to replace. Tucked a silver cross into a lead-lined pocket and silver and ash wood stakes into my bun, and strapped on a few weapons before hoofing it downstairs.

We ate a nice supper, *nice* meaning it was a five-star-type meal: a crisp salad with fresh bread to start; leek, spinach, and cream soup; braised rabbit with wild mushrooms; bacon, fig, and brie tartines; and a lovely white wine. Enough food to stuff a woman watching her weight. Miz Onie served huge quantities for breakfast, but not for supper. There were too many green things and not near enough meat to satisfy a skinwalker with battle—mental and possibly physical as well—ahead. When we left the B and B, all weaponed up and ready to rumble, we made a fast trek to Boudreaux's Meats and ate a *real* meal. Barbecue pig, slaw, and French bread. That crazy coonass witch could freaking cook!

The sun was setting as we left the eatery and meat shop, and Lucky clicked off the lights and locked the door behind us. His wife and daughter were waiting in a car at the curb, engine running, for a meet and greet with the Doucettes, and, amazingly enough, they handled it all themselves, without my help. They had even agreed on a location convenient to all, in the blood bar across the street. Maybe the BO citizens were growing up. We'd meet the two families in the bar after the witches got their circle going.

Eli was dressed in Ranger desert camo and weapons. Lots of weapons. Even Alex was tacked up, with tablets in his pockets and my Benelli M4 on its harness up his spine. It looked strange to me for the Kid to be wearing weapons, but it worked. Fully armed, looking like a high-tech, paramilitary gang, we crossed the streets, weaving between an unused grader and a front-end loader. The heavy-duty equipment was beginning to rust—not unusual in the high humidity of Louisiana.

In the square, witches had gathered, standing in a circle. Back from the witch circle, in clumps of three or four, human blood-servants stood, watching, looking menacing, but not doing anything. More witches appeared. No vamps yet, as the sun began going down behind a fresh bank of clouds moving in off the Gulf of Mexico.

I checked my cell. No one had gotten back to us about the wreath. The Kid had worked all day and still had nothing from historical archives, museum archives, or law enforcement archives about a missing *corona/ wreath/breloque*. None of the photos he had found were a match for the one in BO. Nada. Nothing.

It was hard to tell for sure, but the sun was nearly gone when the last witch showed up, rushing in on a bicycle, which she dropped in the street, and raced into place, heaving breaths. She managed a gasping "Engine trouble. Bike. Water." Another witch handed her a bottle of water and she drained it, still gasping.

Solene, who was standing in the center of the circle looking cool and maybe a little bored by the presence of the blood-servants, bent and placed the wreath on the pavement. The waiting humans tensed, every single one. Preparing for something. Three in one group pulled extendable truncheons and snapped them open. I drew the M4 Benelli shotgun from Alex's back and slapped the barrel into my palm with a resounding *smack*. "Think twice!" I shouted.

Eli laughed, the scariest sound I'd ever heard him make, and said, "Leo Pellissier's Enforcer will have no trouble making mincemeat of you untrained coonass idiots." They shifted, finding my partner in the falling dark. His voice softened now that he had their attention, and I could practically see their bravado melt away. "And I'll be pissed, because that means I'll have to clean up the blood and guts." His voice went conversational, but with an edge, a little crazy-sounding. I liked it. "It's hard to get blood off asphalt, know what I mean? Of course, brains are the hardest. They're sticky; they adhere to the tar like sourdough and Elmer's glue."

In the scant seconds that the servants hesitated, Solene said, *"Hedge of thorns."*

The words surprised me, because that was my BFF's family's spell, but it seemed to have gotten around, even to this backwater.

An inside circle flared up, reddish and sullen in the remaining daylight, the ward enclosing the wreath. A half second later she said, *"Electric dog collar."* The outer circle, looking like little more than a pale shimmer, raised up. The witches were protected. I had the feeling that Solene hadn't needed my help anyway. I had a feeling she had all sorts of offensive and defensive spells ready to toss at the humans, some of them deadly.

"Where the heck did you get that laugh?" I muttered to Eli.

"Borrowed it from a Taliban commander who thought he had us pinned down one night in Afghanistan. He didn't. But until we filled him full of holes, he had the Bela Lugosi laughter down pat."

"Gave me the shivers. Keep it in your repertoire. I like it."

Eli gave me a lip-twitch grin.

The front doors blew off the blood bar.

I dropped to a crouch, Beast slamming into me. Eli dashed for cover. Dragging Alex by the collar. The humans in the street screamed, ran, or were knocked off their feet, depending on where they were positioned relative to the blast. The witches turned as one and looked at the bar, then, while the humans were still reeling, turned back and continued whatever the heck they were doing. The sign that had hung over the bar, LECOMPTE SPIRITS AND PLEASURE, landed in the street and bounced. I couldn't hear it over the concussive damage to my ears, but it splintered and broke. I snarled and sucked in the wet night air, over my tongue and the roof of my mouth. The smell of explosive magic was an overriding stench filling the street, nearly hiding the smells of blood, sex, and liquor, and the stink of vamps.

Overhead, thunder boomed and the skies opened, not droplets, not drops, but bucketfuls. A deluge like something from Noah's time, solid sheets of rain like standing under a waterfall during a spring flood, the rain pounding on me. Instantly I was drenched. "Well, crap."

Night fell with the rain, the world darkening. Beast's vision flared over mine, a greenish silver overlay of energy and life, everything clearer than my human vision. The Gray Between rose around me, from within me. Pain flashed through my flesh and sizzled through my neurons, intense and blinding, lighting up my nerve endings, searing my flesh. Then was gone. I stood from my crouch and growled, stalking to the door of the bar.

At the first hint of trouble, Eli had shoved his brother into a hidey-hole under the second-floor gallery and Alex crouched there, arms wrapped around himself, hiding his laptop from the mist that sprang up from the ground as the huge raindrops hit and splashed, creating a saturating mist along with the soaking rain. The Kid's long curls were wet and dripping, plastered to his skull. But he was safe.

I got a glimpse of my hands. Pelt-covered, knobby knuckles. Beast had shifted me into my half-puma, half-human form. But there was no pain, and the change ground to a halt before my bones cracked and split, incapacitating me for way too long in the midst of a battle. Beast was getting good at this.

My hearing was already healing, and I made out screaming, the wail of a vamp dying, the nearly ultrasonic pulses that made my healing eardrums shudder.

From the bar doorway, flames flashed. Witch magic. Had to be Lucky.

I pulled on Beast's strength and speed and jumped. Shoving off from the street and landing twenty feet away, just inside the door. Impossible for a human. Piece of cake for a *Puma concolor*. When I touched down, I instantly pushed off again and landed, rolling under cover of a pool table. It was on fire but only on the felt top and one leg.

I took in the fight. Vamps in the corners of the room. Witches and humans in the center, the remains of a protective ward scorched into the floor. The vinyl floor tile was on fire, melting. Draperies on a low stage were blazing, the flames not just licking up the rotted fabric, but roaring up. Smoke filled the room.

There was a burst of thunder inside. Magic parched my nostrils. A human-sounding scream was quickly cut off. Something heavy landed on the pool table over me and I heard an ominous *crack*. The top of a pool table is made of quarried slate, and it's strong. I bowed my body in and rolled. Across the burning floor. To the feet of Clermont Doucette, fully vamped-out. His fangs braced at the carotid artery of a furious Bobbie Landry. A threat not yet carried out.

A shotgun boomed.

Everything went still. Silence vibrating with the gunshot. For an entire second that felt like an eternity.

A baby's cry broke the mute waiting.

I swiveled my head, locating the sound. Gabe stood at the edge of the stage, vamped-out, lips curled back from narrow, pointed fangs, eyes blacker than the pit of hell, set in pale pink sclera. Still starving. *Idiot.* And then I realized he was holding a baby in his arms. A witch I didn't know was at his feet, bleeding. Unconscious. And somehow he hadn't fallen on her to feed. Gabe had unplumbed strengths.

Shauna was standing in a *hedge of thorns.* Staring at her husband and baby. She wasn't afraid. Something I didn't have time to examine.

Lucky Landry was inside a triangle, a ward I had never seen before. He threw something at a vamp on the stage near Gabe. The unknown vamp screamed, an ululating howl of pain, and started bleeding from his nose and mouth. He fell, writhing on the stage.

Eli raced across the room, heading for the stage. Lucky threw a second spell. It hit Eli, bowling him across the room, against the far wall, so fast it was a blur. I saw him hit. My heart stopped everything, went into some kind of no-thought-no-feel mode as Eli's head conked the wall and he slid down it. I growled and aimed my M4 at Lucky. "I don't want to kill you. Don't make me do this."

Lucky swiveled his head to me and his eyes widened.

Clermont, within inches of me, his speech impeded by his fangs, said, "What you are?"

Lucky's eyes slid past me and he said, "What *dat*?"

I followed his eyes to the pool table.

Atop it was this . . . thing.

I swiveled and fired. Six shots, silver fléchette, hand-packed rounds, silver for the creatures of the dark. As I fired, Lucky threw a combustion spell at the thing. Flames rolled around it and off, onto the flaming felt of the pool table. Mud, dried by the flames, cracked and dusted down. If my rounds had done it harm, I couldn't tell.

Part frog, part boar, part alligator. Frog body and back legs, boar tusks and bristly hair and little twirled tail, a frog mouth and snout, full of alligator teeth. And arms muscled like a gorilla but covered in horned scales. The thing was dripping mud and foul gore. Whiffs of tar, the tart stink of rotten lemons, and the perfume of the grave came from it, fish and dead birds and rotten gator meat, *days* dead. A demon from the deeps of the darkest hell. I had seen one before and it only took seeing one once to know them all. And from Lucky's face, it wasn't one he had called.

With strange double pops of air, Clermont disappeared and reappeared, this time holding a sword with a slightly curved blade, not quite a broad sword, too wide and curving to be a dueling sword. The blade was black except along the honed steel edge and point. The cross-guard was a swirl that swept back, protecting the hilt and his hand, to knot around the pommel. A Civil War–era sword, old and dependable.

He rushed across the floor and cut a long slice, deep into the swamp thing. The demon screamed and black blood welled up. I had a half second to notice the dark magics within the blood, then the wound clotted over like tar cooling.

I retreated toward Lucky, which was also closer to Eli, lying unmoving against the wall. His eyes were half-open, the whites showing. His chest moved as he drew in air, and something inside me unclenched, sending relief shivering through me. He was still alive.

The demon spread a grin, half its face opening to reveal teeth no frog ever had, spiked and barbed and curved back. It should have roared, but instead it flexed its shoulders and laughed, a deep, dark reverberation. The notes made Eli's laugh sound innocent, a schoolboy at a silly prank. This was the laughter of a devil with a torturer's joy of blood and misery.

Clermont's eyes continued to vamp-out, growing blacker than I had ever seen them. Gently he put Bobbie Landry behind him and said to her, "Take Shauna and Gabe and Clerjer. Door to left of stage and down, into lair. Make my fool son drink from my primo and my secundo. Tell dem all, *Sacrement!* Dey know what to do."

Bobbie shot a look at Clermont, then at Lucky, her eyes wide with fear, the calculating kind of fear that can keep its head in the midst of bombs and explosions and even demons from hell. As if it wasn't there, she reached through Shauna's *hedge* ward and shoved the girl. Hard. Shock on her face, Shauna stumbled out of her ward, toward the door. "Mama? How . . ."

With one unladylike fist, Bobbie roundhoused Gabriel, catching Clerjer as he dropped the child. The baby over one shoulder, she grabbed a handful of Gabe's long hair and tried to haul him across the stage, not bothering with gentleness. My kinda woman—take no prisoners, no back talk, and no stupidity. Shauna, seeing what her mother was doing, took her baby, laid him across her own shoulder, and added her strength to Gabe's deadweight.

They disappeared behind the stage just as the flaming draperies lit the ceiling overhead with a wind-whipping roar. The heat flowed like a burning wave across the ceiling, seeking the air at the doorway, the flames billowing and rolling like a boiling, upside-down river, like water gone mad. The entire ceiling was afire, the heat so fierce that I crouched to get my body an inch or two lower. I smelled wood smoke and burning hair. Mine. The smoke raged down, black and suffocating.

Into the inferno Edmund raced, two long swords flashing in the red-scorched heat. He and Clermont attacked the swamp demon. If I'd had the time, if my partner weren't down, I would have stood there slack-jawed, watching them. Edmund Hartley with swords was a thing of utter beauty. Thrust, whirl, lunge, lunge, lunge, thrust, whirl, the cage of flashing steel so fast that, even with Beast-vision, I couldn't follow it. It was a glittering, flickering dance of death that slashed gobbets of mud off the demon and sent them flying. They hit the walls and quivered, orienting themselves back to the battle, as if the mud gobbets could see the demon, even without eyes, as if seeking a way back. Lucky tossed preprepared workings at the dismembered parts and they drooped into flaccid nothingness, sliding to the floor, where they lay inert.

Satisfied that all were safe-ish, for the moment, I raced to my partner. Kneeling, I rolled Eli up across my shoulder and back, and raced to the doorway. I dumped him there in an ungainly pile and shoved him into the street, into the rain. Freshly wet, I raced back inside, the rain so cool it felt delicious on my charred scalp.

Lucky was coughing, but he and Clermont were moving with purpose around the swamp thing, staying out of Edmund's way, flanking the creature. The three warriors scarcely looked at one another, but seemed to read intent, matching maneuvers as though they had worked paramilitary tactics together for decades. Clermont surged forward and hit the floor, rolling under the pool table. As he ran, Lucky spun to one side and pulled something from his pants pocket; he threw it, spinning, red-hot, and smoking. It hit the thing under the arm, silent. Just like a ninja throwing star, but one that had been in a furnace all day, glowing with fiery magic. The star disappeared inside the swamp thing with a sizzle of sound. The creature hissed and laughed again. It licked its lipless mouth with a wide, brown frog tongue. Lucky tried the preprepared working that had been successful on the dismembered body parts, but on the bigger mass of demon, the spells simply rolled off it and went out in poufs of broken energy.

Edmund spun his body in again and this time cut off one of the thing's hands. Black blood bubbled out of the stump. The hand landed across the room. Lucky's spell disabled it and the fingers melted, the hand liquefying into water and runny mud.

In the open doorway, I saw a form jump into the room, and time slowed. Not the Gray Between, the new power I had learned to use, not the one that was likely to kill me one day. No, this was the slow-down of time that warriors experience in the heat of battle, where the human body goes into overdrive and is able to see, hear, feel, and evaluate at hyperspeed. I studied this new thing as it leaped, while it was still in the air. Slight yet bulky. Small yet managing to appear hulking. Hairy, apelike. *Weaponless. Not a threat.* I ruled it from my attention before it landed.

Still with that battle speed upon me, I saw the demon on the table as it bent its knees and jumped to the floor. The old floorboards shattered beneath its weight, its bizarre feet buried in fragments and shards of wood that pierced its flesh. Its blood splattered into the room, reeking of acid, black as tar. The thing roared in agony, but it didn't leap out of the hole it had made. It just stood there, ankle-deep in splinters of pain.

The other, smaller form had landed, flat-footed in the smoke, and was searching the room. And I knew who it was. If I hadn't seen her in the camo uni before, I might not have recognized her. The ensemble was homemade, a one-piece, hand-tied, quilted outfit of green, brown, black, and tan strips of thin cotton cloth. Each strip was attached to the base garment with thread or knots. Irregular lengths of green yarn rippled from it in the hot wind of the fire, with rare pinkish, strawberry red, purple, and blue bits of thread interwoven. It was Margaud's lightweight ghillie suit, made for wearing in the heat and wet of Louisiana, but this time it was soaked from the torrents pouring outside and hanging weirdly, the strips of cloth flapping wetly, her boots making muddy puddles. Around her was a glow of power, a pale reddish light of a ward, the kind witches sometimes make and sell to humans, a one-off spell contained in a charm. A miniward. Short-lived and weak, but better than nothing. And it also seemed to have some don't-see-me properties, as no one looked her way but me.

Lucky shouted and threw a flaming blast of power at the frog thing. Nothing happened to it, the fire parting and rising to smack into the smoke overhead. Adding to the heat. Edmund crouched from the heat, his swords still flashing. Vamps were highly flammable. Ed had to get out, and soon.

Margaud lifted her legs and mimed stepping forward, without leaving the circle of the ward's energies. The thing echoed her movements, but stepping out of the hole. And it all came together for me.

The first time I saw Margaud wearing the weird ghillie suit, I had wondered what she needed the suit for. At the time, I figured it was something she had made to celebrate her sharpshooter days, something she wore when hunting in the swamps and bayous, despite the occasional brightly colored bits of thread. Now I realized the uni was something more, something magical, a suit that she wore to protect herself and to . . . to call the thing in the bar? To *control* the *demon*?

Wondering if I could die from fire, from burning to death, I inhaled to shout, and started coughing. I hacked out the words, "Lucky, put out the fire." And he must have understood.

The witch wrenched his attention from the swamp thing to me, then to the ceiling. His eyes widened in surprise. I don't think he had noticed the flames until that moment. He pulled something from a pocket and threw it with one fist, up into the ceiling. It stuck and the flames twirled around it, whirling back the way they had come, toward the metal star stuck in the ceiling and the slight hole it had made there. Cool, wet air rushed into the room from the busted door. The roar of the fire diminished and was gone in seconds. But so was the light, the electricity ripped away, along with the flames. I saw the room in overlays of green and silver, and hot spots that continued to smolder.

The creature unsheathed claws from its muddy body and swiped at Clermont.

The vamp sidestepped the claws, the motion beautiful and neat, no wasted movement, no wasted energy. He cut again. Sidestepped. Cut. Sidestepped. The creature roared each time, but its wounds clotted over.

Clermont stepped back and Edmund stepped in, cutting, cutting, cutting, lunging over and over. Just before each of the creature's motions, Margaud moved, its body following hers in a peculiar, macabre dance.

Lucky was watching her, as I was, and he reached again into his pocket and withdrew something that sparked when it hit the air. He threw it hard, a baseball pitcher's fastball. It smacked into the ghillie suit and stuck. Flames licked up, burning, even in the wet cloth.

The creature stepped forward and backhanded Lucky. The witch spun through the air and cracked into the pool table, bending in ways no human body was intended to. His ribs splintered with brittle *snap*s. The table was no longer on fire, and Lucky gripped the scorched felt, curling his fingers into it to stay upright. But I heard the bubbling wheeze when he tried to inhale. He had lung damage. He grunted and his face went white.

Margaud's ghillie suit roared up in flame, and she screamed. The swamp thing walked to her. It wrapped her in its arms and the flames sizzled out, smothered in mud and swamp water. I could hear Margaud gasping and the stink of her terror was clear and sharp, even over the reek of burning homemade ghillie suit.

The demon turned from her and it seemed to have found its way. It stepped forward and struck at Clermont, its claws gouging deep into the vamp's belly, sending him flying too. Edmund danced out of the way. The other vamp, the one who was down on the stage, groaned, catching the demon's attention. The creature fisted its hands and raised them high. I tried to fire the M4, but it clicked. *Empty.* The mud thing brought its fisted hands down on the unconscious form. Bones splintered and cracked.

I reloaded the M4 with regular shot, my movements efficient and spare, Beast fast, but still too slow. I raised the shotgun and aimed at the thing. Then shifted my aim for Margaud. I had never killed a human except in defense of my life or in defense of another. I hesitated, uncertainty filling me. What if Margaud wasn't actually directing the thing? What if I had it all wrong? I fired. The round hit the ghillie suit and spread. But nothing penetrated. The shot stopped, hot and smoking. And fell to the floor with *ping*s. Her ward, which had seemed so weak, was more than it had appeared. Much more.

From the doorway came a crash and a deep rumble. A blackened claw bigger than the opening busted through, burned wood snapping and splintering. A yellow arm pushed the claw through. No. Not a claw. A shovel, with steel teeth along the bottom. What the drivers of heavy machinery called a bucket. It was the front-end loader that had been parked in the street. Jerking the bucket side to side, the loader ripped out the old entrance. The ceiling above shuddered, the weakened second floor trying to drop through. The creature and Margaud turned to the heavy vehicle. Edmund backed away from the mechanical claw, laughing with delight, his head thrown back with joy. Dang vamp. He was having fun.

For the first time in the fight, I could also see Margaud's face clearly. She was perhaps the most beautiful woman I had ever seen, even in the silver gray of Beast sight, even with her face twisted in hate. The ugly expression was darker than the hell the swamp demon had been called from, foul, dreadful, seeking only pain and death.

The huge bucket with its steel claws jerked and tore as it worked its way forward, the tractor tires gripping on the damaged wood floor. The yellow machine was forcing its way inside like in some child's film about sentient machines. The loader rolled inside, revealing Eli sitting in the glassed-in cage, his face like stone, his hands working the controls. The demon attacked the loader, throwing itself against the clawed bucket, Margaud's body a mirror image, fighting an invisible menace. The bucket jerked forward and up, picking up the demon, the steel claws catching it at its middle and tilting, lifting. The swamp demon roared, its voice matching the sound of the huge engine. Eli carried the demon, rushing to the wall beside the stage. He slammed the bucket into the wall, the claws ripping through the demon and cutting into the plaster on the far side. Black blood sprayed.

The demon shuddered and screamed. Lucky hit with one of his dissipate spells. And the demon melted into a puddle of mud. Clermont whirled to Margaud. But she was gone. He clutched his middle, which was bleeding, and caught himself on a chair, holding himself upright, amazingly still whole, in the middle of the ruined blood bar.

Clermont gripped his side and belly, holding in what passed for guts in vampires, and made his way across the wrecked floor to the vamp on the stage. He rolled the unconscious, broken vamp over and tilted back the bloodsucker's head, as if opening an airway. But . . . vamps don't need to breathe. I understood when Clermont's fangs snapped down and he bit his own wrist, holding it to the vamp's mouth. The blood flowed fast for several seconds before the vamp's eyes snapped open and he swallowed. He gripped his master's arm and pulled it tight to his lips, sucking.

Lucky groaned and rolled over, clutching his side and ribs. He activated a healing spell, one I could see in the dark of the bar, which was probably red and orange, but in big-cat vision looked green and silver, shot with blue, in the weird colorblindness of the feline.

Edmund made a quick whip/slash motion and sheathed his swords. Elegant and beautiful. And if I was guessing right, he was a better swordsman than Leo Pellissier's Mercy Blade. Better than Leo. Maybe even better than Grégoire, who was known to be the best swordsman in the entire United States. Edmund had been hiding things from us all.

The clatter/roar of the front-end loader changed to a cough and went silent. The plasticized glass door opened, and Eli stepped out of the loader cage and dropped to the floor, where he caught his breath and held it for a space of heartbeats. He moved away from the machine, his body stiff and slow. He was badly wounded to be showing any sign of weakness.

"Honest to God," he said as he stepped to the wall where the bucket was stuck. His voice was just a hint breathy as he went on, "I thought Vin Diesel as Riddick had it all wrong, but there *are* movie mud monsters. And worse. This one melted on a wood floor and disappeared."

"It'll be back," I said. "Its maker or controller, or both, didn't get what she wanted. And she got away."

"Who?"

"The person in the homemade ghillie suit. Margaud."

Eli frowned, pulling the name out of his memory, making associations with a demon and a bar fight. "The sister of the two Hulk wannabes with the Amazon this afternoon? The one that made all this small-town, love-triangle, witch-vamp shit happen?"

"Yeah." I couldn't argue about the estimation or the language. Sometimes *shit* is the only word for a particular situation.

He looked around the burned blood bar. "Margaud. Makes sense."

"Questions to ask Solene if we can break the circle. Or in the morning, if we live that long. You need vamp blood to heal. Edmund?" I called, looking around. He was gone.

"You need to shift back," Eli said, as if we were debating. "And I don't know where the slimy little bloodsucker is. I never saw him in the battle."

"He was there. We'll talk about him later. How long?"

Eli frowned, a downward quirk of his lips. "It lasted one-twenty-seven seconds."

One hundred twenty-seven seconds. A little over two minutes. It seemed like an hour. But my partner was right. Where was my vamp helper? Why had he taken off after facing a mud demon and fighting our way out of a mess?

Clermont snapped his arm away from the healing vamp, licked his wound to constrict the fang holes, and stood. He walked over to Lucky, still lying half under the burned pool table. He knelt close to the witch and said, "We been played. Our children been played. Or entire peoples been played, by a human what can call her up a demon. We been enemies a long time. We been friends only since our families join. I say we stronger dat little time when we joined. I say I sorry I din' see what happening to my boy and to your girl. I say I sorry I such an ass, even if you don' take my sincere apologies."

Lucky put his hand into Clermont's and let the vamp pull him to a sitting position, his legs stretched out and his back resting against a blackened pool table leg. "I accept. And I offer you my own, how you say, sincere apologies."

"We not much leaders we not able to see a common enemy."

"Divide and conquer work best on dem what blind to dangers," Lucky agreed.

"We not some dumbass politicians. We leaders. And right now, we need our strength. I offer you, Lucky Landry, father of my daughter-in-law, gran'father of my—of *our*—gran'boy, Clerjer, blood of my veins, to make you strong to fight."

"Long as I don' got to kiss you, I accept."

"I'm told I kiss real good. Maybe I'm insulted, yeah?"

Lucky chuckled and his face wrenched in pain. "Okay. I kiss you. Hell, I kiss dat ugly frog demon if it fix my ribs. And I thinking I got lung problems."

"Got you pneumothorax, you do," Clermont said. "I hear air leaking and blood gurgling."

I remembered the vamp leader was a surgeon, back in his human days.

"To fix you, I gone stick a needle like a tenpenny nail in you side right here"—he touched the witch's side—"and den I'm gon' drain my blood inside. Heal you fast. Den you drink some my blood and be heal for real."

"I not gon' wake up dead, am I?"

"No. You still be pain-in-de-ass coonass witch, what walk in de day."

"Do it, den, wid my thanks."

"Lucky? Clermont?" We all turned to the stage door where Bobbie stood, holding her grandson on her shoulder. "The vampire you sent to protect us says the fight's over."

"Vampire?" Lucky asked.

Edmund eased Bobbie away from the door and stepped out. Behind him came Gabriel, looking pink-skinned and healthy, and behind him, a gentle hand on his shoulder, came Shauna. So that was where Edmund had gone. To check on the people downstairs. *Go, Ed.* I nodded at him, a slight inclination of my head. He nodded back, his gaze serious and intense. Weirdly, Edmund walked to me and knelt at my feet, his swords back and behind him like wings. I looked down at the top of his head in confusion. What was this? I looked around in growing panic.

"Ed?" He didn't answer. Just knelt there.

Whatever Ed was doing, no one else seemed to notice or care. The others—witches, humans, and vamps—ignored us and gathered at the pool table where they huddled together with their faction leaders in what was probably a group hug/blood-feeding/bloodletting. Eli, who was still moving stiffly and clearly needed to feed on a vamp sometime soon, looked over Edmund and me, chuckled softly, and turned his attention to the room, evaluating entrances and exits and possible close-quarters fighting. Not looking at the hugging. No longer looking at Ed.

From the doorway, Alex walked into the bar, saying, "Just gag me with a spoon and get it over with. All that huggy, kissy, mommy, daddy crap." The brothers fist-bumped. *Idiots.* Every single one of them. And the worst was Edmund, still at my feet, his head bowed. I wasn't sure what gave me the impression, but I had a feeling Ed was laughing at me.

I considered my vamp helper in light of the battle, the problem with humans, witches, a starving vampire, and a baby locked together in an underground lair, all afraid and angry, and decided it had turned out much better than it might have. "Get up," I said, hearing a long-suffering note in my two words. Edmund stood with a flair that might have come from the Middle Ages or a Hollywood set. "Ed, I take it you taught the young vamp idiot how to feed without sex?" I said.

"Yes, *my master,*" he said, sounding quietly subservient and yet somehow managing to convey his hilarity.

"Having fun, are you?"

"More than you can possibly imagine, *my master,*" he said, with heavy emphasis on the last two words. He was determined to call me *master.* To get under my skin. Or to bind himself to me in some way I couldn't comprehend.

"Teaching proper feeding habits doesn't take long when one is experienced in such matters." He added, "My master."

I narrowed my eyes at him, thinking, *No freaking way.* I had enough responsibilities to deal with. "Once you get over the chuckles," I said, "would you be so kind as to heal my partner? Eli's hurt from when that thing knocked him across the room."

"Yes, my master."

"And since you can heal without sex, make sure you don't annoy him with any come-hither pheromones or whatever you do to get sex. Because I'll let him shoot you if you do."

"Spoilsport," he said, wandering over to Eli.

I watched as Edmund spoke quietly to the Youngers, and then presented a blade, hilt first, to Eli, and lifted his other wrist to be cut. Satisfied, I walked over to the huddle of BO citizens. "Okay. Get your crap together and meet me at the bed-and-breakfast because I need to know everything you know, and can guess, about the demon and about Margaud, and about her brothers, and everything about that dang wreath. Because no way is it all disconnected."

In the corner of the room a flame flared up. With a pop of speed, Gabe raced for a fire extinguisher and put it out, kicking the smoking remains of drapery away.

"Fine," I said. "First we make sure the fire is out. *Then* we talk."

I got a good look at myself in my mirror as I changed out of my wet, smoke-damaged clothes, and the pelt I wore in my half form was pretty awe-inspiring. Knobby joints, retractile claws on my fingertips, narrow waist, no boobs to speak of, feet shaped like huge paws that had ripped my sneakers into ruined shreds, and a body of solid muscle, covered by a golden pelt. I shoved the cell into my jeans pocket and inspected myself closer. The brown/black nose looked a little odd, but the gold shining eyes totally made it work, especially with the gold nugget necklace. I had never thought this about myself before, but pelted? Even with the jeans and T on top, I looked hot. Weird. But hot.

Beast and Jane are not hot. Beast and Jane are best hunters. Beast and Jane are worthy of best mate. Beast and Jane are best at everything, Beast thought at me.

I chuckled under my breath, grabbed a robe, and went to shower off the smoke stink.

It was two a.m. before everyone was finally healed and the fire was deemed completely doused. The rain had drained to a drizzle, though water still shushed through the magnolia leaves, swirled in the streets, and pooled in the ditches and low-lying places. The witches were still encircled, studying the wreath, and not much had changed with them, except this time they weren't wet. Seemed they had figured out how to add a water-repellent aspect to the *electric dog collar* ward.

Leaving human blood-servants to keep watch for changes in the witches' activity level, others to keep watch for the demon and Margaud, we gathered in the living room of the B and B. I had quickly made notes on the things I needed to know, and I started the little tête-à-tête by saying, "The vamps of Bayou Oiseau never had a formal parley with Leo and his peeps. The witch coven never met with the New Orleans witch council. I thought both parleys had taken place. Honestly, I don't have a crapdang care why they didn't take place. They *will* take place next week. Lucky, Clermont, nod if you want to keep your heads on your shoulders."

It may have been the honest agreement that the meetings needed to take place, or it might have been my pelted and glowing-eyed aspect that forced them into compliance, but both nodded. Beast chuffed, feeling her power over the gathered. *Beast is good ambush hunter.*

I smiled, showing her teeth.

Clermont cleared his throat, laced his hands over his stomach, stretched out his legs, and crossed his ankles, every bit the relaxed gentleman. He was tall, lean, and gangly at nearly six feet, with dark brown eyes and blondish hair, a combination that seemed common in this area and had been replicated in the genetic makeup of his son. Somewhere he had found clean apparel and changed out of his smoky, bloody clothes. Now, like the first time I saw him, he was dressed in worn jeans, an ironed white dress shirt, a gray suit jacket, a narrow tie, and boots, which were ubiquitous in Louisiana. His reading glasses were perched on his head, reflecting the light. "Lucky and I been talking, we has. Already confirm appointment with New Orleans' councils."

"Good," I said.

"Share, we do, all intelligence we know 'bout dat wreath. *Corona. Breloque.* It first appear in 1927, day de blood bar open. Professor be playing piano, lady singer singing, though I forget her name, it be so long ago. My sire, he dancing wid a local gal, blood-slave, she was, and thunderstorm outside. Rain pouring down like what it done today. Hard falling, it was. And there be a crack of thunder. And, like *poof.* It appear in middle of stage. All by it lonesome."

Lucky said, "The witches heard about it. My family ancestors, the Bordelon sisters, asked to see it. The vampire said no. We not see dat *breloque* until my Shauna took it and brung it to us."

Clermont frowned. Maybe Shauna would be considered a thief in the eyes of the courts, providing that the *corona* belonged to the vamps under some form of finders-keepers rule of law, but I couldn't let that topic become the center of the discussion. Before anyone could accuse Shauna of stealing, I said, "And were either the vamps or the witches ever able to use it?"

"No," Clermont said, his mouth forming a totally human smile. "Back before de electronic revolution, *la corona* sat on top my TV for years. Best rabbit ears dey ever was."

Lucky laughed. So did I. And if there had been tension in the room, it dissipated. "Okay. So where was it kept when Shauna and Gabe got tricked into causing all this trouble?"

"It in my gun closet. Locked to keep the young 'uns out. Key hanging on my bedpost on leather thong."

I looked at Shauna, who was pretty as a picture, sitting beside her husband, snuggled on the sofa. She looked abashed and tucked her head down under her husband's chin, snuggling their child up close in her arms. The silence pulled like a long length of taffy, and she finally spoke into it. "When I saw Margaud and Gabe together in the bar, I went home, packed, got the key, and took the wreath. Then I strapped Clerjer into his baby seat on the airboat and went home to Mama and Daddy." She turned her clear, blue gaze to her hubby. "I was a fool."

"No, Shauna, my love, I was de fool," Gabe said.

"You were all fools, but we don't have time to list the ways," I said, thinking Shakespeare, with the height, breadth, and depth of foolishness. "So what does the wreath do?"

"I can tell you that."

I swiveled on my satin-upholstered chair to Alex, standing in the doorway. His skin looked darker than its usual caramel, and his hair was kinked high from the rain and the humidity. Except for the laptop, he looked like a nineties rapper, in boxy pants and oversized T-shirt. "I found it in the new database."

That meant Reach's database, the one he was still learning how to use. Alex turned the laptop around, and on the screen was a picture of a marble statue of a man wearing a wreath—laurel leaves standing up at attention—but this wreath was stone, not metal, and it was missing the lower part, the part with the writing. I started to say that, but Alex said, "It's a statue of Julius Caesar, commissioned in the seventeenth century for the Palace of Versailles. And he's depicted wearing what was called a civic crown. The civic crown, also worn by Napoleon and other kings, is the laurel leaf part of the *corona*. The lower part is what I'll call a band crown, as seen on Greek kings and consorts, like you see on this silver coin, called a silver tetradrachm." He displayed a picture of a coin with a woman's face on it and then zoomed in with his fingertips on the touch screen. The crown was a narrow band and did indeed seem to have etchings on it that might—or might not—have been a match to the ones on the corona. "I haven't actually seen one of the band crowns, but they were worn by queens or consorts in the BC era. And it shows these little marks. See? Here." He pointed.

"Fine," I said. "I see the marks and I acknowledge the research, but—"

"Someone combined the two crowns, a laurel leaf civic crown and a band, worn by a consort. A witch took the two concepts and melded them into one. Like this." He punched a corner of the screen and a picture came up, which matched perfectly the corona in the street, surrounded by witches, standing, dry, in the rain.

Alex was tired, I could see it in his face, and beneath the stench of smoke and blood in the room, he smelled of caffeine and testosterone and adrenaline, a combo that said he had been bingeing on energy drinks. "Okay," I said quietly. "We have a theory about what the *corona* was made from. Now we need to know where it came from and what it does."

Alex heard the word *theory* and his shoulders slumped. Then his face brightened. "My research says this: '*La corona* does one thing and one thing only. It allows a misericord to attain human form.'"

I stood slowly. "Oh crap." I looked at the windows. Outside, lightning flashed and distant thunder rumbled. "We might be in a bit of trouble."

The misericords were Mercy Blades, the creatures who made sure that vampires didn't keep their children alive after a decade, two at the most, in the devoveo. In other words, they administered the mercy stroke of death to the chained, insane killing machines that never made it through the vamp turning into true vampires. They were also Anzu. Storm gods. And . . . I had recently been struck by lightning during a storm. *Holy crap. What am I missing?*

"Jane?"

I jerked my head to Alex, who looked oddly concerned. I stood, digging in a pocket for my cell. "Yeah. I gotta make a call."

I walked outside under the gallery roof into the drizzle that had started again. I pulled up my address list on the official cell, the one that my boss could trace, listen in on, and read texts from. I found the name Gee DiMercy, who was also known as Girrard DiMercy, aka Leo's misericord, or Mercy Blade. An Anzu. Once worshipped as a storm god. Like a blue and scarlet Big Bird with a bad attitude. A storm god . . . I hit SEND and waited. The cell rang. Rang again. And then I heard a calypso dance number behind me.

I pulled a vamp-killer, spinning on one toe. Ducked the sword strike that was aiming for my head. Threw my body into a forward roll, tucking, landing on one shoulder and sliding under the swing hanging on chains. Gee laughed, and his laughter was exactly as I remembered from the first time I heard it—joyful, like a kid in a park, and I found myself smiling with him, even though I was hiding behind a swing, in the dark.

He didn't attack again and I saw him sheath the sword, the steel a silver gleam in the porch light. "What are you? Kato?" I accused.

"That would make you the Green Hornet. And . . . a sidekick? Have I fallen so far in your estimation?" He swept a hand to his chest. "My heart breaks. However, I am not likely a secondary character, and I much prefer your first appellation—Zorro, the swords master hero."

Gee DiMercy was standing under the porch light, his very-milky-chocolate-colored flesh cast in a slight yellow tint from the bulb. A V of chest hair was framed in the opening of his shirt, and a faint film of pale energies ran on and under his skin. His black hair was dry and longer than when I first saw him, loose and curling around his pretty face like a cap. His skin looked Mediterranean or Middle Eastern mixed with a hint of African. His features were utterly beautiful but full of mischief, like an angel who was pushed out of heaven for laughing during prayer. He was dressed in a draped-sleeve, open-throat navy shirt and blousy pants with boots to his thighs, but now he also looked younger, maybe fourteen years old in the poor light. But since it was all a glamour, he could look like anything he wanted.

I stood up, keeping the swing between me and the Anzu, no matter that he looked like a dance student rather than a swords master. Slight, delicate, and smelling of jasmine and pine, the commingled scents fresh, lovely, and dangerously disarming on the night breeze. I sheathed the vamp-killer, which would have been useless against the longer sword, even with Gee's shorter reach. I had been taking lessons, but I mostly sucked with a long sword.

His gaze swept me from my feet to my head and said, "The pelt is lovely, but feathers would have been beautiful. Remember that you owe me a hunt."

"I remember. Why are you here?" I asked.

"I am here for *le breloque*. It is mine."

"And how do you figure that?"

"It was made for my kind by my goddess and friend. It was lost when one of us died unexpectedly. Until now, we did not know where it had landed."

"Uh-huh. And how do you intend on getting it, seeing as the witches have it warded and protected?"

"Their magics are child's play to one such as I."

"Hmmm. And if they have a steel blade and stick you with it?" Anzus—Anzi?—could be wounded and even killed by steel. I had seen that myself. Gee scowled.

"Right," I said. "And if they decide that 'finders, keepers' is a more appropriate method of deciding ownership, and they attack in a coven of twelve, could they singe your tail feathers?"

His scowl deepened.

"Come inside and talk to the leaders I've managed to get in one place. The coven leader is"—I waved a hand into the slow, misty rain—"otherwise engaged."

"She tries to use misericord magics, stored in *le breloque*. She cannot."

"Whatever." I opened the door and went into the bed-and-breakfast, pausing by the front door. Gee passed me, altering his apparent age to midtwenties before assuming a fists-on-hips, aggressive stance, like a sea captain, or maybe a pirate captain. All he needed was an eye patch, a parrot, and a stein of rum. "I bring greetings and a warning to your people. I am here in peace. But I will have *mon breloque* back or you will all die."

If I'd been close enough, I'd have head-slapped him. Fortunately the witch and Clermont laughed at him. Edmund stood and pulled his swords. He stepped in front of the others and said, "I will not permit—"

The front window blew in and a mud demon shaped like a frog stepped through. Everything went to hell in a handbasket.

Eli fired two handguns, backing into the hallway.

Lucky dove across the room, throwing a fire spell that simply disappeared into the frog's wide mouth, where it sizzled as the demon swallowed it, treating it like an appetizer. When he landed, Lucky flipped a table over on its side and ducked behind it. Clermont, Edmund, and Gee all turned on the thing and attacked, swords flashing. Black tarry cuts appeared on its sides and it roared with anger. I still had my shotgun, but the Benelli was useless in such close quarters. I'd hit one of the swordsmen. I checked the hallway and Eli was gone, and so was his brother. Eli had to have some toys in his room. He'd be back with military reinforcements.

The demon picked up the sofa where they had been sitting and threw it across the room. It crashed on the table hiding Lucky, and the table cracked, splintering. The furniture collapsed on the witch.

The demon's arms extended two feet. It grew claws. It attacked the swordsmen.

They didn't have a chance.

But . . . they were all using steel. I pulled a vamp-killer, with its steel edge and silver plating. "Ed!" I shouted. I lay the long knife on the floor and spun it to him. He bent and picked it up while making two cuts in the demon. No. Make that four. He was . . . Edmund Hartley was freaking fast. Seeing him fight next to Gee DiMercy made that abundantly clear. Holy crap. The vamp who was on the bottom of the pecking order in vamp HQ was amazing, a skilled, talented swordsman.

So why is he the bottom of the bunch in vamp hierarchy? Why did he lose his control of his blood clan? How did this guy lose a blood duel?

Before the thought was fully formed, Ed dashed inside the demon's reach and cut a long gash in its belly with my vamp-killer. The black blood cascaded out. And this time it didn't clot over. Go, me!

"Silver!" Edmund shouted at me.

I pulled two more silver-plated vamp-killer blades and slid them across the floor to Gee and to Clermont. They put their lives in danger of his long reach, dashing in and back out, but the demon squealed as they all began to make headway on bleeding the thing to death.

I whirled and went back outside into the rain. Looking for Margaud.

She was standing under the magnolia tree in Miz Onie's front yard, leaning against the trunk of the tree, half-hidden in the low branches. This time she wasn't guiding the demon with kicks, fists, and maneuvers. She was standing still, running with rainwater, a sodden mess. Shoulders hunched, she was staring into her cupped hands, shielded from the elements. Staring at something that had her total attention.

I pulled a small knife, one with a wide pommel and short blade. I drew on Beast's stealth abilities and her speed. I bent and leaped across the ground, landing on a mossy patch of ground. Instinctively keeping downwind, in the shadows, I leaped again, landing beside the girl. Raised the knife. And bonked her on the head. She dropped like a stone. I caught her hands and picked out the thing in them. It was . . . a gris-gris.

Time slowed all by itself, the bangs and thumps from things breaking inside growing deeper in tone. The raindrops seemed to decelerate, not hanging in the air, but falling at half speed. My stomach cramped. This was not gonna be good. In fact, it was gonna be very, very bad. I could tell.

Gris-gris were small leather bags that had originated in Africa and were believed to protect the wearer from evil or to bring luck. Or to provide the wearer a method of birth control. Lots of things, depending on what the wearer and the maker wanted. They had become part of New Orleans' voodoo, or vodoun, subculture, and they looked a lot like a Cherokee shaman's medicine bag at first glance. This one was made out of leather covered with red silk fabric, tied with undyed hemp. It was about four inches long, less than three inches wide, a little large for a gris-gris. Like the shaman's bag I had begun to wear in my soul home, gris-gris held herbs and small animal bones. And when used in dark magic, the spells they powered could become unstoppable.

I touched the leather, which was bumpy and rough—tanned alligator skin. There was a swatch of bristly hair tied into the hemp. I held it to my nose and caught the scent of wild boar.

I toed Margaud with my foot paw and she lolled limply, sluggishly. Still out. Moving through the abnormally slow rain, I carried the gris-gris to the porch and stood under the light. Inside, the fight was still taking place at half speed, and I could hear grunts and the sound of more breaking furniture. In the distance I also heard sirens. The light-sleeping Miz Onie must have woken even with the sleep spell, and called the county law enforcement officers. I wondered if they would fall sway to the sleep spell as they entered the city limits and if they'd get the unit stopped in time. The thoughts were useless things, mostly background, so my subconscious could worry about the real problem while my hind brain kept me breathing and my heart beating. A lot going on at the moment, and there were, after all, priorities.

One shouldn't open a gris-gris.

It might unleash many things, even worse things than the demon inside the house. Or . . . maybe the gris-gris bag had *been* opened and that was how the demon had gotten free? Or . . . maybe there was something even worse *still* inside the bag.

I had the answer to any gris-gris. I pulled my silver cross from the lead-lined pocket in my jeans. I untied the hemp and pressed the cross into the gris-gris bag and shook it. Black smoke boiled out of the bag, tarry and sour-smelling. When the smoke cleared, I dumped the contents into my knobby-knuckled palm. Fragile bones, mixed dried herbs, a tooth, and three clay tiles fell out. The demon was part frog, part boar, part alligator—frog body and back legs, boar tusks, bristly hair, and a little twirled tail, alligator skin, frog mouth full of alligator teeth. And arms muscled like a gorilla. Using my index finger, I pushed around the contents. There was a jawbone of a very large frog or toad. The boar hair was tied with a string. The white tooth was probably an alligator's. The tiles were rough, etched with figures of a frog, a boar, and an alligator. I rubbed one and it felt like dried mud.

Of course. I held it to the yellowed light and decided the mud had been mixed with sacrificial blood before it was shaped and dried. Something had died to make the gris-gris. It was black magic.

But Margaud wasn't a witch. She was human. So where had she . . . ?

Things began to pop up and slide together in my mind, like some weird puzzle forming all by it itself. Margaud and her brothers were Moutons. The brothers had shown up at Lucky's with Solene, the coven leader, who was Lucky's sister. The Moutons were vamp haters from way back. Lucky was a vamp hater from way back. Solene hadn't seemed any too happy to be sharing the town with suckheads. Solene and Lucky were related to the Bordelon sisters, one of whom had been their grandmother, and the sisters had fought the vamps to a stalemate in the town's vamp war.

Had the Bordelon sisters used a gris-gris? Had they called up a demon?

Through the window something flew, slowly, ungainly, tumbling through the air. Gee DiMercy. But he didn't fall, tuck, and roll. Blue and pink and lavender magics boiled out from his slight form and in an instant he sprouted feathers, spread his wings, and caught an air current. He glided across the yard, barely maintaining altitude above the ground. He flapped once as he crossed into the street, trying to make it over the witch circles. He wasn't successful. His wingtips brushed the top of the *electric dog collar* and the *hedge of thorns* where they met at the top. Black and silver sparks flew, slightly faster than the rain. The acrid stink of burned feathers filled the air.

And the wards exploded.

The Gray Between caught me up, and time simply . . . stopped. The falling magics looked like slowly burning paper, blackening and scorching in arcs of heat, with flaming lights at the edges. Raindrops hung in the air. I didn't look at the droplets. I knew better. They held the possibilities of future timelines, spreading out from this moment, from the decisions I made in this moment, possibilities that affected everything and everyone. If I looked at them I could be paralyzed, unable to act, afraid that anything I might do would mess up everything for everyone else. So I didn't look. I didn't even want to.

I dropped the gris-gris' contents to the porch floor and crushed it all between my paw pad and the old, painted wood. It made a strange grinding sound, the tiles breaking. The cross hadn't stopped him, so that meant that even this might not stop the swamp thing, but it should do *something* to the demon. Weakening it would help, at the very least. As I ruined the spell, my guts twisted horribly. The pain felt like someone was dragging my intestines out of my abdomen and braiding them into a long, plaited coil.

Nausea rose, tasting of blood and bile. I gagged. I didn't have long.

When the tiles were dust, I walked back inside, where the fight was still taking place, found a small escritoire with paper and pens inside. I wrote a note to Eli explaining what I had figured out, about Solene Mouton probably helping Margaud, trying to drive a wedge between vamps and witches. I folded the page and tucked it into Eli's hand, where he'd feel it in real time. Then I stuck the mud monster with a silver-plated blade about fifty times. Surely that should do it.

Satisfied I had done all I could do in here, I shoved off from the porch, leaping through the air, faster than time, splashing through raindrops hanging still in the night. Racing toward the center of the street. Seeing the wards as they fell, breaks appearing in long striations of fractured energies. Seeing, *knowing* the weakened places in the magics. I bladed my body through a tear in the outer ward, my pelt sizzling and stinking. I raced between witches and spun through the inner ward. It bent and gave and fell beneath me.

I took two steps through the center of the circle, stooped, and picked up the wreath. *La corona. Le breloque.* I pushed off the asphalt and landed on the far side of the witch circle. Moments later I was half a block away, bent over, retching. Blood pooled on the wet pavement beneath me. Time had returned to normal. Or I had returned to normal time. It was confusing.

I gripped my middle and kneaded the twisted steel of my muscles. And once again the heavens opened up and rain assaulted the earth.

I looked up and saw, in the distance, Lucky Landry, Edmund Hartley, and Clermont Doucette walk from the ruined house and into the street. The vamps were no longer sporting swords, so crushing the tiles must have killed the demon, or sent him back where he came from. Whatever. I'd take it. The witches in the circle were screaming. I could hear them in the distance. The rain that had started above me raced across the street and hit them too. Lightning jagged down, the sound booming. It was close. I had no desire to be hit by lightning again. Once in my lifetime was enough. I looked around for the Anzu, wondering if he had called down the current storm.

I pushed up from the water-runnelled pavement. My other hand was . . . gripping the wreath.

I have the wreath.

I have stopped the demon.

And I might live.

I hid in the storm, walking away from the clamor in the main intersection of town and into the first weedy lot after the row of businesses and shops. The last business in the row had a newly applied sheet of plywood on the side wall, half-hidden by weeds . . . covering a hole. I remembered when the hole had been made. Lucky had thrown a bowling-ball-shaped keep-away spell at me and missed, trying to kill me when we first hit town. The nails holding the plywood in place didn't hold up to the strip of metal I used like a crowbar to expose the hole into the beauty shop. It was tight, but I was able to step through and I shook myself like a dog, my pelt shedding water that went everywhere. Following the trajectory to the inside wall, I found another piece of plywood and pried it off too.

I ended back in Lucky's shop and raided the beer cooler. Three beers later, even my skinwalker metabolism was feeling pretty good, if hungry. So I raided the refrigerated meat counter and settled to a table with a fourth beer, a beef roast of some unknown cut, a dish of pulled pork barbecue, a half loaf of bread, and some slaw that smelled heavenly, even to my Beast. And I ate most of it before Eli managed to pick the lock on Boudreaux's Meats and get in out of the rain.

He closed the door behind him and switched on a small but powerful flashlight. He caught the broken plywood first. Then me. I figured Alex had found me by tracking my cell phone. I had hoped the rain and the magic had shorted the thing out. No such luck.

"You leave any for me?" Eli asked.

"Not only that, I made you a sandwich." I pointed to the last sandwich, one I had really made for myself, but this was much better and made me sound unselfish. Maybe even noble, since it did involve food. Eli grabbed a beer and straddled the bench beside me. He gathered up the oversized sandwich and took a huge bite. I hadn't known his mouth could open that wide.

"Not bad," he said as he chewed. "But with Lucky's meats, even you couldn't make a mess of it."

"Ha-ha." I pushed over the open container of slaw. It bumped the edge of the flashlight and sent the beam rolling crazily for a moment. "I left you some, but there was only one fork."

"You don't got cooties, do you?"

"Yup. Girl cooties. But I'm pretty sure you can't get them from eating after me."

Eli chortled and nearly choked. When he got his airway clear he asked, "You got the wreath?"

"Yup."

He nodded contemplatively as he chewed. Pulled his cell and sent a quick text before putting the phone in his pocket. He ate a bite of slaw and made appreciative noises that might have been *This is good*, if he hadn't been chewing at the same time. He swallowed and said, "The demon melted into a puddle of mud and Margaud was unconscious under a tree outside. You do all that?"

"Yup."

"That's my girl." He lifted a fist and I bumped it, but he wasn't done. Carefully expressionless in face and tone, he asked, "You bleed much?"

"Not as much as last time. It was pretty bad until I got some beers into me."

Eli looked over the table and onto the floor where I had started placing empties inside the wreath. "Eight beers?"

"So far."

"You drunk?"

"Oddly enough, pretty much. I'm thinking that bending time does something wonky to my metabolism."

"You're still pelted."

"Yeah. I noticed."

"You and Bruiser ever—"

"No. Do not go there. *Ewww.*"

Eli chuckled and ate more of his sandwich and I realized he was teasing me. Through the bite, he asked, "What are you going to do with the wreath?"

"I don't know. But for sure the vamps and the witches here won't see it again."

"And where's the Anzu?"

I ate some meat, using my fingers to stuff it in. Licked my fingers. The paw pads felt weird on my tongue. I opened another beer. Drained it halfway. I kinda liked having a buzz, even if it meant I was going to be an alky and go to hell, according to some of my housemothers as I was growing up. "I haven't decided about that," I said. I picked up *la corona* and placed it on my pelted head at a jaunty angle. "Gee calls me *little goddess.* I think I'll wear it for a while. You know. All goddess-like. With a crown. Before I decide." I ate some more meat as Eli finished his sandwich.

"I guess we should pay for this stuff," he said. "Think forty will cover it?"

I shrugged and Eli tossed two twenties into the light of the flash.

"You did it, you know," he said. "You got the vamps and witches talking and the Moutons will be brought under the watchful eye of the newly appointed Bayou Oiseau Citizens' Council."

"Self-appointed?"

"Yeah. But it's a multiracial, multispecies, multigender council, so it's a start. And it's better than what they had. Which was nothing."

I pointed to the wreath on my head. "It's what we goddesses do. We fix stuff."

"True," Eli said, his face amused. "Do you want or need to go back and accept kudos from the citizens council of BO?"

"No freaking way." I scowled at him. "But I need to go back for my stuff and get the guys."

"Already taken care of."

"Swwweeeet." I boxed up a mixed six-pack of cold beer and stuck it under my left arm. Picked up the M4, which had somehow ended up on the floor with the wreath, which had somehow found a way from my head to the floor. I nearly fell when I stood.

"Am I going to have to carry you to the SUV?" Eli asked.

"I don't know. Things are kinda whirly right now. How far do we have to walk?"

"I texted Alex and your vampire babysitter earlier. There's an SUV idling out front. It's most likely them."

"And if it *isn't* them?"

"We'll shoot our way out."

I grinned at him, showing my blunt human incisors and elongated big-cat canines.

Eli said, "Edmund. He's pretty good with a sword."

"Yeah. I saw. Maybe better than Grégoire." I placed the crown back on my head and adjusted my grip on the shotgun. Steadied myself on the table's edge.

Eli was watching, not helping, which was good. He said, "Ed's too good to have lost a Blood Challenge for clan blood-master. Too good to be wanting to be an Enforcer's primo. Something's up his sleeve. You got any idea what?"

"Plans and schemes and tactics and strategies all layered up with some hubris into a nice, neat plot to take over the world? Or at least the vampire world."

"Think we can shoot our way out of that one?"

I tried to take a step and the world whirled slowly. "Pretty sure we can do anything, partner." I put a hand on his shoulder to catch my balance. "Let's go home before the delegation from Rome gets here and stirs the pot."

"And where are you gonna hide the wreath until we figure who it belongs to?"

I already knew who it probably belonged to—the Birdman of New Orleans, or one of his kind. But I wasn't ready to hand it over. Not yet. Maybe not ever. "Looks like I'll be renting another safe-deposit box. A big one this time. And we'll need to wrap the interior with lead."

"You're getting quite a collection of magical trinkets."

I grunted. I knew that. And I didn't like it one bit.

"We'll need to come back and gather up the principals for a parley with the NOLA fangheads and witches," Eli said.

"You think you can get the helo? I could go for a kidnapping and forced negotiations at knifepoint if we could do it fast."

Eli nodded. "I can make that happen. Are you going to shift back into human anytime soon? Or are you too drunk?"

"I am not drunk," I said. "Not exactly. But I don't think I can shift back anytime soon. And I probably shouldn't let the witches see me like this." I pointed to my face and body in a little twirling motion.

Eli's mouth resisted a smile. "You think they'll try to take you prisoner?"

"Witches can try," Beast said through my mouth.

Eli led the way to the door. "We'll get out of here before anyone knows what's what. The lead foil came in last week. We can line your bank boxes anytime you want."

I nodded. "Let's go home."

Bound No More

Author's note: This short story takes place (in the JY timeline) after *Dark Heir*.

"Your goddaughter is driving me out of my blessed mind," Molly said, sounding frustrated and more Southern that she usually did.

Funny how the seven-year-old became *my goddaughter* when she was being difficult. I grinned into the cell, knowing Molly wouldn't know I was laughing at her. With her. Whatever. My voice solemn, I asked, "What am I supposed to do about it? If I'm reading the time right, you're still laying over in Atlanta, which makes me still about six hundred miles away. "

"Talk to her. She fell asleep on the first leg of the flight and— *Stop it*, Angelina Everhart Trueblood, or I'll turn around and take you back home." Into the phone, she said, "What I want is for you to tell her it was a bad dream and nothing is wrong."

Something in my chest squeezed tight for a moment. "Dream?"

"Son of a witch on a switch," Molly cursed in witch vernacular.

"Aunt Jane, you there?" It was Angie Baby, aka Angelina, my oldest godchild and the love of my heart. The stress in my chest eased away and the smile was real this time. Angie didn't sound distressed or afraid, she sounded angry.

"Yup. It's me." I leaned on the couch and pulled a soft, fuzzy throw over me. The Kid had turned up the AC and it was freezing in here. Outside, rain fell, splashing into the puddles, pounding on the roof, trickling down the rain gutters, rushing toward the street and New Orleans' storm water drainage system. Taken together, it made a melodious sound, the varying and harmonious sounds of rain. I had learned to love it. "What's up, Angie Baby?"

"You gots to get up outta your sofa and protect the scaberteeth lion bone."

I was on my feet so fast the couch nearly flipped over. A half second later, Eli, one of my partners in Yellowrock Securities, rounded the corner, a nine-millimeter handgun in each hand. "Backyard," I said, taking the weapon Eli slapped into my palm.

"Round in the chamber, safety on," he said. "Whadda we got?"

"Don't know. Angie"—I held up the cell for him to see—"had a dream about the sabertooth lion skull, which I hid in the boulder pile."

Eli grunted and pulled a vamp-killer. My partner was a two-handed fighter.

"It could be anything." *Or nothing*, but I didn't say that. Eli already knew it. Angie had strong witchy powers, for sure, but she was barely in school yet. She was a kid. Kids make mistakes.

Eli opened the middle door from the living room. Half juggling the cell, I pulled open the door closest to the backyard. All the doors out of the living room onto the porch were new, and mine stuck, swollen by the rain. I yanked, and when it opened, it nearly hit me in the face. I slid out onto the slick porch floor a half second behind my partner.

"Don't hurt it, Aunt Jane!" Angie demanded, her voice tinny, so far from my ear. "Just stop it! Quick! Hurry!"

But I couldn't hurry. I stopped, breathing fast and shallow, staring out over my backyard. Beside me, Eli stopped too, his breathing even and slow, his scent charged with testosterone and adrenaline. "Is that what I think it is?"

"A mostly naked teenage girl kneeling in the mud, digging under my rocks? I think so." The girl was dark-skinned, with long, kinked, black-, copper-, brown-, pale white-, and silver-streaked hair plastered to her shoulders and back. My Beast pushed to the surface and took in the girl. In Beast sight, she writhed with energies, powerful, supercharged, magical strength. All in rainbow shades of light. "I think she's a juvie *arcenciel*, playing in the mud. And Angie says we can't hurt it. Her."

Eli made a soft grunt of acknowledgement and holstered his gun. Standard ammo didn't hurt *arcenciels*, the term for dragons made of light. Neither did silver. Only steel. Angie could say we couldn't hurt her all day long, but if the *arcenciel* was a threat—and my experience suggested that they often were—we might have no choice. Eli would stay armed. He kept the fourteen-inch steel and silver-plated vamp-killer in his right hand and drew a black steel KA-BAR Tanto knife with his left. He wasn't wearing a shirt or shoes. The steamy air landed on his taut chest with a misty sheen.

"Aunt Jane! *Hurry!*"

"Okay, Angie. I got it. Love you." I disconnected and placed both the nine mil and the cell on the wet porch floor. The juvenile *arcenciel* couldn't have missed our entrance to the backyard. We hadn't been covert or quiet and were standing within feet of her in what passed for broad daylight in New Orleans in a rainstorm. But she was ignoring us thoroughly, as she clawed with her hands beneath the boulder and pulled out a rounded mound of mud. She was slicked with it. Leaning down, she reached back under the boulder, into the muddy little cave, and began to scrape more mud to her.

Behinds us, Alex, the third member of Yellowrock Securities, said, "Camera's running. So far she shows on digital footage."

When *arcenciels* were in human form they photographed fairly well on digital and film. When they were in their light-dragon form, digital was often nearly useless and film only slightly better.

"Angie says she's after the sabertooth lion skull," I told Alex.

"She say why?"

"No. Just that we can't let her have it and we can't hurt her."

The *arcenciel* whipped her head around at my words and hissed at me the way vipers do, mouth open, showing teeth. Lots and lots of sharp, pointed shark teeth, glinting like pearls. So she knew English. Interesting. No one really knew what *arcenciels* were or where they came from. Just shape-shifters, time benders, and not from around here—as in not from Earth.

"And the skull's out *there*?" Eli asked.

"Not usually," I said, lowering my voice so that the rain muffled it. "But with Angie on the way, and her being so nosy and having access to everything inside, I put a bunch of stuff in the yard. In hindsight that may have been stupid."

"You should have put it in the safe room."

"No. Angie mighta spotted a magical signature in the safe room, and then she would have known the room was under the stairs. With all the things that kill people."

Eli grunted his understanding. "Whadda we do?"

The *arcenciel* pulled another armful of mud from beneath the boulder, or what was left of the boulder from the last time I had borrowed mass from it. I'm a skinwalker, and when I need to take on a form that is bigger than my own mass, I borrow it from something with no genetic material of its own. Hence, boulders that get busted.

A storm front had stalled over the gulf region, and it had been raining for so long that the earth beneath the pile of rocks was muddy, and the stone was slowly sinking. In another twenty years, the pile of once-massive stones that I had managed to break and crack and shatter would disappear beneath the surface of the alluvial mud. Faster if the *arcenciel* kept up her digging. With a sudden move, the boulder rolled toward her and dropped into the trench she had dug, trapping her hands, wrists, and lower arms. The creature screamed and writhed, jerking her body, and I had a spike of visual memory, intense and sharp, of a . . .

A fox caught in metal teeth, trying to rip off its leg and be free. Stinking of fear and blood and death. A man was above it, watching.

Trap, *strange thing inside me thought.*

From high above, saw weapon crash down on fox, shattering fox skull. Blood flew. Man's back paw stamped down, pushed down hard beside metal teeth. Trap opened. Beast's eyes went wide, staring. Interested. *Man pulled fox free. Man stood and stuffed dead fox into bag at waist. Reset trap and put small piece of meat in center. Scattered leaves over it. Man walked away, boots loud in brush.*

A white man. *Yunega.* A trapper, *strange voice thought.*

Man stank of whiskey, blood, unwashed body. Beast studied steel cage of death. Trap. *Remembered the way* yunega *had freed dead fox.*

Beast can do that. Free trapped prey. Eat those that Beast wants. Others go free, *strange thing inside of head thought. Strange thing with strange thoughts. Should not be inside with Beast. Strange thing that struggled to be free. Struggled to see through Beast's eyes. Struggled to be like alpha in pack. Beast should be alone. Beast pressed paw onto strange thing in mind and it went still. Beast leaped from rock ledge and landed beside trap. Picked up stick and dropped onto trap. Steel teeth clanged shut.*

Beast reached in and sniffed stinky meat.

Bait, *strange thing inside thought.*

Bait, *Beast thought back, testing meaning. Ate scrap of meat. Beast hungered. Keeping paws on matted leaves, Beast followed* yunega. Will eat all bait. Will not hunger.

"Jane?"

I blinked, the world whirling around me. Eli had my upper arm in his fingers. Steadying me. "Sorry. Tell you later," I said. Stepping carefully off the back end of the porch, I placed my feet on the wet grass. Rainwater squished up through my toes, cool and fresh. The *arcenciel* whipped her head to me and her eyes glowed. She hissed again.

I showed my empty hands. "No steel," I said, thinking of the trapped fox. "I can help you get free."

The juvie went still, the way water goes still on a full-moon night, reflecting everything, black and white and harsh with shadows. "Free?" Her voice was raspy and coarse, as if she hadn't used it in a while. "Free is . . . safe. Free is . . . desired."

"Uh-huh. Right." I had no idea why the *arcenciel* didn't simply change shape and get free that way, but she didn't. Body balanced, knees slightly bent, I took a step toward her.

The *arcenciel* said, "I will never be free." She shifted shape into light-dragon form, rainbows sparking off her like sparklers and fireworks. Her dragon form was feathery, luminous shades of the rainbow sparkling with brighter motes. Her cotton candy hair flew on an unseen wind, white, stripped with red and black and brown.

In the instant she shifted, I realized several things, all of them what Beast had been trying to tell me: The *arcenciel* had been luring me in. *This* was a trap. The skull was bait for *me*. The *arcenciel* had come for *me* as well as the skull. And I was too stupid to figure out what the ancient memory had meant. Deep inside, I felt Beast chuff with delight. *Beast is best hunter. Good fight with light predator.*

The light dragon launched herself at me. But before she hit, she was back in human shape. She slammed into me, elbow to my gut. I *oof*ed in pain and flew back with her, feet in the air, to the ground, into the mud. She landed atop me, the elbow still in my gut. Something tore inside.

Drawing on Beast, I wrapped my legs around her waist and rolled over in the mud, loosening her hold, hitting her with a bare fist as hard as I could into her nose. And with Beast so close, I could *hit*. A human nose would have cracked and flattened beneath my knuckles, but her nose gave way in a shower of sparks and seemed to suck my entire hand into her face with a slurping sound and a cascade of sparks. The inside of her was painful, like a mild electric current enveloping my hand. Hot and gummy. Which was gross. Until I realized two things. Rainbow dragons might pack an electrical punch as big as one of those electric eels, five hundred volts. Enough to stun a human. And I had recently been hit by lightning and nearly died. Every nerve ending across my entire body crawled at the thought of being hit again.

Beast fast, I ripped my hand free and rolled again. Punching her mouth, her eyes, her temples. Nothing seemed to faze her. Worse, I had no weapons. No gun. No blades. I risked a glance from the girl to the porch. Got a glimpse of Eli moving, bending.

If the *arcenciel* bit me, I'd be poisoned, and it wasn't as if I had immediate access to the antidote. No. That was hanging in Leo's deepest subbasement, literally a heartless bag of torn flesh and bone riddled with silver ammo. But the light dragon didn't seem to be desirous of biting me. Instead she hit me back, and if I hadn't turned my face at the last instant, she would have broken my jaw. I backhanded her and got a good handful of her hair with my other hand. I wrapped her hair around my fist and around her head and yanked.

We rolled through the mud, and I slammed her head into the boulder she had been digging under. Her skull hit with a satisfying *crack*, and she went still. I was gasping and hurting and managed to stand, one hand on the boulder. She wasn't moving. Didn't seem to be breathing. I had maybe killed a dragon. *Oh man. No.* I nudged her with my bare foot. Her head lolled. I bent to check for a pulse, but there was nothing. Did an *arcenciel* even have a pulse? They were full of a sparkly ectoplasmic goo, not blood. No internal organs that I could recognize. I lifted her eyelid to reveal an opalescent eye with a slit pupil that narrowed when the dim light hit it. Assuming she had reflexes to light, she was still alive.

I started to drop the eyelid when the pupil sharpened in focus. I leaped back just in time to avoid a slash of rainbow-hued horns. It shifted in an instant and I jumped back again. Its body was vaguely snakelike, iridescent scales the color of tinted glass and thick storm clouds, with hints of copper. It smelled like green herbs burning over hot coals and the tang of fish and water plants. The *arcenciel* vanished in a sparkle of light and a spray of harsh magic that burned on my arms and dried the mud into a brittle crust.

I stepped to the other boulder she had been digging beneath and pulled on Beast-strength to roll it away. My gut heaved from the elbow it had taken, and my breath came fast and faint. Beneath the boulder, in a hole I had dug the day before, was an oversized plastic Ziploc bag containing a waterproof vinyl bag full of magical stuff—the few things not under lock and key in various safe-deposit boxes—and the skull. I slid the bags from the muck and removed the vinyl gobag. I slung it over my shoulder and around my body to my back, where it gave a satisfying *thump*. So much for all the plans of mice and Humpty Dumpty.

I slapped the mud off my arms and legs and kicked it from my feet in big clumps. Holding my aching belly, I stood as straight as possible and looked at the porch. Eli and his brother sat in matching dented, rusted metal garden chairs, rocking back and forth on the bent-metal-tube frames. Eli was sipping a beer. Alex was sipping an energy drink. They both were grinning and broke into polite applause.

"Chick fight," Eli said.

"Chick fight *in the mud*," Alex amended.

"Thought she was gonna take you for a minute there, babe."

The sky opened up and spilled half an ocean onto me. At least it washed away the mud. I made it to the porch through the downpour, where I managed to climb up to the wood flooring and fall into the remaining chair. Eli had picked the old, rusty chairs up at a yard sale for five bucks each. Twenty dollars for the four. I had thought it was waste of money until now, when the chair bore my weight and settled me into a comfortable rocking motion. I was still breathing painfully, and I pulled up my T to reveal a bruise starting to form, just below my ribs and above my navel. This was gonna hurt.

The rain fell so powerfully that it splashed up when it hit, the microdroplets forming a mist similar to fog, obscuring the boulders and the brick fence beyond. Eli opened a beer and passed it to me. I put the vinyl bag on the floor and swallowed down half.

"Lemme have my cell. I need to call Soul."

Eli handed me the official Kevlar-armored cell, and I flipped it open, tapping the image for the PsyLED agent—a tiny, multicolored gecko. Soul answered on the third ring. I heard her say to someone else, "It's Jane."

From a distance I heard an unexpected voice say, "Hey, Jane."

"Jodi?" Jodi worked with the local PD, in charge of the woo-woo team, my term for paranormal cases. PsyLED was a federal woo-woo agency under Homeland Security. The two law enforcement officers shouldn't be in the same place at the same time. Then I put it together. The Witch Council of the entire U.S. was happening in few weeks. Both the president and the governor—usually fierce opponents—had expressed an interest in the Witch Conclave and the meeting between the witches and vamps that would happen on the last day. It was to be a parley, a vamp term meaning to negotiate and come to a legal agreement, like a peace accord. The powers that be wanted the witches and the vamps to sign a treaty and bury the hatchet, and not in one another's backs.

Making certain that everything worked out well and that nothing outside interfered with the attempt at rapprochement required that the entire city be secure from hate groups and terrorist groups, homegrown and imported, paranormal and mundane. Security for a whole city might involve PsyLED. Yellowrock Securities was concerned with the micro parts—the security of the mansion where the big weekend-long affair was to take place, security at vamp HQ, and security during travel times, when the witches rode the streetcar from their hotels to the mansion hosting the event, and later, when Leo Pellissier was limoed in. "Are you out of town with Soul or is Soul in New Orleans?"

"We're eating at Coop's Place on Decatur. We just got here. Come join us."

I looked down at myself. Thank God I had put on a bra, or I'd look like I belonged in a wet T-shirt contest. But I'd still need to change. "Order Eli and me the gumbo with extra seafood and we'll be there in twenty." I tapped END and looked at Eli, who still wore a faint smirk. "I'll get dry and change and meet you out front."

"I take it I'm driving?"

"Until I can breathe without pain, yes."

Alex said, "Bring me a shrimp po'boy with extra lettuce and tomato."

Eli stood and followed me inside to put on a shirt and shoes. Even in the Deep South, the "no shirt, no shoes, no service" protocol reigned.

Five minutes later I was clean and dry except for my wet hair, which I braided in a single long plait down my back. It took too long to dry as much hair as I had, but I'd have to get to it soon. Wet hair in this weather could get rank. I strapped a set of small throwing knives to my calf, which I could reach under jeans. I'd rather be better armed, but with cops around, even cops I knew well, no gun and no obvious, oversized bladed weapon was my best choice. I slid into loose jeans and a T, with the long sleeves pushed up to my elbows.

I set the vinyl bag with the skull in it on the floor in the closet and removed a small wooden carving of a crow. It was carved from ebony and had been brushed with some inky stain that darkened the knife cuts even more than the smoothed wood. The crow contained Molly's new, modified, portable working—what nonwitches called a *spell*—an updated version of her *hedge of thorns* ward. I tapped the crow's claws with my fingernail, which opened the hedge over the crow and the vinyl bag, protecting it and everything inside. Even the *arcenciel* would have trouble getting to it without a major singeing. I no longer had to spill blood to set such a prearranged ward—except the big one out back, which I hadn't used in months. Satisfied that no one could get to the skull and the spelled charms Molly had made, not without getting hurt badly in the process, I headed out.

Coop's advertised itself as the place where the not-so-elite ate. It was a renovated old building so close to the Mississippi that I could feel the faint vibration of the river moving beneath my feet. It was bar dark inside and smelled of beer and drunks and excellent food. Today it also reeked with excitement because someone had just won it big at one of the video poker machines.

Our food was waiting when we got there and I slid into a booth next to Jodi. Eli took the place next to Soul and said, "Ladies."

We dug into the food and when my appetite was moderately appeased—mud wrestling with an *arcenciel* used up a lot of energy—I held up my glass so the waitperson could see that I needed more iced tea and said, "I had a visit from your old friend, the chick who always wears rainbow dresses."

Soul had been reaching for a French fry and she made the faintest of flinches. *The chick who always wears rainbow dresses* was an unmistakable code for an *arcenciel*. "When?" she asked, sounding unconcerned and maybe even casual. I'd have totally bought it if I hadn't seen that tiny flinch. "I wasn't aware she was still around."

Eli looked at his watch and said, "She showed up thirty-three minutes ago. She and Jane had a four-minute-and-two-second mud wrestle in the backyard and then she took off."

Jodi laughed. Soul didn't. I didn't know a lot about *arcenciels*, but the fact that an *arcenciel* stayed around for a battle she didn't have to fight seemed unusual. That she fought in human form seemed unusual. The fact that she didn't draw on her ability to alter or bubble time to win the fight seemed unusual. Pretty much everything about the situation seemed unusual, including Angie's prescient dream and the call to warn me. I had to address that too—soon, but not in front of present company.

I asked, "So, you didn't know she was in town?"

"I knew. She was spotted by a CI, but I haven't had *time* to *see* her," Soul said, with subtle emphasis on the words *time* and *see*. Soul was an *arcenciel* too, and when one of her kind bubbled time, she would know it if she was paying attention. More stuff Jodi couldn't know.

"CI?" I asked.

"Confidential informant, which means she won't tell either one of us. Who the heck did your CI see?" Jodi asked. "Girl in a rainbow dress? Some kind of code word?"

"No. A distant relative," Soul said, shoveling a spoonful of boudin onto a sliver of toast made from French bread. "The only one of her generation in the States."

Which explained how she knew which *arcenciel* I was talking about. *Arcenciels* didn't bear young easily or often, and the presence of a young one would have been noted and observed, at the very least.

"Her name is Opal," Soul said. "She is . . . young and creative and willful. I understand that she has taken a shine to Jane and has dropped in unexpectedly. Twice now, once on the other side of the Mississippi, once at your house, for a sparring session, yes?"

At which I nodded, realizing that Opal had to be the rainbow dragon who had attacked me in my SUV not that long ago and nearly managed to get me killed. "Sparring match, my butt," I said.

"I am truly sorry at her intemperance. She is innocence personified, but manages to be a troublemaker." She took the bite and gave me a look that told me to drop it, and that we could talk later, when a human cop wasn't present.

I wasn't exactly sure what *intemperance* meant, but I shrugged and said, "Nothing I can't handle." *Maybe. Hopefully.* "So fill me in on the city's security for the Witch Conclave and Eli can fill you in on YS's part."

Eli shot me an indecipherable look and asked, "Why can't you fill them in?"

"If I had intended to talk, I wouldn't have needed you here. I'm eating." And I did, all through the boring and tedious discussion of traffic and buses and streetcars and hotel security and stuff I used to have to handle. Having partners had freed up a lot of my time and let me take on bigger and better jobs. The job as security had come through Molly, and thanks to my partners, YS was making a lot of money for the one weekend, freeing me personally to be Leo's Enforcer at the same event. Couldn't beat getting paid two times for the same job.

As soon as Jodi finished the debrief, she slid out of the seat and was gone, leaving a twenty on the table to cover her tab and tip. The moment she was gone, Soul said, "Tell me everything that Opal did and said."

I pulled up my shirt and showed her my bruise, which was starting to turn a bright, spreading red where all the small arterioles and capillaries had been damaged by the elbow. I told her everything that had happened, excluding Angie's part. In this version, we were sitting on the porch having a beer and enjoying the rain when Opal appeared and started digging around in the backyard. I finished with, "I had hidden a few of Molly's magical trinkets out there along with a skull Leo gave me, a sabertooth lion skull used by the sabertooth vamp I killed when I first got to town."

"What do you think she was there for?"

"I've had the spelled trinkets in the house for months, and the skull had been buried out back on other occasions, so I can't say." I stopped, my tea halfway to my mouth. "But I've never had them all in the same place at the same time before. So . . . maybe some kind of magical energy symbiosis? Something that drew her attention?"

Soul sighed and slid from the booth too, tossing down a second twenty. The waiter was going to have a good tip day. "I don't know," Soul said. "Keep me in the loop." And she was gone too.

Eli helped himself to their boudin leftovers. I ate the leftover fries. When Alex's to-go bag was deposited on the table, we each tossed a few bills on top and went back outside into the drizzle and the unexpected cool from the storm front. Autumn wasn't far off and the slightly cooler temps of the chilly eighties promised that the frigid seventies were not far behind. Molly would be here soon, and the cooler temps would make her visit more pleasant. Molly hated hot, humid weather.

Little Evan and his dad were still in Asheville, which proved that Angie and Molly weren't staying long, just long enough so Molly could meet with the NOLA witches and assist with the final group workings that would be used as the witch part of security. Witches were coming from all over and Molly and Lachish Dutillet, the head of the New Orleans coven, had a big job to prepare for. But even short stays in New Orleans were expensive, and so my BFF and goddaughter were staying with us. There was plenty of room in the five-bedroom, three-bath house for them to each have their own space, but this time they would be sharing the bedroom over mine, because the boys were painting the other guest room, which we ordinarily used as a workout room.

I'd had the entire house cleaned, had new linens put on the twin beds, and made it clear that the werewolf who spent some nights in Alex's room had to stay downstairs and not scare the guests. I was pretty sure that Brute understood me, but when a were-creature spent too long in his animal form the brain began to lose its human characteristics and spoken language was one of the first things to go. Since the angel Hayyel had touched Brute in some metaphysical manner unknown to the rest of us, he hadn't been able to shift to human. Brute wasn't very human at all anymore.

I was watching out the front window when Mol parked her rental car, a nifty Ford Fusion, a block down from the house. I was out the front door before she got the door open and gathered her and Angie and the cat travel box into a big group hug. I didn't hug many people, but Molly was family from way back, as much as I had family from way back. Kids raised in children's homes usually had limited family ties, but the Everharts and Truebloods were family of the heart, if not of the blood. "It's so good to see you both," I said softly into Angie's strawberry blond curls as I crushed mother and daughter and cat box to me. Angie's feet dangled off the sidewalk. Molly smelled of perfume, which she didn't usually wear around me, tart and sweet, flowery and lemony, like roses and lemongrass, a strange combination that made me want to sneeze. My inner voice held a hint of growl as Beast laid claim to Angie, with the thought, *Kitssss* . . .

"I missed you so much!" I growled aloud.

"I know, Aunt Jane," Angie said, her feet kicking. "You and your Beastie big-cat love us, and we love you. Now lemme down! I wanna go inside!" She kicked, her knee narrowly missing my tender belly, and I set her on the pavement.

"Door's open. Your room's ready," I told her.

Angie took off for the house and I grabbed the luggage from Mol. Being a skinwalker meant being stronger than I looked, and Molly usually packed light. This time was no exception, although the cat cage was getting heavier. KitKit was asleep inside, heavily drugged. And there were scratches up Molly's arms.

I tucked the cage under my elbow and the two bags in each hand.

We were halfway to the house when I heard Angie scream.

I leaped the distance and inside. Dropped the luggage. The suitcase, tote, and cat cage didn't fall. They hung there in the air. I had bubbled time—or Beast had—and I hadn't even noticed. Silver mist and silver-blue motes of power danced around me, coming from within me. Time vibrated and wobbled and my gut twisted tight. Acid rose in my throat. Angie's scream hung on the air, a deep warble, like a siren.

Alex was half standing behind his modified desk in the living room, his eyes wide and fearful. Eli was midleap in the doorway to the living area, drawing his nine mil, his face expressionless. I looked where Eli was looking—into my bedroom. I stepped inside, the deep sound of Angie's scream thudding into my eardrums.

It was coming from Angelina, which I had known, but not the *why*. She was in my closet, on her knees, her hands on and in the *hedge of thorns*. And the hedge, newly modified by Mol, had manacled the little girl's wrists and was giving her a mild electrical shock.

Part of me was horrified and lurched toward her. Another part stopped me. And sent me a shock of vision, of a puma kitten tottering on the edge of a ledge. And my/our clawed paw reaching out to her. Swiping her back inside the ledge. A little too rough. But making a point. *Teaching kit,* Beast thought at me.

Child abuse, I thought back, kneeling beside Angie.

Beast chuffed at me in disgust.

Not now, I thought back at her. Mountain lions and the Cherokee had very different feelings and instincts about how to raise their young, and I wasn't going to argue with my other soul. I studied the hedge, its energies a dull red of smooth shimmering light. In most wards, the energies were a coruscating light pattern, a roiling of thick and thin, fluidlike, waterlike power, or banded like an agate, or ringed like Saturn. Sometimes even a licking flame. But always there were weak spots in it. Not this time. The hedge was a ruby red, smooth as polished glass, except for the manacles that had trapped Angie's hands at the wrists. That was actually a second working wrapped inside the first, blue energies sweeping up out of the hedge and coating Angie's skin. I could see the tiny sparks of electric energy arc out and snap at Angie's flesh.

This was new. Entirely new. Which was important, but it was more important to release Angie from the discomfort it was causing.

Molly's family had created the original *hedge* spell and taken the unprecedented step of sharing it with other witches. They had given it, free of barter, to the New Orleans coven. I had thought it was to cement relations with the different covens, but now I realized that the gift had been an easy one to share because the Everhart sisters had already devised an update. *Hedge of thorns 2.0.* A better, faster, sneakier working. One I couldn't figure out how to break, once it had been initiated, even seeing it out of time.

I saw Angie's pinky finger move. The tiniest little tremor, a quiver of a fingertip. A black light arced out from that fingertip to zap the manacles.

Black light. Black . . . black *magic* full of darkness and prism sparkles. Something I had never seen before, or at least not like this. Black light with a hint of purple, a trace of blue, a faint reddish tinge around the edges. A second arc of black light zapped out. And a third. And the blue manacles began to fail, to disintegrate. Angie was using a type of magic I had never seen before, except once when a crazy vamp clan was about to sacrifice witches to accomplish a blood-magic working. Sacrifice Angie and her baby brother.

This was bad. This was very bad.

Angie was way too young to have access to her magic, which wasn't supposed to manifest until puberty. She had been bound by her parents, her magic tightened around her like a second skin, still there, but not available to her. It was a binding that had been explained to me, how they'd done it, how it worked, like knitting magical swaddling clothes around her. I had seen them renew it as she grew, and it had to be renewed often, but it was a binding she had begun to notice, and probably fight against. And clearly that binding had stopped working. Again.

My gut tightened and twisted again and I pressed a fist against the pain. I hadn't done anything but walk while time was bubbled, but that was enough. Bubbling or twisting or bending time made me sick. If I didn't stop soon enough, it made me vomit blood, and it wasn't a sickness that my Beast was able to heal. My Cherokee Elder teacher, Aggie One Feather, *lisi*, had told me that if I didn't listen to my magic, and kept pushing its boundaries, it would one day kill me. I had a bad feeling that she was right, but I wasn't always in control over it. Sometimes it was instinctive, like if I was in danger of dying, or someone I loved was in danger, then, sometimes, the magic itself took me over. At such times, my own life, *our* own lives, no longer mattered, and Beast would take over our magics and send me into the Gray Between. And bubble time so she could move outside of it.

I started to knead my belly, but the bruise stopped me fast. Pain doubled me over and the acid rose again. I swallowed it down. I didn't have long. I dropped to the floor beside Angie, crossed my legs guru-style, and studied what she was doing. Yeah. Angie was definitely analyzing and breaking the hedge. The manacles weren't hurting her, not like they should have been. She wasn't writhing in pain, she was *mad*.

Pressing my belly gingerly, I let time snap back.

The echo of Angie's furious scream assaulted my ears. The luggage hit the foyer floor. The cat screamed and yowled and the cage tumbled with the cat's acrobatics. Eli landed inside the room. His eyes went wide at the sight of me there. Molly blew in and caught herself with both hands on the doorjamb, her body bowing into the room and back out. Her face was full of fear and shock to find me there. Molly's lips moved tentatively, but no sound came when she said my name. *Jane?*

Eli put away his gun and the vamp-killer he had drawn without even noticing.

I turned to Angie and said, "If you don't stop it trying to get into the hedge, I am going to turn you over my knees and tan your little backside." Empty threat. I'd never hit my goddaughter, but still.

I didn't know what Angie saw in my face, but she finished breaking the manacles with a snap of sound and a flash of light. She jerked her hands away from the hedge and scooted out of the closet, her back still to the door and her mother. Her cheeks were red apples of anger, her eyes flashing with fury. "It's not fair! It's dangerous. It's gonna hurt Mama."

"There is nothing in that bag that will hurt your mama. She made most of the spells."

"Not the *workings*," Angie said, thrusting out her bottom lip. "The shiny lizard that wants to hurt Mama. She's gonna use the scabertoothed lion bone!"

And that shut me right up.

"I have to bind the bones," she said, "like Mama and Daddy bind me. Or the lizard will find it, and that will be bad! Very, very bad."

Molly's eyes had gone dark with the realization of what Angie was saying and what her words might mean for Angie's future. Keeping Angie bound was a way to keep her safe, and Angie wasn't supposed to be able to sense the bindings, let alone bypass them or turn them off.

The witch gene was carried on the X chromosome, and due to the scarcity of male witches who lived to adulthood, Angie was one of only a very few witches to ever have received the witch gene from both parents, one on each of her X chromosomes. If PsyLED or the Department of Defense or any other government agency, or worse, some terrorist group, discovered how powerful Angie was likely to become, the fear was that she would disappear into their clutches forever. The development of the psy-meter, a device to measure the magic used by a person or a spell, had made it easy to detect witches. If one was ever used on Angie and she wasn't bound, her secret would be out.

Molly sucked in a breath that sounded strangled and said, "She's free of the bindings."

Angie jerked and whirled all in one motion, her eyes wide at her mother.

"Might have been free for a long time," I said, "and her magic is different from yours. Black light with some purple and a trace of blue." I paused and took in Angie, whose eyes were full of guilt. "There's a faint reddish tinge around the edges. Arcs of black light were zapping out. *Black* light." It was raw power, which was unstable, dangerous all by itself, and needed to be soundly reined in by training and the proper workings mathematics. Her parents had made her bindings impregnable, keeping her magics under lock and key. Or so they'd thought.

Angie's mouth fell open in an O. She looked terrified, her shoulders rising, her head ducking. "Uh-oh."

Molly stood straight and dropped her arms from the jambs. "Come here."

Angie looked at me and I shook my head. "Forget it." She was getting no protection from the consequences of her actions, not from me, not when the real consequences of breaking her bindings and using unstable, untrained magic were beyond anything she could imagine. She could harm herself, burn herself, kill someone by accident. She could be taken away, disappeared into a secret government program, and never heard from again.

Angie put a hand to the floor and stood. Her wrists were red where the blue manacles had trapped her, though the signs were resolving rapidly.

"I'm sorry, Mama." Angie burst into tears. And every bit of my resolve crumpled with her. She threw herself at her mother and wrapped her arms around Molly's waist, hugging her tightly.

"Your room is ready, Miz Molly," Alex said. "The one directly overhead. I'll bring up the luggage and put it in the hall outside your door." Which was a terribly polite way to tell Molly she had a private place to take her daughter. The Kid was growing up finally. I gave him a nod of approval and his shoulders went back; an expression that might have been pride swept across his face and vanished. He shrugged and then gave me a faint smile, one slight enough to be Eli-worthy. I gave him one back.

Molly and Angie trudged up the stairs, Molly reprimanding her daughter in angry hissed sibilants, anger that was also suffused with fear. Alex gathered up the dropped bags and followed them at a distance to give them more privacy.

Eli came into my bedroom, his expression noncommittal. "How bad do you feel?"

"Bad enough. But Beast can mitigate some of the problems, now that"— I attempted a joke—"I'm back in time."

"Not funny," he said.

"I know."

Eli held out a hand and I let him help me to my feet. He said, "Let me see your belly."

That was a lot more intimate than we usually got, but Eli had been a Ranger, which meant that he was a lot more knowledgeable about medical matters than your average Joe. Rangers and other special forces types often did their own battlefield medicine, saving lives on the run. I raised my shirt hem to the bottom of my bra and looked with him. The bruise delivered by the *arcenciel*, Opal, had spread across my belly, dark angry red with a purple point in the very center, spreading to paler red, and then to pinkish beneath my ribs.

Eli pointed to the spot between my ribs. "The xiphoid process is a little spear-shaped bone right there, just above where that thing hit you. If the process gets hit in just the right way, it can tilt in and puncture your liver." He stepped closer and put a hand on the back of my head and pulled down my lower left eyelid. He frowned, a real frown, with wrinkles on either side of his mouth. "Your lids are too pale. You've lost blood. You need to shift. Now."

Eli pushed me toward my bed and said, "Now, Jane. I'll sear a steak and slip it in when you tap on the door." He closed my door, leaving me alone.

I looked back at my belly. It didn't look that awful, but I did feel kinda . . . weird. Tired. Playing with time on top of fighting an *arcenciel* was probably stupid.

I pulled the T off and tossed it and the jeans and the undies to the floor. Sitting on my bed, I thought about Beast. I used to have to wear my mountain lion tooth or be holding mountain lion bones, giving me access to the RNA and DNA in the marrow, using it as a guide to find the proper shape and form. But since Beast and I had merged on a deeper, more spiritual, metaphysical, and purely physical level, I hadn't been stuck with that limitation. Now, though I still needed genetic structure to work with to shift into other animal forms, I could shift into Beast form most anytime I wanted. Easy-peasy.

The silver energies rose around me and I closed my eyes. Reached inside, to the strands of RNA. Once upon a time, I'd had a double strand, just like all other humans, and when I shifted into another animal, it was into its double strand. Now, Beast's genetic makeup and mine were inextricably paired into tripled strands, each coated with silver and blue-green energies, each sparking darkly.

The change was almost, but not quite, pain this time, as my bones bent and snapped. Pelt sprang out on my arms and legs. My back arched, then threw me forward. Air wheezed from my lungs.

In a matter of seconds, I was Beast, crouching on the bed. I stopped Beast from extruding her claws. *My linens do not need holes.*

She snarled back and stood, stepping slowly to the floor. On the hardwood, she extruded her claws and stretched, almost sitting, to pull on shoulders, then lifting up to pull herself forward, her belly scraping the floor. She extended her back legs and lifted the right one, stretching from front paws to back toes. Then she did the other leg. Languid and svelte, she moved to the door and lifted a paw.

No scratches!

She snarled again and deliberately extended her claws, dragged her paw down the doorjamb, putting deep grooves in the paint.

Oh crap. Eli just painted the moldings.

She chuffed with amusement.

When he gets mad at you, don't blame me. He's the one who brings you steak these days.

Eli is good hunter. Brings good cow meat. She stared at the damaged door. Her appetite was growing at the thought of bloody meat, a totally different kind of cramping in her belly, the cramping of hunger from the energy used in the shift. *Beast needs sharp claws. Eli will not see.*

Eli sees everything.

A knock came at the door and I/we stepped back. The door opened and Eli bent inside, placing a platter on the floor. As he was rising, he stopped, his eyes on the scratches. For a long moment he didn't move, halted half-bent-over. Beast looked away, offering to him her profile in a cat's utter disinterest. "I'm going to let it go this time. I'm going to repair it. I'm even going to make a scratching post for your damn claws. But if you ever do that again, I'll start cooking your steak well done. *Charred.* Are we clear on this?"

Beast sat, front paws close together, as if posing, but she snarled at him, eyes slit, lips pulled back, showing killing teeth.

"I'll take that as a yes. Jane, are you better?"

I dropped my head down and back up in a human nod, which felt all wrong but was the best way to communicate with Eli in this form.

"Good." He closed the door.

Beast maintained the disinterest and indifference until we heard Eli's footsteps recede to the kitchen. Beast then picked up the largest chunk of raw steak and half chewed it before swallowing it and taking the next.

Back in human form, I felt much better, except for the hunger that raged through me; I had used up a lot of energy on the second shift. I dressed and got a step stool, placing the vinyl bag on the top shelf of my closet behind everything, and initiated the *hedge of thorns* ward back over it. It looked weird up there, some ten feet off the ground. I had never set the super-duper ward on anything up high, and the energies had formed a sphere around the bag and through the shelf. It wasn't easy to see in the dark of the closet except in Beast-vision, though I was certain that Angie would be able to see it if she got high enough. I took the step stool with me and inspected the room to see if an enterprising and determined little witchy girl could stack furniture and climb up there. I didn't see how, and I was pretty sure that levitation wasn't part of the witch repertoire.

When I came out of my room, I took the stool with me and deposited it in the butler's pantry. On the top shelf was a mad cat, her tail tip twitching and her eyes slit nearly shut. "Sorry about dropping you, KitKit." She managed to ignore me with utter disdain.

In the kitchen, I could smell oatmeal cooking, and my mouth watered. It was cooked just the way I like it—old-fashioned oats dumped into boiling, slightly salted water. Cooked for a minute, two at most, then re-dumped into a big bowl filled with enough real sugar to bring on a diabetic coma, and lots of milk. The absolute best. I practically inhaled it and felt the sugary energy and complex carbs start to work on me immediately.

Molly joined us and looked from the empty bowl to my hair, which was now unbraided and hanging to my hips in a black swing. And was dry, which was nice. "How's Beast?" she asked, putting together the signs of a recent shift.

"She's good. How's Angie?"

"Pouting. She's currently in magical time-out, which makes her angrier.

I don't understand what's going on or how she . . ." Molly shook her head in frustration, her reddish mop bouncing. I only now noticed that she had cut her hair. The short, curly style looked good on her, professional, smart, and chic, but I bet Big Evan had not been happy. Molly added, "I don't know how she did what she did." She lifted her cell. "I have a dozen phone calls to make, including one to my husband about that child. I smell tea steeping, and I'd love to have a cup."

"You want a shot of whiskey in it?" Eli asked.

"Actually that sounds amazing. I'm sure it's five somewhere in the world. But just a dribble, please." Molly turned and left the kitchen, already tapping calls into her cell. My eyebrows went up. Molly accepting alcohol in the middle of the day? That was another strange part of an already strange day.

Eli took my bowl—a mixing bowl that had held twelve cups of oatmeal—put it in the sink, and ran water into it while he poured tea for Molly and me. He put my mug on the table beside my elbow, along with a tub of Cool Whip and little cup of real cream, and carried Molly's tea, with its drip of whiskey in it, to her. I looked at the Cool Whip and the cream. Cool Whip in tea was comfort food, but it only worked with cheap tea. This smelled like the good stuff, and so I added a teaspoon of sugar and a dollop of the cream. It was perfect. I sat, sipping, listening to Eli as he tiptoed up the stairs and checked in on Angie and then came back down. He took a cup from the espresso maker and sat across from me, his dark eyes even darker with worry. "What happened?" he asked.

I held the warm mug for a moment and set it down, leaving my fingers lightly circled around the ceramic heat. "Molly had sent me a portable hedge and I activated it over the vinyl bag holding the skull and Molly's charms. It was a new working that was geared to not only stop a regular thief but also a magical thief. *Most* magical thieves. If the *arcenciel* had gotten to it, I can't guarantee that she would have been stopped. For all I know she might have swallowed the whole thing and taken off." I waved that thought away. "Anyway. The new working has manacles built into it so a thief can't get to the bag, and also can't get away. They're trapped there. When Angie touched it, the working grabbed Angie's hands and wrists with the manacles. When I was outside of time, I watched as she shot little black light magics into them and into the hedge, trying to get loose. I didn't turn off the hedge. She used raw magics to get free."

"Black light magics? I thought you said most magics are blue or green. Or red." He thought and added, "Sometimes purple."

I nodded. "Yellow, orange. Prisms of the rainbow, light and energy as used by a witch. They work like a signature to people who can see them. Angie's used to be white. Blue sometimes. Rarely with little motes of black power in them. Except the very first time I ever saw them manifest. She was barely out of diapers, and she got mad, and a whirlwind of her magics ripped through the mobile home they were living in. The magics were dark, like an angry cloud. She could have killed her parents. Instead Beast calmed her and stopped the attack. Molly and Big Evan bound her that day for the first time."

I drank more tea, trying to put it all together in a cohesive timeline. Working with long-lived vamps, I had learned that timelines were important. "When Little Evan and Angie were in the witch circle waiting to be sacrificed by the Damours, Angie was surrounded by dark magic. And when she freed me from the head Damour, there were streaks of dark motes in her magic. I had never seen her magic up close enough to get a good look, and back then I couldn't bend time, slow it down, to really study it, and I didn't understand . . . but I think her magic became dark that night. I think she learned something and has been using it. Or was contaminated by it. Maybe not black magic, not blood magic, but something that can go either way." I looked up from my mug. "This is going to be hard on Molly and Evan."

Eli nodded. "You want me there?"

I shook my head. "No. Yes. I don't know." I thought some more. Having Eli with me would be cowardly. I was *not* a coward. Or not often. "No," I decided and stood. I refilled my cup and added more cream and sugar, stirred it, but then left it on the table. I walked out one of the new doors to the side porch. Molly was sitting there in one of the rusty chairs, rocking, her dress full-skirted and flowing out and down to the decking, chatting on the phone. Her red hair was flopping to one side, and the curls followed the same line as the dress. She looked as if she were posing for a painting by some famous watercolor artist. The thought was way too artistic for me, and I shook it away.

Molly's tone informed me that she was talking to Big Evan, her hubby. I walked over and sat at her feet, my legs curled up guru-style in a half lotus. It was an intrusion as well as an act of submission unusual for me and especially for my Beast. Her perfumed scent was too strong for me, augmented as it was with my Beast senses, and I resisted the desire to sneeze or wrinkle my nose.

Molly's voice trailed off and we could hear the dripping and tapping of rainwater and the ever-present sound of traffic. "Jane's here," she said.

"Would you put me on speaker?" I asked.

Molly tapped the screen and said, "Evan, you're on speaker. Jane has something to say. And she's sitting at my feet. Like a house cat."

I managed a smile. Molly understood what my position and posture meant.

Evan said. "I'm not going to like this one little bit, am I?"

"Probably not," I said. To Molly, I asked, "You already told him about Angie?" Molly nodded slowly, then shook her head. Mixed signals meant he knew parts. Slowly, I went on, knowing that I needed to say this in a special way, with compassion and tenderness and all that crap. But I didn't know how to do things like that, and hadn't figured out how during the walk out here. I was a bull in the china shop of my friends' emotions. "You know I can bubble time. So when I heard Angie scream, it just kinda"—I shrugged—"happened. And I ran inside. She had her hands buried in the hedge—that's the new and improved hedge, by the way—over the saber-tooth lion skull. The trap part of the new hedge had been activated, and she was stuck. But I was standing outside of time and I saw what she was doing. She was zapping the manacles. And her magic was like black light. She's using her power raw, without maths to give it form. Controlling it just with her mind and will. And I have a bad feeling that she saw me bubble time, which means she might know how to do that too."

Molly closed her eyes. Her face went a paler shade of cream; clearly she hadn't told Evan yet. I caught a whiff of her reaction, which was all tangled and twisted and broken.

"Thanks for sugarcoating it, Jane," Evan said, the sarcasm so thick even I understood it.

I shrugged and stood, patted Molly's hands, and walked back inside. I was still barefoot, the wood floor smooth but with the rolling surface of a very old house. At the table, I picked up my tea. "That went well," I said, lying.

Eli chuckled, and there was no amusement in the sound at all.

Supper was a quiet affair, though Angie didn't seem to sense it. Angie had sat Ka Nvsita, the Cherokee doll I had given her, on the chair beside her, and was telling the doll about her day, omitting her time-out and concentrating on the flight and KitKit, who was still hiding on the top shelf in the butler's pantry. According to the doll chat, Angie had enjoyed a stellar day.

Molly stared alternately at her daughter and at her own left hand clenching in her lap. She ate with determination, but I could tell she wasn't enjoying the salmon and black rice Eli had made, nor the mixed greens salad—which wasn't bad for green leaves and veggies and nuts and stuff.

With nothing settled and no decision made about what to do with Angie or the skull, Molly pushed away from the table and called Evan again, her voice low and worried. Together, over the cell connection, they warded the house, Molly's incantation and Evan's flute playing following her from door to door and window to window. When the house was protected, Molly took a pouting but seemingly obedient Angie Baby upstairs. I followed and watched as Molly and Evan put their daughter to sleep. They used a new working that Angie wasn't expecting, a sneak attack that they didn't announce or warn her about. The little girl's eyes flew open in surprise and she resisted for some five seconds before she fell back on her pillow, eyes closed, and her breath even. Asleep. Molly looked from the little girl to me and said, "We had to."

I nodded, relieved, and Mol turned back to her daughter. The music and chanted words of the new magical binding sounded through the house, the energies shivering along my skin and through the soles of my feet, sweet and dangerous and tight as thorny vines.

When Angie woke up, her powers would again be bound, more constricted than ever. I had a feeling that she was gonna be one ticked-off little girl. But safer. Much safer. When Angie was bound, Molly said some sweet nothings to her hubby and I pulled on Beast sight. The little girl's body looked as if it had been wrapped in a cocoon of blue and red magical strands, with a touch of bright sunlight energies thrown in to seal it. There was no way she would be able to break this one. The bright yellow magics would cancel out her nascent dark magics. I knew next to nothing about how magic actually worked, but I understood this one on some basic, intuitive level.

Satisfied, Molly and I took the stairs down and joined the card game waiting for us at the kitchen table. Poker. Five-card stud. It seemed that I had a natural advantage in the game, because I could smell the difference between players' excitement at really good hands and their change in scent when they were bluffing. Alex wanted to take me to a riverboat casino offshore in the Mississippi for some high-stakes gambling. I wasn't interested in risking the money I had put aside, but the Kid wasn't to be denied his experimentation and, with Molly here, he had another subject to test me against. I won every single one of the matchsticks we bet. Later, the Kid told me that if it had been real money, I'd have made about fifty grand, according to his own geeky conversion mathematics based on a terribly inflated value for the matchsticks.

I still refused to go gamble. Repeatedly. Watching his avaricious eyes go blank each time was priceless.

At nine sixteen p.m., I was holding a perfectly awful hand of a pair of threes, but it beat the other players' hands if I was still reading the scents correctly.

A *boom* shook the house. Inside, the lights flickered twice and died. A drawn-out *zzzzzz* sizzled outside, in front. The sound resembled a transformer exploding and sparking. Or a small bomb? In the next second I realized that it couldn't be a bomb, because Eli didn't throw himself on top of the rest of us, but he did draw a weapon and vanish into the shadows. I didn't remember seeing electrical transformers close enough nearby to make the sound we had heard.

I stood in a crouch so I couldn't be seen through the kitchen window. Looked out into the street. The houses across from my house were still lit.

Eli's voice sounded from the living room. "Lights are on at Katie's." He craned his neck, visible as a silhouette in the window, which was brighter from outside lights. He added, "And both neighbors have light."

Molly said, "Y'all? We have a problem." Her voice quavered on the last word. Her body smelled of sudden sweat and the acrid, bitter tang of terror.

The sizzling, slapping *boom* came again, followed by the electrical *zzzzz*.

I pulled on Beast-vision from where I stood at the front window and saw the energies of the ward over the house. It was an older model, one Molly had used before, the spell muted blue, green, and silver, the energies growing up from below ground, as natural as leaves and plants sprouting up from fertile soil, but this time the fertile ground was Molly's earth magic, augmented by her newer, more deadly death magic. The ward was powerful, self-healing from most mundane (meaning nonmagical) attacks, was resilient, and air permeable, covering the house and most of the grounds. And it was sparking blue and red, like sparklers on the Fourth of July.

"What is it?" I asked her. But she just shivered, her eyes lost in a distance I couldn't see. "We're under attack," I said to the Youngers, "but I don't see anything. Alex, the exterior cameras have battery backup, right?"

"Yeah, working on seeing what we have now," he said, his voice distracted, coming from the darkness of the house. "I had to turn on the inverter and get everything going. So far I don't see anything. Bro, get the fridge unplugged."

Eli moved to the kitchen, following orders.

"Jane," Molly said, the word garbled as if she was choking.

I raced to her, but I didn't make it in time. The *boom* was massive and the windows rattled as the entire house shook. The ward sent out a shower of sparks, like bloody water falling over a waterfall, the red energies blooming light. Beautiful, but also taking power from the ward. The broken magics smelled of char and burned herbs, sunlight on linen, and the dark of the moon on a winter garden. "What is it?" I asked Molly, slipping an arm around her shoulders. "What's attacking us?"

"Jane?" Alex said. "It's an *arcenciel*. A young one." He spun the tablet to us. "And this time I can see the scar on its side."

So could I, though the scar was nothing more than a dark shadow along its snakelike side. She was in the visible range, a rippling of light and shadow, with a human-shaped head, showing small, budding horns. Her mouth was open displaying rows of shark teeth that glinted like pearls. Her transparent wings glimmered in all the colors of the rainbow, and a frill around her head was scintillating shades of copper, brown, and pale white. Her body was snakelike, bigger than the last time I had seen her, with iridescent scales the color of tinted glass and thick smoke and hints of copper. As before, she smelled like green herbs burning over hot coals and the tang of fish and water plants. The shadowy scar ran along her side, healed but a potent reminder that she could be hurt. This was the creature we had wounded in Leo's basement gym. This was the light dragon who had attacked me before, but at least now she had a name.

Did that give us power over her in some way? Could we use her name to defend ourselves? "Her name is Opal," I said.

"That isn't its real name," Molly whispered, her eyes faraway as she studied her ward and what was happening to it, "that's just its English name." She ducked her head and slid from beneath my arm. "I've been doing research. Her real name will be a lot of sibilants and *crack*ing sounds and an explosion of light in the correct wavelength. I can't even recognize it as a name, let alone reproduce it or use it in defense of us." Yet her hands rose and I saw the power of her magical working—what the mundane and lazy, including myself, called a *spell*—as it sparkled from her fingers and raced to every window and door, building up the ward in the most probable weak places.

"Molly, you don't have a circle," Alex said softly.

"I'm using the ward where it enters the ground as my circle," she muttered. Which was news to me. I hadn't known that was possible. Magic was tricky, as tied up in the practitioner's belief system about the practice of magic itself, as it was in the practitioner's actual ability. A witch who believed she had a lot of power probably had a way to access more than she might have otherwise. And a witch who believed she was powerless likely was, regardless of her magical potential. And Molly was a freaky-powerful witch, and had become more so, when, in defense of her life and her sisters', her magics mutated from earth magics with a hint of moon magic thrown in, into death magics, which she couldn't use without killing something. Or someone. She had found her way back to earth magics, but her hold on them was tenuous and delicate.

There was little any of us nonwitch types could do to help her battle to keep the wards in place, but if they faltered, I'd need to have a weapon, and steel hurt even *arcenciels*. I accepted the vamp-killer and the small KA-BAR-style knife Eli handed me and strapped the double sheaths to my left leg. The vamp-killer I adjusted for a right-hand draw, up near my waist, and the smaller knife I set back for a left-hand draw nearer to my left knee. As I worked, nothing more happened—no *boom*s, no house shaking, no nothing. Maybe it had gone away to lick its wounds. Or maybe the *arcenciel* had gone for reinforcements. I'm such glass-half-full-of-blood kinda gal.

I pulled my cell and tried to call Soul, the only other *arcenciel* I knew, but the call didn't go through. I had no bars. The sat system Alex was setting up wasn't working either. I slid the units across the kitchen table, where Alex was tapping. He jumped up and raced to the hardware under his desk in the living room and switched off some of the gray boxes and then switched them back on. Little green and yellow lights glowed. He ran back to the kitchen to work by the light of two tablets. I hated technology sometimes.

Whatever was happening outside, Molly was using the time to spin reinforcements on the ward. Her feet were shoulder width apart, knees slightly bent, almost like the footing for a martial arts move, rooting her body to the earth beneath the floor, balanced and stable. Her fingers were flicking and snapping and the smell of rosemary grew on the air, a strong, intense scent that seemed to wend down the stairs from her room overhead, mixing with the scent of her fear and that awful perfume. When it came to magic, Molly was a battle witch, standing between her child and danger, and I could see the Celtic warrior women of her genetic history in her stance, fierce and tender and unyielding.

From the corner of my eye I saw a flicker as something leaped out of the shadows. I whirled, Beast fast, and caught it, whipping it out of the air. And got lines of scratches for my mistake. KitKit yowled and hissed and did some kinda ninja move and bit my thumb. I dropped her and she landed with another yowl, a whirling cat move, and a faster-than-sight leap to Molly's feet.

The scent of fear Molly was exuding instantly eased. Her not-familiar had helped her control her death magics. KitKit was a *not-familiar* because familiars didn't exist. They were myth. KitKit's abilities were a big secret, the revelation of which would subject Molly to ridicule and embarrassment. But she couldn't be without the dang cat.

Disgusted with myself for reacting instead of letting the cat reach her mistress, I went to the sink and washed my wounds. My skinwalker metabolism would heal them faster than similar wounds on a human, and they would heal instantly the next time I shifted into Beast. For now, however, they stung like crazy. But unless KitKit was rabid or had cat scratch fever, they weren't life-threatening. I stared out at the night. In battle sometimes the hardest part was waiting for something to happen.

A *boom* shook the house. A *zzzzzzzzttttpowpowpow ssssss* sound, ending this time with a slap on the tail end of the sizzle. The *arcenciel* seemed determined to get inside the house and was probably injuring herself on Molly's wards.

Alex muttered, "I guess you already figured out that all coms are down. I don't know what that thing is doing, but it's affecting more than just the power. It's like a mini–electromagnetic blast. I can use the tablets—ah shit. Now the *tablets* are down."

Eli promptly head-slapped him. In his battlefield-mild tone, he added, "Language."

Alex cursed again, but I think it was Klingon or Elvish or some fictional language, and no one else reacted. I was worried that the juvenile *arcenciel*'s light show would attract the attention of the cops, who would then descend and possibly get hurt. Or worse, attract the attention of a larger, mature creature, not Soul, but a stranger, and that the larger one would think the humans, the witch, and the skinwalker were the aggressors.

The *arcenciel* hit the house again and again; the floor vibrated under my feet. The ward beyond the windows spluttered and shuddered, the energies showing signs of cracking. Molly was sweating now, her perspiration full of adrenaline and its acrid breakdown chemicals. The cat was wrapped around Molly's ankles, purring steadily. The *boom* sounded, harder, deeper. I shook my head and set my feet, oddly reminiscent of Molly's stance.

I wasn't going to have a choice. I was going to have to risk the Gray Between. I was going to have to bend time so I could be fast enough to fight the *arcenciel*.

But the Gray Between would allow all similar creatures to see me working outside of time, and again, that might result in other *arcenciels* showing up to help the juvie rainbow dragon. I hesitated. Eli walked through the living room and into the little-used laundry/storage room on the back of the house, behind my bedroom and bath. He leaned to see out the windows.

And I heard Angie's voice, coming down the stairs. "Hey. You're pretty. All sparkly. Wanna come play with me?"

Before Eli or I could move, Alex was flying up the stairs. His flip-flops came off and bounced down the stairs. Eli and I raced up after him and into his room to see Angie Baby standing outside, on the second-floor gallery, her body outlined in the ward's light, the *arcenciel*'s huge head reared back, only inches from her. The light dragon was horned and frilled, its long hair copper and brown, and this time, traced through with red and a hint of sapphire. Its teeth were longer than my hands, sharp and pearled and glistening like the opals for which it was named.

And Angie was gripping a small steel knife in one hand, holding it behind her back, where the *arcenciel* couldn't see it.

Alex skidded out the long, narrow doors of his own room, out onto the gallery, and grabbed Angie up under his arm. Dragged her back inside, one hand ripping away the knife. Slammed the French doors closed and twisted the finger latch.

Angie struggled in his hands and tore herself away. "No!" she shouted, her face hidden by shadows, her hair standing out in a halo of static power. She snapped her left hand at Alex and screamed, *"Tu dormies!"*

The Kid's knees folded, his body dropped, and Alex was instantly asleep. As he fell, Eli snatched the tumbling knife out of the air and glared at Angie. Alex's head bounced on the rug at the foot of his bed.

"Angelina!" I shouted, furious. And frightened. Angie shouldn't be able to do that. At all. Angie was supposed to be bound.

Angie whirled on me, her white nightgown furling around her. "I'll put you all to sleep if you don't let me talk to the shiny lizard!"

"Angie. No," I said, trying to find a calm tone. If she put us to sleep, she would be all alone with a creature who could kill her in a heartbeat. "Angie. Baby, please don't."

"I tolded you that the scabertoothed bones was calling to it," she screeched, her hands fisting in front of her like a boxer. *"You didn't listen."* Magic coiled out of her fists, not as strong as before, but clear and bright, a blue laced with black that looked scary in ways that magic had never looked scary to me before. She took a step toward me, and her voice lowered. Slowly she said, "And you let Mama and Daddy put me to sleep." Angie sounded furious and dangerous.

I had never seen her act so badly, not since . . . I stopped, trying to remember. What had I smelled? When Molly first arrived. Flowers and lemongrass and that awful perfume . . . "Oh no," I whispered.

"Yes!" Angie shouted, raging. "I'm a big girl, not a baby! I can kill my own snakes," she said, using a phrase Molly used sometimes.

"Angie," I said, "you can't kill this snake. That's not what that phrase means."

Angie whirled and beat the bed, her fists pounding into Alex's pillows and rumpled covers. "No, no, no, no, no!" she screamed, her words muffled in the covers.

The house *boom*ed again, as I tried to figure out what to do. And again. And again. The old timbers were creaking and the windowpanes of the French door behind us shattered. A fireball burned through the door and into the house, the flickering flames momentarily brightening the room. Angie flicked her fingers at it, the way she might if she was flicking water off her hand, and it stopped, the fire snuffed out in a puff of black smoke that stank of flaming rosemary. It all took maybe two seconds. In Beast-vision, Angie's magics floated around her like a diaphanous veil, brighter and hotter than only a moment before. *Holy crap. Just . . . holy crap.*

I looked back at the French door and the circular hole that was burned through it. Molly was throwing fire spells at the *arcenciel*, and one had bounced off and come back inside. And Angie had broken the energies of the working as if she were popping soap bubbles.

Fire wasn't Mol's strong suit, but it was all she had left unless she loosed her death magics. And if she did *that*, and if Angie tried to grapple with *that* form of magic, she would die. We might all die. And that would kill Molly as surely as taking a gun to her own head.

Eli had glanced up at the fireball and then back to Angie. He said, "You hurt Alex. I thought you liked him." The tone was like a kid, finger-pointing, but Eli crossed his arms and frowned hard. Eli. *Frowning.*

I checked to make sure my partner hadn't grown another head. Outside, the *arcenciel* head-butted the house. The room shook. Opal hit it again. And again. Something fell in the bathroom and shattered. Angie jerked at the sound and lowered her hands slightly, her fists slack, her face flushed but uncertain now. Her hair still stood on end, and her magic radiated out as if on the verge of explosion.

Eli ignored it all and dropped to one knee, one hand extending to Angie. Sadly, he said, "Alex thought he was saving you, like a prince saves a princess."

"I don't need saving," Angie shouted at him. "I'm not a stupid princess. I'm a snake killer and a witch!"

Eli looked surprised for the briefest moment and then he said. "Right. Alex thought he was helping you. He didn't know you could save yourself and"—his voice dropped low, a gentle and wretched tone—"you hurt him."

Angie tilted her head and looked down at Alex, her breath blowing hard. She fisted her hands again, as if teetering on the edge of something. Something catastrophic. She sobbed once, and hiccuped and swallowed. Her magics went cooler and calmer in color, fading the way a rainbow bleaches out of the sky. In a calmer tone, she asked, "He was helping me? But Alex isn't a witch."

"True. But he thought you were in trouble and needed help. And . . . *you hurt him. That's wrong.*"

Tears started like a fountain, and Angie's face was suddenly shining with them. They fell in rivulets onto her nightgown. She sniffled. "I didn't mean to hu-hu-hu-hu-hu . . . " She inhaled, taking tears in with the air. "Hurt him." Eli smiled, showing teeth, looking charming, said, "True. And Alex knows that. But when a prince sees someone in danger they always go to the rescue."

Angie nodded, staring at Alex as her magics settled. Tension flooded from me like Angie's tears, in a flood, and I sidled to the damaged door and looked out. The creature just beyond the walls was banging itself bloody (if the clear goop that was dripping from her jaw could be called blood) against the ward. Angie said, "I'm sorry." She frowned. "Uh-oh. I don't know how to wake him up. I haven't learned that one yet." Angie blew out a breath that puffed her cheeks. "I been bad again. Mama's gonna be mad at me."

Relief surged through me. "But Alex will be okay, and we learned something, right, Angie?" I said, my voice remarkably calm, considering my racing pulse.

The little girl looked at me, and her shoulders slumped. "The light dragon is gonna break through if Mama doesn't get some help. She needs my daddy."

I walked to Angie and bent, lowering my arms. Angie lifted hers and I gathered her up, standing. Her arms wrapped around my neck and she huddled close. She smelled of a confusing mix of pheromones: anger breaking down, magic dissipating, tears of frustration and fury. And not a little shame.

Outside, the *arcenciel* stopped her attacks on the house, and I had to wonder if Angie's magic had excited Opal somehow, and then when Angie calmed, quieted her. Where *arcenciels* were concerned, I was flying by the seat of my pants. Feeling better about things for the moment, I carried my goddaughter down the stairs.

As I left the room, Eli knelt, picked his brother up in a fireman's carry, and dumped him on the bed. He could hide the visual cues to his surprise at his brother's weight, but not the olfactory ones. Alex may have topped out at around five feet, eleven inches, but he was putting on weight, all of it muscle, which until now had been hidden beneath his loose clothing.

Molly still stood in the middle of the living room, but now she was hunched, her fingers still flying but looking stiff and less coordinated. She was stinking of fear sweat and that awful perfume. Molly never, ever wore perfume around me because she knew my sense of smell was so much better than a human's, and I hated the stink of synthetic scents. So . . . why did she . . . I studied her in her full skirt, the bodice pulling across fuller boobs. And at her waistline, I recognized the small but firm baby bump. Molly was pregnant.

I asked Angie, "Do you want the skull to help the baby?"

Angie pouted prettily, her lips swollen from her tears. She said, "Yes." She glared at me. "Yes, damndamndamn!" Which was Molly's swearword when she became frustrated and too angry to take life anymore and was hiding behind the closet door, where she cussed in private. Somebody had big ears. If the *"tu dormies"* spell was any consideration, *very* big ears.

It wasn't the right time to fuss at Angie, but I had to. "Language, young lady." Her pout deepened, her eyebrows scrunching down, and I managed not to grin. "And the creature? Why does it want the skull?"

"To stop Mama's baby from being born. It's gonna try to go back in time and stop her."

The amusement went out of me and I bent, placing Angie on the couch. My arms free, I studied Molly, confused about what the little girl might really be meaning. How could an *arcenciel* go back in time to stop something that will take place in the future? How could Angie know what the *arcenciel* was thinking/planning/wanting?

Several things occurred to me all at once and my knees gave way, lowering me to the couch beside Angie. *Arcenciels* might have much stronger powers over time than I understood. What if they could see the possibilities of the future, and then go back in time to stop a certain thing from happening tomorrow? What if they could go back in time to stop anything they wanted to, no matter how far in the improbably distant future it might be? Based on Angie's statements, maybe Opal wanted to keep Molly from getting pregnant? Or, much worse, stop the Everhart sisters and Evan Trueblood from ever being born. "Holy crap on crackers with toe jam," I muttered. I had been thinking too short-term about time. "Angie, I get part of that, but how does the skull fit into it all?"

Angie was concentrating on my face, hers serious. "They gots to have a focus. A focal thing." She grimaced, trying to find the proper words. "If Opal goes back in time, she gots to follow a thing that went back there too."

"Ahhh. So if she has the skull, she can follow along the skull's timeline back. To what?"

"To stop you from being given the skull."

"Okay. So Opal would go back in time and stop me from getting the skull."

"And that will kill you, Aunt Jane."

I remembered back to a time when I had been on the verge of death and Beast had drawn on the skull's DNA and RNA and taken mass from nearby stone. She had shifted into the sabertooth lion's genetic form, even though he was a male big-cat, which I had thought wasn't supposed to be possible. Not that I knew a lot about the process, as my skinwalker training had stopped when I was five or so. But the shift had saved our lives. Without the skull, that shift would not have been possible, and I—we—might have died.

Like my father had died in midshift, his injuries too severe to survive. And if I died, Molly's death would eventually follow, on the timeline created by the *arcenciel*. And I still didn't know what was going to happen on the *current* timeline. Dealing with time, thinking about time, made my brain tie up in knots. Thinking about *changing* time was so confusing that it gave me mental vertigo.

Eli passed me, checking the windows. He stepped out onto the side porch through one door and back in through another. He was carrying a subgun, a small, fully automatic weapon, in one hand and his full-length flat sword in the other. No shirt, no shoes. Brown skin catching the shadows and throwing back the light as muscles flexed and relaxed.

He said, "I think the *arcenciel* is gone."

Molly's hands quivered and slowly relaxed. She fell into the nearest chair, dripping with sweat, red hair clinging to her face. Angie left the couch and stood beside her mother, taking her hand; with her other hand, Angie pushed back her mother's damp hair. "I gotta get this mess cut again," Molly whispered to Angie.

"Daddy will have a cow again," Angie said back, startling an exhausted laugh from Molly.

Molly stood and pulled her eldest up the stairs. "I need a shower, and you, young lady, have some explaining to do."

"Tell your mother everything, Angie," I said. "And I mean *every*thing. Including about the skull."

Angie gave an exaggerated sigh, an omen of what they would sound like when she hit her teens. "Okay, Aunt Jane. But she's gonna be mad."

"Yeah. Probably." The two disappeared up the stairs, Molly's footsteps sounding exhausted.

"That little girl is gonna be nothing but trouble in about ten years," Eli said. Which echoed my own thoughts. Eli made the best partner.

"How's Alex?" I asked.

"Still out. He'll be okay. Pupils equal and reactive. Breath is even and slow at twenty."

At the same moment, the lights flickered back on and my cell rang. I raced to the kitchen table to answer. It was Evan, his voice frantic and babbling. He had been unable to reach Molly and had clearly been thinking the worst. Which was not far from the truth. I said, "Molly's okay, Evan. They all three are."

Evan stopped talking and then stuttered ahead, "Sssshe told you?"

"No. She didn't. Angie told me."

"Angie doesn't know."

"Yes. She does. And she's been carrying a big load of worry. We need to talk, you, Mol, and me. But first, let me catch you up." It took a while. At one point, I heard the shower come on and then stop upstairs. And later a moan drifted down the stairs as Alex woke. Eli, and later Molly, joined me at the table, and I put the cell on speakerphone and switched on the camera so we could interact. Otherwise the house was silent.

When Eli and I had given Evan all the info we had, he frowned and said, "What if Mol and I bind the skull so the *arcenciel* can't see it?"

Angie peeked around the wall and said, "That's a good idea, Daddy." I managed not to *eep*. Eli managed not to shoot her. Molly managed not to drain her of life. I thought we all did pretty well.

"Angie?" Evan said. "When did you—"

Molly interrupted with "Son of a witch on a switch. What are you doing downstairs? She's supposed to be in time-out," she added to Evan.

She told her father, "You can do to the scabertoothed bones what you did to me. It worked until I grew up and undid it."

I said, "We didn't know she was here, Evan. No sound, no scent." Evan breathed in, a soft sound of shock. Molly looked terrified. Angie had spelled herself in ways I wasn't sure her parents could do, at least not without a lot of prep time and testing and frustration. Eli, who might not understand what had happened, but did understand that we were all upset, looked bored but intent, the way he had when we were trapped inside while outside a dragon made of light and magic raged, wanting to eat us.

"But I can't undid it if I'm mad," Angie added, taking her place at the table like the big girl she proclaimed herself to be.

"Angie," Evan said, "how did you know about the binding?"

"It tickled. And then it hurt, the way my purple heart jammies hurt when I try to put them on."

"She's outgrown the purple heart pajamas," Molly said thoughtfully.

"She outgrew our binding?" Evan asked. "Literally and physically or metaphorically and metaphysically?"

"Yep," Angie said cheerfully. "Can I have a peanut butter and jelly sam'ich?"

I stood and got the almond butter and the cashew butter out of the cabinet and some homemade muscadine jelly. I made sandwiches for all of us, including Alex, who was clomping down the stairs, a cold rag around his neck and a plastic bottle of pain meds in one hand. I used Eli's new sprouted grain bread, which tasted a little weird but worked well with the nut butters and jelly.

I poured goat's milk—another of Eli's new passions—into glasses and passed the food and drink around while Molly and Evan experimented, putting Angie into her binding, watching as she loosened it and stepped out of it, almost the same way she might unknot a too-tight bathrobe and peel it off. Then they put her back into it and let her unknot it again. And then they wanted to try a binding on the skull, all of which sounded terribly boring to me and to Eli as well. He took his and Alex's snacks to the living room on a large sterling silver serving tray he'd found in the butler's pantry, leaving the family working in the kitchen. I got the cause of all the trouble, touched the crow on its beak to remove the ward from the skull, and placed it on the kitchen table, to the delight and awe of Angie Baby and the wide-eyed disgust of her parents.

Leaving it there, I took my plate and glass of milk to the back porch, where I could be alone with my thoughts. It was raining, a soft *plink* of drops, and I sat with my back against the house wall, staring out at what passed for darkness in a city, and ate. The scents were clean and mildly ozoney, wetwetwet, falling from the sky, flowing along the ground, draining into the storm sewers. Between downpours, mosquitoes buzzed everywhere, though most of them were locked out of Molly's ward, butting the energies and making tiny sparks before dying. I'd have to tell her she could patent the ward as a house-sized bug killer/security system/light show.

The repaired ward was a haze of shadows that lit up in silvers and greens in Beast's vision, glowing a rich and mottled blue, green, gray, and lavender, like a psychedelic dream from the sixties or an animated fantasy magic movie. Few humans could see the energies of magics, except for the presence of unexplainable lights, which made it easy to pretend there was nothing there, nothing happening. Even I couldn't see magics well without Beast helping. I worked to combine our vision and tilted up my head to watch the rain falling in the security lights of the house to my right. The drops hit the ward and ran down the wall of energies, picking up the reds from the ward, looking like blood falling from the sky and dripping downward.

I thought of Beast and found her sitting in our soul home, the cave dark and silent, her eyes golden and bright. *We couldn't fight today,* I thought at her.

No, Beast thought at me. *Was trap/cage. Beast remembers trap, steel mouth filled with steel teeth to break bones and make prey bleed.* Her ear tabs flicking, she added, *Have been inside cage. Do not like cage.*

That was a lot of concept for my Beastly self. *Yeah. It was a cage. A protective cage.*

Like den?

I smiled and thought, *Yes. Like a den.*

Ward is cage den made by Molly. Kits and littermates are safe in cage den made by Molly. She sounded pleased with herself for understanding the concept of a cage that was for safety and not for capture. Satisfied with that understanding, she looked out into the rain through my eyes. *Jane needs to go into Gray Between. See what* arcenciel *sees in time.*

No thanks. I'm not overfond of being sick and throwing up blood.

Beast wasn't in a mood to let me avoid it. Faster than I could stop her, she raked a clawed paw on the stone of our soul home and pulled the Gray Between out of us and around us like a cloak.

But that's where she stopped. There was no entrance into the slo-mo experience of time stoppage, no bubbling time so we could act outside of it. More slowly than usual, time began to tighten and grind down, something I could follow as the rain began to fall at a more leisurely pace than atmospheric conditions and gravity usually permitted. I could see water droplets slowing and slowing again. When they hit, I could make out the rounded teardrop shape and the splatter they threw as they landed and broke and then gathered into the pooled water closest. *Capillary attraction,* I thought, remembering that from some high school chemistry class.

Time and the rain slowed again. And then halted. This gradual dipping into the timelines made the experience easier and I felt none of the nausea I usually experienced. My belly didn't cramp or burn. Relief replaced the tension that had built in me.

In each droplet that hung in the air, a tiny vision of the near future was captured, a moment in time, each different, though sometimes only in minuscule ways, of the captured possibilities of the next moment. In the water on the ground, in puddles, were the ruined possibilities of the near past, possibilities that had almost happened, but hadn't, changed, destroyed by the choices made. In one was a distorted vision of Angie being eaten by the *arcenciel,* her blood running down its jaw. In another puddle the *arcenciel* had crashed through the side wall of the lower floor, the one that now was composed of doors. In another was a ruined vision that might have been Eli, dressed in camo pants and T-shirt, killing the *arcenciel* with his sword, a possibility that had never been, perhaps because of one simple decision—the clothes my partner had chosen to wear prior to the attack. Could a timeline be altered by such a seemingly simple choice? Or was there more that affected that discontinuity in time?

If Angie was right, then *arcenciels* are able to see time as I could while in the Gray Between, but see back along a timeline into the more distant past. Unlike me, while working in the Gray Between, they could move forward and back in time along the possibilities.

The idea was way over my head, and it made me nauseous thinking about it. But at least I wasn't throwing up blood. Maybe just looking at time wasn't quite the same thing as altering time or moving and acting outside it. Or maybe Beast had found a way to halt what I had come to call the timesickness. But I wasn't holding my breath. Life was seldom so easy.

I looked out into the droplets of rain that were still hanging in the air just beyond the ward. In one, I could see myself, looking out into the rain. In another, I could see myself on the cell phone, my face like a thundercloud. In another drop, farther out, I could see Angie sitting in front of me watching me, my eyes closed in meditation, but the background was different, not on the back porch. A brick wall was behind me, perhaps out in the garden. Another was me asleep in my bed. I strained my eyes and drew more on Beast's vision, seeing out into the droplets. The futures there were much more odd, as if the area around me contained the most likely possibilities and as if the possibilities of the more distant future lay farther out. So the things I did in the here and now could make the potential futures more likely or unlikely.

If I walked in among the falling droplets, might I see enough of the potentialities, enough of the possibilities, to chart a course for a future I liked? And if I spent enough time looking into the puddled droplets, would I see decisions I had made, that others had made, in the past, choices that had made today what it was? Was that what Opal had done, looked into the past and the future and seen a disaster that she could avert? Could her kind walk among the water droplets of the future and the past both, and see what dangers and disasters awaited there, and then go back onto the puddles of the past and *fix* them? If so, that was a power and talent more terrible and vast and profound than any I had ever heard of. *Arcenciels* had the power of *time*.

No wonder vampires wanted to ride them. That kind of power was unimaginable.

And what happened to the memory of the one who altered time? Did they lose the memory of the time they had changed? Or did they keep the memories that they destroyed? There was one person I could ask, but if I asked, then Soul would know that I knew the secret of the *arcenciels*. Might the future show her something, some decision I might make, some action that I would or might do that was bad for her or another *arcenciel*? If so, would she feel the need to kill me to stop that action?

All this meant that *Soul* knew the potentialities of the future, if she wanted to. If she looked. I had a feeling that Soul didn't look at the potentialities as often or as deeply as Opal did. But it was just a feeling. One that said that the adult or mature *arcenciels* made conscious, or perhaps unconscious decisions, to view the future seldom, decisions that came from age and experience and the memories lost. Or worse, the memories of a present unalterably violated and destroyed.

Something had changed in the air around me, and I opened my eyes. They had drifted closed, bringing me close to sleep as I meditated in the Gray Between. Now, rain was falling at a normal speed; time had sped back up, as if a natural part of the experience of the Gray Between. While I had been bubbled in time, the rain had fallen off to a sprinkle of widely spaced drops and I had relaxed, my muscles feeling more calm than I expected, as if I hadn't sat still all this time and had instead been stretching and loosening up. The ward over the house included most the rocks in the garden, and I stood, stepping off the porch into the mud left from earlier in the day. It was drier now and didn't squish up between my toes. The rocks were clean and dry, and I climbed to the top of the one closest, careful to keep from cutting myself on the sharp edges of the rocks I used when I needed to borrow or lose mass to shift into a bigger or smaller creature.

Sitting cross-legged, back relaxed, I continued my meditation. This time I entered the Gray Between, I was in my soul home, a real place in the real world, seen once long ago, but reimagined in the darkness and shadows of my mind. I was squatted before a fire pit, cold and flameless, but the darkness wasn't absolute. Rather, a pale, soft illumination seemed to emanate from the stone walls, throwing dim light but no shadows. From what I could see of myself, I was dressed in the new garb of drab cloth leggings, unadorned moccasins, and a blue tunic tied with a long scarf.

My green-and-black leather medicine bag hung from a thong around my neck, swinging slowly back and forth. My braids moved as well, two of them, one to either side of my head, as if I had been standing and had just now squatted at the ring of cold stones.

I looked up at the center of my soul home, the stone dome high overhead. I had learned that it changed as my life changed, reflecting known and unknown truths about me and the possibilities of multiple futures. At the very top, there was a bird, what looked like a dove with white wings outstretched, spreading, improbably large, down the stone walls of my home. The flight feathers spread and lengthened until they touched the stone floor. I wondered if the dove symbolized the angel Hayyel. And if it did, had the celestial being who had so altered my life and its timeline marked his territory over my soul?

I couldn't decide whether to be ticked off by the marking of territory, or feel blessed and protected. Briefly I wondered if the wings could keep me from becoming *u'tlun'ta*. I wondered if the wings in my soul home were a result of being struck by lightning. I wondered a lot of things, none of them useful in this moment or contributing to a decision about Angie Baby, Molly, her unborn child, and the *arcenciel*.

Directly overhead and to the side of the angel, there was a black dot or spot or mote. It was positioned near the heart of the dove but to the side. It looked like a black blood splatter, one dropped straight down, not flung or slung or thrown. It pulsed like a tiny, dark heart.

Hayyel's heart? Why would an angel have a dark heart? But it did nothing, just sat there, unmoving except for that strange pulsing. It was curious but not worrisome. For now.

A bizarre notion sped across my mind and skidded to a halt, lingering. *What if the blood diamond, buried in the new weapon, the one made by lightning and the battle between Hayyel and the dark thing he had been fighting in my last vision of him, might allow me to "ride" an arcenciel? And see what Molly's baby might do in the future?*

Which would mean taking a slave. The thought jerked me out of my meditative trance and I banished it. "No way," I whispered. "No freaking way." If temptation was real, then the idea of slavery was a temptation direct from the heart of a demon. Almost all of the tribal peoples of the

Americas had been sold into slavery, had toiled and died in chains, for centuries before the first African slave had been brought over. Like our African brothers and sisters, we knew slavery.

Silent, abashed, and more than a little ashamed, I stood and went inside and closed the door behind me.

Molly and Evan had bound the skull, keeping it from being used by anything magical—including me, I assumed—and Mol told me that the skull was much like an ensorcelled teapot she had seen recently, one that moved along a timeline following a vampire. Which just sounded weird, but most things magical were weird. I hoped that with the skull bound, the *arcenciel* would stay away.

Angie was put to bed and the lights in the house went mostly dark before I smelled Molly outside my room. She had showered off the stinky perfume and the sweat, but her own Molly scent, augmented by the pheromones of pregnancy, flowed under the door as she stood outside waiting for something. I knew she could see the light under the door, so she was standing there, indecisive. Uncertain. I could have gotten up and made her decision for her, but I left it to her. If Molly wanted to explain everything, she could. Or not. Finally she walked away and I went back to my reading on my tablet, going over Alex's research on *arcenciels* and other things paranormal.

Half an hour later Molly came to the door again, and this time she knocked. I smelled some of her herbal tea, the stuff she drank when she was pregnant, along with some herbal spice tea, the stuff I sometimes drank at night. Most drugs have no effect on skinwalkers, but caffeine was one that worked on me, and quite well, so real tea at night was something I usually avoided.

"Come in, Mol," I said.

The door opened and Molly entered. Mol usually slept in a nightgown like Angie, but with the guys in the house, she was wearing chaste flannels. Pink. Her red hair was curled in a disordered mop all over her head. Her feet were in pink slippers with rubberized soles. And she wore a serious face, devoid of makeup.

I patted the bed. I was sitting up, the sheets folded down, pillows plumped against the wall to make a chair. I was wearing loose, thin pajama bottoms and a T-shirt, all in charcoal tones, so that if I needed to move through the house in the dark, I wouldn't stand out from the shadows. It's sad, the things that people like me think when we make the smallest decision. Death, danger, dismembering, threat, menace, dark magic, gunshots, bombs, and peril. All while buying pj's.

Molly placed the tray beside me on the bed and crawled up on the other side, pulling the sheets over her legs. I smiled at her and accepted the mug of tea, which had a dollop of Cool Whip on it.

"I made a mess of things," she said.

I didn't reply, just watched her over the mug's rim as I sipped, the ceramic warm on my fingers.

"I've made a mess of a lot of things over the years."

I still didn't reply, and she frowned.

"I made a mess when I blamed you for my babies being taken by the Damours. I made a mess when I let fear drive me away from earth magic to death magic. I made a mess when I didn't trust you to do the right thing. All the time. Every time. Always." Tears gathered in her eyes. Pregnancy was making her weepy. "You always do the right thing, even when it comes back and bites you in the ass. And I'm sorry for biting you in the ass."

I smiled and took a cookie off the tray. They were Eli's cookies, kept for special occasions, and no one had permission to open the bag. They were his to disperse as he saw fit. Like prizes. He had found them at a local candy store—though Alex and I had never figured out which one—and bought them by the dozen, usually taking them to Natchez to his honey bun, Sylvia, the county sheriff. More rarely he'd bring a bag home and dole them out as treasures. Caramel and white chocolate and macadamia nuts and walnuts all in a gooey soft cookie, with a single dark chocolate button in the center, melted flat and soaked into the dough as it cooked. I ate, and didn't tell Molly that the cookies were "hands-off," which was evil, but comfort food was always nice.

Molly scowled. "Are you gonna forgive me?"

I shrugged and pushed a loose crumb of cookie from my lip into my mouth. "Did that a long time ago. Just like you forgave me for not keeping your kids safe from the Damours."

"That wasn't your doing or your fault. It was their fault. I had no reason to be mad at you. Neither did Big Evan."

"Where their children are concerned, parents aren't exactly logical. I knew that going into our friendship."

"But it seems like it's all going one way. All you, giving to me and to mine." Her tears, which had slowed, flowed harder again and dripped onto her flannel top. Her voice had gone tight, with tears clogging her sinuses and larynx. "Letting us stay here. For free. Every time we come. Bringing danger to you. Making things harder on you."

I handed her a tissue from the box on the bedside table; she set down her mug and dabbed at her eyes. "Sometimes," I said, "with family, the attention all goes one way for a while. Then sometimes it reverses and goes back the other way." I shrugged and placed my empty mug on the tray. "Life is like that."

"I didn't tell you about the baby."

And Molly had hit upon the one thing that had wounded me. She hadn't told me about the baby. I dropped my eyes. "No," I said evenly. Just because I thought of Molly as family didn't mean that she felt the same way. And even if she did think me of family, some things were private. Or time sensitive. "You didn't."

She looked miserable but inhaled and blew out the breath, seeking an emotional equilibrium she clearly didn't feel. "Okay. I want to explain. There were two reasons. One, we wanted to keep it secret until we know if it's a witch."

If the baby was a girl she would definitely be a witch, because she would get Evan's X-linked witch genetics. If it was a boy, there was a fifty percent chance he would be witchy because he would get all his X genes from Molly, and she had only one witchy X-linked gene. Or gene packets. Whatever.

"Two," Molly went on, "we didn't want Angie to know for a while. We were going for eighteen weeks. Just to be sure that . . . well. That everything was okay."

And then it hit me. She was worried about losing the baby. Witches lost more babies to miscarriage than humans and way more witch children to childhood cancers than humans. It was something that I had never had to think to about. "Oh," I said, feeling flummoxed. And stupid.

Molly looked at her hands, holding her mug. "It didn't seem fair to tell you until we were more certain about everything." Tears slid down her face, not the drenching waterworks that Angie could turn on, but a lot of tears. I passed her the whole box of tissues. Molly sobbed, a single heart-wrenching note, sounding a lot like Angie.

I said, "So . . . we're okay?"

Molly nodded and her throat made a horrible wet tearing/sobbing sound.

"The real problem?" I said. "Was that *awful* perfume."

Molly blubbered out a laugh in the middle of her tears and inched closer on the bed. Using my foot, I pushed the tray out of the way and Molly moved to my side, putting her head on my shoulder.

Littermate, Beast thought, sending me a vision of a pile of cat bodies curled up together against the cold. *Should have littermates. Like this. In den.* Warmth, cat warmth, spread through me, and I had to blink away my own tears. I restrained the purr that started to build in my chest and tilted my head to rest it against Mol's. *Kitsssss,* Beast thought, the scent of unborn baby and pregnancy filling my/our nose.

"So," I said. "How far along are you?"

"Almost eighteen weeks." She bumped my head with hers. "I've been eating like a horse and gained a lot more weight than with the others by this time." She patted the baby bump and molded her hands around the mound. "We get the ultrasound next week." I felt her lips turn up against my shoulder. Hesitantly she asked, "Want to fly or drive up for the ultrasound?"

Deep inside, Beast stopped purring, her ear tabs high and her gaze piercing. *Molly can see kits inside of Molly? Magic?*

No, I thought back. *White man medicine.*

Beast hissed with displeasure, her thoughts on seeing kits inside of Molly containing blood and guts and dead kittens on the dirt. *It's not like that,* I thought at her. But the vision persisted.

"Jane?" Molly asked, her voice hesitant. "Do you?"

A smile pulled at my own mouth, wanting but uncertain. "You mean me? In the ultrasound room? With you?" My happiness slid away. "What would Big Evan say to that?"

"It was his idea. He said that he wanted his baby's godmother to be there."

"Oh . . ." My lips stayed parted, and I blinked at the tears that had gathered all unknowing, in my eyes, but they came too fast. One rolled down my cheek. I sniffed and wiped the back of my wrist across my face.

Molly jerked away, twisted on the mattress, and extended her neck like a turtle, her eyes searching mine. "I made you *cry*," she said, incredulous. She passed me one of my own tissues.

"Yeah." I chuckled unsteadily and patted my face with the tissue. "Crying's contagious, but this is ridiculous. All these teary-eyed females in my testosterone-rich house. The boys are seriously outnumbered."

Molly grinned, lighthearted, showing teeth and wrinkling up her eyes, a smile that I remembered from the earliest days of our friendship. "So come and stay with us for a few days. We'll have an estrogen-filled household there too, and we'll eat fresh-baked bread with olive oil drizzled over it and fix fresh stuff from the garden and Beast can hunt in the woods on the hill nearby and we'll shop—"

"Oh no. Not shopping." I gave a mock shudder. "Girlie stuff. Next thing I know you'll have me getting a mani-pedi and a perm."

Molly fell against the pillows and put her head back on my shoulder. "Baby shopping. Once we know the gender of this hungry little munchkin." She patted her belly harder, as if giving the kid a head slap for eating too much. "So, will you? Come and stay for a few days?"

"Yeah," I said, the warmth still filling me, like heated air filled a balloon, rising from the ground, so much bigger and more powerful than it seemed. "I'll come. Thanks.

"Now," I said, "we need to talk about you staying here. The thing found you here and attacked, and there's no saying when or if she'll be back. Should you catch a flight back to Asheville? Should you move to a hotel?"

"And get knocked out of the sky by a rainbow dragon, killing us and everyone else on board? No. *Doofus*. Move to a hotel and try to get a ward around that? Again, *no. Doofus*. I'm safer here. *You're* not safe here with me here, but *I'm* safer. And with the baby and Angie, I'm staying where I can ward and you can fight. Which is utterly selfish, but it's the way I feel."

"Not selfish," I said. "Motherly. Understandable. And we're honored."

The talk degenerated then from friendship and kits—babies—to the *arcenciel*, and I explained my theories about the light dragon being able to see timelines. And about Molly needing to protect herself at all times.

Molly nodded. "There were stories, way back when, tales my grandmother told, and she said her grandmother told her, about one entire family of Everhart babies disappearing from the cradle, each time following a flash of light. I wonder . . . if witch babies are dangerous to *arcenciels* in general or if it's Everhart witch babies in particular. . . ." Her voice trailed off, and I could smell sleep coming. She yawned and asked, "What was I saying?"

I stood and pulled my BFF to her feet. "You were saying that it was bedtime. Go upstairs and go to sleep. We have stuff to do tomorrow, and the fight wore you out."

"Yes. It did." She yawned again, hugged me with one arm, and turned for the stairs.

I stood at my doorway and watched Molly climb the wide staircase, lifting her feet as though they weighed a ton each. She was exhausted and her balance was wobbly. I would have carried her if I thought she would let me. But as it was, it was time for her to go. Otherwise it might have occurred to her to ask what her baby might mean to the future. She might have begun go wonder why the *arcenciel* wanted the baby to have never been conceived. And I had no answer. And I might never have one.

When I heard Mol climb into the bed, I closed my door and turned off the light, wondering and worrying what might happen if Soul came into contact with Molly and her baby. Which was certain to happen at the Witch Conclave, if not before.

Just before dawn, the *arcenciel* attacked the wards again, with a *boom* so loud and hard it threw me from my bed, into a roll, and down. A big-cat move. The moment I hit the floor, I dashed on hands and knees into my closet, where the long sword was kept with the steel-edged, silver-plated vamp-killers. As I drew the weapons, I felt Beast rising in me, lending me her strength and power, her vision of silvers and greens and charcoal shadows where before there had been only shades of blackness. And this time a border of gray energies spun around me, close to my skin.

Eli and I met in the foyer and I steadied him when the house shook. Showers of red sparklers fell in front of the house to the street. Opal was concentrating on the upper story and I didn't know why. Or even if there was a logical reason.

"Molly?" I asked him. My voice was a hint lower, a Beast growl caught in the single word.

"In the hallway, working her magics."

All this stress and magic couldn't be good for the baby. "Alex?" I asked. And this time my voice was a full octave lower, an unmistakable growl in it.

Eli's eyes pierced me, evaluating even as he answered my question. "Told me he had a work-around to keep coms up. He hasn't been to bed."

"In here, guys," Alex called from the living room. Just as the *arcenciel* rammed down again on the top of the *hedge of thorns* ward, possibly its weakest point, assuming the ward had a weak point.

The *arcenciel* slammed down on the top over and over, the attack physical as well as magical, and I heard Molly yelp softly. Already she stank of fear. She was afraid she wouldn't be able to hold the ward. *Kitssss,* Beast hissed deep inside.

At this rate, the house would be a pile of matchsticks in no time. Dark humor welled up in me with Beast. "I hope the insurance is paid up. And that it covers acts of magic."

There was a trace of humor in Eli's tone as well when he said, "Yes. And no. We'll claim that a tornado came down and hit just this house. That is if we can't get it stopped. And if we don't get eaten."

In the living room, Alex was at his small desk, lit by the faint lights of batteries and electronic stuff. He said, "No cells, but we can text out on a tablet. I piggybacked on Katie's Wi-Fi. Plus Evan wasn't able to figure out a way to shackle the creature, but he sent us a melody that he said would work on the ward, would help Molly, if Opal came back tonight. And we have enough battery power to last a few hours if you unplug the fridge again." Eli was already moving to the kitchen to follow his brother's orders.

The *arcenciel* hit again. I lost my feet for a moment, and Alex's table and chair scudded across the wood floor with deep scratching sounds. Molly shouted, "Jane! I can't hold the ward!"

Kitssss, Beast thought at me. *Save kitssss.* And she pushed against the gray energies that were swirling about me, drawing on more of my skin-walker magic. I looked to the kitchen table where the skull still rested, glowing with energy in Beast-vision. It had been double warded by Molly and Evan, and the *arcenciel* shouldn't be able to sense it, but it seemed that no one had told the rainbow dragon that. I raced to it and carried the skull and the tiny charm that contained the *hedge of thorns* spell back to the closet. Not that it would do much good. If the *arcenciel* could break through the house ward all it would have to do is look for the bit of magic in the matchsticks, pick up the warded skull, and carry it off someplace safer, where it could dissect the energies undisturbed. Being handcuffed to the hedge by the built-in shackles would probably present little problem to a creature made entirely of light and magic. And that would be the end of everything.

Opal hit the house, the attack rhythmic as a jackhammer, if slower and far more powerful. I could hear the house creaking beneath the battering. Without the ward, the house would be splinters and dust by now. After a dozen blows, Opal backed away, her rainbow lights filling the house from outside. I had to wonder why the neighbors hadn't call the cops yet. Or maybe they had, and the cops had decided not to get involved with this particular situation. Not that I could blame them. Or maybe only we could tell that there was a problem at all. Magic is freaky weird sometimes.

"Evan's song, coming up, Miz Molly," Alex shouted.

Music flowed out of the speakers that the Kid had wired into the entire house, a haunting yet jagged-edged melody played on one of Evan's wooden flutes.

"Yes," Molly said, gasping. "That helps. But it isn't going to be enough, y'all. This thing is figuring out my magics as fast as I can alter them. I need Evan *here*, with me, if we're going to beat it." Opal hit again, this time from near the front door. The windows rattled. Molly said, "Jane?" her voice wavering with uncertainty.

I remembered my worry about what might happen if Soul came into contact with Molly and her baby. But we had no choice. "I got this, Mol," I shouted. "When I give the word, drop the ward, take a break, and then try to get it back up."

"Okay," she said, breathless.

Softly I ordered Alex, "Get in touch with Soul. Tell her we're under *arcenciel* attack. Tell her to get here. *Now!* Tell her that I'm going out to fight it and if I have to kill it to save us, I will."

"That'll get her here," Eli muttered.

Alex started keying in the text. "No armor?" Eli asked me.

Outside the *arcenciel* hit the side of the ward, at the second-floor gallery. Red sparks of broken energies scattered through the yard. The reek of scorched paint and burned wood and desiccated herbs came from the sparks. The ward was close to breaking. I was almost out of time.

"No. Beast is close. I'm going out in half-Beast form."

Instantly Beast shoved through my skinwalker energies, pushing and pulling. Which was crazy because my life wasn't in danger at this particular moment. I had plenty of time to shift. Like, whole seconds, which was unusual for me. Pelt roiled out of me; my bones popped. Pain that was more than physical slammed me to the floor. I landed with a gasp, spine arched. I wasn't sure why it was so painful to shift sometimes and so pain free at others, but this was one of my more painful times. My hair tumbled around me; it had come unbraided, which happened from time to time in a painful half shift.

When I could breathe, I levered myself up off the floor with the fist that still held the vamp-killer. My knuckles were knobby, my feet were wide paws, my claws were all out and glinting in the dull light of Alex's tablets, grinding and tapping on the wood floor as I found my balance. My hips were lean, my belly narrow and flat, my shoulders too wide, my clothes hanging at the waist, stretched tight across the back. I was pelted all over, my amber eyes glowing. Unbraided black hair flowed to my hips, in the way. But I was energized with Beast's power and strength.

Eli pressed my shoulder, turning me until my back was to him, and gathered my hair into a tail. His fingers awkward, he slid three elastics onto the ponytail, at neck, shoulder length, and midback. Then he tucked it all into my collar and down my T-shirt, out of the way. At my ear, he said, "To be a really good second, I need to learn how to braid hair. But being a ladies' maid would get me laughed out of the special forces, so this will have to do."

I chuffed with amusement and tossed the vamp-killer into the air, the blade whipping and shining with greenish light. I caught it by the hilt. I felt strong and swift and a bit reckless. "Keep them safe," I growled to Eli as I stalked through the side door onto the side porch. And I screamed out a challenge.

The *arcenciel* stopped its attack on the second-floor front gallery as I leaped out onto the damp earth where we had fought earlier. The partial shift had healed me, and the dull pain of the elbow to the gut was gone. "Come and get me, you dumbass lizard! *Now*, Molly!"

The *arcenciel* rose high in the air over my house, her body a snaky, tessellated, whipping light, her tail barbed and coruscating, flashing with scales and tasseled flesh, her wings held wide and thrashing forward as she hovered. She darted her head in, her horned skull frilled and patterned with bony plates of light, all in shades of copper and bronze and browns. Her teeth, like long, curved tusks of pearls and diamonds, chomped at me. Her tail whipped and snapped. She was seriously ticked.

The ward fell in a shower of light and power that burned where it shattered over my pelt.

Opal reared back and came at me, striking cobra fast.

I bent my knees and leaped, steel sword high in the air, an upward lunge, whirling, cutting, in motions that were still unfamiliar and graceless. The vamp-killer to the side, I aimed for the tail-like body that slashed at me. I scored two long gashes, one in her belly and the other in the side of her tail. Opal screamed, lights boiling from the wounds, clear goop splattering out.

I landed in a bent-kneed crouch, weapons circling over and around me in the vamp's version of the Spanish Circle method of sword fighting. The blades a glittering cage of death.

Opal spat at me. I leaped to the side, a big-cat move, my sword whirling slowly, doing the job of a puma's long tail in the leap, keeping my body stable, my balance rooted to the ground, and keeping the movement itself steady and controlled. The saliva—acid? Poison?—which was surely a weapon, missed me.

The *arcenciel* back-winged, her eyes glowing. I had no idea how to read the body language of an *arcenciel*, but I'd have said for an instant that she looked triumphant. She pulled her frills tight and her wings closed. I landed and leaped again, to the top of the shattered rocks near the back wall.

Faster than I could follow, Opal slammed into the ground where I had stood and vanished. I was heaving breaths. The fight had lasted perhaps five seconds.

"What the—"

"Jane!" Eli shouted.

Lights prismed off the walls. Inside the house.

I raced to the porch and inside, to see the light coming from the kitchen. A long, narrow beam of coiling, writhing snake made of light. It was now much smaller, perhaps two inches in diameter, bright as a torch beam and pouring out of the kitchen like a sea serpent. Eli was cutting at it, but it moved faster than he ever could.

The *arcenciel* had gone into the ground. Now it was in the kitchen, in a different form. "Molly," I screamed. "Ward yourselves! She's coming inside!"

Molly raced to her daughter's bed, and I felt the magics snap into place above me.

And I felt the Gray Between again, a yank that pulled on time and space and matter. And me. I screamed as Beast forced me into a second shift. I fell to the floor, dropping the blades. Which hung in the air, even as I landed in a writhing heap. Gagging and strangling, unable to breathe. And I was tasting blood in the back of my mouth. *Beast bubbled time. Dang cat.* The internal bleeding that seemed to be a part of this state had started earlier than before. I coughed and covered my mouth. Blood filled my cupped hand. I spat to clear my mouth and throat, and wiped it on my shirt. Trying not to think about the four big tusks that made up a large part of my lower face.

I stood slowly, carefully. My gut cramped as if a huge fist gripped it from inside and twisted. Ripping . . . something. I pushed up from the floor and took the hilts that were still hanging there. Tugged the swords into the bubble of time with me, their weight transferring, the swings they were in before pulling my arms into motion. I stalked into the kitchen.

Eli was standing, his blades high, in the act of cutting Opal's elongated face, nostrils and horns twisted and trailing, her frill still captured within the drainpipe. But Eli missed the narrow ribbon of light. Not the right size for an *arcenciel*, more snaky than dragony, long and lean, like an LED cable, and a brilliant dark red. This red light was coming from the kitchen sink. As I moved closer, it pulsed once. A moment later, in time as I understood it here, it pulsed again. The light shifting from deep red to paler red, and paler again, into orange, light going through the prism in slow motion. It *was* Opal, coming up through the sink's drainpipe. Or trying to. She was moving slowly through stopped time, not speeding through time as she could in her normal dragon form.

She must not be able to manipulate time while shifting to a form like this, one abnormal to her natural state, stretched out and . . . Suddenly I understood. This house was old and so were its pipes. Old enough to have lots of iron in them. Maybe even *made entirely* of iron, rusted and corroded. They had to be causing the *arcenciel* pain.

I studied the shape of the creature, how the light flowed through it, a rippling, ripping, singing note of light. Its cells were weren't like a mammal's, one cell touching others, but more like the neurons in a brain, bulbous and spiked with long, linear filaments that shifted with light. Light that came from them and flowed through them.

I could see everything about her. She looked like sunlight, as if her light was created, stored, broken, then reflected. As if Opal got her power and her body from the sun alone. I wondered how long she could even stay alive in the dark. As I watched, her wings were pulled through the drain, a glistening rainbow, so thin that I could see through the membranes. She was beautiful. And she was deadly.

If Opal stayed alive she could come after Molly at any time, past or present or future. Anyplace. If Opal lived, Molly or her child, or both, might die. I flipped the long sword, thinking, my blade catching the light of Opal's beauty. Thinking about time and memory. About changing time itself, both in the future and in the past, like plucking one bubble of possibility out of the timeline and breaking it up into molecules and atoms of nothingness. Could Opal also change a memory of the future, of an event yet to be? Was changing the memory of a future event even possible? And if she could, would that be an evil of the worst sort? Or would it be worse if I killed her, a creature so beautiful she had to make even God weep? I didn't know what to do, but I had a bad feeling that no matter what I did it would be the wrong thing, ruining everything for everyone in the process.

I slowed the movement of the sword and held it low, tip near the floor. Took a breath. Smelled Molly's panic, stagnant on the air. I turned to the stairs and saw Angie Baby, peeking around the corner of the stairwell. She had slipped free of Molly's warding. The little girl was watching, her eyes on me. I had stood still long enough for her to focus on me, even bubbled in time.

In this state, I could see the energies that once bound her magic. They were nothing more than a broken magical garment that she could put on and take off. Worse, as I watched, Angie reached out, her little hand moving faster than she should be able to. Her fingers threw tiny sparks of raw magic, and they raced away from her, as if searching. My breath caught. *Holy crap.*

Angie was seeking the Gray Between.

She must have seen me bubble time. And learned how by watching me.

If she figured that out, Angie would be more than dangerous. If she learned how to enter the Gray Between, she could be deadly to herself, or to me, by accident or in a fit of anger. She was a little girl. Little kids had no control or wisdom to know when to use, or not use, a gift or ability. Worse, if she figured out how to bubble time and alter it as the *arcenciels* could, there was no telling what that ability would do to her morality and ethics. She could abuse and alter timeline probabilities at a whim. Angie could easily become a weapon of mass destruction.

My choices were limited, and all of them were dangerous to Angie. She could see me kill the *arcenciel*. See me die at the jaws of the rainbow dragon. Then get eaten herself. See her mother die. Then get eaten herself.

"Crap on crackers," I whispered as little sparkles of black light power flickered and a small tuft of the Gray Between opened in the cup of Angie's fingers. I walked to her as the *arcenciel* went through the blue and green spectrum of light, throwing the kitchen into lovely colors of sky and water. Another foot of Opal's energies had flowed into the kitchen. Her wing tips were still inside the drain but the upper portions had partially unfurled.

I stopped at Angie and watched as her fingertips spat tiny ribbons of black light, moving slightly faster than the *arcenciel*. I studied the tattered robe of magics she wore, the energies broken and frazzled but still active. If I weren't in the Gray Between, in the no-time place where magic was visible as pathways of power and interactive energies, I couldn't see where the breaks were. But since I could see it maybe I could also fix it? I had never been able to create magic, but I could sometimes disrupt the magic of others. And once, not long after I came to New Orleans, I had manipulated magic by accident. Molly had later told me I shouldn't have been able to do that at all, and I had never been able to do it again, but maybe when I was in this state, I could do magic . . . mechanically.

I set my blades at Angie's feet on the bottom stair and slipped my knobby fingers into the tattered energies. I began to tie them off, one by one, using the tiny spurts of black light, Angie's own magic, to secure each of them. It wasn't pretty, like the knitted energies of the Everhart and Trueblood workings. The knots I was making were downright ugly, the way a painting I had done would look when held up next to a Rembrandt or Michelangelo. Childish and inept. But it was working; the binding was coming together.

I didn't know what the effect of my actions would have on Angelina Everhart Trueblood and her magics. Out of fear, I didn't tie her as tightly as I might have, stopping when the garment of bindings was connected to her own magics but wasn't constraining her in any way. When there were no more black light energies spurting from her fingertips, I tied off the last stray thread of bindings and stepped back. If she figured out that I had done it to her, would she hate me? Something to worry about later.

I returned to the kitchen trying to figure out what do, how to fight Opal away without killing her outright. I couldn't kill a sentient child, not even the child of another species. But my body was spasming tightly, an electric charge of pain that shivered along my nerves and burned in my fingertips. Eli was at her side, so I positioned myself where her head was growing wider, back into its real shape and form. And because the pain was growing so fast, I reached for real time, knowing that if I made a mistake, Opal might kill me. But because Angie was watching, I had to get the fight back in real time.

I whirled my swords and forced the Gray Between to fracture and split around me. The fight slammed back into real time. The *arcenciel* slithered through the drainpipe and into the kitchen in scant seconds. Her wings billowed open. Knocked by a wing, the kitchen table and everything on it went flying or sliding across the house to crash into the back wall. The kitchen window blew out into the street as the other wing encountered it.

Eli cut the dragon in a half dozen places. Clear goop splattered. She roared, mouth open, long tongue lashing. I lunged with the long sword. Stabbed her in the mouth with the sword, the blade piercing her tongue to the roof of her mouth. She jolted back at the last instant. The steel missed her brain, if her brain was located in her skull.

The *arcenciel* screamed. In a single flash, she flew through the broken, unwarded window and into the street. Taking my sword with her. I grabbed a frill and leaped with her. Slamming my shoulder into the window jamb on the way through it. I heard and felt the *crack* of my collarbone. My right arm went numb. I lost my grip on the rainbow dragon.

That's not good.

Jane bad hunter. Stupid kit to ride prey through small hole.

I landed in the street, tumbling. Rolling over the injured shoulder with a pain that screeched through me like a predator's fangs. As I rolled, Beast sent a blast of pain-deadening adrenaline through me, and I caught a single breath that didn't hurt. I made it to my feet fast, still holding the vamp-killer, left-handed.

Molly rushed through the front door, throwing jagged bars of blue and green power-bolt bombs at the dragon. They quickly went from sharp-edged energies to crumpled slags of dying power. The bombs that didn't bounce off her, the rainbow dragon seemed to simply absorb, taking in all the magical attacks.

Eli joined the fight with a steel sword, but the *arcenciel* hit him with her tail, sending him flying. My sword was still pinned in her mouth. Steel keeping it in the present flow of time, which was what I had hoped. Guessed. Whatever.

And up until now, excluding the broken collarbone, the fight was going the way I had hoped. From the uptown side of the street, lights glided into long streamers. Soul. The cavalry to the rescue.

She whipped faster than my eyes could follow, wrapping Opal up in her much greater energies. Molly saw what she was doing and turned in a circle, her arms wide, both hands open, sketching a circle in the air around her, and then around Opal. Together the witch and the mature *arcenciel* wrapped the juvie *arcenciel* up in magic. When the writhing, angry rainbow dragon was secured, a light flashed and Soul appeared in the street in human form, her long skirts flowing in a breeze I could see but not feel. Deftly she pulled the sword from the creature's mouth and tongue and tossed it toward me. The captured *arcenciel* made a keening sound of anguish and woe.

I stepped back, hitting solidly against Eli's chest as he caught the sword out of the air. My partner secured my arm at my waist with his, wrapping himself around me, holding my sword upright at an angle near us in his free hand. "Broken collarbone," he said into my ear as Molly and Soul stood together in the street, studying the tangle of energy that was Opal. The two magic workers walked back and forth, speaking in low voices. I didn't particularly like the way Soul's eyes kept dropping to Molly's baby bump, clearly outlined in the pajamas, but there was nothing I could do now. The water droplets of time would have to figure it all out themselves.

Opal stretched and bit at the energies. Acid rose in my throat at the thought of having to fight again right now. "Yeah," I said, struggling against the nausea of the broken bone, time bending, the fight, and now, the fear. "Kinda figured that." My words were slurred by the tusks. Shivers wracked through me, making the pain much worse for a moment. When I got a second breath I smelled Eli's blood.

"You're hurt."

"Just a scratch."

I pushed him away with my good hand and caught a spurt of blood into my face. "I don't think so," I said, blinking fast. I followed the blood to his upper arm and wrapped my knobby, über-strong fingers around his biceps and tightened them into a pressure bandage. Then I chuckled, though it wasn't anywhere near my usual laugh. He was holding my injured arm in place. And I was holding his.

Soul walked over, her arms crossed over her ample bosom, her gauzy, flowing gowns no longer fluttering in a breeze I couldn't feel. She looked me over, and I realized it was the first time that the PsyLED agent had ever seen me in my half-Beast form. Some people might have been taken aback, but Soul seemed composed in the face of pelt and big-cat fang tusks. She said, "Thank you for making the right choice."

I probably should have kept my mouth shut, but I had never been very good at that. "So . . . ," I said. "You had been sitting around watching the fight between Opal and me for . . . a while." *Though bubbled time makes that term insubstantial at best,* I thought. "Watching and probably judging." I frowned at her, wondering what Soul would have done had I taken another road. As part of PsyLED and also as an *arcenciel*, she had a wide scope of power. If I had killed the *arcenciel*, would she have had the rule of some arcane, possibly prehistoric law to kill me? Or go back in time and kill me before I killed Opal?

Soul pulled a scarf from a pocket and pushed my bloodied good hand away from Eli. She tied the scarf around my partner's wound and immediately the pulsing arterial blood stopped. Eli's face, which had held a hint of pain, eased back to its neutral, natural mask of nothingness. "This scarf has a healing working in it," she said, adjusting the knotted scarf. "It's self-renewable and powered by the sun, so when you finish with it today, simply wash it out and hang it in a window."

"What about me?" I asked.

"I haven't a thing for broken bones or timesickness. Your skinwalker energies will have to help you there."

The fact that she knew I was sick from bending time reaffirmed that Soul had been watching the whole fight. I pressed against Eli's helping hand and wrapped my bloody good hand around my own elbow, keeping it close to my side. I could take care of myself. Eli was holding my unsheathed sword. Not the smartest thing to do while in close proximity to another person. That thing was sharp.

Soul walked to Molly, who was now sitting on the low steps of the front porch, her sock-clad feet on the sidewalk. "I'm sorry Opal attacked you," Soul said. "Free will is something my kind believe in, and I will make certain that she doesn't repeat her actions against you and yours. But you should know that the child you carry has the potential to change the timelines for Opal and her progeny, and the closer that timeline gets, the harder it will be for her to restrain her survival instincts."

Molly raised her head to Soul, emotions I couldn't begin to name moving beneath her skin. Her face was pale and wan in the dulled streetlights, but her expression firmed when she said, "Do you have some kind of evidence for that speculation, or are you just trying to make me mad?"

"I would never attempt to anger an Everhart."

"Damn skippy," Molly said.

I smiled slightly.

"So how did you know about my baby?"

Soul tilted her head and her long silver hair slid forward, the waves catching the meager moonlight. "I see your child in the timelines. There is significant data to suggest that the baby will be a witch and will ride Opal, trapping her in a crystal at a time when she is carrying an egg. And the egg will die. And so will Opal's line. There is less evidence to suggest that your child will partner with Opal to some end. That is the way you should bring up your child if you wish it to live long and prosper. Agreement and harmony, compromise, understanding, a mutually beneficial bargain."

"That's the plan," Molly said sharply, obviously stung that her parenting and witch-teaching skills were being called into question over her unborn baby.

Soul nodded once and made her way to the *arcenciel*, tapping it on the snout and leading it back up the street, changing as she moved into her own *arcenciel* form. No one looked out the windows, no cars attempted to drive down the street, nothing disturbed them or us. It had to be *arcenciel* magic, something put in place by Soul while she watched us fight. Nothing else made sense.

The glowing lights of the rainbow dragons faded and died, but not before Opal swung her head back and looked at Molly and Eli and me. Her glowing eyes were baleful and full of promise, half-hidden by streamers of reflective frill and horns bright as crystal. I had a feeling that Soul wouldn't be able to keep the young dragon in check for long.

Back inside the house, I stood in the foyer watching as Eli and Alex made sure the house was habitable, plugged in the fridge, got the coms and cameras back up on the city's grid, put the skull that had caused all the trouble back into my closet on the high shelf, and started an early breakfast. The smell of bacon quickly filled the lower story. Molly was curled on the couch talking with Big Evan on her cell, discussing magic and ways to fight light. I heard her tell him that Angie had been a perfect angel and hadn't even gotten out of bed. "She's still asleep, the little darling. I think the binding is going to stick this time. . . . Yes. We done good." She laughed, her happiness like crystal tones on the air.

I pursed my lips, tracking my goddaughter to my room by scent. Angie had done something magical to her mother, to keep her from knowing that Angie was up and around. And then I had . . . interfered. Now Angie's scent was angry. Maybe tantrum angry.

Eli had put my weapons on the floor. I took both by the hilts and strode into my room, totally ignoring the little girl sitting in the middle of my bed, looking mutinous. I sheathed the weapons, double-checked that the skull was back where it belonged, and finally turned to Angie.

If I hadn't been hurting, I might have crossed my arms, spread my feet, and stared her down, but I was feeling more pain than I had expected, now that the fighting was over and the effect of adrenaline was wearing off. Every breath ached like lightning, and I knew exactly how *that* felt. So instead of trying to look stern, I leaned my weight against the wall by the closet and slid to the floor, to sit with my back against the wall and my knees bent up. I reached out to Beast and sought my human form, what little of me was left in the tangled mess of our coiled and twisted genetic structures. I teased the human strands out and let myself fall into my human form, hearing my collarbone scrape and snap back into place. The pain of the healing was stabbing, grinding, and electric, and for a moment, it seemed to fill all of who I was and all of who I might ever be.

And then the pain drenched away, fast as storm water sliding down a gutter. I held up my hands and made sure I was human. Eight fingers, two thumbs. Thin shavings of Eli's crusted blood dusted into my lap. I touched my face—skin—and touched my teeth—human—and pulled out my T-shirt to peek down at my chest. I was always afraid I would come back only partway and have furry boobs, but I had skin. Good.

Angie was watching, silent, her face red, but her scent was less angry than before I shifted. This was the first time I had shifted in front of her, and she understood that it was a measure of trust. My shifting in front of her was a proclamation of her maturity and of our friendship.

"So. What's up?" I asked her. *How lame? Stupid!*

"You can do . . ." Her hands made little circles in the air. "You can speed up. You can move faster than I can see."

"Yeah."

"I tried to do it too."

"Yeah."

"Did you stop me?" Her face started to flush again, and I smelled her beginning anger.

"Yeah. You want to know why?"

Angie narrowed her eyes at me. I placed one hand on the floor at my hip and propped my weight on it. With the other hand, I kneaded my belly. It growled loudly. The two half shifts and the fighting had left me weak and starving, but sometimes there were more important things than food. I watched Angie, reading the emotions that flashed across her face as she considered my question.

"I guess," she said, as if the words were dragged out of her.

"Because I get really sick when I move fast. The last few times, I threw up blood."

Angie sat up straight. "You puked blood? Ewwwww."

"I know, right?"

"Did it stink?"

"Yeah. It did. And I was so sick afterward that I had to shift back to human to not end up dead."

"You think I would puke blood and end up dead if *I* moved fast?"

"I think it's possible. And because you're my godchild I had to stop you from doing something that would hurt you. The same way I'd have to stop you if you wanted to jump off a cliff to see if you could fly." I cocked my head at her and my hair, still trapped under my shirt, but no longer bound in the scrunchies, slid forward on my shoulder. The scrunchies dropped to my waist in a little nest of knitted material that itched, but I'd have to wait to scratch that one until Angie was pacified. "You know what being a godmother means? Not a fairy godmother like in fairy tales, but a real godmother?"

"Daddy says it means you can spank me if I'm real bad, but I don't believe him. You would never hurt me." When I didn't reply she asked, "Is going fast being bad?"

"Can you fly?"

Angie tucked her chin at my seeming non sequitur.

"Let's say you had a spell that you thought might let you fly, and you wanted to jump off a cliff to see if it worked, instead of testing it by jumping off your back deck. I'd have to stop you from jumping off a cliff. And if you were really grown-up enough to test that spell, you would never have thought of testing it by jumping off a cliff in the first place."

Angie thought about that for a while as I kneaded my belly and breathed in the wonderful bacon smell that was wafting under my door. "You mean that if I was stupid you would have to stop me from being stupid?"

"Yep."

"I was stupid to go fast?"

"There might be a cliff at the bottom of *go fast*."

"Did my magics get messed up because I tried to go fast?" Tears gathered in her eyes and spilled down her cheeks, and I felt like crap because of them. "I can't use my magics no more." She sobbed and buried her face in my pillow.

Thank God, I thought.

Kit, Beast thought. *Pull kit in to nurse.*

No way. Ick. But a good cuddle, maybe, I thought back at her. I managed to get to my feet and went to the bed, where I sat on the tangled sheets and pulled Angie to me. She was overheated and sweaty and smelled like . . . like Angie. I placed her on my lap and positioned her head on my healed shoulder, my nose in her hair. She smelled wonderful, of little girl and happiness, even over the scent of anger and tears.

"You didn't mess up your magics trying to *go fast*. At least not permanently. But you did get snarled back up in the binding while you were trying to figure out time, and now your magics are tied in with it. Meaning that you can't use your magic until your parents say so. You won't be able to make them forget things or not see you doing things."

"Not fair!"

I chuckled. "It's fair, it's just not what you want. There's a difference."

"*You* jumped off a cliff."

My breath caught at that accusation. Because she was right. I jumped off cliffs all the time. "I guess I did. But I've jumped off cliffs for a long time and I started with little cliffs and I know how big a cliff I can jump off of. And I also know that, sometimes, it's better to jump off a cliff and risk death than the alternative."

"What's *alternative*?"

"What's it mean?"

Angie nodded her head, bumping my nose.

"Saving you and your mama and the new baby is worth jumping off a cliff. Worth risking my life for." I nuzzled her head, and she repositioned herself on my lap and sighed. "Some things are *worth* fighting for. Worth dying for."

"But if you died, then what about us? We might have died too."

I nodded. "I knew that was a risk. And if I'd had lots of time to reason through it, I might have taken the selfish way out and gone fast and changed things to my benefit. To all our benefit. But making things turn out the way I want can have unintended consequences. You know what that means?"

"It means that I plan for a good thing to happen with my magics, but my plans make a bad thing happen. Mama says that's witchery one-oh-one."

I grinned against her head.

"And I'm not supposed to say that to other people who aren't witches because it might *creep them out*."

She was quoting Molly and my grin grew broader. "Right. Even something good, if it's done in the name of selfishness, always results in evil. Only good, done in the name of unselfishness, results in good. Most of the time. *Sometimes*. It isn't guaranteed, no. But it sometimes works out.

"When I fought in real time—instead of going into fast time—it allowed your mama to wake up and get down here. To help. It also allowed Soul to get here. Doing the right thing doesn't mean good things happen. But it does keep my spirit clean and pure, my soul home clean and pure. It does mean good things are more likely, and not selfish, bad things."

Angie pulled away and looked up at me, scowling. She'd gotten really good at it, and I had to fight not to laugh in the middle of what had turned into a deadly serious discussion. "Are you trying to say I shouldn't undo Mama and Daddy's magical bindings? That I should *stay a little girl* forever?"

That was a sideways slide from one subject to another subject, but I followed it. "It's up to you whether you fight the binding or not. I guess it has been for a while now. But the bindings have let you mature and grow and learn to use your magics slowly, at a pace—that means speed—that lets you grow into being a witch and an adult at the same time. So yes. I think you should wait until you're eighteen, like I did."

Angie flinched and her eyebrows went up fast. Her scent spiked with the sharp pheromone of surprise.

I said, "I grew up without a mother and father, in a children's home. With humans. No witches, no skinwalkers—no people like me. My magics were bound by a thing called amnesia."

"That's where people forget stuff!"

"Yeah, it is. And I forgot everything, even how to speak. And my Beast—"

"Your big-cat?"

"Yes, my big-cat. She made sure I didn't remember how to change into my big-cat shape until I was grown-up. Until I was eighteen years old and had learned enough to figure out how to use my magic properly."

"That sucks."

I couldn't help it. A giggle came out between my lips with a sound like *shurffle*.

Angie giggled with me. "Don't tell my mama that I said a bad word."

"Trust me, I won't. So, are you going to let your magics be bound and not jump off a cliff?"

"I guess so. Since you did it. But only biscause . . . because . . . I'm letting it happen, not because Mama and Daddy are making it happen to me."

"Mmm." I decided in an instant not to tell Angie that I had bound her magics. The less said the better, or the better part of valor, or the likely detail that I was chicken. Whatever.

"When you grow up, you can be bound no more, your magics yours to use."

"Okay, Aunt Jane." Angie sighed, her whole body getting into the deep breath. "But it still sucks."

With that momentous decision made, I carried Angie to the kitchen and managed not to crawl into the platter of bacon. I ate steadily, knowing that the coming discussion with Molly and Big Evan was going to be difficult, because of my chat with their daughter and the things I'd told Angie Baby. I still felt I'd made the right decision, but as I'd told my godchild, doing the right thing can have difficult consequences.

But for now we were all safe and alive, and tomorrow had come with a golden dawn and a chance for a future for all of us. There wasn't much more I could ask of life.

ABOUT THE AUTHOR

Faith Hunter is the *New York Times* bestselling author of the Jane Yellowrock series, including *Dark Heir*, *Broken Soul*, and *Black Arts*; the Soulwood series, set in the world of Jane Yellowrock; and the Rogue Mage series.